The Baltic Falcon

by

Lynn Williams

Published in the United Kingdom in 2014 by
Cambria Books, Wales, United Kingdom

2

1919

In the immediate aftermath of the Great War, the Baltic became a highly contested territory between those who sought independence, the imperialistic old guard, and the new Bolshevism which threatened to consume all before it. Into this frenzy of civil war poured the German Freikorps with its own agenda, though some viewed it as a liberating force.

Within its ranks were mercenaries, like Kessler, and secret patriots like Steiger, both of whom contribute to the narrative of *The Baltic Falcon*, which is more than just a novel of their time.

It is a story common to all wars and a romance without physical boundaries, or borders of time.

Dedications:

For Robert, who sadly never saw it.
For my, wife Margaret, for putting up with it.
For David, for his unswerving support and belief.
For Gunter Bronsart v. Schellendorff and for Thies Eisele,
for their valuable input and for correcting my German!
For Walter Mitchell, the original Fabian von Schneer,
a brilliant, unpublished author who fell in the hour of
his triumph. For John, who taught us how to
live our lives, then left us all too soon.

And in fond memory of Richard, Klim and Harry,
who inspired those same characters within, without hyperbole.

CONTENTS

It Begins...   6

Part One   17
Chapter 1. *Thus Spake my Father*   19
Chapter 2. *Interview and Introspection*   25
Chapter 3. *Confronting the Abyss*   41
Chapter 4. *History and Home Truths*   51
Chapter 5. *Emma*   61
Chapter 6. *A Secret*   69
Chapter 7. *Clarissa*   85
Chapter 8. *Grimwich 'twinned' with Koidanov*   97
Chapter 9. *The Baltic Falcon*   113
Chapter 10. *The Cold Moon in Full Majesty.*   127

Part Two   139
Chapter 11. *Funeral in Berlin*   139
Chapter 12. *Obsession and Seclusion: James's Story*   163
Chapter 13. *Layers of the Onion*   181
Chapter 14. *Visions of Hieronymus*   187

Part Three   201
Chapter 15. *Great Yarmouth 1921*   203
Chapter 16. *Confessional*   225
Chapter 17. *The Road to Glory: 1914*   235
Chapter 18. *The Linden House*   251
Chapter 19. *Graczyna, Nina and some Baltic History*   267
Chapter 20. *The Graf, his Daughters, their Tutor and their Nemesis*   281
Chapter 21. *The Call of the Wild*   293
Chapter 22. *The Bull, the Cat and the Cosmos*   311
Chapter 23. *Katya and Old Kaiser*   325
Chapter 24. *Following the Horse of the Morgan Bloodline*   341
Chapter 25. *Out of Africa*   355
Chapter 26. *Into the Firebreak*   363
Chapter 27. *Albania 1917: an Old Adversary*   371
Chapter 28. *Homeward and Revenge:*   397
Chapter 29. *Fragile Gifts*   423
Chapter 30. *Kat*   433
Chapter 31. *Death of Klammersdorf*   443

Chapter 32. *Death of Dragunavicius*   453
Chapter 33. *Berlin, Swinemunde and the VI Reserve Armeekorps*   473
Chapter 34. *Kampfgruppe Wiking:*   489
Chapter 35. *Return to Liepus Namas*   519

Part Four   523
Chapter 36. *Frankfurter Hof Memories*   523
Chapter 37. *Act of Mercy*   545
Chapter 38. *Rolf's Story*   567
Chapter 39. *Culturing the Bacillus*   589
Chapter 40. *It wasn't personal …*   599
Chapter 41. *Fighting - with Flares*   611
Chapter 42. *Albanian Justice*   617
Chapter 43. *How to Crash!*   631

Part Five   635
Chapter 44. *Paranoia and Parallel Histories*   635
Chapter 45. *Wolfgang, Zubr and the 'Little Prince'.*   641
Chapter 46. *Farnborough: Late Summer 1988*   669
Chapter 47. *Unternehmen Alberich*   695
Chapter 48. *With the RAF Expeditionary Force*   705
Chapter 49. *Arkadi: War Hero*   709
Chapter 50. *There is no God!*   713
Chapter 51. *Hostages to fate*   727
Chapter 52. *The Siberian Eagle*   747
Chapter 53. *Aktion Direkt*   757
Chapter 54. *Ninja*   781
Chapter 55. *Véles & Véjas: Spirits of the Dead,*   811
Chapter 56. *Coda*   837

Captions to illustrations   839

It Begins

She stands, still as a tree 'neath a snow-laden sky. From the overcast an iron mask stares earthwards, expressionless. Winged shapes in echelon move dark against the clouds. Silently she utters the word, *'Walküre'*, the title of her dreamscape expressed in oils, omitting the definite article, perhaps for the 'Slav' in her. After all, she had once been named Natasha.

The first time she'd lost her reason it had been to puerperal psychosis, extreme post-natal depression that stalked her like a gypsy's curse. At its worst she'd come to believe her husband was an agent: *once a spook* - she'd later rationalised. An assassin, sent from Herod to liquidate her firstborn.

She'd shot him.

Mercifully, like the threatening faces on the wallpaper her handgun was hallucinatory. But her intent had been real. Paradoxically she'd also believed her daughter to be evil incarnate and Natasha herself had come close to harming her.

It was all in her notes.

In time she'd recovered, resuming normality as she'd known it: for fourteen years, exchanging Wandsworth for a Surrey postcode, separation, divorce, and the lingering illness of a mother who'd remained as distant unto death as she'd been in life.

Now, months into her stay in this bar-less cage; in *durance vile* at a one-time Gothic workhouse and infirmary, she's told she might *not* have late-onset schizophrenia, but Dissociative Identity Disorder. That good old-fashioned term, 'Multiple Personality Syndrome' is no longer in favour, Dr. Metz informs. *She wonders if she shouldn't feel cheated that he lacks an obvious Central European accent, though to his credit he affects a beard and on his bookshelf sits 'Der Kobold im Kopf'. In the comfort of his surgery Natasha gives tongue to her flight of ideas; fixates on a wanton Klimt smiling at her from the wall.*

If MPS were the result of some unaccountable misery she'd suffered in childhood, the associated night terrors had appeared only in later life. And she didn't believe suicidal tendencies had been an ingredient of her core personality despite her slashed wrists when they'd found her. So maybe it had been one of her 'others' he's conjured from this couch.

The condition, she's learned, can be brought on by life-threatening disturbances, neglect or abuse, perhaps emotional abuse at a sensitive developmental age.

Metz, dwarfed by his armchair is a hermit crab half out of his soft leather shell that wheezes and pops as he shifts his weight. He appraises her; a magus with deep-set eyes, a sorcerer: the raven that had haunted her old Suffolk farmhouse. *And once, insubstantial as a soap bubble, a transient memory of Asian eyes, dark and mesmeric and the faint shudder of U-Bahn traffic rattling down Berlin SW, reminding her there was a world outside her fearful cellar where she'd shivered in withdrawal.* When *was* that?

Everything flows from instability. Had she suffered childhood physical abuse or sexual trauma? Inwardly recoiling she'd replied that she didn't know and Axel's professional eyebrow had registered no disbelief. Part of her thinks she might; a memory in her girlhood, of falling...a cut flower. From what little he's said perhaps one of her several personalities holds the clue. Memories and images tumble through her mind she cannot explain. Someone had suffered somewhere in secret sensory deprivation, shrieking its silent counterpoint as its victim fought hysteria. A ball gag choked the screams to a whimper. Her imagination? A horror film?

Subsequent to her recent mental and physical traumas, deemed unfit to plead and remanded for psychiatric reports, 'irregular' rendition to the UK had unexpectedly followed assisted by a police officer: an intercession, smoothed by some sharp lawyers in the European Court of Human Rights for whom she had every reason to be grateful. This was why she was here under her new name. *Where at least they speak English, Anna,* Slater had said, not rotting in a Greek jail while her case was postponed midst Foreign Office disclaimers and passport queries. From the conference notes she'd glimpsed - no FOI Act for residents - borderline schizophrenia had *not* been ruled out, though those notes had been compiled shortly after her admission. Despite whatever daily compulsive rituals she's driven to perform that keep evil at bay, or from what paranoia she might be diagnosed as suffering, it didn't change her belief that 'they' were out to get her. A night-long low frequency growl...piping infrasound or muzak into the plate in her head? Tinnitus, insomnia. Indeed she was fearful of sleep after her insulin-induced coma. LSD flashbacks perhaps? *'Is she a labrat? Should she genuflect before the technician in his white coat; roll over for him, play dumb? Play along with whatever spins his wheels? In here where is volition? Only in the mind, and where was that if we are but cellular illusions?'*

'So, Anna, you attacked a member of staff?'

A statement shaped like a question.

'Why would you do that?'

Casual dress, intended to be unthreatening, softens the nature of such secure units as these. But the tee shirt had provoked with, *'Lithuania? Hmmm…where's that?'* Mind games during exercise; Natasha right in the bewildered woman's face offering a short roller-coaster ride through some recent European history. But wasn't that part of her disorder: random, unexplained violence, though normally expressed as self-harming?

People! Weekend tourists with their stag and hen mentalities…what happens in Vilnius stays in Vilnius, yeah. Right. And screw the architecture. Anyway it was verbal not physical. She smiles faintly. *Physical* was whacking a bailiff stuck like a cork in her Godalming kitchen window trying to serve Natasha a warrant of execution, courtesy of her feckless ex. But she *had* shot Slater's Albanian, hadn't she? Or was he a Turk? The 'no-slogan tee shirt rule' was enforced more rigidly following the exercise yard confrontation; a 'setback' preventing her being transferred to a different sort of prison, which suited Natasha for the present. Manslaughter is a refuge if she wants it; the next to last refuge for those who cannot plead they didn't do it, but that the balance of the mind may be called into question.

So they do talking therapy or some sort of role play with a member of nursing staff present - she can never remember the details, just the anger which sometimes conceals her despair. Metz favours hypnotic regression, through which sessions she's tried ineffectually to lock eyes with the gilded dominatrix, Gustav Klimt's voluptuary, flanked by diplomas attesting Axel's competence in psychiatry. Disturbing manifestations have been invoked, each a distinct personality with their differing memories, some seemingly having lived lives pre-dating her own birth. Frequently they've divulged fearful and emotional events. Classically each has his or her own sex, temperament, posture and accent. Free to speculate she might have been persuaded towards her late father's delusion on cluster re-incarnation. But that would have meant putting all her rotten eggs into one metaphorical basket-case, accepting that these individuals were interacting in real time; unaware of previous serial existences and connections. So she talks compulsive flimflam while Axel listens and she hopes she's not been indiscreet, babbles unstoppably, *perhaps it's the meds,* staring at the seductive print through heavy-lidded eyes. She has no idea if anything she says is true, too exhausted or too drugged for her volcano of rage and despair to erupt.

So thank you Dr. Metz. I'm drifting on this dark whirlpool thanks to your psychometric drugs that breach the blood/brain barrier to my central nervous system, 'Please, Anna, call me Axel.' I will if you will, Herr Doktor. Call me by my own name. My other name. But hey, it's been real! An experience I wouldn't have missed for the world. Anything is better than that electroconvulsive shit.

She wonders who he's reporting to apart from some official judicial-forensics department where her file is archived for review. When was it she signed up for this procedure? When did she slide over from patient to victim in Metz's egotistical discredited experimentation which, she is reassured, is in her imagination? More mind games? So, is it sadistic punishment or just a quaint old fashioned remedy for temporal lobe epilepsy? Is any of this even remotely *legal? What do you say, Doktor Metz? Or is it Metzger? Mengele perhaps?*

But her protestations are muffled by the bridle, like the ball gag in her nightmares. Leather restraints at wrists and ankles, she's strapped into a close relative of Old Smokey. Only her eyes would tell of the fear, desperation and bitter hatred she feels, directed beyond the clinic walls.

Metz's professional opinion is of course that I'm delusional and dangerous, though he refrains from stating the latter to my face; so none of what I believe to be real exists outside the scaffolding of my mind. 'Nothing is as it seems' is as good a definition of 'reality' as it's possible to achieve. Perhaps then I should welcome pain; at least that has a reality of its own.

Later, from a dreamless sleep, she wakes; perhaps physically rested after ECT, but with that recurring sense of loss, of the jigsaw pieces of her past. Of personal identity among the many cyphers that inhabit the labyrinth.

Maybe we were all mad in our family, she sighs. Her neurotic mother had been, unless she'd simply seen life for what it was and her overwhelmingly addictive personality was her way of coping. If she could but re-boot her life, wipe out the viruses; disturbing ideas swimming in parallel streams of consciousness... But she was hostage to her fickle memory. *Could that be better than no memory at all, eh Daddy?*

~-~

The art room seats six comfortably. Heather, the therapist, is about Natasha's own age, so middle-forties, greying; good bone structure softened by the years and she's sitting with Fran, fresh-faced but older who is painting one of her angels and wearing the smile of an enraptured nun. Heather is looking enquiringly at Natasha's work; despite helpful comments for Fran she's been intrigued by what's emerging on Natasha's easel, Payne's Grey and white, heavily applied with a palette knife.

'Anna,' she says. 'How are *you* feeling today?'

Heather might have avoided the tripwire of how are '*we*' today but she's already asked this question once. Despite the anti-depressant cocktail Natasha's forced to swallow each morning she manages, 'I'm fine thanks and how are you?' though she's pretty damn far from being fine. She has her usual headache and the kitchen waste disposal system is striving to deal with the failure of Natasha's struggle with conformity, the objectionable wig that had hidden the cranial pins and sutures while the stubble re-grew. She's wearing a headscarf this morning to hide the spikiness. Like a Russian peasant.

'So… what's the symbolism? Grey swirling clouds. Surreal birds with masked faces?'

Natasha smells the linseed oil and turpentine, hears Heather's abstract question hanging in the communal silence, but her mind is far away. *She'd fought like a tigress when she'd eventually regained full consciousness; had been immobilized in hospital for her own safety. A titanium ring had been fixed to her head after the operation, forming a sort of metal halo which removed any pressure on her brain and held the fractures together with the riveted plate. She knew she'd fight again given the chance.*

That question. A mysterious Magritte? But were it to turn its face, the figure might have more in common with Edvard Munch's screaming and tormented soul. Heather would have seen stranger artwork from troubled inmates over time, she thinks.

Natasha continues painting her rear view of the statue in the snowfield, the paint applied boldly and thick. The statue's arm is raised. Maybe it's saluting the Valkyrie. It's somewhere distant in place and time, thought Natasha. A distorted image that was perhaps once another reality in some parallel dimension? A war party, frozen in the moment to man's natural default position. The archetypal warrior, in this case wing-ed. The observer standing, judging. Solitary witness or victim?

'What's that's one carrying - under its wings?' Heather's voice seems distant.

Bombs to smite the ungodly, she replies in her head. And before you ask that's not a fascist symbol there. Not political or anti-Semitic. That was later. It's Sanskrit, Ancient Greek, Amerindian, what you will. A good luck swastika. Unlucky for some, obviously.

Oh give me a grey and gloomy day. A high dismal view over wet Welsh slate where I can hide away from myself; isolated from the world and its unanswerable questions, writing letters to the dead, which Axel says is cathartic, though it's the loneliest occupation plumbing such depths, the dark ravines and oubliettes of my mind.

'Can't think what it all represents.' Heather is smiling sweetly.

The transom window of her room only opens so far and no further – god knows she's tried - over steep roofs and black Victorian chimneys. She's finger-tip searched her cell without success for the suicide watch camera she feels sure will be there. A transom on the adjacent granite has revealed Fran's medieval sleeve, fingers searching for a pigeon feather to add to her collection of angels' wings… else she's channelling Joan of Arc, Mary, Queen of Scots or Hildegard von Bingen, as is her wont.

Those voices, castigating, condemning. Faintly perhaps, among her accusers, there will yet be one she longs for, *'Natasha, I am still here; always…'* But no. No such balm, never so much as a consoling whisper comes to ease her torment. A scratch has appeared on her shin; self-inflicted maybe, very sore. It looks like two ragged capital letters, *'AL'*, and perhaps something else. For a dread moment she imagines another voice breathing in her ear that, *'I am forever with you.'* That goblin in her mind. *Der Kobold im Kopf.* Unsettling. Beyond strange.

Later they'd come again and search her room, find the palette knife she's sharpened on the window sill. They think she may cut her wrists, but it's only to let the blood run free on her arms. So she can feel closer to Emma.

Heather's smile is fixed.

She's come back after her transience: daydreams sometimes re-classified as petites-mal, the episodes of minor epilepsy she'd experienced following 'the event'.

'I'd assumed that interpretation of dreams, this art therapy stuff was the reason for this annexe. You know, oblique examination of the roots of our depersonalisation and disconnection. Fran's religious mania obviously. Psychotic revelations in paint by Axel's performing seals.'

Heather seems flustered. 'Not at all, Anna. It's supposed to be creative, a way for you to express yourself and relax. Taking you out of yourself.' She smiles unconvincingly.

'Out of … *myself?* Natasha, astonished, removes her headscarf. 'What do *you* think lives beneath this patchwork shell? *Anna*, my so-called 'host identity'? Or any one of…how many other…*demons?*' She was groping for words to express herself, self control wavering. Heather tries to calm her, maintaining an even expression, not reacting to the ugliness of the 'cradle cap'. She is unsure whether this is 'theatre', a prelude to a contrived emotional event or the real thing.

12

'No I shouldn't get upset. Here at Her Majesty's pleasure. Better than being banged up in Rampton or somewhere for who knows how long. For a crime I didn't commit.'

'Anna……'

'Perhaps I'm not Anna today. Perhaps I'm one of the others. God forbid I should be Nikolai Sergeyevich. Do you happen to know any of these Germans and Russo-Balts hosting their reunions in my head? Because I don't. I have traumatic amnesia, I'm told.' *She'd been stretchered, broken and comatose from her coil of blood below the villa. An oily signature immortalised on cotton had materialised in her underwear drawer, a Turin Shroud of evidence that matched the silhouette of the weapon found on the terrace.*

'Anna, please stay calm.'

'That woman there with the beatific smile, she poisoned her husband. Confesses it, yet she's at peace with the knowledge, painting saints and angels.'

'Please, Anna. I'll have to call for someone…'

'*She* committed murder,' Natasha stands, close to having a crisis as Heather would report later. 'But I didn't. And my daughter… it was…' The incomplete phrase is a cracked whisper; a papery rustling; like dry dead leaves scuttling on the lid of a tomb.

She hears the controlled desperation in her voice, a playback from someone else's life who's maybe trying to accustom themselves to grief; not as Natasha will be, flagellant, visiting that spectre in denial one bitter bite at a time each night in her room.

If standing coolly outside of self is a public function of MPS then Natasha has it in spades. *Some* of the time. Unless it's no longer *Natasha* that she wakes to, remembering to become Anna before breakfast. Even if in here the witness protection is third class, it's all she has now.

Fran passively continues her angel's wing as if nothing *is* happening nor *ever has* happened since time began, the smile unwavering. Heather buzzes for Security but Natasha has already departed and stands again, tearful in her yesterday.

She'd marked her own *fin de siècle* on the Minoan terrace. Her indelible story would stain that Mediterranean strata, for a thousand years.

Flower meadows sweep to the road where blooms meadowsweet, like asphodel gathered; paler than lilies for the dead. There grows sedge, willow, and ripe wild raspberry. Gentle breezes caress the grass, riffling wildflower on rolling pasture and birch leaf in the woodlands of my distant memory. The scented air is warm, murmurous with hum of insects and a twitter of birds. A small figure comes into view for whom these sensations do not exist. There is only the road, the picture in his mind and denial in his heart.

He is running hard, breath rasping through clenched teeth, throat dry, chest an iron cage of pain in which his heart flutters: a terrified bird. Tear-blind, he looks neither right nor left. The rhythmic slap of his feet and involuntary whimpers of distress are the only sounds of which he is part aware. His legs ache. His side hurts, but he drives on; through the ornate iron gates, pounding down the wide lime-shadowed carriage sweep to sanctuary.

Without pause he hurls himself up the wide steps of the Linden House: the Lamb of God entering the portal of Hell.

~-~

Time passes. Wars and seasons. Hope's new dawning in the heart of man.

The girl has woken to the smell of burning. Something is pinioning her, restricting. It's an effort to get moving. The night around is filled with fire and crackling, a dead weight pressing full upon her. She struggles mightily, remembering fingers closing about her neck: kicks and fights to release their grip.

Flames illuminate the creature lying on its side and smouldering. She can see now that it's breathing and recoils in panic and revulsion, her body racked with sudden retching, vomiting the drugs. She staggers upright, explores with bloody fingers her wounded neck. Her world is spinning. She wanders from the carnage, adrenaline pumping; the ground about her faintly trembling: recalls with wild terror those tasered convulsions at a one-time place of safety.

A gargantuan creak, a groan, like the earth's mantle cracking. Masonry collapses in a shower of sparks. The creature stirs. There are shouts. *More of them!* Throwing off her nausea, she runs from the flames into the enveloping dark; breathlessly down dim pathways. Through the

14

trees, a faint glow. Perhaps it's a road or the lights of civilisation!

She hears the rasping breath of her pursuer, risks a glance over her shoulder and trips headlong, landing with jarring impact on outstretched arms. The pain in her wrist is sharp, but she blocks it, gaining her feet and running hard. The panting now is louder; a growling between the short, hissing breaths. Her glance has confirmed that it's gaining despite that it's definitely on fire. With an involuntary scream she jinks left as a black shape looms out of the darkness, holding what looks like a weapon.

She hears another shout, from her left, '*Azu, kur ji?*'

And a response from near at hand, '*Saugokis! Gauk ji! Shoot!*'

The ground seems to be opening out. Behind she hears a grinding rumble then the close thudding of her pursuer's footfalls. That glimmer ahead – it's a lake, its waters part obscured by pale mists that glow in the darkness! She hesitates, but has nowhere else to go. The creature is upon her as she dashes headlong into the shockingly cold water. Then she's under, swimming for all she's worth; comes up for air to hear a splash behind her, something entering the water. The surface of the lake is luminescent; vibrating and bubbling. She can feel the trembling through the water as she goes into a fast crawl, urged on by the echo of her mother's words, fighting the agony in her arm. Voices are calling along the shore.

'*Danu, ar matote jos?*' Then in English. Her name, 'Emma! It's OK!'

But it's not. Something has grabbed her legs and forced her under, no matter how she struggles. Her lungs are bursting and her head is full of noise. She fights strongly. Then weakly, but her arms have no power. Then fights not at all: surrendering at last to the primitive urge to breathe; to the will - of the Water Goblin.

Part One

She is the dreamer and the dream.

Clothed in mist she sails, o'er lake and forest, following a dark valley in her mind; embraces with shamanic wing the half-familiar landscape of her dreaming soul.

She inhabits its limitless horizons, explores its remoteness; the mysterious topology of her psyche.

In the drift of her imagination she stretches languidly upon the current: spreads her primal feathers on the ancient wind, rests upon the rise and fall of her nocturnal opiate.

Her body, invaded, is flooding with endorphins as with silent cry, she surrenders to Sibelius.

~-~

In wonderment she's drifted, star child voyager of Brückner's interstellar distances, her mind swarming with visions: a grey glacier's gleaming and a thousand quicksilver lakes. So too with Brahms' joyous optimism she'd strode, confident upon the sweep of alpine meadow; caroused with journeymen poets at the *Red Hedgehog*, heard their laughter.

It's not the voices in my head it's the things they say, these German Romantics!

Though music be fortifying wine, her choice falls to a strange vintage; an uneasy repertoire distilled from bitter fruit. One such, served chilled: Shostakovich's portrayal of Ivan's *Dread* successor.

Yet music is escapism, from the mythic thing that stalks her sleepless twilight. It has many names: among them, *Raudongevklis*, one of the multitude of spirit beings that populate her father's narrative setting, from his mysterious, adopted Lithuania.

Surfing, pre-sleep on a wave of sensual release, her demi-reality is realm to things unbidden that surface and tumble in the penumbra of a secret history; cold-blooded, floating stealthily into recollection: the crocodilia of her cryptopsychy entwining the souls of two dead-drowned women who each mourn a child.

~-~

Her father's legacy was a passion for symphonic music. But *this* 'memory', filtering through half-dreaming paralysis, has an insidious vocal coda. Disturbing whispers borne on sibilant hiss. Of carrier wave; tinnitus in her ear, white noise and EVPs. Background mush that should not be audible on her CDs, even if they *are* old von Karajan recordings. *Hush, Princess. Precious petal of my pure white rose. I will return.*

Natasha is awake and moving. Momentarily a child: terror struck. Emma's *Walkman* thudding to the carpet: Karajan's Sibelius, *digitally re-mastered*, killed in soaring flight, wings folded. *Icarus* falling. Horror…..had she responded with unconscious sensuality beneath the sheets, seduced by the secret voice in her suggestible mind? Some pestilent incubus squatting in the dark; a suckling fish on her dormant breast, like a vision of Hieronymus Bosch. What voice had it uttered in mimicry? What defilement fears she to recall? A memory that should be buried in hell, its corpse rotting on the windmills of eternity.

It's the things they say.

I watch her in my memory, that other me: watching coolly now, from another place.

Back then the doors had been double-locked: shreds of memory, fleeting shadows in her room: among them a blind-folded Natasha undergoing her arcane test: feels the metal, cold to her touch - then it's gone.

But a shocking memory of more recency strikes like a physical blow. A spray of red on whitewashed walls, like a Jackson Pollack. The dead dogs. Blood thick upon the kitchen flags. Clarissa in the Land Rover, the engine still running, a fan of blood on the windscreen where the wipers squeaked and shuddered. Smell of burning.

Emma is with friends outside Grimwich. Safe for the present. Natasha reaches for the whirring CD player. *Hush…*With dread she feels her returning paranoia. Another sound had intruded. She listens keenly, heart thudding, pulling her robe tighter.

It had been animal-like; snuffing and snorting from the rear of the old farm house. Natasha moves across the landing. Light streams through the nets. Mill Farm's new photo-electric intruder lamps flood the yard with a million candlepower. A scrabbling sound. Trembling, Natasha pulls the curtain aside: steels herself against the image in her mind.

Raudongevklis? Red Throat or his blood relative?
Only a badger disappearing into the undergrowth.

18

Chapter 1. *Thus Spake my Father*

Upon the landing her heart began to slow. 'Why am I so honoured?' she wondered. Is this staged just for me, events in which I am both observer and participant? An actor in my own production of blurred reality and dreams. If so it features childbirth – that was reality enough, made hideous by forces beyond reason. And my child, with whom I'd failed immediately to bond, she'd suffered too. Betrayal…history repeating itself in a single generation.

Her reflection glowers in the kitchen mirror. 'Who the hell *are* you, Natasha?' She picks up her father's dystopian fantasy; some five hundred pages now printed. *His* Baltic journal; but how much of it was true? She should keep this in a wall safe, if she should keep it at all. 'After all,' she thought, 'What do I owe him when all is considered?'

You come over as a bloody hero in your own legend. But what's the sub text, Daddy?

Yarmouth. A co-incidence that she'd moved to be within comfortable travelling distance of that old port, considering it featured so prominently. To that first page she'd added her own underscored dedication. Appropriately, given her father's obsession, in German:

<u>Also sprach mein Vater</u>

Shorelines, Natasha, are places to think. They seem to bring you to conclusions about life, sometimes even delivering messages to your feet - if you can believe that co-incidence is fate disguised………

Shorelines draw the soul to wander between the restless slumber of the sea and the angst-ridden consciousness of the land. The changeling light and patterns on sun-bright water dazzle and obscure, but their open horizons can clear the mind of clutter; beckon it forth. Thomas Mann had his fisherman's hut on the Curonian Spit. Dylan Thomas his boathouse on the Laugharne estuary: Mahler his lodge on a Tyrolean lake. For my sins the view here is an ocean of blowing grassland.

At Great Yarmouth, our hero *Rolf*, whose life is the fragile filament that binds these stories, had walked the strand, clutching his head that bore too great a burden for his skull. A creature of torment: Munch's *Scream* personified. Or perhaps that troubled figure at Rügen: Caspar

David Friedrich's *Monk by the Sea*? A cipher, a symbol of anguish. Solitary: a romantic.

My father had included a little watercolour sketch based on Friedrich's original, inscribed, 'Der Mönch am Meer'. The image evidently held some special significance for him.

Like a beachcomber monk Rolf had scavenged and searched his damaged memory for the truth - determined to confront or release his silent tormentor, that goblin crouched behind the locked door in his mind; the unknown thing that had haunted his Norfolk exile, that seemed tantalisingly closer following the interviews at Whitehall Court.

Some things had come to him coincidentally, unbidden. The old captain who stared seaward had answered some of it; triggered by that other thing, the 'horn-headed flotsam' drifting in darkness upon the Yarmouth tide.

~-~

In his Baltic retreat her father had tapped his cryptic story.

I have a bird's eye view from my tower, Natasha. As if I've climbed a mountain and in some ways I have, seeking among high places for a truth that is within. Elevation distances the writer from his subject, provides a loftier view of the struggle; excludes him from the society of men and the common fray - more keenly to observe. A pilot's view in truth. When I fly over this same tower now restored, I see how it must have looked before the Revolution. I imagine seeing through a patriot's eyes, how it must have been, fire-blackened and besieged when he'd returned here near ninety years ago. In this place now I could not be more in the midst of things, separated only in

20

time.

Is it only coincidence that twenty years later, the same courageous agent, Natasha, secretly flew this very aeroplane across the North Sea to the Norfolk coast? That was sixty-eight years ago.

But to make sense of the 'here and now', I fly westward in my mind from the Yare estuary: fast forward by the calendar: 1943. War, and another shore.

Ginst Point, the eastern end of Pendine Sands, South Wales. In the 'twenties Campbell, Segrave, Parry-Thomas… all made their successive land speed records on the seven-mile stretch. Here a gruesome find was made by a cockle-picker loading her cart at ebb tide. Was that a discarded sack of shellfish jammed among the rocks? Or the body of a man, washed ashore: pummelled, wrapped in seaweed, black with estuarine mud and part-decomposed. Two days on and further north, two others had rolled in on the flood at Cardigan Bay. All three appeared to have been in the sea for the same length of time.

The police investigation found no identification in what remained of their rough working clothes. Similarities were their Slavic caste of feature, numbers tattooed on the left forearms and a 7.62 mm round lodged at the base of each shaven skull.

Neither Navy nor Coastguard could shed light on the discoveries. Nor was any connection made to a recent sinking of a target identified as a Type XIV U-Boat by depth charges from a patrolling Liberator of RAF Coastal Command.

The bodies were interred as 'unknowns'. Verdict: victims of murder. Jetsam of war.

~-~

For much of my information, Natasha, I am grateful to Herr Hans-Peter Neumann, deceased: late of Luftwaffe Intelligence, a gentleman whom I came to know quite well, though our meetings had been sporadic over twenty years. With his dwindling contacts among Kriegsmarine, Abwehr and SS Intelligence sources, some creaking Bismarckian *Ancien Régime V-Manner* - and a one-eyed *Freikorps* survivor he'd tracked down in Switzerland with a mistress half his age, he'd begun to piece this tale together. He knew that when in doubt you should always follow the money.

And of course there was old Harry. A true hero in every way. He provided the sort of detail you couldn't begin to imagine. And vitally, held the key to it all.

~-~

Friend Hans-Peter spent more time and effort than would have been sensible, beginning with an attempt to identify an obscure civilian aeroplane that had been hidden on a Norfolk estate. Of pre-WW2 German origin, it had been discovered in the '60s by an Englishman, an aviation enthusiast - perhaps a little eccentric by 'conventional standards', who'd contacted *Peter* (as I knew him) for assistance. But by the time I met him, Natasha, he had the bit between his teeth; had slipped again into the harness of his old intelligence officer self, hot on the trail of something deeper and intriguing.

It fell to me to regroup and add a writer's gloss - judge that how you will - to his valiant fieldwork. I may say that I found it disturbing to the extent that I felt it necessary to take certain precautions. But I acknowledge my debt and he'd already collated most of what I have since transferred to compact disk, including events prior to and following the '14-18 War. After which nothing would be the same.

~-~

Peter's success arose from his readiness to turn over stones, to dine out with unreconstructed one-time *aides de camp* to the mighty: colleagues and old enemies who'd worked under Dept VI *Sicherheitsdienst Einsatzkommando*. Killers. Men to make you shudder, like Steimle and Rapp, based at Berkärstrasse 32 and fellow *Wilhelmstrasse Ministerien*; among them such dark ministries as 8 Prinz Albrecht Strasse with a torture chamber in its basement. The information that three mysterious corpses had been among ten *Ostfront* Russian or Polish ex-coalminers, un-named prisoners of the SS, eventuated through confabulation. Below the parapets of the New Germany. Sneer in place and monocle screwed tight, his enquiries had stretched across the South Atlantic to the terminals of the *Odessa* ratlines, Otto Skorzeny's *Organization der ehamaligen SS-Angehörigen:* Nazi escape system, to the Argentine, with rumours that involved Reichsleiter Bormann and the ELA; the second-generation *Eiserne Legion Ausland.*

Among his contacts, a more conventional veteran was an ex-Luftwaffe air-sea rescue seaplane pilot, name of Kühling. His crew had recovered bodies from a sunken U-Boat in the Bay of Biscay - survivors there were none. *But it was not from the deck of that submarine that the executed men had been dumped, Natasha.*

Following orders, an SS contingent serving aboard a conventional Type VII U-Boat had disposed of the bodies *two weeks previously.* SS-style undoubtedly, all lined-up on the U-Boat deck. Without ceremony. Bullet in the brain stem. That boat had sailed from the submarine pens at Kiel harbour and had obediently returned to Kiel.

The *sunken* boat had been a *Milchkuh,* a submarine tanker designed for refuelling *das Rudel,* the *Wolf Pack*: Admiral Dönitz's U-Boat fleet while it remained at sea. *At this period of the War, Natasha, the German submarine blockade was still a serious threat to our survival.* But on that voyage that specialised Type XIV had not been carrying fuel oil.

She'd been sailing for La Rochelle – a diversion port, when she had been detected. Her captain had responded to a radio signal encrypted by a six-rotor *Enigma* machine, which message had been intercepted and decoded through ULTRA at Bletchley Park's Government Code and Cipher School - the British code-breaking centre. The signal intercept had been a warning to the 'tanker' U-Boat captain, that the entire Type VII's crew had been arrested by the Gestapo upon their return to Kiel. The arrests were on the orders of Reichsführer Heinrich Himmler, chief of the state security apparatus, head of the SS.

Commander in Chief of the *Kriegsmarine* Admiral Karl Dönitz had been outraged at the arrests and had protested to Hitler, but in a 'matter of state security' he'd been over-ruled. The Führer, reeling from the terrible losses of Stalingrad had brushed away his favourite admiral and left the matter with Himmler himself to resolve. Cogent reasons demanded that the U-boat crew be held for questioning; security matters over 'naval signals' and possible fraternisation with the enemy in the Scillies. So Hitler swept aside the protest, certain that his faithful *Heini* would get to the bottom of it.

La Rochelle would have provided no immunity from arrest by the SS, but short of heading for neutral territory, it would have put a little distance between Germany and Himmler's unquestioning security apparatus, acting to protect the Reichsführer's cabal: perhaps offering an opportunity to go to ground, or else seek some sort of hapless negotiating position. Given what they knew, it was obvious that they were now liable to elimination. After Kiel, even the small SS task force among the *Milch Cow* crew would have realised that they were not exempt.

Fatefully and possibly due to that message intercept by British Intelligence, none of them made it in any case. Corpses of some German submariners had been recovered WSW of Belle-Ile at 47N, according to Leutnant Kühling's surviving Heinkel 115 logbook.

But Peter himself would not see the fruits of his extended investigation.

~-~

She glanced again through the first pages. She'd started her own journal since, as a way of making further sense of it and to leave some sort of record if …well she didn't want to speculate on that. Perhaps she should have been more cooperative with the police. But if this was some massive conspiracy...? And the twins. She couldn't believe they were in any way responsible for murder. In fact the police didn't seem to know of their existence.

She picked up another file to reprise what she'd most recently written. It began with the police interview in Ipswich.

Chapter 2. *Interview and Introspection*

There was an unpleasant smell of stale cigarettes, I recalled. Someone smoking in here despite the ban? Maybe it just hung about one of the two police officers sitting opposite; the sour-looking DI from his fingers.

'Friday, February fifteenth, 2008. Interview Room 3, Ipswich Police Station. Present are DI Slater. WPC Hamilton. Mrs. Natasha Stuart-Hedges. For the purposes of the tape Mrs. Stuart-Hedges has not requested a solicitor at this time. Interview begun at 0945 hrs.'

What did he mean 'at this time'? Am I to be re-interviewed as a suspect?

'Tell me from the beginning, Mrs. Stuart-Hedges. Or do you go by the name of Morris?'

Slater had a disconcerting way of not quite meeting my gaze, seeming to focus on a point above my right shoulder. A 'turn' in his eye perhaps.

'I prefer Natasha Morris.' *Ms* Morris will do if you wish to be formal, I thought.

I no longer remember the beginning.

At the worst I did not then think that I was suffering from paranoia, nor experiencing the evil flowering of late-onset schizophrenia. I had after all refrained from illicit substances at university - perhaps the only edict of my father's which had survived unabrogated through my tempestuous years. *So what was it that I had carried with me like a virus when I'd flown home with him by my side?*

'Can you be specific – about the 'beginning'. Beginning of what?'

'Beginning with what led you to settle in the village of Grimwich. Almost into Fenland.'

I flushed a little. Slater's off-centre focus hadn't flickered but his slight smirk had irritated me. I hadn't recalled having heard the banjo theme from *Deliverance* whenever I'd crossed the border. And said as much.

He looked blankly at my shoulder. Damn, I thought, that was provocative and immature. I'd taken issue with his comment as an implied prejudice against Fenlanders, crude gossip about in-breeding: web-footed Morlocks. Not that I'd felt the need to defend incestuous practices: he'd just chosen the prickly part of the Lunar cycle to question me.

He seemed unruffled.

'Are you aware of or do you know anyone locally with a congenital malformation of the hand?'

I blinked, still thinking of Fenlanders: Clarissa's joking admonition that it was *verboten* to offer strong liquor to the natives hereabouts - and wondering what he was driving at.

'What specific malformation?'

'Ulnar hexadactyly,' he said, referring to a typed sheet. 'An additional finger, situated beyond the little finger. Normally tied-off at birth.'

Gimme a 'high six', I thought, shaking my head.

'Still,' he said, folding the sheet with slow deliberation. 'Bit of a rural backwater, Grimwich, for a young woman from leafy *Surbiton*. Wouldn't you say?'

An open question. In other circumstances I might have been flattered by the tag 'young'. But I couldn't imagine 'other circumstances' with someone who had the knack of irritating the hell out of me. His manner had suggested that I must know much more about the case than I seemed prepared to reveal. Despite the boredom of routine that permeated, stab vests, all the quasi-military paraphernalia worn on station duty by the worker bees, implied a threat of siege within the hive. A few years previously such a view of an English police station would have been unthinkable but chimed now with my impression of a broken society. *No, not 'broken', Chrissie had said passionately. Divided, that's all. Poor Chrissie.*

Somebody once said that if we sentimentalise the past we are failing to see it correctly. But in achieving the wisdom of years we may directly compare what was then with the now, each generation shaking its collective head at the indulgences, the inversions of values and common sense in favour of judicial cowardice, now more than ever, under the onslaught of political correctness and moral collapse. It seemed most evident in the young, without the old restraints: the withering of good manners and public decency. God, I thought. I'm thinking like my father.

The female officer sat in cool appraisal, at ease in her perfect make up. She could have been anywhere between 'work experience' and thirty, blonde hair scraped back in a 'Croydon facelift', *roots dyed dark* perhaps? *Some ironic statement* I thought, waspishly. But she radiated a confident air of knowing more than either was prepared to reveal. Which was nothing. Standard Operational Procedure I was sure. I wondered if this was a sort of 'annoying cop, bimbo cop' routine. I wasn't under arrest so I hadn't been swabbed but was fairly certain the station teacup would be whisked away for a DNA match from Grimstone House – not that I'd for a moment denied having been there recently. Undoubtedly they'd obtained samples from the Land Rover too. How long before we have a DNA database for the entire population; and biometric ID cards? Or be 'chipped' at birth, as Clarissa had prophesised?

'Marital break up would be the short answer.'

My ex-husband's habit had made up for both of us. It had been one of the several things that had placed me in my present situation. Perhaps that was the 'beginning'.

'And it was Godalming.'

'Ah.' DI Slater looked at the folder again. A contrived lapse to lull interviewees into lowering their guards. More SOP.

'Nice is it, Godalming?' His mouth twitched again.

To my shame I realised that his occasional smirk was a facial tick, exaggerated by a lachrymose expression, the sallow lacunae of his cheeks. Like his strabismus, it might be another weapon of distraction. I wanted to laugh at how surreal it seemed, but his armoury of combined afflictions could make him a dangerous interrogator.

'Nice enough. With the income,' I said coolly. HM Revenue and Customs don't take prisoners, I considered.

I cannot rid myself of the sense that everything, I mean recent events, seem strangely connected. Occurrences, which at one time I might have brushed off as mere coincidence, seem rather to be pointers: signposts along the way to a greater truth. Or they mark the falling dominoes of Fate. I am willing to believe that there are 'more things in heaven and earth, Horatio,' than might be dreamed in my own philosophy. But I had not been ready just those few months since to take a first step into the occult: embark upon a journey from which I might not return without a struggle - and who knew what risk to my sanity.

'So how did you come to know the Blundell sisters?'

'They were my neighbours,' I said. 'It was almost inevitable that I should meet them in due course.'

'How long had you known them?'

'About three months. I'd been resident at Mill Farm for about six weeks before I got to know them at all.'

'And your relationship with them?' He'd transferred his attention to another file. I took it he was fingering the SOCO's report. The questioning seemed deliberately monotonous, mesmeric perhaps, designed to lead the unwary down pathways to eventual ambushes: else he was bored and on auto pilot, wishing he had a cigarette.

I reflected on my state of mind when I'd sought them out. After the discovery of my father's diaries and the subjects of his particular researches. I'd felt then rather as he must have done: 'an old prospector-journalist', paraphrasing his own cryptic journal. *'….standing at a bend in Time's River, who's glimpsed at last the gleam of a 'golden tail' within the pan.'*

My cosmos was in disarray and I'd been uncertain then and anxious. Perhaps suggestible. I sensed that I might find council with them. Maybe I'd trusted my instincts too much in a one-time flight from reason. Emotions, along with the imagination, may run riot at difficult times. Time of loss. I remembered vaguely thinking that I'd intended to ask Clarissa what she'd thought was happening at sub-molecular level: that is if she weren't part of the plot. What was it she'd said? *The closer we get the more distant everything appears.'* She'd been talking about the world viewed through an electron microscope. *Poor Clarissa.*

We are told that parallel lines never meet. Therefore as with much in life, things are not always as they seem. So perspective is a lie: or rather a construct of the mind that enables us to make sense of a three-dimensional world. *Ergo* a philosophy. Most of our information comes to us through our eyes. The Bayeux 'Tapestry' tells an embroidered historical truth without recourse to such artifice. But what of parallel *lives?*

'They were neighbours. They were friendly, though not friends of long standing. I was new in the locality.' I supposed I'd craved companionship. That my life had gone to ratshit. But I wasn't about to admit that. I was guarded.

Nature, I mused, is governed by chance and probability. Our lives are hostage to uncertainty. Part of my mind wanders from the interview room. I am wondering if the 'heavenly twins' had been ciphers. Their appearance seemed so …convenient. But Tania's uncontrollable shaking in the passenger seat of the Volvo had been real. I'd wondered uncharitably then why they hadn't become high class hookers like other beauties of Eastern European persuasion. Instead they'd been underpaid drudges fallen on hard times and thankful for a soft landing at Grimstone House, whose jagged silhouette floats unbidden in my mind, a sash of chequered police tape denying entry to the natives.

But that's to judge people by my own cynicism - with a narrow, bitter irony that I could not then have guessed at. They are unimaginably identical and of such symmetrical beauty that I wonder if they are true mirror images, whether one or other's internal organs are reversed. I remembered thinking I should check to see if one was left-handed: a sinister sister on a Möbius strip.

Though the forensic team would have pored over the burned-out caravan with their UV lamps, searching out fluorescing flavins, I was sure their names had not appeared anywhere in connection with the Scene of Crime Officer's report.

Yet, I think then the *Grimwich Coven* seemed benevolent. My dilemma resides in my own worldview, of things you can touch and feel, and a half-remembered grappling with Lenin's *Materialism and Empirio-Criticism* which I was urged to read as an impressionable student; a work that hotly defended dialectical materialism, tearing away the theatrical veil draping the 'hovering sphere'. Mysticism, Metaphysics and Marxism. Are *we* the ghosts in another dimensional reality? *Discuss!*

Faintly I hear again the words of my lecturer in modern history.

'The theoretical geometry of a non-temporal fourth dimension which physicists and philosophers had increasingly debated before the turn of the twentieth century, became, to Lenin's fury, a philosophy usurped piecemeal by the 'heretical cult' of the *Otzovists*, the 'God-builders'. That Bolshevist faction had, following the crushing of the 1905 revolution, colluded in fostering peasant superstition, weaving it seamlessly into the cultural background, postponing social revolution 'til the auguries should proclaim it propitious.'

I'd hurriedly scribbled my notes: a serious student......

'Lenin, the revolutionary, exiled in Geneva, was enraged that the proposition of a fourth dimension might encourage a belief in spirits, ghosts and the afterlife; anxious lest it bolster religion, become part of a theosophical reaction against the juggernaut of material sciences then busily de-mystifying the spiritual ideas of the universe. Upon such dialectics he'd hitched the coattails of a modernizing cometary zeal, dragging the people towards the liberating ideal of a socialist, secular state. To paraphrase the author: *while mathematicians hypothesized the existence of four dimensions, the Tsar would only be overthrown in three.*'

New discoveries then seemed to bear out such polemics. Radium itself demonstrated that matter was not immutable and energy was its other form. It marginalized those seers, charlatans, mediums and illusionists; their smoke and mirrors, which, with their spirit confidantes, existed quite apart from we lesser mortals, comfortable in our Newtonian universes.

For a while, after the hideous appetites of two world wars, instead of within the hushed darkness of theatre halls, apparitions, apports and table turnings were confined in private: behind closed-curtained drawing rooms on wet Saturday afternoons. Have we again, I wondered, in our failure to keep faith, in our Western godlessness, retreated into New Age superstitions for the Twenty-First Century? Embracing *Feng Chui*, reading our horoscopes.

For myself, a little voice of reason had always held me back if invited to indulge in necromantics by some freaky flat mate, or whoever was goth-tripping on the occult. I was aided in this by the comic thought of a black-caftaned Margaret Rutherford swooping to the rescue with her crystal ball. None of this could be of the slightest interest to the police in the investigation of suspicious death.

But just those few short weeks ago....whether it was cosmic disorder or loneliness, I felt an attraction, a need to confide that magnetically drew me back to the 'fallen angels' and to the residents of *Brimstone* House as I secretly named Grimstone and its little cell of necromancy. There *was* an energy there and a superficial, uncomplicated openness.

They make jam and welcome me within. Clarissa, ex-GCHQ mole as she described herself: an early retiree, redundant due to strides in computer science with her fine mind is foil to Chrissie, fey earth mother versed in Wicca: unwitting follower of Aleister Crowley. A coincidence that she should now be my neighbour. I remembered her as a role model in my youth with her Blackfoot dream catcher, shaking her tambourine, and singing round the campfires at the Greenham Peace Camp. She's in remission: to be fair she's not sure it's the herbs, but the Weed does dull the pain. Each contributes to the dynamic. They are two pillars of as unlikely a quartet viewed from the outside ..... closer to the inhabitants of some freethinking quasi convent or sect than of a Cold Comfort Farm. But nothing matched them up close, in the animal warmth and unstructured comfort of their home.

A coincidence indeed that I should have bought the freehold of rundown, leaky Mill Farm, complete with its own smallholding, just next door by rural measurement, and had possibly been among the last to see them alive? Traditionally that now placed me under suspicion. A different approach might have been to 'get on side' with me: the sympathetic, faux social worker approach combined with cynicism. *Look, we appreciate how much pressure you must've been under, etc. People snap, right? So just cough for it, darling!* But no. Slater played the slightly bored suburban plod, perhaps hoping I'd dig my own elephant trap. At no time did he lose his rag and spit out that *this was a murder enquiry and I'd better damn well take it seriously.* But for sure they were struggling for a motive and doubtless leafing through my past. I hoped they'd find it intriguing. Perhaps they'd even fill in a few of the blank pages for me.

There were signs of a struggle, I am gravely informed. I already know this of course. But we need to go back to the beginning as I saw it.

~.~

Natasha's Story

When I was a little girl I had a glass paperweight, a present from my father. Inside the globe upon a snow-white field was a painted wooden church with a green roof. The globe was water-filled and had little white particles that flew around like snowflakes when it was shaken. It looked so pretty. My father told me it was Russian. When he and my mother fought I used to shake it and hold it up against the pale light from my bedroom window, my eye close to the glass, watching the little church stand brave against the blizzard. I imagined myself warm and safe inside that wooden church where everything was calm. I told myself that if they stopped arguing before three snowstorms settled, everything would be alright.

~.~

The word *stroke* evokes terror and compassion in equal measure. In my father's case, it resulted in dyspraxia, the inability to speak and perhaps to understand language. In a writer, this was possibly the cruellest blow.

I had received the letter dated from the previous week, forwarded from my old Surrey address, written in correct English and signed by the hospital manager in Vilnius. He had received prompt treatment following his CAT scan after the housekeeper's discovery, but still he had quite possibly lain a whole night and half of the following day before he was discovered. By then the ischemic brain injury was profound with obvious implications for long-term recovery. I'd flown Lithuanian Airlines to the capital to accompany him home from his Baltic retreat and for the time being he was lodged at the Cedars Nursing Home, near Westerfield, on the outskirts of Ipswich along with some of his effects, the remainder of which was to be shipped.

It had been a hectic time for me: marriage in tatters. Emma making it even more difficult, sulking in her room, texting her friends, planning her escape and resisting the inevitable house move on all fronts. Simeon had defaulted in every imaginable way, not just with the affairs and drinking. That fantasist, Piers, with whom he'd shared a cocaine habit and at least one mistress in a simultaneous menàge I suspect, had helped compile his investment portfolio somewhere along their mutual path to destruction. Now in absentia not even the massed ranks of the CSA could ensure that maintenance would be provided. It should have been obvious that he'd been suffering some sort of a breakdown and we'd even discussed his leaving the firm for something less stressful than the City.

So I bade farewell to our beloved *Cottage-in-the-Woods*, Godalming, to find a state school for Emma at the critical time for her GCSEs, an NHS dentist for adjusting her brace - and she was being absolutely bloody. I'd decided to abandon Surrey, make a clean break and return to my Norfolk roots, though I'd eventually settled for Suffolk, where my house-hunting had turned up a sorry looking detached property with some land that I could afford: a smallholding outside the Hamlet of Grimwich close to the Norfolk border, between Great Livermere and Thetford. It was grandiosely titled Mill Farm, but possessed no mill that I could find, though it was certainly secluded enough to give me breathing space, which was part of the plan. Time to think.

Probably I was as crap at choosing houses as partners. I told myself it might scrub-up to 'shabby chic', but at least it was somewhere to regroup, to settle my affairs and consider renewing some long abandoned legal training. Last I'd heard Simeon was in Crete with Piers and an Old English sheepdog, sharing a fishing boat and God knew what else. Probably snorting the white butterfly of happiness through a rolled 100-drachma note. No it's *Euros* of course. Whatever, good riddance and damn them both.

At worst, if I came out with enough money to rub along, maybe I could sell some watercolours and become a character in the local community; take up campanology: grow a beard and embrace the real ale culture; break away from my unconscious obsessive doodling on shopping list or note pad: a half-face that disturbingly peered from behind the curve of the moon. I must be *really* messed up, I thought. But at least Emma would have somewhere to keep her bloody pony. And now Dad….. I mean, bloody hell, talk about multi-tasking.

In fact the telephone had yet to be connected which meant no Internet for Emma and her course work was suffering, *she said*, but it was a blessing that she wasn't spending hours being 'groomed' in teenage 'chat rooms' and anyway why couldn't she make new friends, real friends not cyber ones?

So it was my mobile that had rung with the news that he'd died.

Why had I set off so fast for the Cedars? Dead is dead. That was a fact. Killing myself by speeding through tall-hedged country lanes in the Volvo that I hadn't then sold for something more practical was the reaction of a distracted woman of forty-four summers - not that suicide would ever have occurred to me as an option; except in circumstances of unbearable agony of body and mind - and I'd already known that once….. So I let up on the accelerator; which was just as well.

The next bend revealed a hay cart and the brakes barely saved us. A solemn yeoman stare; me flushing redder than his mutton-chopped cheeks; a contrite wave as I looked straight ahead smiling tightly while the tractor squeezed past with its load, Volvo pressed against the hedge. There was already a small dent in the driver's door that would need pulling out, if or when I tried to sell it. That and a deep knife blade scratch down its length.

I drove more slowly from there, reflecting on the recent turn of events. Until his sudden incapacitation I hadn't seen my father in a long time. My parents had split more than ten years before. John, my father, had been a journalist and aviation writer, consultant on technical matters, and a moderately high flyer in his field. My mother, Karen, was uncertain of her role. Dad was frequently away and when he was around seemed obsessively busy, although he always had time for me, an only child. I had adored him but we seemed to spark off each other increasingly. Especially when I reached puberty. I found myself regretting some of the things I'd done in adolescence having discovered with Emma how difficult it can be dealing with a teenager. My student days saw me running with the most vociferous of the vituperative Left, but always I looked to my father for his approval, even when I knowingly set my face against his own moral and political leanings, which I considered were to the *Right of Attila the Hun*, a common phrase then. He felt I took our country for granted. I felt he was part of the old regime. Part of the 'problem'.

We'd lost touch and I suppose I'd sided with my mother in the divorce, although I could see that he'd somehow outgrown her. To me she'd seemed 'all at sea', adrift in her Valium swell while my father tugged against her pull: a ship, dragging a sea anchor. I recalled an unexpected and rather strange letter from him a few years before where he'd described his wind-blown Baltic *Schloss*. I never knew whether it was some sort of hotel or sanatorium, but assumed he was a paying guest. He seemed to have had the run of the place and now that I understand more

I realise he had decided to make it his home, though just how he'd made enough money to afford the lifestyle was a mystery to me then. I did know that with the collapse of Communism you could pick up a derelict, graffiti-daubed country mansion for a song in those countries. If you could sort the dry rot, the urine-saturated stucco, find reliable labour to put it right, handle the bureaucracy… well, it might be possible to return one to its former state.

I'd remembered being so angry when I'd received his letter: full of condemnation for my flirtation with Marxism in my long ago student days, as if *he* were re-living the period. He'd just disappeared for years and as far as I knew he had no idea how ill Mum was and what a strain that had put on my own marriage. I'd been ill too with what had been diagnosed as 'mild' OCD, Obsessive Compulsive Disorder. I'd suffered with some sort of hyper-agitation from time to time, as far as I could recall, since giving birth and all that had entailed. It manifested itself by my being obsessively protective of Emma after my recovery from the mental chaos then enveloping me. Now of course she was rebelling, much as I had done.

Mill Farm was relatively remote. You could see quite long distances across the flat fields of plough in winter, the leafless trees with their old rookeries and open farmland to a wooded horizon. Despite the sense of peace here and the quietness I loved, I'd found myself double and triple-checking that doors and windows were locked. Even if I was just working in Blaze's paddock in broad daylight, as a break from being indoors, though I'd told myself recently that I had good reason for such caution.

I'd written to my father in Lithuania following my mother's death in Godalming but had received no reply at that time. And he hadn't turned up for her funeral.

~-~

From Vilnius I headed north on the A14 to Utena where I turned northeast into the National Park, driving amongst its lovely lakes towards the Belarus and Latvian borders: a minor road that climbed gently among low, wooded hills. It was as he'd described in that letter, although so much more beautiful than I'd actually imagined.

'A portal'd doorway offers into an expansive reception hall…vaulted ceilings, flanked by twin sweeping staircases leading to spacious sitting rooms and the many bedrooms.'

I found myself recalling it in my mind, like a description from an estate agent's brochure, which was how he'd written it. You never knew

34

with him: his prose, aside from his technical writing, whether his descriptions or diatribes were intended to be ironic, tongue-in-cheek or just matter-of-fact. I still don't know whether this was a weakness or its strength.

'Comfortable reception rooms and a spacious dining hall downstairs…barrel-vaulted corridors convey the visitor to drawing rooms, library, study, gun and tackle rooms…. so to the kitchen, servants' quarters, parlour, laundry, cold stores with a view of the inner courtyard. Screening this is a lilac-scented walled garden and a wide patio upon which the music room (in which a Steinway Grand is re-installed) and conservatory open, revealing stone eagle-studded steps that fall to delightful tree-shaded pathways with formal gardens beyond.'

How unlike your last tawdry resting place, I fear. I really am sorry, Daddy. If you'd waited 'til the house was ready…..

'All around are swathes of blowing grassland, rivers, trees, lakes and towering cloudscapes to delight the eye from any one of four score of windows. I wonder how much of it is still irradiated. There is a portico of stags' antlers and other hunting trophies that range through the corridors. Lord knows where they all came from as I am informed that they weren't here in Kosygin's time. Nor Podgorny's, nor Brezhnev's, when it was a local KGB headquarters.'

So his letter had run.

~-~

It was a lovely day in early autumn that I'd brought the hired Audi to a stop before the iron gates of the *Linden House*. I'd identified myself to a microphone grill and the gates swung silently open. The sweep of the drive, the tall lime trees moving in the wind, the sunlight-dappled lawns extending hundreds of yards on either side and the glimpse of the fine house beyond took my breath away. I moved off gradually; the grandeur of the mansion, its glittering windows reflecting the cloud-studded sky unfolded from the foliage as I drew nearer. The house seemed to exist in its own bubble of time, like my little Russian church in its secure glass dome, as far removed as was possible from the brutalist post-war Soviet blockhouse architecture that seemed to infect European Russia and its satellites.

I parked next to some other cars, a couple of sleek Mercedes and a Porsche, on the paved area to one side of the flight of wide steps.

One of the black painted doors framed the steward who had been waiting for me. He was dressed in a green-gold liveried jacket with white lace at his throat, wearing red breeches with leather gaiters. Very

Nineteenth Century. I knew that Czechoslovakia had revived the *Ruritanian* image for tourism but hadn't realised such kitsch had spread quite so far north.

I was ushered inside to meet a blonde-bearded secretary of some kind with a tanned, open face. Broad-shouldered with a seaman's gait, he introduced himself as Julius Jankaitis. Jankaitis had expressed his deep sympathy in heavily accented English at my father's sudden illness and offered his most sincere good wishes from all the staff for his speedy recovery. He explained that the House was actually run as a trust and my father had been an executor of a fund: a position of some importance, which would now need to be filled with a vote of the trustees.

The purpose of my visit was to exercise power of attorney as his next of kin, to collect some of my father's effects, including his passport, any cheque books, personal letters and other precious items, photographs or monies that might be in his desk and in his chambers, and to investigate what investment portfolios, deeds, will or covenants that he might have made that might be lodged in a safe or local bank vault: in a word anything that should be properly looked after and not left to chance. I assumed he had a lawyer who represented his interests here in Lithuania but had no clue how the system worked. Nevertheless I felt that the quicker I could take stock the less likely it would be that things would go astray. Jankaitis provided me with the appropriate legal details, with the address of a law firm in Vilnius and was happy to let me go through my father's possessions, giving me a key to the desk in the tower room and the combination of his personal safe which Jankaitis had unearthed.

Ancient maps of Lithuania, Estonia, Latvia and Belarus hung along the oak panelling. Upon the desk stood a particularly striking bronze sculpture of a vigorous stallion with flying mane that I recall as the most compelling focus of the room. I felt the strong associations for the open landscape of the Baltic, with the wind and the freedom of movement that the running horse symbolised.

How long I'd stood there I didn't know, but from the doorway Jankaitis caught my eye - I'd forgotten he was there - smiling wryly, almost as if he'd read my thoughts.

He said, 'In Russia the horse, in art, is symbolic of apocalypse: of war and tyranny. Perhaps from race memory of Genghis Khan.'

'I read somewhere that Stalin had kept something similar on his desk.'

He smiled disarmingly. 'In Lithuania we just love our horses.'

The windows were closed and I detected the slight stale smell of combustion. Gravitating to the leaded windows I discreetly glanced at an empty metal waste basket behind the desk, noticing a slight discolouration of the paint. I wondered vaguely about that as I stared at the gently blowing trees; the patterns of sunlight on the mown autumn grass. For a full minute my eyes drank in the beauty of the distant woodland, the rising hills with the skyscape of sun-splashed cloud; underbellies of soft blue-grey in drifting formations diminishing in hue to the horizon. Such a sense of space. An ancient landscape of breadth and untold history. Somewhere you felt you could breathe at last. My father had spent a lot of time here, I thought. How he must have loved it.

Distantly, in the corner of my eye, something bright moved on the wind. I turned to look across the fields. Among the moving shadows between the trees, a fluorescent windsock. So there was an airstrip here. Given he was a keen flyer in his younger years, he would have loved that too. But it did not occur to me to investigate further in that direction.

In the bedroom I felt his presence very strongly. I selected several shirts, sweaters and casual clothes to take with me, socks, underwear and a soft pair of shoes of my father's. Two small wooden wall plaques, bird paintings, took my eye. These I packed along with various files and other effects thinking they would be a comfort to him, while Jankaitis lent a hand. I arranged with him for the rest, including at the last moment his guitar in its battered case that at first I'd thought to abandon, to be forwarded. Perhaps the goal of re-learning the instrument in time would be an aid to his hoped-for recovery, however unrealistic that might prove. Jankaitis seemed eager to accommodate even given the circumstances. In retrospect I formed the opinion that anything sensitive to the operation of the Trust among my father's papers would have been scrutinized and removed.

Jankaitis gave me the tour. House and grounds, everything lovingly restored, he told me, to match its pre-Revolutionary splendour. Atop the staircase I remember the most distinguishing feature; huge and dark and ornately framed; a medieval oil painting of a knight on a white charger slaying, by light of a full moon, a crowned black double-headed eagle with a sword: a symbol of Lithuanian independence. Carried upon his shield, the *Vytis* double-cross of Orthodoxy.

It reminded me of a giant Tarot card. Something from the 'Suit of

Swords' from what I'd read somewhere, and on the stair I'd felt suddenly cold, shivered as if 'someone had just walked over my grave' as the expression goes, regretting having left my wrap in the car.

In the sunshine it was surprisingly warm despite a strengthening breeze from the west. I remarked on the wind and the way the grasses rippled 'almost like flowing hair'.

Jankaitis gave me a keen look and told me that my father had made the same comment. He said that in Lithuanian mythology such ripples were caused by the *Lauku Dvasios*, spirits who run through the crops and the fields. When the wind blew, people in ancient time identified this as their passage. Lithuania, he said, had been the last great pagan stronghold of Europe, that there was still a deep down belief among older folk that we are always in the company of the *Véles* - the spirits of the dead. Among the myths of this mysterious land he said was a powerful spirit called *Véjas*, who stirred up a mighty wind that blew the wicked into oblivion.

He mentioned another name: *Raudongalvis*, a free spirit with long red hair, an association I was later to remember.

We took our leave on the steps. 'Look!' he said, pointing to the sky. 'The storks, they are coming home.'

I watched as two black and white storks floated over the roofs and settled onto a huge untidy nest on one of the chimneys.

'Had they been away?' I asked rather stupidly.

The storks flexed their necks with improbable sinuosity, clapping their bills in a courtship display.

'In a manner of speaking. Birds with light plumage that lay relatively large eggs suffer most from caesium 137. From Chernobyl, about 250 kilometres to south east. They are coming back again. Maybe they are immune now, who knows? I hope. They are lucky birds,' he smiled, flashing a gold incisor.

A strange philosophical blend of scientific analysis and superstition. Did that begin to explain the Lithuanian character, I wondered. Or was Jankaitis teasing me with his Viking humour?

I loaded the boot with suitcases and piled boxes of files and briefcases on the back seat, including one that looked part-cremated. Most of this I'd intended to ship from Vilnius via their freight depot to simplify travelling; anything remaining at the house Jankaitis would send. Preoccupied, or perhaps in a 'senior moment', I had found myself confirming to him my previous Godalming address: but, impelled by some intuition, I'd checked myself before I could correct my mistake.

There was room in the garage and the Abercrombie's would be good enough to keep anything for me, until I could collect it.

It was in pensive mood that I drove back to the capital. Only later did I recall looking perplexedly into the rear view mirror. Not so much as if I was expecting to be followed, but almost as if there was some presence I'd hesitated to acknowledge amongst the folders stacked upon the back seat.

Chapter 3. *Confronting the Abyss*

Next day I'd accompanied my father home, or at least to Emma's and my home initially at Grimwich with me as carer for two days until he could be admitted to hospital. But it was quite obvious as we'd just moved in and so much needed to be done that it would be much better for my father to have professional care in a residential home, once his treatment in the Ipswich stroke unit was completed.

Enough money was made available from the mysterious Trust, agreement for which was reached between Vilnius and a local firm of solicitors, covering my father's needs for the foreseeable. I'd already had years of caring for my mother. She'd confided once that she wasn't made for motherhood which she'd discovered too late. While mine were of shorter duration (thank God because it was a truly horrible time) her own 'baby blues' had perhaps extended through infancy into my mid-childhood.

She revealed to me those nurturing years were laden with resentment for mind-numbing boredom spiked with moments of panic and desperation. Our bond was never strong and she'd pressed her own self-destruct button early. It had only been two years since her death and I really didn't feel I was ready to repeat that shipwreck with a house to refurbish.

A physiotherapist called twice a week at the Cedars and I'd visited each day in between scraping wall paper to reveal cracked plaster that would need hacking off, tearing up skirting to find more black rot and woodworm, treatment for which had not been carried out - *contrary to what I'd been assured by my surveyor, damn him.* And investigating the damp patches in the bedrooms I'd crawled into the attic space to discover strategically placed pots and buckets brim-filled with rainwater where the ridge tiles had cracked only to be severely startled by the intelligent eye of a raven regarding me through a broken tile.

There was a large zinc water tank up there and it was with some distaste that I'd fished out the floating corpse of a decomposed pigeon. *That act seemed to raise troubling thoughts, as elusive as they were disturbing.* I remembered later that a single raven in a house was an omen of death.

My mobile had been ringing on the kitchen table, the buzz carrying faintly from below as I was painstakingly crawling across joists, afraid of

putting my knee or trainer toe through the crumbling lath and plaster -
which I nearly did in my hurry to shin down the ladder: racing down the
bare wooden stairs to breathlessly answer the nurse's final ring.

*So sorry, would I please come? The doctor was there and an ambulance had been
called but had not yet arrived.*

I looked a wreck. I'd been working, wearing tattered jeans, trainers
with ankle socks and a big shapeless sweater over just a bra. I'd never
been big but I had lost weight in the past few months and it hung on me
more than ever. Damn, who'd care? I stopped to drag a comb through
my hair and noticed a flick of grey in front of my ears. Damn again. A
quick dab of lipstick, *for Dad* I thought, moving quickly but still in a sort
of daze, first forgetting to lock the kitchen door, then trying to start the
car with the house key. Emma was at school. Exams were starting in a
week. It would wait until she got home for me to tell her. And damn
again: *Polish Fred* was supposed to be coming this afternoon to assess
what repairs needed doing to the render. I dashed off a cryptic note
apologising for not being there, wedging it under the door knocker.

At the Cedars rooks were calling and squabbling in the eponymous
trees. Patients were sitting outside in dressing gowns, enjoying the
sunshine. No ambulance had yet arrived, or if it had there must have
been a damn quick turnaround.

In reception the battle had been lost between the wilting fuscias and
carnations against the stench of urine and disinfectant. I supposed that if
you worked there long enough you wouldn't notice. I found the matron
and the silky Mr. Khan, proprietor, talking to a man introduced as Dr.
Mitchell. The doctor was tallish, in his middle 'forties I guessed, with
'pepper and salt' hair worn too long and a ready smile which he'd wryly
inverted as he expressed his sympathy for my loss.

'Your father died in his sleep,' he said. I detected a slight accent that
might have been Scottish border or Northumbrian with just a hint of
something else. 'There was no pain. He just lay down on the floor
listening to music and drifted away.'

I didn't know how true was this statement but I appreciated what he
was saying and that he was showing me an act of kindness in telling me
this. There's no accounting for the way the mind's computer works. His
words soothed. I was treated to a snapshot revelation of a citadel abbey, a
thousand-year bastion of faith and tranquillity off the Northumberland
coast that the voice had somehow projected. Some people have such
poise at times like this, I thought, that gift for healing that permeates their
being.

42

'Thank you,' I said. 'May I...?' I hesitated.

We entered a wall of sound: the vibrating bedlam of the residents' lounge with its booming advertising, 'no-win-no-fee' legal aid for contrived accidents; a dozen pair of old eyes riveted on the giant television, the minds behind them somewhere else entirely: the immaculate Khan deftly deflecting a pale harlequin in a dressing gown who'd made a beeline for me nursing a teddy. He led the way to my father's room with Dr. Mitchell following.

The room was small and fairly spartan, although my father's papers were all about; boxes and briefcases which he'd evidently opened, contents strewn as if he'd been looking for something.

'It was his heart. He's lying just as we found him,' said Dr. Mitchell. 'No need to disturb him to carry out my examination. He looked... well, *comfortable.*'

I appreciated that. He had apparently lain down on the carpet, full length next to an old record player, a scatter of vinyl LPs alongside him.

So there lay my father, the closest human being to me next to Emma now that my mother was gone. He looked peaceful. His eyes were closed or had been closed, and I could imagine that he was just sleeping. I dropped to my knees, my lip quivering. I felt a tightness about my throat. I reached down to touch his cheek. *Lindisfarne* fading....the grey seals and cormorants. A flash of memory: running along the three-mile causeway from Holy Island with Emma, ten years old, the sea racing to cut us off. *Emma run or we'll be swimming.* My fault. Failing to properly check the times of tides. Mother, asleep in the car park at Bamburgh Castle. Oblivious, adrift in her inner sea with an empty wine bottle. Simeon already adrift somewhere. A tear splashed onto my extended wrist. A failure as a mother, failure as a wife. As a daughter I've failed my father again; for the last time. Yet a little voice murmured something other in my brain, opening up that dark valley of the mind, full of rage, fear and repulsion: and guilt that's a canker on the soul.

'We'll leave you for a while.' said Khan.

Alone, I brushed the questions away; gave way to honest grief. Much that we'd shared, all that was good about my childhood when he'd been there came flooding back. It seemed that my rebellions were borne out of my perception of his withholding love from me, when he'd only been away by force of circumstance, not wilfully, like a straying husband. Except for later when he and my mother no longer spoke. In my teenage years I saw him less, and in fact repudiated him and the *petite bourgeoisie* as I then so smartly called the class into which I'd been born and so despised. Agitating with my Left Wing comrades and anarchists. Throwing cobblestones at the shields of oppression in Germany, perhaps in some vicarious, rather pointless anniversary of solidarity with those other students at their Parisian barricades, trying to revive the earlier brilliance and glamour. That memorable summer when I'd lost my stupid virginity for *The Cause* to a disciple who extolled the orgasmic example of Comrade Kollontai, associate and confidante of great Lenin and of Stalin. She was, he told me, the Bolshevist high priestess of free love. He wore his *Che Guevara* beret in the sack. It was his identity.

I was overcome with sadness and guilt and already keenly felt my father's loss with his corpse right there before me. I knew later, when he would be forever incommunicado, I'd feel it more. Although we'd scarce spoken for years, at least I'd known he'd been out there, somewhere. It had been a shock some twenty years before that I'd discovered he'd been burned in a horrific accident in Germany; as a spectator, covering an airshow for his magazine. His injuries had not been serious but it had provoked the realisation that one day I would lose him.

Later, when my marriage was heading south, although that was something I would deal with in my own way, it gave me solace: that knowledge that he was still out there and in extremis he could be contacted, though to my great disappointment his no-show at my mother's funeral was one case that had proved the contrary.

The irony was that when I returned with him, communication was still one-way traffic. His eyes had been the solitary communicating beacons and I didn't always get the message.

~-~

The turntable was still revolving when the care worker found him, Mr. Khan had said. It wasn't my father's record player. Nothing so bulky had yet arrived from the Baltic, nor was anything like that expected. It was a *Marconi* and evidently belonged to the Cedars, but was of an age that meant it would have been contemporary with my father in his twenties. Moreover it was straightforward to use, with no small buttons or knobs. Something a dexterous man might have managed even with his cognitive skills impaired, using his left hand: the unaffected side of his body.

I lifted the lid. It was Shostakovich's 4th Symphony. I knew it to be one of my father's great favourites. Dmitri Shostakovich had exemplified my father's view of heroism. A brilliant composer writing in a hostile milieu, who might have been damned, or worse *liquidated*, for composing music that might not find favour with the Politbüro, criticized by the Union of Composers. Yet he remained his own man. Had he fallen foul of Stalin, his name would have been on a death list and his family's too. He'd slept with his case packed under his bed every night, awaiting the knock that would announce the KGB. *The gulags were stuffed with dissident intellectuals: composers, writers, artists, scientists and poets, in medieval torment, denied the most basic humanities, Natasha. Dying inside. Dangerous criminals I'm sure you'd agree.*

I had haughtily, unwittingly given aid and comfort to the *meat grinder*, paid lip service to inhumanity. Helped Comintern in its fight as long as it would smash Capitalism. Maintaining that view I am ashamed to admit required the *double think* of some of George Orwell's allegorical works writ large. My very name, *Natasha*, made me a natural for targeting in my student days. I often wondered why my parents chose it. *Little Miss Natasha Morris.* It really *didn't* have a 'ring' to it. But it seemed to ring all the bells when I changed it in a spectacular *volte face* to Mrs. Simeon Stewart-Hedges. *Natasha* Stewart-Hedges, *née Morris* erstwhile spinster of this parish, photographed for a glossy air-head magazine by one of Simeon's glamour photographer friends. There'd been a spoiler in reference to my romantic Marxist past, snidely by-lined in the gossip column on a preceding page. But that was dealt with in the way of such journals, as if I'd been found *in flagranté* after too much plum brandy. Or mooning from the back of a limousine at some debutante's *coming out glitzfest.*

I dabbed at my eyes. Something caught my attention. A folded piece of paper was wedged under the record player. I reached across my father's body and retrieved it. It was a sealed envelope addressed to me in my father's one-time clear hand.

I scanned the contents with my blurred vision. To my surprise I discovered that apart from the recent date it was a re-hashed copy of the letter I'd received from my father three years before; essentially that same letter which I had reacted to angrily back then. Same old *Re-Action Man* soapbox polemic, or so first it seemed. Perhaps he thought I hadn't received the earlier one as I hadn't dignified it with a reply.

Kuznetsova,
Aleksandras Apygarda,
Summer,
2007

My dear Natasha,
You are probably wondering what has happened to me if indeed you give your father a second thought nowadays. I am sitting at a fine oak writing desk tapping away at my laptop with the morning sunshine slanting through the windows of this mansion, a sort of grand Scottish hotel and European hunting lodge combined.

A miniature Versailles formality invests the gardens to the rear but round about is riding country without equal: somewhere to fill your lungs with clean, fresh air and stretch your muscles. You'd love it. Or do you ride now, I wonder? Perhaps you still regard that as an indulgence of class privilege. I'm sure Emma is still keen and would not politicise such wonderful natural enjoyment and beauty as may be had from an equine relationship. Hopefully pig-headedness will have skipped a generation.

I am writing to you as much as for myself at this time. I know you didn't care much for history at school: British history, not the socialist worker viewpoint, was still being taught then I believe. Perhaps you lived too much in the moment, although you were as political as anyone at uni if I remember. You espoused those causes that were fashionable with others of your generation, naturally — calling on the masses to tear down fossilized tradition and bring low the false gods of capitalism. You were soon quoting Engels and passing out pamphlets condemning the government's defence policies and believed you could change the world, sweep 'real politic' into the history books; so you will probably have stopped reading this by now, thinking, as usual, it's just your father ranting about the young, hectoring you about 'old values' and what's wrong with the youth of today. Well, I am a bit. You know me, a 'right-of-centre fascist' I think was your affectionate tribute whenever I was home.
You might recall that soon enough you had capitulated in favour of the worries common to modern mothers, that whilst you were balancing your career and family, in the final decade of the Twentieth Century the Soviet state was rotting from the head. Like a fish. Without overt help from the West.
So, if you are still here, as a statement of clarity I feel I have to resort to some brief recent history, as I recall it. It's a tough message and can stand some re-telling in these uncaring times.

This was pretty much the tenor of the letter he'd sent me three years previously. I'd read it angrily then and probably tore it up. Or shoved it into the back of a drawer. There was much in it that I recognised of myself and was ashamed for. But it was old territory. I'd grown up and too much hassle had been going on in my life to take on board any more guilt or contrition at that time, let alone follow the strange and meandering pathways that my father was wont to wander.

In that last decade, Natasha, the monolith that was the USSR was fissured and crumbling, the 'buffer states' of the Warsaw Pact by then breaking away like icebergs from an old glacier. A democratic Rumania had begun the year full of hope, albeit bloodily as far as the Family Ceausescu was concerned. Czechoslovakia looked forward to a new Prague Spring, as they emerged, the countries of Eastern Europe, blinking like animals in the sunlight from their long winter hibernations. One by one they stood up and shook off the detritus of that communal grave where the corpse of Communism soon would lie. So who was 'the dinosaur' in the end, Natasha? Rather stole the thunder of the Greenham Peaceniks you'd joined up with for a while, except you and they rather claimed it as their doing. Smoke and mirrors perhaps, considering many were actually in love with 'The Great Experiment'? Perhaps you're doomed always to kill the thing you love.

Stalin himself might have said it though, had he lived, Natasha. 'I've yet to see the tambourine that would stop a bullet!'

Poland's, Hungary's previous moves to self-determinism, alas had failed. And that other Prague Spring had been crushed before it could blossom into summer in '68, when you were just an infant, my dear. The televised newsreel broadcasts had seemed unrelenting. You might remember from later documentaries - Prime Minister Chamberlain's return from the Munich Conference thirty years before: that piece of paper waved in triumph from a windswept Heston tarmac marking the shameful dismissal of '... a distant land of which we know little...'. We would learn its hard lesson, 'Tasha: why tyrants should never be appeased. Though for Britain it heralded our darkest hour, it was no thanks to pre-war defence, not foreign policies, nor peace movements that it then became our finest. A truism: if you want peace; prepare for war.

I looked down at his sleeping face. In my head I heard his voice, clear and strong as I'd always heard it in my mind, proclaiming for the Defence of the Realm, *Pax Britannica*, bemoaning loss of Empire, all that. Well perhaps not, but he was *dyed in the wool*. Speaking those same words now, telepathically, brain to brain; age to age, never the twain.... and yet...I wonder, do we mellow or become more entrenched with the years? Are we still the product of our early associations: mine those exciting young student agitators with whom my fellow revolutionaries of either sex were all so obviously in love? And we were so angry, weren't we, who saw things so much more clearly than your generation? When no one over 30 years of age was to be trusted with a political thought, obviously. Except dead revolutionaries and radical thinkers on the Left. *Obviously.* However much we later tried to conform, or *sell out,* as they'd have called it. No more the anti-war blue stocking would-be saviour of the world. Who were we all now? What am I now, Dad, apart from an orphan and mother looking into the abyss?

Chamberlain, dying, was doubtless unaware that it was Czech-built Panzers that outflanked the Maginot Line, threatening us with what then seemed an unstoppable force. After Dunkirk the image of a Nazi standard planted on mainland British soil had become a real and frightening prospect.

Yeah, Dad, I thought. Same old 'drum and trumpet' polemic. Ancient, fossilized history from your very own pulpit.

The Ribbentrop-Molotov non-aggression pact had given Hitler and Stalin a breathing space and the Führer his free hand in Europe. Remember from your history lessons, if that was mentioned, Stalin would share the spoils of a prostrated Poland, which would cease to exist as an independent nation, putting the Baltic States under immense pressure until they too were re-assimilated into Russia. But both men understood the inevitability of the final test between their political ideologies, however that contest might be postponed, while fellow travellers and sleepwalkers nodded sagely or looked away.

Same old, same old thing.

Even as new evidence comes to light of the manifest cruelties of that ruthless regime there are those old Communists who look back nostalgically to the glory days of the Cold War, with the consensual selective amnesia that was the secret to survival back then still prevalent, bred into the Russian soul: the forever muzhik.
Then, in the nineteen-nineties, there was a new sense of freedom in the air. In Berlin the Wall between the two Germanys was coming down; attacked with hammers and chisels and with the bare hands of the common people. I sent you a souvenir of it once, in a plastic bubble: a time capsule glued to a postcard of the Brandenburg Gate. Remember?

'Yes, Daddy, I do. I do…….' We'd been once so close and the step-change to the personal struck an emotive chord: that shabby little piece of painted concrete with a smudge of graffiti held associations of human contact across a divide no less real than that which now separated me

48

from my father. Except that in the long run that divide had been breached and I checked the sob that was rising again in my chest. My emotions lay scattered, like casualties on a battlefield.

Though in the months from Tienamen Square to Timisoara, from China to Europe, the freedom to peaceful protest had still been bloodily denied, the 'nineties had been a watershed. In Lithuania fourteen martyrs had died defending the Vilnius television tower. After the Singing Revolution and the Baltic Chain, it had marked the last murderous act of a discredited regime in the Baltic. Soon the move to vote the Communists out of office would be irresistible while the Free World held its breath that Europe might at last know Peace for Our Time. A vain delusion.

Free World? I couldn't decide if this stuff was as sentimental as it might sound over a coffee with some of my literary friends in West Ken, even though one or two had been parliamentary researchers in their youth. Long on law and protocol, they saw revolution as something that happened elsewhere among the lesser breeds. They'd never sold out because they'd never believed anything, deluding themselves that they were more than leggy eye-candy for puffed-up politicians. But here, in this room with my father cold by my side, I was no more a pretend insurrectionist. I was vulnerable, with no beliefs and no clear hope. A weathervane. A child again.

'Dad, I don't know where you are, but I hope you're alright.'

Chapter 4. *History and Home Truths*

I was given to momentary reflection that political success, other than of the Left, was, I had to admit, relentlessly trashed by the left-leaning liberal intelligentsia with its ready armoury of moral propaganda and accusations of conspiracy - now deep-threaded within our society. Else they'd close down the argument in the typical vilifying ways that I'd have recognised from my past life as a 'useful idiot'. Back then I'd ignored the immoral realities of corruption, oppression and the resulting misery or saw them as exclusive to the reactionary Right. Of the union-crushers, warmongers and profiteers lining up for their knighthoods. But I'd long watched party apparatchik *Svengalis* at work from behind entwined barricades of logic and dialectical obfuscation, the lovelight of endless revolution in their eyes and concluded in the end that they fucked with your mind. Certainly with my own suggestible mind, as I'd realised it in my own time but didn't like reminding of it. It still stung a little. No prude like a reformed whore though, eh Daddy? Part of my reformation was ultra conformity, or so it might be perceived. I married Simeon, merchant banker, rhyming-slang intended. On the rebound from make believe political activism. Remember? How had that happened? Damned if I knew and damned if it hadn't been a *really* bad idea.

Except for Emma.

Just like you married mum. You married Karen on the rebound from your dead Angel, didn't you? I see that now at this moment like a flash of light, for the very first time. Next to your corpse so you can't confirm it. Angelika. An early victim of aerial terrorism. A PLO bomb in the baggage hold and you've carried a torch for her memory until now.

The worldview has changed again since 9/11. The brave little convoy of Trabants winding smokily out of East Berlin to wild cheering was a milestone that has passed with its lasers and the Ode to Joy celebrations. But the tribulations of Germany and of Europe as a whole have not lessened with immigration from whatever direction. Nor from corrupting influences within and close to governments, nor from organised crime spreading from the east: from child beggars to people-trafficking, extortion and the rest.

Some of these lines are definitely not those that I'd recalled.

I muse on recent events, Natasha, from my 'safe house'; a restoration with fine views around about this old Folwark fiefdom wherefrom I administer good works to alleviate suffering where I see it, thanks to the beneficence of the fund which I am pleased to call, in private, the Anastasia Bequest, although its official title is more prosaic. The Internet provides the anonymity vital to my personal security and the charity's protector and trustees provide successive cutouts from 'arm's length' investment advisors. The staff, by the way, are excellent, as if service has been revived from the surliness of the old socialism.

I certainly don't remember this part.....

I think on balance that the outcome has been fortunate even though my personal safety is still in question. Sometimes I feel I'm looking at eternity from the far end of the grass runway among the trees…but when I open the throttle and climb into the Baltic sky I feel again the old rush; the living on the edge, viewing the world through a whirling kaleidoscope. There I am content; at ease in the air and captain of my fate. Or thought I was…. I have recently tried to re-master my 'mother tongue' by the way, and with some success, aided by a charming tutor who visits twice a week. I am sure that that sentence will astonish you after all we are English are we not? I believed so until I began to dig past one generation and uncovered Pandora's box. Anyway, that can wait. At last I have found the time and energy to write again. So first I write to you.

This is all new, not to say bizarre….

Putin now invites us to review the glory that once was the USSR, not dwell upon the errors of the past, those necessary evils and growing pains. Like the gulags and pogroms. Surely the internal Russian holocaust has few enough memorials to the millions of innocents that suffered and died. For what? Inefficiency on a gigantic scale. Poisoned lands and poisoned minds: broken dreams and broken spirits, unknown graves across the tundra.

So what's changed? Stalin had his Trotsky ice-picked in Mexico. 'Someone' (the present incumbent?) has his irradiated in London. An 'enemy of the people': that old catch-all! What was it he'd said I wonder? A rhetorical, 'Will no one rid me of this turbulent priest?' People need new heroes. Mother Russia wants her standing in the world restored: her self-respect back.
So what's new really? Nothing's changed? Fraud was always the curse of the Russias. Russian billionaires? They're nothing new either, just the 'come back kiddies'. Thanks to Yeltsin. Just like in those stinking pre-Revolutionary

Azerbaizhan oil fields. Billionaire oil moguls, oligarchs and their mafiya minders: they're not fashion statements. Not such strange bedfellows when you think about it either, with that other essential ingredient, the corrupt government official. The Iron Triangle. It's a Kleptocracy: they are raping Russia all over again, only this time the click of a mouse can transfer millions that could once only have been moved by the trainload. The long-suffering muzhiks are suffering again. The pensioners without pensions, Natasha. The young without jobs, without hope. Girls sold as sex slaves on the Internet. Drugs and bootleg samogon vodka ever the refuge of the masses.

Oh yes and the long arm of the FSB KGB NKVD OGPU CHEKA call it what you will, it's still there for the flexing. Its fingers still pull the trigger, drop the poison from the phial, its nerves still pulse, still obey orders from Moscow Centre. Putin himself said it. 'There's no such thing as an ex-KGB man.'

This is not what was previously written. About *Litvinenko*. This *is* this year's news.

It may sound strange but I feel I have resumed my true identity and found peace, both in my spiritual 'homeland' and within myself and reflect that there is no stronger bond than between old comrades who have a history of shared hardship. I like to believe (does that sound delusional?) that the Kameradschaft of the Jasta is absolute; such kinship that is nowhere stronger than at squadron level, no matter which side you happened to have been on, though perhaps that too is all bravado and born of fear of being alone. Of looking too much inwards or 'whistling in the dark'.

Historically, perhaps many have fought for their perception of right as have unquestioningly followed orders, in all wars, in all epochs, none of which may claim exclusivity for monstrous half-truths, lies and political expedience. You prepared and distributed propaganda pamphlets for your friends at the LSE. I wandered the earth, a hack for the Telegraph and the aviation press, everything carefully edited, so the freedom of the press was certainly not free to jeopardize Middle Eastern arms sales nor report the London lifestyle of the pampered sons of sheikhs, their glossy hookers, Masers and Lambos, losing a king's ransom at the tables without the flicker of an eye. Not my brief, Guardian stuff. Your young idealistic student stuff, ignoring how the world worked. Working just one side of the street; on this side of the Curtain reading the Socialist Worker that extolled the lie that the Workers' Paradise lay on the other side. But we were both young and foolish in our time, though I was perhaps corrupted by the need to eat. You had the luxury of a stable home and a mother's love.

Now Putin's Bears and Blackjacks are out of mothballs and testing our perimeter again, just like in the good old days of the Cold War. How nostalgic is that?

You are always part of me, Natashka. If I'd excluded you from this chimera, it's not because my love for you is any less, but I believe our souls belong to other spheres, yours and mine. I think you will have to go on your own journey to find your 'complete self' and then maybe we can again communicate like father and daughter: instead of political rivals with your mother sitting there like Belgium.

I'd tearfully smiled at that despite myself.

Perhaps the fancy that we re-incarnate in 'clusters' to work out our karmas and to interact with past friends and lovers holds some truth. Role-playing the old associations of previous lives. After all, where does consciousness lie? In the nuclei of atoms? Is memory in the electrons? They are immortal apparently and recognise each other in their orbits, so perhaps sentience devolves to the subatomic. In any case I think I may have truly found myself fallen among comrades, far flung though some may now be.
You must think your old man's lost the plot, eh? No matter. Just remember, in extremis, it's just a house of cards.

I was nonplussed and suspected that he'd been eating the local mushrooms. What *was* he alluding to in his 'homecoming', and kinship of the bloody *Jastas*, whatever they were?

But this is a serious matter. The evil that men do lingers and so I proceed with caution. Polonium may be one of the carcenogenic constituents of tobacco smoke, for all I know, but I've never indulged. So if anything happens to me, anything: don't assume it was other than premeditated.

Half of this is definitely not that same letter which at the time I'd considered little more than the raking of old history and a Right Wing rant. It is an extended form, much of it, and was evidently written earlier this year, 2007. The previous sentence for one was most certainly not included in the version he'd posted to me. To paraphrase:

'Don't assume anything that happens to me was other than premeditated. Anything?'

Then this.

One man from that troubled century remains an enigma. It is his life I have tried

54

~-~

Why for heaven's sake had he signed this copy, *Johannes'*?

I considered that maybe he'd 'gone native'. After all those lands had been German-owned once, I was sure, before they were Russified, and Swedish before that. And Litho-Polish for centuries before extending into Ukraine and Belarus. That was one little bit of history that had stuck and some of that was courtesy of Lithuanian Airways' passenger information kit stowed in the seat pouch in front. But that's all I really knew.

In a previous existence I would have been encouraged to consider it all as legitimately belonging to the USSR, won through patriotic toil, blood and sacrifice fighting Fascism. I knew better now, I reminded myself.

Why not the whole hog and include the Stahlhelm, Madame Blavatsky. Anna Sprengel and the Hermetic Order of the Golden Dawn? Multinational imperialism, corporate resource piracy, crop circles and the conspiracy of the Illuminati? Polonium 210, for God's sake. Did he even know how much that stuff cost to make? It had to be a joke.

~-~

Shostakovich's 4th. It ends with the longest and most hauntingly beautiful coda in all music.

a few pinpricks of illumination moving against the lovely twinkling backdrop, the lights and dusky domes of Saint Petersburg. Moving in slow majesty into the Gulf of Finland, the Imperial Yacht of the Tsar of All The Russias with her lights blazing, a ghost ship sailing in state, towards the distant empurpled gloom of the sea and the Scandinavian coastline: sailing under the ice cold evening sky set with little darkening clouds, like a mackerel shoal. Sailing for the very last time. Hear the muted pulse of her engine, fading out into the night, and the long drawn out moan of her siren floating on the breeze. Gone now forever, yet her echo remains as the music moves slowly on a sustained chord that hovers, brooding in near silence and lingers upon the ear like an eerie memory: that beauty of sound so close to silence resonates in the mind long after the last soft beat of the engine, the muffled drumbeat and the deep lowing woodwind has departed. The conductor is now conducting silence, his baton still raised commands it: head bowed in awe and admiration for the master of all symphonists. What genius.'

My father, the Romantic. He held no particular candle for the Romanovs, of that I was certain, though they've since been sanctified in their martyrdom by the Russian Orthodox Church. It was all that continual spilled blood, the waste, the terror, the suffering that so repelled him. The pogroms. The gulag: the grinding years of fear, hopelessness and toil.

Dad's copy had a repeating groove that allowed the coda to run on like the sleepy murmur of some secret Russian lover. For an eternity he'd listen with eyes closed and a wistful smile as if in memory of a kiss, imagining the glory of Russia before the Revolution while my mother smoked herself stupid and watched TV in the living room. Maybe it's not what Shostakovich intended: perhaps, for all I knew, the symphony wasn't even programmatic, but that's what was conjured in my father's imagination and so, as a child, in mine. It was the one thing we'd agreed on, the perfection that was the output of the great classical composers, even if I'd become a neo-Bolshevist myself in my rebellious years and forgotten the fabulous Imperial imagery, a beautiful *Fabergé* fantasy that was my father's legacy from such works.

I considered there must be at least three of *me* in me. Inhabiting my mind like three Dickensian ghosts. The *past*: my childhood, when I viewed my father with uncritical eyes: the rebel: and now, always on the threshold of the *future*, the uncertain penitent and mother. The metaphor was slightly out of phase because we are always in the *present*. Aren't we, Clarissa? Vibrating on a visible wavelength.

But what was the *Baltic Falcon*? What did it mean?

~-~

Outside the sound of voices. The ambulance had arrived and gone away. There seemed to be some confusion. Suddenly there was someone at the door to my father's room, looking in: a harlequin in a pink dressing gown, pyjamas with slippers to match. *Alice* I think Mr. Khan had called her. She seemed swift on her feet and it seemed odd that she was in night attire in the middle of the afternoon, but then so many of them were.

'Hello,' she said solemnly. 'Have you met my daughter?' She lifted the teddy bear for me to see. 'Isn't she pretty?'

She held my gaze and deigned not to notice the dead man on the floor. 'She's my baby.'

I felt a deep well of sympathy for her despite my own bereavement. Perhaps she'd never recovered from the loss of a child. Perhaps she'd never had a child. Her eyes were china blue like a baby's themselves, quite without guile: without understanding, as if she were trapped in an enchanted cocoon of infinite childhood. The work of some malevolent spider in a fairytale, spun by the brothers Grimm.

'Lucy would like you to come to tea, please,' she said in a six year-old voice. The bear was actually a pillowcase. Not even a real teddy then, to represent her unreal daughter. How very sad.

I thought of Emma.

~-~

Mr. Khan made his gentle capture in the doorway and with his mouthed 'Sorry,' Alice was ushered away.

Dr. Mitchell appeared. He was sorry too. Sorry the ambulance was called earlier and Reception failed to cancel it. Did you want them to contact a particular undertaker or use the one that the Cedars usually use?

Usually, I thought. Of course this must happen all the time. It's more than usual with an aged, demented and infirm clientele. Just not thinking straight.

'Please, Doctor. Whatever's necessary. Whatever it is that's usually done in these circumstances. I am new to the area, so that'll be fine, I'm sure'

Someone taking on part of that responsibility for now would be just great with me. I was rewarded with a reassuring smile.

'Just leave things with me,' he said. 'And please call me "Mitch".'

My smile must have shown my relief. The matron walked over to me.

'Cup of tea, my dear? You can sit in my office.'

'Thank you,' I said. 'That would be lovely.' Unthinking middle class reflex.

~-~

The office door remained slightly ajar. Psychologically immobilised, I stared absently as an elderly man in a vest vainly sought an armhole in a bath towel.

I don't recall whether it was quite an hour before the undertaker arrived. He and his assistant were swift and professional in removing my father's body and wheeling the coffin along the corridor to the waiting hearse. The residents were playing bingo, sealed off in their lounge, a care worker calling the numbers through a karaoke microphone.

I returned to the room to collect his papers, the inevitable research documents of his profession amongst them. They'd been scattered and shuffled at random, unlike the meticulous way he'd have organised them in sound mind. Dr. Mitchell had left the premises. Khan and the matron were occupied elsewhere and I was alone with my thoughts. *Matter....not immutable. Transmutable, and energy its other form. So where was your energy now, Daddy?* I'd managed to fold and sort the papers into appropriate folders as far as possible and was making the second of my trips to the Volvo with his briefcases and box files when a silver-maned cadaver with a Zimmer frame beckoned from a doorway.

'That's two already this month,' he wheezed enthusiastically. 'And we're only 'alf way through!'

'Oh dear,' I said. Sympathetically, I hoped.

On my way back I saw that despite the Zimmer he'd collected a wheelchair containing a tiny hairless creature. Her mottled hands were shrivelled tarantulas in her lap.

'Do you know how old I am, dear?' she asked. She could have been a hundred-and-twelve. 'Ninety-nine and a half!' she exclaimed, before I could think of an intelligent answer. 'In the mirror every morning, I says, "Good Gawd, I'm still bleedin' well 'ere."'

'Never mind, Millie. Won't be long now,' he wheezed.

I smiled, lost for words.

I'd removed everything that had belonged to my father and was about to take leave of matron. Mr. Khan was nowhere to be seen. Apparently I owed for the rest of the week. Policy. But that was taken care of the by the Trust. I'd email to inform them I thought, then damn! BT hadn't connected me and I still had to get a modem.

I failed to make a clean getaway. Alice spotted me and she and teddy followed me to the car. In the clean fresh air amidst the somehow comforting sounds of the calling rooks, the sight of a sudden squirrel on the grass, there was something fawn-like and fascinating about her. She was straight-backed and moved silently in her pink slippers with an almost oriental grace. I thought for a moment that she would get into the Volvo but she only looked inside, as if expecting to see someone.

'He liked Lucy,' she said, still six years old. The youngest by far of anyone here I thought. Perhaps everyone else at the Cedars looks terribly old to her. Maybe I was a fresh face although God knows I didn't feel very fresh, or young.

'Lucy's very nice,' I said, thankful to see matron descending the wheelchair ramp.

'Will you come to tea soon?' she asked, eyes begging, paler blue now that the pupils had contracted out of doors.

'I don't think that will be possible,' I said as gently as I could, slightly ashamed at my own embarrassment.

'Come along, Alice, lovey,' said the matron taking her unresistingly by the arm. 'Sorry about that. She wanders all the time. Worse than a toddler.'

'Goodbye then,' I said. 'Bye-bye, Alice.'

Alice turned her head as she was led away. Such blue eyes I thought. She's trapped in there in that old woman's body that seems so light and moves so easily. I had a sudden impulse to call after them. 'Yes, I will come to tea with you, Alice. You and your baby.' After all what would it cost me but a little time? Time that I hadn't given my father. God knows I've given time to less worthy criteria.

But I didn't.

The sound of the rooks seemed suddenly intrusive and their collective noun sprang to mind: a 'parliament', very appropriate based on what I'd seen televised at PM's question time. But I realised that I'd subconsciously sought the collective noun for crows. A 'murder'.

The choreography to the north of the Stowmarket road was a mighty thumbprint hovering in the sky; ten thousand starlings swarming across my windshield, intruded on my bleak mood, patterns changing in a heartbeat; dividing like primitive cells in a microscope. What was the collective noun for starlings? A constellation?

Don't assume anything. His words.

'*He liked Lucy,*' Alice had said. Past tense. So somewhere in her confused and childlike mind she'd come to an understanding that my father was dead. Her studiously ignoring his corpse on the carpet might have been a defence mechanism.

Mitch had told me that it was 'natural causes' and not to worry. He'd do the paperwork.

Damn, look at the time, I thought. *Emma will be home.*

I'd already made up my mind to contact the coroner's office to see how I might arrange for a post-mortem. I knew from my early legal studies that I had the right to be represented at the inquest by a legally qualified medical practitioner. This would not be Mitch as he'd already certified the cause of death but he'd be called to give evidence. It occurred to me that he might be offended by such a course of action and I felt a pang of regret as even on short acquaintance I'd felt drawn to him. I immediately thrust the idea aside. Whatever was I thinking? Just couldn't help myself. I didn't need another entanglement now or for the foreseeable.

I didn't even know if he was married.

Chapter 5. *Emma*

Emma had let herself in and was playing some thuggish 'rap' in her room.

I called her downstairs. She leaned opposite me against the living room wall, half a head taller and growing fast - graceful but stooping; blonde as I was dark, rebellious in her 'St.Trinian's school uniform' as I'd once referred to it. She'd no idea what I'd meant by that and cared less. I told her about her grandfather. She looked at me once under her brows, to see how I was taking it I suppose, nibbling the skin at the edge of her thumbnail in her perpetual sulk. I didn't expect much in the way of an emotional reaction as she hadn't seen much of my father since she was eight or nine. About the same age as I was when I'd been closest to him myself, I guessed.

'Can I go now?' was all she said. No eye contact. I wonder about autism and her MMRs.

'Of course,' I said, biting my own lip metaphorically to avoid correcting her with: *Emma, may I go!* 'But aren't you hungry?' I asked of her mute, disappearing back.

Quite right, Emm. Society's glossy mores. *You can't be too thin and you can't be too rich* to quote Mrs Simpson.

Her music resumed, shaking the ceiling. A grating snarl had replaced the mobster rap; the battering-ram signature delivery of the German 'heavy metal' group: *Rammstein.*

'*Eins....Zwei....Drei....Vier.....* *Hier kommt die Sonne....*' The gutteral, stone-crusher language. Visceral. Shocking. *Vikingly* macho and seductive. It made me think of swastikas, flame-throwers and steel helmets. Someone, I forget who - perhaps it was Riedel, once said of German that 'it was the language of hate and of anger'. Maybe also of conquest. While I could imagine the testosterone-charged sexual appeal for rebellious nymphets, it was numbingly loud so I shut myself in the kitchen where its thudding beat was muted. No doubt she was dealing with things in her way, dancing and stamping in her room.

Maybe she was burning still from my having dropped the boom on her all-night rave last weekend. She'd told me that her friend, Alicia, would be going and promised to be home by midnight. I told her *no.* She'd wheedled expertly, reckoning that she was in a negotiating position, the plea drawn out for several beats, a semitone higher; her *'whys?'* remnants of childhood's grasp of how arguments are 'resolved'.

I'd been calm. Perhaps I'd overwhelmed her with the sum of my fears… permanent damage to her hearing ….. legally under age. *Rohypnol.* Triple vodkas splashed into her rum and Coke. GHB. Skunk. Horse tranquiliser. Plant food. People smoking God-knows-what. Fear of Ecstasy tablets, galloping Chlamydia; the increasing AIDS epidemic that nobody talked about anymore.

Fear of teenagers without the remotest sense of responsibility and their designs on my barely fifteen year-old daughter.

'It's not simply a matter of trust, Emma. You may find it difficult to avoid a situation you might fail to assess clearly ….. the excitement, the music. Experienced older boys looking for a soft target. Especially if you'd had more to drink than you realise.'

'If you don't trust me it's hardly, like, a *vindication* of your parenting,' she snorted. 'Like I'll be wearing *beer goggles?*'

My mind veers away, selecting its file, a photo-fit parody of her incisive logic and whimsical slang. *Pellagra,* the 'spectacle disease'; pearlescent rash ringing the eye sockets caused by lack of specific vitamins in a poor diet. Or famine.

The human brain is capable of processing millions of bits of data per second via synaptic connections, but it's a mystery why unhelpful visual prompts occur. Maybe it's a memory short-circuit. Had I seen such a thing in an old medical textbook? Perhaps.

'Drop the attitude,' I say. 'We both know what's happened before. Only your age saved you from prosecution for *aiding and abetting!*'

'I *so* don't need this!' Emma's addressing the ceiling. 'It was a *TWOC.* He got like a *caution?*'

Habitually her voice rose in interrogative inflection, even making a statement. I held back on the matter of criminal damage and a broken society.

'What's Alicia's mother's 'phone number. See what she says.'

'They're not on the 'phone.'

'Oh gimme a break, Emma. What are you trying to pull? You've got Alicia's mobile number. Ring her and ask to speak to her mother.'

She just glared at me under her brows.

'If you've got a date with another drug-pushing car thief,' my threat tailed off. 'Where's this 'barn dance' supposed to be? I'll drive you there and pick you both up at eleven. You *and* 'Alicia'.'

'Get lost! I'm not having my uptight *mother* pick me up!'

'Uptight? Oh how *'sixties*. How *swe-eet*!'

You could surf off that lip curl. Suddenly she was *Gogo*, the mini-skirted Yakusa assassin in Tarantino's '*Kill Bill*'.

'Try being nice, Emma. It's the only option on offer. What's Alicia's number again?'

She glowered at me. 'Like, what's the point? You are *so* not going to let me go.'

Like was an introduction, a preposition, and an adverb. It was a random received mode of speech among teenagers and twenty-somethings. I suspect it made her feel 'cool', amusingly superior, in control. Providing an extra half-second's thinking time. Something to hide behind; part of the code.

'I'm trying to be reasonable Emma, but you're not exactly 'creditworthy'.'

'Like *you're* the best role model. *Ev-er*!'

I was crushed. 'What do you mean by that?'

'You were like a *wino* for about six months!'

'How dare you!' I flushed.

'Know thyself, Natasha!'

I remembered well enough. I wished I could forget my days of misery.

'I was struggling with a lot of things. Trying to pay the bills.' *Qui s'excuse, s'accuse,* I thought, guiltily. 'How would you have reacted if I'd stopped your pocket money?'

'That's just control freakery,' she said emphatically. 'Violating like my human rights! You're basically a *fascist* anyway! You should, like, join the BNP!'

Blake came to mind: *What immortal hand or eye?*

'You don't even know the meaning of the word. Or about real freedom.' *Echoes of other arguments with Dad concerning moral relativism.*

'I know more than you think.'

'In that case you should know that you're not going to win this argument.'

'Just because *you* don't, like, have any friends you don't want *me* to go out.'

My God. Was there any truth in that?

'Sorry Emma. My decision's final. And will you for God's sake stop saying *like*. It's infuriating and stupid.'

She scowled, uttering further abuse.

'That's it, Miss. You're grounded!'

'Bring it on!' she sneered. 'I'm ringing *Child Line*!'

'Why not? You sound about bloody *six* and you don't act any older!' I was angry and ordered her to her room.

Am I now the Victorian nanny? She'd been difficult enough as a pregnancy, draining me of iron and calcium, but next thing she is a Philadelphia lawyer with her own biochemistry degree demanding a test of my mitochondrial DNA! I didn't know a thing about symbiotes and maternal DNA when I was her age. Perhaps its study was in its infancy thirty years ago. At least she was learning something at that school.

'Do you think I'd have put up with your bloody nonsense if you *weren't* mine?' I'd asked in a choking voice.

'Why did you have me then?'

'I didn't think it was actually going to be *you*!' I snapped. *Sometimes I wonder who the hell* 'you' *are. But then sometimes I wonder that about myself, don't I?*

'Anyway it's like your fault I'm *at* that bloody school! I mean could we be more remote? Just 'cause *your* life's a toilet why should *I* have to live in this *hole*?'

'Sue me!' I hissed, biting on my rage.

'Anyway, how am I supposed to get good grades if we aren't, like *on* the Internet? I *am* dyslexic.'

More guilt. She'd been taught in the insurrectionist way of modern education with its demolition of *rote* and the times table, encouraged to see words as symbols associated with their meanings in picture form. Remove the picture and you have a pictograph. Take away the ability to multiply mentally and you disempower. She'd been effectively brainwashed by revolutionary teaching, to the extent that by age nine she'd resisted all my attempts to redress such toxic social engineering aimed at who knew what literary competence. We'd both been exhausted by the tussle.

I'd taken the school to task over their New Literacy and New Maths camouflaged as progress but might as well have saved my breath. I'd been made to feel like a Luddite: curmudgeonly and old fashioned, ironically even *Rightist*. They knew best how to draw out of the child what was already there, innate; seeded in the womb like a pearl of wisdom. Moreover, I was informed, education should be a tool for radical political change, to challenge traditional notions and raise a generation that would subvert the prevailing institutions: raw Marxist dialectic. The language was changing organically. Standard English and correct grammatical usage now marked you as elitist: old guard, part of the dominant culture.

Such a structure 'flattened imaginative and creative writing' and was a thing of the past, of Empire. Multiculturalism had rendered all that obsolete by the variegated and colourful contribution it had made to the burgeoning New Britain and its lingua franca. This sat comfortably within the guidelines of the Government's education policy and its level playing field for the new integrated society, modern and cosmopolitan. I considered that 'flattening' was already endemic and was embedded in the *Newspeak* where 'deferred success' was the PC alternative to failure. One result was that a high proportion of school leavers were effectively illiterate. It was not always thus.

My resort to phonic teaching based on the sounds of twenty-six letter recognition, the traditional teaching methodology as trashed by the educational establishment, finally paid off with Emma. I compared the staggering rise in the diagnoses of dyslexia to the parallel implementation of their new methods but they argued that hitherto dyslexia simply wasn't recognised as a condition and that great strides had been made. Government figures showed that forty-six percent of children were dyslexic, they said smugly: as if that was some kind of vindication. Probably they needed to massage their ratios to improve their standing in the League Tables.

I still didn't believe her brain was wired differently: rather she was a victim of a child centric-wonderland in which the role of teacher had been redefined. Where it seemed it was more important that our future citizen should to learn *what* to think, rather than *how*.

At school, I too had been a casualty of experimental teaching, but my father had led me out of the labyrinth to appreciate literature, for one thing. For that I thanked him still. I saw the parallels too with the New Order that I'd zealously embraced at university, to my father's chagrin. A brigade of revolutionary teachers in the grip of a dangerous dogma can cause havoc, the extent of which society may not yet fully comprehend. My political leanings hitherto had guaranteed that Emma would go to a state school but I couldn't wait to get her into private education after my exposure to the Orwellian alternative. The parting shot across my bows was of 'relevance'. In the prevailing political ideology, the teaching of any of the positives of British history had to be counterbalanced by the execration of our forefathers for Empire; for enslaving and polluting the Earth. Perhaps Dad had been right.

Through my coaching, she too had mastered reading competency, but so far had failed to appreciate reading for its own sake and never managed to overcome her fear of mathematics. Perhaps success in those areas was merely *deferred*.

After a period of home tuition, abandoning work on my own degree via the Open University, we'd enrolled her in an expensive school, only to have her education interrupted by my separation from Simeon. Considering the subsequent drastic change in our living standards it was fortunate that I'd found this address within the catchment of a reasonable state school for her final important years.

Since our move, her frustration repeatedly surfaced in her superior manner, combined with teenage sarcasm in toxic reaction. I was now the enemy through my failure to make learning 'fun' as it was officially represented in the canon of formal education, and was spoken to as if I were an imbecile, when she could be bothered. Maybe she just plain held me to account for our 'reduced circumstances' and her forced removal from the privileged society of her wealthy friends.

'This argument is not about your schooling,' I said. 'It's about behaviour. You're too young to go gallivanting at all hours.' *Gallivanting. That word? My father's voice uttering from my own throat.* 'Don't you understand what can happen to young, vulnerable girls?'

There I go, implanting my own fears. It was only natural that she'd want to meet boys. Did I want a timorous recluse for a daughter?

'I thought it was your generation, like *pioneered* the 'sexual revolution.'

'No, that was your granddad's.' It sounded wrong even as I said it.

With a jibing inflection on my given name implying it was an affectation of my own, I was invited to 'talk to the hand'.

'You're so conventional, Natasha. I'm not a child! I can get the *morning after* pill from a pharmacist without your consent, so chill!'

'Rights imply responsibilities. You're a minor in law and you don't call the shots.'

'I'm old enough to decide for myself and you can't stop me,' she said defiantly. 'Ain't gonna happen to *moi*!'

Fifteen, going-on thirty with mood swings to match. She reminded me so much of me, when I was young, stupid and hormonal. 'It can happen to anyone,' I said, 'Even if you take precautions.'

'*Whad-ever!*' she drawled in a phony accent. 'I'm going to Greece. I'll live with Simeon. He lets me do stuff.'

Could frame thy fearful symmetry? Simeon was in there too. I had loved him, had I not?

She might have won on 'door damage' collateral, but I'd got even on points when I'd had a minor panic attack. She'd looked almost

66

concerned.

'What's the matter?' she'd asked with just the vestige of a scowl.

'Nothing!' I said, although an iron band encircled my chest. 'Just that... if looks could kill you'd be, *like*, half an orphan.'

'OMG,' she mocked. 'That's like *humour*? Only *different*!'

We were so alike but doomed to fight. How much protection is stifling nowadays? How much is even possible? Tomorrow she could be lovely. *Might* be, I corrected myself.

~.~

But now my dad was dead and Emma didn't even seem to notice.

I threw on my old Barbour and walked to the end of the garden to see to the pony's feed. Blaze ambled over in his paddock, nodding his head and greeting me happily at the gate. At least he hadn't got out again so my baling wire fence repair must be holding. I rubbed his muzzle and fed him a sugar lump. Damn, I thought for the umpteenth time. This should be Emma's job. I walked him over to his shed absently kicking some straw over an exposed patch on the hard earth floor.

I remembered a glossy magazine I'd flicked through in my doctor's surgery. A four page article on a one-time TV celebrity and her near-identical sixteen year-old daughter: *Stepford Twins*, shopping together. Best of friends. It was easy to sneer, but why was it such a battleground with Emma? I felt a sudden loneliness. Perhaps I was just a bad mother. It ran in the family after all.

A week before she'd been quite normal, calm and chatty. 'We have a barn owl,' she'd said, with a slight smile. 'They're like protected aren't they?'

'Yes, I said. That's nice. Perhaps she will help Quantum keep the mice down.'

'Cool!' she said and smiled again, her disposition almost sunny, then thrust a blade of ice into my ribs. I saw the razor stripes on her arm.

Emma, milking her lifeblood again to release unbearable tension.

Chapter 6. *A Secret*

I looked up the number of the coroner's office and planned to ring them first thing. Then I'd get onto the undertakers to tell them that an autopsy might have to be arranged. I needed to ring Dr. Mitchell too, out of courtesy. Meanwhile I needed food. It had been an emotional day but I thought I'd handled things well; no histrionics in public. My stiff upper-lipped Dad would have been proud of my performance.

On the kitchen television the 6 o'clock news was the usual fare of suicide bombings. In the Sudan a story was running that an English teacher had allowed her primary school kids to name the class teddy bear *Mohamed (peace and blessings be upon Him)*. The news item suggested that she might be given forty lashes and jailed for some time midst rising hysteria and calls for the death penalty. Someone, Orla Guerin perhaps, stared out of the cathode ray tube, reporting with unsmiling intensity. It was getting so mad I wouldn't have been surprised if they were to put the bear in the dock. Perhaps we should respond, carpet-bomb the Sudan with pork scratchings?

I'd rashly suggested to Emma that she should be careful with Iqbal who seemed to me all 'flash'. She'd raged at me for an Islamophobe; called for a public stoning. Contemptuously she'd asked me how I justified my own life; told me I had been brainwashed by the Daily Mail and its editorial line of Islamic demonisation: I was ticking all its readers' boxes on the issue of race. I said that it wasn't about *race. It may have been my blonde daughter speaking, who never read a tabloid newspaper, but ventriloquism seemed more likely.*

Part of me was mortified, having always encouraged Emma to view all as equal, until he'd wrapped a stolen car around a tree with my daughter and two other youngsters aboard. I felt vindicated that my intuition had had nothing to do with race *or* religion. I'd perceived arrogance and a thinly disguised contempt for women in his attitude, not least to myself, and considered a degree of prejudice was a justifiable tool in our armoury for survival. Like a sixth sense. More than that, I felt I'd recognised the beginnings of mind control, and feared the radical politicisation and oppression of my daughter. History repeating in one generation more tragically than Karl Marx' *farce,* I thought. Or, as he'd have posited, *first* as tragedy, *then* as farce.

Emma confided that he'd carried a knife, a dagger - for protection of course. It was a religious thing, cultural. I countered that that was *Sihkism*. Well then, a 'family tradition' she'd argued. What sort of family? I'd wondered. I felt that her mind had been infiltrated and she was fully-primed for overthrow from within.

I had fought off my demons in my own way and in my own time. Post-natal depression and worse. Those memories were confused, but at least I'd had some sort of help. All sorts of agencies were out there preying on the vulnerable, radicalising the young and the victims seemed to get younger; pre-university. That institution was still the favoured fishing ground, though as many monkfish as cod were attending following government policy. But it was ever a bottomless resource for recruitment, as I should know.

Emma's injuries healed but she'd remained grounded for a few weeks. Meanwhile her friendship with the Class A-dealing narcissistic *king of bling* dissolved. Fading with it, to my unashamed relief, the image of a future Emma, her blue eyes regarding me from inside a *niqab*.

~-~

Why polonium? I thought. If the KGB wanted to 'disappear' someone they just disappeared, unless he was a high profile whistle blower living in London, and Dad had been anything but. I surmised that if Russian Mafiosi were involved in whatever it was my father was mixed up with, their methods would have been equally unsophisticated. Bodies would be found in skips and so on if warnings were intended. Or so I presumed.

So perhaps the polonium was a symbol. Shorthand for, 'I'm worried that something is going to happen to me and I just want you to know that.'

But why?

As I sat down to eat I caught my wrist on something in my jeans pocket. My Dad's letter. I unfolded the envelope and placed it on the kitchen table, upside down by chance. I noticed something then that I hadn't seen when I'd read the letter at the Cedars. Not in the letter actually but on the back of the envelope, faintly… something very small in pencil. It was scratchy, erratic writing of some sort, or a drawing. I wasn't sure which. It was my father's right side that was, *had been* affected. I got up and walked over to the hob and switched on the light over the kitchen worktop and squinted at the envelope. Capitulating, I fished out my reading glasses.

'*Sie ist der hellste Stern von allen.*' A rare lyric passage from Emma's bedroom. *'Kann verbrennen, kann auch blenden....'* before *Rammstein's* blistering heavy metal sun became molten again, threatening to burn its way through the ceiling.

I could make out a capital 'A' so I thought. The rest of that word was unclear though it sprawled across most of the flap. Below this was a very crude, *what I thought of,* as a 'smiley face' with ears. It looked a little like a cat's head. It had been drawn twice as though my father had been unsatisfied with the first left-handed attempt. I struggled to identify that word beginning with an 'A'. There seemed to be about five letters altogether with a spidery line joining them as though getting the pressure right on the envelope was tremendously difficult. I imagined my father trying to hold the envelope down onto a flat surface- possibly even the top of the record player and with an immense effort writing an illegible message or cipher that he must have felt was of tremendous importance.

And failing heroically.

Like the message in his eyes that I was not receiving when I brought him home. When I'd visited him. I was remembering his agitation and how I'd tried to calm him, quiet him, when all he wanted was to communicate something to me that was vitally important to his peace of mind.

I saw something else, an almost Neolithic 'arrow' now that I'd looked hard enough. Part of this cipher was an arrow that seemed to point from the word and became part of the 'drawing'. Or was pointing from the word to the drawing of the 'cat'. Or was it a cat? Somewhere in the distant past, from my childhood, I recalled my father drawing little doodles for me, illustrating poems that he made up about animals. He was very good at this. I'd then copied the sketches, sometimes with hilarious results until my drawing skills improved, which they quickly did I remember. There was one about a rhinoceros, a pastiche on Hamlet, *'To Biff, or not to Biff'.*

My eyes opened wide. I looked at the kitchen wall where I'd hung some small, framed pictures, pressed flowers behind glass and a copy of Max Erhmann's *Serenity Prayer.* There were others, a couple of originals I'd kept all those years, signed JM. The one that caught my eye was a cartoon of a smiley whale, blowing a jet of water from its blowhole.

The poem was entitled *'The Cetacean'* and parodied Hillaire Belloc. How things become invisible to us through familiarity.

I walked over to it and read it again, though in truth I'd remembered it word for word since childhood. It was one of his didactic fun poems, to encourage me to read and learn more about the natural world. I read:

> *I beg you prevail,*
> *Consider the Whale,*
> *Hi Magnitude,*
> *His Origins,*
> *His IQ, and Tail!*
> *Or Flukes as they're called,*
> *And not nearly so bald,*
> *As appear at first sight,*
> *But are covered with Hair,*
> *And his teeth are not Teeth,*
> *But are Whalebone,*
> *So there!*

But this other little smiley face that I recognised on the envelope, for all its torturous execution, had been a regular thing. I was looking at one again flickering on the cathode ray tube: the concluding BBC news item from their correspondent in Khartoum. In my memory it had featured in a serial, within the anthology of poems my father had written: a sort of *Winnie the Pooh* or *Paddington* character that had appeared again and again. *Mohamed - peace be upon him.* A bear.

And at once I saw the word in its entirety. It was '*Alice*'!

'*He liked Lucy.*' '*She wanders all the time. Worse than a toddler.*'

Alice, and an arrow pointing to a bear that was also a pillowcase.

I would have to reconsider that kind invitation to tea.

~-~

My father had died in the late afternoon: a Thursday, so I'd had the weekend or I would have blamed myself for my hesitancy in ringing the Coroner's Court for a day or so. That Monday the clerk at the office that dealt with my request for information said, if the proper procedures had been followed in establishing the cause of death, that I'd need more than my concerns that he had died of something other than natural causes following a stroke for an inquest to be held. If I wished to make a representation in person or in writing to the court then this would be considered. In my father's case his death had been recorded with the Registrar of Births and Deaths within 24 hrs., before close of play Friday.

Very efficient, Dr. Mitchell.

There was no way that I could use that rambling tract that was my father's last letter as evidence. I could hardly abstract passages concerning his fears about foul play and withhold the rest. It would be regarded as a reactionary blast from a man in late middle age against the world and politics as he saw it, yearning after an England that had long past into history; not least, dubious evidence of extreme paranoia about some fantastic international conspiracy. I shut my mind against memories of my own paranoia, happily done with. But perhaps such conditions had a hereditary basis.

But how could I build a case for a forensic investigation without more to go on?

I delved into his papers. It was a jumble: things filed randomly, partly my fault obviously, but no particular pattern had emerged after several hours of agitated sifting and two glasses of supermarket plonk - I already knew better than to be as free with the bottles of Blundell's Elderberry that had been thrust on me. How many government health warning units would that amount to after a week for a woman of my reduced Body Mass Index? I caught her reflection in the kitchen mirror. Still attractive but a shadow of her former self. Perhaps we have a yet untested addictive personality and might become one of the three million alcoholics in this country. Three million and one? Something to watch.

Unsurprisingly most of the documents revolved around historical aviation matters and I was beginning to nod by the witching hour. I'd looked in on Emma: gently removed her CD player headphones. The *Rammstein* CD had migrated from the music centre and was still running in the portable.

I held the phones to my ear for a moment. ' *...und aus der Erde singt das Kind...*' And the child sings from the ground.... From *under* the ground? Macabre. And why was everything in German suddenly? Was this some unconscious irony of hers, a pastiche on my love of the German Romantics? I switched it off then, after thinking how angelic she could look, she with her intense *Save the Tiger and Polar Bear* issues; clicked off her table lamp, remembering how she'd once put her tiny fingers into....... *Emma, oh Emma. My Dad is dead. He was my rock, even when he was out of sight. A distant, flawed rock, but out there still..... until now. Emma you could sleep through an earthquake.* She was a teen zombie on school mornings and it was a battle to get her up and pointing in the right direction.

I had a happy knack of being able to reach out and cancel my alarm clock seconds before it would have buzzed me into wakefulness. It didn't really matter how much sleep I'd had. I'd just tell myself to wake up at

06.45 and I did, rendering its existence futile except as an indicator of my prophetic prescience or more likely of a fine-tuned biological clock. With old wind-up alarm clocks, even from what I thought of as a deep sleep I'd find myself pressing the button just as it clicked, before the first stutter of the alarm. I'd read somewhere that it was the result of my circadian rhythm responding to *Zeitgebers* or subliminal clues. The click of a releasing escapement on the alarm clock would be enough. But that didn't explain my response to pre-empting an electrical alarm. Anyway I set the timer to give me that ten minutes or so to review my day or my life to date while luxuriating in my warm bed, not missing Simeon at all, as I reminded myself.

What is love? *Kann verbrennen, kann auch blenden…* it can burn, can also blind you. Where had I heard those words before?

Ah, Simeon. *'If it doesn't scare the crap outa you it ain't worth doing!'* Now there was a statement! I'd thought he was an original but his bad boy image was copied from his Type A Personality associates. Weekend *Hell's Angels*. Sky diving party animals, ex-*Ruperts* some of them I'd thought perceptively, perhaps from the Paras or other good regiments: refreshingly dangerous and seductive, brash, fast, living on the financial edge, riding the bubble……good looking with that stain of vulnerability that made him boyishly irresistible, seeming sometimes awkward and standing apart from the ruck as if he didn't really belong…. For a while there had been *BS* and *PS*. *BS* was the bullshit of *Before Simeon*, I'd told myself into my wineglass. Everything else would be *Post Simeon*, at least that's what I'd thought when first he'd deserted me: part gadfly, a weakling, owned by his habits. It was *he* that had been full of *BS* and anyway I'd since cut down on my drinking, finished with guilt and self-loathing. Sick with turning from the reproach in Emma's eyes.

Her self-harming was at issue. I'd made an unworthy, somewhat drunken and oblique accusation, or perhaps Simeon had taken it as such, that he might have been some way responsible for her behaviour, based perhaps on my own sleepy, fugitive, unsubstantiated recollections of a once beloved father's hands lifting the bedclothes…. putting me, Natasha, 'his own special princess', to bed. Simeon had vehemently denied that suggestion, called *me* the twisted bitch.

'Who was it threw our week-old child across the bedroom, barricading herself in and trying to shoot me with the TV remote? You were round the twist for weeks, so don't you *dare* accuse me of interfering with….of harming her.'

I'd noticed he'd stumbled on 'interfering' which further narrowed my suspicions, whereas 'harming' carried a psychological connotation, embodying perhaps the lesser construction of a 'personality flaw', excused by one's being over strict, 'wanting the best' for the child - tripping over into the 'lesser evil' of mental cruelty – all this analysed and pre-judged by a 'mother tigress' in a microsecond. But later I had taken time to consider that his emotions, his reticence to confront such a thought levelled by someone he'd professed to love, could make even a candid utterance of denial stick in the throat.

Now the ache was dulled. But the anger was still there when I scratched at the scar. There was the Valium-induced *nepenthe* for a while, not unlike a trance-like state I'd known once before *BS*; when *they'd* tried to control my mind. *Bits missing. Waking up in strange places. Unbidden images of a blindfolded younger self, a sexualised image.* It gave me the shudders. Who the hell were *they* anyway? *Move on, woman.*

Too late for Simeon and me now, in any event.

~-~

There was a lot about the Baltic States too, equally unsurprising as Dad had lived there for a couple of years at least. Doing what he always did: researching and writing I suppose and acting he'd said, with others, as an altruistic counterbalance to what he described as *Coca-Cola Capitalism.* It was already well into the early hours of what had been another exhausting day of work: talking to my solicitor for advice since my father had died intestate it seemed, and how I should proceed with an application for an inquest based only on what might be regarded as paranoia; asking the undertakers to please keep him in the chapel of rest a little longer and just before I called it a night I stumbled on something.

In a plain brown A4 envelope with the letters *FSV* scrawled in the corner were some early German magazine clippings with pictures, a few dozen dog-eared photographs of people and aeroplanes. Old aeroplanes. Nothing unusual there: nearly all my father's photographs were of old aeroplanes. Along with these there was a translation of German text: a cutting from a 1927 *Sportflieger* magazine. It concerned a senior flight instructor at the *Sportflug GmbH: Mittelfranken und Oberpfalz* at Fürth near Nuremberg and showed an old biplane flying low around a snow-covered racetrack, overtaking a motorcycle combination and a stripped-down Bugatti racing car. I knew it was a Bugatti because my father had been almost equally interested in vintage cars. He'd pointed out the distinct horseshoe shape of the Bugatti radiator pictured in his collection of motoring books when I was a child and still susceptible to his enthusiasms. It's surprising what sticks in the mind of the young.

Reading the transcript I found it was indeed a Bugatti Brescia and that the pilot of the biplane was a man called Udet. There was also a picture of a leather-coated man in a short-peaked First War German officer's cap leaning on the wing of the same aeroplane talking to a man in flying gear who was wearing a parachute. The pilot was smoking a cigarette. The aeroplane was painted a dark colour with a white letter 'D' and the number '822' on the fuselage side. The pilot identified in the caption was Captain Udet. The other man was unidentified but underneath in red ballpoint pen was the name *von Moritz* followed by a question mark.

It looked like my father's handwriting but meant nothing to me and I moved on. I soon found another picture of the same biplane, described as an Udet U-12 *Flamingo*. This time the same man was in the rear (pilot's) cockpit and the transcript stated that 'Ivan Morizhov', known as 'The Baron', stood in for Udet at some airshow performances in Europe, later joining him on tour in the United States. The article named 'von Moritz' as the flight instructor mentioned as based at Fürth and that he also flew as a film 'stunt' pilot in some of the four movies that starred World War 1 flying ace Ernst Udet. Connecting the two articles I could only speculate that the title of 'Baron' and the name 'Morizhov' might have been a sort of professional name for Moritz like a 'stage name' for his performances in front of the crowd, maintaining his own name for the more prosaic and serious business of teaching pupils to fly. But why the interest in this character with his highly dubious alter ego from the early days of flying?

In this same envelope there was a faded sepia *Daguerrotype* of a small sea biplane suspended from a crane hoist, the jib attached at the stern of what looked like a large trawler. The seaplane had the letters DSV painted prominently on the nose. On the back of the photograph was written, 'D692, *prototype?*' and in another hand, '*Deutsche Seefischerei-Verein, Nordmeer.*'

Another photo was of what appeared to be an identical biplane, but this time with a landplane undercarriage and a curious *oblique* chequered flag scheme on its fuselage. It bore the registration 'D', again presumably for 'Deutschland', followed by a number, 698 - D698. On the back was written, '*Hääcke motor replaced by 60 hp. British* ABC *Hornet*', in my father's hand. There was another picture of it in a cutting from a German magazine, but this time with no caption translation although the man sitting in the cockpit was identified as 'The Baron'. In both pictures the tail bore a macabre device: a black 'pirate's flag' in the form of a painted pennant: a skull and crossed bones in white that seemed to flutter defiantly, contrasting with the white-painted fin and rudder: a death's head in a black cloak.

The Staaken logo commemorates the E.4/20 airliner built in the Zeppelin sheds and destroyed by order of the Inter-Allied Military Control Commission.

Von Moritz's Staaken Z-1 Flitzer at Staaken Aerodrome, Berlin, 1927. The fuselage bears the blue/white diamonds of the *Bayerische Wappenschild*. (Archive Neumann)

So what did it amount to ? An obscure (?) understudy of a famous fighter pilot (it said Udet had been credited with 62 victories in one of the articles) ie. a First War flying ace had employed a flying instructor and itinerant exhibition pilot who in turn used a 'Russified' version of his given name for airshows… retaining his own name for his more professional aviation work? It might indicate that the showbiz side of flying, stunting and barnstorming was by then less than respectable. Such a conflict of careers, I speculated, might impact on his more 'professional' flying, training crews for rapidly growing European airlines at a prestigious flying school - management and shareholders distancing themselves from the thrills of the flying circus. Hence the *nomme de ciel*. Or was it actually a 'bona fide' *nomme de guerre* from the Great War? What would that have made him? A *White Russian*? God, I thought, there are more things in heaven and earth, Horatio, than you could shake a stick at.

One thing I'd learned is that in life things are seldom what they seem. People are chameleons. They draw their cloaks from their surroundings, like octopuses: they blend. They are adept at camouflage — even if it's only an expense account or membership of the golf club and driving the right car. But Baron Morizhov? What a bogus name? It had connotation's with the English comic-sinister tradition, like a hastily written character for a rural melodrama: a production having a caricature international financier: a wicked, top-hatted capitalist, fictitious title and sinister laugh, given to seducing innocent maidens and gleefully evicting the poor from their hovels.

But wasn't I looking at a turbulent Germany emerging from the shadow of defeat? And what was so important about his identity that so interested my father?

Tucked into the bottom of the envelope was something hard. I tipped out a thick square of cardboard, folded and stapled. I rummaged in the kitchen drawer for a knife to remove the staples. Inside was a minidisk: a small DVD. On the front was written *Udet &Co.* in green CD marker pen.

Consumed with curiosity I crossed to the lounge and inserted the disk in the DVD player. The film was a bit scratchy in black and white but there was a commentary that had probably been added sometime later, when newsreels had sound. The language was delivered 'rapid fire' in clipped narrative style, like our own English newsreel commentaries from the same period. To a stomping '20s jazz accompaniment the Flamingo looped and rolled, manoeuvring very near the ground. I understood enough German to make sense of it all. At one point the commentator broke in excitedly to say that Captain Udet would pick up a handkerchief from the grass with a wire hook on his wingtip. He concluded his display with a long sideways-slipping manoeuvre, propeller stopped, Udet straightening the biplane at the very last second to touch down first on one wheel and then the other, rolling to a safe halt with a shriek from sax and trumpet; a long dead pilot living again courtesy of a DVD-transposed film.

A feat of precision flying for its day, but just what would *he* have made of the antics of the *Red Bull Air Race*? I'm wondering, when the words *Kunstflug mit Flitzer* appear on a clapperboard. I realise the disk has more to offer; another film grafted on. I recognise the chequered scheme and the black pennant of the Baron's biplane. The phrase, *form following function,* occurs to me.

The propeller is swung. The camera pans the crowd, pulling focus momentarily on smiling *Berlin chic*, be-furred, cloche-hatted flappers on the damp tarmac standing in front of an *UFA* film studio sign. Their escorts in plus fours cluster near the hangar. There's an impressive open Mercedes, big headlights and flowing exhausts. *Staaken Berlin* appears in large letters above the giant doors and again embroidered on the shoulders of the white-overalled mechanics before the film cuts to the moving aeroplane.

D698 rips through the grainy film, racing its hurtling shadow on the grass. The commentator is talking about someone called von Schleich and Gerhardt Fieseler. His voice lifts a semitone as he mentions that the 'Baron flies!' before the vibrant brass and clarinet resume.

The aerobatics are vivid — almost as if the pilot can hear the music. He flies level for no more than a few seconds. Compared with the bigger Flamingo, 'Flitzer' D698, is a swift: making vertical zooms, darting and twisting, looping, rolling, flashing in the sun, spinning - recovering at low level. The pilot concludes his display by bouncing the wheels in an exaggerated ballistic roll, wings whipping through the vertical, followed by a gentle touchdown into wind. Hurrah! It was breathtaking, even by current standards of what I'd seen casually on TV.

The 'Flitzer' taxied slowly towards the camera, the nose swinging from side to side under the pilot's direction: ruddering like a tacking yacht, forward view evidently obstructed by the nose due to the ground attitude. Udet could be seen walking towards the cockpit, still smoking followed by hearty young Aryans and their flapper consorts. I thought naked lights weren't allowed around aeroplanes - proof that Health and Safety had yet to intrude in the 1920s. The propeller flicked to a halt and the pilot jumped easily onto the grass. Udet shook him by the hand. A broad wing strut briefly obscured the pilot's features as he peeled off his helmet, but then he grinned into the camera. Sharp focus. My tiredness drained away. The room seemed suddenly to close in around me and my hair literally stood on end.

The look in the eyes, that engaging smile I knew so well. My flawed 'rock'. Unmistakable, despite the quality of the film stock. That smile I'd see no more on the face of my father. The same. The very same.

I re-ran the DVD ten times that night. The impression never wavered. I was awake. Not suffering some hypnopompic fit. I was not hallucinating, or if I was the hallucinogenic effect kicked in every time. The face wasn't my father's, but it could have been his younger brother. Or maybe his *grandfather*, given the date of the *Sportflieger* magazine article, which was most probably contemporaneous with the film footage. That seemed possible. But my late grandfather, Arthur Morris, had lived in Islington. Served in Palestine in the Army: driven a Sherman tank. My gran, Amy, had died just before my mother, had lived in sheltered accommodation after my granddad had died, and both were as British as could be. My great grandfather then? Or great uncle at least - on the *German side of the family*? But there *was* no 'German' side to the family - as far as I knew. Moritz. A 'von'. 'Stage name' *Morizhov*? Anglicised to *Morris*? My father had been born just after the War. Christened John, a popular name then, *Ivan* being its Russian equivalent.

And he had, bizarrely I'd thought, signed himself *Johannes*.

~-~

I found the relevant passages in his letter.

I have recently tried to re-master my 'mother tongue' with some success, aided by a charming tutor... I am sure (this) will astonish you ...we are English are we not? I believed so until I began to dig past one generation and uncovered Pandora's box.

And later:

It may sound strange but feel I have resumed my true identity and found peace both in my spiritual homeland and within myself..... no stronger bond than between old comrades who have a history of shared hardship....the Kameradschaft of the Jasta is absolute.......Perhaps the fancy that we re-incarnate in 'clusters' to work out our karmas and interact with past friends....role-playing the old associations of previous lives.....I think I may have truly found myself fallen among friends.....

Delusional? Off his trolley? They were his own words. Like something out of Kafka. When does co-incidence leave off and fate reveal itself? When do things that seem innocuous start to form patterns in the mind? When do these things trigger paranoia or descend into schizophrenia? Would we recognize it in ourselves or would we just think the whole world was wrong? Should I accept such evidence or just leave it in a drawer where it would grow in power for every day that I tried to ignore it, like that one unopened bottle a recovering alcoholic keeps, to remind him of his vow?

There was a soft 'thud' just behind me. I jumped like a startled rabbit, but it was only *Quantum*. Uneasily I realised that I must have left the kitchen window slightly open.

She was a small tortoiseshell cat that had adopted us soon after we'd arrived and settled in happily, even before we had. We called her that because it was shorter than *Heisenberg*: neither a *wave* nor a *particle*, she seemed to have the facility to be in more than one place at a time. So we'd see her in the garden and then she'd be found curled up in Emma's bedroom or we hear her on the roof of the lean-to kitchen just as she walked in through the open door. It was only that we'd yet to see *two* such identical cats together that inclined us to believe there weren't in fact a matching pair. She purred and rubbed against my legs and I recalled guiltily that I hadn't put food down for her this morning. She seemed to be able to survive though and had evidently done so before we arrived. So either she was hunting mice in the fields or she belonged to someone

80

else, eating at more than one establishment.

I opened a tin of cat food, and on impulse, my *Pears Cyclopaedia*, to the page relating to Heisenberg's *Uncertainty Principle* in Quantum Mechanics. I found that it was published in the same year that Fritz Lang's modern Gothic film *Metropolis* was released with its bleak view of a de-humanized robotnik future of science and state control, co-incidentally made at the UFA film studios in the old Zeppelin hangars at Staaken, 1927. The same year that Charles Lindbergh flew the Atlantic Ocean solo in the *Spirit of St. Louis*.

Of course, no mention of a contemporary race between car, motorcycle and aeroplane, with one *Johannes von Moritz*, a possible ancestor of my own, joyfully stunting his 'Flitzer' at an unnamed event in Germany? I fumed at our lack of a landline that would have enabled me to make an Internet search for Udet, von Moritz, *Flitzers*, et al. I determined to call BT again on my mobile tomorrow. I looked at my watch. It was already 'tomorrow' by two hours!

~_~

The next day I called at the chapel of rest. I explained that I was intending to apply to the Coroner for an inquest into my father's death. If they thought this was unusual they gave no indication of it. I asked to see my father's body. Alone with his corpse I felt a wave of emotion. I steeled myself to lift his eyelid and saw what I was afraid I might: a light speckling, now fading, of what had been a bloodshot eyeball. The pages of a forensic textbook I'd retained from my curtailed studies raised the possibility of anoxic death, a fading indictor of petechial haemorrhaging on the surface of the eye suggesting at least the possibility of suffocation.

~_~

To my amazement a post mortem was allowed. I almost withdrew my request at the last moment. Guilt: that my father was to be slit and his innards dissected: weighed out, like on some butcher's slab, pored over and examined. But that was the price of truth and ultimately justice had there been foul play.

The inquest took place in Ipswich the following week. Mitch gave his evidence. He glanced my way as he stood down. I wasn't sure if his expression revealed what he was thinking; if I detected sadness or pity for my irrationality.

The pathologist's report followed after an interval: the subject being a 'well-nourished Caucasian' male of middle-age….. No contaminants or foreign substances detected in the gut or the haemoglobin although there was a slight increase of seratonin evident in the intestine. Hyoid bone intact, etc. The report continued for about five minutes. The evidence was weighed. Nothing conclusive could be determined.'

In lay terms, asphyxiation indicators, such as the blood blotching of the eyeballs, would have dissipated by the time of the autopsy. Given the weight of evidence regarding his stroke and the not uncommon heart attack that followed, the hearing concluded that death was from natural causes.

The Coroner was kindness itself in addressing a few words of comfort to me. I felt hot, unconvinced still, despite the forensic evidence to the contrary. Some little neo-medical upstart inside me told me that they would have used undetectable toxins that probably caused his stroke in the first place but they'd failed to kill him then. Later they'd succeeded either by the simple expedient of closing the mouth and pinching the nostrils of a helpless, part-paralysed man who could not even cry out, or by the administration of another toxin, possibly a neuro-toxin injected into an orifice - the ear perhaps, so that the hypodermic mark would be undetected. It was too horrific to contemplate.

I was now able to proceed with the funeral arrangements and told myself that I had done what I could to assuage my concerns. But that same night I dreamed I'd stood alone in a graveyard, wringing my hands by moonlight, hooded and veiled. Withered flowers disintegrated in the wind, leaving a smudge upon a headstone that revealed no inscription. Perhaps, I thought, dreams were about past conflicts or messages fundamental to current purpose. I recalled snatches of Mahler's *Symphony of Resurrection*, the first, troubling movement, at the graveside…. Clearly there were unanswered questions here, but something else as well that disturbed me.

Maybe I should look for that work on the interpretation of dreams by Carl Jung.

~-~

My conscience still bothered me and would continue to do so for some time. I felt the sudden need of someone to confide in with my concerns. I knew few people well enough close at hand. Emma was too young and too vulnerable and her exams were looming.

Mitch had been an ally I'd thought at first and in any other circumstances I would have taken the step of approaching him, except it was he who'd pronounced my father dead and signed the certificate. Given that he would hardly have suspected the skilful assassination of a stroke victim in a care home for the elderly infirm, to resurrect my worries and place them at his door would be adding insult to injury. He might view it as a persistent attack on his professional competency.

I abandoned the idea of ringing some of the West Ken *fashionistas*, my erstwhile *botox set*. Even those not now addicted to Danielle Steele would assume I'd been reading too many spy novels or that I was suffering some paranoid obsession from lack of sex, shopping or other nostrum of Twenty-first Century living. They'd demand I visit them for a trawl of Knightsbridge and beyond, prescribe that I *shopped 'til I dropped* and I'd return home with killer boots and an expensive outfit that I couldn't afford and I'd never wear with nothing resolved. Besides, I was done with all that and Emma, like an annoying fly always buzzing against the window you *didn't* open, would be arranging texted assignations with old boyfriends and trying to give me the slip. It was difficult enough trying to keep her from the local 'raves' and the STI card-carrying hoodies that hung around Ipswich of an evening. Too stressful. Too dangerous.

Who did that leave then for 'Natasha No Mates' as Emma had called me? In a previous incarnation there'd just been professional working relationships, a chat over coffee and a Danish. No sharing of addresses or 'phone numbers. So who did that leave?

The Blundell 'sisters' on the adjoining smallholding.

Chapter 7. *Clarissa*

Grimstone House and its surrounding meadows and herb gardens had been part of a larger acreage but much of it had been sold piecemeal to one of the bigger producers, and so with Mill Farm. Clarissa was fearsomely intelligent and interesting and not the sort of person you'd expect to find living in a run-down Suffolk farmhouse. Before it closed down, post office gossip alleged that Chrissie, her younger sister, had changed her surname by deed pole in a distant, less sexually-liberated era, despite the flakiness of the 'sixties. And there were the young 'tenants'. I'd not met any of them to begin with, except for a brief first meeting just with Clarissa. But it was the second occasion that had broken the ice in more dramatic fashion.

~-~

I recalled the first meeting.

I'd intended to call for a while to find out if Quantum was perhaps their cat. I am solitary as a rule but while I was wondering if cat ownership was pretext enough for an introduction, Blaze solved the problem for me by returning with Clarissa holding his halter after he'd got into their cabbages.

'I think he just wanted to make friends with *Serenade*,' she said.

'I'm sorry?'

'Chrissie's *donkey*,' she smiled cheerfully.

I apologised again and we lead the pony back to the paddock. 'My name's Natasha, by the way,' I said.

'What? Not another bloody Pole!' she said amiably. 'Place is a Baltic suburb already.'

Clarissa Blundell was an iron-haired, solid-looking, once handsome woman in her late sixties, I would guess. With jeans, green wellies and a body warmer over her roll neck sweater she looked every inch a countrywoman.

'Well of course they are flocking-in now they've got EU membership. Can't blame them,' I said. 'I hear they work very hard on a minimum wage.'

'They work *bloody* hard,' said Clarissa vehemently.' Mostly for the bloody gang masters. I've got two staying with me. Poles I mean, not gang masters! Most of the local jobs you see advertised in the community newspapers are in Polish now.'

'For my name,' I said. 'I have to thank my father's love of nineteenth-century Russian romantic novels; the lure of that enigmatic country. Ian Fleming too perhaps. My father was a fan of his. The books are far better than the films of course. The early James Bond films were good though, don't you think, when Sean Connery was in his prime?'

She was studying me keenly. Had I been waffling?

'Was?'

'Pardon?'

'You said that your father *was* a fan. Did he change allegiance to Graham Greene, or….?'

Perhaps I'd given her the impression that I was an orphan.

'Oh, I think he outgrew that sort of novel in his twenties,' I smiled. 'No, he's living abroad at the moment. In Lithuania.'

Living his own romantic fantasy, I thought.

I did invite her in but she said she had to get back though we chatted for a few moments more and I brought up the subject of Quantum. She seemed quite amused by the name and suggested that it might be *Schrödiger's* cat.

I looked a little bemused until she mentioned Heisenberg and the allegory of the hapless feline which was the subject of Schrödiger's hypothesis. This was way over my head as I'd only heard the theories expressed at dinner parties and hadn't studied Quantum Mechanics at all. Why would I?

'Come and visit us any time. We're always at home, particularly to someone interesting. It would make a change from *Soduko* while Chrissie tunes the wireless to background radiation.'

I must have looked as blank as I felt.

'From the Big Bang,' she explained.

Probably I'd looked as vacant as a schoolgirl.

'Listening-in for EVPs?' Clarissa's mouth demonstrated a half smile.

'Pardon?'

'Electronic Voice Phenomenon. Chrissie's bonkers, but she's not alone in thinking that spirits try to communicate from beyond using electrical apparatus. Speaking through 'White Noise'.

'Oh, I see.'

Only later did I discover that schizophrenia can manifest itself in hearing phantom voices through radio static, sometimes induced by use of cannabis which Chrissie smoked freely.

'Chrissie bakes and we make our own wine,' she said. 'She makes delicious goat's cheese pizzas. And the girls have brought they're own cooking specialties to our table.'

'The girls? Your children?'

'Heavens no! Not *my* sprogs. The Polish twins, Lili and Tatiana. They're great little cooks. They've got an old caravan in the corner of our vegetable garden. Is mother still with us?'

She sounded like a country doctor. 'Er, no, sadly. She died a few years ago.'

'Shame. Well the offer stands. Open house at Grimstone, despite the name. Just pop over.' All very jolly.

That encounter seemed an age ago. Turns out she was a doctor: Bachelor of Science, a gifted mathematician and one-time GCHQ code specialist who was convinced that she'd prove *Riemann's Hypothesis* given time and a following wind. I was in no position to judge if that was a delusion.

It seems I'd met her on one of her 'good' days when Clarissa's old 'black dog' was safely sleeping somewhere else for the time being.

Chrissie called it *Churchill.* As in her whispered, 'Rissa's got *Churchill* with her today.' And Clarissa would not move from her room for forty-eight hours, never speaking, barely eating while the mood lay upon her. Eyes turned inwards on her mind, curled up with her 'black dog'.

The week prior to my father's death I'd been to a builders' merchants in Stowmarket. I was day-dreaming down sleepy country lanes humming *'Take me home, country road'*, the Volvo Estate packed with materials for the next stage of the renovation and reflecting on a strange framed print I'd seen in the window of a local art shop: *'Nightbird'* by an artist named Kutz. With its sad, haunted expression a carved wooden owl seemed to grow from the tree branch on which it sat. Above shone the orb of a polished wooden moon.

The irony of that paradox; intuitive wisdom enclosed in wooden immobility, symbolised now my father's inability to communicate, but held mysterious other resonances for me, evading my recall. Something wraith-like and sinister loomed behind the amnesic barrier which by now I'd decided I had personally erected in order to protect myself. Some repressed memory that was too shameful or terrible to confront. Perhaps I needed professional help to abreact whatever I was concealing. Or most likely all I really needed to do was to throw myself into restoring the farm house and then look for a job to occupy me before my overdraft limit was breached forever.

I shrugged off the image, looking forward as I was to getting things finished in the living room now that the kitchen was reasonable. The bedrooms were damp on the north-facing walls but they'd wait until I could afford to have the roof sorted. Emma's room was cosy again with the space heater going for a day and night to dry things out after a particular rainy spell. I'd had a plasterer lined up for the following week. But in the event I had to cancel.

I rounded a tight bend and saw what I thought was a white Transit-type van parked in a field and a figure on the road who seemed to be grappling with someone, before that person was pulled through the gate, the pair disappearing peripherally as I passed by.

It was broad daylight and if people wanted to fool around it was no business of mine. But there was no denying the movement. It had had the appearance of something 'desperate' and made me slow down and think about what I'd really no more than glimpsed. I was sure that the running figure I'd seen for no more than half a second was female. Perhaps because of the clothing or the way the figure moved. I don't know.

I reversed the Volvo to the open farm gate. I could see the van. Both cab doors were open, the rear door closed. I left the car with the motor running. I could hear a man's voice: threatening, exasperated it seemed to me and although I couldn't hear the words clearly I was putting together a fairly obvious scenario in my mind. I had my mobile which I switched on as I cautiously entered the field keeping close to the hedge. My phone bleeped at me. Battery low. Dammit.

A well-built young man with very short hair, dyed blonde-white, aged about twenty-five was holding a young woman. He was wearing jeans, trainers, sweatshirt and had a spider tattoo on his neck. She was dressed in jeans too and an embroidered blouse. Her arm was locked behind her back and she was obviously distressed. He was grabbing at her breasts and she was struggling and pleading - not in English.

'The police are on their way,' I shouted, deepening my voice; employing as much authority as I could manage.

'Yeah?' Seeing that I was alone his reply was one of sneering contempt. 'How long d'you think before they get 'ere, sweetheart?'

We were in rural Suffolk and police resources were stretched. He stared about theatrically. 'No security cams,' and as an afterthought, 'See you after then. Pork anything with legs, me. Old bag like you'd be *gagging* for it!'

I seethed with anger. The girl looked up at me under a fringe of fair hair. 'Please. It's ok. He is drunk. I'll be all right.'

'Leave her alone!' I shouted as loud as I could.'

'He will hurt you,' she said. 'Please go.'

My courage in my hands, I moved towards them without a clear idea of what I was going to do. As a kid, aged ten, I was quite good at Judo. I'd been lithe and light and had no fear of falling. But I'd drifted away from it in my teenage years. It's practice saves you and I was out of it: my training had been long ago, but he was preoccupied with holding on to her and effectively he had only one arm free. So it was back to basics – female fighting technique. Without more ado I ran at him, circling behind, so he had to turn and wrench the girl around with him to keep me in his eye-line. I was pleased to see that she didn't make it easy for him even though she screamed with the pain from her twisted arm. I regretted not looking for some sort of weapon in the car but I couldn't think of anything that was suitable. The carjack handle would have been ideal but I'd have had to unload tile cement, coving and plaster to get at it.

'You pathetic piece of shit!' I yelled, lunging at him, raking the side of his face with my fingernails. They weren't very long unfortunately due to the work I'd been doing on the house but I had the satisfaction of hearing him yell as he ineffectually grabbed for me but I kept away. The girl was struggling but he refused to let up on his grip. I circled them again, staring into his narrowed eyes which glared back in fury and hatred, like the eyes of a panther. I had time to notice how lovely the girl was despite her expression of anguish as she twisted helplessly in his grip. His arms were bare, empurpled with some endermic crassness: a serpent and a naked girl by the look.

'Bitch,' he swore. 'I'll bloody 'ave you.'

I noticed that the free hand was now behind his back. I had a sudden realization that there was a knife there, in a sheath.

'What's your name, dear?' I called to the girl.

'Tatiana,' she panted, her breath coming quickly with the strain. 'Tatiana Raczinskya.'

'Shut your mouth!' He snarled, pulling her arm higher so that she cried out again.

'Ok, Tatiana. I'm going for help. Be brave. The police won't be long. I'm going back to the road. I can't help here.' I was walking quickly towards the gate.

His eyes bored into mine. 'No you bloody don't. You fuckin' stay 'ere or I'll stab the cow.'

'No you won't,' I said as calmly as I could. 'I've got your van registration and I can identify you.'

I walked over to the van. I heard the deep growl of a dog in the back and the clink of a heavy chain. 'And I've got your ignition keys.'

With a cry of rage he dropped the girl and ran at me, roaring.

'Run Tatiana! Across the field. Go to the hedge by the road.'

Tatiana ran like a deer as the assailant rushed at me, knife in hand. He was fast but the field was muddy and slick near the gate and he slipped which gave me a little time. The adrenaline had really kicked-in and I hurled his keys into the bushes, although in retrospect it all happened in a series of disjointed snapshots: me trying not to lose my footing, fumbling with the door handle - but thank God I'd left the engine running. I gained the wheel of the Volvo, slammed the door and hit the accelerator as he banged on the roof and tried to rip open the rear nearside door while the car slipped out of his hands.

The rear wheels screeched as I accelerated down the lane, slowing only to look for the girl, hoping there was a gap or a thinned-section of hedge that she could squeeze through.

I wound the window down.

'Tania!' I yelled. 'Tania!' Her full name was too long.

I could see the white of her blouse as she ran along the far side of the hedge above the road. Then she was fighting to get clear of twigs and wire – had half-made her way through but was snagged on something. The man was coming. I could hear his breathless swearing over the sound of the Volvo engine. I swung open the door and leaped out. I could just reach the girl's out-stretched arm. I grabbed and pulled with all my strength. She came through the hedge with a cry of pain and her blouse ripped across the back. Then she was on top of me in the ditch, both of us struggling to get to our feet. I bundled her into the driver's seat and screamed for her to scramble to the passenger's side so I could get in. I wasn't sure whether he'd run down the lane or followed Tatiana through the hedge but as I sat down a strong hand grabbed the door and the other came around with the knife. His face was partly obscured but his teeth were bared in triumph. I jammed the gears into reverse to get away from the blade and it scraped down the glass and along the door skin. The tyres squealed again and the open door crunched against the hedge and the man was forced to let go or risk being dragged into the hedge or under the front wheel.

I reversed about twenty yards then grabbed the door and slammed it. He was walking determinedly towards the front of the car with the knife held out threateningly. I revved the engine. He stood in the middle of the lane in a show of bravado, mockingly cupping his hands in a beckoning gesture: a bullfighter, daring me to charge. I thought he's high on drugs as well as booze. Suddenly, a deep thumping sound! A Golf hatchback, stereo booming, tore round the corner causing the wretch to leap into the ditch for self-preservation. The car swerved to avoid the Volvo which was on the wrong side of the narrow road, its young driver flipping us his middle finger in salute as he roared away.

I took the opportunity to make our getaway. Alongside me Tatiana's legs were shaking. I floored the pedal. He erupted from the ditch and lunged towards the car with the knife, an almost suicidal gesture. I obliged him. Volvo doors are very heavy. I unlatched it, swinging right then swerving left, braking at the last moment. With the inertia the unlatched door hit him hard on the knife arm. I felt the thud as his wrist or forearm snapped. His scream was shut off as I slammed the door shut and gunned the engine. The last I saw of him he was on his knees, holding his arm in my rear view mirror until the tightening bend hid him from sight.

'Where are we going?' asked Tatiana.

'The police of course,' I said. 'My phone wasn't working back there. It was a bluff.'

'No. No police,' she said emphatically.

I was incredulous. 'What?' After what he tried to do to you? A rapist with a knife.'

'Tried to do. You said it. He don't rape me.'

'Tatiana. He is a potential rapist. Possibly a potential killer. You are not the first one he's attacked, you can be sure.' The media had been full of the recent murders of prostitutes around Ipswich.

I wasn't one of those 'all men are rapists' feminists, but he'd really got to me and I too was shaking with the reaction. We were half way to Stow Upton and I suddenly realised I wasn't sure where the nearest police station was. Probably it was back towards town - the way we'd just come.

'He is Willis,' she said. 'Shane Willis. Works for Polish gang boss as driver, mostly.'

'Tatiana? Are you one of twins?'

'Yes, and I know *you*. You are Natasha Morris, yes? Clarissa told me about you.'

'But Tat…'

'Call me Tania. Everybody does and I prefer.'

'Tania. That man is dangerous. He must be arrested at once.'

'I cannot. It cannot be. He knows me and I will be in trouble.'

'What trouble? He tried to rape you didn't he?'

'Yes. And you broke his arm.' She gave a hint of a smile at that.

'Yes. I did, didn't I?' I giggled and put my hand over my mouth in mock horror.

Her blue eyes widened in complicity.

Suddenly I started laughing out loud and so did she. We'd just passed through Grimwich. I was laughing so much I had to pull over on the verge just before the lane turn off to my entrance. We were both laughing hysterically in reaction to what had happened and tried to recall bits of it, incoherently, and we gripped each other and hugged like old friends and laughed until we cried.

'Natasha. I can tell you I think. I cannot report this. I am illegal. Not Polish. Belarus. From Minsk, me and my sister. I work with team at big agricultural business. Lilia pulls from chickens feathers at factory. Even on minimum wage here I earn more than both our parents earn at home between them. They are qualified teachers and work full time. I am teacher also, like Lilia. The same. But we have to be 'low profile' here. It is hard there, for family. Under Lukashenko, is like old Soviet Union….we are not in EU. Please. I send home money for brother who is sick – his digestion system. I cannot go back.'

They say that there is no such thing as coincidence, only fate. That it is an opportunity in disguise if only we see it. Or a warning. The Mafia traditionally didn't believe in coincidences. Nor anyone who'd ever been involved in state security, of that I was sure. But Belarus reminded me it was getting late and I should visit my father before teatime at the Cedars.

I sensed that Tania wanted to tell me more but it wasn't the time.

'OK, Tania. I'll take you home.'

'It's OK. I walk from here. It's only half kilometre. Thank you.'

'If you think I'm going to let you walk home just one metre after the shock you've just had….. I'll drive you home.'

Then from somewhere the whispered adage, *no good turn will go unpunished* came into my mind.

~-~

Upon the flagstones of the Blundell's warm chaotic farm kitchen I am drinking tea and leaning against the Aga stroking one of three black and white Border Collies who stares up at me intently.

Outside is a garden of scented herbs and a rather cluttered yard with a fenced compound to the rear. A small donkey keeps company with a nanny goat and the squat white shapes of beehives stud the field beyond. Columbine grows against a brick wall and duck nesting boxes sit close under some bushes. Sycamores and lilacs threaten to undermine the farmhouse whose kitchen faces south. Chickens peck about the door and its boot scraper. The half-timbered 'hen house' is Clarissa's old 'shooting brake': a rust-brown Morris Traveller set up on concrete blocks in a corner of the yard.

Tania is sitting at the kitchen table with a mug of tea, fussed over by Chrissie while Clarissa listens grimly to her tale. There is a rattle of the door and Tania's photographic double enters looking flustered. She ignores us and goes to Tania's side, gripping her shoulder speaking breathlessly, excitedly in some Russian dialect as the dogs fuss around her feet. Her eyes are big and animated. Tania strokes her hand and soothes her like a mother. I am captivated by the beauty of the Slav accent in the smoky voices of these two pretty girls and touched by the scene. The dogs remain agitated and Clarissa shoos them out.

Lilia finally calms down. Tania looks around the room and fixes me with her blue eyes.

'Lilia, my sister knew I was in danger. She was shopping in village and ran all way here. She always knows. We are one organism, she and I,' she says almost wistfully and looks tenderly at her twin.

Lilia turns to look at me for the first time. Something, a cloud passes before her eyes it seems, but she quickly summons herself and rewards me with a gracious smile. It is like looking at Tania. There is no difference.

She reaches for my hand. 'I would like to most sincerely bless you for saving my baby sister. I am, we are, most obliged to you, Mrs. Morris, for your great courage and for your presence of mind. My sister says you were 'brilliant'!'

'Not at all,' I said. 'Anyone would have done the same.' Typical trite middleclass answer.

'And please call me Natasha.'

'Natasha, good. But no, not anyone. You are *warrior*, Natasha,' Lilia smiled. 'Brave, like *Ruskii Vitiaz*.'

'Russian Knight,' said Tania

'You said *baby sister*. I thought you were twins.'

'Sure, Natasha,' Lilia smiled. 'Tania was born ten minutes after me. So I am big sister!'

'We would like you to come to dinner one evening, please,' Tatiana said. 'It would be honour.'

'Of course she must,' said Clarissa. Invitation's always there. Come soon. Tomorrow if you like.'

'Please come. I will make for you special *bobka*!'

'Thank you. I really must go now and see my father. He's at the Cedars, near Ipswich.'

I hesitated just for a moment. 'Perhaps I could give you a ring for an evening next week.'

'Ah yes,' said Clarissa. 'We'd heard he was taken ill in Poland. How is he?'

'Lithuania. Not much improved, I'm afraid. He can't communicate and his writing arm is affected. I've tried a sort of question and answer thing with a nod for 'yes' etc., but he gets terribly frustrated after a few minutes and won't play.'

The kitchen door opened slightly and the trio of enthusiastic collies scampered back inside, tails wagging. A man's voice called, ' Hello?'

'It's Fred,' said Chrissie.

'Fred, come in,' called Clarissa, 'We're in here having a 'powwow'.'

'Oh, then I come back again. I saw the car. I should have realised you had company. Stupid me!' His accent too was foreign. European.

'No that's alright. Come on in. Meet Natasha. She's our newest neighbour complete with another Russian name. Natasha, meet Fred Pig.'

'Oh, how do you do?'

I shook his square hand. Fred was a tanned, thickset man who smelled of the barnyard. Eighty-plus at least but looked fit as a fiddle. He wore overalls and a beret, which he removed to reveal cropped, snow-white hair. He must once have been taller, straighter. He gave me a gap-toothed grin.

'So, you have bought Mill Farm?'

'Yes. Needs a lot of work doing,' I said.

'Call me if you need help mit fixing stuff. I have plenty off time.'

'Fred's a good mechanic, Natasha. He's been lusting after my 'Mock Tudor hen coop' for years. Never gives up. He restores old Volkswagens and Morris Minors for a hobby,' Clarissa explained.

'Sure I am total 'petrol head'! I ask always the 'girls' to sell to me their Morris Traveller,' said Fred with another smile and a wink at the twins. 'Timber frame is good and it's not so rusty. Vould make fine collector's car, and I make you brand new chicken shet mit good timbers.'

'I know, Fred,' smiled Chrissie indulgently. 'But the chickens are settled where they are and laying well. Maybe later, when these 'peg out'. Tea?'

'Thanks but no. I must go, so I leave you in peace,' said Fred. 'See you round, everyvun.'

After he'd gone I asked if I'd heard right. If his name really was Fred *Pig*.

Clarissa smiled.

'No, he has an unspeakable Polish name, like *Piekzowiczski* or something. So everyone calls him Fred Pig. He doesn't mind.'

'That is correct, Clarissa,' said Lilia severely. 'His name is Hans-Frederik Piekzowiczski. It is not unpronounceable. But he is *not* Polish.'

'No, I know that. He's mostly German. At least he was born in Silesia, whatever that made him in the 1920s.'

'*German*?' I asked.

'Yes,' said Clarissa. 'Ex-POW. Stayed on after the war. Much preferred it here in Suffolk. Keeps a few pigs so the name fits perfectly. Told you it was a Polish suburb, well *Baltic* anyway, as some aren't *actually* Poles.'

She looked meaningfully at Lilia.

'Yes, old Fred,' she continued. 'Salt of the Earth. Luftwaffe. Got an Iron Cross from Göring. Flew in Dorniers. Bomb-aimer/gunner or somesuch. Shot down in Kent in 1940. Only survivor of his crew. Never went home. There was nothing to go home for in 1945.'

~-~

Time was getting on. I said I should be leaving, but then I noticed the twins looking at each other and back to me.

Tania spoke.

'Your father, Natasha.....if we can be of any help to communicate. We don't wish to....er.' she struggled for the right word.

'*Intrude*,' said Lilia.

'Intrude? Da! *Interfere*. But sometimes, well you know.... we can read minds.'

'If it's of any help,' said Lilia and Tania simultaneously.

'Thank you,' I said.

I'd left, wondering what kind of specialised weirdness I was getting into.

Chapter 8.
Grimwich 'twinned' with Koidanov

That weekend I visited my father three times at the Cedars for an hour each time. Physically he seemed a little better and he'd tried his best to talk, but only gutteral sounds emerged that must have distressed him as much as they did me. The physio had left a message that she could see signs of improvement, but if there were any they were invisible to me. I slept fitfully on the Sunday night, tormented by night terrors. I felt pressure on my chest but was unable to move or open my eyes. My mind conjured a classic image of Fuseli's incubus, the grinning hobgoblin of my half-dreaming state - but suddenly very real and somehow I screamed myself awake, terrifying Quantum who was kneading me, administering some sort of feline CPR. He jumped down, wide-eyed in the sudden lamplight with a piteous cry. Emma slept on soundly in the next room.

The following Tuesday I'd arranged to visit and have dinner with the Blundell's and the Raczynskya's at Grimstone House. I'd left word with them to ask *Polish Fred* - I couldn't bear to use the 'Pig' appellation bestowed by the jolly *Grimwitches* – to look at some small jobs I'd gladly pay him to do: the *help mit fixing stuff* as he'd volunteered. Emma was staying over with Alicia Roberts' family in Ixworth who were glad to have her company. She could be charming when it suited and at least she'd made one good friend at that comprehensive. She had her schoolwork ready and she'd be ferried to school in Marcia's 'cool 4x4': better than the Morris's ratty old Volvo, evidently.

So it didn't matter what time I rolled in. I'd fed Quantum before I left and Blaze had his feed and a bucket of water in his stall. I'd had a relaxing bath and I was looking forward to the evening and a chance to wear a dress for a change. I was pleased to find that a black frock I hadn't looked at for years had ironed well and still fitted me perfectly. I was as good as new with a bit of jewellery to show off my good neck, matching earrings and some heels. Was I trying to impress? We were all girls together and two at least were undoubted lesbians of late middle age, but to heck with it, I thought. Forty is the 'new black' give or take four years. I hadn't dressed to please myself in a long time and it was about how *I* felt not whether I could attract. That was a given. I checked my bum in the bathroom mirror. I didn't expect that I'd be fighting off *Sapphic* advances and was entirely relaxed for the first time in an age.

In fact I thoroughly approved of the way I looked and didn't feel a bit divorced or 'second hand' that cool early winter's evening, as I threw on a warm jacket and scarf in the hallway.

Outside, motion caught my eye. There were the distant starling flocks again, sweeping across the pale grey sky in incredible whorls and arabesques, as if choreographed by some super computer. *Murmurations*, yes, that was the collective noun. Somehow *constellations* had seemed better, I thought, as I drove the 'half click' to Grimstone House.

~-~

They'd made an effort to tidy the farmhouse and we enjoyed a spontaneously hilarious dinner with delicious fare provided by the twins, colour-coded in divine blue and green dresses that revealed their elegant white shoulders. *Charity shop in Bury St. Edmonds, Natasha. Very cheap. Reproduction in 1950s style, nyet?*

Clarissa wore what looked like a safari outfit with a broad leather belt and a cameo broach on her lapel as a stab at femininity. Chrissie had picked a fresh pink cardigan to which she'd pinned a large topaz flower and wore striped woollen tights under a leather miniskirt. She'd discarded her flat shoes for comfortable slippers. She wore big glasses and her hair in a grown-out 'bubble cut'. I wasn't sure what effect she'd been trying for unless she was planning to run away with the circus.

They'd made little place names in the shape of cardboard butterflies in those same vibrant colours so I'd know which of the twins I'd be talking to for the rest of the evening. In fact we all had them, though mine was cut out like a knight on a charger. Clarissa's was a cat which had $E=MC^2$ written on it and crossed out, that she said was *Schrödiger's* and Chrissie's was a hen. Chopin was softly playing, the table was invitingly dressed and the lighting soft.

It was warm in the house with the Aga going strong and the fire in the lounge was fierce if you sat too close. The old walls were thick and took a long time to heat up but retained their warmth even when the fire began to die down. By 9.30 I began to realise how tired I'd been and I confess I was nodding after the *royal consommé*, the tarragon lamb and several vegetables prepared the Belarus way, with delicious sweets including a chocolate *bobka* followed by a glass or three of Chrissie's home-brewed wine, with which we'd toasted the downfall of all rapists, ex-husbands and men in general, most of them.

After a while I realised I must have dropped off and apologised for my rudeness. I needn't have bothered because Chrissie was snoring quietly with *Quark*, her tortoiseshell cat, on her lap by the fire, Clarissa half-slumbering opposite her with a collie each side of her chair and another one on his back stretched in front of the fire, the picture of contentment. Was it just another coincidence that I should have casually given the name *Quantum* to our stray while at the next-door smallholding there lived an identical cat (which Clarissa had failed reveal to me on the occasion of our first meeting) named for the smallest theoretical particle of matter that I'd personally heard of? Was it the same cat, or was there going on, at some level of reality, things that were totally beyond me? Is this evidence of paranoia or am I missing something? Was it the wine, or like Heisenberg, was my recognition and observation of such things affecting outcomes of an experiment: one in which I was beginning to feel I was an unwitting participant? Or was I a player in a video game in which I had no idea of the rules or how many levels there were to attain?

The twins had drawn up small leather stools with cushions and were sitting either side of the settee on which I was snoozing, each mimicking the other's posture in perfect symmetry, like guardian seraphim. Tania gently removed the empty wineglass from my hand and put it on a low table to the side. Lilia was looking at me intently.

'What?' I said a little stupidly. 'Did something happen?'

'No,' said Tania, in the green dress. 'It's ok.'

They both looked at me with their sky-blue eyes, their inscrutable faces glowing in the firelight. They were both young and old at the same time. Their cheeks were smooth and perfect but their eyes seemed full of wisdom and the sadness of ages: oracles of a once-revered aristocracy. In ancient times they might have been branded, burned as witches for their telepathic gifts. Then, in Belarus perhaps, their knowledge of herbs and potions might have seen them highly regarded, as healers: or strangled by edict of a spreading theocratic, patriarchal autocracy that ruthlessly broke with animism and the natural world, for penitence and by control of the spiritual authority vested in man.

'Lilia had a dream,' Tania said.

'Oh? Did she fall asleep too?' I smiled, stretching a little theatrically.

'No. Not this evening. We have stayed awake. Watching,' she said rather mysteriously.

'Watching! Watching what?'

'Things,' said Tania.

'Sometimes it's better than satellite TV!' said Lilia with a grim smile.

~-~

'Lili had a dream,' said Tania. 'The first time she saw you she saw something. I was too pumped with adrenaline myself, because normally, if you can use that word at all, we both see same things. Not *exactly* the same, but we are both aware. She more than me perhaps.'

'What do you mean?' I asked, remembering the 'cloud' that had seemed to pass over her face. 'What kind of things?' This was a little unnerving, but the crackling fireside, the wine, the feeling of childlike contentment and the sense that the Suffolk winter was slowly making its presence felt beyond the heavy drapes created an atmosphere of companionship within; almost a sense of hibernation from the nights of the *Cold Moon*.

All should be well with the world if we could be just like this with Christmas not so far off. I felt I was a not unwelcome guest at the fireside of Badger, with Mole, Ratty and the carol-singing field mice sitting round, but part-transposed - to *Howling,* Sussex with its watercolours of chickens. A witch who dowsed her animals for 'hot spots' with her quartz pendulum – *'original spin'* as Clarissa called it, affecting an Irish accent and mock fervour, like the Reverend Ian Paisley on full song: massaging away their cramps, listening enraptured to static on the wireless while she rolled her joints, ear cocked for spirit messages from the Big Bang; her quartz pointer spiralling to the ancient dance of the electrons.

~-~

Chrissie, it seemed, possessed a keen sense of humour, earlier directing me to look at the blue unicorn in the corner. I looked in amazement at the beautiful creature as it slowly faded from view.

I was speechless.

'You see, Natasha, not all we may see is real. Or else, what is reality?'

'What...*was* that?' I managed at last.

'Nothing. An illusion,' Chrissie smiled as her pendulum slowed. 'It's simply that you are very suggestible. You have been hypnotised before.'

~-~

The very fact that these 'interesting' neighbours were welcoming and seemed, if not quite 'normal' at least warm hearted and kindly disposed

100

towards me made for a sense of security. Community. 'Things', whatever *they* were had no business intruding here in this 'niceness' but perhaps should have been confined to the *wood shed*. Especially things that were invisible to me but seemed real to others, to two of the coven who seemed to be otherwise rational human beings, even if they were foreign and a little strange: but for all, along with Fred Pig up the road, characters that Stella Gibbons might have considered too unlikely even for her *dramatis personae*.

~-~

Lilia spoke and it was as if an eloquent sprite had descended and given her tongue in a language that was not her own. As if the spirit of a Conrad rested lightly on her white shoulder and whispered in her ear. Sadly she spoke, yet clear as if delivering plain verse while entranced, possessed by a memory that shimmered still in her mind. I cannot recall her exact words as I offer them here, but the sense was that a child's loving spirit had suffered a great wrong at a time of great historical upheaval, in which random acts of unspeakable cruelty were commonplace and the 'reality collapse' that followed was her only escape:

> *Once I had a dream,*
> *That some dark defiling thing,*
> *Ravaged below.*
> *While I, terror struck,*
> *Climbed. A* tarsier,
> *Stripped of my intellect,*
> *And shrunk to foetal mind,*
> *Looked down from the canopy,*
> *With passivity and detached interest.*
> *For pity was there none I could afford,*
> *And keep my sanity.*

Lilia looked at me. 'What is *tarsier*?' she asked.'

I told her it was a small nocturnal tree-dwelling insectivore with an opposable thumb, thought to share a common branch on the evolutionary tree with a distant ancestor of mankind: facts retained from my eager reading of natural history as a child.

'Like a *bush baby*, Lilia. But a native of Indonesia with a cry like a human baby.'

'Ah yes. I have seen picture. Cute, with big, big eyes.'

Cute as a *sci-fi Gremlin* I thought. I was recalling a night-time flash photograph of one with its mouth full of grasshopper.

She paused. 'I also dreamed that cripple gave to me a book. Do these things mean anything to you, Natasha'

I shook my head.

'When did you dream these things, Lilia?'

'It was after we met. But I also see something. The first time you were here, in kitchen, last week. It was 'with' you and not with you.'

I was puzzled and intrigued by these statements, resisting a growing sense of superstition.

'Our little mother…*grandmother* was fortune teller,' said Lilia. 'Psychic, like us. Some of these things we see are from long time ago. Sometimes in future. She talked sometimes about things that happen in Russia, beginning of last century. Bad things. *Spanish 'Flu, The Terror.* Always war. And famine. When people eated dogs….'

'*Ate* dogs, Lili,' Tania gently corrected.

'And dogs *ate* people. And people *ate* people. Terrible times, Natasha. And after, in Great Patriotic War, many dreadful things happened. There was massacre in our village. One thousand six hundred people, Jews. All murdered.' Her hands are clenched I notice, and the knuckles white.

'Murdered. By the Nazis?'

'*Nyet*, Natasha. Some say it was Latvian fascists. But my father say it was Lithuanian special police detachment, Jew killers, but yes, with Nazi overseers. German SS *Einsatzgruppen* used all nationalities for murder squads. Latvian SS was *very* bad.'

She stroked a fist distractedly with her free hand, passing the palm over the knuckles: a defensive blow withheld. The word 'very', though emphasised, was also short, as if she would rid herself of a thought. The hand gesture to my mind represented an act of symbolic *washing*, as if she had suddenly developed OCD, which I knew enough about already. She was much too young to have been so directly affected by the events of 1941 or '42. Tania turned her head and with gentle eyes becalmed her sister's restless, inner sea.

'I thought you were from Minsk. That's a city isn't it?'

'We lived in city of Minsk,' said Tania. 'But were born and lived in *Dzerzhinsk* until we were ten. It is twenty kilometres to southwest. Named for founder and head of Cheka, later NKVD and KGB. It was very sad place. Its name was before *Koidanov.*

'There was Soviet epitaph in big open space. Overgrown,' said Lilia. 'Was written, officially 'sixteen hundred patriots by fascists murdered', from Patriotic War. No mention that all were Jews. It happened everywhere. '

Blonde, blue-eyed, I did not think the twins looked remotely *Judaic*. *Nordic* perhaps.

'Was full of ghosts, Natasha,' said the twins, simultaneously.

'I also see something strange.' Lilia was speaking again. 'Black tatters at crossroads, dangling, with things - crows clustered upon it. There is poem pinned to it, in my mind. For me. For 'it', there is no poem, no epitaph. No 'mind' there. It just twists in the night wind. Perhaps is symbolic.'

I shivered despite the warmth, but smiled indulgently, I'm afraid, slightly intoxicated though the sleepiness was gone.

'I dowsed map for this thing,' said Lilia. 'I used Chrissie's pendulum on atlas of Baltic States, Poland and Belarus. Pendulum rotated strongly over north east of Lithuania, mmm…where border projects into Belarus.'

Tania produced an old atlas. It opened readily on European Russia and the Baltic. Lilia pointed to the irregular Lithuanian-Belarus border and the protruding salient. The nearest town on the Belarus side of the border was marked *Vidzny* situated on the Disna River. Ignalina was situated on the Lithuanian side.

Clarissa had joined Chrissie in a gentle duet of snores but soon rose to dominate before subsiding, smacking her lips and mumbling in her sleep. A log popped softly in the fire. The supine collie's ears flicked. The snoring resumed.

'Who do you think it was, upon those gallows?' I asked.

Lilia looked at me with that unnerving candour that probed and questioned me, entering through the windows of my soul. Were the crossroads also symbolic? A choice to be made with death in the wings?

'I do not know who or what. But was long time ago.'

'So. Lili. What was it you saw that first time, when first we met?'

She looked at me with a faint smile.

'I saw a good person I think. The saviour of Tania whom I love as myself, who is part of me closer than anyone could be. We are two chicks from the same egg!' She smiled.

'A *blighted* egg perhaps, sister,' said Tania softly, pursing her lips at Lilia's warning stare.

'And what else?' I asked in puzzlement, ignoring the sudden cooling. 'What else was it that you saw?'

Lilia gave a great sigh. 'Something I don't like to see. Something I have seen maybe twice before. It makes me think there should be exorcism.'

Exorcism? I'd seen the film.

'What d'you mean. Of this house?'

'*Nyet*, no! Not of house.'

'Of *me*, then. Do you think I am possessed?' Almost none of me believed any of this, but the little bit that did was clamouring for attention.

'No, Natasha. I don't think you are possessed.'

'So…what?'

'I think you are being followed.'

'Followed! By *what* followed?' I could feel my responses getting more Yiddish by the minute.

'By demon, Natasha.' She was emphatic. 'By *demon*.'

~-~

Two days later my mobile had rung on the kitchen table at Mill Farm and I'd rushed down from the attic, from under a raven's piercing eye, to learn that my father was dead and all of this occult stuff was forgotten for the time being. Certainly the twins had given me no inkling that they'd seen the future for me even two days hence. They'd said they might be able to understand what it was my father was trying to express, but although they said they could do this at a distance, by using their energy together and perhaps with something of my father's for them to touch, we'd not discussed it further.

Two nights before, in the cool of that evening's visit, I'd walked home from Grimstone to my own modest farmhouse, snug enough in my warm jacket and scarf. I remember deciding that it was better to leave the Volvo until the next morning. The fresh air revived me even though I wobbled a little at first. It was only a few hundred yards to my lane and then the narrow dark drive to my own front door. Emma was staying in Ixworth so there was no-one at home. I'd forgotten to switch the porch light on before I'd left so it was very black once I'd turned into the Cypress-lined walk to the house with only a little starlight amongst the broken cloud. The driveway was in desperate need of repair with potholes and puddles so I had to take especial care in my heels not to turn an ankle in the dark. I proceeded with caution and trod very gently.

I had been reviewing the evening's conversation on the 'big things' randomly discussed among our coven of mostly childless women. Life, love, war, economic migration, people-trafficking, politics: what, if anything distinguished organised crime from disorganised government, bank deregulation and corruption in the present age. Post-*Thatcherism*, was there still such a thing as Society in the wider sense? Broken or otherwise; where City croupiers and short-sellers, shell-gamers and cardsharps in red braces, gambled with vast sums, not their own; celebrating with thousand-pound bottles of wine, *his 'n her Ferraris*: sustaining the bloated, unsustainable credit bubble, taking huge risks for their rake-off. And what an adrenaline rush when they pulled it off! People will be eating out of skips when it all crashes, she'd said.

I realised how much I'd missed stimulating conversation, even if some of the contributors held eccentric views inflamed by a *splif* or two. And so to false memory syndrome: mental illness, the environment, the war on terror: the ultimate questions of supersecular belief and the afterlife – one topic flowing into another as if we were all on a 'high'.

Clarissa had been forthright and pragmatic. We were only animals and the Carbon Cycle would continue, or as Chrissie put it *Gaia* would be replenished whether we offered our dead through sky burial, Tibetan style - the lammergeyers to crush our bones for their marrow; offered in missionary position to the worms in prescribed C of E fashion; buried at sea to feed the fishes, or cremated: our last carbon footprint. What was death but a long dreamless sleep? Chrissie said it was all a continuum of energy fields. Clarissa said that the wisdom of all ages had yet to reconcile religion and rationality and preferred to engage her mind full-on with complex mathematical problems and we'd find out soon enough. Besides a long sleep wouldn't go amiss. The heavenly twins were convinced of the hereafter but said there were many pitfalls for the unwary and would not be drawn on the concept of Heaven.

Tania said, 'Natasha, memories are *not* lost on higher plane. The spirit unites the risen souls into one consciousness on spirit level. These souls are like jewels connected, like on string of necklace. That string is *memory*. It is unbroken. Sometimes these memories return to you in dreams, or in sudden flashbacks to past lives. It can explain irrational fears.'

'So what then is a ghost?' I asked, pushing away a disturbing flashback of my own: sitting up in bed with the door barricaded, rocking Emma, just a week old, gripping something hard and cold to my side - revisited over time during occasional sleep apnoea. I considered it had to be stress-related.

'It's like in 'real world', Natasha. Things don't always work perfect!

Sometimes ghost is a grounded spirit that failed to reconnect. Perhaps like *Kelvin*.'

Who was Kelvin I wondered? But then Clarissa interjected and asked what *I* thought happened when we 'flat-lined'.

The idea absolutely terrified me, I admitted. I had some vague notion of 'coming to' in a limbo of crepuscular nothingness in which we 'see', but there is nothing *to* see, not even our outstretched hand. A grey *Nibelungen* fog in which we move, or think we move, drifting spatially with maybe other spectres of the stricken for dismal companionship, perhaps a 'quark-like' sense of 'up' and 'down'. But nothing tangible at arm's length. An eerie mournful eternity of despair as punishment for a life of sin in which to contemplate our failures. A Catholic view of Purgatory.'

'Sounds like a *ganzfeld* sensory deprivation experiment,' commented Clarissa, 'J.C. Lilley's hobbyhorse taken to extremes!'

'Hell is perhaps just that. Something which you most fear: forever,' I said.

Somewhere I believed I'd already tasted it, just as I'd described. Some recurring nightmare whose recall was just out of sight, furtively lurking in the corner of vision, disappearing as soon as the eye would confront it? Or was it something from my childhood, concealed by the cloak of time? I could not say.

'Is it possible to sustain 'fear' indefinitely?' I wondered aloud. Pain was a different matter. Wasn't it the Incas who'd kept a tortured soul alive for years, limbs broken and re-shaped, in perpetual agony: expiation for the sins of 'society' and its false but terrifying gods? Like those sacrifices to the sun. Or a brick-entombed medieval virgin to whom an imperfect society would bring its woes, unburdening in confessional: Mao Zedung keeping a political dissenter sleep-deprived for years, enjoying the spectacle of the disintegration of his victim's mind. Wasn't that hell?

Was this the grim shadow of what I really believed? Does each of us, I wondered, sublimate our own hell which we are then forced to experience: a cruel joke programmed into our subconscious and no redemption? Do we each of us within carry the seed corn of our inevitable destruction: the outline draft of our mind's own theatricals? *What the hell are you remembering, Natasha?*

Immediately I felt that my thoughts, expressed through the un-inhibiting influence of the wine, had added gloomy footnotes to the evening. I'd left clumsy footprints in the *Sea of Serenity* which I'd not intended and broke from my depressing monologue with a sudden sense of déjà vu, as if a parallel videotape had been running in my mind: pictures from my cryptic psyche illuminating the words even as I spoke them. It was as if I were repeating some pre-recorded mantra. I sensed claustrophobia and desperation: some greater will than my own, pressing for ownership of my divided soul.

Clarissa broke the ensuing silence, quipping that though 'hell just might be *other people*', all life had eventually emerged from the constituent elements billions of years after the Big Bang. So we are all effectively sidereal dust, gas and fatty acids; glycines essential to all organisms for creating protein, borne here encased in the ice of inter-galactic comets and asteroids, possibly including viruses (comets were classically harbingers of pestilence and famine); carbon–based, with shared electrons and that the chasms of distance between our subatomic particles are vast. We are not, then, as we seem to the human eye, but largely made of empty space. The cosmos itself is a hologram. Would we one day implode and return to that cosmic singularity as with all matter, as if some temporary act of will keeps the electrons in their orbits, eventually to collapse: to implode and then re-explode, again and again, endlessly, like a *cosmic pulse*? Or does the universe forever accelerate as it expands into the vastness, ultimately to rub shoulders; to merge in fatal incandescence with other universes?

~-~

I picked my way carefully, head spinning from the conversation, the wine and Chrissie's joints. I remember thinking that in winter time especially, it was important to have some lights strung along the driveway in the trees. Tonight with thickening cloud and no moon it was hard to see anything, no matter how accustomed to the dark one's eyes might become. You'd have to be a bush baby or perhaps a cat to negotiate this path, I thought, then started as I felt something brush against my legs.

'Quantum?' I called. 'Quark? Is that you?' I noticed that my voice was wavery and uncertain.

Truth to tell the evening had spooked me more than I cared to admit. I stood in the dark porch fumbling for my door key, wishing I'd thought to put my little penlight in my handbag as the cat twirled around my legs. It occurred to me, not for the first time, what a dangerous enemy I might have made in the person of Shane Willis. He might have some ugly friends or family who could use a night like this to take brutal revenge on someone they'd blame for physically injuring their kin in a hit-

and-run. It would be unlikely that he'd have actually told anyone the truth about what had happened last week. His sort of people rarely used the law to sort out their squabbles, of that I was certain. I didn't know how many old Volvo estates there were in the locality, but it wouldn't take too much detective work to find out where I lived if he was determined. Especially as he'd be looking for Volvos with the driver's door panel dented and a knife blade scratch along the side. He must have gone to a hospital with that arm though, surely? Perhaps it would be possible to make some discreet enquiries in that area to try to make some assessment of the risk he might pose. It was a fuzzy idea. My one obvious choice of reporting the incident to the police was excluded because of the illegal status of Lilia and Tatiana.

Society's broken, I thought.

I wondered how Willis had extricated himself from the field with that wrist I was sure I'd snapped with my car door. Had he a spare key to the van, or had he been able to hot-wire it and drive with one hand? Had he called for help on his own mobile? I felt vulnerable now just shopping or getting petrol from the local service station.

I found my key, stumbled into the hallway and switched on the light. Everything was as I'd left it. I really was getting spooked. Demons! Who needs demons, I thought, bolting the door, with the likes of Shane Willis stalking the parish?

I slept, but my slumbers were laced with dreams which I could not then remember, although I woke several times in what was left of the night with a feeing of unease and glanced towards my bedroom window. The moon's mournful face had looked in on me once and then I heard an owl.

Der kalte Mond in voller Pracht,
Hört die Schreie in der Nacht.

Why was I remembering snatches of German poetry? At seven o'clock I got up and made myself a coffee. I didn't see any possibility of getting further sleep and a meagre daylight was anyway creeping reluctantly into the carcass of the old house. I didn't expect to see Emma until later in the day, probably teatime if I knew my daughter.

I sat in a state of half-sleep as the coffee boiled and I pursued the shreds of a dream I'd been having that trailed away like rags in the wind. Strange though, remembering a moon. I'd thought the night was moonless. The word *Tokarev* came back to me. Why, I wondered, would some Russian name be in my mind, tumbling from the fissured tissue of my folded brain, from God knows whatever labyrinth it had laid in or for how long: retrieved unbidden from the system? Were these real memories? Or false? Who can fathom the human mind in its vagaries? God knows who wrote its crazy software.

I would chase up that telephone connection. I had to get a modem. Today, I decided, the gloves are off with British Telecom.

~.~

The events of that week had naturally obliterated that resolution from the forefront of my mind. Only following my father's death, the inquest over, had BT carried out the work and Emma was back on-line gathering information for her course work and no doubt e-mailing and spending time in secret chat rooms. It was a couple of weeks later, after the funeral, that I had given some thought to returning to Westerfield and the Cedars, to find out what, if anything, was secreted in Alice's teddy bear.

If Mr. Khan was surprised to hear from me his voice did not betray it. I explained that I'd felt rather badly about excusing myself from Alice's plangent invitation. He assured me that it was perfectly all right and that she always asked *everybody* who visited to 'come to tea', and seemed to assume that my conscience would be sufficiently assuaged by that reassurance and again sympathized with me for my loss. I rather thought he was suspicious that I might want to resurrect enquiries via the back door about the circumstances surrounding my father's death, but I warbled-on happily and insistently and said it would make me feel *so* much better to give her a little treat and a new face to talk to.

He was sure that Alice would be pleased to have a visitor, although he didn't much sound it himself. But he did admit that she had no one other than her carers at the Cedars. He did say that he had a professional duty of care to Miss Bowen and that while she was an adult she was obviously incapable of looking after her own affairs, so he needed to be certain that everything was entirely above board.

We left it that he would put the proposition to her. I suspected that he might try to influence her to turn down my belated acceptance for reasons one could understand given that my father had died in his establishment and I had requested and obtained a post mortem. That is even if he intended to let her know.

I surmised that she probably received no more attention than she needed on a day-to-day basis, nothing 'extra' I imagined, and apparently no family to visit her, so she would probably wonder what was going on at some level if her routine were to be broken. That was assuming my late response to her invitation had been proffered - or that she would even remember me. I did consider that I was 'using' a vulnerable adult but could see no alternative if I was to lay this mystery by the heels and I hoped I'd not need to resort to more nefarious methods. Such as invading, disguised as both wave and particle.

It transpired that Mr. Khan did transmit my RSVP and indeed Alice remembered me, but nonetheless, it was with trepidation that I presented myself two days later, armed with cream doughnuts, trifle and chocolate éclairs. Otherwise Alice Bowen had been allowed to choose her own menu but I insisted on providing some of the dessert based on what the staff told me on the telephone of Alice's likes.

I wore a skirt for this visit and an informal top with a simple necklace that I had chosen to demonstrate a demure ordinariness and lack of 'motive', creating, I thought, a soft, low-key femininity - together with cream shoes and a generous matching leather handbag.

On impulse I plucked *The Friendly Yak'*, a small framed poem of my father's from the kitchen wall to present to Alice as a *quid pro quo*: satisfying the principle of fair trade.

Alice wore quite a young dress for her age, white, with a bold red floral pattern and neat ivory-white low heel shoes. The staff had done her hair, and she looked amazingly different with a little make up, so that one would have placed her perhaps at a well preserved fifty.

'Thank you so much for coming,' she said, her voice inflected like a child's still, but older than six this time. I'd hoped that a private tea might have been arranged in Alice's room, but a tea table had been set up in a corner of the dining area, with discreet lighting that emphasized the shadows but softened her skin tones so that she seemed even younger than hitherto. Here, the smell of disinfectant lingered but those other smells were thankfully fewer, replaced by the less mephitic smell of cooking. That, or like the staff, I supposed I might be getting used to it. The other residents were wheeled or had shuffled-in, rubber-necking into our alcove, but I avoided eye contact. The noise level increased. A carer sat a few feet away feeding an emaciated creature with distant eyes, never moving out of earshot. Alice had left Lucy in her room, to my initial dismay, so just the two of us, without her inseparable bear, sat down to a slightly awkward repast while the banter, the cajoling and the noises of the elderly infirm from all walks and societies who were thrown together, perhaps unwillingly at mealtimes, rose and fell about our ears.

I had worried about how the conversation might go, but I'd used the framed poem as an effective ice-breaker. Alice read it aloud.

The Friendly Yak
When you've lots of 'nicks' to pack,
And you haven't got a van,
Call upon a friendly yak.
He will help you all he can.
And he won't expect a tip.
Just a pound of best plum jam.

The poem was illustrated with a little cartoon drawing of a yak burdened with all manner of luggage, eyeing a pot of jam with anticipation. Alice was delighted and thereafter chatted away happily, swooping between maturity and a childlike charm that so disarmed that I warmed to the personality that was viewing me through wistful blue eyes. She sat with perfect posture and glanced about occasionally to see if the other residents were observing, seeming to take pride in her status of 'one who has a visitor at teatime'. Indeed, she reminded me of that other Alice: an innocent in a looking glass world that was hard for her to understand. She told me about people in another life and spoke of them as if I knew them too, and I confabulated with this stratagem and made the necessary noises of encouragement.

When opportune I fed into the rather lop-sided conversation that there was one important person missing at the tea table. She looked at me in puzzlement.

'Lucy,' I prompted with a ready smile.

'Oh,' she whispered conspiratorially. 'They told me she couldn't come.'

'Oh dear, why on earth not?' I asked.

'They said it was 'inappropriate',' she whispered, as if this were a great sin.

'How can your teddy…your little girl be inappropriate?' I asked.

'Well, they said she was.'

'Nonsense!' I said encouragingly. 'I'm sure she'd like to join us for the pudding.'

'Do you think…?' she asked, smiling, eyes bright. Gum recession was the only indicator of age.

'Why not go and get her? I'm sure nobody will stop you if you're quick!'

Alice trotted off with alacrity and was back with Lucy before the 'alarm' was raised, although the nearby carer gave our table a sour look. I smiled dismissively at her, averting my eyes and she looked away. I nursed the teddy bear for a while, careful that it was at Alice's suggestion and eventually managed to slide the pyjama case zip down at the back. The bear was well-padded internally – otherwise it would have flopped unnaturally, with just enough room for folded pyjamas and something small and flat concealed within. The only thing it contained, however, was my arm. I felt all around inside up to the neck and armpits, into the padded bulge of its belly and into its crotch. Na-da! The torso was empty.

'Alice,' I said, handing her back the now zipped-up bear. 'Did Lucy have anything inside her tummy?'

Alice looked at me with a startled expression, then hung her head.

'How did you know that?' she asked, eyes downcast.

'I didn't know for sure, Alice. I just thought there might have been.'

She looked at me again, with a penetrating stare, trying to understand who I was and what I wanted. What I knew.

'It was a picture of a buzzard. I stuck it on my wall.'

'Could we go and get it, Alice? You see, I think it was meant for me.'

~-~

At Mill Farm I examined the picture, much more closely than I had in my distraction: when I'd packed it with its companion back in Lithuania. It was indeed a bird. A powerful raptor. A Great Icelandic Falcon or *Gyrfalcon* if I was not much mistaken, that fixed me with its fierce eye like the raven on my roof. It was pictured sitting on a rotten tree stump, aloof and proud, with the winter snows of Northern Europe depicted beyond. Executed in oils and heavily varnished with some cracking evident, it had been painted onto a round wooden base about six inches in diameter, three-quarters of an inch thick, with a raised perimeter. Despite a brass hanging bracket on the back, Alice had attempted to use 'Blue Tack' to stick it to her wall paper. It had fallen to the carpet and rolled under her sideboard where I'd bent to retrieve it; hearing someone admonished through the thin wall to, 'Take your *opening medicine* and be sure and have that bloody bell handy'.

So leaving Alice clutching her *Friendly Yak*, marooned among her looking glass ghosts, my Judas promise to return sealed upon her cheek with a shameless kiss, I'd stolen away from the Cedars with the *Falcon* in my grasp.

Like so many characters in this play, I thought, I'd become the spy. Wittingly or no.

112

Chapter 9. *The Baltic Falcon*

The back of the picture was covered in aged, foxed paper with what I presumed was a lot number label gummed to it and indecipherable writing in brown ink. The painting was signed by *V. Kestautis* with the date '1908', so I presumed it was by a Lithuanian artist. It seemed perfectly ordinary though quite professionally painted, but I could not begin to guess at its authenticity or value.

However I knew that it contained my father's secret. A kitchen knife soon stripped away the paper to reveal a smaller diameter plywood backing insert below the rim, which I was able to prise out to reveal the computer disk concealed within. It bore the title *Funeral in Berlin ~ a Prelude*: and in brackets *(The Baltic Falcon)* written in CD marker pen in my father's hand.

Over the next few days I read and re-read the entire tale with a growing sense of mystification. Some of it was entirely rational: his own experience of a growing intrigue which became more real with a series of compounded events and one particular accident with which the narrative begins. But then the coincidences that seemed not to be coincidences and evidence of my father's obsession with the characters of eighty or a hundred years ago seemed increasingly bizarre. As the story expanded he seemed to merge seamlessly with first one and then another, writing in the first person, or transcribing directly from Neumann's own rambling account, based largely on the incomplete diaries within. Even the *Kameradschaft of the Jasta* began to make a kind of fascinating sense to me. And, if you believe it, the concept of our 'reincarnating in clusters'. I began to wonder what that implied for me, for my own character and impulses. Perhaps for my very existence. And the existence of those people into whose society I had unwittingly drifted, for good or ill. Were they also part of this conspiracy? Or were they witting guides, mediums or illusionists? Were there already among them persons to be feared in this world, motivated by avarice? But how could they possibly know anything? I was new to the area.

Or was it a matter of revenge? Was it would-be rapist, peroxide Willis, *tattoo man*: he of the broken wrist that stalked me? Was he my *Nemesis*, or something else?

I really did not know what to do with this story at first. There was the further consideration of a considerable fortune that may still be out there which was presumably being tapped for the 'Trust', and which the Russian Mafiya and maybe third generation Nazis and others might be seeking, including some ex-*Spetsnaz* hired guns. Like the one that may have killed my father if you bought into the theory. People even more dangerous than a small time drug dealer and sexual predator among the *illegals*.

I'd made up my mind to call into the local surgery to ask for an appointment with Doctor Mitchell, even though I wasn't on his list. My first instincts had been to trust *Mitch,* as he'd asked me to call him. The matter of the post mortem I felt needed to be addressed. I didn't want him to think that I bore any ill-will and wished to ascertain that there was none borne on his side. I had felt an attraction towards him that I couldn't deny, but primarily he was the only link that I thought might be able to help with discreet enquiries about a broken-wristed individual that might have received attention at a local emergency hospital, or even the surgery.

More confusion when the receptionist told me on the 'phone that Dr. Mitchell was no longer with the practice and had only been taken on to cover for Dr. Sheila Grant. Dr. Grant had been involved in a serious traffic accident the month before. The post had since been filled by another doctor. Dr. Mitchell had been a locum.

I seemed then to lose my moorings and drifted in a sort of preoccupied daze that weekend towards Grimstone and the 'coven'. There I explained some of what I had learned from my father's account, though not the means whereby I'd come into possession of the narrative.

I felt that the story had the elements of a long fugue: in musical terms, 'a flight'; and *flight* played a leading role in the saga. In medical terms, a fugue was an 'absence', a transient epileptic event where the victim's eyes are open but the mind is elsewhere. A *'petite mal'*. The main character, subject of my father's researches had been tormented by a determination to recover his own 'missing time'. But much remained unanswered from the document. Moreover, what had I been expected to do with it? The disturbing feelings returned; that there had been 'absences' in my life too.

By day I watched while I worked, my consciousness tuned to sudden noises, like the croak of the raven that seemed to haunt the place. At night I circled within the house, checking and double checking the doors were locked.

Neither Clarissa nor Chrissie had been able to ascertain the whereabouts of the man Willis let alone whether he was out for blood. Tania said he had not reappeared as a driver at the farm estates.

I was frankly fearful after recent events, still jumping at shadows at Mill Farm. I'd had no proper rest for days. Emma was sleeping at Alicia's over at Ixworth this weekend (their 'phone now 'working' evidently) and the place seemed lonely. A wind had got up and the house was full of creaking, with sudden gusts under the eaves. A panting in the attic, like a blowing *narwhal* I thought inexplicably; peculiar sharp fluting noises: a wooden ship pitching in choppy seas to the sound of Tritons.

Had the twins been able to communicate with my father in the special way their alleged talents allowed - as they'd indicated their willingness to do, it might have explained what other dangers I might face and what was wanted of me. So must I have looked at them with a sort of hopeless gesture, capitulating to their beliefs for solution to my angst. It was something I'd promised myself I'd never get involved with.

Thinking of twins, I wondered what had become of the second plaque, the other bird painting on its oaken disc. *The Baltic Falcon* had been one of a matching pair. I thought I remembered having put both in the suitcase at the Linden House. But I'd searched through my father's things since. It wasn't in anything retrieved from the Cedars and I couldn't find it anywhere at Mill Farm. Emma denied having seen it. A mystery.

~-~

'It can be done, Natasha,' Tatiana was saying. We sat in the parlour of the house at Grimstone. 'Death is no barrier if we use ouija board and planchette. Chrissie is adept and so are we. Perhaps Clarissa will join us for more energy when she comes back.'

Clarissa's ancient Land Rover was chugging up the drive as she spoke.

To my surprise Clarissa seemed quite ready to join in a séance. I suppose I expected someone with a doctorate in mathematics to dismiss such unscientific mumbo-jumbo as beyond what she'd countenance, but she seemed perfectly happy to experiment, which I felt was evidence of an open mind. Indeed I myself was the most reluctant participant, yet I'd instigated it. My curiosity at least to attempt to gather evidence with regard to the death of my father and what it was he was trying to communicate — beyond the retrieval of the CD - had been reinforced by the gripping story that was *The Baltic Falcon* itself. This led me back to Grimstone House, outweighing my old reluctance, suspending for the time being my natural disbelief in the occult. A pragmatic decision I told myself. Whatever I might learn, if anything, just *might* be advantageous if it worked. So what if it didn't? What harm could there be in it?

They'd insisted I eat with them first. The winter afternoon had become early evening by the time we'd cleared away and seated ourselves around the kitchen table. By turn, Lilia and Tania both held the round tablet by Kestautis, their eyes closed, fingering the carved decorations of the rim.

Chrissie sat absently shuffling her Tarot cards and offered me a reading. I shuddered at the thought. I considered that the proposed séance would be enough for one night and declined, but not before Chrissie had turned over the top card. It was a dead ringer for the painting on the stair at Liepus Namas. I stood rooted to the floor, my expression of shock for all to see.

'It's the 'Knight of Swords', said Chrissie. 'Lord of the Winds and Breezes, King of the Spirits of the Air. The archetypal warrior. Someone good to have by your side, Natasha.' I remembered Jankaitis and the mighty Lithuanian wind spirit. The *Véjas*.

Chrissie had retrieved her ouija board from behind the sofa and there was an expectant air about proceedings. I was reminded of an amateur dramatics evening or the excited anticipation of a childhood film show, before we had VCRs. Somewhere in my memory I heard the faint whirring of a film projector. But my thoughts were still tinged with anxiety.

The ouija board was black-lacquered and decorated with an ornate gold pentacle. The letters of the alphabet and numbers were arranged in two sweeping arcs as well as the words 'yes', 'no' and some common phrases to assist communication.

'Before we start, Natasha,' said Clarissa, 'You should know that I believed that the *novelty* that is the ouija board, which sold in their thousands, particularly in the USA where it was invented, was *just* that. A late nineteenth century parlour game. What you see on TV is nonsense. Any messages that were received were due to small, involuntary ideomotor reflexes and the unconscious will of the participants to 'get a result'. That naturally tended to reinforce latent beliefs in an afterlife and the immortality of the human spirit in otherwise rational human beings.'

I recalled Lenin's arguments on materialism. The twins looked at each other in silence.

'Rissa,' Chrissie said, 'Let's not spoil it for Natasha. She's a truth seeker. We are just the channels to this place we inhabit. Mere conduits to our own dimension.'

'You used the past tense,' I said, looking straight at Clarissa. 'You said 'believed'.

'I *did* say that. It's because I now don't know what to believe. Everything from snowfall to the crystal structure of a snowflake can be expressed mathematically, Natasha. Even those things too weird to imagine exist as mathematical concepts. Better mathematicians than me have calculated that there are multiple dimensions: ten at least, folded into space time. Who is to say that other entities do not inhabit these regions, invisible 'transients'. Rubbing shoulders with us right across the electromagnetic spectrum? From 'DC to daylight and beyond'!' she smiled.

'But whether they are the realms of those who are 'dead' to us, who can say? Anyone who is not shocked by Quantum physics doesn't really understand it, so perhaps we should see what happens when we try such an experiment as this, to see if we do unconsciously influence the result, as Heisenberg hypothesises. Physicists have become increasingly open-minded since Nils Bohr's generation and the Copenhagen Protocol, though Quantum Mechanics itself was at first too 'occult' even for *Einstein.*'

Scientists will forever study the *nature* of Nature, but while some secrets may be unveiled, she will endlessly withdraw, only revealing further mysteries. Einstein commented that human inadequacy of thought and our inability to comprehend Nature ensured that inconsistencies will always exist in any scientific proposition. Each time an accepted formulation is re-examined it broke down somewhere, leading to a modified or new proposition which itself is subsequently found to be inconsistent, and so on; infinitum.

'But,' said Clarissa, 'Regarding *our* experiment, only if we gain new information that is 100% provable and *not* known to any one of us, can we say that using a planchette to divine knowledge has any validity. But that assumes that such knowledge wasn't unconsciously revealed from our subconscious without the participant realizing that she is the unwitting source.'

'Is there any evidence that the 'collective unconscious' can work together?' I asked.

'In studies, yes. Electronic Random Event Generations seem to be connected to human consciousness. All sorts of insects seem to operate using collective 'intelligence', pre-programmed, pheromone-triggered.'

I recalled the instantaneous formation changes of vast flocks of starlings on the wing.

'But blind trials with ouija boards,' Clarissa continued, 'Have resulted in gibberish. Uncertainty is built into the tiniest measurable quanta. So what price messages or predictions on a grand scale?'

Chrissie interrupted. 'What about Mill Farm's own ghost, Rissa?'

I looked at Chrissie in astonishment.

Chrissie explained. Terrible injustices had been visited on country folk running family farms. Healthy poultry and cattle had been slaughtered in their millions after self-serving ministers had made loose statements which were arrogantly held to, despite contradictory evidence or lack of real evidence; *mind you, she said, wars have been declared on the basis of lesser evidence.* There'd been no health risk of bovine-human transmission of 'New Variant' CJD, *or so we're now told.* Dubious tests had been carried out in an attempt to prove that BSE had crossed the species barrier. Rapid and unjustified legislation based on so-called expert predictions soon lead to our Government caving-in to the threatened consequences from the EU.

'Just like the salmonella-infected eggs scare, Natasha,' Clarissa added.

'Driven by hysterical media. It was the usual feeding frenzy. When it all died down, livestock and poultry farming was laid waste.'

'Our egg business never recovered.' Chrissie's eyes were moist behind her lenses. 'Kelvin lost his entire herd to 'ring fence' the disease. That was his livelihood gone, despite the 'compensation'.'

He had been recently widowed and the destruction of the prize herd he'd nurtured and built up over years was the final blow. His cattle were shot and burned in his fields despite no evidence of disease.

'Of course corners were cut,' said Chrissie. 'Vast sums were made at taxpayer's expense, allegedly. Inflated costs being submitted by those charged with the 'clean up'. The animals too were supposed to have been shielded from the massacre of their kin, but they *knew* what was going on, Natasha. Huddled together, making a terrible commotion as the shooting went on; a bovine holocaust behind canvas covers. They aren't stupid animals. Kelvin had wept openly and cursed the righteous idiocy of government.'

Clarissa spoke with increased intensely.

'There are exceptions, but those behind government agendas seem to work just to keep the public in a permanent state of apathy and anxiety, to exercise control. Look at the authoritarian legislation on 'Terror'. The one thing they're competent at – frightening us with apocalyptic warnings. Bird Flu: Anthropogenic Global Warming, re-branded as 'Climate Change'- for which read mega-taxation to fund outrageous, flawed Green technologies. Shutting off the oxygen of dissent by discrediting the alternative view, hiding and manipulating the facts. Dismissing research that doesn't fit the fundamentalist 'political consensus theory' of their myopic coterie or meet their plans for 'renewables' with God knows what future for industry, unless it's a part of their wind energy scam.'

'Four thousand climate scientists…' I began.

'You might as well say "four thousand hairdressers".'

Clarissa then dismantled my accepted view on 'climate'.

The earth had been warming gradually since the last Ice Age, she said, and average temperature has remained constant for the last ten years. She questioned whether our climate was so unstable that CO2, a mere 0.033% on average of the entire global airmass, could cause runaway global warming if it *doubled*? We in the UK only produce 2% of the world's manmade CO2 from our shrinking industry, and that is a *minute* proportion of that in toto: yet we paid the highest price. Ice core samples show an 800-year *lag* between temperature rise and subsequent

CO2 level increases – a tiny proportion of which is actually generated by industry. The IPCC was a discredited organisation, openly infiltrated by political activists, its PC positions filled by UN quotas on gender and equality.

'People who think of CO2 as a pollutant, Natasha! Those who speak out and disagree with the Climate Modellers are smeared by the Eco-Nazis as representing Big Oil. Don't forget, in the 'seventies, these same experts were telling us we were heading for a new ice age.'

Clarissa paused to light a cheroot. Until then I'd seen no evidence that she'd smoked. She dragged deeply and went on.

'If the Government's aim, with a complicit media, was to keep us repressed, docile and uninformed except by their relentless propaganda, it seems to be working. Our 'head-in-the-sand strategy' means we've missed the bus on nuclear. The future will see us all shivering in the dark.

'We'll be seeing massive energy hikes next. We are already paying for hundreds of thousands of bureaucrats in the world's 'energy departments' while climate 'scientists' torture the data to match their climate model and justify their existences. Kyoto was a travesty. The Czech president only signed up to it due to extreme pressure, much like his predecessor faced in 1938 when it seemed the whole world was against them.'

'But wasn't a Nobel Peace Prize awarded for that docu…'

I thought Clarissa would explode.

'*That*…propaganda video, and those cartoons to frighten the children – how long before they rid themselves of what they've imbibed, like under Goebbels, with their mothers' milk; melting polar bears and drowning bunnies. We're fed filmed Power Point presentations stuffed full of assumptions, blatant conflation, half-truth and distortion, exaggeration and flawed analysis.'

The 'non-aligned' BBC, she said, only ever presents the political consensus viewpoint. It was partly as a result of its slow drip of Green propaganda that we're now seeing onerous Green taxes, loss of economic freedom, the march of wind turbines across our green and pleasant at a cool million pounds a mile to connect them to the National Grid. We sit on abundant cheap energy that we could burn efficiently. China builds two fossil-fuelled power stations each *month*. 'We'll be buying windmills from *them* next; the ultimate irony! Like the bloody Opium Wars in reverse.'

She stubbed out her half-smoked cheroot on the kitchen table with a savage jab of her thumb.

'But renewable energy *is* important, isn't it? I asked.

120

'It's the destruction of the rain forest that has to be stopped,' broke in Chrissie. 'Of course if you write about that in parts of South East Asia you'll be losing all your fingers to a chainsaw gang!'

'Yes, renewables are *vital*,' said Clarissa. 'But tidal energy will always work while the moon stays in orbit, which at its present drift will still serve us for millions of years yet. It's costly, but nothing compared to what's been wasted already. We are governed by spineless, know nothing politicians who take their orders from Brussels. Its tentacles are spreading across what was once part of the 'Free World'. Its root system is stealthily expanding to complete centrist control. Social engineering for the benefit of the very few; Marxism as we've now come to understand it.'

I hardly knew how to react. My sentiments were wavering under that remorseless tirade and I was feeling intellectually defenceless. Rather lamely I ventured that we still lived in a democracy. Clarissa gave me a pitying look.

'Since when did a career politician care a damn about what you thought, except when out on the stump, gathering votes?'

She said that after the then Chancellor had raided our pension funds of £100 billion, with desperate consequences for the future (which Clarissa for one said she was glad she'd not live to see), we were then lied to by government, in '99, when they said they were only selling off 3% of our 'reserves'. They'd included in that tens of billions borrowed on the currency markets. It seems now to be pushing credibility to its limit that they would actually have sold half the country's entire gold reserves *after announcing it to all and sundry*, which promptly drove down the price, in *real* terms, to a low of $275 per troy ounce. Today it's $1000 and there's every indication it'll keep climbing.

When the present incumbent first clutched the reins of power in his fists he deregulated the banks, she said, leaving us wide open to some gigantic fraud – which is what this toxic debt scam has become. He then says we're *best* placed, as a country, to ride out the recession and then had the hubris to boast he would 'save the world'! The banks are bailed out by the poor benighted taxpayer but still they deny business the credit it needs to trade, hire or expand. Viable firms, livelihoods, all are destroyed while bankers are rewarded again and again.

'Million pound bonuses for overall *failure*, Natasha. Meanwhile the politicians are raking it in with all sorts of expenses scams, flipping their primary residences, claiming for non-existent mortgages. They desperately tried to hush it up under the cloak of parliamentary privilege. Thankfully someone had the balls to expose the corruption.'

'Well to return to the point, Rissa', said Chrissie, who's heard all Clarissa's tirades before. 'Fred discovered his friend Kelvin's body. I'm sorry to say he'd committed suicide in your kitchen.'

I was aghast.

'Death duties, debts meant that his son had to sell up, and the people who then bought the farm sold most of the land to agribusiness, just as we did here. They themselves sold up and left Mill Farm after six months. Perhaps because of 'The Haunting'.'

'I never saw anything, Chrissie,' Clarissa said flatly, 'And nor did you.'

And nor had I in the few months I'd been there, thank heaven, I thought. Emma wasn't settled though, but there were probably several reasons for that. However, she disliked our kitchen intensely and had told me so... She'd also started that horrible cutting again.

'So...Clarissa,' I said hesitently. 'Please tell me *honestly*. Do you believe in what the rest of us are trying to do here? Can any of this 'experiment' be relied upon. In other words can it be *real* – at any level, in your opinion?'

'It's fruitless to probe the *reality* of reality, Natasha,' she sighed. 'Your perception and mine will be different We create our own realities. Take colour. My collie dogs see a flower in shades of grey. My eyes convert the image to colour – in the brain. Whose reality is right, the dogs' or my own? Does the flower actually have colour? The *bee* sees it in UV. Whose is real? Perhaps it's consensual, our belief in what we perceive as real: the way it *trends* in human consciousness, our perception of the universe, based on acknowledged precepts. A flowing tide of social constructionism - until the next big idea arrives; scorned at first as it always is, then, grudgingly accepted, it takes centre stage. The latest paradigm shift of an ever-shifting 'established truth'.'

'So why *are* you participating, Clarissa?'

'Because.... you all want me to. But be warned, people who dabble lightly in such things have been known to suffer unexpected consequences and reaction. Possibly their subconscious minds bring things to the surface that they'd rather not confront. Something from the *Id*, or the reptilian cortex. The participants most probably already know the answers to their questions on another level but the answer may not be something that they want to face. It does not prove life after death, Natasha.'

She looked me in the eye as if to test my determination to proceed. As if she'd shone a light into the dark caverns of my troubled mind and glimpsed paranoia lurking there. Her expression was similar to that of the twins' when I caught them looking at me.

'There's a million dollar prize waiting for anyone who can unequivocally prove the existence of the mind beyond the grave. People who have overactive imaginations, or who've experimented with drugs; the psychologically fragile who've played with the board…some have gone bonkers.'

I fell silent, remembering Margaret Rutherford. Just let there be no *ectoplasm* I thought.

~-~

The stage was set then for the drama. Curtains were drawn against the winter night. The kitchen was warmed by the Aga and lit by a few discreet uplights under the wall cupboards. The collies slumbered in a corner. Chrissie asked us all to place our right index fingers on the planchette, a little, cast-alloy three-wheeled castering apparatus with a vertical pointer underneath, black like the board. The tip of the pointer was painted white so that there could be no confusion about where it was pointing.

My own index finger joined the four fore-fingers resting on top of the device and we prepared ourselves for whatever might come. The twins had closed their eyes seemingly on cue. Clarissa gave me a look which said I don't really believe this stuff, but I'll go along for now.'

She'd felt the need to further clarify her position, elaborating on the occult and citing the effect of positive ions that could induce the mind to hallucinate.

'As strata shifts, Natasha, piezo-electricity is produced, effecting changes in magnetic fields. This is sometimes associated with earthlight effects, piezo-luminescence, which can cause mist to glow. These seismic disturbances create 'magnetic anomalies' impacting on the brain and influencing the human nervous system. These could create 'supernatural phenomena' which have been reproduced in the laboratory,' she said.

'Though….' she hesitated. 'I might consider a hypothesis that fragments of human energy *might* survive on some wavelength. We are, after all, only standing waves of energy. We're only visible as solid to our limited human eyes. On a molecular level we're mostly water. On an atomic level, we're 99.999% empty space; hardly more than holograms. Self-aware perhaps, but illusory. On the other hand, if our atoms are immortal, then so are we!'

We were as illusory then as the mythic constellations of the Ancient Greeks in the vastness of the universe.

Was it possible, I wondered, that 'four thousand hairdressers' engaged in a common effort to prove that anthropogenic gobal warming was real, and so, as Heisenberg hypothesised, could they influence the result? — or at least influence the climate modellers' conclusions? Perhaps by some morphic resonsance thing: Jung's 'Collective Unconcious' at work? But I refrained from sharing this seditious thought with Clarissa...

~.~

Chrissie began the session. Breathing deeply with her head slumped forwards she asked, 'If there is anybody there please come forward. Come forward from the shadows where I know you can see us. Please come forward if you can hear me.' And the immortal words 'Is there anybody there?'

I suppressed a giggle from nervousness as much as anything. Tatiana must have known because her eyes flashed their blue brilliance at me in the dim light: not a warning, just an acknowledgement of my nervous tension, and a half-smile of encouragement to sit tight.

'Is the spirit of John Morris here?' intoned Chrissie. 'Is there anybody there? Anybody? Please, if there are any spirits here, I beseech you to reveal yourselves to us.'

The planchette remained inert.

Chrissie was not about to give up. She asked again and again for some sign, implored the spirits to join with us, to move the pointer to make their presence known. 'Is there anyone there? Is there anyone there?'

I could feel the trembling of tension from the others, or perhaps my own, through the planchette and wondered if involuntary action would set the thing in motion.

As I suspected might happen it began at first to slide in little arcs and whorls about the board, in seeming random swoops. Everyone's eyes were on the planchette, my own probably wider than most. I 'knew' it wasn't me controlling the planchette, so assumed that it must be at least one of the other four. I wondered who was doing it and if it was a 'conscious' manipulation. I wondered too if they, or at least Clarissa, wondered the same thing.

The swoops and arabesques seemed to get wilder, like the murmurations of starling flight, with our arms whirling about the board as the planchette wove and scurried, controlled by our subconscious or something else. Upon the wall our heavy shadows swarmed in ghoulish parody.

'Is there someone there?' Chrissie's voice had assumed a higher tone. There was a sense of her using her psychic powers to communicate above the invocation to participate through the board.

Suddenly the planchette moved sharply and definitely to the word 'yes', and stopped.

My heart beat like thunder in my breast. Tania looked at me again and Lilia to my right caught her twin's eye and held it. I was faintly aware that one of the collies had started moving restlessly.

'Please identify yourself to us,' said Chrissie huskily.

For a long moment the planchette remained motionless, then it slowly began to revolve around the board. It seemed to be considering something, almost, I felt later, as if the transliteration of words were a factor.

It slowly spelled the letters which we all parroted as the pointer stopped. Z-H-A-I-L-A-I-Z-N-I-I-V-A-L-K. Total gibberish, as Clarissa had said, but this was with our eyes open.

Clarissa looked at Chrissie. 'Just what is that supposed to mean, anybody?' she asked.

But I was looking at Tania. Her eyes had been fixed on the planchette following its movements, as all our eyes had done. 'It is Russian,' she said quietly. 'Sounds of letters made, not exact from Cyrillic, but is *definitely* Russian.'

'So what *does* it mean?' I asked.

'It is two words,' said Lilia. '*Zhailaiznii Valk*'. It means *Iron Wolf*.'

I was stunned by this. Unless Clarissa and Chrissie were secret Russian speakers, only the twins could have influenced the planchette to spell out Russian words. But why would they?

'I think,' said Lilia, 'Is name of your demon.'

Suddenly the planchette began spelling out again.

S-M-Y-E-R-T

Chrissie had a coughing fit, holding her throat.

Even I didn't need that one translating. I had read Ian Fleming.

It meant 'Death.'

Chapter 10. *The Cold Moon in Full Majesty.*

Simeon had always been totally dismissive of the paranormal, an assurance I'd envied in him and something I'd too adhered to, remnants of my Lenin's *Materialism*.

Problems had started in Surrey with four-year old Emma's somnambulism, once putting her fingers into the bayonet contacts of her bedside light bulb. We'd rushed into her bedroom at her frenzied screams. She'd been burned. Perhaps it even heralded that later pattern of self-harm. A child psychologist had been consulted but could get no further than to repeat in bafflement what Emma herself had said; that *they* had told her to do it which raised the question of a schizophrenic event. But surely she was too young for such a terrible condition to appear. It was amazing to us that she'd been able to extract the bulb which itself must have been hot. It took a determined effort for an adult to remove the bulb from its bayonet, pushing down and twisting it to release. No one would attempt it with a hot bulb. We couldn't believe that she could have removed the bulb and *then* switched the lamp on, so looked suspiciously at each other. I knew *I* hadn't consciously removed the bulb. But given my medical history I knew that Simeon suspected me of something terrible.

We'd eventually bought a negative ioniser for her room. It seemed to calm her but she continued to sleepwalk for some years.

~-~

A few days after the séance I'd picked up a local newspaper in Grimwich and glanced at a story on an inside page, titled *Gruesome Find in Suffolk Ditch*. A pensioner walking his dog had come across what he thought might be the latest victim of a killer who'd been targeting prostitutes in the Ipswich area. The naked body had been discovered half-submerged in a ditch only three miles from Mill Farm. There was already someone in custody for these crimes, a forklift driver named Wright, so the article sent a shiver down my spine until I read on and found that the 'body' was a discarded shop window manikin. Typically the story had suggested a more sensational find before coming clean that it was a dummy. And really, I thought, the insensitivity of people fly-tipping something like that in the countryside, considering the horrific local murders. Unless it was some moron's idea of a sick joke. The story concluded with the information that the head was missing. Or else it was one of those models that had simply never had one: like the dummy that dumped it there, I thought.

~.~

My plasterer's van was still there when I'd driven into the yard. It bore the legend *'Spam's the name and Plastering's my game!'* on the sides. Spam had seemed a little thoughtful when I'd returned, my having left him happy in his work. I made him tea and a sandwich and asked if everything was alright. He said yes, but then asked hesitantly if we had a gardener. In winter time? My blood ran cold as I thought of Willis.

'No,' I said. 'There's just me here when Emma's at school. Why, did you see someone?'

'I thought I did,' he said. 'Through the kitchen window. Just a glimpse, like. I thought he might be looking for the lady of the house so I went out to find him. I hadn't heard a knock but then I had the radio on. There was no sign of him outside. I shouted and went round the other way. I was worried in case it was someone casing the place, like. A 'gyppo' perhaps, but there's no *travellers* camped locally as far as I know. I didn't hear a car or nothing.'

'Can you describe him? Was he elderly, with a beret?' I was hoping it might have been Polish Fred.

'No. I mean it was a fleeting impression, like. But I didn't imagine it.'

'Yes?'

'Short - below medium height anyway, but not a kid. Stooped, sort of. Long black coat. I thought it was strange on such a mild afternoon, like, for the time of year I mean.'

'So what colour was his hair?'

'I don't remember.'

'Well, was it very blonde, *dyed* d'you think?'

'Oh, no. He was bare-headed so I'd have noticed that. But…..'

'Yes?'

'Well there was something….or probably it was nothing, but he seemed to have a red rag held at his neck. Sort of a dirty scarf, like. Come to think of it he did have gingery hair.'

A phrase comes to my mind.

'Tis the eye of childhood fears the painted devil.

Wasn't that *Macbeth?* I had a sudden terror-struck memory of barricading myself in our bedroom in Surrey, straining to pull the chest of drawers across the bedroom door and bleeding from the effort. The child was not yet five days old and I had to protect her with my life.

~-~

The Blundell 'sisters' murder and alleged suicide came out of a blue sky. A medical document had indicated that Chrissie had no longer been in remission. I'd understood that Clarissa had been prone to depression and confirmed this to the police. DI Slater asked me what I knew about people-smuggling: anything about *Tongs* and *Triads* and if the word 'Snakehead' meant anything, which it didn't. I denied any knowledge of who if anyone might have resided in the incinerated caravan. Slater gave me an old fashioned look but they didn't charge me with anything and couldn't hold me but I knew it wasn't over with them. The 'angels' had vanished into the ether leaving no trace. For some reason the police were hinting at something much further east. I didn't want to think that the twins had had anything to do with foul play; that might have meant that the whole 'attempted rape' thing had been 'street theatre' not to mention mind-manipulation by planchette, but either way I was in no position to assist the police further.

The last conversation I remember having with Clarissa had been about Russia which she told me was being robbed blind by financial criminals. She spent hours on the Internet following the money markets and she had kept in touch with some of her GCHQ contacts. Her eyes were bright as she warmed to her subject. The legitimate financial and commercial services in an open market economy, she said, were corrupted by the dark side of the network. That's the price paid for millions of transactions per day on the international money market. Shell bank accounts and cut-outs were staging posts on a disappearing paper trail and virtual banking had created a conduit for an endless outward cash flow, where $100 billion dollars can pass silently through a trading shack on any bankrupt Pacific phosphate island. One that'll play host as a major offshore banking centre and virtual financial services agency.

'Your confidentiality guaranteed for a Swiss fee of $18,000. Banks' computers have millions transferred from one hard drive to another in mouse-click laundering operations, Natasha, where stealing and forging bank credits is a daily occurrence.'

She said that mega crooks, like dollar billionaire Semyon Magogovich, stand astride the Iron Triangle of gangsterism, supported by corrupt government officials. And all the finance minister can do is wring his official hands.

'Who knows what pressure he's subject to? But it's the poor that suffers, the pensioners without pensions, the young without hope, without jobs, as Russia's wealth is bled away. Putin expresses justifiable outrage at these billionaires – there are none within the ruling coterie of course.'

'It explains the growing militant position.' I said, subconsciously quoting my father.

'A cynical gesture to deflect awkward questions at home, run the battle flag up the pole! Pressures for revolt are resurfacing, so they look for external targets: refuge of all governments - foreign policy. Old enemies. Scapegoats. Interventionists. The usual suspects. The Mafiya are closely bound into society, into business, the banks and institutions. Chechnya or Georgia are troublesome so they will do nicely. The handling of the school massacre.....that was bad. But they are the new Jews out of Egypt, people who would be independent and therefore must be taught a lesson.'

'What about the others? The stay-at-home *Yeltsin billionaires*?'

'Example: Vlad banged up Mikhail Khordorkovsky in a Siberian jail for tax evasion and other irregularities. Regarded as a political threat to the crypto-fascists: charismatic, a popular following with dangerous democratic leanings... that he'd also controlled the largest private company in Russia may have had something to do with it.' Clarissa smiled ironically. 'Eight years in the Chita prison garrison, Natasha, in the best Russian tradition and his company taken over by state-owned Lukoil. If you *Google* him you could get a shedload of semi-literate *Naija* spamming-locusts clogging your mailbox with breathtaking offers of fortunes that you'd make by assisting them in laundering his billions ....for a handling fee: praise God and I pray for your indulgence.'

'Naija?'

'Nigerian. The '419s': those smiling entrepreneurial honest-to-God Lagos boys with their escalator of 'advance fee frauds'. Very enterprising, those kiddies. Always ready to capitalise on human misery and natural disaster.

~-~

And it seemed almost as if Britain was a happy hunting ground for 'enemies of the people.

'With all the leverage they can muster around the world, Natasha,

130

they can find anyone who they regard as a thorn in their sides and liquidate them easily. Ex-KGB heavies. Or the Klyuev Group, Russo-Mafiya assassins. Make it look like a fatal heart attack or something. Not only that...' she paused as if uncertain to go on. 'I have my old contacts and others besides. They're into phone hacking just as the under cover agencies are. Just as some news reporters are if the truth be known. It's easy if you know how. It was once part of my job, officially.

'The more obvious Mafiya methods of 'disposal' might lead to embarrassing investigations and unwanted publicity, Natasha, except when they want to send a message. Then the body would likely be found in a skip. Mother Russia's soil is inviolate and while London provides a safe haven for hundreds of gangster entrepreneurs there's bound to be reciprocity in diplomatic circles when some major crap hits the fan. Tit-for-tat expulsions. Ratcheting-up of international tensions.'

Clarissa looked at me keenly, as if probing the extent of my historical knowledge.

'Just like before the 1917 Revolution. They had every sort of revolutionary group resident in London back then. Gun fights in London streets in the early nineteen-hundreds. You've heard of the *Siege of Sidney Street?*'

'I've heard of it, yes.'

'That was January 1911. Latvian revolutionaries and bank robbers. Winston Churchill was Home Secretary then. Had to go down and see for himself what was going on. Got a bullet through his topper for his trouble.' Clarissa smiled. 'Questions were asked. Order papers were waved. Of course, not all were murderous anarchists. Many saw that the only hope for Russia was to rid it of Tsar, Church and feudalism. But as many latched onto the movement for their own criminal ends and for power. Just like now, Britain was a safe haven for Russo-Balt and Georgian extremists.'

'My father's post mortem was inconclusive,' I say tentatively.

'Perhaps they're just getting better at murder, dear.'

She looked pensive.

'You may remember the incident on Waterloo Bridge. Giorgi Markov? An outspoken Bulgarian journalist in London. Murdered with a ricin pellet. Fired from an umbrella tip. I knew him 'professionally' so to speak. Before I went to GCHQ full time.'

I tried to imagine what that 'professional' relationship had meant, but she was not forthcoming, continuing to stare out of the window into the walled garden with its Morris Traveller: the 'Mock Tudor' hen coop, and the caravan of the heavenly twins.

She'd said that in the years since *perestroika* there had been some very pally meetings between old KGB hands and old CIA. It would be ingenuous not to credit that Mafiya-Russ billion dollar scams and money laundering hadn't seen some shared enterprise, business opportunities, facilitating investments in the Middle East and elsewhere and in safe financial havens round the globe. Financing million dollar warlord apartments in Dubai out of the public purse. Perhaps, she'd hinted, without further elaboration, there'd been joint operations too, with retirees nearer home, from all agencies, who felt their pensions needed boosting. She intimated that her contacts had provided a list of some rather public and other lesser known personalities, multi-millionaires to a man: not all ex-pat Russians.

There'd been several cases of Russian millionaires disappearing recently. A rather brilliant young ex-colleague from GCHQ had died in horrible circumstances, on the face of it during a perverted sex game that had gone wrong. That he'd been working on some important leads to Russian money laundering operations involving some very respectable banks was not intended to be in the public domain nor deemed to be in its interest.

'Don't believe all that you read ,' she said softly. 'Crime scenes can be cleverly faked. I didn't trust some of those erstwhile colleagues at GCHQ…we had exchange postings with the NSA and others. God knows who some of them were although their security status was three tiers above impeccable. But I never dropped my guard. Don't raise your head above the parapet, Natasha'

Clarissa, it seemed to me, was staring deep into her past, into a sad place.

'As for the CIA,' she continued, 'They'd developed a number of assassination tools which induce heart attacks. They used it effectively in Latin America on a number of occasions, camouflage for their "wet jobs".'

It closely mimicked an allergic reaction and caused a delayed clotting cascade, inducing cardiac arrest. The compound was extremely difficult to detect even using sophisticated forensic methods.

'Can't remember what it's called now and *Googling* for the information won't help, Natasha. It's been 'surgically removed' from the Internet. Meanwhile there's every reason to suppose that the Russians - by that I mean the FSB - possesses equally sophisticated materials. Yet, ricin's an Old World favourite still. Took just 425 micrograms to kill

132

Markov.'

It too was very difficult to detect in the bloodstream. In Georgii's case it was only revealed because the ricin pellet itself had not properly dissolved.

'Yes, my dear. Always adept at murder, the bloody lot of them.' She gave me an intense look. 'It's a paradox that those lovely girls, Lilia and Tatiana, could spring from such a place as Dzerzhinsk; *Ivan's* own 'Porton Down.'

I gave her a quizzical look.

'It's where the USSR's top chemical warfare establishment was based, you see. All sorts of deadly poisons were experimented with there. The water table was polluted with god know's what even before….'

'Before what?'

'Before *Wormwood*: the star that kills; poisons the waters of the world. From Revelations. Translates as *Chernobyl*.'

We were silent a moment while I absorbed that. Clarissa stared out of the window and I stared at her back, recalling the undiagnosed stomach condition which the Heavenly Twins' younger brother suffered from.

She turned back to face me.

'Be very careful, Natasha,' she said, searching my face for lack of resolution, or so I felt. 'Don't assume now that your phone isn't tapped and don't think your mobile is any safer.'

I said that I thought it took a legal and ministerial ordinance to sanction a phone tap. Clarissa gave me a pitying look.

'The fact that you are associated with me might be reason enough after what I've seen in my old job. And what I've researched and discovered since. I am trying to find a way of blowing the whistle without revealing myself. I don't want to suddenly fall under a train or anything, you understand!'

She'd gone quiet suddenly. I looked at her eyes and saw the tell-tale stare from the abyss. *Churchill* was roaming near; her black dog, loping towards her in her mind.

~·~

Three weeks later I read newspaper accounts of the death of a one-time business associate of Russian billionaire Boris Berezovsky, one Badri Patarkatsishvili, a Georgian businessman, also known to ex-KGB agent Lugovoy. Lugovoy had been identified as the prime suspect wanted for questioning in connection with the London polonium affair. The tycoon had died of natural causes, allegedly, at his luxury mansion in Leatherhead, Surrey. A billionaire six times over he had funded an opposition campaign to the Georgian ruling party. A covert tape recording had been made of a meeting between a Chechen 'warlord' and a Georgian interior minister which allegedly indicated a plot to assassinate Patarkatsishvili.

A heart attack it was said. Like my father's.

Yeah. Right.

~-~

Blaze has been slashed with something sharp. He'd lost a lot of blood and Emma is beside herself. I am very upset too. The vet has stitched the wounds and applied some anti-bacterial spray. No internal organ appears to have been ruptured, thank heavens, the fee being big enough as it was. Maybe I'd made a mistake in selling the Volvo for a pittance and buying a beat-up Citroen 2CV in 'jeans' blue with a 'Jesus Fish' in the back window. I should perhaps have purchased something less conspicuous if I wanted to hide; made of something stronger than a bit of corrugated tin and striped canvas. But it was so different from the Volvo estate I thought it would put the bad guys off my trail. Perhaps it hadn't. Had it been a warning or prelude to something worse?

Reporters from the Eastern Daily Press push cards through my letterbox. Vultures. I hide, pressed against a wall until they go away.

Tatiana had told me that she'd found out that Willis was occasionally shacked-up with a woman who worked at an unnamed caravan park, and this was likely to be somewhere within a reasonable operating radius for his work as a driver for the gang masters: information which I quietly filed away for future reference.

Clarissa's last act was to give me two email addresses from her GCHQ cyber-tracking days. She'd said, just in case anything happened. I didn't know what she'd meant. She told me not to write anything down but commit them to memory, just like a real spook Their IDs were roadkill@anonymous.com and landfill@baitline.com : ironic handles I thought; almost fatally prescient if it was true that these wireless network surfing nerds regularly hacked into the emails and even bank accounts of the very rich and not so famous as well as big corporations despite 'un-breachable' firewalls, wireless intrusion detection systems, passwords and other security cut-outs, inserting their little bits of computer code…But apparently they did and a code of conduct was adhered to by them with a few select others, wedded in unbreakable trust. Honour amongst hackers, crackers and radio silent "sniffers" who skimmed enough to fund lifestyles that were sufficient unto their geeky needs for the latest electronics, without they're drawing attention or being traceable in any way, seamlessly re-configuring the balance sheets. Out-thinking the best launderers that Organised Crime could field in a visceral multi-dimensional game of international below-the-parapet money transfer. Computer geniuses of whom SOCA's E-Crime dept. was only academically aware. These were not just teenage hackers from Anonymous International but dedicated professionals whom the CIA, FBI, NSA, Homeland Security, SIS or even the FSB would be well advised to employ on top salaries, if ever they were to offer themselves on the jobs market…which of course they never would.

The addresses provided the initial route only to access their email addresses, which required another password to contact via a tertiary stage cut-out which opened on a short timer. You had to know exactly what you were doing to gain entry and it was by strict invitation only. They were living on the vertiginous edge, just sitting there at their consoles. Experiencing the adrenaline rush of all time.

I recalled standing in my kitchen where Kelvin had hanged himself, looking vainly for the moon, which at that time of the year is named for the wolf, *Wolf Moon*: wondering what darkness her far side was concealing from me. The name *Hecate* had surfaced from somewhere. Wasn't she the goddess of the moon's dark side and of magic? My heart leaped as something wild in the night gave vent to a sharp, unearthly scream; a vixen surely. A shiver went through me and I stood again in the Linden House upon the stair; that sense of malevolence invading me. Inexplicably I'd felt that there had been something 'not right' about the painting that was so dark where there should have been light, except for the light of the painted full moon that shone above, glinting on the shield with the Vytus cross; on the helmet and uplifted sword of the ancient Lithuanian knight on his white charger.

Came that scream, closer now. Then rose the pitiless moon; freed from the branches of the clutching thicket, huge in her full majesty.

Der kalte Mond in voller Pracht.
Hördter der Schreie in der Nacht.

The cold moon in her full majesty...

Something bright moved very rapidly across the sky; a shooting star perhaps. I remembered the night, the last time I'd said goodbye to them; Chrissie, standing at the door, Clarissa sitting in the kitchen with the dogs. We watched as a star moved smoothly across the heavens set on a steady track until it was lost among the trees and the light pollution on the horizon that was probably Ipswich.

'What do you think that was?' she asked.

'Man made. A satellite.'

'But how can you *be* sure?' she asked. 'They manipulate gravity. If they wanted to hide they can bend light; cloak themselves. Or pretend to be satellites. Or reveal themselves, when they care to.'

'Who's they?'

'The UFOs'.

'Flying saucers?' I said. 'Oh *please*!'

'Not necessarily flying saucers, Natasha. Flying triangles, flying shapes of all kinds.' That was Clarissa from the interior.

'You believe in 'visitations' then?'

'You only have to ask two questions, Natasha. Are they seen and are they simultaneously tracked by radar? If they're here then they have an agenda, I believe.'

'What agenda?'

Chrissie answered. 'When I worked part time as a craft therapist in mental health in Wales and the Borders, before Care in the Community took hold, I had a client, a disturbed young man who'd developed a sort

136

of 'crush' on me. He said he or his spirit could travel on the astral plane and visit me in my flat at night while I slept, travelling down, what he described as a 'tube-like conduit' - a sort of birth canal; a lightspeed super highway to anywhere he wanted to be. Arriving there almost instantaneously. Rissa would say it was like a wormhole in the fabric of space time, but travel in the mind was 'real', just as it was for the remote viewers.'

'And that had been proven to the satisfaction of their US and Soviet military Black Ops handlers in the recent past,' said Clarissa.

I waited to see where this was going. Chrissie continued.

'He accurately described many things in my flat, the furniture and a book I was reading, *Edgar Cayce*, as it happened. Anyway he told me one night he'd seen a flying 'Dalek' above a mountain road. Except it wasn't from 'Doctor Who'. It was big and fast and fire droplets dripped from it as it flew overhead, glowing capsules or probes descending that vanished into the dark hillsides. He was mystified by this thing and made a model of it in our craft group. It was disturbing behaviour. Rather like that driven character in 'Close Encounters'.'

'You did imply he had mental health issues.'

'Yes, and an alcohol dependency. But after that night he suffered nightmares in which he dreamed he was being abducted by giant black-eyed mantids and that they were demonic abstractions rather than *Extraterrestrial Biological Entities*. He died in a pentacle of fire when his flat burned down. He'd set a candle at each of the five points of the star for protection and fallen asleep with a bottle of whisky.'

'And you believe this?'

'It's no stranger than the concept of life after death,' said Clarissa behind Chrissie's shoulder. 'Why not alien life on the sea bed or in Earth orbit with bases on the dark side of the Moon. We are just standing waves of energy and our atoms are immortal. The visitors are built the same way, if they're real - or so one is led to understand… But perhaps they've always been with us and can shape-shift like shamans, or slip-slide between the dimensions.'

'Sometimes I think I hear that boy's voice, in background radiation, imploring me to release him.' Chrissie looked bereft.

'Ok, so what's the agenda?' I asked.

'Well star people bringing hope and a warning to the peoples of the earth is balony. That's more about *Humanity's* needs; 'surrogate parent syndrome'. A New Age take on an old religion. No, I believe there are several possibilities. One would be technology transference. The biggest secret in possession of any government, very many levels above top secret. Massive advantages for a nation state's black projects department. It's so big the presidency would be well out of the loop. Small price to pay for turning a blind eye to their experiments, human and animal: but they are deceivers.'

'What do you mean?' I felt overwhelmed by these ideas.

'We live on an over-populated spaceship, vastly out-numbered by the downtrodden of the Earth. The 'haves' fear the inexorable march of the burgeoning 'have nots'. While mass economic migration is inconceivable and there aren't really enough Kalashnikovs to go around, those terrorists who claim to represent the poor and needy *can* still make a difference, especially where mineral wealth may be in jeopardy and strict religious observance is a useful moral launchpad. So, taking a wider view…a worldwide pandemic right now might be just what's needed. Big international corporations may have already formed an unholy alliance…You can draw your own conclusions.'

I tried to take this in, but Chrissie interceded.

'Oh, Rissa. You're such a conspiracy theorist! "Antibiotic-resistant Black Death anyone?" You'll be frightening the poor girl. My theory is we just fascinate them, the *EBEs*, I mean We are self indulgent and have volition. We are vibrant and unpredictable. We don't have the 'hive' mentality. But I'd make a guess at a breeding programme which involves our DNA.'

'Don't they have any DNA of their own?' I asked incredulously.

'I don't know… but Matt, my dear dead contactee, told me that there's one thing we have which they don't. Something your demon lacks, I fervently hope.'

'Which is?'

She offered a wan smile.

'An immortal soul.'

This might be Clarissa's and Chrissie's *reality*, I thought. But I'd make my own, thank you. And 'visitors' had no place in it. I had enough trouble as it is.

~-~

I closed the curtains against the face of the moon, resisting the urge to check the doors again.

It is my father's continuing story I have transcribed here in his own words. In the 'first person', just as they appeared on the first disk.

138

Part Two

Chapter 11. *Funeral in Berlin*

There is a suggestion of thunder in the air, the promise of rain on the wind. That would be a blessing after such heat.

Though defiant gargoyles stare stonily from the eaves, the copper-domed Lutheran sanctuary retains an air of abiding serenity. Windowless for decades, it had weathered thousand bomber firestorms, survived armies of occupation and bears with dignity the loss of its transept arms; *Venus supine*. It rests now in suburban quietude, far from the contorting schist of the German economic miracle. For this moment, on this day, flanked by the stone sarcophagi of Teuton crusader knights, Peter's flagless catafalque softly gleams within.

Pastor Kleiber's sermon comforts the living, assuring us of the certainty of resurrection, while beyond the hermetic sepulchre, beyond the church of *Sophienfriedhof*, the *Glass-und-Metall* strata of the new West Berlin, the world spins; unaware of the intonation: *requiescat in pace* for a repentant Nazi.

I am sitting in a forward pew near the chancel. The usher rises; solemn and professional. The coffin lid is replaced and decked with lilies. That it had remained open at all is a tribute to the embalmer's skills. I follow the procession as Peter begins his final journey down the aisle, like *Siegfried's* down the Rhine; indeed this is the Wagnerian tribute whose sombre strains now accompany the procession. I felt that Peter would have approved my choice, or been amused by it. After all he'd attended the funeral of General Udet in '41, in which the same music had been chosen, by Göring on that occasion.

Those scattered shadows of which I'd been conscious take form and substance, but of Weissgerber, actuary, who had professed friendship for the departed there is no sign. Instead sits an old woman in rapt preoccupation, head-scarfed, her mouth moving in silent prayer, else communing with her ghosts. For a moment of panic I think she is the same demented crone at the bus station in Kaiserslautern who'd grasped me by the wrist and cackled that I would wed my own grandmother. Thankfully, she is not. Another figure slumps in semi-shadow: a derelict, or perhaps a seeker of brief sanctuary from the rough and secular. A spattering of others, mourners or penitents, sit apart. Strangers. No Herr Weissgerber, but backlit from the doorway, straight-backed, her iron-grey hair cut short, sits Alexa. Undisputedly. In severe black, eyes averted, which I take as a signal that I am not to acknowledge her.

The oppressive weather has broken. The pavements are wet and there is a hint of ozone. A slight press of figures clusters about the door as the coffin slides into the elderly hearse; another survivor. So when I find the slip of paper in my pocket I am not surprised.

In the quiet cemetery, bareheaded in what seems a balm of drizzle, I search for sight of her at the grave. Among ancient headstones, the crow-black pallbearers and professional makeweights. Under the trees, huddled with the gravediggers. Down on the yew-lined road with the drivers. She must be well into her sixties but she'd looked fifteen years younger in the church.

Something noisy, possibly an aging *Caravelle* climbing out of Tegel drowns the graveside peroration as the coffin descends.

For a brief moment I feel the pain of another loss. Someone I had loved and from whom I'd had a difficult parting. The note, '*Schatz, vergiss mich nicht. Be happy.*' The last chance phone call and her tears of indecision had me racing to Frankfurt; too late. The bomb had exploded at 4000 feet, severing the elevator controls. The pilots kept the Caravelle flying for 20 minutes on the throttles before it finally went down. In the Rheinland, near Trier. Twenty years ago.

I brush the memory aside, but neither am I listening to the service. I am searching for Alexa. In vain.

~.~

I had flown to Germany at short notice to cover some exhibitions and an air show or two for my magazine: post-Falklands, from an asset-stripped Britain of miners' strikes and the 'me' generation running wild without brakes. By contrast, those who'd claimed to care for the planet and world peace with a socialist agenda were fighting a rearguard action for unilateral disarmament, savaging the old positions that had created the decades-long nuclear stand-off. A week previously I had been harangued by tambourines at Greenham Common. I'd watched a Memorial Flight Spitfire performing a graceful roll over the air base; a poignancy lost on the *Peaceniks*: then found their complimentary pamphlet under my windscreen wiper calling me a warmonger and demanding the removal of US cruise missiles. I bemoaned passing glory

140

to Justin, my sub-editor.

'That's nothing,' he said, leaning forward to make himself heard. We were propping the bar in a crowded pub with the door wedged to let in some air. A slow procession of westbound traffic crawled towards the Hammersmith Flyover. Justin had mounted his favourite hobbyhorse.

'Those deluded harpies are already claiming success for SALT while *actually* prolonging the agony: providing comfort to the enemy. You can hear the Kremlin old guard laughing from Whitehall. What a coup!' He was shouting above the din. 'Friendly exchange of letters and a delegation to Moscow, my arse. Who *do* they think is listening?' He was ex-RAFVR, on his third pint and there was no reining him in. 'Probably ten percent of them are KGB, not to mention *lezzers!*' It was difficult to decide which affronted him the more.

Arguably, it was the Reagan-Gorbachev Reykjavik summit: the Strategic Defence Initiative Talks that had actually started the landslide towards a new reality in the USSR and its satellites. That and their defeat in Afghanistan. *Perestroika* and *Glasnost* were the latest buzzwords. *Solidarnosc* and Havel's *Velvet Revolution* were newly established. But the 'Wall' was still intact, and what 'futures' gambler would then have prophesised that, in a land where once to sell a knitted shawl would have been punishable as 'speculation', successor Yeltsin would usher in the new decade of the Russian billionaire?

With twenty-twenty hindsight one might have surmised that of the several hundred *Spetsnaz* who'd burrowed deep into the fabric of Western society, who watched their years of cover squandered: summarily stood-down - put on permanent 'hold'; that one or two deep-penetration agents *might* have sought more lucrative latter-day careers; even tipped-off by Moscow Centre via some moderately high level archivist......making connections through their controllers, who *also* wanted a piece of whatever action was now going down. A little something, *tovarich*, to compensate for parallel lives you field men had lived. In shadow, dissimulating. Waiting vainly for the call.

But nothing was further from my mind as I climbed the crumbling steps to Madame Kara's Hammersmith flophouse, chosen for its convenience to Heathrow, because it was cheap, and because it was one of the few such establishments likely to have a room at short notice late on a Friday night. The usual pantomime ensued with prolonged knocking to rouse the house, and shouts of *'Go 'vay'* via the letterbox.

'Madame Kara, I telephoned you earlier. Morris.'

'Don't know Morris. *Go 'vay.'*

'Sure, you know me. I've been here before.'

'You bin here *before*??'

I could hear the rising incredulity in her voice, as if she were about to add, 'And you came *back*!'

So after we agreed the price I stuffed fivers through the letterbox until she opened up. Like the last time she was dressed head to foot in layers of black formlessness. It was hard to tell just which part of Europe or the Near East she hailed from. I helped her drag a wardrobe across the darkened landing revealing a hidden bedroom door, the raised room number painted over, perhaps to conceal its identity except from guests adept at Braille; as if this was a secret room, revealed only for the late night traveller. I wondered fancifully if she would drag the wardrobe back again as I slept. *Kara, Black Goddess of Asia Minor: collector of men.*

~-~

In Herr Alois Weissgerber's well-appointed offices in Bonn I had been questioned in a casual sort of way about the last actions of his recent client. My prime concern was to the funeral arrangements over which he seemed to be assuming control with his power of attorney. We both agreed that Berlin was the appropriate venue, where Peter had lived these last years. And there were colleagues who would wish to attend. There was no family. The actuary's telephone call had come as a surprise to me; the second such call I'd received in as many hours since I'd checked back in. I'd no idea anyone even knew of my temporary lodging at the small Frankfurt hotel, other than the receptionist and a few clerks in the hospital from which I'd been lately discharged, which was the presumed link. And that explained a later visit from a Community Liaison Policeman, a post I never knew *existed* in the *Rheinland-Pfälzische Polizei*, and a female social worker. Being fully ambulant and foreign I'd not even anticipated a *health visitor*.

Like Weissgerber, they were solicitous about my well-being following my ordeal, which was as nothing compared to the suffering of others. Like Weissgerber they'd expressed their heartfelt commiseration at the sad passing of my 'good friend' Herr Neumann and I could quickly see that the questions were all pointing to my association with him. Hans-Peter's briefcase was hiding under the bed at the time and I was very conscious of two pairs of eyes ranging around the compact en-suite room. Co-incidentally it was broken into while I was at dinner the next evening, enjoying the seclusion of a quiet alcove away from the stares at my bandages and burns.

The collateral burglary involved some neighbouring rooms and the hotel safe. Luckily, my wallet and passport were in the jacket I was wearing, but a pocket book was rifled and some traveller's cheques were taken. My Nikkon and tripod were not stolen though the carrying case had been forced. By this time the *other* case was speeding elsewhere by taxi-courier, courtesy of *Stephanie's* warning to '*Get rid of it, safely somewhere. Right away.*' Police arrived, the staff was interrogated and statements were provided while a thorough search was engaged in; a forensics team dusting for fingerprints. A young immigrant kitchen assistant fell under suspicion and was taken away with what I considered to be great show, like an arrest in a theatrical melodrama: only for him to be released a few hours later. I wondered: how much had Germany really changed?

~-~

This still lay in the future as I'd cleared customs at Frankfurt Main, though it was clear that the Germany of my last visit *had* undergone changes. The *Rote Armee Fraktion* posters were gone, Ulricke Meinhof and Andreas Baader fading from the public mind. My first impressions as I'd got off the bus from Kaiserslautern with my camera equipment was of the sweltering heat. The stalls selling parasols and sun hats at Ramstein were doing a roaring trade. What a difference a few hours would make.

~-~

It was three days later. The banner in the two-day old *Süddeutsche Zeitung* that lay on my hotel bed headlined the lead story with graphic pictures taken at 'ground zero', Flugtag '88, Ramstein AB.

The symbolism is ironic enough, and the bigger story has a pathos and irony that comes first with the 'piercing of the heart', *Cardioid*: the *Frécce Tricolori's* closing manoeuvre. Such a romantic idea, the team splitting into two elements from a pull-up in opposing downwards half-loops, trailing their long ribbons of pretty coloured smoke, completing their 'heart' in the sky, each element heading apparently straight at the other, crowd front. The solo 'Arrow', as if from Cupid's bow, plunges dramatically though the smoky image. A tiger through a flaming hoop towards the massed spectators. *Bravissimo!* Such daring. Such skill. Such timing! The crowd loves it and a collective gasp of admiration is audible even above the sound of ten screaming jet engines.

In aftermath, I found it hard to piece together the events in exact sequence, it had happened so quickly. Yet at the time everything had slowed right down. There remained an element of disbelief that such a thing had or even *could* have happened. But after I'd been released from the cottage hospital outside Kaiserslautern it was beginning to sink in. By then I'd been able to view and review the whole thing on TV news bulletins from the comfort of a hotel room. There was so much 8mm cine footage taken by spectators there had been no difficulty with the *Luftfahrtbundesamts* Air Accident Investigation Department deciding on the cause, though no official comment had yet been issued. Even uninformed media speculation in a rack of newspapers, each banner headline a variation of 'Ramstein Horror!' was implying 'pilot error'. That and the filmed evidence seemed to confirm my own impression of the moment.

I had been in shock for a while, and not a little pain, but after a day or so I'd found the motivation to investigate the briefcase. I recalled the last words he'd uttered, hissed, through lips that refused to co-operate. 'Trust no one.' It would have been impossibly melodramatic even if he hadn't died just afterwards.

~-~

It seemed that *Piotr* or Peter von Strelitz, whoever he was, had gone to the bad, through dissolution to perdition: five years before the mast on windjammers, the boy having 'run away to sea', eschewing his inheritance: a lover of art, women and green dolphin seas, only to prodigally return to the Baltic to receive a dying father's blessing and the title of *Graf*. Or so the contents of the blackened briefcase told once the heat twisted lock had succumbed to my Swiss army knife.

But what had these motley contents; the charred-edged reams of old hand and typewritten notes, scribbles from different periods, to do with the agitation that the late Hans-Peter Neumann had displayed, before the engulfing horror of Ramstein?

There was a photograph of an old Albatros fighter biplane on skis sitting in a field of melting snow, its pilot smiling from the open cockpit: the name *Kessler* and *Viipuri* written on the back, and a date: *1922*. Old envelopes bearing the *Deutsche Feldpost* stamp, dated 1920 and the *Grenzschutz Ost Feldpost* mark containing censored letters. A photograph, a *Baltische Feldpostkarte* of something called the *Freiwillige Flieger Abteilung* showing an impressive line of *Siemens-Schuckert* rotary-powered fighter biplanes in the snow; *'Freikorps Litauen, 1919'* in black gothic script on the reverse. Magazine clippings; an old sepia recruiting poster with a great claw-like hand reaching from the horizon over a German-Balt farmland idyll complete with church spire. *Freiwillige für Grenz-Ost*, it exhorted. Recruiting office Friedrichstrasse 112a, Bln: extolling ex-officers, NCOs and men to join the Border Defence Force against rapacious Bolshevism. More translations and ephemera.

~.~

Kessler's Kobold Archive: Hans-Peter Neumann

Another tattered picture, this time of a very compact little biplane with a balanced rudder and no fin; and that name again, *Kessler*, to which its design was attributed. I remembered some of these pictures from my informal visits to Hans-Peter. And the conversation.

'You know, Johann, it's strange the pathways we follow when engaged in other research. It's fascinating and one can easily be distracted from one's course. Take *goblins* for example!'

I'd looked at him in bafflement, seeking vainly for a smile on his lips.

'I mean the *Wasserkobold*, the water goblin of myth made flesh, that decapitates its half-human child.'

'Was that Hans-Christian Andersen? Or something 'Grimmer' still?' I'd quipped, quite pleased with the pun.

'Neither,' he'd said. Serious still. 'It's a Czech fairytale. But it was perhaps also an event from recent history. I mean also the *abstract* Goblin that hides behind a locked and barred door in the labyrinth of one's memory. The creature that guards a terrible secret. A door that you are compelled to break down, but which you storm at peril and risk to your sanity.'

Hans-Peter had turned to a cabinet and rummaged for a file. From an envelope he'd withdrawn that same photograph.

'This is a more tangible goblin I found. It's Kessler's first design. *Der Kobold*. The Goblin. A challenging little aeroplane from what accounts I could discover!'

'So who was Kessler?' I asked.

'Who indeed?' asked Hans-Peter enigmatically. 'The other half of Steiger, perhaps. One's Yang to the other's Yin? His *Eusebius* to *Florestan*, complimetary, symbiotic. Schumann's invented twin; a separate and impetuous personality.'

It made little enough sense at the time, Natasha. But later…well you will see.

~-~

From his illustrated diary, that *other* Peter, Strelitz, had been a poet and a writer of lyric prose, even given Neumann's translation first into German and then much of it, avoiding too literal a mind set, into rather formal English. But that could not disguise the vitality of the thought: the timeless evocation of a starlit night under sail at the turn of the century: or the way of the albatross, driven on a solid gale through the *Roaring Forties* that had been rendered first in Polish, or sometimes when it had taken the writer, in French. He may not have been Conrad, but those nineteenth century diaries rang with the sounds, were heady with the fragrances, of Hawaii, the harbour: the smells of Rangoon, of ships and seafarers; palpably an impression of an adventurous life lived full under sail. Still it was a solitary soul whose spirit drifted through the pages, almost every one with some bewitching Indian ink sketch or delicate watercolour, scenes from life ashore or on deck, spindrift, clouds, ultramarine seas, flying marlin and leaping dolphin; dynamic movement masterfully captured.

Reading the transcriptions, I gained an impression of a cool observer, popular with the crew perhaps, but reserved, the internal life glimpsed through his rapid jottings, and a biding of time. Among the sepia photographs of iron ships, four-masted barques and steamers,

146

loose-limbed dusky girls and Europeans drinking in rattan-roofed bars, a tallish, handsome man appeared more than once, either moustached or with a 'full set' in RN terminology: a figure with the languid poise of an aristo, quite at ease with life at his temporary station. In one he stood beside a giant marlin suspended on a hoist, another with a white-tipped reef shark. As a collection of South Seas memorabilia they'd probably have fetched a modest sum at auction, but for the rest, it was baffling at first.

It all seemed quite unconnected, and although my grasp of German was reasonable, I wondered at the accuracy of the translations from time to time, many of the original documents being written in several languages including Cyrillic Russian and, I assumed, Lithuanian, in various hands. Unverified. To be marked with an *obelus* perhaps?

It was a miracle that it had survived at all and it was probable that the compacted tightness of the documents had prevented their total combustion when the briefcase itself was aflame. Came 'Stephanie's' warning, and considering what happened later I wonder if it would have been better had it been totally consumed in the fireball.

For *Stephanie* I read *Sophie*, surname *Clapham*. Both of which I knew were aliases for the remarkable Alexa. Surname then unknown. I'd recognized her voice, which was still clear and authoritative and had hardly changed in more than a decade. I also recognized its urgency. *Werden Sie es schnell los!* She'd rung-off without another word, which emphasized the alacrity with which I assumed I was now expected to act.

~-~

But my concentration was lapsing. Although I was drowsy from the painkillers, I found my mind kept returning unwillingly to the accident. It is not in my nature to dwell on 'what if' scenarios, but it had been a close call. I thought I'd come to know the man who'd owned the case, who'd briefly shared a corridor with me, each of us on a trolley, a scene repeated all over the Palatinate due to the overwhelming number of injured: but suddenly he was an enigma. He'd once said to me that 'to know the heart of another is to enter a dark place'. I think now he was quoting a Russian proverb.

~-~

I had met aviation author Hans-Peter Neumann at the Biggin Hill airshow some eighteen years previously where I was covering events for the aviation magazine I then wrote for. As in '88, the crack Italian aerobatic team, the *Frécce Tricolori* was performing. Different pilots, different aeroplanes, but with the same zest and the same attitudes. At that time they'd exchanged their American F-84F Thunderstreaks for the then relatively new Fiat G-91s, and were obviously proud to be flying an Italian product in the UK for the first time. I'd rubbed shoulders with them at the Surrey and Kent flying Club bar after their pre-show practice and when I'd finally stumbled out at 2 am to find my way back to the hotel, a roaring party was still going on with the Italians on top form with beer flowing, music and girls. I remember wondering at the stamina of the Latin pilots who showed no sign of flagging.

Next morning, heavy-eyed and contemplating black coffee in the hotel lounge, thinking about getting back to the show by bus, a gentleman with greying hair asked if the adjacent seat to mine was vacant. I indicated that it was, though my head was hurting too much to relish conversation.

There was a commotion on the stairs and we glanced up to see a handsome Frécce pilot making a rapid descent to a waiting taxi. A girl followed, still half-dressed as they scrambled into the cab. Grey hair exchanged my look with a slight smile. 'They never change!' he said. I recognized a German cadence. The pilot was young and youth's a stuff will not endure.

If I fast-forward those eighteen years I find myself on the parched grass at *Ramstein Flugtag '88* at the USAF Air Base, Rheinland-Pfalz on a blistering August afternoon, heading for the refreshment or press tent, I couldn't recall which, but with a cold beer definitely in mind. I'd encountered Hans–Peter again, by chance, and we'd chatted over a brew. He'd been expecting someone on the display line so we'd headed back outside. He walked over to the hot dog stalls and the ice cream queue where he thought he might recognize someone, so I sat down on the grass to watch the *Frécce* taxiing out - then in their smart, black Aermacchi MB-339s with the traditional tricolour arrows on their sides.

Over the years I'd formed a friendship with Peter, as he preferred to be known. We were in the same line of country and he was a fount of knowledge on German aircraft in particular. Wartime and pre-WW2 were his specialities, as well as modern Warsaw Pact equipment and rocketry with which he was very up to date. He spoke almost perfect, cultured English and along with Gert Heumann, Peter was one of the first German resources I'd ring if I needed some background details or historical/technical data of any kind, especially where things were rather vague or classified in the UK. Unsurprisingly we shared some friends and acquaintances. We both admired and in some cases had worked with many of the same aviation technical writers and commentators. It was a small world in which Gunston, Braybrook, Ramsden and Fricker were as well known as had been that dogmatic *éminence gris*, the late C.G. Grey; doyen of the Royal Aeronautical Society and the *G.B.S.* of the aeronautical editorial and the critical essay.

I had seen Peter from time to time around the shows and called on him at his Berlin studio on a couple of occasions. His wife had died during the wartime bombing and there were no children. After a spell in a Russian internment camp then working in civilian jobs, he'd officially retired and now lived for his research. He undertook this for his own interest and on a modest fee basis on behalf of others, though he freely gave of his time when approached regarding subjects dear to him. He was an assistant curator of the growing archive at the air technical library associated with the *Berlin Luftverkehrsmuseum* with a vast and growing data pool from global sources, frequently ex-Luftwaffe and Lufthansa veterans, with many from the Americas. He was himself in receipt of a Luftwaffe pension. In about 1970 when first I'd met him he was compiling a mass of data on wartime German jet fighters, *Turbos* as he referred to them, to fill in the blanks following the destruction of artifacts and data, initiated first by the *Luftwaffenamt* itself as well as the *SS* as the capital was surrounded, and then via the wanton and wholesale destruction of everything possible by Russian troops, before the GRU and their technical people could get in and stop the damage, to salvage whatever secrets they could find, along with many examples of gas turbine powered aircraft scattered through eastern Germany while the Americans salvaged everything they could elsewhere under *Project Paperclip*, including Wernher von Braun!

Still, the Russians got their share of scientists and jet technology.

Britain, last in the queue, acquired the *Zaunkönig* : a small, wooden single-seat parasol monoplane powered by a 50 hp. Zundapp!

Peter had opened up to me on one of my visits. I'd called at his modest Berlin address by arrangement and was looking in fascination through his collection of photographs and drawings of advanced Luftwaffe projects from the very last days of the war. He also had a charming collection of tinplate model aeroplanes from the 'thirties, including a Junkers 52, a Dornier Wal and a beautiful Focke-Wulf Condor. Later we sat in the leather furniture of his comfortable study warmed by a log-effect gas-fire, snug among his books with pictures of service personnel here and there. There was an oil painting of his late wife; a beautiful woman with her hair in the 'forties style, evidently painted later from the silver-framed colour photograph alongside. As a young man, he'd been captivated by a lady flautist at the *Musikverein, Wien*. He'd attended a Mahler concert, fallen instantly in love and bought tickets for the whole week by which time he'd plucked up courage to speak to her. They were soon inseparable. He'd never recovered from her loss.

He showed me his album of signed glossy black and white pictures of movie stars and celebrities: Marlene Dietrich, before she left the Reich and a later image of Zarah Leander stepping from the runningboard of a *Mercedes Kompressor* with the poor physical specimen of propaganda minister Goebbels at her elbow. Peter told me that the *Giftzwerg*, as he referred to him, by then a devotee of Leander, was quite dwarfed by her height and had advised Hitler never to allow himself to appear so vertically challenged whenever cameras were about - hence the Führer's refusal to be photographed in her proximity. There too was Garbo and Leni Riefenstahl, and informal photographs of people I recognized, such as Udet playfully dunking the formidable Marga von Etzdorf in the Heinkel factory swimming pool. Pictures too of Peter in Luftwaffe flying kit, and as a young man in the cockpit of a glider.

He said that as youngsters growing up in Germany between the wars, he, his younger brother, and their friends had been dazzled by the pervading messianic *Zeitgeist* that was to deliver them all to destruction. Afterwards he experienced a bitter and bewildering sense of loss and betrayal, followed by the pressure to sign up to a collective guilt. The bit in between was hell on earth for millions and has been written about ad nauseam, but five years of internment in Russian labour camps had done nothing to persuade him of the superiority or egalitarianism of the Communist system. He'd returned to Federal Germany, resettling in West Berlin but not in good health. That was before the Wall, when the burgeoning fruit of the 'economic miracle' tempted many crossings from the Eastern Sector.

In the '30s, for him, the *Hitler Jugend* had been a boisterous yet disciplined scouting association, although later he had to acknowledge its brutality. Pitched battles with the established German Scouting movement were common, finally resolved by an expedient Nazi government ban on the latter. 'Later on, Johann,' he said, 'The DLV, the *Deutsche Luftsportverband* enabled me to achieve my dream, to reach for the sky.' He always called me *Johann* instead of by my given name of John. It

150

was a sort of avuncular epithet, his way of accepting me with my halting German as a would-be student of the culture, despite the rawness of the recent war that had wounded that concept. His passion for the composer Mahler's music, a Bohemian Jew who'd adopted Roman Catholicism to preserve his career even before the rise of Naziism, matched my own; perhaps was an indicator of the journey he'd made since *Mein Kampf* had been his required reading.

'Was just a 'rant', Johann, immature, full of anger, malice and general distortions and it took another fanatic, Alfred Rosenberg to refine it, try to justify and make some coherence of it, though Hitler also manipulated him in his intuitively clever way. But as a boy… one is easily brainwashed. We were starry-eyed and worshipped the Führer. As the Jesuits say, give me the boy when he is seven…… Only later, much later was revealed the malignant narcissism that drove the man. But then it was too late. By then it was already a… a 'train wreck' as the Americans say.'

So with Brückner, Brahms, Beethoven – particularly the late quartets; and Schubert: *'Ah, the String Quintet in C, D956… If he'd written nothing else, this work would have marked him a genius…'* Our tastes coincided and such was the background of the few evenings we spent together. He found much solace in Bach, the Brandenburg Concertos and the Cantatas, for their purity, their measure, a 'civilized kindliness' and of the unselfconscious grandeur of the great fugues that gave of the whole of Bach, it seemed, avowing such humanity that could never have prefigured a Third Reich as it was to emerge, even at long range, despite the foreshadowing of the all too recent Inquisition. 'To think he was once considered *second fiddle* to *Telemann*, Johann!'

Peter, like me, was also a devotee of the sensual collaborations of Lenya and Weill, sung by a relative newcomer, Ute Lemper, whose smoky voice and rolled 'rrrs' rendered me helpless with nostalgia for a Berlin I'd never known, whose album cover had me riveted by her vampish look which out-Dietriched Dietrich.

He described his early experience of soaring flight, how he'd become a keen glider pilot, passing his certificates.

'I loved the hiss of the slipstream and the comparative silence and contemplation of it all. There was great natural camaraderie. It was a brotherhood and of course flying was intoxicating. That and the sport we played kept us fit and happy. Germany was the most advanced in this field then of course. Still is actually. And the spectacular scenery over which we flew from the Wasserkuppe, it was literally uplifting. We felt special and privileged, we youngsters, even without the rhetoric.'

I'd done some gliding myself and knew exactly the feeling he described. The elemental one-ness with the atmosphere, the dependency and skill in finding wave and thermal, the sense of triumph when the vario indicated 'up'.

His eyes were half-closed, his wineglass stem became a control column as he spoke of the transition to powered flight, roaring engine up front. 'At last I was able to emulate the heroes from my childhood's books: Udet, Boelcke, Almenröder and Richthofen. Later,' he said, 'I met General Udet and feel now that I had glimpsed the coming suicide in his eyes, if they are indeed windows to our souls. If the old proverb, *To know the mind of another is to enter a dark place,* is correct, indeed there was a deadly conflict therein. You only had to look again at *Mein Kampf.*'

Yes, I thought. Pull on your jackboots. Hang up your humanity with your civilian clothes.

'But you were Luftwaffe Intel. At least you didn't bloody your hands with that *SS* stuff.' It wasn't meant to sound as patronizing as it possibly did.

He looked at me. 'We all have blood on our hands, Johann. The girl in the factory who makes the fuse. The riveter who skins the fighter's wings. Pacifists in the Third Reich were lined up with Jews, trades unionists and homosexuals. Before long they just weren't heard of; quietly forgotten about. Never spoken of, not even in private.'

He gave me a long look. 'You know, Johann, Hitler chose to believe that the Jewish race stemmed from a different branch of evolution entirely to that of humans or Cro-Magnons. He once stated that they were further removed from humankind than the Neanderthals. Himmler spent money belonging to the German people, actually much of it from the property of German Jews, turning the truth inside out to fit the theory. He sent expeditions all over the world: Finland, Tibet, Mexico, India to find the origins of a lost 'Aryan' race of Proto-Indo-Europeans through the common root of language. Equipped with facial-profile gauges. Looking for an ancestral super race of proto-Germans. We were all prepared to believe that stuff, God help us. It seems astonishing now.'

He stared into the fire. 'Thomas Mann said it well as he prepared to leave Germany; New Year's Eve, 1937. They'd burned his books and property. "God help our darkened and misused country. Teach it to make peace with the world and with itself."'

'But we were mesmerised. You can't now blame those youngsters who joined the Hitler Youth. Everybody did. We'd imbibed Nazi propaganda with our mothers' milk.'

He was silent for a while. There was just the popping of the gas flame and from the lounge, a brooding saxophonist successfully conjured, for me, an image of dark, rain-wet streets, sling-back shoes and tacky neon.

'*Im Ufergras,*
Zu früh getrennte Liebe.
Nah liegt ein Pferd,
Schreiend.'

He half-spoke, half sang the verse softly, almost to himself.

'What's that?' I asked, assuming he was quoting something from the music, which, though it had a hauntingly human timbre, was purely instrumental. I half thought that it was from the wartime jazz scene, with its resonances of Kurt Weill. It had been vehemently condemned and outlawed by Goebbels, only to be promoted eventually by the Nazis on a selective 'if you can't beat 'em, join 'em' basis', bent to their own satanic purpose.

'Oh, do you like it?

'Yes,' I replied. 'Is it from *Heine*? I would hazard a *Schubert-Lied*. I can imagine it sung by Dietrich Fischer-Diskau.' It had a haunting sound, although I couldn't follow it all. 'Something about a horse?'

'*On a grassy bank,*
Love leaves too soon,
While nearby a horse lies,
Screaming.'

The last lines came as a shock, jarring with the dreamy image that I had begun to create in my mind's eye.

'It's a *Haiku*,' he said. 'But a *German* one!' he smiled enigmatically. 'It's just something I'm working on. It fulfils the perfect seventeen-syllable requirement in English too, but I haven't translated it back into Japanese yet!'

I didn't quite follow. It seemed to have both a positive and negative charge. Yin and Yang.

'It's also a kind of *leitmotif*. It recurs over and again in…' he stopped mid flow. 'Forgive me,' he said, 'Perhaps I've been drinking too much.'

But those four stanzas had evoked a feeling of ineffable sadness, though perhaps it was the wine - as Peter himself had hinted. The discipline was that any thought could be refined in seventeen syllables. A very oriental idea, but intriguing.

He was speaking again. He seemed far away and the subject had changed. 'When I was an officer cadet I had rather a bad accident in a

Focke-Wulf *Stösser*. Entirely my own fault if I think about it even though the Board of Enquiry didn't come down too hard. I'd been side-slipping over trees after a gunnery exercise when the engine faltered as I opened up to arrest too swift a descent. I landed hard, buckled an undercarriage leg and turned over, breaking two vertebrae in my neck. Broke the aeroplane too. When I recovered I was taken off flying and with my engineering degree I'd worked for a few years in the Luftwaffe Intelligence Branch in Berlin, specializing in foreign developments and being lucky enough to travel on several overseas missions, up till 1940. There, Johann, I met many interesting people. After the war several crossed my path from time to time. They were a useful fund of information whenever I needed to check a fact here and there, as an aviation journalist then with *Der Flieger*. You see, many pre-war and wartime records were destroyed in the bombing, and later by our own people. Then more thoroughly by the occupying forces – the Russians. For the Soviets it was a matter of policy, amounting to a crusade, to obliterate as much German military history as possible, along with anything pertaining to German culture immediately after the surrender.'

A reputation for assisting several British aviation historians and authors had led to his doing some research for a young Englishman named James Delcroix, he informed me later. He asked me if I knew the name. I had to admit that I did not. It transpired that he'd been involved in some long lasting saga of research and had drawn a blank in identifying a pre-war German pilot and some obscure aircraft that he'd flown. That was until Delcroix had himself turned up an old pre-war copy of *Der Sportflieger* at *Beaumont's* in the Holloway Road, London. It had contained a rather faded picture of the aircraft, taken in Kassel, and a clear image of the pilot's face. Peter had received a Xerox of the article and with a shock realised that he had known and worked alongside this individual during the war, when they'd both served in Luftwaffe Intelligence. He'd looked up the library archive for the issue and was lucky to find a single copy to confirm the identity, but to his amazement the relevant page was gone, not torn out, but carefully excised, probably with a razorblade so that a cursory examination would not reveal that a page was missing.

Moreover, this officer had, it seemed, been involved in a crusade of his own; as great in its import as any historical epic in terms of world events, and in the early part of the war Peter had himself been an unwitting pawn in that enterprise. That story would culminate, *if ever it had ended at all*, in a determined act of heroism and daring.

'It was an attempt by one man in the *Siegfried* mould, yes I believe

154

now a kind of *innocent*, Johann, to change the course of the War and thus the history of the latter half of the Twentieth Century, but who was doomed to drag with him the restraining grip of others' mendacity and corruption, and was to suffer ultimate betrayal.'

Peter paused before he spoke again, choosing his words very carefully. 'But then along with most other good Germans at the time, I would doubtless have considered him a vile traitor to the 'Fatherland' for whom the hangman's noose or a firing squad would have been no less a fate than he'd deserved, though the military were required to swear an oath of allegiance, not to their country, but to Adolf Hitler himself.'

I recalled that long ago conversation as I sat and contemplated the scorched briefcase in my hotel room. I got up slowly and went to the bathroom. I had burns around my eyes and my eyebrows were singed. My hair, which usually fell forward over my forehead was burned close to the scalp for a few inches back, giving me a crinkly 'widow's peak' and there were some scabs forming, like a baby's 'cradle cap'. My forearms too were singed of all hair and altogether it looked as though I'd had a powerful dose of sunburn. It was very hot and painful still and I poured cold water into the basin to splash on my face and then soaked my arms in it for ten minutes or so. I was really not fit to be seen, but many other victims, about five hundred, had suffered far more serious burns. Seventy or so had died according to reports. It had been the worst accident in airshow history, including John Derry's De Havilland DH 110 accident at Farnborough in 1952.

~.~

It seemed we'd been in the corridor on the trolleys for hours, although when you are in pain time can drag unmercifully. In the ambulance Peter had been slipping in and out of consciousness and it had taken the driver an age to find this hospital. It seemed that there had been so many casualties that both the base and the Kaiserslautern emergency services had been overwhelmed so that less severely injured patients had been taken to smaller hospitals in the Palatinate countryside. As we were found close together and the initial assessment of our injuries was such that it was considered that we could make it, we'd been placed in the same small vehicle, just the two of us, with our saline drips and a worried looking nurse who spoke no English. We were luckier than some. I discovered from newspapers later that a busload of severely injured people had arrived at Ludwigshafen hospital 80 km away, three hours after the accident, unattended, the driver being unfamiliar with the area.

The doctor had asked me if I knew who Herr Neumann's next of kin might be. I said I knew of no one. I was now holding the briefcase that with a supreme act of determination, he'd thrust into my arms with his blood sausage fingers, as his trolley was about to be wheeled into the little operating theatre. I'd had a momentary impression of his eyes as he'd part risen, but his blackened face was an inscrutable mask, a red slash for a mouth. He'd pulled his oxygen off and his breath rasped through the swollen lips.

'Trust no one.' he'd gasped.

Earlier, still in the ambulance I'd heard him say 'Find Delcroix!' thickly, and something else, followed by a bout of coughing: something like *'MacHeath'* which was itself a kind of cough. Though why he should be saying the name of a serial killer from *The Threepenny Opera* I couldn't imagine. I'd assumed he was delirious. It was obviously extremely painful for him to speak. I now think that he was trying to say *Macbeth*. But his last words had been a wheezy stage whisper from his smoke-damaged lungs, and those words at least were clear enough. *Trust no one.*

Regretfully, the doctor explained a while later, that Herr Neumann had succumbed to a fatal heart attack whilst undergoing emergency treatment for burns.

~-~

Just a few hours before I'd seen Neumann, in grey flannels and a white shirt, wearing a dark blue tie and steel-rimmed shades. He was standing on the crowd line near the dart-like shape of a Luftwaffe 'widow maker': an F104 that was shimmering in the heat. He'd looked slightly agitated and was clutching a heavy briefcase. This seemed a little unusual for a man of retirement age who was a spectator at an airshow hosted by the United States Air Force in Germany - given that it was predominantly an 'open day'. It was not a trade fair as such where aerospace representatives might be making contacts and exchanging company information. I suppose my journalistic antennae were aroused by that as I'd hailed him. At first he'd looked a little startled and a slight shadow of disappointment had crossed his features, quickly covered-up as he greeted me with his usual *Berolina* warmth.

He had been guarded at first, but then probably he'd remembered our conversations of a few years previously and became more open about his scheduled meeting, which was with Delcroix, though it was obvious that the rendezvous had not worked out. I ventured that he was perhaps stuck in traffic somewhere, but he made no reply and continued to scan the crowd. We were soon onto one of our favourite topics; ramifications from the cancellation of Britain's Saro 177 programme, which depended on the German order, in favour of Starfighters; Lockheed F104s. Lockheed had an orphan fighter and was desperate for foreign orders. Dark mutterings had circulated about bribes paid in high places. Later there were shocking losses among young Luftwaffe F104 pilots, due in part to the additional roles forced upon the design and the inevitable weight escalation.

After a while, me watching the display and Peter mostly watching the crowd, the heat took its toll and I suggested we retire to the refreshment marquee.

'We can keep an eye on the rendezvous area from there if we position ourselves near the entrance,' I said. He reluctantly agreed. While we were there he was never more than a foot from his briefcase. When we'd sat and drunk iced lager it had stayed in full view on a folding chair next to him, his arm resting protectively on it, and when he'd gone to the bar, it had gone with him. I didn't ask but my curiosity was off the scale. I guessed it had something to do with the discovery of the aeroplane data that Delcroix had been researching in the late 1960s, and the identity and of the mysterious Luftwaffe Intel officer who was at the centre of it.

Peter decided to go back out and search through the crowd again. To be companionable I went with him, although the heat was fierce. I considered that if this meeting and the briefcase was that important I should at least take a look at the dogged Delcroix who'd presumably paid for Peter's valuable time on and off for over twenty years. What kind of secret was so important that you spent that long on its study? Fanatics had spent that long looking for the Loch Ness Monster the Holy Grail and the Yeti, but so far the existence of all three was unproven and it seemed like an alibi for doing nothing: a way of idling away an unproductive life, camouflaging it under the heading of 'Research'.

~-~

Alexa

A few years before, at the Hannover Airshow in the early 'eighties, Peter had introduced me to a fascinating woman, a striking beauty: Alexa, Prussian, blonde with blue eyes. In her early sixties by then but still a knock out. She had all sorts of contacts and had worked for German Intelligence, directly for Admiral Wilhelm Canaris, head of the Abwehr. She'd been parachuted into Norway ahead of the German invasion with a radio transmitter on her back and a shovel strapped to her front. She'd ended her spying days in Alexandria where she posed as one Sophie Clapham and lived above the New Zealand Officers' Club where her main job was counting ships, gathering what other information she could and then radioing the data back. The British couldn't prove she was a spy, but kidnapped her anyway and transported her to Palestine where she spent the rest of the war. She told me she'd had eight brothers, all officers, all killed in the war. She insisted that she wasn't a Nazi, un-reconstructed or otherwise, and also that Canaris had advised her early on to put all her earnings into a Swiss account as it would not be safe in the Reich. I recalled meeting her for several reasons, one being her magnetic personality, physical presence and vigour, the other being how terrifying it was being driven at breakneck speed around Hannover one evening in her BMW while she told me her life story, or a version of it, and seemingly was never sure quite where she was going. But she said that by driving fast she'd be certain to get there that much quicker!

We'd finally arrived at our mysterious destination where she'd taken me to an upstairs apartment to meet another contact of Peter's. It had been a strange meeting and some of the experiences that 'Harry' had had were worthy of a novel in their own right. Later I was to learn a lot more about this short, tough-looking individual. He was ex-military, Polish, or so I'd assumed by his accent, and highly decorated. It was evident that he lived alone, was either of modest means or cared nothing for luxury. The place was reasonably tidy but had a 'temporary' look, with suitcases and overstuffed rucksacks just shoved into odd corners. No ornaments or pictures: certainly no female touch. A base camp for his personal Everest. For some reason Peter had wanted a 'cut-out', that is not to meet Harry face-to-face. Or maybe he didn't want to be followed to the apartment, for his own or Harry's sake. Harry took it all with equanimity, and handed to or received from Alexa whatever document could not be sent in the mail.

Returning by a different but equally circuitous route I suddenly realised that Alexa was not remotely lacking in a sense of direction, but was deliberately throwing off any car that might be trying to tail us. What my role was supposed to have been I never knew. I hardly saw myself as 'muscle'. But it seemed to prove something. Peter trusted me.

I looked again at the scatter of typed A4 sheets, foolscap drafts, pictures, notebooks and letters. I suddenly realised there were codebooks and flying logbooks among the documents. There was a hard-backed diary written in a neat female hand, property of a Miss Claudia Hammond of Cheriton Cottage, Grove Farm, Nr. Wreningham, Norfolk. And there too was the fabled Xerox from *Der Flieger*. And a familiar looking *Stratford Shakespeare: The Complete Works* 1923 edition, well-thumbed with an introduction by St. John Ervine and a frontispiece by Sargent, R.A: Miss Ellen Terry as Lady Macbeth. *The very person who'd handed him this publication two years previously was yours truly, Natasha, having carried it from the Persian Gulf via the UK in my luggage.*

A more thorough examination would have to wait. The open-fronted bedside cupboard revealed a local telephone directory under a Lutheran Bible and a sheaf of travel brochures for Die schöne Landschaft von Rheinland-Pfalz.

I had evidently to get rid of this thing for the time being. If Alexa said so, then it must be so. Natürlich.

After that long ago first meeting at the hotel in Biggin, Peter and I had taken the bus to the airshow together. By now my head felt better and he proved to be a very amiable well-read companion and we found a lot to talk about. When we watched the *Frécce Tricolori* crews arriving on the apron I remembered commenting that they must have been on full oxygen from the start to clear their heads as they taxied out for their display. Like many pilots before them they used the 'Biggin Valley', and although they didn't descend into it, (later banned for safety reasons) they flew a low approach across it which meant zero feet and level, their coloured smoke dropping down into the valley behind them. They'd arrived at the airfield right on the crowd line, impossibly low, deafening and asphyxiating everyone with red, white and green-dyed diesel-tainted smoke as they thundered past. They approached again across the valley and two were seen to clearly touch wingtips, which caused a momentary wobble at very low level. Luckily they only removed some paint on that occasion. Their flying was dramatic, a little ragged, and *very* Italian. And so it proved at Ramstein eighteen years later.

~-~

Peter and I step out into the sunshine mingling with the spectators. I've no idea what James Delcroix looks like so there's no point in my searching for faces in the crowd. Peter has a young man's stride and carries his sixty-eight years well considering the tough time he'd had in Russia after the war. His broken neck, sustained forty-eight years previously has recently stiffened due to arthritis, so he's obliged to turn his upper body to look right and left, but otherwise he's as fit as anyone could expect to be when they're approaching seventy.

Like all such events things seem to happen in ultra-slow motion as the brain goes into instant 'turbo', as Peter might have said. He has seen someone in the ice cream queue and is moving in that direction. I stand aside on the grass, off to the left of the van to wait to see if he's found Delcroix. Somebody, I think it was Proust, says something about death coming at the most ordinary moment. When you stoop to tie your shoes. When you are stepping out of a shop doorway admiring the new hat you've just bought. Queuing for an ice cream on a blisteringly hot August afternoon in Germany in a happy holiday atmosphere. Perhaps just as you reach out to touch the sleeve of the man you've come to meet.

I am distracted by the two converging flights of Aermacchis sweeping together. I've seen it all before, but in practice things had seemed a little more ragged than usual, with the solo performer using airbrakes to correct his penetration-timing for the 'heart' manoeuvre. Nine jets converge low level at crowd centre, the two flights of four and five moving head-on at a closing speed of about 600 mph, apparently fanned to interlock from the crowd's perspective. In reality each element is safely staggered a wingspan or so apart at closure, but the intention is to shock the crowd with an apparent 'near miss'.

When the dark young Italian aviators had walked out to their aircraft - with a *little* of the swagger of seasoned Roman gladiators, I'd wondered half-aloud, 'Weren't gladiators *lionized*?' And I'd quipped to Peter, 'The *Red Arrows* make the easy look difficult, and the difficult impossible. But the *truly* impossible they leave to the *Frécce Tricolori*!'

Peter had grinned, adding a pithy comment in response. He was very aware of the potential for disaster that the team's repertoire contained. The feted Italians had dash and flair in abundance, flying with a showy verve that lacked the ice-cold, laid back precision of the *Arrows*. But they too were steely-eyed, fit and practiced professionals, weren't they? Sky-gods in their own right! The *Regia Aeronautica* of old had been famous for the skill and dash of its pilots, whose panache reflected the fire of the national character. I remembered pre-war photographs of their vivacious Fiat fighter biplanes flying their unique zigzag formation, reflecting the Warren-braced strut arrangement of designer Rosatelli's CR.32s. What could possibly go wrong with their better-trained successors in their sleek jets? Yet there had been an almost 'ad-lib' quality to the recent displays

160

which lent the proceedings a visceral anxiety; an 'edge' that worried the old hands, even if the crowd was generally oblivious on such a lovely summer's day.

~-~

Eins.

Peter has just moved away from the ice cream queue. The ice creams are free, courtesy of the USAF. A little girl is following behind carrying three cones, one for her little brother in his pushchair parked next to the van, one for her big sister. A teenage boy and girl are next in line to be served, his arm loosely around her waist. From this distance I cannot determine from Peter's expression whether the man he has spoken to is Delcroix.

Zwei.

The solo element is running in towards the crowd, fast and low. Lowering its undercarriage in attempting to slow down, it collides with at least one crossing aircraft and the nose breaks away in a cascade of debris and bounces onto the main runway, complete with ejector seat and its dead occupant. People are standing, filming as if everything is normal. The still-flying centre-fuselage and wings pitch-up as the weight of the nose section and cockpit are brutally sliced-off.

Drei.

For a heartbeat I hear no sound. I stand like everyone else in open disbelief. The pitching fuselage is still moving at a few hundred miles per hour but falling towards the crowd, a stream of fire trailing behind. The unstable flight path reminds me of nothing so much as a balsa chuck glider I'd made as a boy, fluttering and falling after losing its lead nose-ballast. Except this time it weighs several thousand pounds, contains a jet engine and is full of highly volatile *Avtur.*

Vier.

The now cart-wheeling fuselage and wings strike the ice cream van and a red Avis truck thirty yards away from me and plough on into the seventy-odd people queuing in a snake behind. A massive orange and black fireball blossoms into the sky, obliterating all else in view including the other crippled aircraft hit by the 'solo' machine which crashes onto a *casevac* helicopter.

Fünf.

People have started to run, but for those in the immediate vicinity it's already too late. Something staggers out of the fire ablaze, but the jet fuel fans out and others are engulfed; human candles in the tumbling inferno whose inchoate lava core has momentum enough to travel many yards, the rolling mass felling and incinerating those twisting too late from the scene.

Sechs. Der hellste Stern von allen.....

I have been knocked flat by the heat and the pressure wave, but I lift myself up to see Peter staggering on the periphery, his shirt on fire. My face feels hot and my hair is burned and coarse where it's singed. I climb shakily to my feet aware of the fierce heat and the smells of burning oil and something else as the soundtrack suddenly cuts-in…. screams, wails, a siren starting up. Agonized cries for help and someone nearby shouting, 'Oh my God!' over and over and over again. I stumble over to Peter and roll him on the ground. The shirt is sticking to him and he's suffered deep burns. His face is black and I can't see the features.

I'm only sure it's him because he's still holding the briefcase.

Chapter 12.
Obsession and Seclusion: James's Story

The view in the fading light beyond the curtained window is of a Norwood Hill garden off the A217 south of London en route to Crawley. The garden has returned to its natural state with meadow flowers and a screen of dark trees including a group of yews clustered like nuns giving the cottage a cloistered look and an air of mourning. Nettle and rhododendron have claimed ownership from the dying fruit trees in the modest one-time vegetable plot at rear. A few sheds and outbuildings extend to a leylandii boundary grown tall and tassled. To one side a shadowed carport conceals my rented Ford Escort. The place is well overdue for development given the ramping of house prices and the desirable locality.

Cooking is via electricity, presently from an illicit meter by-pass. Lights are restricted to a table lamp with a 40-watt bulb and a bedside lamp, lit only when the heavy curtains are drawn.

I am at what James refers to as one of his 'safe-houses', an empty, fly-blown property complete with dry rot and disconnected telephone on the books of an estate agent acquaintance, whose *For Sale* sign lies low in the tangled flowerbed, who owes James' friend, Mike, a favour or two. A rather unsafe arrangement I'd have thought if the stakes were as high as James, Alexa, more recently alias *Stephanie*, and co. had intimated. A sticking-plaster security system. The police weren't involved at any level, which at least made it safer than any sort of witness protection scheme as far as James was concerned. He is reaching back twenty years to when he, James, was a young man still, with his ambitions on 'hold' and a pending on-off divorce.

~-~

James is slightly older than me: sandy hair going grey. His clothes look as though he's lost a little weight recently. Late wartime birth, although we're the same generation. We've known the same sort of upbringing, which means we have a quick understanding of each other. I find that I like him on sight, and what's more I feel I can trust what he says. He seems on edge, however. It must be said he has excellent recall and an eye for detail. We are making good headway with some cans of beer while he describes for me his own first meeting with Harry, in

Frankfurt: the Book Fair, and later at Harry's hotel.

Harry, he says, is breathing deeply. James notes that his agitation has been increasing with the hour. Harry paces and sighs, sometimes wringing his hands, mostly staring out at the Frankfurt night, the lighting soft in the rented apartment. It is not easy for James to witness, to wait so patiently for the legend to unfold; piece together the sporadic thrust of the narrative's false starts, to attend a difficult birthing from the damaged, locked soul of Arkadiusz Piotrkowski, known to all as *Harry*.

And it's Harry, even to those of his intimate circle, the Polish community at their émigré Club, *Ogniezku*, in Kensington. Stiff-collared and ramrod straight old officers polishing their monocles, saluting each other punctiliously, Harry swapping stratagems from the depths of a leather armchair, looked down upon by hawk-like generals in double-eagle frames. Harry, at the Baltic Society in Bloomsbury, and at his West Coast home in Pacifica, Cal., bought before property prices hit the roof: gentle deer wandering his garden on golden reverie mornings, dappled in sunlight like dreams of his childhood.

Harry, publisher. Harry with a killer smile and flint in his eyes. Harry, who if he likes you is your best friend, lends you his last dollar who's known hardship and the good life too. Harry, who'd married more than twice; who did something in the War that he never discussed. Maybe too painful, like this other, older memory he will regurgitate at some cost. Not *shameful* though. There was a straightness of back to this dapper, compact soldierly man, whose intimates hold him in high esteem. As does James, on short acquaintance, and not just because Harry is near four decades his senior, John. This is the same Harry I met half a decade later, and then again briefly after the funeral in Berlin. Peter's funeral. Each time the meetings were strange and I seemed to be there as a supernumery, welcomed with a granite handclasp and that million dollar smile that Harry reserved for those of his intimate circle, which meant pre-war or wartime confidantes mostly. Or those who'd known the inside of soviet labour camps, although they were by no means always welcome, so James intimated. It was a shadowy world in 1966, even if your surname wasn't Lime but Piotrkowski: with an 'i' not a 'y' *mark you well*, and it was no different at 'street level' in '88. But though I was welcome, I played no part. I was 'outside' the clique, and did not presume to ask dangerous questions of old spooks who were still 'at it' so it seemed.

~.~

164

James had just overhauled an MG roadster, a cream TC two-seater in the pre-war style. Red leather seats, chrome as good then as when she'd rolled her spoked wheels off the Abingdon production line fifteen years before, in 1949.

Restorations, objects of beauty are James Delcroix' *thing* as a one time professional restorer of antiques or sometimes their *creator.* In his Clifton workshop, paint still tacky on the bonnet: he answers the telephone call from the local flying club. Stead, enthusing about some old aeroplane in Norfolk

He was short of capital: the divorce had seen to that. But Mike Stead's tone arouses James' interest.

'It's a *Jungmeister!*' he declaims breathlessly. 'At least I *think* that's what it is,' he adds.

'The place is due to be sold and that includes *all* contents. Everything's up for grabs. There's a Panther motorcycle and sidecar too! And.... a punt!'

Mike had driven to Norfolk to view the property; a worse for wear but still imposing Georgian pile. Neither estate agent nor property entrepreneur, he'd helped out an old friend with a drink driving conviction who is both those things: Mike volunteering to chauffeur him pro tem in the big Bentley straight-six. They'd spent an hour looking over the house and extensive gardens. There had once been quite a big adjacent farm that's no longer part of the estate, worked now by a relative.

Recently widowed, Lady Barrington is selling up: *lock, stock and elderly servants;* cook-housemaid and the cook's husband, chauffeur-handyman-gardener. Her ladyship intends retiring to Bournemouth, so the tied cottage is for sale. Tough on the help.

James hears himself saying that he can't possibly afford it, even as he comes to the decision that he'll at least go and *view* the dismantled biplane at a mutually convenient date, which turns out to be two day's hence. Just time to be sure that the MG's new paint has hardened. Time enough to mull over what it would be like to own a benchmark pre-war aerobatic classic, worth maybe £5000 or more, restored. If indeed that is what it *is.*

Twenty years since the end of the War there are few Bücker *Jungmeisters* left. Built at Rangsdorf, near the *Rangsdorfer See,* a kidney-shaped lake south of Berlin, there were a couple he knew existed in the UK, and a handful in Germany and the USA, privately owned. Most were in Spain, or Switzerland: those licence-built by Swiss-Dornier at

Altenrhein still served with the Swiss Air Force as aerobatic trainers. They'd survived due to Swiss neutrality, whereas most German examples had been destroyed during or after the War. It was nowadays outnumbered by the two-seater *Jungmann*, basic trainer. Widely used since the mid 1930s by Hitler's Luftwaffe, both types were exceptionally well-engineered and in design terms far ahead of the RAF's then contemporary Tiger Moth.

One reason for Delcroix' fascination was that the *single-seat* Jungmeister was particularly exotic, being a legendary mount for the 1930s aerobatic élite, Rudolf Lochner and Graf Hagenburg to name two, and powered by a beautiful 160 hp. Siemens radial engine. *I could have lusted after one myself, Natasha, but they were damn rare and out of reach.*

'So,' James tells me. 'I collect Mike from the flying club where he's lodged for the summer season, freed for the day from his job as dogsbody/assistant flying instructor.'

The CFI was happy to release him, so saving paying his assistant a wage for not doing much; what with a pupil away on a solo cross-country in the Hornet and the Tiger unserviceable again, James says. A worn-out tailskid and a buckled aileron, according to Mike. James is long on detail. We're both on our second cans by now and this quest is becoming so involved that, to follow the thread, each twist seems significant. It is as if James is at pains to weave a detailed tapestry to convince me of its veracity, given the eventual leap of credulity I will be asked to make.

I slip into the evident reverie that James himself is experiencing in the re-telling. I can relate to it, my own motoring back then consisting of blasting about in a TR-2 – three of us jammed tightly in, singing *Money Can't Buy Me Love!* Top of our lungs at 100 mph.

The long drive to Norfolk commences with hood down but side-screens in place for convenience. It's breezy and satisfying on a summer's day in light traffic. The sports car is 'surrogate flying' for James and evokes imaginary 'memories' of wartime RAF stations he's never known. RAF units *without* an old MG being parked somewhere around were, he felt, 'incomplete'. After all, Bader drove one. In post-war films of the genre, like *The Dam Busters,* James is never happy until he's spotted one!

~-~

'Place is a bit overgrown.'

This is Mike, lounging comfortably on the padded leather, recounting the recent 'reconnaissance' visit, having to shout above the song of the engine. He's uncomplicated and twenty-two, James guesses. Fancy free: lives for flying.

'The old boy climbs up to check the tiles after gales,' he shouts. His delivery is clipped, in part due to the slipstream. 'Better off out of it at his age, really. It's hard luck. Told me they've no savings. Nowhere to go. Probably paid them a pittance.'

James changes down to pass a lorry near Andoversford, on the A436 Stow road.

'Hall's full of badger masks. She's as dotty as they come. Well over eighty.'

He describes the wind-up gramophone in the conservatory with single-sided 78s and piles of yellowed newspapers – mostly 1940s. Pictures of the major in uniform with Sam Browne, and in another wearing a blazer; punting on the Cam or somewhere.

'We'd surveyed the house. Tackle and gun room; dreadful oil painting of a regimental polo match. North West Frontier. Outbuildings and gardens very run down. A prehistoric P&A motorcycle combination out in the weather, next to a punt. And there's an Armstrong Siddeley *Sphinx* in the garage.'

'I'd question the *Sphinx*.'

Mike looks puzzled. 'Why?'

'It's traditional. Well, never mind…..'

'Anyway, the son was RAF. Pilot Officer, killed flying a Spit from his OTU in '41. Left his bedroom exactly as it was! Model Gipsy Moth hanging from the ceiling. Used to fly one, apparently, before the war, so he wasn't a novice. Shot up the homestead, lost control somehow and pranged. Full view of the North window. Big fireball, right in front of ma and pa!' So the gardener'd said.

Simultaneously they chanted the RFC catechism, '*Stunt not over thine own domicile, lest the earth rise up and* **smite** *thee!*' James swerves to avoid a Standard Eight.

'Major and Lady B. never got over it. There's a third place set at table ever since. Last month the Major collapsed in the arms of his handyman: "You've been a good servant, Evans," he said, and expired. There were *two* empty places set when we left last week.'

James pictures the old dowager, flanked by her silver service and her ghosts. And so do I.

'Now she's heading off somewhere with a sea view…. her own last *months* probably. Wonder if she'll take her ghosts with her?'

The road straightens out and the MG gathers speed. 'Tell me about the aeroplane.' says James.

'Last thing we looked at was an old pump house. For irrigation, near the boundary wall. Seemed hardly worth looking inside but we got the door part open and then the roof sort of dropped and jammed it. There was a dismantled aeroplane inside, four wings stacked against the fuselage. Decades of dust and owl crap. Its shape was a dead give away.'

'How?'

'Deep-stringered decking, fabric-covered, very hunch-backed shape of the Bücker. Those long undercarriage legs.'

'Yeah, if you know what you're looking at,' James agreed. 'And the engine?'

'Didn't see an engine.'

'What d'you mean you didn't see an engine?' James was aghast. 'Why didn't you tell me this before? What's the point in going all this way if it hasn't got an engine? *Siemens* don't grow on trees. It's not like you can just install a *Cirrus Major* instead!'

'Calm down, will you? All I said was I *think* it's a Bücker *Jungmeister*. Never actually seen one except in pictures.

'Well, did you look for the engine?'

'Of course I *looked* for the engine. Just didn't see one. That doesn't mean it isn't there under some old sacks or something. Place was dark, it was late evening and everything was a mess. I did see struts, though. And a fin and tailplane. Interior was filthy - birds' nests and spider webs. Dammit, I was wearing my only suit. I didn't really *expect* to be looking at a derelict aeroplane.'

James had driven on in silence.

'It was too late to turn back now, John. Besides, I was intrigued to find out if it *was* a Bücker. Or if it wasn't, what the heck it *was*. It could hardly be any more exotic and rare than a Jungmeister, surely. Not in Britain.'

~-~

Outside the cottage rural Surrey was now in near-darkness. James rose and looked out through a slight gap in the curtain. The dark caste of the leylandii, lowering cloud and the dull amber glow of distant Reigate was all that might be seen. I'd murmured something in sympathy when he'd told me in passing about his ex-wife's drinking, about his elfin daughter, Manda, who was living in a communal squat with a '*scrofulous Peckham Trot*', already carrying his child and hardly eating – some morbid sitology - and she had cut away from her father completely. His square hands curled slightly at this and I found myself imagining an unwashed throat in their grip. In fact he offers me another can from the stash beside his chair. He was afraid that his other daughter would go the same way. Amelia was staying out and dropping lectures at college according to Audrey's increasingly incoherent night time phone calls. Here however he was strictly incommunicado and worrying about the girls. I recognized the bitterness.

I was recently divorced. *Natasha, you had veered Left too, had your fling with Marxism.* 'Went AWOL for a while.' I tell James. 'Before she landed her stockbroker!' I offered the information as if it might make him feel better in some remote way. He just stared at me without seeing; already planning his next chapter.

Returning to the fireside and the middle 'sixties, James explained distractedly that lack of an engine would devalue the project. There'd have been considerable difficulty in finding a Siemens-Bramo even back then at a sensible price. Besides he probably wouldn't be buying it himself. He'd made some telephone calls before leaving and established that there would be a market for either an unrestored original Bü 133c, or a fully restored example at a good figure. So if the old bat wasn't clued up on what it might be worth, it could still be viable. There was the matter of title. She might not own the machine, but presumably by fact of its storage it had something to do with her late son's aviation interests.

But if that rare radial engine was missing it might all be a waste of time and money.

~-~

Somewhat mollified, James is talking to Stead again.

'I have always dreamed of finding a classic old aeroplane in a barn one day.'

'Maybe today's that day,' says Mike, after a while.

They'd continued on the 425, Daventry and Northampton in heavy traffic, breathing diesel, cursing Beeching!

~-~

James pauses. He leaves the next sequence of the narrative deliberately, returning to Harry, his current obsession. Through James, Harry is talking again, and James has leaped forward to Frankfurt, early 1970s. Harry's unburdening is piecemeal. The old urbanity gone on the flood along with both definite and indefinite articles, syntactic orthodoxy ebbing in a swell of Slavic glory.

'You know '*Slav*', it actually *means* 'glory', James?' he'd said.

He stares into the busy street, bright with red tail lights and shopfront neon, leaning forward on the windowsill. An evening breeze moves the net curtains tentatively, one each side of his straight Polish back, like approximations of angel's or ancient Polish cavalry 'wings' of the Holy Alliance, perhaps by *Chagal,* now blue, now amber by the luminescence of inert gases. The uplit features, half-turned, change on an instant; first to the colours of the old Ukrainian flag, then the Polish. Later, James will learn that this was the unifying dream of Henryk Jozewski's sweeping reforms. James suppresses a trivial thought; ignoring the temptation to look for a fiddler on the opposite roof! There will be little enough levity here tonight, of that he's certain.

'James. You know what it is to be *blooded*?'

'Sorry?' The question was so unexpected that the word seemed meaningless, unless it meant that you had scored a victory of some sort. 'An *initiation* you mean?'

Harry looked at him bleakly. 'Yes, exactly. An *initiation*. Like when you kill a fox... or shoot a boar.' He still seemed reluctant to spit it out, whatever it was. That journey he'd been on in the mind must have been long, and followed a hard road, James thought. A rocky road. A *soldier's* road, like in an old Polish song he'd heard somewhere.

'I was a boy only. Ten I think. Lithuania......more than fifty years....' The sentences trailed off. The discourse rambling, the delivery terse. Bite-sized, except he couldn't *bite* or *swallow*. He seemed on the verge of choking on the very words. He'd opened a bottle; vodka, and he'd been drinking already, before James had arrived. Now he ignored the glass and took liberal swigs – offering it to a declining Delcroix, a comradely yet distant gesture for this shared experience that was unfolding – except that it wasn't to be shared in the breach, or not yet awhile: those things too awful to dwell on in the detail. And yet that's where the devil dwelt, in the minutiae. In the nuts and bolts of things. In knife and bayonet ... these were the instruments of his remembered details that separate lamb from wolf, James, innocence from malevolent, brute evil.

'You know the old Jesuit claim....?' Harry gives him a sharp look. 'That's of course if you're not of the Lutheran belief in Pope as *Antichrist*. "*Give me the boy when he is seven and I will give you the man!*" You've heard that, right? Well, I thank God I was ten and not younger when I was .....well, who knows how I would have turned out? You've heard of Stockholm Syndrome? In all the papers since Patty Hearst.' Another swig, another tangent. Another pause.

'I saw a lot in the War, believe me.'

James believes him. James also guesses he means the *Second* World War now, and they have jumped ahead some twenty years in this narrative. 'Same bastards. Same robotic idiots, following orders from people unfit to command, and who anyway don't have to look at results. You may think, James, in your smug English utopia of muffins and cricket, that interface between new and old ideology; syncline and anticline, could be argued through amicably by intelligent men, giving ground where common sense tells you conflict will result in *more* stress and tears. Bargaining hard in conference, especially following 'war to end all wars' (James is sure we've leaped back those other twenty years again) is sensible. Letting loose worst criminals to wreak Red Terror on unarmed civilian populace is hardly *idealistic*, and yet that is what was *sanctified* in name of bringing forth Marxist 'equality, liberty, and power' to the masses, by sweeping away privilege, and Lenin's hated bourgeoisie: as well as making mockery of rule of law or reason, and bringing enslavement and death to millions. Suffering that *Ivan the Terrible* might have blanched at.'

Harry pauses and lances James with a look.

'But this you already know, unless you are some kind of closet communist who *maybe* admits that 'mistakes were made', like bloody Kruschev, but *maybe* game was worth it, in long run, to drag proletariat out of damn feudal ignorance. I don't think so. Lenin didn't give *shit* about people. Was driven by hatred, not ideals of humanitarianism; fatally lunatic revolutionary ideas and hunger for power. But mostly by hatred. Baying for blood like a mad dog. Who turns monastery isle into slave camp: Solovetsky Island – Mother of the Gulag! I don't believe that anyone in the West really has *clue*. You had to be *there*. Had to *be* there, James.'

~-~

We are now drinking coffee. James's face is in shadow. The small bulb in the table lamp does not show me his eyes in that room. Just his voice and the retelling. As if Delcroix must tell me all, now, for the 'record'. Almost as if he doesn't think he will have the strength or perhaps the time to tell anyone ever again. Nor the energy to write all this stuff down, presuming it was important for him to do so. It is the 'victors', after all, who write the histories.

It is two days prior to their meeting in the suite at the Frankfurter Hof. They are just off the Apfelweinviertel, neatly pedestrianised, at a small pavement restaurant on the Sachsenhausen side of the river Main, across from Frankfurt town.

It does an excellent *Eisbein mit Sauerkraut,* and seems worlds away from the German Economic Miracle; the growl of its traffic softened by the neat cluster of buildings with their steep roofs and cobbled walkways. Away too from James' hotel lounge with its televisual horrors of gameshows and close-ups of the Vietnam War. From Che Guevara tee shirts, and Rudi Dutschke firebrand student agitation. The wanted poster for the *Rote Armee Fraktion* was perhaps the only sign here that in its shiny corporate skin, sleek new Germany, divided, still hid a beating revolutionary heart.

Though with anger and fearful contempt, successful business in its purring Mercedes dream, impatiently brushed aside as aberrant these incendiaries; it really *didn't* want to admit to Lenin's old trope: that Berlin, his *Powderkeg of Europe,* and with it Germany, could again explode. Right in their faces.

~.~

They are dining together following their initial meeting in Frankfurt after James' had sought information on his 'find' via an *Aeroplane Monthly* advertisement, a magazine chosen for its worldwide readership, had apparently struck gold. Or at least *pyrites.*

Three months before Delcroix had stopped off at the Aviation Bookshop in Holloway Road, and had flipped through a rare pile of tattered but highly priced copies of *Der Sportflieger* that were newly in. Buried in a copy for 1932 was a photograph of an unidentified radial-engined biplane, with a dark lightning-flash painted along the fuselage. This terminated in a stylised *striking raptor,* a falcon or an eagle, talons outstretched to strike down its prey. The faded image showed a youngish, smiling man in a white flying overall leaning on the *Heine* propeller and holding a winged trophy. His eyes were fixed not on the camera, but on a young woman, a real honey who'd been edited partly out of shot. Picture editor should have been sacked, Delcroix thought, but he was immediately attracted to the design of the aeroplane itself, whose identity escaped him. But when he saw the name on the caption,

172

his heart had literally raced.

Meanwhile a Swiss magazine reader with whom the aerobatic connection resonated had liberated that same issue from the *Aeroklub* lounge at Bex and, knowing his history, passed it to a recently retired LAE, name of Meyer. Delcroix' advertisement for information had given rise to a name linked to *Steiger*, with a suggestion that the Polish Club in London might bear fruit. Both the Polish and the Baltic Society establishments had departments dedicated to the tasks of trying to locate old soldiers, their relatives and further dispersed families and friends.

Meyer had been a Heinkel's He 64 European *Rundflug* team mechanic; the official German entry, for those events that were held on Polish soil in the early 1930s. Repatriated by 'amnesty' after many years of Russian slavery, Harry had joined the Polish Army and had volunteered for stewardship as part of an official reception committee for the international guest competitors. It transpired that both he and Meyer had had connections with the *Baltische Landeswehr* and *Freikorps* back in 1919, despite Harry having been a mere boy at the time: younger by ten years.

'Over a couple of evening sessions, after the competing aircraft had been tied down and quarantined, that sort of thing, they'd shared a bottle, swapped yarns. Meyer himself then had relatives in Cracow. Names had come up when reminiscing about *Kurland.*' says James. 'People they'd known then had risen later with the arrival of the Nazis and the shiny new Luftwaffe: a chance meeting stirring memories that Harry would rather have forgotten, but they'd parted friends. Just never found the time to keep in touch afterwards, you know how it is.'

That of course was from a different time, before the meaning that such words as *Blitzkrieg, Katyn, Auschwitz-Birkenau, Holocaust, Iron Curtain, Gulag* had come to symbolise, and which would sunder such fragile human bonds, it seemed forever.

'Next thing they were on different sides again,' says James, uttering my thought.

Nonetheless, in that pre-Internet decade, by such tenuous leads were old connections remade. After numerous letters and telephone calls the eventual contact had been quite brief. Long distance: from the USA. The voice had merely said that he would be in Europe for a week, and attending the Frankfurt Book Fair, if Monsieur Delcroix would care to make his way to Germany, he would make the time to see him there.

~-~

The waiter arrives as James hands Harry a Xerox copy with the picture of the *Sportflieger* biplane. Harry had already said that aviation wasn't really his subject, not any more but.......as a youngster he'd been around aeroplanes for a while. Helped out as a volunteer. A sort of supernumery mechanic's assistant and 'gofer'.

Harry tells James that he deals internationally in rare books as well as publishing; text books, glossies on art, architecture and archaeology, though it is his modern novelists in paperback that have begun to impact on Eastern European markets. Recent literary conquests behind the Curtain were opening up a New Frontier in book sales. 'Like pushing at an open door, James. The Warsaw Pact is hungry for the English Detective Novel.'

But, like Delcroix I am beginning to wonder if anything is just as it seems. And as James had done over the intervening years, whether that CV was just cover for an old 'spook'. Books can contain any number of microdots, but if trade was one-way, unless I was doing Harry an injustice, who was supplying whom with what? Considering that *I had myself acted as Peter's unwitting courier* of a package originating in the Lebanon: Dubai-London-Berlin, that I'd practically forgotten about, was I being unbelievably naïve?

Somewhere close a café jukebox is playing a compilation of Beatles' songs.

~-~

So, in Frankfurt an apparently relaxed Harry P. and James Delcroix are exploring their world's views, discussing contemporary German politics and history. An orphaned copy of *Der Spiegel* left on a nearby table reveals the florid face of the Chairman of the *Nationaldemokratische Partei Deutschlands*, Friedrich Thielen, *owner of a Bremen cement factory*, the political journalist informs them. The NPD is keen to repeat its successful percentage increases in the polls following earlier Schleswig-Holstein and Bavarian gains. Of the 18 members of the Party Executive, the magazine reveals, 12 are former Nazis, half of whom were high in the ranks of the SS.

Thielen's face at the podium is a scowling mask flanked by familiar crimson flags, each of which bears a plain white disc; an incomplete heraldic image, flaunted like a naked full moon upon which the mind's eye cannot fail but to superimpose the outlawed black ghost of a spidery cross.

The heavy face in the photograph contrasts sharply with a younger

174

black and white Thielen, in uniform, photographed in the 1940s, which James at first takes for Eichmann.

'The same dead look in the hooded eyes, the same oval face and youthful chin. The same cold aloofness, John,' he tells me in the quiet of the Norwood night. The fleshy jowls of the stout middle-aged man with the middle-distance stare make him now more of an angry butcher, like a *Cummings* caricature of Göring wielding a bloody cleaver. There are also recent pictures of Neo-Nazi torchlight processions and of men in dark shirts, marching in formations – goose-stepping, with banners; arms raised provocatively in the now *verboten* manner.

Listening to James, I reach back for a memory of those times, those 'sixties years and the resurgence of Nazism without the name; old men beating their war drums in cellars in the cause of national identity and secret denial. Old men with the same anger in their hearts, like the disinherited rabble-rousers of the earlier period of poverty and strife that had spawned its Hitlers, Röhms and Ribbentrops. Then it had seemed another generation of young men was spoiling for a revolution of the *Right* to counter a young, agitating and vociferous rising *Left*.

Frustrated, I recall merely frivolous images from that time. It had been a new decade that had broken the rules and had distanced us from the post-war austerity. I remembered *That Was The Week That Was*, free love and Angel of course, my one regret. Lost in the Rheinland, a victim of another evil ideology expressed through a fanatic's bomb. Drugs were never my scene, but like they said, if you remembered the 'sixties, you weren't there; though my latter memories were quite as blurred seen through the bottom of a glass. After Angelika.

Callowness and innocence. Their superficiality invests the yeoman British male, allied to a deep mistrust of intense political activity in his youth. With no hereditary memory of an invading army since 1066, separated by the Channel, our *Maginot Line*, we are divided from the continuous landmass and the otherwise unstoppable marching boot. Hence liberals and Stalin's 'useful idiots' had cleaved to the idea that we might just sit still and watch developments 'over there'.

The phenomenon of those coeval tyrannies, Nazism's and Communism's 'almost civilised' way of coming to a sort of dialogue with the world were viewed as necessary growing pains, indulged at opposite poles by opportunistic Black Shirt thugs and the Intelligentsia of the Left. "It's all so new and brave, dear boy. Can't make an omlette, blah, blah!" But Orwell's retort had been straight to the point. 'So where,' he'd asked, referring to the great slave camp of the USSR, 'is the omelette?' But in the 1930s that could have been said of *both* plaguey houses. And for the rest, perhaps if we just kept looking the other way, why, it would all pass us safely by.

Except that at home there was the peoples' armed response to Fascism with the forming of the International Brigade to fight their 'just war' and Moseley raising a para-military rabble of his own, and his arm in mimicry.

I recalled in a mental aside, that Moseley's wife, Diana Mitford, her sister, a deluded minor aristo, Unity Valkyrie Mitford, had been obsessed by Hitler. She had shot herself in the head in a failed suicide bid after the Führer's attention had been diverted, following Eva Braun's own attempt. The man seemed jinxed in terms of the suicides or suicidal gestures among the teenagers and women he'd been close to, like some sort of cursed rock star. His own niece had succumbed. Winifred Wagner might have considered herself lucky that her 'Wolfie' had looked elsewhere for what intimacy he was capable of, though she'd carried her own guttering torch to the grave.

'The Iberian affair was no simplistic good versus evil conflict,' said James, bringing me back to the political table.

The popular view had the Republicans capturing the moral high ground but the readiness of the USSR to come to the aid of Republican Spain had nothing to do with equality and freedom since neither virtue was evident in that oppressive, totalitarian regime. It was rather an opportune moment to demonstrate its power and reach in the face of the ever-growing threat of Nazism; a testing ground for new weapons, particularly their air weapon. Not to mention the flood of political commissars.

Those naïve heroes of the International Brigade, he said, were prepared to sell their lives for an ideal while their passports were sent to Moscow for 'safe keeping' (along with the entire Spanish gold reserves), doctored with new photographs and distributed to soviet agents who slipped into those identities. Presumably the volunteers were not expected to survive the conflict.

'Unhappily for Stalin, Franco won. But Spain could whistle for its gold!'

I considered that Spain had stolen most of it from the Aztecs in the first place, so what goes around comes around; but refrained from saying so.

Thus was fielded Germany's new Luftwaffe, the air weapon of the Condor Legion; Heinkels and 109s. The Russians had their I-16s, and the British upheld the arms embargo.

176

It had been long since a Civil War had happened here in Great Britain; though a '60's Class War had left wounds that were weeping still, picked at by a confrontational press and de-scabbed in the oft-used right to strike. In Spain Orwell saw through it but was then cold-shouldered and castigated by the Metropolitan Left for betraying his socialist roots in *Homage to Catalonia*, denying the paradigm of the great liberating gift that Stalin was offering the poor and disfranchised of the Earth. He'd been there and seen it and fought as a Republican volunteer; read the official lie and observed the true colours of Stalinism. His experiences coloured everything he wrote afterwards, so James said.

But James describes it well. 'Back then, as ever, although sometimes under the surface, John, Germany, Red or Black, was still a cauldron of passionate extremes.'

~-~

A strident *Doppler* of two-tone sirens blares down the cobbled alley - a two-tone flash of green and cream of a *Polizei* BMW saloon, and two motorcycles in a hurry rouse the ire of a passing septuagenarian who glares in the direction of the sirens. 'Verdammt, Ulrike Meinhof! *Slutkiller*,' he pronounces, waving his stick and muttering something about 'Rosa Luxembourg's stolen mantle.' Harry continues to examine James's Xerox copy.

It's no surprise that hectic police activity will raise the suspicion that they are witnessing another terrorist atrocity. Frankfurt had been the first target for a bombing, in '68, when Andreas Baader and Gudrun Ensslin firebombed the Kaufhaus Schneider department store. Baader was assisted in breaking out of police custody by Ulrike Meinhof, whose names were now inextricably linked, as *Baader-Meinhof*, the new German portamanteau bywords for urban terrorism in the West, rather superseding the *Rote Armee Fraktion*. 'That very year, John, the US barracks in Frankfurt am Main was bombed, leaving one dead, thirteen wounded.'

But in the Frankfurt of the 'sixties, Harry, since he's re-appraised that Xerox, is apparently oblivious to the cacophony of the here and now.

'*Steiger*,' says Harry eventually. 'You did say *Steiger*?' Harry is peering at the paper through a pair of slim *pince nez* for the rather difficult to read caption. It is blurred on the copy.

'Yes. *Climber*. Not too uncommon a name, is it? Does it ring any bells?'

'It does if, well.....,' he hesitated. 'I was just thinking of something else. Couldn't be the same Steiger,' he added distantly.

'Which *Steiger* were you thinking about?' James asks after a pause. 'Rod?'

'Rolf, actually.'

'So was I.'

Delcroix' grasp of the language, confirmed by Harry, informs that there had been an obscure aerobatic competition in Kassel, Spring of 1932, and this Steiger had won. He'd bought the magazine on impulse, determined to learn more, and has brought the photocopy with him to Frankfurt on the strength of the *Meyer* connection: the retired ex-Luftstreitkräfte, ex-Freikorps, ex-Heinkel, ex-Luftwaffe engineer from Bex in Switzerland connection. James is more than somewhat intrigued by Harry's reaction to the name *Steiger* from the photocopy. However, any attempt to steer the conversation back to *his* Rolf Steiger is expertly fielded, as politely, resolutely, he declines to be drawn.

But something is on his mind. Ever since he's taken the second long look at the photocopy, Harry, who uses English like a Conrad, has reverted to the old Slav habit of neglecting 'definite' and indefinite' articles of speech, and even the occasional possessive pronoun. Though they continue to converse warmly and easily throughout the pudding, James believed he'd mostly gone somewhere else. 'Into his past, John. Into the long ago dead and buried past of one of the Twentieth Century's most horrific periods, from a century awash with monsters.'

~ - ~

'Do you remember the name *Peter Fechter*, John?'

James is looking at me closely. The 40 Watt bulb gives the shabby room a kinder, slumbering look that helps hide the peeling paper and the damp but does nothing for the smell. An electric fire is lit which provides as much light as heat, certainly more than the bulb, albeit at low level. The unmade bed is redolent of the sort of dismal existence James is living, how temporary I am not able to guess.

I do remember the name and the indelible image that indicted the USSR in the eyes of the Free World, and those unfortunate countries with which the Soviet Union was aligned.

In that Apfelweinviertel café, in companionable silence, Delcroix had thumbed idly again through the magazine, leaving Harry to his '*petit mal*'. There are the usual stories about the Red Army Fraction, and the

178

latest attempt to tunnel under or scale the Wall. Although there have been many atrocities committed against those who sought freedom in the West, it is still young Peter Fechter, whose crumpled body in the Death Strip, shot by a border guard and left to bleed his life into the ground that comes to James' and so now to my mind. Viewing that image was a seminal moment for the millions who saw the picture over their morning coffee or on the evening news programmes. They knew they would never forget it. A young man left to die, like all the others Harry had probably seen down the years. In the wars of his mysterious European past.

Then Harry is speaking again, out of his trance. He lifts *Der Spiegel* so James can see the cover. A finger indicates the blank white discs on the red *swastikalose* flags. The *Hakenkreuzflagge* is rightly censored, for all its rallying associations. But, Harry says, with sudden acerbity, 'Armchair socialists, the soft Left, blind theologians who'll not hear a word against those bastards, Lenin and Stalin, *revere* the bloody Red Star. There is no difference in either of those two *fascisms*, James. *Arbeit macht frei* from your Kapitalist chains! Commissar Kruschev – himself a hit-man apparatchik toady: thousands of bloody corpses on his conscience - said, "When I hear that word *Kultur* I reach for my revolver!" What hope is there in a brutal society like that? Beautiful, ancient churches used for artillery practice. Government by souless gangsterism. Philistine bullies. Killers. Gaolers. Enslavers. Cynical hypocrites and despoilers.'

Harry is breathing deeply, fists clenched under the table. He seems to be struggling with something within and begins almost to tell what has been on his mind, dragging it out of the trawl from the submarine depths where it had remained. Locked-down in the ogygian sediment at the bottom of his soul. Even after the intervening years it was a memory from among the very worst of bad times then and sickens now in its recall. The detail, whenever it will come will be sharp, un-gilded by the soft-hazing of time. But the critical moment passes, like a rigor's peak. The storm that was brewing would wait.

But still he has a salvo to deliver.

'Actually, James. I must tell you. Rolf Steiger, whatever he became...... he saved my miserable soul - a long time ago.

Somewhere John, Paul, and George were harmonizing enthusiastically.

'You don't know how lucky you are, boy. Back in the USS... back in the USS... back in the USSR!'

Harry was still somewhere else, deaf to the irony.

'Come and visit me. Thursday evening, at the *Frankfurter Hof*,' he said eventually. 'I will tell you more then.'

Chapter 13. *Layers of the Onion*

'On the stroll back to the hotel, John,' said James. 'I must consider that here at last is someone with a direct link to this puzzle – not the mysterious aeroplane itself, but the intangible mind perhaps behind its arrival in Britain.'

Harry had years before met this character, Rolf Steiger, whose old biplane now lies safely in James' garage/workshop back home in Britain, where it has remained for more than six years, gradually being restored to as-new condition; when time and money allowed. Not only that but, *if* it was the same Steiger, he'd apparently saved a young Arkadiusz Piotrkowski from harm. Saved his miserable *soul,* Harry had said, not his *life.* What ever did that mean? Was there a religious dimension to Steiger's life – had he put Harry back on the 'straight and narrow' somehow? Had he saved his *life* too? Is that what he meant? Harry was a Pole or a *Lithuanian* – perhaps. James had just *assumed* he was Polish. Whichever, Lithuanian or Polish, he was possibly a Catholic, and for them suicide was a mortal sin. Perhaps that was it. Maybe Steiger had prevented a suicide…. It was a very circumstantial presumption based on one briefly spoken sentence, yet there was a lot of conviction and emotion expressed, not only in the words and the way Harry had couched them, but in his body language too. He had looked for a moment very like a lost child, bereft of family, adrift somewhere in time.

Something else. When he'd met the elderly Lady B. back in 1964, and bargained for the aeroplane 'remains', there was a sudden reluctance on her part to sell, almost as if she'd forgotten all about it. She became very tense all at once, and said that it was no longer for sale. That it wasn't really part of the estate, and that it was probably dangerous and should actually be destroyed. It was as if a shadow had suddenly passed over her face.

She'd moved away to the coast before the property changed hands and only her death some months later and the sale of the estate to a developer provided the opportunity for Delcroix to purchase the collection of 'dusty old aeroplane parts' that nobody knew anything about, and which 'didn't even have an engine with it', before the bulldozers moved in the next day.

'The other thing was, John, Mike Stead had been wrong.'

Had it been a Bücker Jungmeister, he explained, it could have fetched James a very good price, restored. This was the same legendary mount of Rudolf Lochner, the Rumanian Prince, *Buzz* Cantucazene, and the Graf von Hagenburg, who had crashed in '38 when demonstrating *ultra* low-level inverted flying during his scintillating act at Cleveland, Ohio's *National Air Races*. Who went on to complete his display in another Jungmeister borrowed from a fellow competitor, Rumanian ace aerobatic pilot, Alex Papana.

Hagenburg had continued with his head in bandages, flying inverted again only inches above the ground, and followed this with an honour lap in a Cord Straight-Eight convertible to ecstatic cheers. Such an historic type would have been a jewel of a find.

'But it wasn't, John. It *wasn't* a *Jungmeister,* although there were broad similarities. For a start it didn't have a chrome-molybdenum steel fuselage frame. I was made entirely of *wood;* spruce, with birch plywood and fabric covering.'

The fabric was rotten but the timber structure had not suffered the ravages of damp or wood-boring insects. It *did* have an identity, however, but not one that was on file with the German equivalent of the British CAA, the LBA, with their *incomplete* registration department's records dating from before the War. They were incomplete because the Russian occupying forces had attempted to destroy all records that they could find, to eliminate military histories where possible, and do any other damage they could which would confound the restoration of any sort of indigenous organization, the bureaucracies even, within the Soviet sphere of influence in immediate post-War Germany – East Germany and East Berlin.

But James had found the evidence on both the stainless steel manufacturer's plate in the cockpit, *and* the aircraft registration number, engraved on the plate and still visible on the decaying fabric *under* the dark over-spray, (*confirmed both by that much later, lucky magazine find at 656 Holloway Road, which not only named the pilot as Rolf Steiger, but showed clearly the same registration number, in 1932, and from further researches by Neumann, Natasha, which revealed a better, original photograph which you may find here.*) This was some two years before the system changed from a combined initial letter 'D' and the old numerical registrations, which dated from 1919 - commencing with 'D-1', to an all-letter grouping, still pre-fixed by 'D', for *Deutschland,* to provide for different aircraft classifications, with four basic categories, based on maximum weight - a very logical system introduced by the Nazis.

James had actually rung the LBA and spoken to a very helpful officer who spoke perfect English but who could shed no light on the aircraft type. They had no remaining record of its existence, although there was certainly a gap in the *Luftfahrzeugrolle,* the civil aviation records that corresponded to its 'D' number. According to the lists, its identity had been lost, its empty space flanked by the ghosts of a Klemm 26 registered at Adlershof and a long extinct Messerschmitt M.28.

Lying on his hotel bed, Delcroix had stared at the ceiling. He'd summed up what he now knew about 'his' aeroplane.

It *had* been registered D-2058 sometime in 1932, confirmed by the fading numbers on the silver fabric (which had been over-sprayed 'flat' black) and by the stainless steel identity plate in the cockpit. This was further confirmed by the magazine's photographic evidence.

The identity plate also told him that the aircraft had been built by the *Kessler Flugzeugbau: Entwicklungsgesellschaft und Werft, Kassel. Zulassung April 1931. Eigent. Steiger, R.*   Or, the Kessler Aeroplane Mfg., Development & Repair Co. Ltd. Owner/Operator: R. Steiger, identified as 'Rolf' from *Der Sportflieger* 1932. A smaller brass plate on the firewall bulkhead stated, *Motor: Siemens 160 PS.* with a serial number.

The other evidence was from *Sportflieger.* The photograph caption referred to it as a KFZ-1 *Tigerfalk*. A Tigerfalcon! Which at least explained the 'savage raptors' on its flanks!

So it was operated by one Rolf Steiger, certainly in 1932, and with it he won an aerobatic competition at Kassel that year, fighting off competition from a couple of Raab-Katzenstein biplanes and some type of Messerschmitt sports plane, according to the article. Steiger was known to his friend Harry, and had aided him in some profound way when a much younger Harry, Arkadiusz, aka *Arkadi*, had been in some distress – so far unspecified. But it turned out that it was another pilot, name of *Kessler*, (Harry was adamant) also known to Harry from his *Baltische Freikorps* days, who'd flown it in the *Rundflug* aerobatic competition in Poland. Harry had been part of the stewarding committee.

Was this the same Kessler as on the manufacturer's plate? The Kessler of *Kessler Flugzeugbau*? Had the builder/designer been the same one-eyed pilot described by Harry on that occasion. It seemed likely. Designers and aircraft manufacturers were much more 'hands-on' in those days.

And Rolf Steiger. What was it Harry had said? *Whatever he became later.*

Whatever did he mean? Did it imply that Steiger, sometime 'stunt pilot', to use the clichéd terminology of hack journalism, was also some kind of a crook, embezzler, a thief, a procurer of women. A killer. Some sort of monster? Had he been something to do with the *SS* maybe?

As to the aircraft, somehow, the *Tigerfalk* had arrived in Norfolk, been dismantled, carefully by the look of the fittings and undamaged bolt heads, then apparently forgotten for a quarter of a century.

After Hitler came to power the system of civilian aircraft registration in Germany had been re-organised and a new five-letter code had replaced the chronological numbering system, still retaining the initial 'D' for country of origin but followed by a four letter group; for example 'D-EABC'. From the fabric evidence, the aeroplane had never been re-registered in the new five-letter code, which would have been the case subsequent to 1934, the second letter 'E' in this case being the second weight classification identity letter, for aeroplanes with an all-up weight of greater than 500 kg.

So maybe it had not been flying subsequent to that date. If so there seemed to be three possibilities.

That the machine was brought (flown?) to the UK before 1934.

That it had been stored, maybe dismantled, having ceased to fly for some reason, *before* 1934, and then shipped to Britain already dismantled, maybe without the engine.

184

Or it might have been stored, retained the earlier numbered code, and been flown to the UK, possibly clandestinely; nocturnally (the black paint?). What reason for that to have happened, James was unable to fathom.

But it well might have had something to do with a roll of photo paper, now locked firmly in a bank safe under a false name.

He'd found it hidden, rolled up in the hollow fin structure when restoring the tail group; a list of names of prominent personages, including several of the British aristocracy, some members of parliament from before WW2, 'captains of industry', as far as he was able to ascertain, even members of the judiciary, many of the above now being deceased, all of whom were listed alphabetically – some 80 names in total, and all of whom had signed the original document against their printed names, of which this was a photographic print only.

The document was dated 1938, which seemed to indicate that, if it was in the fin of an aeroplane then perhaps it had needed to be moved rapidly, and in secrecy, otherwise why take the trouble to hide it? So maybe the aircraft was actually *still* flying, possibly 'illegally', or at least *flyable* in '1938, '39, or later. But perhaps its existence was by then secret, so it had not been officially re-registered. He lay on his bed and stared at the light above his head for an answer.

Either way, that roll of paper would have been political dynamite back then, and probably just as lethal in the early 1970s, for anyone to start waving that list around, especially in the direction of Fleet Street. Based on the list of British names drawn up by Unity Mitford in 1939, the '*Valkyrie List*', those people had evidently been approached. Many of them, each a signatory (at least one still sitting in the House of Lords) had vowed their total and solemn allegiance unto death to the then German Chancellor and Führer, Adolf Hitler. Potential *Gauleiters* of a Nazified Britain.

There was a section of folder photographed along with 'Valkyrie' with dates and scribbled signatures. Beginning in 1937, it looked as if it was part of a card index system with a heraldic eagle gripping a swastika in its talons: stamped *Streng Geheim* and a label beneath whereby secure personnel would have had to sign for access to the document. There were a few blurred and barely decipherable signatures including what might have been the name of the head of *Abwehr*, Admiral Wilhelm Canaris. There were two others that James deciphered that meant nothing to him then. *Walter Schellenberg*. And another, almost in block letter form, that seemed to spell *Klemenz Auer*.

Chapter 14 . *Visions of Hieronymus*

In Norwood James Delcroix is conjuring that 'sixties vision for me again, the Frankfurter Hof room of two decades ago: its curtains blowing in with the sounds and smells of the city night like the flags of heralds. James is sitting patiently. Harry is talking again, looking beyond the window and the city lights. Harry's pose is anything but relaxed. He seems gripped by something ugly that is swimming back towards him from a dark and bloody past. Harry gave James a long distance penetrating look that interrogates and looks through him at the same time.

'James. You know *Bosch*?'

'Electrics?'

'*No!* Hieronymus Bosch. Painter.' He hesitates. '*I* didn't, James. Not when I was ten. But I saw it all, James. You know, like an allegorical picture? Like dancing bears and mad goblins, whirling weasels and idiots. But more savage. Troglodytes and rats. That was my childish impression, and much as I see it now. Was 'collapsed reality' - not quite accurate for *Bosch* – but maybe my mind was creating these images because reality was too horrible. Wolves, and great mooses of men. Roaring men, all drunk, bearded, stinking of battle, beer and piss. Munch's *Wampüren*. *Moroi, varcolaci* foul things, mythic goblins gorging themselves on *everything*, James, human suffering and flesh.' He was trying to describe humanity seen in the floodlit exposure of its worst depravity.

'There I was in its midst. A child, lifted up high, spun around and around in the light and the dark, while tormentors shrieked with laughter. Shaken, thrown from one to the other like a doll, although I kicked and bit. Held by my feet and swung round and round until I was violently sick and thought my head would burst. And I cried because then I knew my father was really dead. And my mother and sisters would not be saved.'

~-~

The boy, Arkadiusz, is running to the Big House, as they called it. Running for help, screaming hoarsely. In his mind's eye are images of his ashen-faced mother and sisters being rough-handled, with vile oaths and threatening actions, by heavily armed men in greatcoats and short peaked caps, not *shakos*, your Excellency, as he tells *Kapitän-Rittmeister* Rolf, and with red arm bands. Russians and Balts together as far as he knew. The image extends to his father's inert form and a dark pool of blood slowing and thickening on the kitchen flagstones.

The big black doors to the mansion stand wide. Horses are milling about the entrance. Horses even inside the house! He runs in, terrified, but with his courage held tight in his fists. There is a flurry of movement and confusion. Nothing makes sense to him. The hall is filled with noise, whoops, yells, coarse laughter. The sounds of smashing glass and crockery, a heavy pounding and the splintering crack of breaking furniture. The smells are rank: the stench of blood and ammonia, and something else.

As he becomes accustomed to the inner light, another horror. The apparition of an eyeless woman, dressed in white who unsteadily descends the staircase. She proves to be a gilt-framed full-length portrait of an elegant princess, ripped from the landing, the painting slashed across in several places, eyes and breasts gouged out. Between her legs a dirty finger protrudes from a strategic bullet hole. It moves suggestively to a chorus of hooting, jeering and uproarious laughter from the body of the hall.

A great blood-muzzled Carpathian beardog lies dead. His tally is three of the 'soldiers', one of whom still gargles in half-life through his torn throat, sunk upon his knees, ignored by his intoxicated comrades who are too distracted to care. The painting falls with a crash and a smallish, wiry, red stubble-bearded man stands before him at the foot of the staircase, glaring at him with fierce-eyes. Arkadi is transfixed.

'Oh, ho!' says a rough Russian voice from behind the boy. 'What have we here? Little soldier, eh. Come to fight us all!' Arkadi is spun round to face a gap-toothed giant with several necklaces dripping from his pockets. He throws his head back and laughs fit to burst at the idea, which seems equally hilarious to the other ten or twenty, Arkadi cannot tell or now recall as he is seized and whirled around and around by his arms and then his legs until he is too dizzy to stand when they set him, head spinning, keeling over on the floor and retching bile from his empty stomach. There is the bizarre image of a bearded lady and then a crash and he is showered with glass crystals as someone blasts the chandelier with a carbine. Another roar of approval from the gathered swine.

The fierce-eyed little man walks over to Arkadi at what seems a crazy angle as for him the room is spinning uncontrollably off its gimbals.

The little man lifts up his hand for silence, which is not long in coming.

'I have an idea,' he says hoarsely, in what is no more than a stage whisper. 'Let's see if he can *get it up!*' Arkadi is lifted, still swooning, and effortlessly carried up the staircase to a white bedroom with fine architectural detail, the centrepiece of which is a large four-poster bed. Held above the floor, his boots and breeches are pulled off leaving him naked, and if it were possible, still more terrified. The pack howls with laughter, rolling with unfocussed eyes, crowding around the bed. Shaking, he is brought near. Voices croon a traditional Russian wedding song of celebration. The 'bearded lady' is among the crooners, a silk petticoat worn over his shirt.

Someone pinches his cheeks and roughly shoves the neck of a wine bottle into his mouth, causing Arkadi to gag again. 'You got to have drink before your wedding night! Don't you like? The Graf keeps good cellar, *nyet?*' More laughter from the gargoyles.

On the bed he sees a shivering, bruised and blood-caked form, a naked rib cage rising and falling rapidly, stretched tight as on a rack, her frame semaphoring the letter 'X', wrists, ankles held fast by leather belts to the posts, eyes rolled up under the fluttering eyelids, so he can see only the whites, and assumes she is in some sort of shock. Having a fit like Sebastian, a boy in the village who used to fall down and shake. He feels himself lifted up and placed almost tenderly upon her pale abdomen, centre stage for the main event.

'You cannot understand what went on. You'd have to have been there to know it all, James. And then tell me, could you sleep?'

Harry looks at James again, a withering look: of someone who had witnessed more than his share at such a young age. 'They called themselves '*Wolves*', James. To strike fear. No wolf behaved as they did. Men are far worse than animals and those were terrible times.'

'Can you imagine it, James? Are you getting the picture? I am Catholic, but Rosh Hashanah: Jewish New Year was my initiation into truth about war. Not in clash of armies, but desecration, looting, murder and rapine in their wake. Unreported truth of war and suffering: smeared with blood of innocence I stood trembling in the presence of him who casts a long shadow to this day. Satan's Messenger or maybe Satan himself!'

~-~

I listen to this tale emerging from the testimonial of Harry, via

James, informed by the Strelitz and Hammond diaries and letters, part-confirmed by the voluble prose of a half-mad Steiger: scribbling in his notebooks on the Norfolk coastline as if his remaining sanity depended on capturing it all, so he'd believe it himself, in time. Plucking recollections out of the ether, storming the locked door in a mind swirling with the myths and fabrications of a country of legends; of mysteries wrapped in enigmas.

I was a journalist. So much material was there…so might a biography be published, using as much as was possible in the *first person* as he wrote it? That something like this story *could* be written is not itself a reason for so doing. The vacuum at the end of the First World War in Europe and Russia had filled immediately with brutal struggle for territory and with it fear of zealous communist expansion. While the League of Nations proclaimed that war was forever outlawed, interventionist expeditionaries from Britain and the USA were aiding the Whites, urged on by Mr. Churchill who continued to warn of the dire consequence to civilization of failure: that Bolshevism must be "strangled in its cradle". Newspaper headlines on collectivisation, crop disaster, famine, disease and mass murder had shrieked from the stands in Piccadilly. What I'd heard so far in microcosm of the experiences of young Arkadi, swept up in this maelstrom in some far-flung place unfamiliar to the "Englishman in the street", fascinated and horrified.

The 'eighties. Remember them, Natasha? You could almost smell the greed. The lack of any ethical responsibility or moral self discipline it seemed. That too was the beginning of a growing attention deficit in the population. Would a fickle 'eighties public with changing preoccupations be drawn to such a history, that in England at any rate was little known? Or like a joyless eye might it find the old subject unworthy of its constancy and look for brighter things?

Meanwhile James continued to fill in the philosophical background for me, in case I was slow on the uptake.

The world would change in ways unimaginable, when the infant Harry had been heir to its history. Collated by Hans-Peter, if true, Steiger's story wove a new skein into the weft of unpublished tapestries. Peter, *Hans-Peter,* had gone through a painful metamorphosis, the process of learning that all he'd been led to believe his entire life up to 1945 was a lie. From the stabbing in the back of Germany's valiant warriors in the First World War, to the master race theory: that the Jews were leeches who sucked the blood of Aryan children and the lifeblood of the German race. That most other races, the *Untermenschen,* were fit only for beasts of burden and forced labour. That Germans had a divine right to order the

190

world. 'Did he know,' Harry had asked him, 'That eleven percent of European Jewry was blue-eyed and blond?'

For Peter to recant, to un-believe all that childhood indoctrination and hold onto sanity, was a feat many did not achieve in their post-war years. It had even been possible for him to tell me, in Berlin, that listening to Dimitri Shostakovich's Seventh Symphony now made him want to saddle up a Yak and fly wing-to-wing with Lilya Litvak, defending Leningrad; the brilliant Marshall Zukov then in overall command - spoken with a twinkle in the old Luftwaffe pilot's eye, traitorously and forty years too late.

'Didn't she fly mostly on the Stalingrad Front?' I asked.

'Does that matter?' he replied with surprisingly testiness. 'She is symbolic.'

Perhaps he just admired the fair Litvak, the most famous woman fighter pilot in history.

'But, Johann, what had we that was comparable to arm ourselves with, apart from the usual propaganda?'

'Wagner?' I'd hazarded

His smile became wintry.

'That thing of gloomy myth and misty legend? Of *Nibelungen*. Doomed to *Götterdammerung*. Hitler's own predestination.'

It is indomitable Russia invaded, he'd said, that Shostakovich toweringly conveys. Its honesty is his triumph, untainted by edict of that paranoid monster, Stalin, who'd culled the best of his Red Army command. Whose immediate response to *Barbarossa* was to shoot the commanders of those areas fallen to our Blitzkrieg: those officers whom he'd ordered *not* to mobilise, so as not to provoke our German suspicions by border troop movement; invasion preparations that might be observed by Luftwaffe reconnaissance overflights – to which, *preposterously*, Stalin himself had turned a blind eye.

~-~

Peter leads me to an adjacent room where stands an upright piano.

'Shostakovich gives us first a quirky pre-revolutionary echo of pomp and circumstance, the architecture of Petrograd and its bustling city garrison: the twirling heel of the ceremonial guard, high-stepping with his long *Nagant* rifle, all reeling under a zealous *sozialismus* from which undercurrent...'

Peter sits at the piano and softly picks out a martial tune.

'Beginning thinly on a plucked violin - emerges a discordant marching theme, handed to pipe and woodwind….'

His transcription of the jaunty theme quickly rises in an arrogant pastiche of a triumphal procession. Overtones of a more sinister *Bolero* flash through my mind.

'Look, here comes Field Marshall Ritter von Leeb with his Army Group North and two hundred thousand horses!' The thumping discord has a malevolent, mechanistic drive. 'How happily they march, those lusty boys, singing songs of triumph and invincibility!'

The inexorable drumbeat grows in menace, advancing through the orchestra. 'Panzer filters by now clogged with Baltic sand, no doubt,' he grins mirthlessly. 'Then the long siege: *The Eternal War of the Pauper* they called it on the German side. Under-equipped, in freezing conditions while the city starved despite roads and railways laid over the ice of Ladoga; a siege of near nine-hundred days had begun.'

His right hand smashes wild chords while the relentless tramp of marching armies reverberate under his left. Abruptly he breaks off from his impromptu demonstration and motions me to the other room and the gramophone. Selecting a record from a shelf, he carefully lowers the needle onto the vinyl. Without a word he sinks into his armchair, a hunched shadow in the semi-dark, carved as though from granite. I sink again into my own stillness as Shostakovich's 7th begins. In those first passages in dreamlike evocation the subtle thread is woven. Dah-dit-dit-dit. 'B' in Morse Code. 'B' for *Barbarossa*, Hitler's codename for the invasion of the USSR.

Air raid sirens: shrieking Stukas arch and dive in a charnel sky. Howling in tumultuous crescendo above the rubble of a frozen cadaver city under siege whose heart yet beats, *'In Morse Code!'* Peter says. And then, after a titanic struggle and a period of lyrical reflection, comes the final, horrific conflict, resolving in a major key. Repeated over and over in its last moments, the fateful hammer blows: Dit-dit-dit-dah! *'V for Victory'. Barbarossa* reversed! Hurrah!

Peter's voice emerges from the shadows. 'Like Beethoven Five, Johann, but more *vehement.* As if Dimitri the patriot firewatcher would drive his baton like a *Katyusha* - again and again, like a dagger through the heart of the Nazi aggressor.'

One brings life's experience to the appreciation of great music. I am silent, stunned by the power of this symphony, its ability, with some insight, to convey so much, but taking with a pinch of salt the fine detail that Peter reads into the work. Along with the obvious, Peter invents spurious references that Shostakovich himself might never have dreamed were there.

Meanwhile, Johann, he says, here in Berlin that *sinister* dwarf, Goebbels, was making a prematurely bombastic speech.

'I was ordered to attend, a minor adjunct to the General Staff along with hundreds of invited officers from all services to learn that the War in the East had been won by autumn 1941. We had to sit and listen to this rubbish,' he'd said. 'While the biggest *Katastrophe* ever to face the Wehrmacht was still unfolding.'

If in retrospect Peter seemed passionately to have gone over to the other side at least in musical terms, the non-partisan melancholy of his personal loss seemed undiminished.

He told me he'd lost his younger brother at that time. In the Baltic, where the spearhead troops had rapidly advanced into the wasteland of scorched earth where, strangely it seemed at first, great Hanseatic mansions had remained intact, ideal for quartering senior officers and their staffs in some luxury. Except they'd been mined, most of them; their foundations packed with explosives and artillery shells with delayed-action detonators, timed to explode days, weeks - even months after the Soviet retreat. So perished the young ADC, Walter Neumann, *a truly gifted pianist, Johann,* and a dozen others of various ranks in a mighty explosion when their *Schloss* erupted. Although some hidden mines were detected and defused, for many weeks across the region, explosion still followed explosion at erratic intervals, rendering such stately minor palaces untenable, adding to the nervous tension.

How civilisations rise again, I mused, making good all that's been lost to war, century after century seems miraculous, born of the human will to re-create such miracles through sacrifice. Yet in every decade or so, some evil, power-crazed corrupting force emerges, bent on destruction.

~-~

Looking back, Natasha, one thing Lenin had had right. Bring Germany into the fold and Europe would fall to him, for Germany with its industrious people and technological advances would provide the USSR with the most powerful consolidating foundation for world revolution. Always most favoured trading partner they would morph into one self-sustaining cell, expanding outwards. Those countries in between would exist only in history books and those on its perimeter would fall, one by one. And the history books would be re-written.

For all history is 'spin', *skewed* like a bowler's googly or spun like Ariadne's web, by the victors. Spun in the inscrutable top floors of smoked-glass edifices that reflect the skies of Bonn, Paris, London, Washington, spun for them by their advisors and the spiders of the BND, Stasi, KGB and CIA. Re-spun by fundamentalists, '*original spin*'? And long ago embroidered by *Merlin* by the light of a flickering bulb in a Györ boarding house, as I was to learn, my dear, and you may yet discover under *The Siberian Eagle*.

Historical dissection is essentially a flawed interpretation; its oblique viewpoint is narrow, a focus that ignores the titanic forces that build the Himalayas, *the creeping of the magma and the hydro-thermic vents beneath our feet.* Steiger may have steered early towards the political Right. *Did that mean his testimony should be dismissed, John, assume the viewpoint is biased because the liberal left intelligentsia always retreats to the moral high ground? What is truth but that which exists only in our minds and is lost when our bones are covered by the desert wind?*

Steiger had been indoctrinated at least once by the Left. Was he afterwards rudderless, or playing the long game? There was evidence that at least one underlying medical condition might have affected his faculties. So how much of the documentary material could be taken at face value? What was its value? Was it Blue Chip? Ironclad? Copper-Bottom guaranteed? Harry, Peter, Alexa, James…. How much of this conspiracy could I swallow in one sitting?

I sit there in the gloom, reflecting on recent events, my burns sore but healing, glad of the privacy that darkness affords. The story and Delcroix' telling seemed all over the place at first, but gradually I began to see some crystallization, and if I saw it right, a part-formed structure could be discerned in the amorphous cloud, swirling in my mind.

Like the beginning of things.

~-~

To Know the Mind of Another

I confess that *savant syndrome* was unknown to me then, Natasha, though I have since researched it. I believe that Steiger, or whatever his real name was, had been suffering from it, *if* 'suffering' was the right word. Part of his obsessive writing, which I had myself read with increasing interest, not to say alarm, when eventually I had retrieved and examined the briefcase, seemed manic and driven. I am part persuaded that he wrote from the craving he quite naturally exhibited for learning the truth about the voids that lodged in his brain, the semi-dormant black holes that had fed on his memory, like unsated lampreys that sleep awhile, but may return again to devour more of his once lost identity.

The terror must have haunted him that he might yet lose more of his past than he'd regained. That his memory's return was but an uncertain respite: that he would wake again to a blank void in which his previous existence with its accomplishments, friendships, enmities and loves were veiled, was an horrific and dismal prospect. So he wrote, I'm sure, in an attempt to recall everything that he could so it would be there on the pages of his notebooks the next morning when he'd awake and once more take up his pen. But he also wrote abandoned, seemingly random poetry or lyric prose, and indeed drew rapid pen-doodles of faces and heads, which first I took for evidence of mania; of the *Idiot Savant*, but later made a kind of sense.

Meanwhile the old prospector journalist within me muses silently, like some no-hoper standing at a bend in Time's River, who's glimpsed at last the gleam of a golden tail. If it pans out well for us, I think, it would make a quite fascinating story - with much of the sieving and spadework done.

But then I had no idea where it led, with James's input and perhaps Harry looping in. Alexa had provided the spur with her telephoned warning and her later incognito appearance at the funeral, so I was primed to act with caution. Especially after the over-solicitous concern demonstrated by an untraceable police dept. official followed by the burglary of my hotel room. So when I acted on the cryptic instructions Alexa had magically planted on me, I had taken particular care to watch my back as I slipped quietly out of the hotel and entered the public phone booth in a Hannover street and waited to ring the number, letting it ring twice at *nine minutes past two in the morning, precisely,* as it said on the note.

'Johann!' it was a statement.

'Hello…. Stephanie.'

'Is it safe?'

'Is what safe?' I asked foolishly.

'The item I told you to lose.'

'Yes.'

'Can you retrieve it without difficulty?'

'I… I think so.' I had yet to accomplish this, trusting to the fact that the taxi-courier service I'd used had actually deposited the case, double-wrapped and bulky in stiff brown paper from the hotel's stationery cupboard, in the Brunswick railway storage depository. The key to the bin was currently in my pocket, posted to me in the self-addressed envelope I'd entrusted to the driver along with the generous tip. The paper had helped to disguise the stink of burned leather and flesh as well as concealing the condition of the case, which would otherwise have attracted suspicion.

'Were you followed?'

'Not as far as I could tell.' I was not a 'professional'.

'Johann, get out of Hannover. Get out of Germany fast. Those people, they have a long reach but in England you will be safer.'

'What people? Who are we discussing? What's it all about?'

'Not now, not on the telephone, Johann. Just memorize the name of this estate agent.' She passed me a name. 'In *Guildford*. Go there and ask for Victor. Bring it with you.'

I replaced the receiver. She'd rung off without further ado. It was much as I expected with her, all business, when things needed to be done. But her secrecy seemed over the top given we weren't at war with anyone and things looked pretty good for the blossoming of a new East-West accord, if Gorbachev's enlightened statesmanship was genuine.

~-~

Freedom is a dangerous idea, Natashka. No one owns anything including freedom, increasingly not here, and not *over there*, not then, not now, nor under the striped and starry myth of Freedom of Information. Like how many ex-SS war criminals did the FBI recruit for their intelligence operations after the War. That too belongs to the state, in its gift. In the end victories are personal if they exist at all. It might feel like victory for a while when Johnny comes marching home, but just wait and see.

So why tell another war story? Who would care? But perhaps it was not about just telling a long buried truth.

Why was James putting this burden on me? Because Peter trusted me and I unwittingly became the custodian of twenty years of research? Because James was a 'shot bolt? Peter had said '*Trust no one.*' Did I have the key?

~.~

'All right James,' I said. 'I have been patient. Just who the hell is it we're hiding from?'

'I don't altogether know, to tell the truth. More than one faction for sure.'

'Are we talking about a foreign secret service organization?'

'Bear with me John. It's complicated to say the least. I don't imagine you'd want to be involved, but you are through no fault of your own.'

'Just tell me who. My imagination is working overtime and you're making me nervous.'

'Some of the acronyms might not mean anything to you, but yes the KGB has an interest, not to mention the Stasi, some of whom may be SS or their spawn.'

'Bloody hell,' I said. I'd naturally expected something like this but I'd hoped I was wrong. I was going to have to unplug the barrel of my Colt .45.

~.~

'The railways of Russia were the conduits, John.'

He was back there in the midst of it all again, obsessively. Back in the cold, old Russia standing at the crucible of the USSR, up to his elbows in the bloody and deceitful history of revolution and civil war.

As James relates it to me in the Norwood dawn, after the Revolution poor old Admiral Kolchak had believed in a brokerage between the Great Powers that might save the day for his White Siberian army and the country, had he been able to fight his way west; unhappily for him without the aid of the valiant Czech Legion. Their murderous betrayal by Trotsky ensured they were driven by enlightened self-interest, with a burning desire to return to their newly emerging independent homeland and get out of the god-forsaken bandit hell of Siberia without further delay. But it was a hijacked express or two that had disappeared somewhere along the route of the trans-Siberian railway: that was at the core of it.

'A few hundred million in gold ingots could buy you several nice little wars in 1918.'

Kolchak had thought he'd scooped the jackpot when he'd ambushed Lenin's commandeered Treasure Express on the Trans-Siberian Railway, though History will record that his particular derailment, *if such it was,* wasn't the only one heading out of Petrograd with a cargo reputed to be worth millions. Enough to arm and supply several armies to fight their way to Moscow. In the event, as far as Kolchak's booty was concerned, a Far Eastern economy had become the alleged beneficiary of the Romanov's *and no one was about to tell the truth about that, John. And we're not about to do it now.*

I pretty much knew that post-1945 history books published in the Home Islands had spun their various tales of *casus belli* exculpation for the diet of Honshu schoolchildren. The 'South East Asian Co-Prosperity Sphere' had acquired trillions of dollars worth of loot during the occupation of China, Manchuria and other Far Eastern countries – still unaccounted for, although the Philippines were rumoured as the likely cache.

Meanwhile the official published history, written by the victors, the story of the Great Patriotic War spun north of Hokkaido through Sakhalin, to suit Soviet ideology. Later, History itself, almost obliterated under Mao's *Great Leap Forward,* had been extinguished altogether in the killing fields of Pol Pot's *Year Zero.* Sorting out the truths from the much earlier Russian Civil War would prove more difficult and involving.

'That first 'great experiment' of social engineering in the Twentieth Century could have been strangled in infancy, John, as Churchill had preached. Civilization, with the eradication of old inequalities, might have moved ahead at a different pace with millions spared. The later manifestations were direct responses to the revolution in Russia in a forever destabilized world.' James' voice is low but forceful. 'This Harry believed.'

~-~

But this story begins with an unknown who would pull at a thread to tear the whole of the tapestry apart or die trying, a gesture timed to shred an unholy alliance. It may have *needed* telling even if no one cared to listen, some day. But whilst hiding out in a small village south of London, book publishing was not uppermost in one's mind. Harry was a publisher and owned part of this story, and I was a writer, a technical man not an essayist. When I rang the number scribbled on the little folded slip in my jacket pocket, as requested at exactly nine minutes past two am, *call box to call box evidently,* and spoke to Alexa using her *Stephanie* cover name, I had been baffled as to the meaning of all the cloak and daggery. I wasn't sure that I was any clearer after my session with James, complicated later by

198

the arrival of Zubr and co.... But certain characters were emerging to whose innermost soul-searching I was now privy, through Peter's legacy.

Later, were I to sketch it in, as Rolf had tried first to do with Bell, his mind fighting the trauma, or to 'block it in', painting the legend with broad strokes for Saunders, recruiting sergeant for the firm, one would be inclined perhaps to edit out the ephemeral. But the strengths of this unlikely *corpus* were in the detail; the rivets that held the grisly, half-formed skeleton up to the light of forensic examination, like Piltdown Man. He'd be disinterred whole to dance a lively *courant* for a new, ingenuous generation, since as a species we learn nothing from history and so are forced to re-live it. Meanwhile newspapermen can be bought. So can newspaper groups. The eternal hucksters are poised to crank up the propaganda machinery. The politician polishes his mirror. And as for lies, and Piltdown Man was one, 'If you're going to tell one make it a *big* one,' Hitler said.

Detail *is* where the devil resides, Natasha. So I give you a tale by *Dürer, Albrecht*: a *Northern Renaissance* etching in black and white, every last follicle of it, just as Steiger gave it to Browne. A journey of the mind that led me once to tread the same East Anglian shoreline where Steiger walked and thought and scribbled frantically in his notebook at dusk and watched a 'horned satanic head' loom upon the black Yarmouth tide. Where I dreamed that dream of a *severed* head; recalled almost as he'd recalled in savage pen strokes a painting by Friedrich, in which, like Edvard Munch's *'The Scream'*, the anguished Capuchin, Rolf himself perhaps, wandered the shore, clasping at his temple of thoughts that were too great a burden for his skull.

In time, by last gleam of light am I guided by a Polish giant to seek the ghost of a duplicitous *Myrddin* hermit, wild-eyed at the centre of the web — beckoned westwards into a slate-grey/green Kyffin Williams' landscape, where keening buzzards circle ancient hills and rained-on sheep huddle the ravines, like maggots in a wound.

Part Three

Life and Love

On a summer's afternoon under a perfect sky of fair-weather cumulus two lovers lie upon a grassy bank. The air is thick and murmurous with the buzz and hum of life. The girl smiles through a film of tears. Her cheeks are wet, her forehead cool despite the sun's blessing. '*Ateh*,' she says.

There comes a sudden gust of wind, a sense of urgent motion. He is so close to her uplifted face he can see the flecks in her clouded eyes.

'You must go,' she whispers.

'I cannot!' he says.

Somewhere a horse is screaming.

Chapter 15 . *Great Yarmouth 1921*

There is a saying. 'Nothing either good or bad, but thinking makes it so'.

Imagine, if you will, my fractured inner view. My early life, now that I'm recovering, I recollect in sharp focus. Much of it. Indeed my memory seems to improve daily, helped I'm sure by my compulsive scribbling. This then is my memoire, which I write as much for you, dear Krysia as for you, dear Kat, wherever you are.

My later experiences are blurred. Without my logbooks even events on widely separated fronts have merged inextricably. Sometimes the recall is vivid: wildly exhilarating memories of invincibility and power. Once or twice the hysterical delusion of happiness. But in frequent, darker moments other images appear, unbidden from the subconscious: spectres of horror and loss.

~-~

That morning a concussion had me tumbling out of bed. Something I'd *felt* rather than heard, though it rattled the attic windows and redly lit the sky towards Gorleston.

The flat echo of the detonation had leaped among the surrounding buildings. I felt sure that its reverberation would have been heard inland beyond Norwich, probably half way to Cromer; rumbling the eighteen miles down coast to Southwold, like a drum roll for the departed.

What little I knew of such ordnance was that the contact detonator pistols on their *Herz horn* spikes would trigger the explosion even though the thing was old and rusty. The explosive might also have been unstable and gone off accidentally. Or the bomb disposal squad might have had no choice other than to detonate it at that time of morning, due to the rising tide which could have moved it again: despite the chain net, the *Knallnetz* they'd carefully wrapped around.

No, dammit. *Knallnetz*, a trawl net for exploding mines at sea, was the wrong word. I must think in *englisch*!

Possibly it hadn't exploded on the incoming tide, but had sunk gently into the wet sand without compressing the detonator caps. In any event the sand bag revetment had directed the blast seawards. Apart from a few loosened roof tiles and Mrs. Hewson's prints jumping off the snug wall, no harm seemed to have been done. She said later that it had reminded her of the coastal Zeppelin raids, recalling their silver cigar shapes coned in the searchlights; the anti-aircraft guns banging away, shrapnel tinkling on the roofs.

I knew what had happened as I hit the floor, but something seemed wilfully to scatter the jigsaw pieces of my mind. Images and ideas surged there, dark drowned shapes lost in the undertow of that other consciousness that dissolves on waking; a surreal dream that yet intrudes, seemingly rational 'til brute rationality is superimposed with the dawn, making absurd that other recollection, its rainbow colours fading: a nocturnal flying fish caught in the prosaic rigging of the day.

~-~

That night, in the *Niebelung* of my dreamscape, the terrors had regrouped: winged and noctivageous spectres of occult dimension, my companion riders under leaden skies. Wan light glints on helmet, on swastika; war-painted visors scan an empty land for living things.

I see a figure standing as a tree; a dreaming ghost among fields of ghosts. We drone overhead, emblazoning her sky with our black crosses. I think 'her sky' as I have a sense that the figure is female under that dark, winter clothing: that she knows us too, crusader knights and soldiers of ill-fortune: Viking incarnations in Teuton death masks, searching forever,

204

over gun *mantels* for men and horses, artillery and rolling stock.

Her dream too will dissolve on the ether. Her *Valkyries* fading; bearing their spirits of the dead deep into that glacial landscape; following a dark valley of the mind, where gleam lakes without number, all drifting from view upon the echo of our passing.

Unless… she is a scarecrow.

~-~

Norfolk had been my clear destination following release from hospital. Saunders, now my *official* 'minder' had seen me alright for money and my stay at the Waterside Tavern had been officially sanctioned. We'd agreed that eschewing the more imposing Cliff Hotel would be better all round. And cheaper. My temporary passport had been surrendered at my first official debriefing but apart from that I had the freedom to explore East Anglia until further notice.

The local doctor had been briefed that I was one *Ralph Stygers*, Lieutenant, Flying Corps, Retd., wounded. Dutch heritage. English mother. Dr. Campbell was monitoring my progress towards full health. Meanwhile I had hired a little Vauxhall tourer in Norwich with a driving licence that Saunders had fixed for me, and toured the countryside from my Great Yarmouth base, much like the modestly well-off convalescent I purported to be. Sometimes I think that I am too artfully living someone else's life.

I walk the peat-diggers' pathways among cold salt marshes where lonely windmills keep their vigil; stands ruined church and marshlander's hovel, staring seaward. The wind-rustled rushes speak to me of home. Wild duck fly fast and low o'er mud flat and shingle bar; moraine of ancient glacier, where sleek cattle graze the hard. Creek and meandering waterway lead my eye forever to the sea, presenting that same view I hold in my mind from my Baltic youth.

I stand naked and slightly lop-sided before the mirror, noting here and there the keloid scarring, feeling the cranial suture line beneath the new-grown hair. Lapses of memory and missing pieces trouble my mind each waking hour. Most nights I've laid awake, notebook ready on the bedside table, searching the seaward darkness for answers, dissolving the defences of my humble room. I look daily upon the endless waves, forever on a cusp - falling short of answers that might be soluble in those waters. As a boy I'd looked westward to the sea or sometimes across a waving ocean of grass that teemed with invisible spirit life for those same answers. Now I looked in the other direction, across the North Sea. It seemed to me that Yarmouth was about as close as I could get to that opposite shore.

In the aftermath of conflict, despite the bustle of the fishing villages and the water traffic on the Yare and Breydon Water, poverty stalked the back streets and want haunted the cottages of fisher folk and the families of war widows as much as it preyed on any Eastern European underclass who's plight, along with that of the tormented bourgeoisie, was still more hideous under Bolshevism. All struggled to return to the grind of normality, impoverished and exhausted by four years of total war. Some would say that the spoils had gone to the victors that still enjoyed fruits of Empire, but the mark of toil on the common man or woman was as evident here as on the continent of Europe or seemed worse at this time to me, roaming among the gleaners, fish-gutters, black-footed cocklewomen and net-menders in this land of plenty than I'd remembered in a childhood's idyll upon another shore. The same grizzled men caulked their old upturned tubs or smoked upon their lobster pots, eyes fixed upon a distant memory.

~.~

An application at *Weatherby, Capstick and Billcock* for information relating to the estate to which I felt I might now have some claim seemed to be foundering, turning upon the finer points of my own identity and the fact that the Cheriton property had been sold with a presumption of no succeeding beneficiaries, no legal will, nor claimants forthcoming. Their fees apart, Billcock informed me stiffly, the partners had executed their responsibilities quite properly and all deeds pertaining, property and land had been made over to the Public Trustee. I scented battle, but for the time being I had other concerns.

Here was the churchyard and the inscription.

HIC JACET NADIA VON STRELITZ
A LADY
VICTIM OF WAR AND CIRCUMSTANCE
RIP

I stood awhile, head bowed. But I found no one by name of Hammond.

~.~

As I walked I took stock of my limited choices. It seems for the moment I'm not to be 'restored to point of origin' and my hope remains that I'd be re-summoned to Whitehall for a further explanation of self in the hope that my burgeoning memory would further improve. Thus might I convince my inquisitors that I was now a 'sound bet' for entry into service with a department of HMG's military intelligence; given my other credentials and circumstance of my arrival.

I reviewed that first meeting in my mind: a grey and blustery Thursday morning two weeks gone. Early autumn. The sky at first an unrelenting grey with an opal sea-horizon briefly veined with ruby: a distant flush of incarnadine suffused to mother-of-pearl, before the clouds began to build and the on-shore wind to rise.

I was about early, walking the beach a half mile further each day. Indeed I've always found the process of walking conducive to thought and settling to the constitution. I used once to walk in winter woods near my home listening to Schubert in my mind that I'd learned to love on the family gramophone, my freezing breath for company. But I'd always loved shorelines. I relished the tang of salt on the keen air, watched the familiar surf-trotting birds; found comfort in the cries of gulls.

Mrs. Hewson at the *Waterside* had directed the messenger boy to the strand and with some effort he'd bicycled the foreshore through the soft sand to join me on the tidal flat, ringing his bell, 'hullo-ing' and waving the telegram. The surgery obliged me with use of their 'phone and I rang the Whitehall number that was attached to the brief message and found that I was being invited to London the following Monday - no obligation, although my temporary papers were mentioned along with the other documents that I was requested to bring.

~.~

Then comes Doctor Campbell, limping from his surgery. He calls me *Monsignor*, asks, with a half-smile, if signs of 'stigmata' have appeared. He has never asked in so many words about my wealed back, but his kindly eye betrays a look of almost fatherly concern. He reminds me of poor old Brandt; the same gentle worldliness, the same ability to hold his council. He is widely travelled and experienced with the traumas resulting from floggings: 'cat o'nine's', flails. He knows something of Russia and the terrible knout whose stroke can gouge out gobbets of flesh….. I tell him it was my misfortune once in life. That it was later my very salvation

I keep to myself lest he think I also have a Christ complex.

Brain haemorrhage, I now know, provokes changes in the lobes and can create genius in the arts or academe. Mathematicians may be spontaneously created where there was no prior underlying skill, along with expression of manic phenomena and skills with languages (which I already possessed). Recurring images, in my case *The Scream*, may be triggered in the mind, providing impetus for obsessive drawing or painting, which, also in my case, involved drawing heads and faces, male, female, androgynous: morphing from one sex to another. Ethnic, demonic, oriental, Slav.

Writing I'd rationalized as a means of recording everything I could remember. It was liberating and confining at the same time. It was addictive, overwhelming, burdensome, exhausting: frequently 'automatic' as if something else were driving the pen, and indeed not all of it was comprehensible. I tell myself it will help me to recall, to 'unlock the door'. But Campbell informs me that I have most probably acquired a neurological condition which is causing this mania, generating the urge to repeat an activity which might be regarded as creative and artistic in some, but was due to a frontal and temporal lobe imbalance; a functional short-circuit. It is associated with autism. But he is no specialist, just a country GP. Like my father.

Campbell is a kindly man, interested in his patients, and sees them more than just a collection of ailments attached to mortal bodies, each on its moribund journey. I tell him about a mysterious rash that's appeared on my chest and forearms which I'd scratched at until it bled. He beckons me inside, limping ahead to his dark-panelled, turret room overlooking the shore, a window flung open to the screaming gulls, the fresh smell of the ocean and a cracked leather armchair where I am invited to sit. He examines my raw skin with a magnifying lens and tells me it's psychosomatic; stress from re-living events or perhaps trying too hard to remember. He prescribes an unguent. At least I'm healing well. I button my shirt. He looks across the glinting rooftops at the white-flecked sweep of the sea. A fine brisk day for it, your seaside walk, he comments, and walking will build bone, strengthen muscle. Himself has a gammy leg, a permanent 'Jellicoe Walk': legacy of service under Beatty in His Majesty's Fleet. Seamen were instructed to walk with knees bent to reduce shock to the joints in the event of a mine detonating close to the hull. In his case retirement from the RN had been the result of a fall down a companionway ladder. Apparently it had been some party!

Outside again the wind-driven raggedy clouds have parted to reveal a gleam of white gold. He offers me a hip flask and breathes in the salt air like an elixir, screwing up his eyes at the brightness.

'Best things for you, Monsignor; fresh air and sunlight. The sun will heal that condition even better than the ointment.' He raises his arms to the white gold of Ra. Campbell the Egyptian priest. 'Hail,' says he. 'Giver of all Life!'

'I would have taken you for a *conventionally* religious man,' I say.

'Without the sun we'd not be here to worship! Without us here to ponder it, perhaps it would not exist. But you? Ever been drawn to the cloth?'

I hesitate, my English still imperfect.

'Holy Orders, Ralph. The clergy.'

I raise an eyebrow.

'Me neither,' he says. 'Neither cloth nor silk. Divinity or the Bar. Church nor Chambers,' he smiles, evidently running out of similes.

'But I see you each day striding below, still with some difficulty. Priest-like, tight-wrapped in your British Warm.'

Someone, Katya, had once asked me that. Was I a priest? I really didn't want to think about that time and the chasm that had opened up before me and the Family Strelitz.

'I believe the Sun is a great ball of burning gas,' I retort, returning quickly to the subject. 'A mystery that it keeps on burning.'

'Who said that it was not God himself made it?' he smiles. 'There is a poem addressed to the sun, by I. D. Bush.'

Twinkle, twinkle little star
I don't wonder what you are,
For by spectroscopic ken,
I know that you are hydrogen.

I smiled. 'Ha! The *Burning* Bush? But it doesn't explain why it is undiminished.'

'Sol, the Inextinguishable. But perhaps it *has* diminished over eons of time. Logic would demand it. But the origins of the universe and of civilisation are shrouded in mystery.'

'A mystery indeed, or an allegory. Like the sea.'

'Now that is deep, my boy, like the sea.' I suspected he was humouring me. 'The sea too giveth life. I lived there as a younger man. Indeed it's where all life began.'

'So I've read.'

'But we're just stargazing minnows when all's said and done.'

He has told me that I may have *savant syndrome*, resulting in the freeing from repression of the bicameral mind. The capability of achieving prodigious feats of calculation and memory, leaps of *seeming* insight and strange connections are sometimes bestowed on the sufferer. It seems not unlike a religious mania without a religion to nail it to - always the apostate. Nevertheless I sometimes look nervously for evidence of stigmata myself, for I picture still that monk in my mind and find I am often sketching something very like Friedrich's *Monk by the Sea*.

I must have seen a long ago etching of it in a collection of the Graf's art books. It comes vividly to mind as I walk the East Anglian coastline, notebook in hand. In my room I take up water colours and paint that same image, re-creating Friedrich's agonized Capuchin, sometimes in darker tones, sometimes in vivid colour: a cardinal with robes of blood.

I wonder if he is a victim of the Inquisition, torn between his religious belief and his logical mind, forced to dissimulate to survive. Solitary, like a priest. Like a spy.

~-~

I maintained my morning constitutionals over the next few days but found myself standing and staring at the North Sea without ever meaning to. I'd be walking one minute and then be facing the breeze, looking over the glittering waves for how long I could not have said. There was the shipping to claim my attention of course: once or twice the low smoking profiles of four-funnelled destroyers making heavy weather of their fast passage. But mostly there'd be absences, daydreams even as I strained to see something - I knew not what - on the grey horizon. Always the profundity of loss, some part of which I could explain; but that was not the whole of it.

The old sea captain, if that's what he is, nods in my direction as we pass upon the strand. We have not spoken but I come to expect him now and would miss his silent passing by. We are two vessels, holds full of mysterious cargo. Naturally his vigil, behind his English reserve, is seaward. I wonder at the mystery of his story. Had it been more adventurous, more troubled than mine? His weather-beaten face tells the years without need of words and the blue glint in the old eyes suggests sadness, for a loss. A ship? A woman? A child? What was mine?

The shoreline bestirs more than a painted image portends. Of Man's time. Facing the sea-barrier, decisions perchance thrust on him by pursuers. Or arriving by sea, a refugee, an explorer, *he* confronts the land. A border exists 'twixt those elements; ever meeting but never mingling, except at flood tide or tempest.

A man may patrol the shore on the edge of life or death. The beach, by definition unfertile, displays the flotsam that the sea delivereth. Like the ship's spar or dolphin's jaw, *he* is hardly here from choice, rather to *choose*. Come to some decision. A beach is no sanctuary. He cannot survive here. It is a place for contemplation, not settlement. He is transient, like the artist ghost of Winslow Homer; stands, reduced: a specimen on a laboratory slide. Old Campbell in his turret, or Rolf's own out-of-body self, sees that lone marching figure. Unknowable. A cipher.

Back at eye-level, his beachcomber monk moves along pathways to truth or oblivion, neither of which is mutually exclusive. But Destiny rules and the door is locked to the past. So what does the old captain see? I make up my mind to ask when next I meet him.

~-~

Catching an early train I'd paid off the Liverpool Street cab at Trafalgar Square and walked to Horseguards comfortably by eleven o'clock. I'd had plenty to think about on the journey, but the railway carriage had been stuffy and the chill London air did me good, though not as bracing as Norfolk with the wind in the East. My newly mended fractures ached and pulled as I climbed to the third floor overlooking St. James' Park, but I'd barely noticed. My mind was churning and so too was my stomach. I really had no idea what to expect. I had a bizarre notion that I was to appear before some sort of hastily convened inter-Allied court to account for a mis-spent youth and subsequent other treasons.

The girl who took my hat and overcoat coat asked me if I'd found the place alright and I was rewarded by her smile when I said yes, thank you, that I'd been provided with immaculate instructions by telephone from a very precise young lady. But if she had been my correspondent that remains an Official Secret. I am led to a door at the end of a panelled corridor and ushered into the presence of a smooth civil servant who introduces himself as Browne.

'This is Colonel Rose, who will be sitting-in and asking a few questions of his own as he thinks fit, if that's all right.' Browne is indicating his companion in civilian attire who is rising fastidiously from an armchair in the corner, a man in his forties with a hawkish expression whose hooded gaze remains intent upon me. A *rose* by another name entire, I think, and for the moment re-christen him 'Hawkeye', as I feel certain that Rose will not be his real name and is no more authentic than his rank. There is a dark-browed, sinister air about him which is faintly familiar. We exchange a few pleasantries, then I'm seated and it's down to business with Browne.

'If you'll just tell me your story from the beginning,' he says.

The two of them now sit serious-faced behind the big walnut partner desk. A couple of bank managers, and me the nervous interviewee short-listed for a job in the City. In my eye-line a female clerk is poised with note pad. There is a pot of tea and my worth runs to some Civil Service biscuits.

'Of course, it will help us if you are perfectly frank,' Browne adds with a smile that he withholds from the eyes. The verbal contract was simple and direct, which is *don't lie to us or you will find our urbanity is for the written record only*. 'Mr. Rose's specialty is Russia,' Browne adds unnecessarily, although as it turned out Hawkeye's specialties are legion.

Browne clears his throat primly and turns to the first page of a dossier that sits with other files and reference books on the polished walnut. 'You've already been interviewed by Bell. We have the transcript here. Of course we understand that you were receiving medical treatment; quite intensive from the file. Recovering from a serious accident… that could account for inconsistencies. So we will start with the clean sheet.'

In the corner of my eye I can see the secretary is preparing a shorthand account.

~-~

My Name is Rolfus

I recalled Bell well enough. He had been the first living soul I'd encountered after what had been a very long sleep, when I'd woken in the British field hospital. My other recollections from that time were a lot hazier. Indeed there were ragged bites out of my memory that the medics assured me were temporary absences, traumatic retrograde amnesia as a result of the crash and the blow to the head, and I was not to worry.

'Let's start with your full name.' Browne, the huntsman is leading his interrogatory pack: the handler letting slip the long dogs of, *Who? What? Why? When? Where?* and *How?* — to sniff out the forensic evidence while Hawkeye-Rose stares unwaveringly with his dark, unnerving eyes.

Who are you?

~-~

The strangest thing had been recovering consciousness, but with no memory of my identity.

I recalled floating in embryo, exploring the sensation of weightlessness upon a dark void with the vague remembrance of a long ago titanic struggle in some distant galaxy of the mind. But before that moment of what I took to be consciousness I seemed only to recall a nebulous voyage of anaesthesia, where I'd drifted in amoeba-like disembodiment, aware of motion on a timeless journey of the self that asked no questions and delivered no truths to my encystment. I was aware only of existence, cocooned in the near blissful formlessness of my being. And no demands upon my hibernating intellect.

Somewhere a heavy door had slammed shut in my brain. Beyond it were secreted the meanings of the here and now and behind it all truths were cached, unknowable.

The effort of remembering seemed Herculean. Nothing, not even a glimmer of cognition remained. I had no concept of where or what I was and grasped vainly for a word or a name that might have meaning for me. No graphics appeared in my mind's eye, not a landscape, nor face that I could hold to, just shadows from somewhere in my subconscious that for all I knew were constructs of my own. Simultaneously I recognized both gravity and pressure, and when I struggled I felt I was breaking free from alluvial sludge, the sense of evolving into a swimming night creature suddenly very strong.

Evolving. That word and another, *Metamorphosis,* came unbidden from the matrix. My brain was beginning to work on concepts it seemed, but for the moment I was this nameless, depersonalised, zoanthropic groping-thing that had wrenched from the primordial sediment in an infusoric cloud. Gradually, as seen through watery depths, I imagined the glimmering light that might lead to the surface and a hoped-for newborn realisation of self.

I struggled, aware then of pain in my chest, sharp and stabbing. In my left forearm, a dull ache, matched by another in my right shin. Worse still in my neck, and in my head, which seemed to suddenly expand and open up – with the disquieting impression that the swelling tissue was oozing fluid from a brain-fissure. The back of my skull throbbed, and there was a blinding light across my eyes. I screwed them tight against the brightness, and to my relief it moved away.

For a while I'd been aware of motion. A barely perceptible rocking. A tidal lift with the sound of the sea singing in my ears now emerged as a jolting, noisy passage in some sort of vehicle. It came to a halt and the sounds were then of latches being released, the light 'clink' of chains, and voices. Although I understood what was being said I could not name the language.

The vehicle rocked as someone climbed aboard, moving stealthily closer. I felt an eyelid being lifted and again a sear of pain as the beam of an electric torch shone into my eye. I'd closed my eyes tightly but cautiously re-opened them as the light moved on. Abruptly a Slavic head wrapped in a bloody crepe bandana loomed into my face, a sardonic smile playing about its parted lips and pale eyes stared straight into mine. Horror struck, I'm sure I tried to scream but no sound would come. Torchlight played over it, grotesquely animating the cadaverous features with swarming shadows. But not the eyes; they remained inert in their sockets, their stare fixed, diffuse as blue ice under water.

'Two more!' A gruff voice. Polish…yes that was certainly it. German-accented, I recognized the lilt. Another figure clambered onto the lowered tailboard. 'This one at the end, and that one there,' said the first voice. I saw the stooping figure gesturing towards my smiling dead companion whose torso seemed to be covered in a rough blanket or heavy sacking like the other inert forms I could now see in the wagon.

'Well let's get 'em out,' said the second soldier or medic. 'Make way for those that have a chance.' The corpses were unceremoniously dragged out and two other patients were helped aboard, a third being slid down the centre of the wagon bed on a litter. The tailboard clattered shut and canvas curtains were re-tied. There was movement outside and the smell of petrol momentarily subdued other palpably rank body smells, ammonia and the whiff of iodine in a company remarkable for its quiescence.

A shout, the engine was cranked into life, and we moved off with a gnashing of drive chains heading for a hoped-for casualty clearing station, though where we were geographically I had no clue. Seemingly unrelated shards of information were flitting wraith-like through a crossroads in my mind, but the signposts were blurred. I felt that some would lead me down starless pathways where I would not choose to venture, still I tried to follow. But I might have grasped at smoke for my attempts to catch a fleeting image. Fearful shapes flashed up momentarily, like popinjay targets at a demon shoot, and then were gone. I was both pursuer and pursued through a dark maze or labyrinth where I ran in panic and with each dead-end I would fetch against that locked door. My head throbbed and exhausted, jogged by the motion of the truck, I fell thankfully asleep.

~-~

'So!' said the laid-back voice in French. '*Monsieur Rolf.* Is that who we have here?'

I'd been off drifting somewhere else, inhabiting an alien landscape with a double sun - seeing but not understanding. But now I realized that the bed I was lying in provided a view of two bright lights, lanterns, slung from a substantial wooden post, and these were creating deep shadows all around. The figure was in partial silhouette from the aura of light about his head. Another figure stood by the bed. These stood like sentinels or gatekeepers, guarding the portals that marked the curtailment of a journey to somewhere, a journey I'd yearned to make, but would not now complete. I could see a Red Cross nurse talking quietly to the occupant of a bed opposite my own. A canvas wall was visible beyond. I felt a terrible sense of loss and that I'd been robbed of volition. As if I'd suddenly become aged with no memory of youth.

I was strangely incurious about all of this. I would quite happily have continued lying there drifting in and out of sleep. The name 'Rolf' didn't seem to mean anything much. I thought it *might* be my given name, and on reflection it did seem to fit, with an old glove's familiarity, and I surely couldn't think of any other name that fitted better. I didn't feel much like talking in any event; my head and face hurt like hell and I was certain there was a large area of swelling on my cheek. I could taste blood and my tongue felt huge. My lower jaw ached mercilessly and I'd have been content to take a holiday from whatever other reality was lurking out there.

I sort of assumed my memory would come back in due course. Whatever I'd suffered must have created this temporary lapse. I was certain I'd heard of such things, events that injured the brain, either physically traumatic or shocking to the mind. Somewhere. Sometime.

'Parlez-vous francais? Sprechen Sie deutsch? Sind Sie russisch? Ukrainisch? Tschechisch?

Rolf, if that's who I was, tried to answer. I spoke reasonable French, English and German, of that I was pretty sure. I'd understood the language on the wagon – Polish, too. I couldn't put a name to the other tongues… although, yes. Now I had it, Russian and Lithuanian. This didn't seem uncommon to me. However when I, *Rolf*, tried to answer, nothing came. My head was aching violently and thinking made it worse. My tongue moved thickly around dry lips, the lower being split and exquisitely painful to the touch.

'Nurse, bring some water will you?' The same silhouette had spoken, a different language! I felt a gentle hand under my bandaged head, lifting, re-positioning a pillow so I could sip some water.

'There you are, that's better,' said a soothing female voice. *English*.

'Can you understand me?' The first voice went on in slow French. 'This letter was found in your breast pocket. Nothing else. It was addressed just to *Rolf*. A Balt. Lithuanian, Latvian? The name *Dragunavicius* is mentioned in the text and the word 'father'. Is that you then? It means *dragoon* doesn't it? Are you he? *Rolf* son of *Dragunavicius*?

I, *Rolf*, managed only a croak.

'Qu'est que vous dites?' The figure leaned nearer to catch the words.

'Where am I?' I managed at last, replying in French.

'You're at a British Red Cross dressing station. Outside Duvno.'

The name meant nothing.

'Look, you've had a rather a bad knock on the head, and some other injuries which will need further treatment. Do you understand?'

I tried nodding my head and immediately regretted it. 'Yes,' was my weak reply.

'We need to establish exactly who you are and with whom you were serving. Essentially which side you are on actually, in this godforsaken place. Given that you were wearing a hotch-potch of military kit practically from all combatants. If you feel that you can only provide your name, rank and number, I understand, but you will be passed on to our Intelligence people when you are fitter.'

'Whose Intelligence people?' I thought I detected an accent behind the French.

'British. You're with our Army and Red Cross combined at the moment. I'm David Bell. That's Captain Willoughby, deputy army surgeon next to you.' I took in the congealed blood on the apron the Captain was wearing.

'I have English,' I said.

'So you speak English.' He sounded relieved to be speaking it. 'Care to tell me your name?'

'You said *Rolf*? Rolf ...*Dragunavicius*. Why did you call me that?' I dimly recalled him babbling in French about some letter but I really wasn't concentrating, nor was I much interested.

'As I said a moment ago, this letter is the only document we found on your person.' He was holding it in his hand. 'It's addressed to Rolf possibly related to a Dr. Dragunavicius from the contents, if I'm deciphering the rather smeared handwriting correctly. No address.' It looked as though it had been folded and re-folded a hundred times and dragged through several campaigns. 'It is dated October 1919. Do you remember this letter?'

The iron door in my mind was bolted and barred. 'No,' I said.

'Well do you know whose signature this might be?' He held the letter up, obscuring the text. I screwed my eyes against the pain and the light. The page was soiled and had obviously been soaked and dried out at least once in the past. I could make out a flamboyant 'K' and a full stop.

'No.' My head seemed to be bursting, not just with pain but with sound. My ears were ringing as if with residual noise, an infernal roar and a high pitched hiss combined. Like... something. I couldn't remember what. An initial, 'K', with a flourish. Some semaphores and levers were clicking in my brain, but somewhere along the line the signal had been lost. Too late, the little piece of information had been shunted into some remote siding in a faraway place.

'The letter is in Lithuanian, with some words in French and German. Don't you remember what it says?' I just wanted him to shut up and go away so I could sleep. I could think later maybe, when it didn't hurt so much.

'Look, I know this is important.' The Captain addressed Bell in a weary but firm voice, speaking for the first time. He was tall, in his thirties I guessed, and looked dog-tired. 'However, my patient has suffered some quite serious injuries and needs to rest.'

He turned to me. 'I am sorry to be blunt, but I have others to attend to here quite urgently. You may have suffered temporary amnesia following your crash. I don't want you to worry about this. These things tend to right themselves in time with proper rest and care.' He was reading from a list now. 'Your arm and leg injuries are not complicated and you're young. You look pretty fit and they'll heal well now they've been set. You've broken some ribs and you have a fractured cheekbone, cuts to your face and chin, loosened teeth, *and* you've bitten your tongue. But these are not serious so long as infection doesn't set in – we've picked several celluloid fragments out of your cheek by the way, but there may be more to come. It's a bit messy and the swelling and contusions obscure things. What we are not certain about is your head injury. It may be a fracture. Certainly there's trauma and swelling on the left side of the cranium. You'll have a headache for a while anyway.' He slipped on the earpieces of a stethoscope. 'I'll just have a listen to your chest before I go.' Satisfied, he gave me an encouraging smile and was gone.

Bell was like a terrier with his questions but the nurse rose to the occasion. She suggested with a firmness that allowed no opposition that he should come back tomorrow if he knew what was good for him, for which I was devoutly thankful. I needed time to consider what had happened as far as I could remember which wasn't very much at that moment. There was something so profound that I knew I should address, that I needed to do and was more important than anything else. I'd burned my bridges somewhere. I had to retrace steps to move forward. But when I looked back I'd left no trail in the dust that my mind would acknowledge. There was only the vague, symbolic image of a 'door' to be negotiated so that I could move forward, but to what?

The nurse returned with soup and I managed to swallow a little, with her determined efforts. For the moment the soup was real and she was real. All the rest was terra incognita.

~_~

Next day I awoke with the same dreadful headache. I had slept, but the sleep was not one that *'ravell'd up the sleeve of care'*. My dreams had been populated by phantasms and mindless horrors of the *id*, hideous images like the piratical Slavic head grimacing in my face. Horsemen of a black apocalypse rode on skeletal nags, shrieking foully, gesturing triumphally while I stood helpless amid what I perceived to be the ruin of innocence. Visions that Dante and Hieronymus Bosch might have collaborated on had swept past me 'neath the dark rush of the sky and a sickly moon. Upon a black gibbet a poor, eyeless creature twisted in the wind, and in my hand I held the stub of a broken sword.

So I woke to a feeling of impotence, mentally retaining enough cryptic symbolism for whole chapter of the *Royal Road to the Unconscious*.

And suddenly for the first time, a tiny bell had tinkled somewhere in a locked and faraway room, on some other level in my brain, *Alarum* or *Angelus* where maybe lay some scattered and dusty extracts from Freud's work on the interpretation of dreams.

~-~

The room had fallen silent. Browne brings me back to the present with his next statement. 'We know the contents of that letter and the reported circumstances of how you and it came to be delivered to the field hospital at Duvno. The question is therefore, were you the intended recipient, and if so how did you come by the letter? Was it hand delivered? Presuming it is in the original envelope, all that was written on the front is the name *Rolf*. Is that Rolf, Rudolf, Rolfus, is it short for something else? Are you he, and at the same time whom you now *purport* to be?'

Is this you?

I have a temporary British passport. How temporary it remains might depend on this interview, I feel sure. Rose's eyes are dark pools. Where have I met him?

I was christened Rolfus, I tell them. Known also as *Rolfs* in the Baltic tradition of name endings, but I have generally answered to the shortened Germanic form of Rolf. And as to the *next* question I am the only child of Dr. Augusts Dragunavicius, general practitioner and sometime country veterinarian, and of Hannah, a dark Sephardic beauty; a nursing sister whose crypto-Jewish antecedents had fled both the Inquisition and the Iberian Peninsula.

My free-thinking father had pretty much abandoned all religious ideology, and his wider interests included natural history, psychoanalysis and philosophy. He'd read all that the prolific Freud was publishing in German, despite the ban then promulgated against the Latin alphabet. He said that where Darwin showed us the journey we'd made and Shakespeare expressed the intricacies of human nature, Freud revealed new ideas on the meaning of the self, while Nietzsche showed us where we might be heading. Thanks to Freud we could analyse who and what we really were. It seemed a liberating thought, and his obsessive interest had intrigued me and I'd read some of it myself. In fact I'd read avidly as a child in my father's snug study that smelled of tweed and tobacco, gun oil and polish with Wolfie's gentle head upon my knee. Sitting among his microscopes and other apparatus, his botanical and entomological specimens, I'd pored over books on many subjects extra-curricular to my irregular schooling, and some of it must have stuck.

He'd said some things to me which I remembered on the day that I left home forever; the day I'd begun my journey to Austria: under a cloud.

My father stood at my bedroom door as I was dressing to leave. He held several books in his hand which he insisted I take with me. Works of literature, poetry and philosophy, crammed into my little suitcase with my clothes.

Thus spoke my father:

'Protect your name.'

Actually he'd spoken Russian. A rare thing.

'Beregi plat'ye snovu, a chest 'smolodu!' Which means 'Take care of your clothes when they are new, and your honour when you are young!'

He said that if your good name is sullied it is worse than any theft. That it may not be possible to redeem it in a lifetime.

'Read a book every day,' he said. 'Fight injustice.'

He told me to avoid drunkenness and drunkards, and to try not to smoke too much.

'Speak the truth,' he said. 'Learn from the mistakes of others for you will not live long enough to make all of them yourself. Protect the weak and right those wrongs which are in your power to correct. Speak against evil but be sure of those in whom you confide. Do not countenance cruelty. Stand by your friends.'

He embraced me. I cannot remember his embrace before that time, though I always knew he loved me.

'Stay safe,' he said, holding me by the shoulders. We were the same height now, I suddenly noticed.

'Keep a cool head, and if you must die, my son, sell your life dearly. God bless you.'

There was a catch in his voice.

I remember thinking that he didn't believe in God.

That morning was the last time I was ever to see either my father or my mother. I remember them standing together outside our gate as I was driven away. I craned my neck for a last glimpse of their blurred faces, my mother's still beautiful, though pale and worn and her last goodbye in my ears, my stomach twisted with the thought that Katarzyna had betrayed me.

~.~

That is I tell them *some* of this. My replies are measured rather than terse. The account is fit for purpose, but the account in my mind runs long. Furthermore my history is not without complication and it is simpler to let the story unfold naturally in the way I choose to tell it. The spontaneous surfacing of key facts in a long and bitter saga, like islands of reality, will keep me on course through the ordeal of what now seems the epic dream that I truly wish it were. But the earliest recollections are fonder, though improbably mythic when viewed at the gallop.

~.~

I am taken back to the land where I grew up. It is fourteen years since as a tow-haired dreamy lad I had run wild, barefoot as often as not with the threadbare village boys, shouting loudly in the only recently un-banned Lithuanian *lingua franca*, taunting the Russian soldiery and running for cover in alleyways or the tall timber; often with feral children for whom lack of noblesse inferred scant obligation, yet among whom there was honour, friendship and in whom there was bred a sense of nationhood, and with them I adventured in this *ancient land of heroes* as passionately declaimed in our anthem.

Under towering cloud castles we rode half-wild horses, often bareback like Red Indians, over wide, windswept grasslands where we fought imaginary Teuton knights armed with wooden swords, all in a lush, green, untamable landscape, richly portrayed (though we didn't really know it) in the epic *Pan Tadeusz*, Mickiewicz's lyric poem. Ironically this was in the Polish language given later border conflicts, but is still a patriotic rallying cry for both Polish and Lithuanian aspirations. Truth to tell, we were just as happy to be frontiersmen and wild Indians given the popularity of Fenimore-Cooper, or explorers like Sven Hedin. We gave little heed to our antecedents' victory at Grunewald or the distant echo in the east: the Golden Horde's tidal wave breaking against the Grand Duchy's borderland redoubts, eight centuries before.

I'd slid effortlessly between fishing, swimming in the rivers and lakes, snaring rabbits and cooking them in the open; wildfowling, skimming stones with my urchin friends, searching for amber after rain. Sitting with starched collar, kicking my heels between my parents at high table in the Big House - that fine Russo-Baltic mansion. On Saint's days, trying to catch the eyes of the two Strelitz girls. Later I would escape with the other children and cousins, the servants' youngsters too; bicycling with Marik; he on his new English *Raleigh*, me on my Duks *Russki Vitiaz*, relieved to be out in the sunshine on the sweeping linden drive where we rode like the wind and fell off to limp stoically in with a cut knee or elbow for Nanny to mend. *'Nichevo, Malyutka! It's nothing, Little One!'* she soothed. Once aged only seven I'd come crying up the rose garden steps, shocked from a fall and was held tight to the Governess's bosom while she'd sobbed silently with me, to my discomfiture; my pain melting so in bewilderment that I'd torn myself away running after Marik, through the elegant Edouard André-landscaped gardens that were still 'a work in progress', over the meadows, off to the woodland and beyond to that hyperborean idyll where the *Turk* never stood, who, I'd been told, would:

'Set the seal of Suliman on all things under sun'.

Marik told me that *Black Joshua* wasn't a Turk and had been with the Family 'forever'. But then I was mostly oblivious of *all things* save for the moment in which I'd lived.

And all forgotten until that expectant quiet in a high-ceiling'd Whitehall room with the midday sun streaming in and another question hanging in the air.

~-~

But to go back to that second question. Where was I born? Simple, straightforward question, requires a straightforward answer, and they are waiting, smooth Browne and the Last of the Mohicans. I have a good ear for mimicry and also for languages. Given time and some polish I felt I might assimilate as a bona fide Englishman. Just a wild tendency to lapse into, what? Europe Central, or Scand, with a regional trace which I can drop into and out of at will. I was even, in part, a country cousin English public schoolboy, if you can count two miserable terms and another ecstatically happy when I discovered literature and music boarding at the Conrad von Hippel *Deutsch-Englisches* Gymnasium in Bremerhaven. Before the funds ran out and I was shipped back home. And, well, I must confess that there was an unfortunate incident around that time which had a bearing. Even so, should I then say *England* and be done, surprise everybody and save a lot of time?

But no. My life, as it turned out, was just as full of loose beginnings as of loose ends. So I'll give you the version I gave them, and I gave them their money's worth. As I came to know it myself. Just as it emerged when cloistered with the Graf in the confessional at his own hallowed and stuccoed mansion, steep-roofed, Russo-Balt in aspect with later additions and embellishments more in the Hanseatic style. Knocked about a bit, it was by then – but they were tough times.

~·~

I say 'confessional' because I had done things to survive, well at least to 'improve my prospects' of survival and ambitions, just things. Life decisions of one sort or another that one makes, viewed in retrospect, but some had made me a refugee of sorts. A clandestine servant of my newly adoptive country through *force majeure*, already half way to becoming a spy! This would have unforeseen consequences in the way that, say, modifying a piece of machinery or telling a lie can create knock-on effects somewhere, downstream. In time that lie will jam the works and the human cost will be incalculable. 'Confessional' because the occasion upon which I recall learning the definitive truth about my birth involved a *mutual* confession and some wider revelations to me personally.

Never be ashamed of who you are, Rolf, he'd said.

Chapter 16. *Confessional*

I believe that confession is good for the soul and as the dawn light filters through the library windows I know this will be the day for that confession – and for answers. For my part I must first admit that I once stole something of value and so behaved dishonourably. So I am a thief. In my defence I would claim that my theft was not for monetary gain, that I had acted from desperation, and that my actions intended no harm to anyone, at least none that I would have foreseen at the time of the act. Nor did the victim of my theft suffer any loss that he knew of. In fact my crime had been spontaneous, provoked by circumstances of near despair.

Perhaps worse than this I have taken life. Sometimes hotly. Sometimes vengefully - that old meal best served cold, a maxim with which I will not disagree. Fighter on fighter, when you manoeuvre to shoot an enemy in the back it cannot be called chivalrous, yet, I confessed to my diary, in the grimmest weeks of war, he would do this to me in a trice in our mutual turning combat. So should I feel no emotion? I had been tasked to compile the squadron war diary, which I did in the terse words of a seasoned air fighter. But in private, tremulously, I wrote in my *own* diary: '*So short a moment have we trod that vault of beautiful endeavour, yet have we carelessly sown there the seeds of fire and death. We sully the clouds with maiming and murder though abhor the suffering of fellow airmen. Yet do we enjoy the hunt, for in combat there is emotion, and beauty in the curve of pursuit, in leading your 'game bird' by deflection shooting, undeniable visceral excitement, a thumping heart, legs that shake uncontrollably on the rudder bar after a near collision. And raw fear'*

'*But a human being cannot afford too much fear. It must be pushed aside or it will paralyse him. Too little and he is a hero not destined to tarry long in this world.*'

In the end the greatest enemies were tiredness and the beginning of a blasé or too fatalistic an attitude. That and the pathetic equipment we had, especially at the beginning. It was just as well that the Russian equipment was equally lousy, at the start.

The great exceptions were their four-engined bombers, the big Sikorskii *Ilya Mourometz,* 'square-rigged' biplanes, named for the legendary Russian hero. Operated by Major General Shidlovski's *Eskadra Vozdushnyka Korablei,* Squadron of Flying Ships; the most efficient and respected unit in the Imperial Russian Air Service. Those heavy bombers were long-ranging, tough opponents and on one raid they'd wiped out a German seaplane base on Lake Angern in Kurland. Later they destroyed *General Oberst* von Below's HQ at Shavli, Lithuania, where a squadron of gigantic 'R' plane bombers had come to roost; ash-grey burned and flaking, their remains lay like cast-off exoskeletons of some gargantuan arachnid spring. I remember seeing one collapsed sideways, its monstrous wing spars and blackened ribs naked to the sky, monument both to air power and futility.

Later it got more technical, with generally better equipment and also as reconnaissance duties required more and more protection from the fighter force, the techniques of air fighting grew rapidly with experience and some exceptionally gifted combat instructors emerged; Oswald Boelcke in particular, who tutored his acolytes in fighter tactics on the Western Front.

In that theatre none was more calculating when shooting down his eighty victims than Richthofen. His fame and prowess inspired us on the Eastern Front where I confess to surviving mostly by looking over my shoulder. A cool killing machine, Richthofen with his silver trophy cups was nonetheless a remote figure, whereas Brumowski, Linke-Crawford, Arigi, Kiss and Kessler; these were my local heroes and compatriots on the Italian, Salonika and Galician Fronts. I think of those valiant young men, our brother pilots on both sides from whose departures, though ritually marked, we publicly withheld feelings for the duration. The emotions came unbidden then and later, alone, and at unexpected moments. So too the nightmares. And now they rarely leave me.

~-~

'And your family. Where were they from, *originally* I mean?' By this I am directed to conform to their plodding chronology of my legend, amazed that it's only 12.15 by the discreet clock on the oak panelling beneath which our secretary sits, scratching in cuneiform.

My mother Hanna's family, named *Perez*, had centuries before crossed the Pyrenees and settled in France and the Netherlands before making the trek through Prussia to a demi-paradise known generally as Kurland taking the name *Perchikorwitz*. In still later years one might be forgiven for failing to identify that region on any map, and though all nationalities and creeds rubbed along under a Kurlandian sky the irony was that, over time, Hannah's family, unlike those of other refugees fleeing persecution, whose adherence to their faith was the essential ingredient of cohesion and identity, had lapsed in their devotions, but had not adopted Roman Catholicism, Lutheranism, or indeed Russian Orthodoxy. Freed from gnostic doctrine, although she would later return to her devotional roots, Hannah had married and moved south-east across the border to the Lithuanian homeland of another lapsed (*Ashkenazi*) Jew and humanist doctor, where in a gesture to the powerful spirit world of Lithuanian mythology, she named our house *Ausautas*, from the Old Prussian once spoken thereabouts, for the 'god of health and medicine'.

She was however, not freed from the curse, whose genetic component, as discovered by Mendel and codified some decades later by Thomas Huxley in the textbooks my father owned, had claimed the lives of her mother and grandmother - a predisposition to breast cancer. The good doctor, whose own mother had also succumbed to that disease, had spent a tireless crusade and much of the family's wealth combating it. Consultations and stays in clinics in Petersburg, Paris, Vienna and Berlin, though aided by the generosity of his good friend and near neighbour, Kristian Graf von Strelitz, had practically emptied the family coffers. It is upon the chaise longue of the Graf, twice-widowed baron of the Kuznetsowa Estate, honorary Margrave of Aleksandras Apygarda, in the well-endowed library that I now recline in memory.

The 'now' of *this* part of the telling sees me in a limbo of numbness and heartache in which the physical pain of my situation is the smallest part. My parents are dead, and this knowledge so recently imparted is from the mouth of a Kristian more emotional and human than ever he has appeared hitherto: as a man, rather than 'the Graf', in whose aloof and imposing presence we children had demonstrated the greatest respect and courtesy: when at the behest and invitation of Marik, eldest of the Graf's children, and my best friend in the world, a much younger Rolf had enjoyed the hospitality of the fine House of Linden. *Liepus Namas* in my native Lithuanian – despite the ban. It was albeit under the watchful eye of the governess whose lessons in etiquette extend to Rolf when he is under that roof, and struggling with French, which all the children speak at table.

My injured leg has been expertly dressed by Nina, nanny to the children of the Linden House. She is slender-waisted like so many Baltic women. Of Russian extraction she seems thinner than I'd recalled, but then almost everybody is, including me. She is demurely buttoned to the throat, a dark chignon bobbing above the curving nape of her neck as she works. Nina, surrogate mother to orphans, Anna and Lisa, her little nieces who were the young playmates of Graczyna, exhibits the same sweet-natured disposition as in those happy, easy times; she'd attended to all we children during the not infrequent visits of my long ago youth.

~-~

'So tell us more about this Graf. This von Strelitz. What were his political affiliations? Was he concerned with his personal affairs entirely and the continuation of his privileged position as gentrified landowner? What were his business connections, do you know? Did you know the *man*? What were his qualities, would you say?' This from Rose, the first time he has spoken.

I have not failed to notice the volume of the *Almanach De Gotha* among the literature on the desk, but wonder how you slide under the skin of another human being, especially one who from birth has been instructed in maintaining cover and wears the ermine cloak of noblesse, belief in service to proconsular rule, sharing in privilege through family and connection in a rigid hierarchy of possession and elevation through title. Well might his erstwhile serf, our Bolshevist brother, boil with envy and seek to make him low. Expropriate his wealth and redistribute the spoils unevenly, cynically, among the next brutal enslavers of men. For it is human nature to keep the best back for yourself, despite the mutant doctrines espoused in Marxism-Leninism.

I recall being lifted up in strong arms. I was wearing some sort of tunic and breeches of what I know believe was cut in a military style. I had on a cap and had saluted the tall figure smartly in our hallway, next to the *Baumfroschwetterglass*, which worked amusingly well enough: as if it were an aneroid barometer.

'So, *Jünge*! Are you now with the *ABC Schützen*?' ABC Rifles was a popular term for primary school chidren, the youngest of pupils.

'Yes, sir!' I announced clearly, as I had been taught, viewing the beaming Graf at the length of his extended arms and looking him straight in his grey-blue eyes.

'That's a good little soldier,' he said. His voice was strong and pleasant and he seemed god-like compared with my own father, who was mellow and kindly, not flamboyant, rich and powerful like the Count.

A short while later, or so it seemed to me, I awoke to a cold moon. An owl flew past my window, white in the moonlight and night visitors came to our home in a clatter of hooves in the yard and women's voices whispering in the hall. I remember other faces; concerned faces, his

228

among them, stern and unsmiling. Everything seemed to change then for a long while. I didn't know what it was that I'd done wrong, but the atmosphere in our home had perceptibly altered and I seemed to be spending a lot of time on my own. My parents were still around of course, but there was a different mood or pervading sensation that I learned to accept in time and no longer questioned. But a wordless guilt hung fretfully over my young life that seemed in solitary moments to impart intimations of some original sin.

It was perhaps two years before I was allowed up to the Big House where I made my greatest childhood friend, Marik.

~-~

Ah, but there are none like the 'vons' for glibly dissembling, unless it be the public school educated Englishman, a truism I'd already understood by the time I was finished at the von Hippel gymnasium, and would later professionally re-discover. Both could sum up a non-class member *augenblicklich*, boot you downstairs, and in US parlance, give you the 'bum's rush' with such elegant aplomb. Smiling while they kill comes with mother's milk, and few are equipped like the English upper middle class for the cut and thrusting City and the Diplomatic Corps. In both so-civilized jungles, a deathblow deftly delivered with faultless manners finds the untutored victim outside looking dazed - and he's never seen it coming. Equally either could be suffering a storm force panic attack right next to you at dinner, and you'd never feel a thing. But here is the phenomenon of an unwrapped von Strelitz *without* amour-propre stripped to his epidermis with no hint of *in vodka veritas*, for all I knew despising me, and treating a ne'er-do-well bourgeois rake, seducer of his eldest daughter as he must have seen it, candidly, with apparent equanimity.

This House of Linden had rung to the sounds of children's laughter and hitherto was not that habitat of ghosts it has since become. Now it seemed that furtive and watchful presences have been invoked by agitation and the frank use of names. Hallowed and implacable through suffering and time, they stand as shadows behind a Graf who feels he must unburden now to me as religiously, each night, candle in hand, bends he in mute supplication to the dead saint on the stair. A Lithuanian pilgrim to the Madonna at the Gate of Dawn.

So I'd listened to the lowered voice of the man whom last I'd seen some four years before.

In my memory he is standing tall upon the platform at Ignalina as I board that southbound train. It is as though I am to embark to a caravanserai of exile, although in my case not 'internal' as was traditional in Russia. But it's a regular 'bums rush' whichever way you viewed it.

'Life's a journey, Rolf,' he'd said brightly, shaking my hand as I boarded the carriage.

~-~

It seemed barely credible that more than four years had then passed since I'd prepared to leave home as a young man of not quite eighteen summers. Convicted, guilty as charged. Crime: falling in love with someone above my station in life. Sentence: banishment. Despite the friendship that existed between my father and hers — there was too great a gulf. Through the network of the so called Soldaten or 'Masonic' Bund (*not* the similarly named Jewish Workers' League) with its long military arm, a Teutonic *'Old Boys' Network'*, by baronial edict I was to join a regiment in Austria (why Austria and not Germany I knew not then why) with no 'ifs' or 'buts', decreed through an old feudalistic legacy so recently repealed, yet re-enacted, so it seemed, especially for one disconsolate Rolf, only son. Disobedience of such a directive would, it was being explained to me as I polished my best boots, bring tribulation to my parents. The family coffers were in sorry depletion and mother's ailing health had demanded extreme sacrifices. In short we were almost destitute and were considering the sale of *Ausautas*.

I had been summoned to Liepus Namas and rode there in trepidation. Krysia, whose name was foresworn from that time in our home, had also been dispatched to new fields of academe, to Paris. The Sorbonne. But with no word of what she would be studying.

I stood to attention before the Graf's desk in his study decked with African memorabilia.

'I am sure you know why I've called you here this morning, Rolf.'

The Graf spoke calmly but there was little warmth in his tone. I remained silent, staying in control.

'I have written a letter commending you to my old friend, Major Gerd von Schlieffen, adjutant to the 2nd. Regiment *Archduke Franz-Josef der Erste*, a very famous cavalry regiment based at the Helmsburg Garrison of Angerfurt in the Österreich. He has now replied. He states, on the basis of my fulsome recommendation, that the regiment will provisionally accept you as an officer cadet, that is despite you're having failed to complete your education. Lacking your Abitur, the basic educational requirement for enrolment for officer training, would normally disqualify you from receiving an Austrian commission. However he has promised to take special interest in your progress. If you keep your head down and study hard you may well succeed and a military career could be yours.'

'I see, sir. Thank you, sir.' Confused: with his connections I'd anticipated *Germany*.

The Graf looked at me with his steady gaze. Finally his face broke into a smile.

'Don't look so worried, my boy. A fine marksman and a good horseman like you should do well.' He looked serious again. 'You have good blood in your veins, Rolf. Don't you forget it. Be proud.'

~-~

The Graf would provide funds enabling me to live in a manner and style appropriate to an officer cadet from a good family, contingent upon my performance in training.

There was some mention that, with the caveat of my compliance, funds would also be provided for further treatment for mother, who'd recently taken to frenetically washing, cleaning, and polishing everything in sight, despite the faultless duties in this area fulfilled by the young maid, Daine, of the downcast eye, whose name means 'song' but who moves silently. It was as if Hannah were making up for the loss of devotional years in the cleansing rituals of her faith. As if vigorous scrubbing would rub out her canker.

To my great surprise the Graf himself had turned up bright and early with his pretty Sizaire *torpedo* to drive me to the railway station at Ignalina. This was of course a great honour, though I would have preferred our slow little Benz or the landaulet and my father's company.

So I'd waved my parents goodbye for the last time at our gate, heard their '*Go with God*': twisted my body to keep in view the slight, wasted figure of my mother with my father's comforting hand upon her, his other raised in farewell burned long into my retina after they were obscured by a twist of road and the birches. I wondered when I'd see them again. I wondered if Flitzer would miss his morning exercise. For a moment I thought I saw Vilkie (*Wolfie*), as if I'd left him in the kitchen, standing with his paws on the windowsill watching my retreating back. Alas he lay forever 'neath his elderberry tree. The Graf talked as he drove, fighting with the steering wheel like Mr. Toad as the open car bucked through the potholes, me with my suitcase clutched to my chest lest I should lose it overboard.

We passed the endless walls of his Kuznetsowa Estate and its crenellated lodge through whose iron gates I had unselfconsciously ridden my bicycle or trotted my pony as welcome guest of this man's eldest child, son and heir. Partly hidden by the full-burgeoning foliage flanking the drive I could see the friendly portals of the House of Linden, its pure white stucco bright in the lovely summertime of that year of 1914 with the farmland beyond where I'd spent the happy hours playing and working for the joy of it. And saw Kat, her features indistinct, riding parallel to the road until horse and rider disappeared amongst the trees. Had she been my betrayer or had I betrayed myself?

Along the road the Graf raised his hand. A group of gendarmes saluted. They stood next to a fast-looking black-painted open tourer with the sign *Police* in the windscreen. They appeared to be in conversation with some workmen, one of whom was being held. We drove in silence for a while.

When next he spoke he'd tried to explain then why things had to be the way they were. That Krysia would be marrying the son of a Hanse merchant and ship owner on the Baltic littoral, a business associate who shared his maritime-mercantile interest. That was how it would be and I was not to take it too personally. Any further contact between myself and his daughter would not be countenanced. She was off-limits, had been sent away for her further education and that was that. With regard to my own future, he confirmed the account lodged by von Schlieffen in Angerfurt's Imperial Viennese Bank would gain me modest interest, and at the same time provide for my uniform and the necessary expenses of an officer cadet once I made it through basic training - which he had no doubt I would comfortably succeed in doing. 'Keep hold of your temper, Rolf, and don't give too much away. The NCOs will try to break you. Keep calm: they are only doing their jobs – to make men out of boys. Sometimes the discipline and punishment will seem harsh and unfair. That's *also* the way it has to be. You'll come through if you stay true to yourself.' He paused. 'Good blood flows in your veins, Rolf,' he repeated. 'Never be ashamed of who you are.'

There was much else in this pseudo-avuncular vein. I took it all without much comment. I suppose I was still in shock by this sudden turn of events and not a little awed by his taking so personal an interest in my welfare. I supposed that he thought I needed to hear it from himself, the reason for my exile. I also supposed that he felt a degree of responsibility to make things alright with me given his friendship with my father over many years. That he acknowledged the feelings that I held for his daughter were reciprocated, young though we were, and not lightly to be brushed aside. On that matter, however, he was adamant. I was not to try to write to his daughter, not to *any* of his daughters, nor to any of the Graf's family. At this and the news of her betrothal tears burned behind my eyes and my heart seemed to stumble in my chest. Marik was already in Petersburg but neither was he about to furnish me with details of an address for him at the *Corps of Pages.*'

There was that other darker matter we'd not yet addressed. Another reason for my hasty removal from Lithuanian society which was not at all to do with his daughters' respectability, at least not directly. It concerned the body in the stream.

'Rolf,' he'd said. 'Can you tell me you had nothing to do with that awful business? Hand on heart. I mean, of course, am I aiding and abetting a murderer?'

I was overcome a little with confusion, all my emotions mixed up. Here I was being sent far away from home and the girl I loved with no say in the matter, my mother's health being hostage to my compliance and fleeing the law into the bargain.

'I swear I had nothing to do with his death.'

The Graf gave me a sidelong glance.

'Should I believe you, I wonder?' His voice was just audible above the exhaust.

'We had our differences,' I said. 'That was it. He was taught a lesson. Nothing more. I don't know what happened afterwards. That's the truth, sir.'

He was silent for while concentrating on the road.

'Very well,' he said last. 'We won't speak of it again.'

He'd reiterated that I was actually being offered quite a good career, if I were to take hold of the opportunity with both hands. He handed me the letter of introduction to Major von Schlieffen. His parting shot, standing on the platform as the train pulled out was, 'If you are ever being brow-beaten by a jumped-up *Unteroffizier* who's screaming in your face, don't move a muscle. Amuse yourself by imagining in him naked and covered with tar, with a bone through his nose like a *Schwarzer.*'

I was to find this easier said than done.

Chapter 17. *The Road to Glory: 1914*

I dream of a rain-washed parade ground, beneath a black double-headed eagle that flaps and tugs upon its pole, sixty cadets standing rigidly to attention. They are stiff and uncomfortable, wearing new, old-issue *Hechtgrau*: grey uniforms that prickle and scratch. In front of a saluting base a mounted cavalryman surveys them dispassionately, ramrod straight astride his *Lipizzaner*; a fine animal beautifully turned out, it wears a red shabraque beneath the tobacco-brown saddlery. Though a pale shading betrays its age it remains a magnificent parade horse. The officer wears the uniform of a *Rittmeister* (Hauptmann) of the 5th. Squadron, 2nd. Regiment *Archduke Franz-Josef der Erste*: immaculate in red breeches and dark blue tunic with gold oakleaves on the collar. Water droplets glisten upon his black-crowned helmet with its brass escutcheon. His mount stands motionless, its tail plaited for almost half its length (dressed for the rain) an equestrian statue, man and horse: a heroic study in red, white and blue. The officer has a waxed moustache, and a sharp, intelligent face, though the somewhat haughty look, affected by many of his rank. He is flanked by two mounted *Leutnants* in greatcoats on fine chestnut chargers, and behind stands an enormous *Wachtmeister*: a moustached drill *Unteroffizier*, and two other NCOs, also facially-adorned. *Korporale.* Together it is an impressive miniature Imperial tableau in the non-pareil military tradition, and quite grand enough to awe the sixty eager youngsters from the various duchies and principalities who are there assembled for the first time. Most are in uniform but some still in civilian dress, temporary armbands indicating their voluntary induction.

The statue speaks of regimental honour, of Austerlitz; of battles long ago, and the prizes of Prussian silver still displayed in the officers' mess, souvenirs from a campaign before the friendly alliance of a united German and the Austro-Hungarian Dual Monarchy. He remarks on the diverse nationalities that have proudly served in the Austrian Cavalry. In welcoming them all, he concludes by expressing the hopes that they will each and every one complete their basic training and become brave and disciplined cuirassiers (he uses the archaic term) who will bring honour to the Regiment and serve the Crown and their country with distinction, '…protecting our borders against those grave threats we may have to face in the months and years to come. Be brave, boys. Do your duty. Obey orders without question, and you will be unstoppable. The thankful cheers of the Austrian people will ring in your ears. Hungary will bless its sons, and you will win garlands and know the glory of victory. But,' he paused and looked hard at them for a moment. 'If you should fall, you will have the satisfaction of knowing you did not fail in your duty, and that you will have fallen for a grateful Fatherland.'

At this a pearly radiance suffuses officer and beast; an opportune sunbeam stabbing through the watery layer-cloud beyond the turrets and grey-tiled garrison roofs of the Helmsburg Fortress, upon which celestial cue he turns briefly to the *Wachtmeister*. The Sergeant Major, marches to the front, swagger stick tucked under his arm, and turning with astonishing agility for a creature of his size, crashes to attention. He salutes the officer, who, along with his twin lieutenants returns the salute. Subconsciously I have already identified my tormentor.

A brief, 'Carry on, *Wachtmeister*,' and the hallowed trio wheels left. With a squeeze of the heels to the flanks of their mounts they move away in formation, out of sight of we assembled cadets.

A full minute, that seems more like ten, after the mounted officers have left the parade ground the Sergeant Major stands front and centre, facing our three ranks of twenty. Motionless, apart from his eyes that seem to be everywhere at once. His corporals and the drill sergeant stand easy to his rear. The silence is palpable, broken only by the slapping lanyard and the fretful flapping of the black–on-white spread-eagle atop its white pole. A red-white-red shield flutters upon its breast, the twin gold-crowned heads gape ferociously East and West, then North and South as the wind backs, magnificent and threatening in its heraldic symbolism. Silent nimbus and trailing virga scud overhead, thunder-grey in a yellowish sky like daubs from some animated *avant garde* watercolourist, less real than that flag.

Now, the Wachtmeister from his demeanour seems to say; now you are *mine*.

~-~

Each youth, for most are not yet men, must have similar thoughts to my own in that moment. What will come next? How will I react to what is surely going to be a gruelling period of training? But then what could be finer? Mounted upon our beloved horses, proudly wearing the uniform of a Dragoon, skirmishing on the battlefield with sabre in hand, fighting alongside comrades, the dashing Uhlan and charging Hussar. To wear with pride the medals won in close combat, such things are indeed glorious to contemplate in the vigour of one's ingenuous youth. But is that really how it will go?

The Sergeant Major begins a slow patrol along the first line, pausing occasionally to stare like an unblinking bullfrog in the face of one or other cadet. Each maintains the regulation middle-distance gaze in response, unflinching when the Sergeant Major halts. He reaches the end of the line, and begins his walk, slowly reviewing the assembly.

'My name,' he hoarsely bellows, 'Is Sergeant Major Wöbbe. And *that*,' he stops and indicates the direction in which the Rittmeister has vacated the parade ground. 'Was an *officer.*' The voice strophes like some harsh Greek chorus around the grey amphitheatre.

He pauses. The small eyes flash right and left, perhaps to ascertain if any of the cadets would reveal, by a stifled snigger, the merest flicker of a smile or other signal that they think that this is the prelude to a cosy, soldierly homile, a humorous military anecdote, intended to highlight the differences between the common soldier and the officer class. *Between you and me, boys*, between *us* and *them*, in confidence. Between what each of those sixty cadets aspires to be; what that man would never be *for all your undoubted service, Herr Wachtmeister Wöbbe*. Weighing as much as a small horse, Wöbbe's uniform contains enough material for three men.

'You will have been informed during your induction, even before you was issued with kit, but it is my duty to remind you again, that in accordance with military discipline, courtesy, and Army Regulations, you will address all officers as 'Sir', and only when spoken to, and you will salute them smartly and immediately, standing to attention, or if marching, by turning your head to face them whilst saluting, when you are in uniform. Whether you are off duty or not. *They* do not salute you first. You will address me at all times as *Sergeant Major*, not 'sir', and you will salute me as laid down in regulations applicable to the highest NCO rank. You will address *Unteroffiziere* and *Korporale* as such, but you do *not* salute junior NCOs or other ranks. For your purposes *that* is the difference between officers and NCOs, but you will stand smartly to attention when addressed by any one of them at all times. Is that clear?'

'Yes, Sergeant Major,' we chorus.

'So my fine, young *gentlemen*,' Wöbbe continues, sardonically. 'Some of you, I'm sure, already *think* you can ride. Perhaps you are drovers. Or huntsmen. Perhaps you can, perhaps you cannot. We will see. But whatever you may *think* you can do, it don't matter a Jew's arse to me. I do not give a tinker's cuss! I'll will judge on what I see.'

Hardly *High German*, though my Colonial ear is not tutored enough to place the accent. No doubt the grammatical lapses and deliberate coarsening of the tongue is to accustom we fresh-faced young boys to the 'roughening up' to come.

'Because we *will* train you the *Army* way,' continues Wöbbe. 'The *Cavalry* way.'

I try to imagine the horse, a Percheron perhaps, that will bear the Wachtmeister, but fail.

'And, apart from horseshit shovelling duty,' Wöbbe's voice is reaching a higher pitch. 'Before you even gets *near* the other end of one of His Imperial Majesty's valuable animals, we will train you to *march*. Some of you will *not* make cavalry officers, but you might make the infantry – as common soldiers.'

But, he goes on to inform us, drawing a deep breath, from what he can *already* see of the miserable specimens before him, even *if* we'd had our heads chopped off and were pulled inside-out and skinned with our puny arms and legs tied together, he doubts if any of our sorry hides would be much *crappin'use*. Not even, he continues, as a nosebag for an incontinent drey horse. His voice has been rising steadily in crescendo. He is either reverting to type or deliberately establishing a brutal and profane exterior to instill fearful respect. Probably both, I conclude.

Wöbbe pauses briefly, perhaps for applause, and asks quietly, one eyebrow raised if anything he'd said appeared to us as funny. This is when he is at his most dangerous, as we would discover. 'Did my ears deceive me? *Was* there a titter of merriment?' It is a burlesque performance that both repels and enthrals, but I am rather too bemused by the verbalised cabaret of bawdy imagery to reveal a glimmer of outward amusement.

Wöbbe sweeps down the line and pushes his bulk through to the second rank, facing the cadet on my left. 'Do you think what I said was funny?' Wöbbe asked.

'No, Sergeant Major!' comes the reply, the young man staring straight ahead.

'What's your name, cadet?'

'Kessler, Sarn't Major.'

'Are you absolutely sure you don't find me funny? Because I *can* be funny. Very funny as you may discover."

'Absolutely sure, Sarn't Major.'

'Well you can be *absolutely* sure, *Acting Offizierskadett* Kessler, that I have lots of amusing tricks up my sleeve.'

There is hardly room for the Wachtmeister's *arm* up that sleeve.

Close up, in the corner of my eye I can briefly examine the *Wachtmeister*. He is easily the ugliest man I have seen in all my seventeen and a-half years, even including some of the Russian lepers who worked on the Kuznetsowa Estate. As bad as Shavrovsky, but he'd got the staggers drinking wood alcohol; asleep in the forest, he'd been mauled by an animal. Barrel-chested, with a bulging neck, Wöbbe is shaven-headed under his cap. His features appear to have been forcibly re-arranged, the snout having been inexpertly re-attached by an incompetent surgeon, possibly drunk. Else it was a comic rhinoplasty performed by someone with a malicious sense of humour.

I am sure the Sergeant Major's breath is as foul as his language, and already feel sorry for Kessler, who I had yet to meet, with Wöbbe in his face. I'm impressed that Kessler has 'slurred' his address to the Sergeant Major, as an officer might, in a familiar way, insouciant for a mere cadet. I feel sure that Wöbbe has noticed, but nevertheless, the Wachtmeister moves on.

'How about you?' I am startled, but Wöbbe is addressing someone behind me, in the third rank. Unnervingly, Wöbbe's eyes look in significantly different directions, so that it is not possible to be certain if he were addressing a cadet immediately to his front, or to one side. I recall that Gollub's eye condition had created the same unsettling impression, except that while the schoolteacher's pupils had moved incessantly, Wöbb's were unblinkingly akimbo, like a mesmerizing snake or toad. I note a bristly, but otherwise regulation moustache behind which lurk unnaturally small and dingy teeth. What remains of the upper lip is thin and may actually have been cleft from birth, or perhaps it was from the same facial injury that had so modified his nose. The defect is not successfully concealed by the bristles which reveal his hair colouring as ginger.

'Sir, Sergeant Major!'

'Yes, you, *du Bettnaesser*!' Wöbbe lunges past Kessler and prods the invisible cadet sharply with his stick. I notice that there are notches on it. 'Do you find anything funny in what I was saying, dimwit? Imparting precious observations from my bloody back-breaking eighteen years of service in this army?'

'No, Sergeant Major!'

'Name and number, *Dummkopf*?'

'Steiger, Sergeant Major, sir.' He stumbles over his service number. Steiger is evidently very nervous.

'So, we have a *Steiger* and a *Kessler*. Two good old Austro-German names. That's good. *Steiger*, eh? *Climber*. Does that make you a mountaineer, then? An *Alpini*? Maybe you should have joined the *Gebirgsjägere*. Or are you just a useless *social* climber? Eh? Hah!' Wöbbe's cloven mouth splits into a grin, not prettily, but for the first time.

Steiger makes no reply.

'So, have you any special talents, Steiger?'

'No, Sergeant Major, sir.'

'DO NOT CALL ME SIR! I AM NOT A FRIGGIN' OFFICER. IS THAT CLEAR?'

'Ye…yes, Sergeant Major.'

'So I'll ask you again. Do you have any special talents?'

Just say 'no', I think to myself.

'Well, I studied the piano, Sergeant Major.'

'Ooh! Studied it did we? Did we actually *play* it as well?'

He looks round quickly for signs of smirking. All are too canny to react.

'Yes, Sergeant Major.'

'Show me your hands.' Steiger held up his slender hands.

Wöbbe looked at them a long moment.

'Like a girl's,' was all he said.

Searching my memory for a suitably droll nickname for the *Wachtmeister*, something to reduce the ogre to a manageable size in my mind, I find myself at a temporary loss, warily imagining a more complex, dangerous animal from my natural history library. A scheming *schrecklich* creature beyond the grotesque foolery. Bullfrog seems to fit: *Bufo*. Or something equally toad-like. But as it will turn out, Wöbbe already has a name; the prissy, seemingly ineffectual epithet of *Tante*. Auntie. Hardly an appropriate nickname for a goblin who's expression now reminds me more of Gorbunov's bulldog chewing on a wasp.

'So you want to be cavalry soldiers…. well, time will tell. Time will tell.' Wöbbe seems to be chewing over something else.

He pauses for a moment. 'As you may have heard, those few of you *Scheissköpfe* without cloth ears, during his lengthy address the officer, the *Rittmeister* there, recounted the various nationalities as could once be found in the Austrian army. Swedes and Englishmen, Frenchies, Scots and Irish. We had Polacks, Russkies, Ukrainians, Croats and Serbs, and some polyferkin'-glot odds and ends of legionaries and adventurers from old European wars, or their bastards, and all stuffin' languages heard in the mess, and good luck to 'em. But it was *predominantly* German, French

240

and Hungarian. The Uhlans was mostly Poles, while the Cuirassiers was Czech and the Hussars Hungarian. All good soldiers. Was the Poles saved Vienna. I'll not hear a word said against any of 'em.'

For an instant I thought I'd heard a catch in his voice, and had the awful thought that he might suddenly weep, or break into a sentimental song as part of his charade. Wöbbe had seemed for a moment genuinely moved by the great deeds of the historical battles he was recalling.

'But…. them's time's past,' he says, brisk and businesslike. 'This is the new Austro-Hungarian army, and in this camp it is mostly *German* not Hungarian you will hear. And this, I repeat, is the language we will use in training, and, god forbid, with you bloody lot, in combat, it will prevent serious cock-ups and misunderstandings. Is that clear?'

'Yes, Sergeant Major.' Sixty voices in unison.

'Speak up. I said is that clear?'

'YES , SERGEANT MAJOR.' Louder.

'Yes *what, ihr blöden Hurenböcke?*'

'Yes it is *CLEAR*, Sergeant Major!'

And so Wöbbe proceeds around the intake, stopping here and there to demand a name and sometimes ridicule it, when he could think of a way to do so profanely and to best theatrical effect. Until he comes again to myself in the second rank.

'And your name, *if you please?*' Wöbbe is *purulating* sarcasm now. Having nearly reduced some of the boys to tears, he is on top form.

'Dragunavicius, Sergeant Major.' I now have Wöbbe directly in front of me, and although Regulations forbid that I may look into the eye of a superior while at attention, my earlier peripheral impression of Wöbbe has altered to the point that I now believe that he must indeed be *the* ugliest man in the *whole Austrian Army*.

'Dragoo-*what?*'

'*DRAGUN-A-VICIUS*, Sergeant…Major.' I feel myself becoming a little riled but remember Graf Kristian's words, knowing full well the game this odious creature is playing. Seeing who'd rise to the bait. Looking for any excuse to pounce upon and savage his first victim. Who'd be the first to invite the punishment *'pour encourager les autres'*, as some French sage may have said in my dimly remembered history lessons. Although the pause between *Sergeant* and *Major* was not really intended as a *controlled* slight, it had been just enough to be noticeable. Perhaps not enough to invoke a charge of insolence, for what even as cadets we guessed would prove a serious breach of parade ground etiquette. Wöbbe gave me the long look anyway.

On the short march to the barrack the previous day my escort had gratuitously filled me in on the matter of Major von Schlieffen. Due to the emergency he'd been called to join the Austrian General Staff and was not expected to return, in his humble opinion as a mere Gefreiter. I was to learn in time that Gefreitere and Korporale, as a breed, generally knew more about what was going on at all levels than some of the officers. His parting shot was that Wöbbe and Schlieffen had been about to clash over some of Wöbbe's training methods, which he, the Lance-Corporal said were there to instill iron discipline, a matter that I, Dragunavicius, would soon discover for myself. He said that Wöbbe hated Jews and 'colonials' equally. By the latter he meant Lithuanians in particular. Von Schlieffen, he said with a sly grin, had an estate in Lithuania.

'Dragooooon-avicius… So. You're already a dragoon, eh? Are you?'

'No, Sergeant Major.'

'What? Not a *Dragoner*, with a long-winded pissy name like that? Maybe you're a Frenchie. Eh? Sounds like it might be French. A *Froggie* Dragoon? One of Bonaparte's bastard grandchildren? Speak *French* do we?'

'Yes, Sergeant Major. I'm *not* French, but I do speak French.'

'Ooooh!' Wöbbe pouted mincingly and smacked his lips suggestively, hand on hip. 'So we *speak* French but we're *not* French. How's that then, *du kleiner Scheißer*? You some kind of poxy *interllectual*?' The last word is a snarl drawn out of a sneer. This mad burlesque over-acting is a fascinating display of character repertoire, sliding from *camp* to sinister in a discordant *portamento* made all the more bizarre from his appearance.

I try to ignore the proximity of Wöbbe's puckered lips, and his breath.

'No, Sergeant Major. It was just in common use at home, and at friends'….' But I've said too much and have regrettably provided

242

further ammunition for this bully.

'Oh, *common* use. Bit *above* the common, was we? So what did you use for *un*-common then, may I ask?' He's actually wagging his bottom as he asks this.

'German.'

'Yes, and?'

'Lithuanian, some Latvian and Russian.'

'So that's three more languages. Anything else.'

'English, Sergeant Major.'

'No!' Wöbbe exclaims as though impressed. 'That is, let me see.... ' He pretends to count on the fingers of his ham-like hands. '*Six* languages. Any more while we're at it?'

'No Sergeant Major.' I'm sweating with embarrassment in front of the others, hoping uncharitably, that this will end soon and Wöbbe would pick on another victim.

'So you speak six languages and you're not an intellectual!'

'I've never considered myself an intellectual, Sergeant Major.'

'Well you sound like a poxy intellectual to me, Aristotle. And one thing we don't need in this army is intellectuals. We need men with balls who can fight, not limp-wristed drawing room fops who can worm their way out of trouble with the enemy. Or go over to the other side, either. Like a turncoat. You a *turncoat* Dragoooonavicius?'

'No, Sergeant Major.' Without a clear idea of what a turncoat actually was.

'Seems to me like you speak enough languages to surrender to any bastard outfit we might find ourselves fighting!'

That seemed like a comment that did not require a reply, but I couldn't help responding. 'I'm sure that the Sergeant Major is correct.' Which drew a glare from Wöbbe that was both feral and porcine. I'd seen that same red-eyed piggy-look before, when *Old Kaiser* had charged me.

'So. You're not a turncoat, but what *are* you, Dragunavicius?'

'I'm, I *was* a student and part-time mechanic, Sergeant Major.'

'Oh, my favourite answer. A fookin' student. Of *what*, may I ask?'

'Well, I'd hoped to study mechanical engineering, Sergeant Major.'

'Hoped to? What does that mean?'

'Circumstances meant that I had to cut short my studies, and seek my career elsewhere, Sergeant Major.'

'Oh, yes. What circumstances? Got tired of sleeping with your sister and got some upper class whore up the duff, did we, eh? A *Schlappschwanz* like you?' Wöbbe was jeering again.

These questions were getting too close to home. Wöbbe seemed to be driving towards the truth of my situation in a way that was quite uncanny. Before long Wöbbe would be squeezing out all my intimate secrets, forcing me to admit to all and sundry how my status had decreed me forever unworthy in a world where alliances between sprawling Russo-German Estates over-ruled affairs of the heart.

How she'd been dispatched in one direction and I forced in the other, worlds and nations apart. How the Graf had arranged for my new career - an offer I could not under the circumstances refuse. An offer for which I should be thankful, leading to this chance in life as an officer in a good regiment. It was an opening to a career which had a deep appeal, and for which any other young man in my circumstances might have sold his soul, not to mention saving me from arrest for suspected murder back in Lithuania. But at this moment all that could be foreseen was the prospect of a brutal period of training at various levels, to be followed sooner, rather than later, especially in light of recent events at Sarajevo, by the reality of a European war.

Telegraphed news of the assassination of the Archduke Franz Ferdinand, heir to the Habsburg throne, and his wife, Duchess Sophie, had more or less coincided with my beginning the rail journey from Vilnius where I'd spent the previous night. Many of the passengers boarding the train at Warsaw were full of speculation and rumour about the event, and I'd tried to follow several conversations at once. I failed to get a newspaper on the platform at Czestochowa, but when I'd changed trains that evening in Breslau, I'd bought a hot, meat-filled potato, bread and cheese, and managed to buy a Silesian newspaper, the late edition of which had been selling fast, which set out the bare facts as known. Comfortably seated against the stiff cushions of the crowded railcar, I'd pored over the story in the dim carriage lighting as the night train pulled out, bound for Südetenland, and on through the mountains to Prague.

In the capital city of the Austrian province of Bosnia-Herzegovina, a grenade had been thrown at the open royal car as it passed through the Apple Quay, injuring several of the escort and about twenty of the onlookers. The Duchess had also been grazed by a splinter. The Archduke had insisted the car should stop so that he could personally see what had happened to the injured. He'd then ordered the car to proceed to the military hospital to visit one of the injured officers who'd already been taken there. It was then, as the car stopped to change direction from its intended route that a gunman - 'a boy assassin' the reporter had stated - had stepped from the crowd and shot the Royal Couple. Although they

244

didn't die immediately they were confirmed dead on arrival at the hospital. It was the occasion of their fourteenth wedding anniversary. Everyone was in a state of shock. The editorial speculated on what might happen next.

I stared out into the blackness but saw only my own tow-headed and furrowed reflection in the carriage window and those of the other passengers, many dozing in the congenial warmth, one pretty young mother talking quietly to her sleepy child and stroking her hair, soft-lit, like a picture in a book at home of a painting by Rembrandt. I re-read the article and several other contributory accounts as the train passed noisily through a tunnel, steam, and sooty particles swirling in through a slightly open window, until we emerged into the moonlight. Here, rising ground was sharp and rugged against the moonlit cloud, and the clacking of the wheels step-changed to a more sedate tempo as the train embarked upon the long incline through the mountain pass. Lulled by the motion and tired from the long journey so far, though worried and excited at the same time, I was soon rocked into a welcome sleep. Those last words of the editorial had been full of the talk of a war with the Serbs.

On the parade ground I fix my eyes on the horizon, the turreted garrison wall and the twin-headed eagles atop the spires.

'No, Sergeant Major. I just flunked the examination and couldn't afford another term, so I made a practical decision that a military career would be exciting and more to my taste.'

Suddenly it seemed the rain was getting heavier.

~-~

According to Peter's notes I must break from Rolf's own written account to add this codicil to that first parade. This work in truth comprises a world-wide jigsaw puzzle and these were times when much written evidence was destroyed. So perhaps it was from some later research of Neumann's, via contact with or a document from an alleged survivor of those years. Perhaps it was just an author's licence taken from Rolf's own imaginings, as if he'd been there, in that room.......

~-~

Imagine, if you will, Natasha, *ein Turmzimmer.* A Tower Room, overlooking the parade ground. Stripped of his wet tunic and smoking a *Salmon and Gluckstein* English cigar, Rittmeister Paul-Anton von Kirchstein is staring ruminatively out at the un-seasonal summer weather. Lieutenant Saliger moves to join him with a decanter. 'Sherry, Paul?'

Formalities are dropped off-duty.

'Thank you, Franz. Is the Wöbbe sizing up his first victims for the next six weeks d'you think?'

'*Tante* Wöbbe. Why *does* the Old Man put up with him, Paul?'

'We all know why. He gets results. He's hard on them, but there's no finer troop of *Chevaulegers* and Dragoons in the Austro-Hungarian garrison than emerges from this training establishment.'

'Indeed,' Lt. Wierzejski interjects from the couch where he sprawls with a cigarette and a day-old newspaper. 'But he isn't involved in that. He simply weeds out the unlikely ones during basic training. Same for any infantryman. He ensures that the fittest get through, or so one supposes. But he can be a harsh taskmaster. Breaks 'em down to build em up', moulds them into his own unspeakable image, or so the theory goes. Von Schlieffen would have none of it though. Pity he was posted to *Generalstab.*'

He tosses the paper aside, stands up, stretching his limbs.

The recent newspaper accounts following the atrocity at Sarajevo had created a sense of shock, followed by mounting anger. With Austria in full State mourning, intemperate language in diplomatic circles reported in the press had boiled over in the seething cauldron of public debate as new and ever more damning evidence of plots and conspiracies, sanctioned and encouraged by Austria's volatile neighbour surfaced from the broth. The pathetic figure of Gavrilo Princip, a Bosnian insurrectionist, thought to be a member of a Serbian secret society, had been arrested at the scene. Interrogation revealed that an underlying motive for the attack seemed to be Serb anger at political concessions that the Archduke Ferdinand was prepared to grant to the South-Slav minority resident within Austro-Hungary. Serbian extremists felt that this would undermine their demands for an *independent* South Slav state, so weakening their position as the leaders of Slav discontent. Since the fatal day, just a week before, Serbian press and reported public statements barely concealed the glee felt in that country at the death of two members of the detested Habsburg Monarchy. Austrian reprisals were to be expected. Indeed Austro-Hungary could hardly fail to act in the face of such provocation.

It was becoming apparent to many that the revolver fired by this mere boy might be the spark that would ignite a war between Austria and Serbia, between whom relations were already very strained. Germany would unquestionably come to the aid of the Dual Monarchy, and Russia would be bound to support Serbia for a range of military and political

246

reasons, underpinned by the two countries shared Slavonic heritage of language and religion. Meanwhile it was increasingly evident from the flurry of activity and from military signals that a rapid execution by the Chiefs of Staff of the great mobilization plan had been going on for the past week. The drive to war seemed inexorable and the outlook for Europe was grim.

Von Kirchstein pulls on his cigar. 'Karl,' he says. 'I don't have any problems with Wöbbe's methods, at least not those that I am officially made aware of. He welds the boys into a team, and if they suffer a few bruises - well, what doesn't kill them makes them stronger, as the saying goes. But if I have any complaints about 'the other stuff', I'll be down on him like a thunderbolt. That's a promise.'

'That's the trouble, Paul. Everyone closes ranks, and who wants that sort of scandal? I remember a similar thing in my uncle's regiment. It would be bound to leak out and the good name…. well, we'd never live it down.'

'Nevertheless. If you do hear anything, be sure to let me know.'

Kirchstein looks again through the panes at the glistening parade square, the sixty still figures blurring in the rain, the figure of Wöbbe standing close to one or other cadet, while his NCOs watch from the saluting podium, bored and wet under the flag.

~-~

Although ignorant of the full extent of the emergency, like other young acting subalterns I considered the prospect of going to war on horseback with mixed feelings. We all knew that the road to glory might also be the road to death. In my case home, friends and family were likely to be within the enemy camp, or at least beyond any conceivable front line. My best friend was already serving in Petersburg. Geographically, due to the Graf's influence with the *Soldatenbund*, that old Masonic cadre of former Prussian offers, with its strong influence networked throughout Germany and the Austro-Hungarian Empire, this cadetship, secured at the behest of *Kristian Graf von Strelitz*, landowner, mentor, and friend of the family, has placed me firmly and irrefutably, on the 'wrong side'.

Wöbbe, it turns out, is as vicious a sadist as it would be my misfortune to meet. That first day we were made to run with full packs, an hour in the rain. Many cadets collapsed but were hauled roughly to their feet and pushed on with oaths and dire threats of punishment. When everyone was moving at a crawl we were assembled again in ranks.

'As I thought,' he roared. '*Schlappschwänze*, all of you! What are you?'
'Flat dicks, Sergeant Major!' we replied in unison.

He strutted up and down our lines. We stood straight, trying to adopt a proud military bearing despite being soaked through and exhausted, the packs like ton weights cutting into our shoulders, our muscles aching, knees flaming with pain and ready to buckle. My feet felt as though they were bleeding in my new boots.

'Parade!' Wöbbe's voice rasped out. 'Dis-*miss*!'

Thankfully we began to break ranks when he suddenly shouted again.

'Jewish intellectual-linguists and pianists, *AS YOU WERE!*'

I tried to pretend this didn't mean me, but in an instant Wöbbe's face was in mine, snarling and swearing. 'Stand still when you're ordered, you little *Schwein*. Face front, and you too, Steiger!'

For a further hour we dragged ourselves around the parade square in a state of collapse, rifles held at the 'present' so that our arms felt like lead. We endured press-ups with full packs, barely able to lift our chests from the ground and when we failed Wöbbe's boot would squash down hard into our backs or press into our necks while a stream of invective flowed over us. Behind the bronze equestrian statue of a hero of Austerlitz we 'milksops' were told to lie face down while he climbed upon the plinth. Conveniently hidden from any windows or embrasures in the garrison walls, he proclaimed, 'The Old Man may think he is God and the Rittmeister may believe that he is His representative on earth, but on this camp, believe it, there is no God but me.' A stream of holy urine trickles down, staining the puddles in which we lie.

Towering above our miserable bodies a glistening bare-headed cuirassier stares fixedly at the sky. Heroic, bigger than life and implacable in the rain, he grips the bridle of his tired mount, a defiant sabre in his right hand. His dying comrade hangs vertiginously from the saddle and overall an androgynous spread-winged angel lays its comforting hand upon his shoulder, pointing heavenwards in a gesture of hope; triumph over the grave that waits. This overblown tableau, engraved *Austerlitz, Never Forget,* is set upon a stone battlefield strewn with the weapons of the victorious French and Prussian armies. Austria, glorious in defeat. Grasping a bronze leg, Wöbbe empties his bladder and like others before has kindled an enduring fire within me, humiliation that will burn in fury

248

against ignorance, injustice and brute power and never be extinguished.

Steiger is not moving but I raise my head to look Wöbbe in the face. I see a dark dripping silhouette against the clouds that huddle over the walls of Angerfurt, his bulk hanging from the statue to heroism in defeat like some brute ape. Angel's wings sprout incongruously from his shoulders, like an angel from Hell as he glares at me, buttoning his fly.

'I will break you, boy,' he grates, 'As you've never been broken before.'

There is deep menace in his voice and a wolf in his eyes.

'Now, you filthy pigdogs, get off to your billet and clean yourselves up. On the double!'

He has ignited a hatred in me that cannot be assuaged but I hold my tongue and remember the Graf's warning to keep my temper in check.

Later in the barrack there are hints of ordeals and brutal initiations, worrying whispers of past suicides.

Chapter 18. *The Linden House*

Yesterday. Already it seemed an age ago, the Graf had given me a long look, and then leaned forward in his chair. 'Rolf. I am sorry. It is *really* bad.' His face seemed to sag, and there was deep sorrow and honest suffering in the blue eyes.

'How bad?' I was ice but my heart beat like a drum.

'The worst I'm afraid. Both dead. My friend Augusts, and Hannah too.'

'How?' I was under control.

'Augusts… your father…. He volunteered first for the Tsar's army medical corps, and then, after the disbandment, for the Provisional Government. Later he continued to work after he'd been officially dismissed by the Red Guards for having been a Tsarist officer - even though he was 'medical'. The White forces then took over the hospital, but not before the Reds had looted everything and smashed what they couldn't carry. The Whites had their own wounded to be attended to, and they weeded out any who were deemed of the Left. Many on arrival had tried to destroy their uniforms. Care, or lack of it, was prioritised by allegiance displayed to the controlling political doctrine. There was so much suffering, typhus, dysentery and Spanish Fever; the 'flu hit everyone pretty hard at that time. Wounded everywhere, numbers increasing. Augusts was exhausted, sick and operating the clock round……'

He looked at me with sudden fury.

'Neither Augusts nor Hannah fully recovered after receiving that telegram in 1914. Your mother was mad with grief. She felt she'd not only lost a son but something vital in the man she'd married too.'

He stared at me. 'How did this happen? How did it happen that you were reported killed? *Accidentally*, in basic training?' He was angry and frustrated. 'Tell me it was some dreadful clerical error. You were alive, why didn't you write to correct this terrible mistake? You could have done so via the International Red Cross. Can you *imagine* how much suffering this has caused? For everyone? Not enough they'd lost two other sons to diphtheria!'

I could not take in what he's said. 'Two other sons… I don't understand.'

~-~

Was it only yesterday?

Yesterday at dawn I lay in darkness. I lay quite still, pain coursing through my left shin to the knee where the steel jaws had snapped shut. I'd let out an oath and had fallen forward into the long grass where, teeth clenched, jaw muscles tight, I'd eased into a sitting position, sucking air to stifle the involuntary groan I would have uttered. I listened for any sound that might indicate that I'd been detected while I swore again and again in my mind at this new predicament. I fought panic as first I tried to prise apart with my bare fingers the powerful spring trap that had been buried in the grass. How ironic, at this outpost of childhood sanctuary and fond memory, to which I'd returned numberless times in my mind, that I should be betrayed by the click and snap of this engine of torture.

I felt a warm wetness gathering at my ankle. I'd seen how a trapped wolf would gnaw off its paw and limp away to die. If not bleeding to death it would probably be turned on by the pack, exiled or killed as a liability.

A grim thought occurred. I had the Mauser. If I couldn't use it to prise open the jaws I could always shoot myself. If the enemy came I'd use the last round that way. I expected no quarter.

Swallowing the pain, I examined the trap in the semi-dark with my fingers. The teeth were embedded in the soft leather of the high boot. I hadn't stepped in the exact middle of the spring plate and some of the teeth at one end did not meet, held apart by my shinbone and the muscle, into which other teeth were firmly fastened. They were like shark's teeth, sharp, curving. I could get the pistol barrel between them at this point, but I had nowhere enough leverage to budge those evil jaws. Not one millimetre. I was like a diver held by a giant clam.

Breathing heavily I tried over and again at different angles to lever the barrel between the teeth, but without success. I looked at the dark silhouette of the house. No illumination there. No hint of any habitation. Either the family had fled the fighting or they'd succumbed to it. They might have found sanctuary elsewhere, been arrested, or for all I knew were buried somewhere nearby. And my bones might join theirs in due course unless someone intervened. But I'd already considered all these possibilities en route, so there was little point in further speculation. I re-holstered my pistol and crawled forward a little way to determine if I could drag the trap with me – usually they were chained and pinioned.

I'd made some painful progress with the teeth grating against bone when the chain suddenly tugged and a nauseating pain flamed through my leg and into my back, pulling at the tendons.

For all that I knew enemy troops might be billeted at the house now. I'd lost track of the number of military transgressions I'd committed in the last few days, some punishable by firing squad after the most summary court martial, the sentence for desertion at least. But that worry had been replaced by pressing exigencies. I felt I might easily die of thirst or exposure if I couldn't move overnight. Meanwhile dawn was not far away, the greyness lightening by degrees bringing the façade of *Liepus Namas* into focus. I hardly recognized the long drive, which a few years before had been fringed with beautiful linden trees. Now many were gone, felled. For a moment I thought that I must have made a mistake in my navigation, that this wasn't the Kuznetsowa Estate at all, but the site of some other benighted mansion. In the dawn it still looked as it always had, though there was some damage to the render that looked like bullet scars. Some of the windows were boarded up. It was going to be another grey, overcast day.

I felt for the chain and crawled painfully back to its anchorage. As far as I could see in the dim light the chain was linked via a swivel fitting to an iron stake, hammered well in. I tried to move it but soon lost any hope that I would be able to withdraw the stake by hand. However, the swivel fitting had a threaded yoke, and to my relief I found I could unscrew it.

I began an agonized crawl on hands and knees towards the Big House, which is what we'd always called it as children, dragging the heavy man trap behind me. The action was excruciating, especially when the trap fouled on something and dragged sharply on the trapped limb, but I felt sure that if I were to gain entry to the house or the outbuildings to the rear that I'd find something long enough to use as a lever. I rested a moment. Here, I suddenly recalled, that as a child I'd fallen, riding my bicycle, racing with Marik along the sunlit gravel drive, and had gone running tearfully to Nina who'd bathed my cut knees and grazed forearm.

By the time I'd reached the portals and painfully scraped my way up the steps to the black oaken doors the eastern skies had cleared a little and the sun was well up. I was sweating with the exertion and shaking with the effort. Unsurprisingly the doors were locked and probably barred on the inside. I thought about shouting a 'hallo', but I was at an extreme disadvantage and could hardly depend on the mercy of whomsoever might be on the other side.

I began to make my way as quietly as possible around the outside of the house to the rear courtyard where easier access might be found. Progress was slow and getting slower. The pain was raging in my leg although the foot was numb. I tried standing on the basis that if I couldn't feel pain in my foot maybe I could walk, and managed three paces before I fell, the experiment being accompanied by searing pain in my calf and waves of nausea. I'd had no sense of where my foot was relative to the ground. Back on my hands and knees the trap and its chain clattered and jingled as I crawled along the gravel while the stones cut my palms, so I stopped to wind the chain around the injured leg intending to use the free end of the chain to pull that leg as I moved. This slightly relieved the exquisite stabbing in my tendons and protesting leg muscles, but it took half an hour's clumsy effort, moving like an injured frog before I reached the back of the house through the formal flower beds of what had since become an extended vegetable garden.

I paused there to regain my strength and all at once I recalled another incident not far from here, from my childhood. The sinister arm protruding through the trees towards the unprotected back of little Katya, with the innocent sleeping form of baby Graczyna alongside her. My attempt to raise the alarm curtailed through sudden illness from exposure to *Aconitum napellus*, the Issyk-Kul plant whose venom is deadly, its leaves fatal to young animals and whose heavy fragrance causes nausea, as I can confirm. Later I'd found time to research the species in Navarov's work on the subject of the flora of Turkestan from my father's extensive botanical library.

I remember that suspicion had fallen on old *Cobweb*. It was assumed that he had been skulking in the trees and had committed the assault and so had been driven, wailing and protesting from his island sanctuary, despite my own loud protestations that I'd been unable to identify an attacker. The lock cut from sleeping Graczyna's head had proved that such an assault *had* been made against a child, and it was known that the mad old hermit plaited horse and human hair and that of other animals, working it into *veryovkas*: rope belts, charms and bangles with infinite patience given the limited dexterity left to him.

It fed right into the old Lithuanian myth, Natasha, about an evil spirit called Baubas. A creature with long arms and thin claw-like hands with red eyes that tears hair from human heads. This is the Baltic equivalent of the bogey man and Old Cobweb's character was stretched to fit the profile, despite his digital deficit.

The circumstantial evidence had been weak, but no one was

prepared to take any chances with someone who might molest a child, the Graf's youngest at that.

The iron gates to the carriageway arch were locked shut, but the stables had been burned and one of the rear stable walls had collapsed revealing the chassis and engine of a burned-out motorcar and a view of the courtyards within. A possible place of entry, but a painful climb over the rough stones lay ahead. The car itself would be my salvation. The starting handle was still in place and it seemed that it would be long enough to lever the jaws of the trap apart. Puffing with the exertion of having climbed the rubble with the iron trap weighing me down and biting deeper with every effort, I grasped the starting handle and pulled. It emitted a piercing, metallic squeal of protest as it emerged through the rusty dumb-iron fairing of what I now recognized as the once pretty Sizaire-Naudin *torpedo*.

I paused and listened. The stable door was ajar. Nothing stirred. Sitting exhaustedly on the running board I set to levering the jaws apart, working the starter dog between the teeth with the crank-handle gripped in my bloodied hands.

I'd managed to separate the teeth by just a few centimetres - when I froze. No sooner had I felt the familiar sensation of being watched than a rumbling, predatory growl broke the stillness. I slowly raised my eyes to see a white Carpathian beardog glaring at me from the cobbles only four metres distant. It was a mighty animal. With ears flattened to the lowered head, muzzle wrinkled and fangs bared in the black-gummed jaws, it was an impressive sight. But before I could fully take this in a figure had appeared holding a rifle that was pointed straight at me.

'*Shtoi!*' came the command. 'Stay still. Who are you and what do you want here?' A mixture of Russian and Lithuanian. Beyond, a thin curl of smoke was lifting from one of the tall triple-stacks of chimneys.

I'd barely recognized the old Graf. He'd lost weight and his hair was now completely grey. He looked smaller than I'd remembered and was roughly dressed. But there was almost no one I would have been happier to meet.

Keeping the handle firm in both hands so that the trap wouldn't re-close on my throbbing leg, I managed a smile, though it was probably a sorry effort, but my voice was clear enough. 'Baron von Strelitz, it's me, Rolf!' I spoke in German. 'Forgive me, sir, for not standing!'

'Rolf? Rolf who? Don't know any Rolf.' The gun remained steadily pointing at my heart. German gun. German reply.

'Rolf Dragunavicius. Doctor's boy! It was you packed me off to the military!'

'Impossible!' growled the Graf. 'The Doctor's boy is dead, four years or more. Now who are you really? I give you my word I'll shoot you if you lie to me again. I'm in no mood for more deserters, horse thieves and vagabonds. Nor murdering Red bastards either. So be warned. Tell me who you are or get out. Now, come forward slowly out of the shadows with your hands where I can see them.'

'Sir, I can't move with this bloody trap on my ankle. But it's true, Kristian! *Mano vardas Rolf Dragunavicius.* I didn't die as they said.'

The dog moved forward, sniffing the air.

'*Liutas*? Good boy. It's me. Don't you know me? *Tigras*?' The big dog raised it head quizzically, but after hearing the second name – *Tiger* – slowly, uncertainly, the tail began to wag. 'Ah *Tigras*. It's you! This pup was one of twins!' The tail wagged quicker and the dog moved forward happily, woofing a greeting.

'Papa, papa. It's true! It's Rolf! It is, it's Rolf!' Graczyna came running down the flight of steps straight towards me, throwing her arms around me in ecstasy so I nearly lost my grip on the crank.

'Graczyna. Princess. You've grown so tall!' I said, amazed at how she'd changed physically. She was thirteen I realized. Tigras woofed enthusiastically.

The Graf lowered the rifle and replaced the safety. 'Rolf?' his voice was husky, quiet. 'Is it really you?' He seemed confused and overcome and Graczyna wouldn't let go of my arm and was sobbing so much with a release of emotion that I found myself blinking away tears as well. 'Shhhhhh,' I said. 'It's all right. It's all right. I'm here now.' Although what difference that might make was anyone's guess. 'I just have to get this, this… thing off me before I pass out!'

'Gott, verheizen mir,' murmured the Graf in a daze. Why he'd asked forgiveness of the Almighty didn't cross my mind as a wave of nausea from standing swept over me.

The Graf rallied. '*Graczy*, get old Berg up and tell him to come here at once. Find Joshua. We have to get…Rolf… into the house. Then boil some water. And get Nina!' Graczyna was gone, running like a deer.

~-~

The Graf, with Berg, his bewiskered estate manager and Joshua struggled with the trap. The Graf's black servant was unchanged in my memory apart from some greying at the temples. Between them, supporting my leg and levering with the crank handle, they managed to separate the trap jaws. They helped me up the steps into the music room whose elegant French doors had been re-enforced with wooden boards and nailed diagonal planks. The room was now a wood store I noted, with logs piled along the walls, the parquet scuffed and scratched and a familiar pile of music stands jumbled into the corner with the piano. With the Graf leading, Berg and Joshua carried me through to the library, my arms about their shoulders and deposited me onto a large couch. I was beginning to feel faint again from blood loss and the lacerated boot was soaked in it. It seemed to hurt even more now that the trap was off and the blood was flowing freely. Graczyna brought hot water to clean the wounds that Nina bathed: Nina murmuring words of comfort and distress. Then Grazyna brought me sweet tea: from a dwindling supply I felt sure.

'You were unlucky, boy,' said the Graf. 'We don't have too many of those traps about the Estate. Only twelve or so, close about the house. Of course we know exactly where they are – more or less!' he said with a faint smile. No arteries punctured anyway. Just some bad bruising and deep cuts. You'll need some stitches there. It's going to hurt even more with the iodine!' he assured me comfortingly.

~-~

'I apologise for my lack of courtesy back there, sir,' I said, which was a little old fashioned of me given the circumstances. 'I was a bit familiar with your given name.' I had been helped out of my flying coat and trousers and was comfortably reclined, sipping tea with a blanket over me, and my left leg resting on a towel and raised on a pile of cushions. 'I needed to convince you of my identity before you shot me or something!' Graczyna was kneeling alongside me gripping my forearm for all she was worth, her tear-streaked face beaming upwards.

'Actually we're almost out of ammunition,' said the Graf, smiling grimly. He too was gazing at me in some bewilderment still, understandably having trouble coming to terms with my resurrection. 'We have the sweep of the drive covered with rifles in the upper windows, and mantraps in the grounds, as you know, and in the rear gardens too. But it's a bit *Beau Geste* at best. Apart from a few grenades and an ancient *Jaegerbusch* we have a *Madschlinger*, a couple of *Nagel-Moisants*, two Karabiner 98s and an accurate hunting rifle, and there's my breech-loading double-eight elephant gun on a swivel mount on the top floor for which we make up our own charges. There's a 9 mm *Steyr* and a Smith & Wesson .44 *Russian,* and that's it. So we don't have much in common for what ammunition we've been able to get.'

Arms were officially confiscated, first by the Tsarist army, convinced that the Graf was some kind of enemy alien from the Hanse littoral, despite then serving in an advisory capacity in Petersburg; his son too in service of the Tsar. Military setbacks and enemies at court along with the arrest of brother officers with German family names saw him being placed under house arrest, while at home half his workforce was conscripted. Later deserters stole what they could. The family had managed to secrete a little of what they'd owned pre-war and bartered for the weaponry later. The staff had been ingenious in hiding things when the Graf had been in Petersburg during the War. When he'd returned they were still able to find some boar and with the formal gardens turned over to vegetables neither they nor the little community at Kuznetsowa, in the region of Aleksandras Apygarda, had starved.

'The war raged through here, Russian and German troops advancing and retreating, back and fore. Villages were shelled and homes torched, but Liepus Namas survived; scarred, robbed, but intact. Early on we'd had Bolshevists haranguing the house from the grounds, shooting the place up at night and threatening the staff. Bad enough that some had already gone over to them, seduced by their false promises; peace, bread and land, but others were conscripted by force from the villages, on a 'volunteer or be summarily executed' basis. That results in a 100% effective recruitment drive. We've now dwindled to a tiny staff, working without pay. The economy is in ruins. The banks have been gutted of course. Inflation is mad, even if you can buy anything. Since the National Council convened in Vilnius, Lithuania was supposed to be independent, though linked to the Reich. What rot!'

The Graf, Lithuanian patriot, was on a crusade. I didn't realize that it was a filibuster to avoid darker matters, hiding behind a thicket of words, delaying the dragging of their corpses into the sunlight for my lamentation. He'd not been prepared for their once dead son to re-emerge, like Lazarus, to have after all miraculously survived the deaths of the grieving parents, his good true friends. So he powered on, building up a head of steam to reach the end of the line where the bodies were buried, chivvying their reluctant ghosts for a grim duty call with his back against the buffers.

'No Württemburger *Princelings.* No puppet *Mindaugas* monarchy-in-waiting. No more van den Bruch's *Second Reich* - damned *Deutsches*

Kaiserreich Holy Roman Empire for the German nation, Ducal Kingdom. No more *Prussian Way*. Not here, and never in the East. Although of German blood, Rolf, I was loyal to the Crown. Traditionally we German and Dutch estate owners always have been. But where does that leave us now, with a murdered Tsar? As for loyalty to Germany, signatory to our conditional freedom, where is the succour to our starving population?'

The Graf paused to look out of the window but his mind was turned inwards. He expelled a long breath, looked back at me suddenly as if he'd forgotten I was there.

'Germany, Germany,' he murmured with quiet wistfulness. 'So badly steered, so vain,'

She could have held the alliance with Russia despite the Franco-Russian entente, he told me, and found a solid British understanding had it not been for pride and intransigence.

'The British baulk the re-supply of German forces by diplomacy and naval blockade, so the people starve.' He was gathering way again. 'In Estonia and Latvia the German army in retreat surrendered their arms to and even joined with the demons who assail us, the bloody Bolshevists, spawn of the Tsar's stupidity. We are disarmed and at their mercy despite our much vaunted Lithuanian independence.'

I stared at him. There was a strange look in his eye, almost fearful. I had no answer to the wild rhetoric. I wanted to know the fate of my mother and father. But he steamed on.

'Now there's the Polish 'pressure cooker': the *Polska Organizacja Wojskowa*, stoked up by the French. Pilsudski's dream of a return to a unified Polish-Lithuanian state, with the Poles 'coming to our aid', pushing the Bolshevists out of Vilnius, but holding it by *force majeure*. So that dirt pile, Kaunas, remains our vermin-ridden capital by default. Stuffed with well-fed German troops while the people go hungry in the villages.'

Kovno. 'Govno' the Tsar had called it, 'crapville'. Its Commander, General Grogoriev had fled to Vilnius in 1915 when the Germans invaded and was sentenced to eight years hard labour for cowardice. His fate under the Bolsheviks was unknown but could be guessed.

'Ukraine is in uproar. Now the Freikorps and Rüdiger von der Goltz have fallen back from Riga under fire from the Royal Navy. You must know in truth their occupation cannot be adequately supported or sustained. Not with the sea blockade. I hear that Germany is still in revolt so sooner or later it'll run out of steam and supplies. They can't live off our dwindling food stocks indefinitely while our people starve.

Desperation will cause a bloody revolt. The Red Letts are as unpredictable and vicious as ever in what are now disputed lands. So where are the Allies of the Entente with their promises to intercede? Sure, the British are up in Finland and Murmansk. Ironsides' army trying its best to mop up the blood. A whole British Fleet is ranging through the Baltic from top to bottom. But we need stability here at the Baltic centre. Not in two year's time. A truly independent Lithuania. Now!'

Truly the Graf had nailed his colours to the mast, and they weren't the old colonial red, white and black, nor the Imperial Russian red, white and blue: but the red, green and gold of Lithuania.

'Well we're still fighting in Latvia.' I said. 'Most of Count Bermondt-Avalov's army is somewhere in Livonia, I think aiming for Petersburg, but he's an uncertain ally of ours and his army's undisciplined. Von der Goltz has been told to withdraw by the British and our politicians but he's staying put, trying to operate tactical control through Bermondt-Avalov. But we were being attacked by Lithuanian separatists, Red Lithuanians as well when falling back. Though some have defected, the exhausted regulars are officially retiring in alleged good order towards the Polish border where they're hoping for safe conduct through the negotiation of Count Kessler.'

Kessler, I might have added, *uncle to Ernst, my good friend and comrade*. It had been to his Uncle Harry's Berlin residence I'd hurried midst civil unrest and violent insurrection, to find him there, big as life, recovering from his recent Russian captivity and we'd both impulsively joined the Freikorps – officially the VI Reserve Armeekorps invading Latvia to reinforce the Eiserne Brigade. Uncle Harry, the *Red Count*, so named for his liberal views, would most vehemently have disapproved!

'There remains some hope of reinforcements in order to resume the advance,' I said with feigned conviction.

He looked at me pityingly.

'Advance? What with. And who's 'We' actually?'

'I regret I cannot talk about this in present company,' I said in French. 'But please, what of my parents? Marik and the two girls?'

The Graf spoke softly to Nina in Russian, and taking Graczyna's hand, she curtseyed, old style, and led a protesting Graczyna out of the room.

'*Ninotchka!*' I called out. The woman turned in the doorway. '*Little Mother*, thank you for your kindness and care. That's the second time you've bathed my wounded leg!'

Nina blushed and smiled. 'I remember. You were always getting into scrapes when you were little.'

The Graf followed behind, paused at the door and called to Berg who was patrolling the upper landing with binoculars. Berg answered with an '*Alles klar*!' The beardog lay facing the front doors. Joshua was patrolling somewhere outside. The Graf returned and closed the library door.

'Please, Rolf. This is difficult. Who is 'We'?'

'*Kampfgeschwader Sachsenburg*, originally attached to Major General von der Goltz's army and combined with the *Baltische Landeswehr*. Reinforcing Major Bischoff's *Iron Division*.'

Goltz was co-victor with General Mannerheim against the Reds in Finland. He had made little secret that he entertained wider ambitions for a German Balticum: Estonian and Latvian buffer vassal states and a pro-German government in Russia.

'That was until we were defeated by combined Estonian troops and Latvians loyal to the Ulmanis government around Cesis. It went on for four days until we were pushed back to Riga and Jelgava. Manteuffel was killed taking Riga.'

Baron Manteuffel had been commander of the *Stosstruppen* of the *Baltische Landeswehr*.

'I heard,' said the Graf. 'I knew him only slightly.'

'I was flying *schlacht*, low level strafing and bombing, attacking the part British-equipped Estonian and Livonian front lines, their rolling stock, field kitchens, their supply columns. Anything to slow them down and deny them materiel and sustenance. I am actually with a new autonomous detachment, the *Kampfgruppe Wiking*, a *Freikorps* unit operating on the right flank covering the withdrawal and keeping watch for Latvian and Russian Bolshevist raiders and we've more recently been operating further east, attacking their armoured trains using the Petersburg-Warsaw railway line.

'It's hardly a *Gruppe*, though,' I added ruefully. 'Really only a *Jasta*. A *Kampfstaffel*. I believe we are described as such to sow confusion with the enemy: that our numbers are much greater. We have a limited manifest of diverse machines, suited to a variety of roles, all of which are useful. But maintenance is a continuing problem and we've had to cannibalise some aircraft to keep the others going. The riggers and mechanics perform wonders daily.'

'So does that make you a mercenary? Or do you too believe in Greater Germany: the Freikorps as a pan-German imperialist force to regain Kurland? Trying grab the old Hanse estates for Mecklenburg?

Damn him!'

'Neither, sir. I was only a soldier, obeying orders. We've given everyone a hammering but we can't sustain it much longer. I am disenchanted with what's going on. I came to fight for a free Lithuania on my own terms, although officially with a German flying unit. But now that von der Goltz has thrown in with that Georgian, Bermondt-Avalov - who sees himself as some White Regent......anyway my aim was always to return home to find my family.' I'd left it unsaid, but we both knew that I meant Krystina. My Krysia. I had already seen the burned out ruin of *Ausautas* on the dark night of my arrival. 'Please. What of my parents?'

~-~

The Graf had then given me that long look. Krysia was safe, and so was Katya - physically, as I now knew. Graczyna was safe here with us, of course, but of Marik no news since a letter had come stating that he'd been wounded at the end of 1917.

Now I know that my parents are both dead.

And I have also learned that I'd had two brothers, dead before I was born.

Though my head is swimming I feel that I am yet to acquire the whole truth in this confessional. I am sure that he is holding something back as he sits beside me, on my level, a slighter, stooping figure in his own castle, whose ice-blue eyes, capable of cowing insubordination into wordless submission, now beseech *me* - I know not what. Perhaps *forgiveness*, and yet *for* what I scarce can guess.

For a while upon the night of the first awful day of my return I stir fitfully, frequently awakening disoriented, remembering my loss, but I eventually fall into the deep sleep of one who is mentally and physically exhausted. The grieving has been sporadic, and would be incomplete until I could lay them both to rest, together, as they had been in life, with a marker for their graves. But, all things considered in these deadly, crazy times, that is unlikely to happen, although my mother's temporary grave is now known. As for my father, his unconsecrated funeral pyre was an act of mass cremation.

~-~

'The signature on the letter you carried, a '*K*' with a flourish. It has a savage underlining, like a sword slash, perhaps. Who's signature *was* this?'

This is Hawkeye speaking again.

I know she's out there still. My heart tells me that. A fool that has always followed his heart.

~.~

K for Krystina. Warm, fiery *Krysia* who lay, ethereal, beside my freezing, bruised body in the wild dreamscape of my loneliest nights. My misery lying injured in the library struggling with the knowledge of what had happened to my parents has been leavened with the knowledge that the Graf's eldest daughter, my mercurial and not-so secret lover and the reason for my exile to a crumbling monarchy bleeding freely at its edges *before* Sarajevo… at least she is somewhere safe.

And K for her younger sister, Katya, *Katarzyna*, that other green-eyed beauty of disinterred memory, perhaps the cooler, more thoughtful, but the greater wit of those two glittering sisters, poor Kat, is now reported safe and somewhere near at hand. For sure in my confused slumber it was she who'd appeared in the darkness, bearing a candle to my bedside, or it was ghost or succubus: hair swept back, disembodied face intently staring into mine as I struggle to resurface…. she doubtless needed confirmation that the bedraggled creature on the couch really *is* that erstwhile companion I'd claimed to be – given the report of my long demise – then she was gone, leaving only an intense impression of eyes once so full of mischief and humour gleaming with a new zeal. If I had to choose a phrase describing that nascent light it might be a furious *fanaticism*, the face lit from below like a demon in a staged melodrama, one eyelid raggedly shadowed above. I hesitate to go further. Of relief, or even surprise at my latent resurrection, I recall not a trace, though in my befuddled state I suppose I would have tried to smile. It was only an impression – but then with what she'd suffered, grievously hurt in mind, witness to unspeakable cruelty and such brutal violation, who could say but what her state of mind should be?

This morning, I convince myself, would bring the light of sanity and a fond and tearful re-union with the second sister of the trio who, with the eldest sibling, guide, confidante, blood brother and comrade-in-arms, Marik, I had romped through the happy campaigns and spirited adventures of my blissful early life, perfect in retrospection, roseate in review.

Arboreal escapades, scuffed knees, riverine challenges and rope swings, leafy explorations and glades of secret trysting file past a thirteen year-old's soft-focussed gaze upon a distant wonderland of carp-filled lakes, red farms and glacially flat pastureland. Riding country non-pariel, with thunder-blue anvil-headed cumulus stacked upon horizons empyrean.

My flight of ideas takes me again through the French windows into the music room where I'd swooned from blood loss or exhaustion upon my recent arrival, half-carried by black Joseph and old Berg who is puffing under the strain and suddenly there is a vision of the two sisters straight-backed at their music lesson, russet tresses falling about their shoulders. They could be twins, though just over a year separates their births. Together they play in the theatre of my mind, in the familiarity of a music room seen now as through smoked glass where I am allowed to listen provided I sit quite still and make no sound: beady-eyed little ex-Kapellmeister, Herr Gibeon Klammersdorf and his simian white dwarf *Doppelgänger*, both glower in my direction as he begins the tutorial: one at the Steinway the other on his perch.

Here I am on sufferance, but I am enthralled by Brahms and Schubert. By the shafts of winter sunlight spinning red-gold upon the Titian heads of Krysia, and of Katya, bending to their bows.

It is Christmastide, and I know well those frozen trees, larch and linden, stark black in a grey winter grip, viewed through the French doors that in full summer stand wide, filling the room with the luxurious scents of honeysuckle and lilac, opening onto a broad patio and the informal English rose garden. A flight of wide stone steps flanked by aquiline statuary leads my eye to a tree-lined lake, one of several on the Kuznetsowa Estate. The landscape beyond rolls back in grassy meadows across the grazing backs of black cattle, to a horizon of distant woodland, soft blue in summer's haze on days that are uplifted by the joyous song of skylarks and in autumn sound to the clash of antlers and the belling of stags; a powerful muscular challenge driven from the deep chest cavity that carries for miles in the cool mornings.

Further afield families of boar range freely and are dangerous if approached. *Alas, dear Kat, as you know too well, that is not the great danger that will emerge from those woods.* But in that season which I now recall, the chill is kept at bay by iron radiators plumbed from the big, ceramic-tiled wood stove in the adjacent dining hall. For whenever I think of Lithuania now, it is winter.

~-~

Truth to tell I am feeling a little feverish and fear infection, despite Nina's solicitous ministration. Annoyingly it's the memory of the mannikin Klammersdorf that returns to upset my bittersweet reverie. My only *al fresco* recollection of Klammersdorf is when, with Vladi and some of my more feral compatriots, we had encountered him riding alone one autumn, though whether it was before or after the Christmas that I remember from the music lesson, I cannot recall. I presume it is the previous autumn, in which case I salute his Christian forbearance. Later I would be allowed to sit in on some of his tutorials which widened my knowledge on esoteric subjects and added to my ragbag of seemingly useless information.

But back then we had encountered him riding alone at the extreme edge of the Kuznetsowa Estate, and 'put his monkey up' as the saying goes. The tutor booted and fur-hatted, wrapped in an old officer's *shinal* at least two sizes too large, the little purblind gibbon's face peering inquisitively between the buttons, was mounted on a glum, hunched nag, a *Konek-Gorbunok* straight out of a Russian fairytale. Possibly in a mood of pantheistic introspection and fresh from reading his Goethe, he'd castigated our urchin peasant band at length at his waspish, mordant best, *and* in High German, for our *Unkultur* and raucous trespass of the sepulchral woods. We'd pretended not to understand and jeered him in a coarse street argot, part Yiddish, part *Ukmergic* slang Lithuanian, and waved two brace of plump pigeon in his pale face, victims of my fowling piece, then deftly evading his riding crop, we'd melted into the trees with mocking cries, including my '*Gorbatogo mogila ispravit*' (Only the grave will cure a hunchback!) learned from my Russian-speaking neighbours, an arrogant, cruel epithet, applied to horse as much as rider.

Alas poor Gibeon, for I have seen you swinging.

Chapter 19 . *Graczyna, Nina and some Baltic History*

Morning. The sound of someone chopping wood and probably Berg's heavy footfall on the stair. Doubtless he is still armed and on the *qui vive*. Graczyna knocks and enters with a fine breakfast for me. I wipe the wetness from my eyes. Dear child, she with Galina, the old cook, has made a great effort with what fare they have available, pork with wild mushrooms, a fine *Jaegerschnitzel* considering that further north people are lucky to be eating dog. Old Stenja has arrived with some special eggs from her 'secret chickens', she tells me with a giggle. Graczy is quite the same bubbly little girl I remembered, who'd chuckled with glee as her two sisters and I each took our hilarious turns to read from a first edition of *Wind in the Willows*, trying to translate it into German and Lithuanian as we read, though she is longer-limbed and skinnier and obviously still amazed, touchingly overjoyed at my re-incarnation. She has a special talent for making everyone feel good, a *Pollyanna-lich* capacity for raising spirits when she enters a room, no matter how depressed one might feel.

That same 1908 edition of Kenneth Graham's I recall now in that Whitehall interview room in 1921.

It is held aloft by a hatchet-faced young Commissar who glares fiercely to right and left as he strides slowly through our squatting ranks: a modern Inquisitor, zealously armed as though by sixteenth century papal edict. He holds it in his pale hand, and along with the mounds of other works of bourgeois Western literature that his strictures abjure, piled high for incineration, explains that such decadent poison contains much of the conditioning of class oppression which has corrupted our minds from birth. The odious amphibian of the ruling class, his rodent lackeys; he has studied the text fully and assures us that this is classic Capitalist inspired brain-washing. It promotes the heresy of the cosy family unit that supports and maintains the inevitable pyramid of injustice that extends therefrom. Presumably we should view the stoats and weasels taking Toad Hall as the revolutionary proletariat storming the Winter Palace. This I think, but I do not articulate. The Bolshevist sense of humour is slight and its punchlines are often fatal. We have learned to take their lunacy in deadly seriousness if we are to emerge as reconstructed units.

I am selected, perhaps because of my frostbitten ears - I can think of no other distinguishing mark - to put the torch to the books, a minor Alexandrian library. A crackling bonfire warms us built of ideas, of culture, and poetry. We will not be endangered by their like again, but we are glad of their heat. As we are instructed: the ancient philosophers had tried to explain the world. But the important thing is to change it.' Be grateful,' someone murmurs. 'Comrade General Tukachevsky wants to burn *all* books except the Red Army Manual!'

~-~

My memory returns to Liepus Namas where, alas, I cannot do justice to the meal. I have a sensation in my stomach which I put down to the distress I have suffered more than a physical symptom of some sort – though the nausea is real. Graczyna breaks the spell.

'Rolfie?'

'Yes, princess.'

'Was it you who stole my bear?' This she asks in coquettish innocence, with evident amusement which she barely conceals, awaiting my reply with lips pressed together, dimpling her cheeks, her eyes bright with anticipation. And I have to confess it, hand on heart that I did steal her little bear, with his humpy back and his little button earring.

Graczyna almost explodes with mirth. 'But why? Were you lonely at night?' she asks, *much* too archly for one so young.

'He was my mascot, and he reminded me of you, of *all* you girls,' I inform her gravely. 'Also he looked out for me.' Four eyes are better than two in aerial combat. Even if two of them are beads

Graczyna looks puzzled. 'What, do you mean he flew with you in your aeroplane? In the cockpit. Was he an *observer*? Is that the word?'

'No he mostly flew on my wing – tied firmly to the strut! I was the *Emil*, a mere 'chauffeur' at the beginning, with my *Franz*, that was my officer-observer, in the back directing me this way and that with firm taps on the back of my helmet. Sometimes I don't know which was more annoying, those infuriating raps or the anti-aircraft artillery. That was back in Russia. But later I flew in single-seaters, in Macedonia and later with a *Flik*, that is a *Kampfflieger Einsitzer* unit fighting the Italians. Not quite as big as a *Jagdstaffel*. He always showed me the way and looked out for me in times of danger.' Little *Störtebeker*, my *Bädekker*! My guide, a furry *St. Christopher*.

'Why did you call him *Störtebeker*? '

'It was Marik's idea remember? Perhaps you were too little. After *Klaus Störtebeker*, the *pirate*. We were going to give him a Viking funeral in a toy boat, I think. Or maybe take him as a prisoner to Hamburg – which

268

was the fate of that *real* pirate! We couldn't decide, so I came back and rescued him!'

'Do you still have him?'

'Him?' My mind is wandering a little.

'My bear. *Störtebecker.*'

Lost him. Lost somewhere…..

I remember Josef, a fine combat pilot, and a courageous and good man. My friend.

Czech-born of Hungarian parentage, not an Austrian, Graczy…a mongrel, like me.

It is May 1918. Offiziersstelvertreter Josef Kiss leading, myself and another NCO pilot in loose battle formation, we wade straight into a mixed bunch of enemy aircraft. I am flying my favourite Öffag-built Albatros D.lll series 253 and the other two are mounted on Phönix D.llAs. It is a wild melée but Josef leads brilliantly flying heroically as always. But he is still far from fully recovered; has come back to flying too soon, before his stomach wound has properly healed. He'd been hit when his guns had jammed in one-to-one combat over Pergine four months previously.

253-series Albatros D.III as flown by Steiger on the Italian Front and later in Ukraine: an excellent fighter.
(Archive Neumann)

He is shot down by an Englishman, flying a Sopwith. Killed. I see him go, but I have been fighting for my life and am unable to help him.

He was the only Austro-Hungarian non-commissioned pilot to be promoted to a commissioned rank, Leutnant in der Reserve. He'd never matriculated either.

Promoted posthumously, twenty-four hours after his death in that action.

Such a loss…His fiancée goes nearly out of her mind. Josef, a gallant comrade and so handsome, a brilliant smile – intense, but with such charm. His parents, devastated. My letter of condolence written and re-written a dozen times could not express the loss we all felt, the sadness. Hauptmann von Maier was himself deeply affected. And Julius Arigi, there were tears in his eyes too – they'd been a formidable trio. It was all too much, the war. One soul among millions and he'd himself been responsible for destroying nineteen of the enemy - more no doubt charming, brilliant young men: devastated parents and sweethearts, so wantonly wasted. For what? The re-arrangement of European borders and a sea of souls; a scarred and doubly-decimated generation. With the reverberations already loosening the fragile tectonics of imposed treaties and territorial gains.

My fellow *Flik 55j* pilot got away with his Phönix badly shot up, and my Albatros too suffered combat damage in all four wings, empennage and the fuselage just behind my seat. Graczy's little bear, wounded survivor of Albania, was also a casualty, disappearing into oblivion as the 'Vee' interplane strut was partly shot away which caused the left lower wing to twist and flutter alarmingly so that I had to throttle back to maintain control and get away as best I could. I was unscathed…. physically, at any rate.

But such a loss……

Graczyna is looking at me quizzically.

'Sadly no. I… lost him in that last fight, Graczy. On the Italian Front'

~-~

My mind reaches back to the days by the lakes, the unguarded halcyon summers of my childhood when the ever watchful Governess may have been elsewhere, perhaps reading in her garden chair taking tea among the roses, or under the linden shade with the infant Graczyna. Marik and I, best of friends – though Marik is nearly three years older and knows everything – would move on from archery, catching frogs, bicycling or sailing Marik's impressive model yachts with their two-metre white sails cut like a gull's wing. With these we competed to see how far each would voyage, with the rudders and sails set to drive on the wind, and the days it seemed were more often windy than not.

Often in summer the family would decamp for a week to the coast, the long journey to Soport or to the sunny resort at Palanga with its impressive pier. Perhaps to give my mother a much-needed rest I'd joined them there for one memorable trip where we'd stayed at a grand

270

hotel and we children had made giant sand castles, swum in the sea and explored the dunes. Made the day trip south in a horse-drawn charabanc to the Nemunas River estuary looking for deposits of washed-out amber inside the Curonian Spit where sailed strangely-shaped fishing vessels and the locals prepared the crow nets for the Autumn catch. Hiking along the Spit to Nida with its pretty blue fishermen's cottages and watching out for boar.

Kat said. 'Ugh, Rolfie. How can you eat lampreys?' after I'd teased her with a fine specimen bought at a food stall on the promenade. The trick, I told her, was to eat them before they ate you. She looked cute in her sailor hat. Krysia went hatless as was her style. Marik loped ahead restlessly, eager to regain the beach, bouncing a ball as he went.

'But they're best smoked, not stewed!' I told her.

The Graf had not travelled with us but had appeared later in the week, to the joy of everyone as he'd seemed more invigorated and less bowed down by life than in recent years. Not long afterwards he formally introduced Marik and his daughters to Elenja Roskova, a fair willowy girl with a shy smile and given to quiet moments, but whose personality shone forth when she sang, most beautifully: his future wife.

Graczyna, *Grace* was born little more than a year later, premature, like myself, I'm told: a little flax-haired angel; a joy, inextricably with sorrow conjoined. Such a happy child always, she was mothered and shamelessly indulged by Katya in particular from the very first.

As we grew Marik and I became if anything more inseparable. We would sail in Marik's two small dinghys upon the bigger lake, playing at fifteenth century Baltic pirates from our history books. Often we'd be joined by the older girls who were pirates' mates or sometimes rivals. Boy pirates versus girl pirates, the two equally inseparable sisters with their flying red hair, free *Raudongalvis* spirits, as scary and wild as we were. And there was no need to make concessions to their sex in the matter of fighting off a boarding party with wooden cutlasses. The attacking yachts swooped together like swallows, crewed by lusty lads and fierce red-haired Amazons, while perhaps a passing visitor smiled nostalgically, remembering another childhood.

Extended families, the Strelitz' relatives and wealthy friends make expeditions from the seaboard German and Dutch Hanse towns, estates and country houses and frequently arrive at Kuznetsowa in collections of various exotic motors; quite a trek for an Hispano, Darraq or de Dion. They arrive by carriage: the women elegantly outfitted by Parisian or Viennese couturiers, often via catalogue - that good old British *Frank*

Bentall's stalwart, as much by skilled dressmakers from famous fashion houses abroad, some having been invited to join their households in well-paid positions. They and their well-groomed husbands or escorts are as often collected from the railway station in the family Mercedes, and in Gavrilov's wheezing Züst taxicab - to the delight of the children due to its lusty backfiring, a propensity that Gavrilov never manages to cure despite hours spent fiddling with the timing - this with the perplexed assistance of Schneider, the Graf's chauffeur, during which technicalities a large quantity of vodka would be consumed to the disgust of Black Joshua.

The adults foregather on the patio in chairs, drinking sweet wine under garden parasols. Even the ailing Nadia, ageless invalid sister of the Graf, transplanted from the Kreuzhof, is rugged-up and wheeled out in her unvarying purple on these occasions from her room high in the west wing. She blossoms in company and I wonder why she is so often confined. Kat says she's the only one who 'stands up' to the *Grande Dame* Charlotte who demands, 'Boy, come here. Escort the Countess Nadia round the lake,' which willingly I do, relieving Fräulein Kempfner's maid of wheelchair duty.

And she is a delight, still surprisingly well-informed, discoursing on many subjects with telling anecdotes of European travels that reveal a divine sense of humour and a sharp recollection for detail and people; the stories flowing - a ceremonious uncorking of a rare vintage which I am privileged to imbibe: her personal confidante. In her youth she must have been very beautiful. She still radiates, her luminosity most evident in her eyes of piercing blue, though her candle burns lower. When we pause for her to take in a view of particular charm, her gaze turns to me. Her eyes, intelligent and zestful, shining through a bruised aura of suffering, have a soul-penetrating sympathy.   She asks me gently, to my great embarrassment, about Krysia, but does not judge. Just tells me to arm myself properly against the unfairness and injustices of the world and what joys and sorrows fate will bring.

Glamorous couples stroll in the gardens or sit at a little distance smoking cigars and talking in the shade of the black and gold gazebo, built like a miniature German bandstand. Others may sit at ease in the drawing rooms depending on the weather and the hour. Miss Claudia Hammond would be observed moving among their number with a new assurance; much more than governess or refined housekeeper, rather soul mate and in private the increasingly welcome companion of the Graf's long evenings, entertaining the guests with an easy elegance that befits her. Grown to a striking woman, her *Parisian chic* and amusing conversation at dinner make her companionship a delight and there are those among the Graf's circle who admire her openly. So deft and charming are her rebuffs of unwonted flirtation that their recipients feel that it has been an honour to be so indulged and it is but the consolation of manners that kissing her hand allows their eyes to linger upon her breasts and the perfection of her white shoulder; though some may wish to place a ring rather more than a kiss upon the slender fingers of the sparkling chatelaine. Especially old Major Slansky, widower, according to Kat.

In these summer holidays, with suitable other locals I would join the Strelitz children in team games or in good-natured wars of rough and tumble. These were often breathless, wild with much splashing on the lake shore. Once Graczyna's sacrificial bear had become the pirate *Störtebeker*, 'That Hamburg shall raise your head on a pike!' cried Marik in bloodthirsty glee, ever the good history student. But in the event neither Marik nor the young Rolf could bring himself to perform a cool decapitation, especially as at that moment Nina happened upon the lakeside path, 'dressed for a Sunday', with a big feathery hat, a knowing smile, parasol and perambulator: baby Graczyna sitting up, blue eyes wide under her sunbonnet with little Anna and Lisa trotting alongside. A Dalmation on a lead is a leftover puppy from Great Aunt Charlotte's most recent visit. So the small hump-backed bear was spared, though ritually bound instead to the mast, part-victim, part-figurehead on the little pirate ship, *Goblin*.

But later, when I found out that this hand-me-down bear had first been Krysia's I secretly unbound it and smuggled it to freedom in my knapsack. Really, the first thing I'd 'stolen'. From thence it followed me to the training camp and the cavalry regiment as a good luck mascot and finally it flew, though in bondage again, this time upon the outer interplane strut of my Hansa Brandenburg reconnaissance machine, forever my lucky charm, later transferring with me to single-seaters. And I was by no means alone among fighter pilots back then in taking to the clouds with a little furry cub of the genus *Ursus steiffi* strapped bravely to a wing strut.

'He helped me look out for Italians and Russkies.' I tell Graczyna, as I'd also calmly informed my *Staffelführer* during a morning inspection. When asked if *Klaus Störtebeker* will also look out for the British whose aerial re-inforcements are increasing through the port of Salonika and are also operating in that region of Macedonia, I'd felt my half-smile stiffening. A clear statement of 'I will remain vigilant, Herr Hauptmann,' was my offering, by way of a more formal reply.

But while grazed knees and bruises from falling out of trees were the bounteous crop each evening long ago, to be bathed and unctioned in those days of fond memory, the Great War would massively increase my chances of permanent injury and death.

~-~

'Were you with those dreadful Austrians all that time?' Graczyna rouses me from my reverie.

'Graczyna, they weren't all dreadful. Most of them were rather nice, and so young. You would have fallen in love with some of them for sure! Later I flew alongside a Prussian corps. At least the Jagdgeschwader was *created* from a Prussian regiment. But we had all sorts in there. From all over Germany. They were mostly quite nice too. Gentlemen for the most part. I wasn't the only one from Lithuania, although those others that were came from coastal *Hanse* towns or family estates. Officers to a man.'

'Weren't you an officer then?'

'No. I was an *Offizierstellvertreter*. Acting officer. I didn't get my school matriculation certificate in Lithuania before I left, so I was not really eligible for a commissioned rank in the Austrian Army, and I didn't even finish basic training for infantry or the cavalry – which was my first choice, naturally'

'Why was that?'

'Well some people didn't think that 'colonials' should be cavalrymen at all, let alone aspire to commissioned rank through effort'.

Or enlist as pilots in the LFT.

'Which people?'

Wöbbe, specifically. The name has an appropriately ugly sound.

'It's a long story. It involves one of those rather dreadful Austrians you mentioned. One who was not very nice at all, actually.'

'Do tell, Rolf!'

'I will. I'll tell you. In a little while.'

Wöbbe is closing in and I am feeling uncomfortable.

Co-incidentally my leg is throbbing and I am conscious that it is leaking again, the bandages turning dark brown. It is time for Nina.

~-~

Nina comes and with tender fingers unwraps the bandages. She still looks at me as if she can't believe I'm real. When I arrived she'd stroked my hands and my face like a fond grandmother.

Dear Nina. I remember her laughter with the maids in the kitchen in this house and the several children who helped out, when I would come running in with Marik and we'd be given cakes or a cool drink of lemon and share a joke with the girls before dashing off to play our games of war or exploration. She hasn't changed too much, though like all of us, the real game of war has left its mark. Around her almond eyes, and a tightening of the jaw.

She tells me that at the start of the hostilities, responding to the newspapers' exhortations, as in all households, the servants and the younger girls had prepared wadding and cut up sheets, which they'd rolled into bandages for collection by the Red Cross. These were requisitioned by the German forces who'd occupied the House later. But when they'd left a wider selection of medical supplies had remained, most of which were then taken to a Russian sanatorium that was in dire need – where my father had been *Oberarzt*, chief surgeon. Katya and two of her nieces along with some village orphans had carried them across the border into Latgale. She calmly informs me that her father and both uncles were killed in the war along with her five brothers with one badly wounded and crippled living with an aunt in Palanga. She has one male cousin and six female cousins left and only a few nephews and nieces. Anna and Lisa are lodged with the extended family near the coast too, where it's considered safer. Her mother died during the war, she says from a broken heart.

She is amazingly serene for one who bears such sorrow. She tells me my two dead brothers' names. Max and Witek. The Graf couldn't remember. Dead before I was born, so that I never knew. Diptheria. One of five years, the other a toddler. But why had it been kept secret? She said she didn't know. I wonder if her serenity is concealing a lie.

My knowledge of the events in the Baltic since I'd left in mid-1914, and in particular as these affected the estate and its immediate locality, increased over the next few days. With the absence of Kristian, the loyal Tsarist, in Petersberg in the role of an ex-military mittel-Balt advisor to the War Council for the region, nearly all the able-bodied young men having long gone in service to the Tsar before the occupation, it was left to the older staff and the steward to run the estate along with the stalwart Miss Hammond.

Generals Hindenburg's and Ludendorf's strategic battle plan, overcoming harsh February conditions, had the German 10th Army 'pincer claw' advance sweeping south of the Nemen to meet the 8th Army's claw advancing east from the frozen Masurian Lakes. A section of 9th Army's thrust at Bolimov, south of Warsaw, included the first gas shell attack in the history of warfare, although in the event the extreme cold mitigated the diffusion of the poison. However this feint drew Russian forces away from the German advance from the lakes, allowing the eventual encirclement of much of Russian General Sievers' 10th Army within the Augustow Forest with 110,000 prisoners taken.

Nina's was a familiar enough story. She told me that some of her family had fled the bombardment from the town of Alitus west of the Nemen River. With shrapnel bursting overhead, towns and villages on the route north and east were hurriedly evacuated with pitiful scenes as 350,000 Russian soldiers along with refugees from urban and agrarian communities trailed away with what little they could carry. Though it was frequently halted due to the conditions with up to eighteen horses struggling to drag individual artillery pieces through deep snow, there was neither mercy in the momentous German drive forward nor from the retreating Russians who burned everything as they fell back. Gun-carriages, baggage wagons and refugee's *telezhki* drawn by scrawny *panje* ponies, great creaking carts piled high with whole families, boxes, bundles, barrels and every conceivable piece of furniture and livestock jammed the roads. Hand carts, horse and plodding ox-hauled farm carts with some motor transport sandwiched-in, struggled to make headway.

Sometimes a short, lumbering stampede erupted in the congestion as stony-faced Cossacks beat their way through, torching the roadside villages to deny, they said, the Germans the privilege of looting and burning those settlements themselves. The weakest; small children and the old, frozen, exhausted and sick on their bundles, were thrust aside or crushed beneath the wagon wheels in the surge of fleeing humanity. The Russian scorched earth logic, edict of a High Command, in service to a heedless autocracy was acting in the same imperious manner that built resentment and forever broke the peasant spirit, in war as in peace. *Muzhiks*: sorely oppressed, superstitious, sentimental, the 'tamest animals upon God's earth' fleeing a pogrom of fire and steel, filing through the arbitrary killing ground they'd known as *home*. Though many may have welcomed the German presence as a release from Russian oppression, the poor whatever their ethnicity suffered when their villages were used as revetments against assault.

I picture the action. The crack of camouflaged artillery pieces and the crump of incoming shells create panic along the way, and the skies to the south glow red. Overhead the spectre of the German aeroplane, a sinister angel of death bearing aloft the terrifying technical phenomenon of the airborne machine gun, drone by in ones and twos to strafe and bomb behind the Russian lines, sometimes attacking the refugee columns in order to clog the arteries, sowing terror among the civilians and blocking the retreat. But by 1915 it had all run out of steam, and a static front line had been established between the port of Riga, still in Russian hands, running south-eastwards along the Dvina to the town of Dvinsk, close by, on the Lett border and eastwards to the Carpathians, referred to naturally as the *Hindendorf Line*. By the time *General Winter* had ordered a temporary halt a million Russian soldiers were dead and another million were prisoners.

That this had placed the estate of Kuznetsowa in German hands was evident. Though this was uncomfortably close to the Front, its spaciousness and comforts ensured that the house became the billet for several rather haughty and superior German officers and their staff some of whom, however, flirted madly with the domestics. Its relative remoteness in a landscape of lakes and wooded terrain meant that it was not a natural thoroughfare for transport though the railway line to Petersburg, or *Petrograd*, as it was by then referred to, ran a little way to the east and was a useful conduit for whomever controlled it along any given length. This was inevitably the scene of skirmishing and the sabotage of the lines by one side or the other and though heavy rail artillery threatened the security of the estate, it was thankfully spared more than token heavy mortar shells. The remaining motorcars had been requisitioned, including the little Sizaire *torpedo*, and other local tourers and military vehicles were in evidence throughout this period.

The flat landscape and grounds of the Linden House also allowed the operation of reconnaissance flights. A fuel dump was provided and Rumpler or Albatros two-seat liaison aircraft, as identified by Berg who'd peered into their cockpits at the brass identification plaques - occasionally with a third occupant squeezed into the rear gunner's cockpit, were frequent visitors, bringing a senior staff officer presumably for a two-way briefing on the general situation as the stalemate prevailed and German efforts redoubled on the Western front. Thus Liepus Namas gradually became a minor forward Army HQ run by a fastidious and correct Hauptmann Erwin Kretschmer. Indeed the occupation brought a kind of stability that some thought preferable to the military rule of the immediate pre-revolutionary period. At about that time I would temporarily have been serving on the Northern Italian Front myself, learning the hard way what furious air combats could be like compared with the then relative lack of aerial opposition we'd faced in Russia.

On such occasions when the aircraft arrived, carrying an *Oberst* at least, security demanded that the family, that is the two girls, governess and domestic staff were placed under light guard in a remote part of the house or were confined to the kitchens to help prepare meals for the staff officers. Though telephone links were re-established to Kaunas, and to military camps in the middle and western regions of the country and signals were coded, lines could be tapped and codes could be broken, so aerial messengers were regarded as safer, providing documents could be quickly destroyed in the event of a forced landing from ground fire or engine trouble. Landing in the vicinity of enemy patrols would be fatal - the crews facing possible torture and certain death. Such razzias consisted of hard riding Cossacks that penetrated the lines or outflanked the German positions if they knew the trails through the peat bogs, the great marshes and moors to the south and east that the rains had made virtually impassable, although the locals had an uncanny sense of direction and knowledge of the serpentine pathways. It was joked that they were half-men, half-homing pigeons with magnets in their brains: but could lead cavalry patrols to their objectives, or to their doom, depending on who was paying or how much.

But after the fall of Vilnius three free-ranging *German* cavalry divisions had circumnavigated the moors and swept eastwards through villages, towns and the great estates of Belarus, though they were unable to consolidate any position long enough to create a new Eastern front. The withdrawing Russian troops fired the granaries, villages and factories in retreat, and these actions created severe hunger and deprivation for the population and a massive refugee problem by the following winter. Food supplies were by then becoming seriously depleted. The grain yield across Russia had fallen by 1916 partly due to increasing inflation, so the peasants had been hoarding food and towns that were more remote from agricultural areas were particularly suffering. Although Kuznetsowa had remained reasonably self-sustaining all but one team of plough horses had been requisitioned by the occupying Germans for military use despite the greater demand for production from the surviving estate farms. Military demands generally created great hardship and the pied lepers on the estate provided much of the manpower in sowing and harvesting, and did their best in plough-hauling at this time. But much of agrarian and semi-industrialised Lithuania remained a blackened desert.

Gradually communications began to break down and especially after the Revolution and later German withdrawal, they'd felt very isolated but still held supplies which had come in useful when returning wounded *frontoviki* had been billeted at the house. Frequently local young men had simply turned up, many with serious injuries, on their way home, their armies having either failed to look after them due to the enormous pressure on resources, or they'd simply drifted back and turned up at the welcoming portals of the Big House where they'd received warm food, meagre enough at best, but always graciously provided along with primary first aid as much as could be performed.

The loss of life had been astronomical on both sides. A half million Austrians had been slain or critically injured in one campaign in 1916 alone and tens of thousands taken prisoner and transported east, while the Russians had lost far more than that number overall, but among the wounded there were, loyal to the Tsar, those with serious injuries that needed hospital treatment and who were dispatched by military transport when this was still available, to the medical centre in Latgale. Augusts was by then senior doctor, the *Oberarzt*, and in a hospital which bulged with wounded, many of whom had other illnesses and were suffering terribly from the scarcity of medicines. This was not a Red Cross facility and there seemed to be little interaction between the military and Red Cross hospitals with regard to the supply situation.

My father had been among those who'd volunteered his services as a doctor in the Tsar's army and though after the Treaty of Brest-Litovsk had been officially discharged from his post by the Red Guards, he'd continued to work for the Provisional Government, treating all who came, whatever their nationalities. Many of the medical staff and orderlies were German, Austrian or Czech prisoners who'd given their parole and were able workers, without whom the hospital could not have functioned, but these had understandably been eager to return home after the Treaty had been signed.

In the chaos of revolution the Graf von Strelitz made his way south and returned to his estate to receive the news that Katya had driven across the former front line through the stream of withdrawing troops and some released POWs: former enemies, filing past each other, eyes down in sullen silence for the most part, emaciated and infested with lice. She'd 'illegally' armed herself and run a night gauntlet with a cartload of much needed medical supplies which she'd acquired from the Germans after their staff had abandoned the dressing station they'd set up at the house. For some of the journey the girls were host to a handful of returning *frontoviki*; exhausted, filthy, probably *tif*-ridden Russians whom she feared might have ravished and robbed them were it not for a kindly giant who kept order and politely asked for transport north. She had herself remained at the military hospital which was in desperate need, volunteering as a nurse along with a few of her friends, who were local village girls who'd lost most of their families and were her travelling companions, defending their cargo by concealing it under a thick layer of straw on which they huddled as if they were refugees. For all of them the immediate and 'on the job' training had proved rudimentary at best.

But I must organise my thoughts for this inquiry. In truth the blow on the head I received later has caused me to lose my usually good level of concentration, and I actually did lose my memory for some while, although there were other associated reasons for that as it transpired. It seems that there is a natural protection system in the brain that switches on when the mind can take no more mental torture.

Chapter 20.
The Graf, his Daughters, their Tutor and their Nemesis

My mind returns to happier times before the War. I am sitting lost in the music lesson, when the door opens to admit the figure of von Strelitz. Tall, patrician, in his prime, followed by three dogs; two happy half-grown carpathians, *Liutus* and *Tigras*, and a lean grey wolfhound, entering into that cream rococo interior with its Wedgewood detailing, velvet drapes, a clutter of music stands and the black Steinway grand. A startled fuzzy-haired homunculus poises, hunched at the piano and a dwarf albino gibbon blinks redly from its perch. Upon a window seat, *Gogol*, Katya's amber-eyed *Russian Blue* tomcat gazes forlornly on the wintry view, which makes a change from his gazing covetously at Gagool, the African Grey in the conservatory. Gogol is a *Collector of Souls*, like his namesake, whose corpses he dutifully leaves in neat rows on the veranda, his very own personal Golgotha, which collection would not be complete without the bones of Gagool: a normal Tuesday or Thursday afternoon at *Liepus Namas*.

The Graf is enveloped in local affairs with the added worry of yet another dissolution of the State *Duma*, the debating chamber, usually in uproar – hardly a centre for thought, thus belying the very *meaning* of the word in Russian - First Minister Stolypin's forced reforms, and their impact on the private estates. There is revolutionary propaganda nailed up nightly in Kaunas and Vilnius and the threat of a general peasant uprising in Belarus. Although it's been five years, loss of national confidence following Russia's disastrous war with Japan, the Letts again churning with revolt and tales of Maximalist arson and murder in Petersburg make the blood run cold and recall the horrors of the 1905 'revolution': continuing, with seemingly endless aftershocks of executions and assassinations.

Nonetheless it is the Feast of St. Nicholas at the Big House, and the Graf is at home. He has been both distracted and enraptured by the strains of a Schubert trio floating to his study. Both girls, bows in their hands rise smiling to his paternal embrace. Even though I'd then had limited experience of the company of well-born girls, I felt that, and I know now, that it would be impossible to place these two sisters into any category. They were good natured, funny, witty, especially Kat: beautiful, fearless and I suppose unconventional Baltic 'moderns'; musical, artistic, literate and excellent horsewomen. Everybody loved them, none more than I. I am shyly aware of Krysia's developing womanhood – she is more than fourteen, a little older than myself and entering a growth spurt. Slender Kat has yet to develop in the department of her breasts.

Little Herr Klammersdorf in his frock coat and ill-fitting teeth springs like a spectacled wolf spider from the piano to the polished parquet, successfully maintaining his balance despite the club foot, bowing and almost literally genuflecting, applauding in his fingerless gloves both the divine Schubert *and* the girls, along with the Graf, and, 'Yes my lord it is *indeed* Schubert we are practicing!' He has a wary eye upon the beardog puppies that sniff about his legs, and look in mild surprise at Klammersdorf's long-limbed gibbon on its tall perch. It is tethered at its neck by a silver chain and blinks its pink eyes, grimacing nervously at the dogs while 'his excellency's' plea for *Die Forelle* is met with gusto, though its delivery proves thin from dearth of strings.

Later, Krysia laughingly explains to me that, '*Upetakis*, the poor little trout, has been hooked, over-cooked and devoured bones and all *years* ago, Rolf!' Truth to tell it *had* fallen a little from fashion by then. It had been ninety years since its shining back had surfaced midst the first ripples of the quintet's glittering Viennese success.

The door opens again and a young maid stands aside as a be-ribboned Graczyna trots in unselfconsciously, wearing white woollen stockings and a rich green velvet dress trimmed with patriotic red and yellow embroidery, clutching her little Steiff bear. She is followed by her nanny, Nina, smiling broadly. Some little girls trail behind along with Anna, Lisa and Daine, and the older girls' English governess, Miss Hammond. And who is she, this little flaxen-haired princess?

'A dancer with the Imperial Ballet, Papa!' she cries in perfect French and hugs her father's legs.

The beaming Graf scoops her up and she squeals delightedly as he boosts her ceilingwards. 'Monsieur Diaghilev will not be able to resist!'

She throws up her arms, waltzing her beloved and patriotic bear in space: he too wears the colours of national determinism, a paper tricolour scarf that Graczyna has made herself. Her fingers reach almost to the dripping crystal facets of an electric chandelier, and she stretches, throwing her head back before looking down on him, soldier, prospector, big game hunter, landowner, patriot, cosmopolitan, self-made daddy. Nina is stroking the chattering white gibbon and shushing it to soothe its fear of the puppies that have anyway lost interest. Miss Hammond is taking a keen interest in the score on the Steinway music rest but briefly catches my eye. If she is surprised to see me, standing now in the presence of the Graf, but still secreted in my corner of the music room, I cannot tell. Playfully Graczyna arranges her little *Bruin* upon her father's head as von Strelitz smiles fondly into the perfection of her china blue eyes.

'But, Rolf,' he tells me, when now, years later we are sitting in his study and he calls this moment to mind, acknowledging that I was witness to it. 'As she sings happily to me, I hear echoes of the *Shepherd on the Rock*. It is her mother, Elenja.' She is there, singing with informal precision, who seemed to sing just for *him* that first time he'd seen her. It is an impromptu virtuoso performance of popular Schubertian song in some distant turn-of-century Estonian drawing room where he'd sat spellbound, just Elenja in Kristian's eyes, alone together, oblivious to the gathering of what passed for the local aristocracy.

Kristian had dutifully escorted the *Iron Countess*, Charlotte von Rosen and her 'Lady's Companion', Frau Kempfner to the function. The elderly and outspoken aunt on his mother's side, christened 'The Snapdragon' by the children, had arrived from Vienna by train to stay for a week or two with seven in her entourage; her own maid, Fraulein Kempfner, Fraulein Kempfner's maid, a footman, two Dalmatian hounds and a small unexplained boy. She had tartly dismissed Elenja's performance in private, describing her talent as merely adequate. So Kat had said, she having later chanced to overhear the Countess speaking rather imperiously to her father. She'd said, unfairly in Kat's view, that the lightweight *soubrette* was better suited to the *musical operetta* and was anyway quite unsuitable for Kristian now that the title had been bestowed upon his noble shoulder. He might eventually be excused for abandoning Lutheranism for a Russian princess's dowry; but a slip of a *singer* – in Great 'Iron Aunt' Charlotte's eyes little better than a White Russian harlot - 'And what pray is known of her family?' - was out of the question.

Nevertheless: Love's bright star is like the sun… it burns you and it blinds. Kristian, too long the widower had lost his heart to the twenty-two year-old Elenja Katerina Alexandrova Roskova and he had turned up late at Palanga without his valet to join his children on holiday. He was smiling and fit, looking years younger than when last I'd seen him a month before. The Countess was of the opinion that he'd lost his *head* according to Katya's grapevine from the downstairs scuttlebut, but after a courtship in which he'd pursued the tempestuous *Belarussian Nachtigall* to Prague, Paris and Petersburg, from palace, theatre and salon, they had married in St. Anne's Church, Vilnius's Gothic masterpiece.

Away from the red brick branching traceries weaving organically into sharp towering spires, through a gleaming archway of cavalry sabres, they'd disentangled themselves from among the wedding guests and well-wishers, confetti, and her young *corps de ballet* mignonettes; an animated flock of bright flamingos waving their raucous farewells. From under a torrential carillon of bells he'd driven her himself in the open Sizaire-Naudin *voiturette* in an ecstasy of speed while she clung to her hat, past the cathedral and along the Arsenalo Gatve across the Green Bridge, breathless to their rented pink granite town house for their garden reception. Baroness Nadia, who had rallied for the occasion, the two girls as bridesmaids, also in pink and young Marik in his white junior Tsarist cadet uniform followed in the chauffeured 18/22 hp. Mercedes. The remainder of the happy pack rattled over the cobbles in a cloud of exhaust vapour, the horse-drawn carriages, including the one hired for the Dragunavicius family who'd travelled by rail for the celebrations, trotting well in the rear.

Thence to this windswept, far-flung eastern estate, toweringly dramatic cloudscapes, horizontal rain and the high bright sun between; to his first wife's noble Russian inheritance, where Kristian had guiltily settled to live in determinedly connubial bliss for longer than would have been expected of the most uxorious husband. Guiltily, though certainly not from his abandonment of Lutheranism for a now lapsed Orthodoxy in order then to marry the mystic Sophie.

Elenja, whom he loves in another, desperate way, stands beside him on the landing, coolly surveyed by his late bride, the stolen White Ruthenian princess whose forgiveness and blessing he would receive, for Sophie's beautiful ghost still visits him at moments and owns his heart. Her sanctified image confronts him daily at Kuznetsowa, *Katya had told me*, where too soon her twice-widowed father now and forever would raise his nightly candle in homage on the stair.

Though initial politeness scarce concealed antipathy and resentment from Krysia, the elder girl, yet only half her young stepmother's age, and from Marik, juvenile fascination towards their father's pretty new Belarussian bride, of the *troika* little Katya had accepted her warmly, indulging her father more than her sibling axis. Marik was eventually won over and in truth developed a boyish crush, becoming a little jealous of his own father, for which in Freudian moments he was ashamed. Krysia, as her father's first girl, remained a little sulky though philosophically accepted that a happier father would be a good thing. Katya however did not consciously seek to form an alliance with Elenja in order to secure an advantage and a genuine friendship had blossomed, which proved all too brief. The marriage was to last just one year. Tragically upon that Christmas she gave up her life on the birth of the child he now hugs to his chest. *'"In my hour of supreme happiness," Rolf.'* he would tell me in his cups. *'Which were her final words. Other than to name her 'Grace'. "As she will grace my life."'*

~.~

'Mama!' the thirteen year-old Katya had said matter-of-factly, indicating the heavily framed full-size portrait atop the landing in the Linden House where the wide staircase branched to left and right. 'Painted by the American artist *John Singer Sargent* at his London studio. In *Tite Street,*' she reported knowingly. 'When they were there in 1895. She'd had her wedding dress made there and Papa had commissioned this portrait in that gown as a gift, as he said, "To celebrate her eternal beauty in oils".'

It was a study in white of a striking flame-haired Russian woman and the nervous energy with which the paint had been applied was tangible. Her head set squarely on a high lace-collared *El Greco* neck, the clear green eyes that conveyed intelligence, warmth and sadness too, evoked the strong presence of the person looking at you with a soul-penetrating gaze. The sense of duty that one received from the viewing, the set of her chin and straightness of her pose, impelled the viewer to stand straighter in her presence. A window beyond her shoulder gave onto a cool swathe of green redolent of a Balt landscape with a hint of apple blossom beneath dramatic skies, gilt-mirrored above the mantle where the artist had placed her. Gold, green and red flushed there, the colours of Lithuanian independence. A Red Setter lay adoringly at her feet. Katya says that the Graf looks at the portrait every day and sometimes will not speak for a half an hour after. Evenings too. But his two eldest daughters, themselves her younger spirit, and her image too, must so comfort the Graf, I thought, my gaze drawn back to her eyes, which seemed to change their expression quite subtly as changes the light. Where the Graf in secret searches for a sign, or vain absolution by candlelight, he is scolded for his trouble in Portuguese by *Gagool,* dead Sophie's wretched grey parrot. Now both Sophie and Elenja whirl though his mind unbidden as he holds his youngest high on the eve of her fifth birthday.

A sudden calamity. From my place in the corner of the music room I see the Graf's face change colour. Abruptly he is a deathly pale and seems about to stumble. I fear that he will drop Graczyna.

He tells me much later, under those quite different circumstances to which I have referred, that his head was suddenly swimming. Fearful emotions cascade over him, and he feels as though a great wound has suddenly re-opened somewhere inside. *She had suffered a massive post-partum haemorrage, my father had told me later, for it was he who'd closed her eyes. Elenja was still sitting up in their bed in the home they'd both loved but which she had always felt she was never fully to share with Kristian and his family. Sitting and holding a sleeping daughter, oblivious of her mother's passing.*

The nausea makes him totter. Graczyna abruptly stops her chatter. His heart is racing and he feels both hot and cold at once, holding the startled child against him. His eyes dart involuntarily; an inexplicable premonition, an icy presence of evil has dragged its fingers down his spine as though the room contained some dark entity. As if the dread *Earl King* had ambushed him at a vulnerable moment, invading his unguarded subconscious.

Wer reitet so spät durch Nacht und Wind?
Siehest, Vater, du den Erlkönig nicht?

The two older girls step forward, their expressions concerned and the Nanny is at his side lifting a solemn Graczyna down. Familiar faces are crowding around, speaking, though the words are unclear. The Governess, now part matriarch and senior housekeeper takes his arm and leads him gently to a chair. He sits down heavily, trying to re-focus on the room. A maid arrives with a glass of water.

'Shall we call the doctor?' the Governess asks concernedly, but the Graf, recovering his composure shakes his head, looks for a long moment into her fathomless pale-grey eyes and says they are not to fuss. It's only that he has much on his mind. I volunteer to fetch my father, even though they could simply telephone. My presence is thus quietly acknowledged by the Graf. *Perhaps I could fetch Dr. Dragunavicius he accedes.* Maybe he needs a nerve tonic. Fathers have fears that the young cannot comprehend in their feckless immortality, he later confides to Augusts, who knows this tragic truth too well.

As I stride to the door I see that Herr Klammersdorf's mouth is fixed in a nervous smile. I get the impression that he is perhaps wishing that he could escape somewhere alone. Perhaps again to the winter woods, projecting a younger Pan-like image of himself as *Schubert's Wanderer* in some idealized version of a sylvan idyll and I feel a sudden pity for the little cripple.

I remember now his gruff kindness. He'd spoken to me about my wildfowling but was also aware that I studied birds for their own sake. He quoted Poincaré: *'The scientist does not study Nature because it is useful; he studies it because he delights in it, and he delights in it because it is beautiful. If Nature were not beautiful it would not be worth knowing, and if Nature were not worth knowing, life would not be worth living.'* He also said that truth had a simple beauty, that evolution refined to the present delivered a perfection in form and function for each species. Paraphrasing Darwin; Nature had contrived the convergence of role-specific speciological design in many specialisms, but where competition existed, species evolved to either dominate or co-exist. But no advantage was given in Nature and no niche remained unfilled. So with humankind, except we wasted resources but also enslaved the weak, like ants with greenfly larvae.

Man was also slothful, lazy and easily led. Especially in Russia. It was easy to manipulate the people, but first the manipulators had to rid themselves of intellectuals and the conservative middle class. The intellectuals couldn't organise though the bourgeoisie could be cowed. There was more conflict coming and it was only a matter of when. 'All I know is it will be dreadful, and people of sensibility and of course property would be the ones who will suffer the most. The poor and disenfranchised will think it a triumph for a while, but soon the status quo will re-emerge. 'Fair shares for all!' would prove a hollow rallying cry, I fear.'

He had his revolver he'd confided. A Russian Colt. No doubt fearful and uncertain of his future, whatever his ingratiating manner in the household of the Graf, he was generous and expansive in private, and he loaned me many books which enabled me to continue my studies and spent some of his free time helping me with mathematics, particularly algebra and trigonometry.

Yet I recall too as I led him into Nina's care, placing the revolver carefully on a polished side table....*had he fallen from his nag or just lain there upon the damp moss, to die against a tree?*.....he said he should thank me, he supposed. And looked at me with eyes that might already have been dead.

'What was it Nietzsche said? About when you stare into the *abyss*, Rolf? Eh?'

I looked back at him blankly as I took my leave.

'He said, "The *abyss* stares back!" That's what he said, Rolf. He was right.'

~-~

When the Graf had married that second time those fateful years ago *Iron Felix's* printing press had been secreted in the cellar of the baroque Bernardine Church rising directly behind St. Anne's, where the firebrand revolutionary had churned out his pamphlets and propaganda. There he had plotted Bolshevist sedition and called upon the workers to overthrow the government, destroy capitalism and surrender all to the proletariat. A fanatic who'd coldly had his own mother executed...within a few terrible years he would head the dreaded Cheka, later the NKVD. Kristian had fumed that had he known the whereabouts of that insurrectionist and his skulking rat pack he would have returned from the reception with his revolver and shot them to death in their lair.

But there had been another rodent in the wainscoting that haunted the Graf, a sly and evil menace. Kristian had not gained wealth without risking enmity, and owned to a strange feeling that this premonition involved a person he'd already met: some protean warlock who wished him ill, perhaps through proxy, steered close unseen; apparatchik and lieutenant to Dzerzhinsky and his ilk. Either way it augured woe for the House of Linden.

~-~

I remembered a case history as related by my father.

Augusts had gone to Moscow for a while, succumbing to Professor Orlinsky's, persuasiveness to examine how Eugenics fitted with the theories of Freud and Jung. The subject, Roskov, had a criminal record and a death sentence for his revolutionary activity had already been commuted. Meanwhile arrests and murders following the revolution and terror of 1905 continued, with random killings by the police matched by further atrocities in an escalation of horror throughout European Russia.

He had been released from prison on the very limited freedoms of a 'wolf's ticket': a parole for raskolnik dissidents which forbade them from specified areas or regular employment and had immediately rejoined Dzerzhinsky's coterie, styling himself, ' Wolf of Iron'. Later following a tip from a police informer he was re-arrested, tried and again placed under sentence of death; sent to the prison in Lubjanka Square, Moscow and held in solitary for stirring the inmates with revolutionary rants. His council was appealing the sentence on the grounds that he was now criminally insane.

288

Roskov's crime, with others, was that he had kidnapped the scion of a Jewish financier, a legitimately perceived target for extortion, and held him for ransom — as others robbed banks, expropriating their wealth in an anti-capitalist, political statement, so providing funds for the proletariat revolution. The son had been a star violinist with the Petersburg Conservertoire the previous year and was seen as an up-and-coming virtuoso concert performer with a promising career. He opened negotiations by posting the third finger of the boy's right hand, complete with signet ring, to the family home. There were delays in establishing a satisfactory rendezvous for handover of the substantial ransom, during which period more fingers were dispatched. Thus Roskov's passion for inflicting suffering was wrapped in a political shroud where his avowed hatred of the bourgeoisie, usury, contempt for talent, and anti-Semitism were united in a barbarous and vengeful act, following the parents' frantic ineffectual involvement of the police at a late stage, that culminated in their receipt of a bloody parcel with the remaining digits.

Orlinsky, an adherent of the relatively new science of psychiatry visited Lubjanka, lamenting on the 'barbarism' of confining someone judged clinically insane (Roskov believed himself to be a werewolf) under sentence of death when 'every means should be explored to attempt to establish the medical reasons underlying such aberrant behaviour for the benefit of humankind'. He campaigned that a study should be carried out for the furtherance of science to identify, if possible, the genetic markers (and social conditions) that created human beings capable of such monstrous acts. The paper he would write on the subject of delusional lycanthropy and the lecture tours should see his stock rise enormously in the field of neuro-science, now centred in Switzerland, whose epicentre might well move north as a result.

Roskov was granted stay of execution on medical grounds under the aegis of an enlightened judicial triumvirate, convened especially for this case. The criminal was transferred to the secure psychiatric unit at the Moscow Anthropological Institute where he settled into the regime and became a model patient, in fact a manipulative performing seal. He responded readily and willingly to the psychiatric team's interviews and tests, relating a long and inventive history of childhood abuse, wherein he and not his 'witch of a stepsister' was the victim. The clinic is overjoyed to have such a ready collaborator in every field of study, even unfashionable phrenology: eugenics, experimental drugs, who submits to humiliating photographs to bolster theories of criminal disposition from ear displacement to the skull's meridian, to electric shock therapy, with the docility of a true penitent.

~-~

On the biggest lake on the Estate was the little island upon which we, as children, had staked our claim despite its prior colonization by ducks, and for which we'd embark aboard the little Jacht *Kobold*. Before the ducks it had been a leper colony that might have added a frisson to our childhood explorations had we known, but in truth we had become used to seeing lepers and with care their deformities had become less now than in earlier times and they farmed along with the rest of the community.

Upon that island there still remained one other, encamped for years in a wooden hut away on the northern side with his chickens and a goat, living the life of a hermit, reclusive even among the once reclusive lepers. Old Cobweb, they called him and sometimes we spied vicariously on his comings and goings, but shrank from contact even though he was considered harmless at that time. Sometimes it was our Treasure Island and in a fair breeze the Kobold sped us on our way to freedom with her white sail filled, boys and girls, cousins and friends, sometimes tussling it seems in retrospect, for who'd play Vytautas the Great planting his standard to found the island redoubt and fortress of Trakai; unconscious that such seminal rehearsal in microcosm of a national independent frame of mind would find its expression in the struggle for Baltic identity, with many of those same players at stage front who would fall in the attempt. For even if as the children of German Balts or lapsed Jews, we dreamed in the deepest of secret dreams, like our fathers, of statehood in the land of our birth, we ignored at our peril that we were resented as colonising interlopers by many in or about the borders of the Grand Duchy of Courland, Latgale and Belarus.

But though these seeds may have been planted, national identity was not something openly discussed in the classroom, and for the girls the remainder of the year's grindingly instilled deportment, etiquette, history, languages and the arts by a procession of tutors engaged by Miss Hammond were sloughed off like a lizard's tail in an instant in the holiday; an ecdysis of enslavement. Girls and boys ran bare-armed and bare-legged, bronzed or freckled in the warm sunshine to the shores of the shallow lakes with their towels, armed with mock weapons, balls and rackets and picnic hamper, running their colours up the little masts, to spend all day in joyful exercise, struggling and swimming, with shrieks of innocent laughter, trying to catch carp with the dogs joyfully joining in. In those Dream Days of the Golden Age, to continue the literary catena of those other Kenneth Grahame's works we'd read in English, uncomplicated happiness, especially in our cadre of four, the children's own sense of themselves in firm friendships and in the place, was identity enough.

290

Things became more civilized for a while when the children were a little older and the tennis courts were finished. Organised tournaments and a little more decorum was in evidence. But there was a wild streak in all of them that would find its expression in boundless energetic activity whatever the season, with riding, sledging and skiing wherever they could find a slope.

The first love of one's youth leaves a lasting impression, and its seeds too were growing.

Love of country is love for the people, not just for the landscape, the climate and history however beautiful and valiant. To move even briefly within this privileged circle for me was something wonderful. Here everyone could be themselves and behave in a natural manner, within certain formalities. At home it was less easy. My mother had seemed increasingly distant, pained, distracted and vexed, suffering the well meant herbal curatives while my father seemed to be often away involving himself more with local politics, once or twice as far as Petersburg or Vienna; to medical forums attending lectures by Freud, Jung and others: ministering to his scattered patients, particularly the poor, for which service he charged little or nothing, but was frequently paid in game – sometimes poached from the Estate, to which a blind eye was naturally turned. Money seemed to slip through his fingers, what with his botanical research and the costs involved in my mother's recurrent illness, it seems we were living beyond our means. He seemed tired and though he did not seem to be neglecting his practice, finances were tight. I felt that I would soon have to abandon what education I was receiving and consider permanent paid employment of some kind. In any event school and me never seemed to hit it off.

That wild streak in me no doubt.

Chapter 21. *The Call of the Wild*

'Tell us more about your father's society. Who were his friends? How was he influenced by them, can you say?' This from Hawkeye-Rose, interrupting my Whitehall reverie. I wish I could place where I'd seen him before.

Once in my transition from boyhood, returning home in a dreamlike state of mind and happily tired from riding out with Marik and the girls, I found a landau in the yard and the maid Daine, who advised me of a trio of my long suffering father's friends assembled; Messrs. Troop, Kasparis and Orlinsky: for the purpose it seemed of advising me on a career. I unsaddled *Flitzer* my lively pony, whose name meant *'fleet'* (as of foot) and led him to his stall, watered and rubbed him down before I made my way to the house.

Smells are more evocative of time and of place than other sensations. The sweet hay of the stable, the yard with its elderberry and grasses, the kitchen herbs and onions. The wonderful smell of fresh bread that my mother or Daine had been baking. Apples and flowers in the dining room: the polished leather of my father's study and the furniture polish in the drawing room now mingle with cigar smoke and identifies a particular day as I enter.

My father's one time colleague, Professor Boris Artemovitch Orlinsky, had climbed to a lofty perch as a lecturer in neurology at the Medical Institute. He purported to be a Newtonian physicist who poo-poohed Sir James Jeans' *heat death of the universe* as faddish nonsense. He was perfectly sure of its infinite stability with everything in its place for eternity but held, so my father had told me with a smile, rather to an arcane clockwork *renaissance* worldview that prevailed, and not just in some Lithuanian backwater.

As I arrived, Boris Artemovitch was stooped in the hallway, tapping his fingernails on our baroque tree frog barometer as if expecting the 'pressure' would rise or fall by the unblinking stare of a jewelled amphibian from the forests of Surinam. He turned to enter the drawing room, acknowledging my presence beneath lugubrious lids and sprawled untidily in the window seat, where he smoothed his luxuriant moustaches; satisfied and at ease with *himself, the vodka, and his 'out of whack' paradigm of smug cosmological stasis.*

The frock-coated lawyer, Kasparis sat with my father. Grain broker, Herr Justus Troop stood square before the fireplace, warming his rump and consulting a *hunter* on a chain stretched across his silken waistcoat where an ostentatious emerald pin secured his tie. Re-pocketing the watch, he returned to stroking his scented black beard. My unannounced arrival had caused the cessation of whatever matters of moment were being discussed. Troop, with little ado, launched into a litany of advice for a young man starting out in life as to a suitable career.

It was, 'Economics, not cosmological mumbo-jumbo, that's what makes the world go round, *Junge*, with due deference to professor Orlinsky here. Double-entry book keeping: not some theory of Eugenics nor laboratory research into pre-destined criminality, dogs salivating to a dinner gong.'

Not the nostrums of quackery either – aimed I was sure at my father's seeking of homeopathic cures.

'Business! That's the career for you, my boy. Make your fortune young, spend it at your leisure, abroad preferably, somewhere safe.' His secret for success, as far as I was able to understand, involved identifying a commodity that was in wide demand and deftly acquiring a monopoly on its supply.

'If you can prove you're not Jewish, then I'd have suggested putting your money into *land,* being reliably informed that they're not making any more,' he'd said with no trace of a smile. 'But now, with that damned Peter Stolypin and the growing power of the Great Unwashed, I can no longer advise that.'

Quite how a monopoly was to be achieved without massive bribery and eliminating one's competitors, aged fourteen, seemed to be the sticking point to me, *within the law* in Russia, I told Hawkeye/Browne. Orlinsky was a doyen and luminary of the Moscow Anthropological Institute and a champion of Eugenics. Apropos my father's own flagging career as a down-at-heel country doctor, he'd attempted, before my arrival, to persuade him to join a small research team in Moscow, to observe and help write up his experiments on criminal brains using such Gothic apparatus as Leclanché cells and Tesler magnetos.

I'd caught sight of an album on the dining table with photographs of grim-visaged criminal types, each with anthropometric grid-lines inked on tissue paper. These are overlaid onto their skulls, viewed from every cardinal point, moving on to the actual brains of the subjects, pictures of which he subsequently shows me, proving his theories by default or exclusion when measured against his control specimens: a marble bust of

Ludwig van Beethoven or some eminent Graeco-Roman patrician of suitable gravitas with an allegedly 'normal' brain configuration, alongside those I assumed were pygmies'. Orlinsky casts sidelong glances at my father throughout.

'You've read Madison Grant, Augusts?' he asks. Perhaps, if he can successfully 'captivate' the son by his theories, the father will unbend and join him for a suitable salary.

'*The Passing of the Great Race,*' my father replies.

'Your thoughts?'

'Beguilingly dangerous nonsense if taken seriously. Ultimately unconvincing.'

Orlinsky frowns. Kasparis, the lawyer, smiles. A lay preacher, he'd probably intended to advise me to enter the legal profession but has modified his advice in light of Orlinsky's championing of Eugenics. He suggests that medical jurisprudence might be a lucrative and worthwhile field for study, adding that I might also like to consider my father's one time youthful calling to the church; study for a doctorate in Divinity.

Such intricacies were well and good, I thought for a world without end continuum; but the planet buzzed with revolution and merciless new ideas for change were abroad. I could feel and see it at my then tender age. The villages seethed with it, veritable tinderboxes; small businesses vandalized and striped with agitprop slogans, pamphlets nailed up by small town rabble rousers among whom were agents of the police as outspoken provocateurs. At the local horse fair; rough men with cudgels, their *Vikings'* slit-eared cross-mastiff deterrents in spiked collars, collecting money for 'The Movement'.

'It was obvious that something was brewing again then, though when it would start was anyone's guess,' I concluded.

Change *was* itself a natural law, even according to the restless Marik, who is a law unto himself drawing on one of the Graf's cigars as we sprawled in an arboreal hideout, like Robin Hood and Will Scarlet. Marik always took the obverse of any established ordinance or stricture and on his wise words I hung in my youth: he who had every reason for opposing social ferment. Marik veered sharply in his inclinations; first declaring with the hedonists that pleasure was the sole good, then with monk-like zeal eschewing the advantages of birth, leaving me confused and rocking in his wake.

'Are you comfortable with all this?' he'd asked rhetorically. 'The conspicuous contrast in the way we live with that of the poor in their wretched hovels.' He seemed to forget that I was from a struggling middle class background and slowly sinking into less than genteel penury. I said I could see both sides and that rich was better!

'It takes courage, sacrifice, vision to change society, Rolf. Do you think you're up to it?'

'I'd follow you anywhere, Marik.' Never sure if he was serious. 'But are we not a little outnumbered?'

He looked at the misty hills. 'You know how the Graf made his money? Uncle Peter gambled and whored away his fortune as firstborn: the *Kreuzhof*, our family Hanse estate had withered and died. It had eventually to be sold to cover debts. Before that my father had made a bad investment in that so-called mine in East Africa. Then after paying off some loans he'd acquired a licence to shoot big game.'

Ivory, Marik said, was to have been his father's new adventure. Contract safaris for rich Americans mostly. But all was doomed. Disease had wiped out much of the game and what saved him was meeting Marik's mother to be. The fact that she was another man's wife at that moment seemed of little account. Marik had been conceived and born in German East Africa. The Kuznetsowa Estate itself was the gracious gift of an elderly man along with his blessing and the wish that as his much younger wife had made a new choice, for love, she might live out a happy life free from want. She'd not borne him a child, which had been his dearest wish, but there was no jealousy: just resignation and the calm philosophy of a man himself not far from completing his own journey. Indeed he had hastened his end with a pistol late one autumn having dismissed the staff with generous disbursements on his other estate, far away in the southern Ukraine.

'The 'sainthood' of Sophia, my dear late mother, followed some years after, but I believe my parent's star was cursed from that moment, despite the equanimity of old Count Kuznetsow. A burden of guilt is something that all must bear, don't you think?'

I thought that Marik had a very old head on his young shoulders. But still I did not understand him.

'Everywhere the legal and social prohibitions of church and state spread fear and guilt. Original sin is preached, so the newborn is guilty as it comes bawling into the world to be beaten and scolded until it conforms. If it has the good luck to be born rich, then in the natural order of things it will have power and control over the lesser breeds. Morality is spoken of as if all aspire to it. But what is morality if not another construct of man? *Kantian* morality is sanctified only in the

296

authority of the individual. Animals have no morality. They have survived well enough for millions of years, but are not deliberately cruel like man. Predators kill efficiently, which usually means quickly. Suffering is not prolonged.'

'But Marik we are taught to hunt sportingly. This is our lore. The interpretation of a natural morality, perhaps. Might not the way men treat their domestic animals be a better measure of the health of mankind?'

'Rolf, we both know that men treat other men worse than they treat their favourite horses and dogs. Often worse than their *least* favoured animals, or even their women. What if two children were swapped at birth, the nobleman's son for a pauper's. Will breeding out? Who knows? Maybe it's in the genes, but it's unfair to discriminate so in education, blighting or favouring their chances and the available choices that each one's offspring can expect in life. For that philosophical point alone we can reason that the social order is itself corrupt, that inherited wealth is a pernicious nepotism. That revolution must follow. The knout, poverty, the almighty state with its laws and sanctions and the grip on the masses by the Church will all come to an end. The power of the Word of God, wielded by the metropolitans, that imbues the common man with guilt in the present to keep him in his traces, the promise of salvation after death: that whole concept is under attack on all sides. Privilege and repressive Tsarist rule has had its day, mark my words.'

'Marik! You are either a Nihilist or a Bolshevist!'

'Not at all, Rolf. I'm a *Realist*! If I must bow it will be only to the inevitable unless the reforms gather speed. The rumblings of discontent are loud and reasonable men must make concessions – we may in fact be powerless to do otherwise. We may be forced by Stolypin to part with large tracts of our own estate. He's already gone a long way to meeting the demands of the Bolshevists! Neither the Graf nor I are happy about this and instinctively would take up arms to fight against it. Especially as it is most likely we'll not be compensated, or so the Graf believes. But the army is loyal and we pay our taxes to the Tsar. What if the Tsar is overthrown. What will the army do? Keep close to your raggedy friends in the villages. You may need them, Rolf.'

'But you are my friend, Marik. I stand with you.'

'In a revolution, as it is important in all walks of society, you are identified by the friends you keep and the cut of your cloth. It was not only the French aristocracy went to the guillotine in the *Terror*. In any case I may be going away. To Petersburg.'

'I thought you'd decided against the military.'

'I've not decided but it may yet be the best option, I think. I can't see myself kicking around in this backwater for the rest of my life, inheriting whatever might remain of the estate. Doing the same thing as my father. Dabbling in shipping and politics. Holding council as the Margrave. Understand me, I love the Graf dearly, but I'll be expected to perform the 'ritual of the stair' next, with a candle each night. I need to breathe, to spread my wings, Rolf.'

He smiles, quoting Goethe, *'Und ein Flügelpaar faltet sich los! Dorthin! Ich muss! Göntt mir den Flug!'*

'We've had our little revolutions in the past.' I countered. 'Things have returned to normal. Well *nearly* normal, even after '05. I can't see why you think that a big revolution is inevitable.'

'Can't you? Rolf, those revolutions were dress rehearsals. The preliminaries to the main event. It's bound to happen, and the reaction to excesses will push it through to the point of no return. Old Klammersdorf believes so. A monarchist society's cruel impositions and taxation have created the recipe. It's just a matter of someone stepping up to light the oven.'

'Excesses?'

'Like in Wells, Rolf. *The Time Machine.* Remember how it ends?'

'I think it was with an icy planet inhabited by giant crabs and scorpions.'

'No, Rolf. How it ends for humanity. *Morlocks* eat *Eloi*!'

I thought then that he was simply trying to frighten me.

~-~

For all that my circumstances were profoundly poorer than his, I was the more conservative. Sometimes I thought that the loss of his mother and the Graf's extra-mural preoccupations had left him without a counter-balance: in some limbo in which his moral compass had no 'correction card'. Such was my naïve and parochial view.

Challenge and change, not excluding the apostasy to humanism of my parents had prepared a foundation for my questing need to seek out and decide things for myself, surrounded though we were by the power of church and state. In our world no twentieth century Galileo, 'guilty of following the position of Copernicus', would be forced to recant heliocentricity on pain of death.

Fate too has its ambushes and time has taught me that coincidences are really opportunities in disguise. Coincidence is but a manifestation of fate made clear to us if we will only see it. Sometimes it is that spirit animus that is revealed to us: a spirit of a creature that is more than the creature. It comes to teach us and make us think beyond the obvious and the secular. We crypto-pagan Lithuanians should know that as much as the most spiritual tribes of North America and the northern Lapps with their shamans. It seemed little enough time since I'd lain with my popgun in the reeds and *Vilki* my dog by my side, quiet in the dawn and thrilled to the skeins of geese honking high overhead. The pond system where I lay in wait for duck was narrow with many twists - barely room for a teal or mallard to land, with a difficult approach among the larch and willow: ideal for an ambush.

I was suddenly aware of a great swoosh of wings and a wild goose swooped overhead, low and fast, his neck stretched and head scanning, mighty wing beats loud upon the quiet air. Motionless under the trees I watched him circle once, eyeing the small ponds critically. Without more ado he turned and made his approach into almost no wind. Over the reeds he descended, his tail fanned, wings 'gulled' for stability, arched to maintain lift at a high angle, little feathers fluttering above the curve of the wings indicating flow: emarginated tip-feathers spread like fingers grasping for purchase on the chill air, he slowed, rocking gently as he centred himself on the glide. His webbed feet extended like paddles in the wind, like 'brakes', and in a masterful display of control he settled gently onto the water. His momentum carried him half a meter with the wings acting as giant drogues. Folding them neatly he turned in the water and with a satisfied waggle of his tail he seemed to assess his own performance.

I nearly applauded. I could not think of harming this magnificent, amazing, clever creature and so I slipped quietly back into the trees, feeling blessed, with Vilki, hushed and obedient, so as not to startle the bird, full of admiration for this master class on natural controlled flight that it had been my privilege to witness. It was a little epiphany, one of several such that I would experience in my lifetime. One that set me on an inevitable first step towards my dream of flight which had been growing strongly within me since a few courageous men had reportedly made their first faltering forays into the virgin skies of America and of Europe.

But others there were who would snare free spirits. Church, mosque and synagogue lay in ambush and we self-styled 'free-thinking' young protesters, like Wild West homesteaders, out-faced the Sioux. Real wagon trains that had transported a previous generation of Lithuanian émigrés fleeing from persecution, facing arrows rather than excommunication: escaping impoverishment, exile and hunger; choosing freedom from oppression, taxation, from feudalism by another name, to travel hopefully with their proscribed *Altpreussisch*, their Sanskrit and Aramaic-rooted language intact, to the New World and its constitution for the free man. They carried with them too the sanctuaries and symbols, crucifix and icon, of their faiths.

In discussions with the privileged but thoughtful Marik, inspired by 'Social Darwinism' and ideas of democracy, we'd agreed that before deciding what to do in life, formal belief systems under timely assault should be put aside. We, the young, would not be told what we should or should not believe. We were not alone in making an assault upon religion, though we prided ourselves that we made our case for 'reason and science' and mercilessly mocked the schisms within Orthodoxy that split the Church's Old Believers from the New, based on how many fingers should be used for 'signing the cross', or the compass direction that processions should follow. We rejected Lutheranism as well as the Pope and embraced alternative, half-formed, weathervane philosophies suited to our shifting intellectual positions, age fourteen-and-a-half in my case. I had no clue what I wanted or what I really believed in: where my destiny lay. Nor had I the wit to accept the world as it was, though the conceit to believe I might perhaps help to change it.

But I also had a sense of defection.

Who were we? I was a lapsed Jew, according to my free-thinking parents. So much for my creed: racially of Litho-Slav ancestry with ancient links to Portugal, a real mongrel. Gottfried Herder had defined a nation as the *Volk*. Marik was a minor noble, mixed Germano-Russ, living cheek by jowl in a Russia which still had to shrug-off serfdom, though Napoleon, for all his arrogance, had really sought to change all that.

'I'm with Voltaire, Rolf,' said Marik in our philosophers' tree; this time acknowledging his privilege. 'I believe what I wish to believe based on reason. But I don't believe in such sedition spreading too far among the peasants. I think their belief in a supreme being is important to prevent a collapse of morality. I'd want my lawyer, tailor, valet - even my wife whoever she might be — to believe in God. I think that if they do I shall be robbed less and cheated less!' he confided with a wink.

'But I thought you said you believed in *égalité*! An empowered, democratic educated Russia.'

'Not for all - not yet. It's too soon; the *proles* couldn't handle it. We have ironclads and railways, telephones and the internal combustion engine. Men have flown! But the masses might as well be living in the Dark Ages. Society is not ready. Too much education would threaten culture as we know it.'

'So you'd still maintain an élite?'

'A worthy élite, yes, not based on how much land one robbing bully has managed to acquire compared with the next man. Not the oft-caricatured capitalist oppressor. Not the corrupt official lining his own nest.' He smiled an ironic smile. 'Were I not addicted to comfort, Rolf, I could well adhere to severely ascetic principles. With a few selected servants of course.'

'Based on what then. A sense of the finer things?'

'Yes. To that extent I am of the élite, Rolf. You are an intelligent, but you do not have the natural etiquette of the nobility, the easy grace that comes with history, honour and noblesse. Breeding. Family. To rule should be based on a fitness to govern, to control, to conserve the best in culture, to have an understanding of our history and uphold its traditions, but not to be completely hidebound by them. Nor held to the constraints of religious dogma. *Kultur* must be ring-fenced.'

'But, Marik you are a mass of contradictions. You admit that the Graf only inherited his *folwark* by default, in the gift of an old and gracious man, Count Kuznetsow. Through his bride and her dowry estate. To that extent I find your argument fallacious and your remarks insulting to me personally and to my intelligence.'

'Nevertheless, Rolf. We'd once owned the Kreuzhof Estate. That was our family home for two hundred years. The Princess too was from a fine family. Only my father's drunkard of a brother lost us that inheritance and shadowed our lives. So my argument holds! Like it or not. I am of the élite. Thou art not! Don't take it too hard, you'll always find a place as my trusted lieutenant.'

Such hubris. But we were both afflicted. Although the spectre of the '05 revolution still rose up, and the authorities came down hard, little did I think that while it might be easy to knock down old institutions, we had better have something solid to fill that which nature abhors, else who knows what might rush in and fill it on the tide: a new Bonaparte perhaps, to lay all waste, or some home grown animus; a moving spirit, a nameless beast, a golden calf for the disaffected that Marik seemed to hold so dear.

Informed by a narrow juvenile world-view, we played with alternative homespun egalitarian philosophies and propositions as if we controlled events: children burning ants under a glass. Despite Marik's gloomy predictions, in our sometime rural idyll we were protected by a benign firewall of apparent goodwill, unexposed to whatever white heat of revolutionary ardour consumed my peers and elders in the villages. But the Russian people were growing up. Not much longer would they pray for their 'Tsar Deliverer'.

I'd been too young to understand the political pressures that fired the revolution of 1905, to whose murderous aftershocks we later became almost accustomed. The Little Father's ears had been closed to humble petitioning; the people had been cruelly rebuffed by Cossack and dragoon and the streets had run with blood. This I'd heard with a child's ear, detached from events, slowly beginning to understand the political situation, listening to both sides of the adult conversation. But still it was like watching an incomprehensible play, not knowing the end. Like witnessing the slow collapse of disparate ideologies in a haze of moral confusion. Such policies as were embraced included sharing of resources, reflecting views of others of my wider eclectic circle like Vladi, Grigorius, Tomus and Sasha, that were expressed more vociferously among the underprivileged: the true kindling wood of revolution, awaiting the spark, ever fearful of the *Okhrana* looking over their shoulders: gendarmes, secret police, agents provocateur seeking out the pamphleteers along with the armed and dangerous and those, however young, who by careless word or jest betrayed themselves and their families. Theirs was the real thing, this talk of revolution. Its ignition when it came would see restraint thrown to the wind as Klammersdorf through Marik had prophesied.

While our woolly idealism may have veered towards Bolshevism, to me it meant a fresh start; equality, justice and a common sense stripping away of age-old fetters, religious dogma and animistic superstition which clung to field, forest and river of Lithuania like a prehistoric miasma. I paused at mention of Bolshevism in connection to myself, but Browne and Hawkeye let me rattle on.

Hard work and a system of law and religion had provided a stable plank for Germanic autonomy, settlement and enrichment in these lush pastures and had kept everyone in their appointed place, under the Tsar – like clockwork universe theory. But choice of career depended as in all societies upon class: the church, soldiering, or study for the professions among the bourgeoisie or the lower gentry; apprenticed to some type of artisan if one were of lesser breeding, or even thrown back into recent feudalism to work someone else's fields under the banner of the *dignity of labour*. All was ordained and regulated.

Nevertheless old tradition proves hard to break. When a foul-mouthed village lad crudely linked 'that German whore', the Tsarina, herself a German princess of beauty and refinement, with the disreputable Rasputin I felt obliged to break his nose. Marik meanwhile had left for the Corps of Pages, taking his scary predictions with him. When it came down to it he had inevitably bowed to paternal pressure, the Graf thus demonstrating his loyalty to the Crown, choosing Nikolai over Wilhelm, digging-in the Baltic root. So was proved, if proof were needed, that family, belief and tradition is strong and individuals are weak? Or was it that in the face of a powerful force of nature, like the Graf, we would bend to its will? In the familiarity of its thrall the doomed populations of Pompeii - or Herculaneum - had probably thought themselves masters of their own little destinies.

I suddenly saw Kristian again in his prime; riding breeches and *Loden* jacket. I see him through my younger child's eye, as he lifts me up. His little soldier. His *ABC Schütze*. My eye to his eye in the hallway at *Ausautas* that nudges the estate on the road to Kuznetsowa. I wondered what emotions had been going through his mind then with Peter sculling about the East Indies on his desperate quest. My memory compressed events from those times, so was the telegram or letter already on its way from Java? His brother already lost in the Banda Sea?

'It occurred to me at that young age that when man had felt the need to invent a deity, as he had done many times over millennia, it was essentially a code of moral behaviour enshrining the status quo, be it ever so cloaked in the ancient patina of myth and tradition. It existed to provide a few men with a source of power over others - unless we had somehow remotely influenced our own experiment through the fervour of our observation, given buoyant optimism and a sort of morphic resonance: a collective belief and enough disciples to conjure the spirit. Holy or fraudulent.'

'Perhaps,' said Browne, interrupting a little sniffily. 'That's just what *prayer* is!'

~-~

Back in *Ausautas,* named for a benign if pagan deity, I'd mumbled some sort of comment along the lines that God, if he existed, may be in his heaven, if it existed, but it would make no difference to my choice of career. It seemed I'd either been reasonably articulate after all or struck a nerve.

So I'd suffered frosty looks from churchman and scientist, while the corpulent book keeper stared open-mouthed, black beard bristling like a puffed-up wood grouse. He turned to my bemused father and accused him of wasting everybody's time. Of letting me read Nietzsche. Specifically *Die fröhliche Wissenschaft*, according to Orlinsky, although I hadn't. Hawkeye smiled at this, the first time he had done so since our introduction.

Father still hoped against all the evidence that I would read medicine, eschewing other philosophies. I had neither the aptitude nor the interest. My thoughts turned towards internal combustion theory and the hedonistic lure of speed; the new pursuit of wealthy young men and a seemingly frivolous twentieth century goal in itself.

I could barely wait to escape the confinement of that room, in mild disgrace: re-saddle my surprised pony and with a '*Bek, bek zirgelj!*' galloped away into the evening grasslands, drawn to the green savannah like a sailor to the sea. We slowed to a reflective canter under a vastness of sky whose cloudy vault had dominated my venturing childhood, Vilki as ever loping alongside. Suddenly I dug in my heels, rode, arms outstretched like a bird in flight – *ein Vogelfreier*, in winged embrace of a beloved landscape that seemed timeless and free: mind and spirit reaching for the clouds, shouting my wild challenge to the hills, feeling the tug of nature. My pony's ears pricked to the sound: heels dug in, we galloped full speed 'til becalmed, three rib cages rising and falling in unison midst an ocean of grass and rain shrouded hills, in the quiet of a cyclone's eye. The welkin had echoed my yell '*Flitzer Los! – Go, Flitzer, go!*' that was answered too by a faint keening cry, a whistling buzzard or osprey soaring against the singular beauty of a far off cloud that blushed to the last of the sun. My shamanistic bird spirit!

I wheeled about, riding high upon the moor, where stooped trees were shaped by the wind. Stunted, curve-backed, bent like serfs under the burden of their branches; yet the sigh of the wind through their boughs was the song of freedom. I felt again the need of a spiritual retreat, higher than the highest hills; envied the raptor soaring in the sky, ached to see with his keen eye the edge of my world and beyond. Past lonely salt flats and marshes, to glide with the wickering gulls and whimbrels beyond its shores. Unconfined. Not forever trapped, pinioned to the earth, imprisoned: a domestic animal in my grounded body. I craved adventure, not brokerage nor the law. Not book keeping. Not the church. Perhaps, I thought, I should run away to sea whose distant tang I told myself I could smell upon the wind.

And so like Marik's mysterious, wayward uncle: make my fortune or end my days like Peter Strelitz himself; artist, dreamer, swimming with the Mermaid Queen and her sea snakes in the Banda Sea. Or with the Sea Queen of Sumatra in the Sunda Strait.

~-~

However, I was about to fail my *Abitur*.

After three terms in the Conrad von Hippel gymnasium, that equally prestigious school at the seat of culture in Braunsberg might have been a first step to greater things - had I applied myself and stayed out of fights in Bremerhaven. But I'd stolen away when I was supposed to be cramming for exams, down the Wurster Strasse to the shoreline polder to watch the fishing boats and listen to the *Silbermöwen* calling and chuckling. There I'd hide among the dykes and sit in the long grass eating bread and cheese pilfered from the kitchen: watching sandpipers and herons sailing off the windy sea and the fast, dark cormorants; herring fishers coming in, or stately iron barques towed to harbour by pugilistic tugs. Else I'd slip down quayside to watch the shipwrights and carpenters at work, distracting them with my questions. Strolling the dockside among the myriad jibs and gantries, the clutter of white-masted ships with their complicated rigs, rusting tramps with their sooty funnels. From town via the Ankerstrasse or Argatztsrasse I'd hasten seawards, revelling in the noise of steam cranes, roaring anchor chains, the hoot of tugs. Crossing the sidings to the Kaiserhafen basin, sometimes with a friend, mostly alone, following my star down the long straight seaboard of the Hanseatic port, unconcerned. Lost in thought, a would-be gypsy seafarer, sometimes rapidly sketching ships or dockside machinery; the men at work. With a natural eye for perspective and proportion I could render a scene quickly and satisfactorily. Even sold a few sketches to the stevedores for *Pfennige*.

The sea called me. I looked westwards, my gypsy soul filled with a deep yearning, but all I could see when I climbed to the top of a crane ladder was the smudge of what might have been Wilhelmshaven on the other side of the Weser estuary. With Cuxhaven, Schleswig-Holstein and Denmark to the north, the Friesian Islands and the great sandbanks to the northwest, westwards to Holland and then, a magical name, *England* and the British Empire, the greatest empire the world had ever seen and the mightiest sea power, especially since the disaster that had befallen the Russian Fleet in '05. Behind me lay Hamburg and the railway went all the way to Lithuania and beyond to Petersburg. But home seemed very far off when times were bad.

I fought fierce battles with the other warf rats, befriended some, and my ears were boxed occasionally by the stevedores for my temerity in clambering among the tall ladders, a danger to myself and others.

So, was I destined for some minor clipped-wing bourgeois position, occupying some safe little perch with no view? A clerical post where my modest educational achievements would see my restless soul enslaved, torpid, and half-buried in paperwork; stupefied, enervated? I couldn't bear the idea.

I had considered that by force of will, modest academic endeavour and military service I might elevate my prospects, but in class I'd be off, dreaming, 'somewhere else', to the special ire of my mathematics master, whose merciless penchant for wielding a steel rule was legendary. A solitary, grey-faced bachelor, roosting apart from the other gerund-grinders, he rejoiced in the name of Gollub. He also taught physics, a subject I would rather have enjoyed had we had a more 'balanced' teacher. Known to the boys ominously as *Der Gollub*, this sour *goblinesque*, wisp of a creature suffered from a swivel-eye condition where the pupils flicked side-to-side with great rapidity. I later learned this was called *nystagmus* and met another even more sinister individual with this defect.

Gollub was the subject of much schoolboy humour and chalked caricatures of him looking both ways at once appeared all over the school – sometimes as a manic, uncrowned double-headed vulture: a parody of the Austrian flag. But in truth everyone was terrified of his short temper, his frothing rages; and my knuckles were not infrequently rapped *für Unaufmerksamkeit*: for though I tried to concentrate on my lessons, my mind would run free, like a stag, or I'd be troubled by brooding thoughts. Perhaps at von Hippel they'd been rapped once too often, sometimes for fighting.

The macabre incident that had led to my 'exile' occurred when a boy named Karl Maisch suffered, like many others, the 'Wrath of Gollub'. But his case was the most extreme. Gollub, obsessive about time keeping, had accused Maisch of unpunctuality.

'How dare you be late for my class, boy?' he'd snarled, scowling at his pocket watch, eyes flicking.

Maisch, diffident and respectful, tremulously contended that he was on time.

'You dare contradict me?' screeched Gollub, spindrift flying. 'Put out your hand!'

306

Trembling Maisch did as he was told, and the teacher seized him by the right wrist. The class was silent. Gollub himself seemed in the grip of some powerful force, his eyes almost still for once; glazed. The boy's hand was held hard against the desk and the metre rule was raised high and the edge brought down hard across the fingers. Whether intended the blow was out of all proportion and Karl's eyes popped wide as two fingers were severed as if by a guillotine. The little finger hung by a shred of tissue: only index finger and thumb remained intact, though sorely wealed. Karl turned white and collapsed in a dead faint.

A fine spray of blood on wall and blackboard; a moment of horrified silence, then shouts erupted on all sides as boys ran from the classroom to fetch Matron and the Headmaster. Gollub panicked, screamed for silence….eyes flickering madly, down on his knees picking up the fingers: a goggle-eyed omnivor ape, gathering pieces of a smaller anthropoid: Gollub the obsessive keeper of time becomes Cronos: devourer of children.

Nauseated, I wound my tie round the finger stumps to stem the red spout, which I managed by pulling it very tight. Karl remained grey-faced, eyelids fluttering. A teacher came to investigate, transfixed by the Gothic scene.

'It was an accident!' whined Gollub, eyes swivelling. 'An accident.'

I recalled a red mist rising: grabbing Gollub's arm, the heavy rule in my hand. Inflamed by a sacred fury that I would not have exchanged for the world's riches, I slammed it flat across his face time and again. He dropped, shrieking. Bleeding through his fingers he tried ineffectually to ward off the blows and a few other boys quickly joined in with kicks and punches before the remainder of the class piled-on with righteous cheers and joyful shouts of released tension. Old scores to settle with flying fists and feet, the natural justice of the barbarically civilised young.

A whistle shrilled and the boys scuttled away, crabs from a washed-up corpse, encouraged by heavy blows from other members of staff. Dazed, I emerged from the scrum, and restrained by another teacher and the Head was hauled upright and struck violently across the face and about my ears. My arms were wrenched behind my back and I was frog-marched to the Headmaster's office still yelling death threats over my shoulder at the quivering form of *Der Gollub*, the final nails in my coffin, if any were needed. I was expelled from school that afternoon and sent back to the Baltic with my suitcase, exercise books, a bleeding lip and my ears still ringing. I had lost my self-control and that was alleged to be a flaw in my character that I should address. Indeed the Head had explained this very forcefully to me before I was dismissed.

'You will never amount to anything more than a brute, Dragunavicius,' he'd said sternly. 'You are wild and a hothead. Get you back to your colonial farm. Your place is with *animals*, God preserve them. You've no place here. A civilization cannot function when so-called 'citizens' take the law into their own hands, however young they may be. Usually I would offer a pupil a second chance, but this is not the first time you've been punished for lawlessness and I judge that there is no curbing your violence, truancy and waywardness. It is too extreme, whatever the provocation. I will not have my staff abused. I will be sending a letter with you for your father who, I am sure, will be thoroughly and rightly ashamed of you.

'In any event,' he said after a pause. 'Dr. Dragunavicius is late with this term's payment. That'll be all. Do something good with your life. Pray for enlightenment and a curb on your temper.'

I could see his lips moving and make out the words but the jangling and buzzing in my head made hearing difficult. Anyway I didn't care to hear what he was saying. I was still blazing with indignation.

I reflected on all this and on the train I opened and read the letter with growing fury. I considered it to be heavily biased against me, playing down the true seriousness of the cause of my behaviour and distorting my part in the event, painting me as the ringleader of a vicious attack on a long serving member of staff. So I angrily tore it to shreds and threw the pieces out if the railway carriage window. I'd deal with my father's disappointment when I arrived at Aleksandras station. He wasn't there to meet me, so I began the hike to the northern outskirts of Kuznetsowa and my home. To *Ausautas,* my pony and my dog and all things dearest to me.

My father was surprisingly calm about the situation and arranged for me to go to a local school. Marvellous. I could see Marik again, and the girls too. Month's later, via several incorrect addressees, we received a letter written rather awkwardly and signed by both of Maisch's parents, thanking me for attending to Karl, preventing further blood loss. He was doing quite well at another college learning to use his left hand. They told me that Herr Gollub was about to be committed to a hospital for the insane.

I had no feelings about that whatsoever. I recognized that in a moment of hot anger I had attacked a man that I had seen as a dehumanised creature, freakish and unworthy. My father had taught me that all were worthy of respect and that where respect was given it would be reciprocated. That we had to abide by the law or civilization would collapse. That all life was sacred, although we were taught that our dominion over the animals was God given it should not be abused. Considering that his studies for a doctorate in Divinity had been abandoned for medicine, and that our home was free from religious dogma as existed all around, I consider that we struck to the same moral precepts as our neighbours.

Was I such an untameable creature? How did I appear to others, I wondered? I thought myself amiable, if a little hot headed and passionate.

I have a later memory.

Chapter 22. *The Bull, the Cat and the Cosmos*

Marik had gone to Petersburg with the Graf. Krysia in a shimmering green dress stood straight upon the shore of the lake, *naiad* of her glade, white arm uplifted with the violin bow, barefoot in the grass. I had found a fine saddled mount straying, caught the reins and ridden with the animal to the lake whence strains in that peculiar floating evanescence, the enchanting threnody of a musical instrument played *plein air* was a syren's guide, rising and falling on my ear. A burly, insouciant young baron of about Marik's age was enraptured as the young countess swayed sensuously with the music. Kat was there too, sitting on a grassy mound, staring at the waters, her German Poets or a Russian novel as ever by her side. I'd ridden up with the stray, and slipped from my horse, managing to make a fool of myself by losing my footing on soft ground and falling half into the water, splashing Kat and halting Brahms in full spate: frightening a little flock of dabbling ducks which took off for the island.

'Hey, fellow! Clumsy oaf! Devil d'you think you're playing at?' The young man was on his feet, indignant and ready to take offence, his hands curled pugilistically. 'Apologise to the Countesses at once for this intrusion and then be off with you, clown!'

But Kat turned her full smile on me, shaken at once from her reverie by my arrival, I believe.

'But shall we not *tame* him? Can we not civilise him with human food? Come and sit beside me, you little china shop bull,' she purred, while I flushed intensely at the teasing words, though she meant them in jest and it was her way of pinching the fuse. Clever Kat, though Krysia raised an eyebrow at us both.

But he was not mollified.

'Who is this fool of a peasant?' persisted the baron, whereupon Krysia introduced us formally. I acknowledged him with a slight bow. The baron did not extend his hand and his expression was so sour that I thought in an eyeblink, had I been his social equal, he'd have called for seconds.

'I merely retrieved your mount......sir, which you'd allowed to wander,' I retorted coolly enough, though my blood was up, returning his gaze with sufficient pause between a *less* than customarily respectful form of address and not the downcast eye he'd expected.

'Are you trying to be insolent or are you *merely* an imbecile?'

'No. Are you?'

'What d'you say? Are you accusing *me* of insolence and of foolishness, you whelp?'

'You display arrogance. Perhaps that passes for breeding in your family.'

'How ... dare you!' he exclaimed. He stepped closer and my hands automatically balled into fists. 'Now I know you,' he said. 'It was you we saw poaching on our estate. You and your gang of thieves shot and carried off one of our best stags.'

'Never!' I exclaimed hotly, my anger rising. 'My piece would never drop a stag. It's for pigeon only.' Angry too that I'd felt it necessary to explain myself and my possession of an inadequate weapon: symbolic in retrospect I've since felt.

His hand reached for his plaited quirt. 'You need a severe lesson, you... you pup.'

'Don't prove your foolishness,' I said, but Krysia was between us, a warrior princess, her violin bow held aloft like a sword.

'Stop it, please, Mikhail-Antonovich,' she said firmly, her back to me. Then she turned. 'You'd better go home, Rolf. This is not good for you.'

'I will go, of course, if you tell me.'

'I have not finished with him yet, Krystina,' he said

'Oh, but you have, Mikhail,' said Krysia firmly, her green eyes flashing the colour of her dress. 'Most certainly you *have*.'

The baron was dumfounded and I thought for a moment his eyes would pop, as if from strangulation.

'I'll not stay another moment in such... such *company*.' He sneered at last, placing his boot in the stirrup and throwing his leg over his mount.

'I bid both you ladies good day and suggest that you pick a better class of companion than lives in burrows and buries its food. Word may get about that you're unmarriageable.'

Krystina's face betrayed controlled outrage as she flushed to her roots. I did not take my eyes off the swine to look back at Katya.

'As for you, you will regret your poaching and your damned uncivil tongue when I run across you again,' he snapped, as with a final glare at me he spurred his horse across the water meadow in the wrong direction before galloping off on firmer ground. I was pleased that he was rattled, but both Krysia and Kat, spitting with anger though they both were, warned me not to make enemies of the sons of landowners. In truth I considered myself a free spirit and not bound by outmoded ideas of fiefty. Though my home was battened onto the outskirts of a village set firm upon the giant farm estate or *Folwark*, (*palivarka* in Lithuanian) of von Strelitz, and the baron was the spoiled, youngest son of an adjoining estate, though hardly known to me by sight….still I felt my freedom was inviolable.

For the girls' sakes, though, I made as if to go, but Kat restrained me. 'Come and eat, my little *Aurochs*,' she smiled. 'We have hunting sausage, scones and fruit, and you can tell us a story for the trouble. Or there's green grass and clover if you prefer,' she laughed.

'Dares *Dionysus* to eat with *Titans*?' I joked, thankful that at last those boring Klammersdorf tutorials shared with the girls in the conservatory had provided a pay-off line. Through the connivance of the governess herself, my abbreviated education had been supplemented *ad hoc* by Greek Mythology, amongst other things, Dionysus having been slaughtered as a bull-calf and devoured by those savage deities.

'Dare you not?' mused Krysia, with her provocative smile. Her normal colour had returned. 'Come on, take off that muddy shirt and I'll rinse it in the clear water.'

'No, really,' I said. Then on an impulse, 'I'll do it myself.'

I stripped off my shirt and was about to rinse it in the lake when Kat snatched it from me and with her shoes kicked off waded into the clear water with her dress rolled up to her slender thighs. She thoroughly washed and rinsed the shirt, then wrung and shook it like a practiced washerwoman before hanging it on a branch in the warm sunshine. It was an act of service in defiance of her sister's good offer.

'So you consider me a clumsy bullock, Kat,' I said at last with a smile, settling down to share their hamper, glad that I had 'vanquished' an older rival as I think I saw it then. I was blissfully happy at that moment, with the two sisters flanking me: Kat's *Turgenyev*, *Pushkin* or whatever discarded along with Brahms, and Krysia's violin, both girls sitting close, toasting me with their eyes like woodland goddesses.

We'd discussed *existenzialismus* with the dwarfish talipede, Klammersdorf, whose didactic compass was wont to gyrate alarmingly.

'Perhaps I *am* then an existentialist bull, tiptoeing through a china shop, afraid of shattering an illusion!' I said. 'All breakages to be paid for.' Which drew tinkling laughter from Kat and a bemused smile from Krysia who I knew had little patience with such things.

We spent an hour eating and chatting by the lake beneath the trees with the sunlight dappling the water while my shirt dried and I made up the following short story, on the hoof, such as it was, about a little bull and a cat sitting together by a lake in an enchanted park: a fluffy cat and an English Hereford.

'They watch the ducks at their ablutions and play a game of, 'Do you remember?' or say nothing, mostly, in the companionable silence that exists between quadrupeds. Each with their memories.'

And in my confused memories I wander too, after Whitehall and down the beach at Yarmouth, trying to recapture…what? I see Kat, her red hair brushed from her temple with the cruel bullet furrow, or is it the other…?

'Sometimes the bull, alone in his stall, in an agony of guilt, found he was losing the memory of her features, the topography of her face eroding in time's imperfect mirror, dissolving in the silvered glass.'

I view, as through a photographer's gauze, Krysia and Kat, morphing as one within my imprisoned mind, in the despair of incarceration. Behind the wire of the KZ-Lager and after, like all those unjustly imprisoned, I carry my cell with me. Like those still less fortunate zeks: in Siberia where heroes die in secret. Where memory rots. Where torturers are kings without kingliness. Where zealots rule and good men turn to clay.

'The cat, for her part, with feline fickleness, seldom thought about the bull when he was not there, if he was ever there in her mind. And when he was there she might have wondered who he was, but never where he went when he wasn't there or if he went anywhere at all. For her he barely existed, if he existed, and if he existed she was happy to accept that he was there when he was there. And when he wasn't he might just as well not exist for all the difference that it made to the price of herrings. Not that she knew about the price of fish, or indeed the price of anything, as a concept. Not even the concept of a concept. Her conception was that the world existed for her and existentialist bulls were just one more patently inexplicable figment of the shadowy world of existence, or non-existence that played no part in her circadian cycle. If her fancy or attention were taken by a leaf or a spider, then her focus was fully on the moment in which she existed and idle speculation about bulls evaporated into space.

'The bull, lying in his velvet stall, as spacious as the night, stared up at the conclave of stars, pondered the Milky Way and wondered whether he would find the cat again. He ached for the undemanding companionship he had briefly known and he knew that wherever imagination and philosophical conceptualisation might take him next, there was a little void in his big bovine heart that would be forever cat-shaped.'

I spoke these teasing words to Kat but my eyes wandered to Krysia's face. Her eyes bored into mine like sapphires. Next to me Kat had given a little gasp as the story ended. I looked at her too and her own sapphires were inexplicably moist.

~.~

If violence were avoided on the occasion by the lake I'd felt neither guilt nor shame about my stooping to vengeance in the classroom, nor do I now, though I can see how one can come to regard a victim as less than human, at least in hot blood. I was to find later that doctrine and pernicious propaganda intended to create cultural division bred of envy and prejudice would provide every opportunity for society to implode, and the worst imaginable excesses would then be committed, both in anger and in cold blood.

It took rather less time for my hearing to return to normal, but it was a week or more after my expulsion before the noises finally subsided and I was to have continuing trouble with my hearing later, through exposure to continuous loud noise.

~.~

I was endlessly fascinated by the workings of the cars on the Estate meanwhile and helped Schneider to polish the Mercedes. He was happy to explain the intricacies of the engines: the Otto cycle, the magneto or coil ignition and induction systems, filter, cooling, brakes, suspension and steering – all things mechanical. Although he retained his trap, my father too finally bought a motorcar, a chain-driven 5 hp. Benz-Nesseldorfer and I was in my element, learning to drive it around the nearby fields and dirt roads and to carry out basic maintenance with the tools provided.

The long winter months stretched out beyond Christmas. The Strelitz's spent them in Vilnius, as they often did, while the Graf travelled on to Kreuzhof with Marik, to Kristian's boyhood home, and latterly that of his now mysterious and dissolute elder brother, the late Peter Graf von Strelitz, sea-farer, poet and dilettante artist, so Marik later informed me. They were to arrange for repairs and confer with land agents on the intended disposal of the shrunken estate. I recalled the story later; the one they called 'The Grasshopper', charismatic, an untutored though talented artist n'ere do well, who'd ensured his notoriety gambling away his inheritance, running up debts from Monte Carlo to Rio, who'd gone over the taffrail of an elderly Javanese steamer one evening, in his linen suit. Into an oily green sea off the Sunda Strait, Surabaja or the Flores Sea, still wearing his hat, under the thudding stern deck, as I imagined it; into the creamy wake, Burma cheroot in his mouth, so the mythology went, according to Marik, who knew or thought he knew all the family secrets, and those he half-knew were amusingly embellished.

His uncle Peter, it seems, had simply died of boredom aboard the *SS Ennui*.

When he'd felt he'd lived *quite* long enough, thank you, and had tried everything there was to try, he'd folded his copy of the Straits Times or the Rangoon Chronicle, straightened his tie, and stepped over the stern rail and the last there was to see, if the Lascar throwing waste overboard for the sharks had looked, was a bobbing Panama drifting away in the watery sunset. His effects were eventually shipped and his papers and clothes came to Liepus Namas via the Kreuzhof; a battered steamer trunk smothered with exotic Batavian address stickers and customs labels.

The story had a strange resonance. I seemed to recall a night of sleeplessness and a white owl when I was five or six years old. The sound of horses in the cobbled courtyard of *Ausautas* and hushed yet urgent voices in the house. Two women there; one possibly the Princess Sophie, the other I was not certain of. They spoke, if not in whispers, then quietly so that I stole onto the staircase to listen from the shadows. They were speaking French with my parents and there was talk of a letter that seemed very important, and the word *Java* was mentioned several times with a certain emphasis, which meant little to me then, but seemed important and exotic too, and I was certain this was a place of mystery and adventure. I think I must have fallen asleep on the stairs because I half-remembered being carried back up to bed by my father and other faces looking in on me.

~-~

The widowed Graf, ever an impeccable and imposing figure, riding in his carriage or later sweeping through the lodge gates in his chauffeured open black Mercedes tourer, less frequently in a long leather coat and goggles at the wheel of his white three-speed Sizaire-Naudin with its red artillery wheels, was often away in the weeks after Elenja's death, on maritime business Marik confided with a wistful pride. I detected sadness and a lack of closeness between them; else he was attending trade fairs and conferences with industrialists or playing the Margrave and dealing with local affairs. It was whispered among the staff

316

that he had an exotic mistress in Petersburg, but that sort of thing was never raised openly, still less in earshot of the Governess, who with the assistance of the burly German-Polish manager, Herr Berg, and the Graf's Jewish male secretary, increasingly ran the Kuznetsowa Estate.

Miss Hammond perforce assumed the wider role of part-senior housekeeper while still attending to the comportment and education of her charges, or at least supervising their tutelage, though to a lesser extent with Marik who was then studying for the examination for the obligatory military academy – entry to which was of course almost guaranteed.

Usually the children helped with the harvest, the healthy outdoor exercise suiting Marik and myself, and the girls too, who were close to my age, one younger one older, and banter with the farm workers and casual labourers was fun and it seldom went too far. At least with the older hands who tended towards diffidence and were more guarded, this being expected and understood. But some bumptious and merry lads gave as good as they got and no feelings were hurt or belief systems undermined, even if agitprop Marxists abounded in tavern and town.

'But if you, the privileged, became tired of the toil, you could all as easily drift away or fall into a haystack and sleep for an hour, is that not so?' Browne is speaking, breaking into my thoughts, some of which I'd vocalized in a more or less articulate fashion. Probing my ideology in a very simplistic way, I thought.

My familiar headache, which I had been trying to ignore for some time, wasn't going away. I ask for water and receive it. Since the crash I'd suffer a painful headache for at least a couple of hours per day.

'That the lot of the peasant and the tied farmer is to labour until sunset was not lost on me.' I reply, trying not to sound too testy. 'I am making the point that my viewing platform was a half-way station between the 'haves' and the 'have nots'.' I'd toiled along with the workforce until the job was done, and to their credit the Strelitz children too, determined to show that they could take the strain and with the power of youth they proved that they could stick it out, indeed I'd struggled to keep up with Marik, who was tall and strong, until the last stook was hoisted and a libation was offered to the fields for their bounty, to their own Lithuanian *Demeter*: the peasant girls and women unashamedly incanting a pagan prayer to the hierarchy of ancient spirit gods of field and forest. The peasant farmers who helped work the estate paid the Graf tax in kind at harvest time and he in turn paid his dues to the Tsar. It was ever thus.

My Graf was a Kulak in Bolshevist eyes; worse an aristo, one of the resented landowners, more particularly *dvarininkas* in Lithuanian, a *boyar* if you like, one of the *dwor*, of the nobility. He was of the *Szlachta*, thus doubly and trebly damned and demonised in the Bolshevist propaganda as a profiteering capitalist, crudely caricatured thus in agitprop theatre for the entertainment and corrective education of masses.

'But he was no *Oblomov*,' I declare. 'No languid dreamer, my Graf. He was active and diligent. A self-made man, despite Marik's unworthy character assassination.' *It implied that his mother too was tainted by dishonour. Without that vital spark in Dar Es-Salaam, Marik would not have been born to voice such judgment.* 'In my eyes he was a brave and honourable man. A nobleman.' Hawkeye-Rose had smiled again at *Oblomov*. Or perhaps it was at the concept of honour.

But despite the protestations of Marik's undying friendship, I told them, Rose and Browne, that I could not help feeling rather the poor relation, welcome at the whim of a privileged and powerful, well-established landowning elite. A family of merchant knights whose Hanse house in the west, though run down and infrequently used since the Graf's elder brother, Peter, had died, passing the title to Kristian was linked to the old protecting League by the communicating fire-beacons of a medieval Teuton hierarchy.

Although bordering Belarus, in that vision of transplanted German Imperialism, I, Rolf, was a visitor whose very *language* until as recently as 1904, had been under a complete ban. This Mikhail Nikolayovich Muravyev, when Governor General of Lithuania, had instituted in 1864 following a violent popular uprising against Tsarist rule that had been firmly put down. It had included the closure of the University of Vilnius, a ban on the Latin alphabet, on education and on all printed matter in the Lithuanian language, although such books were printed in East Prussia and the USA and smuggled into the country despite the threat of stiff prison sentences. The German landowners were generally undisturbed by such *fiats* and had consistently supported the Tsar, so their libraries remained largely inviolate, and in any case the Baltic Germans were self-governing to a large extent and peaceable, though Stolypin's land reforms were beginning to bite. However, to the Graf's credit, in the eyes of some he was more 'Lithuanian' than 'landed colonial' in his outlook, though still reluctant to surrender his perimeter. His peasant farmers enjoyed good tenure and received medical attention, subsidised by the Graf had they but known it. But he'd 'gone native' as some of the other families said in secret, and, a speaker himself, allowed the free use of Lithuanian in the household among the servants.

318

But it is the second day on my arrival at Liepus Namas and Katya has not come. And I think I may know why.

The Graf is telling me about the death of my father, Augusts. And about the two brothers whose lives were over before I was born. Max and Witek, so Nina reminds us.

'He couldn't save them, Rolf. A skilled physician; Augusts always felt guilty about that. I thought you knew.'

I was reeling. 'I had no idea. No idea that I'd had two brothers who'd died before I was born.'

'I thought they'd told you, Rolf.'

'This isn't making sense to me. How did my father die?' I felt my lip quivering.

The Graf was silent for a while. 'Dr. Dragunavicius fell in the line of duty.'

'Fell? How fell? He was a doctor, not a combatant. Explain please.' I had finished my tea but my mouth was still dry.

The Graf looked at me while whole worlds of expression passed in muster across his eyes with their processional banners held high. There it was written on the void that separates the reality from the vainglorious ideal; cavalry charges across green fields with the crack of cannon fire and shell bursts all about, that there was in fact little dignity in death. A young dragoon could urge his mount upon the enemy pike-men who break and flee already in his mind, even before the headlong charge to glory, and so the victorious cavalry gains the day. An immortal triumph, and he lives to tell his grandchildren how the foe, with cunning tactics, was routed in twenty hard minutes. Was that the romantic fantasy he'd sold Rolf into? Is that the folly he'd urged Marik towards? But if there was no dignity in death, there were deaths still worse than those upon the battlefield.

'He was working at night in a field hospital in Latgale. Short of medicines, carrying out amputations in desperate circumstances. There was a trench for body parts and bodies that had been dug only fifty meters from the operating tables and an almost constant stream of bearers bringing in stretcher case and taking out what had to be removed. He and the other few exhausted surgeons. At sunset they were surrounded by Bolshevists, irregulars. The foulest scum, the *Wolves of Latgale*. They dragged out the nurses, sealed the building and burned it to the ground with the doctors and their helpless patients inside, hundreds of them – their own Red bedridden wounded too. Extracted only those of their own who could walk and hold a rifle. All else who tried to escape were machine-gunned, while the nurses were made to watch and listen to the screams while they themselves were raped. They then murdered the nurses and threw them into the trench with the body parts. A few escaped since by then the scum were drunk and incapable. Maybe some were deliberately released so that news of the atrocity would spread and with it their infamy which would strike terror into the hearts of those who might stand in their way.'

I said nothing. I had heard of such things. Shortly before our Freikorps broke through to Riga the Bolshevists murdered entire German Hanse families that they'd been holding as hostages. Three thousand innocents. Men, women and children tortured and put to death in the most horrible ways imaginable, the perpetrators escaping us. I recalled the account of a family of four, mother father and two little children that had starved to death: found sitting at their dining table, their hands and feet nailed to the table and to the floor with a meal set before them, inches from their mouths, like the torment of Tantalus. Each of the four reportedly had a Roman letter carved into the flesh of their naked backs: *ALVB*. Freed from all taboos, from the constraining arm of morality, the Bolshevist's capacity for refined torture seemed endless.

Though not without sin, the wrath of our troops too was terrible and von der Goltz barely prevented wholesale slaughter of those locals whom they'd deemed complicit.

'So died Augusts. So nearly died my Katya. The Graf is clutching at words now, almost unable to speak. Rolf… she arrived here, God knows how she made it. Bleeding, starving in rags. Head swollen, half blind. Months later she aborted a child. A boy. She buried it herself, unmarked, without a prayer. She is now full of hate. She will not speak. She clung to Graczyna only, when first she came. No one else can get near her. They'd shot her in the face and buried her alive, but it was dark. They were very drunk and shooting wildly at everything. She turned her head at the last moment and was only stunned when she fell into the trench. The bullet missed her eye by a fraction and furrowed her temple. They threw other bodies on top of her.'

He paused for a minute.

'Some of the nurses didn't die right away. For hours she lay semi-conscious and in pain listening to the moans and crying from the others as they suffered and bled and died, one by one….the crackling of the fire as it continued unabated in the pyre of the hospital. Many hours later she and another girl – an English nurse - dug themselves out and made it to the woods. They travelled south by night, but the other girl was wounded badly and the bleeding would not stop. Katya had to leave her, weak as she was from blood loss, and confused, hardly able to see. She watched over her for a day and a night without food and little water other than what she could suck from leaves or strain from moss. She could hear sounds in the forest that were getting nearer. Terrified, she was eventually forced to leave her friend. She doesn't know whether she was still alive when she left her. With everything else, this haunts her still. This she told me all in a rush. But since the stillbirth she's barely said a word.'

I began to feel a loss of control. Tremulously, 'And my mother?'

'Hannah…. Dead. Grief stricken. She committed suicide, I regret. The Bolshevists burned down *Ausautas* later and much of the village. Elsewhere whole communities were massacred. Rolf, I'm so very sorry.'

Ironically, I learned later that though the expensive treatments had failed, my father's herbal system, based on Hahnemann's methods, appeared to have been successful. My mother's cancer had shrunk away by the end of that year, 1917, the year of Revolution.

~-~

I sit staring at the pale grey sky and the treetops beyond the library windows. My mind is ice but my body burns. There is a hard ache in the middle of my chest, a sickness in my gut and I yearn to kill something or somebody, preferably with my bare hands. It is a primeval reaction focussed on the witchfinder and vile despot who has unleashed his monstrous cohorts in his lust for power.

Each of my questions has revealed a mounting toll. The local population, especially the Jews, have been culled in a bloodfest of savagery and horror, names of families I knew, those of children I had played with have met a dismal fate, turned out of their homes, herded into stinking cattle trucks and tied like kindling upon flatcars, else marched into oblivion, the youngest and oldest clubbed or shot, left to die or to fend for themselves. Slave labour for the New Order? Hostages, or just sent into exile and death somewhere convenient. As I listen my adrenaline surge peaks and I rage at my torn leg. For a mad moment I see myself marching on Latgale, wakening *Vytautas* and riding him one last time to my personal Valhalla, into the firestorm of the Kremlin in my mind - a strangely prescient vision I will recall in time. But it's impossibly far and I cannot even *walk*, though the passion is great, such that I am sick and drowning; short of lung capacity - as if a steel band had tightened round my chest. Finally. 'What of Krysia?' My words are strangled, forced. 'What's happened to her?'

'She at least is safe. She's left the Sorbonne but is still in Paris, staying with Natalia Rosanova – baroness, my cousin by marriage, an aunt of Sophie's. Her husband, Aleksandr Rosanov was at the embassy, a deputy cultural secretary for the Imperial Government. Krysia wrote in desperation via the Red Cross and the letter was couriered through the German lines, weeks' old when it arrived. But she is well and said would try to come when she can get passage. The Gulf is mined although the British Royal Navy has a powerful presence there and last I heard is carving a safe channel to the Baltic ports. To Riga anyway. They were confronting von der Goltz's forces there – your people. I replied that it was not safe to come at present, but I don't know whether she received my hasty letter in reply. Who knows what this continuing war will bring to us? We are too close to Belarussia here. Bolshevist packs like rabid wolves penetrate borders and such demarcations can shift and everyone is looking to extend their territory, opening up all the feuds of the ages to justify their claims, or refute those of the other tribe's.'

'Why didn't you try to escape?' I asked vaguely. My mind was in overload.

'I had no petrol. Only the aviation fuel dump, and that was guarded until recently. I myself had been shot when patrolling with my militia – last year that was, so I could barely walk. In any case the roads weren't safe. Still aren't by God. Nearly all the horses were driven off or butchered. The Mercedes was requisitioned and went when the German troops evacuated. The remaining car was destroyed by arson when the stables were torched. So we were trapped here with a small staff while fighting raged all round. Most of the rail traffic was Bolshie. Sometimes they'd just randomly shell the villages from a stationary train and then pull back. It's probable that we're so far from the beaten track here among the lakes that's preserved the Estate so far from being completely ransacked like so many others.'

It is a sad fact that armies in retreat always leave misery in their wake. The lost territory marked with the indiscriminate fires of spite, revenge and a sheer homicidal brutality against civilians, wreaked at will. *Soldier, have you not a mother, too?*

He looks at me pensively. He says that he believes it is what is left of the goodwill that the late princess generated by her sacrifice that has saved the family so far. 'You may remember, Rolf, though you were very young....'

I only recalled that my father had been away for several weeks when I was a small child. That the house had seemed isolated for a while. However, I later learned that a *cordon sanitaire* had been thrown around one end of the village. I knew the painting well, but somewhere I possessed a half-remembered image of the beautiful flame-haired Princess Sophie, or *thought* I did, who had succumbed in the epidemic. A white obelisk had been erected to her memory in the village square, for her leadership in the care of the victims of the cholera outbreak, whose contorted agony and collective fate she'd shared which had sanctified her.

'And where is Katya now? How is she?'

'She has gone with a servant and a boy to Ignalina for supplies, with two pack-horses. She is armed with the Steyr. I tried to stop her, but you may recall how headstrong she is, Like Krysia, both the same. She's a good shot, and more disciplined than when last she'd tried to bring down a boar, you may recall.'

I'd not forgotten, but had not brought it to mind. Not for a few years. Not since the injustices of Helmsburg and all that came after.

Chapter 23. *Katya and Old Kaiser*

On that cold and crisp winter's eve of memory a breathless young footman from the Big House had lately come, rapping at the door, full of importance with snow in his hair and green-gold liveried jacket askew, bearing a letter from the Graf. My father had reached to take it having himself answered the door, but Jonyas, whom I knew quite well and was but a little older than myself insisted on presenting it to me. My father called him inside and I rose from the table where our little family was enjoying the last of our supper, and took the envelope, upon which my name was written full in the Graf's florid hand. I recalled the content of that single sheet of heavy waxy paper with the red baronial seal. His pressing, *KvS*.

'Master Rolf,

'One of my guests for my Name Day shoot tomorrow feels unable to join us in the field. We are already short of one gun and our day could be spoiled unless we find a replacement. I fear that your dear father's eyesight is no longer good enough, but Herr Berg has told me that you are a good and safe shot. I therefore wish you to join the line tomorrow morning.

'You will be collected by the game cart at half past five tomorrow sharp. Gorbunov will have instructions where to bring you. Make sure that you are properly dressed and equipped.'

It was signed with the Graf's initials. Gorbunov, I groaned inwardly. A rascally giant given to homespun wit. It was alleged that mice lived in his beard and revolution in his peasant heart!

I passed the note to my father who read it aloud for my mother's benefit. 'But you've only your old padded jacket and felt boots,' she cried, full of unnecessary anguish, eyes wide. I know she is thinking that there will be gentlemen there in their smart shooting outfits, possibly ladies too, and I will appear as the poor relation, an upstart middle class supernumery dragged in to plug the gap in the Graf's shooting line. So he wouldn't lose face. It was one thing to have been a child visitor at the Big House over the years, playing discreetly in the background with Marik and the other children. But this was grown up business and 'class will out', or so it's said.

Jonyas cleared his throat respectfully, begging the pardon of both Madam and Sir, and informed us of the Graf's verbal rider, ' To tell young Master Rolf that if he will come back with me to the Big House at once, to the gun room, Ivan Lebedovich, the Head Keeper, will find the right gun to fit him. And Piotr, that's the Graf 's valet Sir, he will be on hand to assist with the clothes.'

I felt flushed and excited but all at once caught sight of a framed and coloured print, *The Huntsman's Funeral,* that had hung long years in our parlour so that it had become 'invisible' to me, until that moment. All the animals of the hunt, rabbits, foxes, deer and boar carried the stretcher high, upon which rested the body of a slain huntsman, as squirrels scampered and birds twittered him to his grave. They gave to him, their old enemy, a respect in death that the true huntsman accords the game, if he fears God and does his bidding, taking only enough for his needs and killing cleanly, abhorring that one of God's creatures should be subjected to suffering.

The imagery gave me pause a moment, before I retired to my bed.

~-~

Next morning at some ungodly hour I was roused from a deep sleep.

'You must salute the game that are always well-brushed, sir, in their 'Sunday Best'. So shall you return the compliment and be as spruce as you can be! Up my lad, the sun is shining!' Much too jocular I thought.

I rose and went to the window. It was as black as midnight still. I was barely shaving then and still at my bleary-eyed worst so my neck stung where I'd nicked it a time or two with the 'cut throat'. I drew on my woollen underclothes and stockings and the unfamiliar garb, which Piotr had selected for me that smelled of camphor but fitted well enough. My mother had prepared an early breakfast, scrambled eggs with game sausage, which I gratefully munched as dreamily I sipped my hot tea, trying to reach a state of approximate consciousness. My father re-appeared in his dressing gown and exhorted me to behave like a gentleman, not to touch a drop of vodka until the shoot was over and address the other guests by their correct titles. 'Make sure you don't poach another man's game by shooting anything that is not heading directly towards you. Above all be safe. Wish I was going with you, although I fear it is a little cold for me today and I have a few hour's sleep yet I might catch up on.'

Pulling on the jacket and tying the boots, I proceeded to lift the gun to my shoulder. It was an exquisitely engraved .350 Nitro Express Rigby.

I sighted the double barrels on an imaginary boar that was charging through our kitchen. Father smiled. 'Well you look the part anyway. Keep that safety catch on until you mean business though. It's not your little fowling piece. And don't load until instructed. That thing can do *real* damage.

There was a shout from outside and I drew back the thick curtain to see the game sled had arrived in our courtyard. Through the frosting on the glass I could just make out the bulky figure of Vassily Fyodorovich Gorbunov, rustic sage, hunched on the box in furs and a *papakha*, a pipe in his mouth.

With the last slice of black bread in my teeth and some hunting sausage in my pockets I crammed on my hat and was out of the door into the cold pre-dawn.

'Lucky you came quick,' said Gorbunov, 'Or I'd have had to rug up horse.' He took a closer look at me as I climbed up beside him. '*Bozhe moy!*' he grinned through his big, irregular teeth, 'What the hell you supposed to be?' His massive tangled beard was flecked with snow. 'I thought you were supposed to be *beater,*' he laughed.

'*Svolkami zhit, po volchi vuyt!* (*If you mix with wolves then you must howl like a wolf!*) Just make sure you don't speak Lithuanian today, boy, or you'll be rumbled for sure!'

I frowned at him and said nothing, wrapping the horse blanket over my knees and sliding the gun in its slip beneath to keep it warm. The horse moved off breaking into a trot as we came to the road, then at a light touch of the whip, it broke into a canter that set the sled humming over the hard-packed snow. The night's snowfall has not frozen hard and was swept like spray from a boat's cutwater as we voyaged through the dark, and the thudding of the hooves and the hiss of the runners would have lulled me back to the realm of sleep had it not been for the icy wind on my forehead and cheek.

After twenty minutes we turned right, off the road and onto snowy banks of meadowland, headed I presumed for the wooded slopes below the Tannenberg Memorial or *Grunewald Denkmal,* as it was also known. This Gorbunov confirmed. 'Best drives on the Estate up there. The Graf has shot there on his Name Day every year since he and Princess were gifted Kuznetsowa estate by *old* Count. Damned cuckold,' he added.

'What?'

'Never mind. On slope down from Monument towards river. It's where they will be waiting, by two big stands of mature pines and five of new plantings; were put in five years ago. They just begin now to get away. Wind is perfect.

'Of course,' he continued, 'They won't give you best position, but somebody may be lucky and get his chance at *Kaiser* today. Big old bastard he is. Must weigh three hundred and fifty kilograms, easy.'

'I've heard of him,' I said. A big old boar indeed. I'd heard he was more than a metre tall at the shoulder. I flexed my fingers in the gloves under the blanket and felt the comforting weight of the Nitro Express, recalling the heady combination of function and beauty. I remembered again its perfect balance when Berg had let me practice mounting and swinging it in the gun room.

'So why d'you think Graf invited *you* today? Scraping barrel, was he?

'I wasn't invited. I was commanded,' I said, bridling slightly. 'Short of guns he'd said in the note. One of his guests apparently declined the shoot.' Gorbunov always brushed my fur the wrong way.

'Hah! Fop from Warsaw with girl's hair. I heard he is happier gossiping with old dowagers and writing poetry to young ladies than standing in sleet with gun in fist. But more to it than that. I reckon Graf has eye on you for while. Old Berg won't go on forever and maybe you could be trained up for manager. Given time that is.' He laughed again, scornfully I thought.

I had a sudden vision of Krysia on a Swiss ski-slope, wintering in a Schloss for a month with the governess. Part of a minor *Grand Tour* or something. I was missing her more than I cared admit to myself.

'Just remember, if you do take up offer, you'll find out who are real friends yours. Don't expect favours from little rag-arses you romped and ridden with and poached Graf's game. They're growing up angry young men. There's *New Age* around corner and we won't always be breaking backs living on own sweat in summer, grateful for few kopeks while noble lords, masters with fine ladies and Petersburg whores lie abed drinking French champagne half day. Strutting about, gambling. And sailing round world to New York and Shanghai. That's *China*,' he added, lowering his voice conspiratorially, as if imparting a secret that must be kept at all costs from the horse.

I preferred to keep silent on this matter. His words could be construed as seditious, but to argue would only inflame him. But he seemed to read my thoughts and went on. 'So, don't come looking for help. You may think you're going up in world, playing young squire, but your future lies with *people*, not damned ruling class. Day is coming, mark words.'

'I'll make my own future,' I retorted.

'Oh yes? When revolution comes history will make and you can be part of, or events will roll right over you, little man! And your upper class harlot too!' he added slyly.

'Hold your tongue!' I said hotly, enraged and dismayed that my secret tryst could be so impugned by this irredeemably impudent peasant as much by the sting of his taunt.

'Ah ha!' he said triumphantly. 'So is true!'

I glowered at him ineffectually, my eyes scarce coming up to his thick shoulder. 'You've been talking treason, *Vassily Fyodorovich*, and not for the first time. There are those who'd denounce you for a few kopeks.'

'*Vilami na vode pisano.* Judas words from your lips, Rolf, for thirty kopeks?'

'So you are the new *Messiah*, then?'

'Not I, Rolf. One comes who is greater. I am but follower. Disciple.'

'So what will *you* do, baptize him?'

'The one I follow needs no baptism. Some say he is *Antichrist.*'

'Who is he?'

'I do not yet know name. But will come. And then all know and tremble. Baptism of fire, everywhere! Is foretold in Russian lore. You can be part of crusade, Rolf. Wipe out injustice that enslaves all, you too. Or else you will meet fate of those you've chosen to worship. In craven servitude.'

'But you serve them too!'

'Yes. For now. But I bide time. For now.'

He was silent a while, chewing on his pipe or his beard.

'But some just follow bandwagon for pickings. And then are another breed of men, make even *these* big bones shudder, evil ones with blood lust in very souls that New Order will seek to harness to its will. These men ready to do that will. Will do anything.'

'What do you mean?'

'Men with no morality. Hard men with no feeling. Wicked men, missing something in head,' he makes a finger-twisting gesture with his mitten at his temple. 'Men who will serve *Beast with no Name*, who show no remorse for vilest act. They are tools for accomplishing great task that lies ahead, force through change at point of gun. But if they become 'new elite', then bloody watch out.' He paused. 'You know, despite what I've said I still believe in God. I have no choice, is how I was taught and I believe as my father and his father too, and his father. Always. Some times I question, but life is hard and short, so why take chance and die sinner. I can still join *Movement* and pray in room, in secret, *nyet?*

Berezhonogo bog berezhot.' (God helps those who help themselves).' He looked at me sideways with a twinkle in his eye.

'You're a hypocrite and a cynic, Vassily Fyodorovich. And a fraud.'

But his words rang true and the future seemed a dangerous place in the assessment of this articulate and thoughtful son of the soil.

~·~

We'd cantered and trotted six or seven versts and now the eastern sky was lightening. The starlit snow, which had led us on our way, changed upon an instant to reflect the rising sun, with a million rainbow crystals glittering in the dawn: the very spirit of *Blizgulis* - he who glitters. The Snow God.

Round the next bend the horse slowed on a rise, taking the measure of the snowy bank, until we stopped overlooking a sheltered hollow where there was a noisy encampment of six keepers and about thirty beaters, some of whom I knew slightly, squatting or crouching around an obstinate pile of smoking kindling. Tough wiry men, each one with a fierce looking wild-eyed dog on a string. They wore reversed sheepskin jackets, felt boots and mostly reversed rabbit-skin caps or *papakhas* tied down with strips of hide. Scabbards for long knives hung at their sides and small axes were slung across their backs. *The Stoats and Weasels of the Wild Wood.* The keepers, whom I mostly knew by name, were attired in the Graf's green and gold-piped livery with a broad-brimmed hat. Each carried a single-barreled shotgun and a curled brass hunting horn.

On our arrival they ceased their cuffing and loud cursing of the quarrelsome dogs and turned their attention to me.

'*Bozhe moy!*' said one. 'If it isn't Doctor Dragun's little boy all dressed up. Come to play 'shoot big boar' with all fine gentlemen, have we?'

'Shut up your mouth, Timotei Viktorovich!' said Gorbunov quietly, but so that all could hear. 'This young man may yet be saviour for all if he can get education and persuade the Graf to farm modern way. Like in Germany.' The bear-like growls and howls of derision did not deter him. 'Pay no heed, Master Rolf.' He raised his hands for quiet and spoke with a respectful tone for the benefit of the encampment. 'These men *foresters*, rough for sure, like damn badgers, but not dumb farm labourers like they employ on some shoots. These will beat straight through wood, not huddling in timid groups like some we know. Some here are Letts. No nerves, fearless. And dogs are tireless. But if you see dogs running out of block have caution, for that means there is *wolf* in there. Maybe more than one!'

'*Oi vey, oi vey! Volkhov boyat'sa-v les ne khodit!*' wailed someone in a tremulous voice, while another, in sneering German, '*Junge, aufgepasst! Der Kaiser kommt!*' the beaters jeering and guffawing on cue as I felt my ears glow hot.

'Quiet, you villains!' laughed Gorbunov. Then throwing back the pile of horse blankets that covered the body of the sled, shouted, 'Come and get it, peasants! Breakfast, courtesy of Kristian Graf von Strelitz, God bless him!'

~-~

The men surge forward happily tucking into the soft-boiled eggs, sausage, bread and cheese while Gorbunov takes me aside. 'Rolf, if you see really big boar, or heaven forbid, old *Kaiser* – and you shoot, and you bloody miss…. fall on your *face* and just let the bastard carve your cheeks until someone bloody else shoot him. He won't retreat. He'll stand ground and fight you to death!'

I step up to help Gorbunov rug up the horse, but he waves me away. 'Stand fast, young Master,' he says, suddenly more formal than ever. 'What would Graf Kristian say if he sees you working as groom in all that finery?'

Somebody gives a shout and we look to see four sleighs draw up in line abreast at the top of the hill. All hats came off as the Graf steps regally from the lead sleigh, dressed in a shooting jacket, plus fours and puttees with a fur-trimmed cloak hanging from his shoulders and wearing a wide-brimmed hat. He walks at the head of his party of guests into the smoky bivouac, where a few beaters hastily smother the fire.

'Good morning, men,' he says.

The men reply with a respectful, 'Your Lordship,' then replace their hats quickly as the wind is colder out of the hollow, and rising.

'Now, Ivan Lebedovich,' the Graf is addressing the head keeper who had ridden the first sleigh with the coachman, 'You and I both now well what we have planned to do, but I will spell it out now for everyone here. The down-slope wind is perfect and not too strong. We will drive each block starting from the top.' Then to the guns: 'Gentlemen, gather round please.' I step forward to join the others at the rear of the circle of guests. 'Most of you will have shot with me before on this ground but let me just remind you of the terrain. We will take these seven blocks of timber and young growth, which you see before you all the way to the river. Our forestry blocks measure fifteen hundred metres across the top and seven hundred and fifty metres on each side, so there is a fair distance for the beaters to cover. We will take the sleighs down to the first cross ride while they spread out along the top boundary. With the wind as it is there'll be no difficulty in hearing the keepers' horns when they start through the cover. Please do not load until you hear that horn.'

He looks around at our Group to let his words sink in. 'As the beaters and keepers come within range of our guns they will sound their horns again. Please do not shoot forwards after that. When the drive is over the horns will sound for the third time. Please then be sure to unload your guns. Our sleighs will collect us and take us straight down to the next ride, so please do not delay us. Unless there is *good* cause for delay the beaters will carry straight on and our game sled will collect whatever you have killed. If you think you may have wounded a beast but did not see it fall, tell one of the keepers and they will go after it on the next drive.' Looking round he continues, 'I see our beaters are ready to go. But before that there are the proper formalities to be observed.'

The keepers step forward with the beaters crowding behind them and on a word of command they raise their hunting horns. At a signal they blow a strident fanfare, the hillsides returning the salute in muted diminuendo and a raucous accompanying recitative from a rookery across the valley. The Graf removes his hat, the indication for all present to do likewise. A slim young guest in a heather mix of tweed who'd arrived in the last sleigh and whose back is now presented to me removes her cap, letting fall a cascade of red hair. My heart leaps like a salmon with the thought that Krysia has returned, but I soon realise it is the second Strelitz sister. I am nevertheless pleased that she is here. I also think that the Graf must have been desperate to make up the numbers for though she is a wizard at archery she has barely handled more than a light sporting gun or air rifle to my knowledge.

Katya winds her hair into a knot and ties it with a snood, turning her beautiful smile on me as she does. For some reason I feel myself blushing as other curious eyes turn on me. Gorbunov treats me to an oafish grin and winks suggestively behind the Graf's shoulder, and I feel hot and foolish and all the worse for wanting to say, *no you bumpkin it is* Krysia *owns my heart.* But I smile sheepishly, averting my eye, and feel the Graf's steely gaze settle briefly on my bowed head.

'Almighty God.' The Graf's voice was clear and strong. 'Who hath made all things, men, women, beasts of the field and of the forest, and all the multitude of creation in the earth, pray give us this day a day to remember, a perfect day's sport. Keep every one of us safe from hazard this day. But we beg Thee also to exalt Thy creations, the game we hunt. Pray give them courage and strength, and for those that must die let them do so honourably with a clean shot. And may those that escape go on to live a healthy and fruitful life, so that we never take more from the forest than Thou in time alloweth in Thy bounty to be restored.'

'Amen,' rumbled the assembly.

'Right! Guns to the sleighs, please.' The Graf was all action. 'Ivan, remember I want you down with the guns so Vassily can take charge of the beaters. Get them on their way now please.' Then turning away to speak in a lower tone to Ivan, his voice is just audible as I happen to draw near. 'Two inexperienced guns out today. Keep an eye - put 'em out on the right of the line where they can do least harm. Mayn't see much action but stand with 'em so that they'll learn how things should be done.' I catch Ivan's expression as I turn away. Not surprisingly he doesn't seem too happy about this, probably thinking of the tips he'll be foregoing from the more experienced guns.

First drive we see nothing. Ivan Lebedovich stands half way between myself and Katarzyna, so there is no opportunity to exchange words, for me to ask after Krysia. In any case we were too far apart to converse and it would have been inopportune in any event with our need to concentrate on the shoot. Then far away on the other side of the cover there is a cacophony of shouts and barking, muffled by the distance. A single shot cracks the morning air, then silence. Some while later the horns blow to signify that the beaters are close and that the drive is ended. The sleighs collect us and whirl us down the hill, again to the sound of horns as we turn into the cross ride. Kat is in front in my sleigh but there is no opportunity to converse. As we assemble we learn that Major Petrovsky had bagged a good red stag and then we are at our pegs in the same order with Lebedovich in between and stand in silence for fifteen minutes, me idly watching a jay circling a tree trunk, alighting now and then, picking his own breakfast out of the bark.

Again there comes a furious barking and the shouts of men, much nearer this time. The cry, *'Djik! Djik! Three, no four!'* Then silence. Until, very faintly comes a soft sussuration of little trotters galloping through crystalline snow, growing louder by the moment. But at that instant came several shots from the centre of the line followed again by silence. Whatever had been coming our way I presumed had been frightened off and had either fled from the side of the cover, or turned about and passed through the line of beaters. I replace the safety and slip the loose cover back onto the trigger finger of my gloved hand.

It is the third drive. The sun has some warmth and the snow is softening in the patches between the trees that drip with moisture. Ivan Lebedovich comes up to me.

'I go to stand with Lady Katarzyna,' he whispers. 'She is good shot I think, but perhaps a *little* excitable so I worry she might fire forward if pig breaks cover with beaters close behind. If I stay close I can knock gun up before she fires. That means I'll be leaving you on your own. Remember what I've taught you and especially what I told you last night. Wait till you see target clearly before you mount gun. You have thicker clothes on than you are used to so throw gun well out as you bring it up. Swing from behind and give target adequate lead. You are clear to right hand side, but be so very careful if you fire to front, and never, ever, swing through line without dismounting gun.' And with a quiet 'Good luck!' he scrunches through the snow to Katya.

Nothing happened at the end of the line on that drive, although shots were heard in the centre and further away on the left. The final horn sounds and I walk over to where Katya and Ivan are standing waiting for the sleigh. I compliment Kat on her outfit and I am granted another of her beaming smiles. She says that the livery jacket fits well and suits me, but then she pouts sulkily. 'Papa may have let me come out today but I know he hopes no boar will come my way. That's why Ivan Lebedovich has placed me out here on the end – away from all the action. The Graf only let me join the shoot because he made me a promise at my birthday party.'

'I am mortified.' I'd forgotten it had been her sixteenth birthday last month. 'How can you forgive me for forgetting?' She smiles again, briefly. She must be aware that my head is still full of Krysia, away these last five weeks. 'But what promise did he make?'

'I am here today because of that fool of a *Prince, Paul von Somebody Very Important,* while obnoxious and very drunk, bet Papa that there wasn't a woman in Lithuania who would willingly face a charging boar. So I spoke up and accepted the challenge right then, but the Prince just laughed at me. So I got very angry and tore up my dance card. Papa tried to hush me but I said that that the Prince was frightened to lose his bet and that gentlemen did not back down once they'd made a wager.'

'That sure was throwing down the gauntlet!'

'First he looked furious, but then he laughed and Papa made his promise - that he'd take me on the next shoot. They shook on it and had other guests as witnesses. This was in the Bristol Hotel in Warszawa. He doesn't mind me shooting other small game.' She smiles, 'He says it's more ladylike than using my ram's horn bow! He says that with it I look like some savage huntress from ancient times! But he's worried stiff that a boar will go for me before I can shoot it. Ha! I'm as quick as any man!'

'And he's right, young lady,' says Ivan. 'But he's also concerned that you might shoot too soon. Beaters have families, you know!'

'I think I know the difference between a beater and a boar, Ivan Lebedovich!' she says haughtily.

'But he's right about worrying for your safety. Remember that boar is cunning and fierce animal. Though easily roused to anger, that doesn't make him foolish. He'll watch for an opportunity to slip past you, but if you block him, or if he thinks you are threat, or maybe he's just in bad temper - which is always likely – he'll turn on you instantly. So watch out. Stand very still and watch for him between trees and thin saplings, but don't shoot. Stand still as a tree until he is in full sight. Then, raise your gun and shoot straight. One smooth action. If you miss, throw down gun and climb tree – high as you can.'

'How you blether on, you old bear,' says Katya, smiling. 'I'll be alright.'

Further conversation is interrupted by the arrival of the sleigh and the heady swoop downhill to new positions. Katya's cousin Boris had shot a sow and somebody else two young pigs, a right and a left, announces Ivan over his shoulder after talking to the sleigh driver.

As we reach the location for the fourth drive Ivan Lebedovich drops me at my peg and I notice that underfoot it's slippery as I climb out, the top layer of snow beginning to thaw. He rides on with Katya to her place about 120 metres away. By now the sun is bright in a clear blue sky although the wind still has some bite. I can see Kat arguing with Ivan as they dismount the sleigh near a stand of birch. Kat feels strongly that she is too far from where the game is likely to run; but Ivan, with the Graf's warning in mind, is adamant.

A distant horn announces the beginning of the drive. The minutes slip past. I stand with my feet planted firm, comfortably apart, facing uphill looking up at a firebreak between thick dark fir trees. I feel strangely alone despite Kat and Ivan to my right and the knowledge that another guest was just out of sight, along the ride in the trees, a hundred metres or so to my left. Though I have been a little keyed-up this has now been replaced by a feeling of calm. I flex my shoulder muscles and then resume my stillness, savouring the feel and balance of the Rigby Express. Occasionally I hear a dog barking at a distance, and when the breeze lessens I can detect the tapping of sticks against tree trunks as the beaters advance.

Something is coming. First small birds fly out, a twittering stream that banks around the trees, crossing the ride in undulating flight to disappear in the undisturbed territory behind the guns. Some perch in the branches above my head looking fearfully back as if to assess the threat, to determine the cause of the general panic before flying on. Then silently, cautiously, slips a fox, out of the trees to my front, pausing a moment to look left and right. It crosses the ride; belly low to the ground its pungent smell drifting on the breeze. I stand stock-still and the animal almost runs over my feet, leaping sideways in fear as it gets my scent then bounding away through the undergrowth as if in a controlled flight from a large predator.

I glance briefly in Katya's direction. She is still talking animatedly to Ivan Lebedovich, swinging round to emphasise her argument. *For God's sake, Kat. Look to your front. There's action afoot!*

With that a large boar trots out of the scrub birch at the edge of the ride just in front of Kat's stand, generally heading their way. Old Lebedovich has seen it too. His shout and my call of 'Katya, Kat! *Djik, Djik!*' has an instant effect. The pig breaks into a gallop and Kat swings around to face it, raising her gun as she turns, but her feet are together, her body off-balance as she fires and the gun jerks sharply, throwing her back. The boar is at full speed but the shot has passed close enough to irritate the animal, which turns hard left on the instant charging towards the stand.

The pig has forty metres to run which it will cover in no time. From eighty metres away I see the snow spurt in front of the beast as it changes course lowering its head, signalling that this is not flight but *attack*.

With my feet apart and my weight well forward I swing up the gun, remembering everything that Lebedovich had taught me, knowing that a hurried shot could be disastrous, but that a delay could be equally so, and would also bring Katya and Ivan dangerously close to my line of fire. Squeezing off my shot when the boar is twenty metres from the stand, the gun recoils against my shoulder and as I check the second trigger for another shot I am aware of the dark brown shape somersaulting onto its back and sliding upside-down, rump first crashing into the bushes hard alongside Kat and Ivan in a shower of snow.

But they are no longer looking at the dead pig. Their mouths are open, shouting, and pointing at something over my left shoulder. I hear the word *sernas*. Boar! I swing back, gun held firmly in both hands, slipping a little in the wetness. Standing motionless across the ride is the biggest boar I've ever seen. Bigger than any boar I could ever have *imagined.* It could only be old *Kaiser*, his furious red eye upon me. I struggle for a good foothold, and then slip, falling on one knee, scrabbling for another cartridge as the boar suddenly bursts into frightening action, pawing angrily at the snow, raking up flakes of ice and dead leaves, exposing the soil like some savage bull, an *Aurochs* in a Roman gladiatorial contest. Grunting and snorting the animal rubs his wicked self-sharpening tusks in the raw earth: shakes his long body, rippling with corded muscle. Thick foamy flecks and mossy debris fly from the long muzzle and the glistening curved razors. The next instant he is in the charge, the stiff dorsal crest standing like a zebra's mane, accelerating instantly to full speed, head down, ready to slash and tear with those fearsome daggers at any part of his enemy. His speed is phenomenal and he already covers half the distance to me as, forcing myself to stay calm, as I've quickly slipped another cartridge into the breech.

Standing erect though still unsteady I throw up my gun and fire a barrel just above the animal's head, into the thick mass of muscle between its neck and shoulders. He's nearly on me, showing no sign of stopping as I fire the second barrel, seemingly point blank with Gorbunov's last words of advice in my ears, then throw myself forward under the sour breath and the grunting, wheezing shriek from the lungs of the massive boar. A mighty blow to my back knocks all wind and sense out of me. I seem to collapse inward and feel myself falling into a bottomless pit of darkness.

~-~

I came to in a world of hurt looking at a bright sky from which the colour had been leeched. I'd been run down by a steamroller and my back was broken. 'At least he's alive!' said a distant voice, and then someone was sitting me up and pouring vodka down my throat adding to my agony as the violent coughing fit I then suffered racked my ribs unmercifully. My head and neck ached and I was sure a tusk had caught my rump a raking slash. There was blood on the snow and on my hands, a few deep cuts and heavy bruising on their backs. Gradually I began to make out figures. Ivan Lebedovich standing upright with a worried look, a bloody sabre in his hand, and Katya, her face very pale, kneeling close to my shoulder. Vassily Fyodorovich knelt on the other side holding a hip flask with some other beaters and their dogs standing silently behind.

Gorbunov is wrapping a blanket over my legs. 'Better to be born lucky than rich, eh Rolf?'

I heard a sleigh arriving and struggled to move but Katya placed a restraining hand on my shoulder. 'Ivan called down the line as soon as we saw you go down. We… we thought you would be dead and Papa would want to stop the shoot out of respect. You've been unconscious for about ten minutes……I expect this is him now.'

The beaters crowded round to stare at me in some sort of wonder as Ivan Lebedovich hurried over to the sleigh where I could just make out a tense-looking Graf seated with two neighbours. 'Tell me what's happened, man,' I heard him say.

'Young Rolfs has just saved your daughter's life – and mine too possibly, or at least saved all from serious injury. And killed biggest damn boar this side of Carpathians!'

'Splendid, splendid; that's all well and good, but why the panic to stop the shoot?'

'Because we thought second boar has killed Rolfs!'

'What do you mean, *second* boar?'

'Well he shot two. Second boar was really big bastard. *Kaiser.*'

Now the Graf was out of the sleigh. 'Shot two? The Graf looked over to the where the dead boar lay at Katya's peg. Didn't Katya shoot that one? It's a long shot from here, I'd say. Where's Rolf? Let me through.'

The Graf and his small group advanced with Ivan. Katya stood up slowly, no longer the tomboy. Her face showed the trace of tears and her hair hung free. 'Papa, Rolf saved my life when my first shot missed and my second failed to fire and then he was nearly killed by the second boar. He had been unconscious since it ran over him and I've been so worried. Please can we take him straight home to Dr. Dragunavicius?'

'Of course we shall, my dear.' To the beaters, 'Cut some birch poles and use some jackets to make a stretcher and take the rugs from the sleigh to keep him warm. Make sure no one gives him anything to drink unless you are sure he is fully conscious.'

Vassily looked up. 'Too late, sir. I gave him vodka. But he's alright. He is strong boy!'

'Let me look.' I'd closed my eyes by this time. It seemed to help ease the pain to shut out the light, but opened them a little to see the Graf peering at me intently.

'Easy, boy.' He said gently, and to Ivan, 'Has he lost a lot of blood?'

'Not too much, I'd say, considering what hit him. And he's young.

He'll heal alright, God willing.'

'Right, be careful putting him on the sleigh, there could well be internal injuries. He's sure to have broken ribs at the very least if it ran over him. Now where's this *big* boar?'

Apparently it had run another fifty metres with my two bullets in him, dead on its feet and still running on adrenaline with vengeance in its heart. Ran straight over me as if I wasn't there but thank God it had stopped thinking tactically when the second bullet joined the first, one through the heart and another as close to as made no difference except it would have died a *little* slower and that would have made *all* the difference in the world.

So instead of slamming to a stop and goring me to shreds with its tusks, it just ran on automatically at full speed in its death rush until it went head-over-heels among the birch saplings and wound up lying on its neck with the hind legs high up against a mature tree that was shaken to the roots. It weighed over 350 kilos. a monster among boars and its hind trotters towered over the Graf and the beaters in a comic posture, *ah, the indignity of death*, when they went to look, even with much of the animal's massive head and shoulders lying in the dark red snow, his throat having been instantly cut by the Head Keeper.

~-~

'You'd have been lucky to have found the heart from such an angle, according to Ivan Lebedovich. But I'd seen the boar at Katya's peg. A perfect shot through the heart. And when we opened up old *Kaiser*, we found your bullet nestling there, remember? Having passed through the right upper atrium, according to your father later, with the other close alongside, *cote-à-cote*, so to speak. Two heart-shots to kill that old monster, a tough beast that one! His mighty tanned hide is still on my study wall, complete with holes! A *pfennig* grouping at 80 km/hr. nearly head-on. That was pretty fine shooting especially given the pressure you were under.' I am back in the Graf's library with my bandaged leg propped up on cushions on the ottoman. 'We all considered you *ein Meistershütze* from that moment on.'

Chapter 24.
Following the Horse of the Morgan Bloodline

It seems now that nearly all my major life-changing events were preceded by an injury of greater or lesser severity. I am thinking this while providing as close a character study of Graf Kristian as possible for Browne and Hawkeye with the other half of my brain. A clatter of many hooves rises to the tall windows and I imagine that a troop of the Household Cavalry is passing below.

There were the little scrapes and cuts as a child and a certain reaction on an occasion that started a buzzing in my seven year-old mind, kick-starting a sort of general belief that something was 'wrong' with the world as I understood it, and my place in it. More than just an accident of birth that later in my youth saw me as the son of a doctor whose impoverishment was increasing monthly. His occasional articles published in learned journals, such as '*The Life Cycle of the Liver Fluke and Other Parasites*' typically those whose sense of freedom was as a component of a bird dropping, waiting for something to eat them may have been an allegory for the lot of the recent Russian serf. Such observations in print from his veterinarian experiences provided little fare: *our pecuniary condition being in part due to his endless researching of homeopathic cures at home while seeking out well-appointed sanatoria in exotic and expensive locations, mostly run by self-styled philanthropists at best, and professorial charlatans at worst; their sole aim to provide false hope for the incurable, as Augusts' friends and peers then considered my mother's situation.*

Already inspired by tales of Lilienthal, Santos Dumont and the Wrights I'd accompanied my father to Germany, a thrilling train journey for me in the autumn of 1908, where he was attending a medical conference in Berlin. On the return journey we planned a detour to pay a short but memorable visit to Lüneburg Heath. There I'd watched in amazement as Hans Grade flew his aeroplane, a bird-like thing of fragile translucence, banking and turning as Herr Grade waved to the cheering crowds and I was lucky enough to afterwards receive a signed photograph of the celebrated airman and his aerial craft.

I'd become increasingly aviation mad and read library books from

Vilnius on the theory of flight and with the de-restriction of the Latin alphabet, my father had been able to openly subscribe to *Flight* magazine, from England. I found I could follow the technical aspects of the text relatively easily, and the language became more familiar along with the increasingly recognizable aeroplane types described in each issue together with thrilling coverage of aerial gatherings and races, and some Polish students' reported attempts, though not widely publicised, were an inspiration.

The summer of '09, with secretly constructed wings of my own, I made use of the roof of a barn for my first and last attempt to fly like a bird and nursed a broken ankle for weeks. The subsequent enforced period of rest, through which I avidly devoured the latest news of Etrich, Sommer, Rumpler, and more distant pioneers like Gabriel Voisin, Glenn Curtis and Alliot Verdon Roe, had been much mitigated by my father's gift of an English-made model kit purchased at some cost from C.E. Richardson & Co., mail order, through an advertisement in a copy of *Flight*: an elastic-powered Blériot monoplane of one metre wingspan: the full-sized machine and its pilot having recently captured the attention of the world with the first English Channel crossing by aeroplane. In exchange I had to make a solemn promise to give up attempts at wing-borne flight on homemade contraptions.

I was fascinated by the model's simplicity that accurately reflected the logic of the original, although it was of a different variant. It was manufactured by the *Finbat* company and I built it with great care on the kitchen table with my leg still in a caste. By late summer the dream of flight had had its long gestation and when the time came that I was able to astonish the village boys with flights approaching a minute's duration, I had already determined that one day I myself would fly like Louis Blériot.

I read avidly still, on science and on flight in particular. Schiaparelli's 'canali' discovered on Mars using the then most powerful telescopes created in my mind an almost visceral thrill. My father was quite as fascinated. That and the discovery in England of the 'missing link' at Piltdown seemed to throw open the question of life throughout the universe and our descent from an ape-like ancestor as carefully postulated by Darwinism in the teeth of religious fervor.

To be fair the Italian astronomer had not anthropomorphized his own observations (it was later revealed that he had an eye condition which striated objects under high magnification) but it led inevitably to speculation, and perhaps opened the door for modern science fiction. So

I dreamed that some day man would fly without limits, even to the Red Planet, with our moon as stepping-stone. Dreaming with Jules Verne that man would stand, feet firm-planted in the rich soil of Mars, *where cataracts that roar raise spectres of cool vapour and drench the dark leaves that hide the spotted tigers in the jungle down below.* With boyish imagination we'd watched from cover the dip and sway of diplodocus that browsed the marshes where we cut bamboo spears at noon....

Later I would lie in the long grass, a half-child, looking at the sky; questioning within my vocabulary those things that were not the certainties they'd once seemed: 'canals', fossils, the purpose of existence, of God and reality.

~-~

I had a mechanical aptitude and was naturally dexterous, aware of the need to make things strong, light and symmetrical and my stick-and-paper Blériot taught me much about proper weight and balance, applied as much to models as later to the real things.

I ventured into the design of other, smaller models built from thin cane, wire and Japanese tissue toughened with banana oil. Based on photographs and basic drawings in magazines these were mostly monoplanes following the Etrich, Rumpler, Blériot and Antoinette types. But one little biplane inspired by a single-bay DFW racer of extreme elegance became my favourite and with several strands of lubricated rubber for the 'motor' and a hand-carved walnut propeller it climbed well and vied with the Blériot for endurance, proving to be extremely tough. This was an instant hit with the village boys some of whom tried to build copies with varying success. So passed childhood in those balmy days.

Then the Strelitz girls thundered past me as I sat astride my bicycle: Krysia on her powerful, jet-black gelding, Katya on her pretty bay. I was suddenly aware that childhood was forever behind me.

~-~

Back from school, I had been languidly dreaming at a crossroads. Such dichotomies as frequented my dreams troubled my waking hours, and here I was, undecided about which direction to choose - as if *volition* could trump Fate. Which route to take on my lonely journey along the Dusetos road on this bright summer's day aged fifteen near enough and watching the world go by: Marik, gone to the Military Academy in Petersburg, already concluding his first year in the Corps of Pages. I'd found part time employment for the summer at a motor garage in Valksarnis where my mechanical skills had found favour and the pay, though meagre, contributed a little to the family income. But today was a Sunday and I'd felt the need for travel. I'd overhauled the Benz, and though officially too young to drive it, still had I looked forward to some clandestine experience at the wheel on a quiet byway. My hopes were dashed when my father had received a call to a farmer whose wife was in labour and the car had been required.

I was out and about in the fresh air, pedalling to nowhere in particular with my mind free-wheeling when I was shaken from my daydream by the sound of hooves and struck by the sight of the two girls riding together, leaping the ditches to clatter over the road ahead of me, making off at a gallop over the unfenced fields far from the Estate. It was as if I was seeing them for the first time, indeed I hadn't seen either for months as I was rarely at the Big House now that Marik was away. Krysia, the elder, led, on *Buran*, her proud horse of the Morgan bloodline: alongside Katya, whose tan riding skirt matched her mare. The now grown Carpathian bear dogs ran out on the flanks, two outriders that no ruffian would dare confront, the wolfhound running wide on point. The girls raised their whips in salute and then were gone where my heart ached to follow.

~-~

A while later, riding my pony, I'd contrived to follow, shyly, at a distance, plucking up courage to join them or to ask whether I could be of service. My perceived status had fallen with the departure of the scion of the Family Strelitz. I felt that I had no further role despite our fulsome friendships of too few summers. I was suddenly aware that their ladyships had grown into young women with suitors no doubt from suitable families who would soon pay court with the blessing of the Graf, the Governess, and all who sat in judgment on such matters: not excluding Graf Kristian's aunt whenever she deigned to visit and whose frosty stare turned men to stone. According to Marik.

It was the autumn after my unexpected happy sunshine hours with Krysia and Katya at the lake. I was riding the long road homeward from a day's duck hunting. It was twilight and I was eager to be home before my father and mother should worry, a brace of duck over my pommel. With Wolfie alongside I was trotting my pony past the black gibbet that still stood at the lonely crossroads and, as always, it made me shiver.

The dog stopped, hackles rising as three figures sprang out from the trees causing my horse to shy, then rear as they grabbed for the reins. My fowling piece was slung over my shoulder and unloaded and while I tried to keep my seat I was suddenly struck hard in the ribs with a cudgel. As I doubled up was struck behind the ear. I could dimly hear Wolfie snarling and barking frenziedly and angry shouts. The next thing I knew I was tied to the gibbet and stripped of my coat and shirt. I'd evidently been beaten hard on my body: my head was bleeding, my face swollen, and I peered through puffy eyes. Low voices were audible somewhere to my left, two or three perhaps and coarse comments were tossed about with a few laughs at my expense.

A figure, peripheral to my clouded vision appeared, apart from the others, where he'd been watching. He was hooded with slits for eyes cut in what looked like dark felt or *Loden*.

'Now you will learn some civility, you dirty poacher. You little Jewish shit!'

I recognised the voice as the indolent scion of 'Oblomov' but did not reply. There was nothing to say. I felt the first stinging slash of the horsewhip across my shoulder blades and hissed through clenched teeth. The lash flayed across my ribs, striping diagonally across my back and curling around my stomach, flicking back with a rain of blood droplets, glistening upon the timbers. I began to grunt after five lashes and then to my shame cried out, but not for mercy, just to exteriorise the pain and give it tongue. This seemed to gratify the torturer. He stopped and, breathing heavily, growled in my ear. 'Did you know that this place was once used for pagan sacrifice as well as floggings? Where they hanged little criminals like you.'

Again I made no reply. But the next time, when with renewed fury the whip bit into my bleeding flesh, I roared with pain. Shortly after I passed out.

Gorbunov found me next morning passing by in his jobber's cart, and brought me home, suffering more than severe laceration and blood loss since the frost had chilled me to the bone. My pony had wandered home before me. Of gun and mallards there was no sign but I was in too much agony to care. But finding Wolfie's body brought me tears of grief. He had died from a head shot. My father gently bathed my welts and they healed in time, but not without some keloid scarring. Of course I knew the perpetrator but realised that I could prove nothing. My father was outraged but he too knew how powerless we were. To have asked the gendarmerie to investigate a rich and powerful family of a neighbouring estate, one might as well have demanded the moon.

Despite my mother's protests I rose from my bed of pain that same night to bury Wolfie beneath the elderberry tree where he'd slept whole afternoons in its summer shade. Faithful unto death. I cried bitter tears and swore he'd be avenged.

Augusts was inclined to bring the matter to Graf Kristian's attention, but I begged him no. My spending time with the two girls had already been a matter of some comment from the governess, Kat had said, now that Marik was away although paradoxically I'd been encouraged to attend their tutorials. For some time, almost for as long as I recalled she'd kept a wary eye on me. Perhaps for good reason where her charges were concerned as I was considered good looking and other girls, forward village lasses, *and* those who aspired to a degree of refinement among the well to do, had acted with coy interest when I appeared, at village dances and horse festivals, when their mamas weren't looking. I suppose I had a reputation for being a budding Lothario, but it was undeserved. I was relatively quiet but enjoyed a laugh with my friends, so it was probably just the look in my eye and a ready smile that caused little feminine ripples.

So I was young. I healed in time, but the wounds were deep in my soul. It changed me in that I trusted less in the innate goodness of human beings. The *Noblesse* did not always *Oblige*. That princely-ness did not always reside in princes. And I also knew I had an unforgiving nature where my enemies were concerned, and would plot a terrible revenge.

~-~

But my heart was still for Krysia, although Katya did amuse me.

Sometimes they rode as a threesome, trotting with the Governess, who rode well, all three straight-backed in the saddles, hair tightly pinned and rolled under their short-brimmed English riding bowlers, or side-saddle, English style — unlike when the girls rode alone, like Indians, loose in the saddles. Less frequently some young gentleman would join them, when it would be without Katya's presence, just the Governess as chaperone. I fumed on those occasions and rode away in dudgeon, slipping into the trees so as not to be noticed, riding homeward or blindly off in random directions, feeling foolish and hot under my collar.

One day I'd secretly followed just Krysia and Katya with their dogs. They were cantering through thin woodland that was alive with birdsong;

346

the afternoon sun slanting between the boles of trees in midge-swirling rays of light and particles of bright pollen dust to confuse the eye. I'd lost sight of them for a while among the silver birch, when suddenly Katya was riding at the gallop in the direction of Liepus Namas. Catching sight of me she'd reined-in her mount to say that her sister had suffered a fall. She was going for help and urged me to stay with Krysia until others arrived. I hurried to the glade where Buran was quietly grazing. My heart pounded when I saw her, apparently lifeless, lying near a low branch across a game trail, the ominous shapes of Liutus and Tigras standing guard, one each side of her body. One of the dogs gave a low growl as I approached, but I spoke softly and recognising me they allowed me to kneel next to her.

She lay serene and fragile upon the grass: Raudongalvis, field spirit of the flowing red hair. But when I'd lifted her head her lips had parted in a smile that was as beatific as it was mischievous. 'Hah!' she laughed. 'I knew if you chased me long enough I'd catch you!' Her eyes crinkled as she smiled. But coquetry was not her characteristic, so her approach to me, a younger though not completely inexperienced youth, was unselfconsciously direct. Even a year was an age of difference and in eager adolescence I trembled on the brink of heaven with both apprehension and desire.

Her control of the encounter was sweet exploration for us both, and we dived into dark whirlpools of sensuality. My body was taught from physical exercise and well muscled: hers smooth, firm, yet tender, shivering to my touch with eyes downcast. Emotions fired by abandoned kisses, breathless passions aroused by whispered words, crashing like surf upon the ear exploded in our brains like urgent lightning bolts as we pressed hard into one another, exploring with tender hands. She was a sudden wild thing, unleashed from her confining corset, offering her soft breasts to my eager mouth. We arched our young backs in turn, to soar, our minds in flight like eagles on the wind, 'til we paused and gazed into each others eyes and I bowed to worship with lips where I hardly dared enter; not yet as penitent, still less the bold lover.

So we tumbled, rolled upon the moss with happy laughter until she lay at last upon me, hair spun in woven cloud to my close horizon; the sun gleaming redly in my eyes through her yet redder tresses.

But in our embrace she saw where the scourge had fallen, there upon my back; tender, though scar tissue had formed. Lightly she traced the raised weals that were in part still livid: turned me over and with sad eyes she surveyed the cruel damage.

'Welikowsky?' She asked softly.

I nodded.

After a while she said. 'I will have to kill him.'

'No,' I said. 'I will have my revenge. You must not endanger yourself. But....'

'What?' she asked.

'But I may ask you for some information about him, if you can discover it. Where he drinks or gambles with his friends. Where he whores when not entertaining at home. When he may be vulnerable.'

'You can rely on me, Rolf, you dear devious creature. Now *lace* me please.'

I was suddenly alert. '*Dear*, what *creature*?' I forced a smile. 'Is that what I am? A pet?'

'Yes, my pet,' she smiled. 'Alas, and more besides.'

'What more'

'My slave!'

'Slavery has been abolished!'

'My *serf*, then.'

'Serf? Never that, *Ladyship*!'

'Well then my lover.'

'That's better,' I smiled, pulling hard the lacing of the medieval torture instrument, her German-made *Ski* Korsett, by the label.

'How do you breathe in these things?'

'With difficulty, my darling,' she smiled. ' It's something we women have to bear to look perfect for our men.'

'Men?'

'Well the ones who are important, according to Papa and Claudia.'

'And they are....'

'Oh, various counts and young officers from good families. *Ouch*!'

I'd pulled the lacing extra tight.

'And you of course, dear Rolfs, most of all,' she gasped. 'Now please slacken it so I can get dressed.'

Mollified, I pulled her to me and we kissed again and again, our passion growing feverishly until we lay on our backs, eyes closed, just touching.

We lay happily together. She stroked my hair and we slept a while in each other's arms content with just our breathing. In a while I woke and drank again the radiance of her beauty with my innocent lover's eyes until the coolness of evening demanded we rise and make our way homeward. I kissed her eyes and she bade me *adieu* and in the now legal Lithuanian, *ateh,* and then she kissed me again. It was by then near sunset in the world that seemed then a very new and wonderful place.

I'd ridden forth as a boy, and was returning homeward not *yet* a man. But felt that I was learning well the arts of secret love and secret warfare.

~-~

I could think of little else until our next encounter. I felt that though I'd regained some poise, becoming more at ease with Krysia than ever I had in earlier times of play, at each meeting a certain shyness lingered still. I harboured uncertainty about her motives; her expressions of desire were not yet protestations of the love *I* earnestly longed to hear; yet for my part, I fearfully withheld. But the delicious excitement I felt in her company overrode all. To hold her to me in some secret glade was sometimes all that was possible though each ardent rendezvous was bliss.

Those were truly *Tristan and Isolde* moments of innocence and arousal, my worshipping body firmly pressed against her softness. Lagoons of happiness gleamed in bucolic memory like oases of ecstasy through days that now seemed barren. Anticipation was unbearable for sometimes she would not, or could not come if eyes were upon her. Soon we arranged a secret mailbox under the gazebo beyond the walls of the Big House so that we could arrange meetings or simply write each other adolescent verse, a 'dead letterbox' as I would come to know such things later. But while letters were one thing, stealing into the grounds at night to deposit or retrieve, it was for her touch and for her voice that I physically ached, for her brightness fuelled my lambent eye. *Liebe, ist der hellste Stern von allen.*

Sometimes in the trysting places, the grand summerhouse by the lake, just the three of us, Krysia, Goethe and me, or sometimes Heine, Rückert, oh yes, and Pasternak: a bottle of ginger ale or even wine. If we were daring we'd meet in the gazebo if it were dark enough, so that Katya could signal with a lantern if someone was coming. Katya was frequently *too* close, convulsed with mirth; in hayloft, or in the shade of the threshing machine on a lazy summer's day, whence she would lure me, and I with pretence of *sang froid* or assumed courtliness would open my dog–eared German poets and stroll with studied nonchalance to where Krysia was decoratively reclined, twisting her hair, looking daggers at her smirking sister until she finally left, to interrupt our rapturous embraces with muffled giggles from not far enough away. Sometimes I'd hear her squirking, concealed chameleon-like in the branches of a linden tree, while I embraced her older sister until we were obliged to go elsewhere to avoid the spectacle of shaking boughs and falling leaves from the convulsions.

'My maddening, half-mad sister,' Krysia said in exasperation as Kat's long *Rapunzelled* tresses, now twisted into ringlets, swaying as she hung by her knees, skirts flopping over her head.

'You are a total *scandal*, Katarzyna,' Krysia shouted. 'Think what Claudia would say if I told her!'

'Think what Miss Hammond would say if I told her about my big sister and Rolf!' came the muffled reply.

'You wouldn't dare tell, Kat, if you know what's good for you!'

'I won't tell if Rolf will be my slave too!' said Kat modestly from under her skirts.

'Slave!' I exclaimed. 'What have you been saying, Krysia?'

'Kat, you cat!' cried Krysia grabbing a low branch and shaking the tree so that Katya squealed in mock alarm.

I joked that Kat really was a shaggy orang-utan with her red hair. But she wasn't as familiar with the fauna of Borneo as I, with my treasured volumes on natural history and she shrieked when she saw a picture later. That may have been when Katya began to behave more decorously; her descent from the canopy, from tree-climbing tomboy to young *Homo Erectus*, a poised young woman was gradual, and she could still slip easily from one guise to another.

But still sweet-natured arboreal *clever* Kat was our trusted go-between when the 'Iron Countess' came to stay. But had she betrayed me finally, wittingly through jealousy or otherwise, or was it our own lovers' carelessness that saw us parted and me in exile?

~.~

Old *Kaiser* had broken a few ribs and left me black and blue with blunt trauma and lacerations consistent with his trotters driving into my unprotected torso and legs to add to those horse-whipping weals - which were barely healed, while I protected my neck and head. I felt, probably foolishly, that I'd achieved a little stature with the Graf and it did no harm to my reputation in the village, nor with the girls. By that I mean Katya, too, as Krysia was away at the time. I felt a little guilty, but we were all such friends... Then there was the later business in Bohemia with the gun limber in training that left me once more with broken ribs and a spell in the sick bay at Helmsburg where I'd witnessed Wöbbe collecting his clandestine phial, and I took advantage of a desperate situation. That this would cause such damage I could not know, but by then my mind was focussed only on escape.

~.~

There were numerous other painful experiences; some dealt me by vindictive, ignorant or clinically insane human beings in positions of power that persons of such lack of integrity and baseness should never occupy. Be they schoolmasters or idealistic leaders, fanatical enslavers, patriots, partisans and witch-finders, depending on your point of view and on who held the steel rule, the gun or instrument of torture: they were *enemies*. Except for schoolmasters, a sort of xenometric argument for the ineffectual response to curbing human frailty, a 'war rationale', can be made in such situations. Wöbbe, like Gollub, was supposed to have been on the *same* side, *our* side. Or whichever tribe one found oneself attached to at any given time, though suspected of alighting from a Trojan gift!

~.~

Then there was the *actual* implement of medieval cruelty, which embraced me with such irony and sanguinary relish upon my painful dawn return to Liepus Namas after four years of war, when I'd re-learned the truth about myself and the passing of those dear to me, hitherto in loco parentis.

~.~

Finally there was the latest crash. Although some six or seven months ago, it had done the greatest damage to me physically, and it must be said, mentally too, if that's where the soul resides. Which I very much doubt. It was that event that stopped me short. And it's hard to function when nothing makes sense, when everything is for the first time. Because that's what it's like when you lose your memory completely.

~.~

'Do savd'by zazhivyot!' '(*It will heal before your wedding!*) was the oafish comment from Gorbunov as I was lifted into the sleigh by the beaters: delivered with a suggestive wink and a insolent grin, his eyes sliding towards Kat, who is not so overwrought by my condition that she does

not notice. Despite my pain I wanted to punch him and say, 'Blast your insolence. It's the *other* sister!' And damn his interference anyway with his big peasant feet clodhopping on such a sensitive flower as first love. Yet I catch Katya's look and I am shocked to see that her smile and brimming green eyes reveal to me something more than just her kindly care and a natural concern for my injuries as she gently strokes my lesser-damaged hand.

~-~

I healed quickly and well enough, as the loathsome Gorbunov had predicted, and without hospital, though most of the recovery period was spent at home in bed, too stiff to move much. After a couple of weeks I was invited to attend a dinner at the Strelitz's given in my honour. Katya had visited me several times in the meanwhile, first time being the morning after the shoot with the Graf, who thanked me very formally and addressed me frequently with a slight smile as Herr *Meisterschütze*. He told me that the boar was the biggest they'd ever recorded at a shade over 350 kilos, and that Ivan Lebedovich had made sure it was quite dead with a sabre slash to the throat – just in case it had decided to get up again! I had a vague memory of being carried on the stretcher to view the animal, still warm and steaming, propped inverted against the big birch tree by its own momentum. Lebedovich had then stabbed the animal again sweeping a handful of congealing blood from the blade with which he then proceeded to decorate my brow, cheeks and nose, in time-honoured tradition.

The Graf was speaking, 'Now you are one of us, a proper hunter. A man of the forest! Respect those that you hunt. Take no more than you need and minimise their suffering. May God guide you all your days.' Gorbunov handed the Graf a sprig of juniper. 'Pity your hat's gone, boy,' he grinned as he tucked it into my hair, 'But I hope your brain is still safely at home!'

The last statement brought guffaws from the beaters, but even in my sorry state I detected a different attitude; no longer was there a jeering edge to the laughter.

'God bless you, Rolf,' said the Graf softly.

'God bless you, Rolf,' repeated Katya, even more softly as the stretcher was lifted.

So I was denied the picnic and campfire-side bonhomie while the arrangements for the collection and transport of the game was arranged, and the vodka and the wine were circulated, and I was placed in the sleigh like some miserable invalid. Driven homewards wrapped in fur and rugs by a silent and disconsolate Gorbunov who belched, munched pickled herring, gherkins and black bread all the way, every muscle and bone seemed to ache in my body and I had no stomach for food at all. *Now you are one of us*, the Graf had said. But I still felt isolation and had no sense that I really belonged to their world. Perversely, though Krysia owned my heart, the memory of her younger sister's expressions of concern aroused strong emotions within me and gave me further turmoil on my journey home.

Little that Gorbunov said on the return journey made sense to me. He related rather a crude story about some young officers at a ball, rushing to pick up the pearls scattered from a broken necklace, dropped by a refined young lady. She'd seemed distraught and embarrassed by the fact and had to be escorted from the ballroom.

I was in too much pain to enquire why, so after a short pause Gorbunov explained that when the officers tried to gather the pearls, they couldn't get a grip on them. They were actually globules of mercury, see, taken as an antidote to venereal disease!

'Dropped out of her knickers, boy! You remind me of those naïve lieutenants. When you are older you'll find all women are same, no matter what their status.' He chuckled evilly.

I again thought about trying to punch him but every part of me ached and all I wanted was to sleep.

~-~

That next day I heard a sleigh arrive – it was too slippery for a motorcar. They'd visited, me propped up in my bedroom with my bandaged hands trying not to breathe too much. The Graf had shown interest in the model aeroplanes hanging from the ceiling, especially the 'DFW' biplane and the old Blériot, which I still possessed, though it had been mended many times, and which I was proud to tell him could be flown for nearly one minute on calm evenings, could circle and climb. Katya had come with some choice cuts of pork which, she said, with the other game they'd bagged, was enough to go around the whole village, still with a good amount for the guests to take away. Everyone was happy and the story of my shooting two boars, with heart shots to each was already legendary. '*As far as Ignalina,*' she'd vouchsafed.

The Graf shook his head and said, 'Two in the heart and another in the first boar's heart too. That was some fine shooting, my boy.'

'There was no deflection with the *Kaiser*, sir,' I said. 'It was head-on. I couldn't have missed!'

'It was a cool piece of work all the same. Older hands might have lost their nerve with that monster bearing down on them. Good work, Rolf.'

I'd felt suitably gratified.

As they rose to leave, the Graf was talking to my parents, Katya returned to say goodbye, and bent to kiss me full on the lips. The sensation of her sweet breath and the tenderness of that kiss of such delicious softness seemed to promise all, and hinted at a powerful passion held carefully in check. 'I hope I didn't hurt you,' she smiled from the doorway. 'I'll have to wait 'til your poor body is a bit better, won't I?' Then she was gone leaving me amazed and in a daydream where she and Krysia circled round me like two red-haired wood nymphs with me as maypole as they wound closer with each turn, their blue-green eyes fixed upon me.

When I was fitter we'd dined at Liepus Namas waited on by liveried staff, the table set with great formality with a wild, gilt equestrian centrepiece that was a rococo frenzy: my parents together with the Graf, Katya and little Grazyna, some local dignitaries and Hermann Berg. The Governess was still travelling with Krysia although they'd received a telegram the previous day from Miss Hammond to say that they'd be returning within a week. That news seemed not to please Katya too well. There was also a letter from Marik – mostly complaining of the endless cold chicken, the only meat they ever eat because the Tsarina is obsessed with it - with an enclosure for me, a photograph of him with his officer cadet intake standing outside the gates of the Winter Palace with the names of his comrades written vertically above in spidery Cyrillic.

Later Katya had shown me again the portrait on the stair, pretending for the Graf it was the first time I'd stood upon the staircase at the Big House. But impressed as I was by the fine architecture, furnishings and other family paintings, my renewed acquaintance with the dominant Singer Sargent proved that the portrait had lost none of its ability to awe.

In the conservatory Katya fed grapes to Gagool. *'Que bonita rapariga!'* said the parrot.

'What did he say?' I asked.

Katya looked at me with a faint smile. ' *She* says *I'm pretty*! What do you think?'

'I think *she's* right!' I said with emphasis wondering if that's what the parrot had *really* said or whether it was a ploy of Kat's.

Chapter 25. *Out of Africa*

'Can you walk, my boy?'

It is the third day since my long journey to the Linden House and my encounter with the bear trap. My leg is mending but I haven't put much weight on it for fear that I will tear the rudimentary stitches.

The Graf is standing at the library door and Graczy is seated on an ottoman while she's been telling me more about how they have managed in the War, and how she is missing Krysia. She hasn't mentioned Kat to whom she has always been especially close, and other than to ask where she is, I have not probed for fear that it will bring more tears. That she has returned from Ignalina with some supplies is as much as I know.

'I'm not sure. I can try.' I reply. I wonder what's in store.

The Graf enters the room. He seems taller this morning, more his old self, composed, controlled. It is as though he has come to some decision and the course ahead was planned. He looks for a moment at his youngest daughter and quietly suggests that she assist Nina in the kitchen. He lowers his voice to me as she leaves the library. 'I pleaded with her to go with Claudia Hammond when she had the chance, until all this is settled here.'

He had arranged safe conduct behind the German lines to Klaipeda and berths on a ship to England exiting via the Red Track, the channel, which was being cleared of mines by the Royal Navy, liaised through his own Landeswehr outfit with an armed escort to protect them both against rapacious mobs, Bermondt-Avalov's roaming mongrel band of Hunnish Russians – our so-called allies, along with the *Greens*, so-called Nationalists, but killers and looters for the most part. But Graczy wouldn't leave. She was determined to stay until Katya and Krysia returned. His true *Cordelia*. The telephone line, restored by the Germans and been cut soon after their withdrawal, so the house was again isolated and without transport their options for escape were limited to say the least.

'You know how strong willed are my girls. Saw it as desertion. Graczyna has her mother's spirit – or perhaps my stubbornness…so Miss Hammond left together with the Baroness - Nadia.'

Was there is a hint of something in the Graf's voice? I recall the pale governess with cool eyes that could search into the secret garden of a child's mind, and wonder if she and Kristian had been lovers after Elenja's death.

I ease myself up, knowing I wouldn't make it far, grateful for the walking stick, which I've been using for my visits to the downstairs facilities.

The Graf affords me a tight smile. 'I'd like you to follow me to the study, if you can.'

He proceeds along the panelling with its military prints and engravings of stern Prussians in uniform along one side and proud bearded Russian officers along the other, facing one another in mute hostility across the gulf of the corridor in their gorgeous finery, rapt in mutual fascination: paranoiac symbols for their countries' symbiosis in trade, war and pre-revolutionary cultural interdependence. The corridor itself with its engravings of martial hostility and suspicion seems to symbolise the delicate furrow the Graf had ploughed in the harness of two masters, Tsar and Kaiser, while nurturing thoughts of his own changeless, inviolate Baltic *Shangri La*.

The symbiosis ran deep.

Peter the Great had encouraged the migration of German subjects to work in the service of the Russian state, a practice increasingly followed in the latter part of the eighteenth century by Catherine the Great, herself a German princess. For some two hundred years German families had flourished in Russia, their members advancing to elevated posts in both civil and military service. Though thoroughly Russified and loyal to the crown, they'd remained a little apart, intermarrying and so perpetuating their German family names, hence many senior Russian officers had borne German surnames; Rennenkampf, Sievers, Scheidemann, Evert, Diderichs: while in the Austro-Hungarian Army, Slav Generals Boroevich and Terszczansky reciprocated with their *Russian* names.

By early 1915, following some early military disasters, many of those in the military with German names were looked upon with suspicion, and some of those within the Russian command were unfairly scapegoated; dismissed, arrested. The Graf lost his advisory position by late 1916 and was held under house arrest in Moscow until the Revolution when in the midst of confusion and blood-letting he'd seized the opportunity to escape. Others were less lucky.

~·~

The gunroom door is sufficiently ajar to provide a view of empty racks and a memory of the boar-shoot. I'm led towards a door with a carved Kuznetsowa coat of arms: the same sword-wielding Vytautas knight that blazons Belarus and Lithuanian heraldry in white and red at its centre, escutcheoned above the frame that offers into a comfortably cluttered, middle-sized room where once I'd stood before, on the eve of my exile.

I've kept up with the aid of the stick. He has been dragging a leg slightly; something I'd not noticed when first I'd arrived with my own preoccupations. He motions me to a leather chair. The northerly outlook is a tree line of dark woodland visible beyond the walled garden. A Biedermeier clock ticks gloomily in one corner, pace-making our remaining heartbeats.

He closes the door and seats himself in the bay window behind a mahogany desk piled with books, papers and silver-framed photographs. I recognize Princess Sophie. In some she is alone, gracefully posed aboard a liner, holding her hat, looking out to sea with the wind in her hair and lace at her throat. Others show her with Kristian, an elegant couple, posing for the camera at glittering dinner parties; white tie functions and plunging necklines. On deck at night with the riding lights of another ship of the line beyond. A smiling Sophie at the wheel of a fast runabout, pre-dating the Sizaire *torpedo* from the archaic shape of the scuttle, and in others, at Palanga perhaps, two small girls and Marik play on the beach or ride ponies. Sophie in formal attire at the reins of a smart gig, with her two girls seated beside her. These bittersweet souvenirs contrast strangely with antelope heads and ivory that adorn the walls and the stretched leopard skin that is hung with spears behind the door. African drums and other artefacts are arrayed, including a colourfully macabre Dahomey fetish mask, something unexpected amongst the memorabilia of German East Africa.

As with the library, glass-fronted bookcases line the walls. Some volumes are contained upon shelves, compressed by ebony elephant book-ends and many more are haphazardly piled on the floor. Some familiar titles: works by Samuel Hahnemann on Homeopathy, a well-thumbed volume by the look and others I remember: medical encyclopaedias and geographical volumes, beautifully bound, both in Cyrillic and Latin script. Darwin's *Origins of Species*, works by the great Nikolai Przhevalsky, more by Semyenov, containing magical illustrations of the fauna of central Asia; several by Sven Anders Hedin: African wildlife with titles by Fritz Bronsart von Schellendorff, all of which had fired my imagination for travel and exploration as a youngster. Some scientific magazines and copies of pre-war aeronautical publications are among them, the latter having once been my treasured property.

'Hannah, your... mother requested that I collect all your father's books after his death and give them safe keeping here. There was much looting and wanton burning,' he says grimly. 'It's still going on. She couldn't bear for these books that were so precious to both of you to be destroyed. It was shortly after that that she ...took her life.'

He stares out of the window while I recompose myself. I seemed to be doing a lot of that recently.

He notices my eyes drawn to the elephant tusks.

'Did you know that a canal existed between the Red Sea and the Nile Delta as early as 1380 BC. Thus the continent of Africa had been separated from its isthmus to Asia and its coastline made entirely navigable for maritime trade until at least AD 800?'

I look at him blankly.

'Of course, since 1869, thanks to the industry and engineering skills of Ferdinand de Lesseps it may once again be fully circumnavigated.'

While I am wondering what this preamble will lead to he pushes a small atlas towards me across the desk. It is opened at a two-page spread of Africa.

'We owe a great debt to Mercator I think,' he says. 'But if you consider the map of Africa, not as a projection but as a *symbol* of a great indigenous animal, turning it anti-clockwise 90 degrees, what is it you see?' A slight smile hovers.

Baffled I do as I am bade, pointing the horn of Africa away from me so that 'North' now lies to my left and I look blankly at the suddenly unfamiliar aspect of that vast landmass. It was shaded into the various colours for the colonial possessions, where the Great War had raged as bitterly, where the heroic tactics of von Lettow-Vorbeck had led the British a costly dance. As an aviator I am used to rotating maps to the most convenient cardinal locations, folding and orienting them to suit a planned route. But this exercise seems to make little sense. *Symbolically?*

'One of the creatures which I didn't shoot. Its horn is prized in the orient for medicinal purposes and is also used for the ceremonial daggers of sheiks. Here the horn has been brutally severed and cast two-hundred kilometres into the Indian Ocean.'

Then I see it. The more I study the shape of 'Africa' on its side, the more I could see the likeness, indeed the individual *species*! I recalled from my interest in natural history that there were five reported species of rhinoceros, White, Black, Indian, Indonesian and Pygmy. It was a Black Rhinoceros, the neck and head, the defined, sardonically prehensile lip of the Cape of Good Hope differentiating it from the wide-mouthed *(weit)* White Rhino, the names Black and White having nothing to do with actual hide colouring. Its ears were Somaliland and its lesser, upper horn, Mozambique. Madagascar, the larger severed horn, lay far offshore. Its eye was lake Victoria.

'I see it,' I'd said, or I *imagined* that I could, but I didn't begin to understand the occult significance of this chimera, this *will o'the wisp* pursuit that I was being invited to participate in. I am irritated, grieving over the loss of my parents, preoccupied and in pain from my injury. Under the circumstances I am even beginning to doubt the sanity of the Graf.

'My story, and so yours, is bound up with this territory. I went there to make my fortune and suffered reverses, but then it presented me with its greatest prize, which in truth I was prepared to steal if that's what I'd had to do. In the end she was given to me, but the burden of such a gift in the circumstances that it was proffered brings with it not a blessing but a curse. I stole her and I am as guilty as if I had robbed a church. I was even driven to change my religion. The house too; a poison chalice. This is why I understand you, Rolf.' He bore an expression of ineffable sadness.

For my part I singularly fail to understand any of it. Not his confession. Not his 'understanding' of my own self, my motivations, or my position, whatever he perceived that to be. I felt, as I had felt from the time he drove me to Ignalina station and left me to my fate with a few terse words of friendly advice, that he'd had a hold over my destiny, and a detached interest in my life for good or ill. As the father of the girl I loved, that was self-evident. But which girl did I truly love?

'Look at the tear duct of Victoria. Do you see it?'

A long narrow lake pointed south starting below the 'eye' of Victoria.

'Do you mean Lake Tanganyika?'

'Precisely. And did you know that there are microscopic creatures that are uniquely found in rhinoceros tears?'

I am now sure that the Graf has gone mad.

'All three people who met in the sinkhole of perversion that is Zanzibar, and mounted a safari along the old slave route to the shores of Lake Tanganyika in 1894 were tinier in the scheme of things than those miniscule microbes in a rhino's eyelashes. And you know what? Nobody gives a damn about that fact other than a few zoologists, maybe. In fifty years from now no one will remember anything of what went on then and there or will be spoken of today in this room. But I will tell you, Rolf, so that you may understand something of the truth. And of who and what you are.'

~-~

'I am trying to tell you something that is difficult; momentously important - for you personally, and will explain much to you, I'm sure. Reasons why certain things happened the way they did. Why things had to be. You were never going to be an entirely free agent, Rolf.'

Despite my searching for some sense in all of this, half my mind is on the current military situation, locally at least. The recent uneasy guarantee from Lenin for the freedom of the Baltic States hadn't stopped the fighting along the border with Belarus, and no one would be naïve enough to think that the aspirations of the Bear ended anywhere short of the entire Baltic coast and its ice-free ports. Perhaps Lenin believed he could relax his pressure on the Baltic States for the time being, no doubt certain that those lands would fall to Bolshevism when the Civil War was ended, as World Communism progressed relentlessly from the centre. Internal unrest still boiled up with the emergence of counter-Revolutionary groups or factions. Latvia had dismissed the attempt by the Socialist Revolutionary Party to recruit an army there and the Red Letts remained loyal to the Revolution and we were still in the middle of it.

The Red Army itself massively outnumbered both the Interventionists and the Whites who were scattered and disunited, plus the Bolshevists held the central and key industrial areas, giving them control of most of the railways and so owned the capabilities for the wholesale production of weapons and ammunition and its transportation to the perimeter. Food shortages, however, were common on every front and the peasant revolt against the Soviet control of food supplies was encouraged by the Mensheviks in coalition with Boris Savinkov's Social Revolutionaries - SRs (*Essars*) who had declared war on the Bolsheviks fifteen months previously, in the spring of 1918.

We'd heard that in the east the valiant Czech Legion remained a thorn in Lenin's side, refusing to be disarmed by force and extending their control along the Trans-Siberian railway although Admiral Kolchak's White Army did not ally with them.

Kolchak, with no talent for land warfare nevertheless succeeded in capturing Perm and Ufa in 1918, but that was the high water mark for his army. He had since been proclaimed 'Supreme Ruler of Russia' despite unaffiliated warlords running their own armoured trains through Siberia, looting and murdering. Within Russia an internal war was still being waged by the Cheka using merciless killers to root out enemies of the revolution both in the Workers' and Peasants' Red Army and in the population at large. On the western margins, hemmed in and harried by the British Fleet, we in the Freikorps were fighting an obsolete war with the half-hearted notion of Balticum, a Grand Baltic Duchy of Greater Germany thoroughly discredited and unrealistic; hanging on by our fingertips, holding the line but resented by much of the population, with extended supply lines and no strategy it seemed to me other than for an eventual fighting withdrawal with a hostile Poland at our backs and on our flanks.

It is apparent to me that a weakened Kristian holds but a tenuous grip on his estate, given its remoteness. Only God and the Norns know the future of Liepus Namas, this once Swedish stronghold and outpost of empire. It is poised at the crossroads of Belarus and Great Russia. It is still fought over by Lett and Lithuanian partisan, those atavistic Brothers of the Sword, and until recently at any rate, the legions of the Duke of Mecklenburg in guise of *Pax Freikorps* Germanism. Whilst other quite vast territories were effectively conceded under 'the duress' of Brest-Litovsk - when the Bolshevists acceded to the peace treaty in order first to deal with internal 'counter revolutionary' resistance - such was clearly viewed only as a 'temporary' situation by Lenin and Trotsky.

Meanwhile, unknown to me at that time, on the north western front, White General Yudenich with 20,000 men, aided by the British, under the command of General Ironside, was poised for an assault on Petrograd.

One thing is sure, in this vacuum, without more firepower the beleaguered inhabitants of the Linden House could be overrun by any one of a remaining half dozen different factions before the rumblings of civil war died away, each more savage in its way than the other, like Makhno's Greens or even by some Anarchist splinter group such as the *Black Hundreds*, who were no better than bandits and murderers. Moreover it is apparent that the Graf's intelligence is no longer up to date and without fate's decreeing otherwise, an onslaught might happen at any time. Kat might have discovered something on her journey but I am yet to see her and I worry about her state of mind.

As for the present, I still have no idea what Graf Kristian is getting at but I'm feeling very uneasy about what is coming. There have been rather too many shocks and horrors these few days.

Chapter 26 *Into the Firebreak*

I recall the haste with which I'd distanced myself from the site of my forced landing. I had blasphemed mightily when at 2000 metres under a grey overcast the engine had stuttered and run rough, as if swearing out loud would convince the BMW to consider its position and restart. Lack of *Benzin* and no other failing was the reason for its distress and for my imminent unplanned descent to terra firma with no options. I was south of the Dvina and may have only been twenty minutes flying time from the fuel cache at *Advance Landing Ground Heinrich*, the designated landing field at *Liepus Namas*.

But it might have just as well have been two hours away. I wasn't even going to make it on fumes. I'd mis-calculated, or the wind component was stronger from the east, or the 185-hp. BMW was burning more fuel that I'd realised, or I had a fuel leak, or, or…it didn't matter. In four minutes, if I did nothing I'd be on the ground. In four minutes if I did something I'd also be on the ground. The difference between doing something and doing nothing was that I might still be breathing in four minutes if I just did two things right.

1/ Fly the aeroplane.

2/ Land the aeroplane.

Well *three* actually. *Find* somewhere to bloody land it!

The big wooden two-blader slowed, wind-milled for a moment and then very gradually stopped, one broad blade with its brass leading-edge sticking up beyond the gun breeches, like a finger pointing ironically skywards. This did nothing for my forward view. I'd eased the stick back to the best gliding speed, and switched off the magnetos. At least now it shouldn't burn. From this point I had to maintain a speed of 100 km/hr to give me the best opportunity to find a reasonable landing space. Southern Latvia is not as flat as Lithuania, but there are worse places for such a landing. However, the terrain of Latgale over which I was now flying was heavily wooded with just a few clearings here and there, and some artificial firebreaks.

Without the din of the throaty engine, which still rang in my ears, the whistle of the slipstream over the metal corrugations on wing surface and fuselage was a novel sensation - were I in the mood to appreciate it. Approximately D# above Middle 'C' I thought, at this airspeed. At least

I'd be able to concentrate fully on looking for a suitable landing field. Whilst that note obtained I knew I was flying at the right airspeed and would not suddenly fall out of the sky through accidentally letting the speed fall too low, while concentrating on my approach.

Theoretically I should fly downwind, to cover the greatest distance and give myself a better chance of coming across a meadow that was big enough to take the Junkers with only one possible approach, turning back into wind and exactly judging the height loss in the turn. Above all maintaining airspeed so as not to stall and spin into the trees.

A minute and a half gone and I was getting noticeably low. If I was forced to make a down-wind landing it could be fatal – although the south-easterly wind hadn't been particularly strong when I'd taken off and hour and fifteen minutes before. *Mission – free-roving reconnaissance and report. Strafe targets of opportunity.* With a serious last look in my direction Kessler had peeled-off and returned to base – before his fuel had reached a critical level. Soon now I will be reported as missing.

~-~

I glance around the horizon. The day has started overcast and hasn't improved. Generally the visibility improves with an easterly but the weather has been strange of late, perhaps presaging an early winter. The thought that I might crash crosses my mind. I push aside the worry that I might be injured and lie for hours or even days in the wreckage with no assistance at hand. Red Letts or worse some of *Roskov's Wolves*, Avalov's raggle taggle mercenaries or some other '*Wild Wood*' revanchist band of so called '*Forest Brothers*' would find the aircraft and make my last hours on earth even more hellish, for their sport.

'Concentrate on the landing, Rolf.' I hear the voice of Greiner, my instructor in Flek 3 at Graz-Thalerhof flying school. A cheery Tyrolean with gold-capped teeth. He had a preference for sitting in the front cockpit to avoid the unpleasantness of collecting a face full of his pupils' breakfasts, which otherwise tended to decorate the occupant of the rear cockpit in rough air. Not that I had ever lost my breakfast in the air. '*Sie haben ein Händchen für die Fliegerei, Junge!*' he'd shouted over the clatter of the 120-hp. Austro-Daimler, and I'd caught the glint of gold in the cabane-mounted rear-view mirror ahead of the cockpits. Greiner. A veteran of many flying hours. Spun in with a pupil in a big old *Lohner*.

I've hooked the bungee over the control column to take some of the load off the stick, to save me holding the nose up. It wants to drop heavily on the glide. *Listen to the airflow and fly with gentle pressures, that's the way.*

Altimeter. I am getting low, 400 metres. There is no future in flying further downwind. I cannot recall any sizeable fields in this direction, which is the way I've already come. I see that there is probably only one chance. Below are gentle hills, wild wooded slopes the occasional foresters' track and frequent small lakes and streams - and the firebreaks; generally wide swathes between the blocks of pine or spruce plantations I see no local huts or farm houses. A firebreak it is then.

The one best oriented for the wind lies on what appears from my altitude to be a slope. Experience has told me that any slope that actually *looks* like a slope from a couple of hundred meters above is very much steeper than it appears. The cross-breaks lie along the rising ground at ninety degrees to the others, and provide the best chance of a survivable landing in my estimation. So here goes.

I drift a little right of the longest firebreak run. It's hard to judge the actual distance between the two stands of trees and the length of the blocks but I estimate 1500 metres is a typical block length, like the ones on the Graf's land to the south. I commence a turn at about 200 metres and continue this onto the approach, allowing for the wind direction. Something is smoking far off to the southeast giving me a clue as to wind and then I'm on my final approach.

Into the firebreak

The familiar effect of an expanding ground plane with the vertiginous ascent of trees and low hills into my periphery returns as I metamorphose from avian to a soon-to-be terrestrial, conscious of rejoining the earth tribe; the twenty thousand generations of humans for whom flight was only the great dream. I can almost see them standing among the tight-ranks of conifers sailing past my wings, watching in silent rectitude the folly of man in this first century of powered flight. *Concentrate, damn you!*

Time to flatten-out. I am now out of wind-effect so I reduce rudder to regain the centreline of the firebreak, which, I'm happy to note is more than twice the span of my Junkers D.1. As I bring the nose up I lose all remaining forward view behind the big square radiator nose and the still upright propeller blade. I touch lightly at first and then it's a jolting slamming passage on that rugged undercarriage as the wing loses lift and the rough ground reveals its lack of improvement. The aeroplane thumps, rocks and bucks over every tooth-rattling rut and a few fallen branches as it runs noisily out of energy like an out-of-control furniture van. I've got the stick hard back and the tailskid is digging-in, doing its best to help things run straight. There are no brakes, not even a claw-brake. The rudder has no effect without the benefit of propeller slipstream at slow speed, despite my efforts on the rudder bar. Just when I think it's over a branch disobligingly wedges itself in the left hand wheel, simultaneously jamming it and causing the machine to veer sharply into the trees. Apart from the mighty thud as the starboard wingtip collides with a tree trunk, I couldn't have parked it better; out of sight of the main drag; except the white-painted rudder and its black cross is projecting out into the tree-line. Just great! Like some ironic flag advertising its hiding place. It'll be far too heavy to move on my own, especially on soft ground. *Dammit!*

I expel a great sigh of relief. I'm down, unhurt, and thankful not to have smacked my chin on the gun breeches. I suddenly remember that wild goose from my childhood. What would he have thought of that landing, I wondered? But what's next? *Get as far away from the machine as fast as possible* is likely the best plan, in case some really bad people have seen my descent. I undo the shoulder straps and the broad lap belt and climb stiffly down. My ears are buzzing with the sound of the engine, despite its demise some minutes since. I look left and right along the firebreak. No sign of approaching danger. Allowing for preparation for travel, given that I would not have been seen from any more than two kilometres away in this sort of terrain, I'd probably be safe if no one has arrived after 45 minutes.

However, I am torn between fleeing in a southerly direction through the woods, navigating to *Liepus Namas* with my folding army compass, which will be very hard going, or using the firebreaks to lead me south eventually, which will be a long walk. Hiding to see if anyone comes and making a decision later is not a particularly good option, but I don't want to abandon the machine. It might be my only means of escape later on - if I can find some reasonably high-octane petroleum. Undisturbed I can spend some of the remaining daylight camouflaging the Junkers, but dithering is a waste valuable time.

Throwing caution to the wind I decide to cut some branches with my knife and camouflage the aircraft immediately, leaving the vicinity as soon as possible. Luckily many branches are scattered about; windfalls and remnants of some recent harvesting no doubt. I gather these and artistically arrange them to look like bushes and young saplings on the perimeter. After a quarter of an hour I stand off to survey my attempts, wondering if a passing logger might fail to notice a bulky grey-green camouflaged attack monoplane nosing into the trees. With a screen of timber around it bearing enough foliage to break up the outline, I tell myself it would have to do – and was probably passable in twilight at any rate. Before I make off I check the tyre marks, and using a leaf-laden branch as a 'broom', make an effort to brush out the evidence my arrival. Especially the swerve into the trees. The tailskid mark is most prominent but there are other marks from dragged tree trunks and horses' hooves, so it doesn't look too obvious but I hope no sharp-eyed forester passes by in daylight. Who am I kidding? Anyone who knows these woods would spot a different look to the locale instantly, no matter what the conditions, short of *pitch black*.

A gentle rain has begun to fall so I climb back onto the thick wing root and drag a small tarpaulin cover from behind the seat that clips around the cockpit. I'm satisfied that it will keep out the rain and the heavier drips from the trees. I briefly examine the damaged right wing tip. The corrugated leading edge has been pushed-in, flattening it for about 200 mm from the tip. It's not serious damage but will disrupt the airflow a bit, creating additional drag and may contribute to aileron vibration. Early handling of these types showed a propensity to aileron 'shudder', and I'd heard a rumour that one aircraft at least was lost when the ailerons broke away. I didn't know how *Junkers–Fokker AG* had cured the problem - if indeed the story was true. But I determine to find some tools; a drill to make a small hole and a steel hook of some sort to pull the metal back into the approximate shape, before I'll consider trying to fly it out.

That decided, I move off, cautiously using the firebreaks but keeping close to the trees, stepping into their cover from time to time to listen, forever looking over my shoulder. Using my army knife I blaze a tree trunk here and there discreetly, every few hundred metres, to help find my way back.

But first I had to find the way *there*.

~.~

I enter the trees on a SSE compass heading. I should eventually come to a cluster of lakes and then I'll find my way back. Back home. To *Ausautas*. To *Liepus Namas*. My parents I hoped I would find in good health, but I had a gnawing feeling in my stomach about that. And Krysia and Kat too. Would they all still be there? Would they be alive even? I still pictured everything as it had been in the summer of 1914, but I knew that picture would have changed drastically. For all I knew no letter that I'd clandestinely sent had ever arrived. So it was entirely possible that they thought I was dead, killed in an accident at the beginning of the war through my desperate attempt back then to cover my tracks reported via the Red Cross.

The woods are full of cadences and memories for me. Strange timbres. Green woodpeckers ….. like machine pistols in the distance. Just like in my other war… Galicia, Montenegro, Macedonia and the Albanian hills. It was a war that had never really stopped around here.

After half and hour or so I come to an area where trees have been felled. They remind me of the stripped branches on that other hillside in the late spring of 1917: the rugged, tribal landscape of the recent Balkan Wars and the Muslim exodus. The Serb POW burial duty standing smoking by the wreckage.

~.~

I'd remembered climbing that hill, pulling through the trees in the dusk: sweating in my uniform and blowing like a horse, to find the twisted remains of my 'kill' – a Nieuport 10 two-seater. That's when I met the man known as Merlin, whose decade was yet to come. Who'd be my guide and confessor, run his agents through Europe and into the USSR: some Promethean creatures of his own creation. But that wasn't his cover name then – he was just a dying war correspondent, apparently. Lying on a bed of pine needles next to his dead pilot, with *Wöbbe* wearing two wristlet watches, rifling through his pockets.

Chapter 27. *Albania 1917: an Old Adversary*

The sun was climbing down a colourless sky beyond the Mali Shpat foothills. I'd hiked back in history into the war torn, ethnically-bled country above the town of Gramsh, driving east of an unnamed tributary of the Devoli River in search of my 'victory'. I'd noted on my map where it had gone down out of control - bandit country. Two hours ago my borrowed car had been left with a steaming radiator in the charge of an armed *Gefreiter* four kilometres south, amongst stunted trees along a dusty track, high above the Cerrik road.

Our adjutant had sent a dispatch to Brigade to determine if patrols were looking for a crashed aeroplane and we were informed that some were recovering bodies from recent skirmishes, searching out drifts of Serbian resistance - engaging the dregs of an army, elements of which refused to concede defeat, scouring the mountains for Albanian 'rebels' and guerrillas. There were accounts of aerial firing the previous day but nothing had been seen in the increasingly cloud-studded sky. They'd had no reports of a crash.

I'd been excused duty as my assigned aeroplane had been damaged following that engagement. It had taken us most of the day to get here, with false leads, twists and detours, where the hills and the poorly made and steeply winding roads looked all alike. Dark gypsies told us they'd seen the engagement but gave fictitious accounts of the combat: where it had taken place and in which direction we should go to find the aeroplane wreck. 'Balkan rules' applied, everywhere being twice as far as we were informed and of course many of them simply lied for payment or cigarettes, though they spat contemptuously on our German brands as we left. We considered that we'd have to barter with our Bulgarian friends to get quality tobacco from occupied Prilep! But mostly the natives misled us as a matter of course.

My motive was not morbidly to view my bloody handiwork, but to confirm the kill - my third. I needed five to be called 'ace'. Not a worthy ambition in retrospect, but I was young and competitive then and a natural 'hunter'. I'd been held back from what I considered my destiny, posted instead as an instructor for much of the second year of the war: ironically for showing too much natural piloting ability. If my Flik commander had known what I was about I'd have been confined to base for sure as it was considered more dangerous to move on roads that were under the alleged protection of our troops than to fly over enemy territory. My driver was armed to the teeth but could not conceal his nervousness.

~-~

In bright sunshine on the previous morning I'd lifted the Brandenburg KD off the temporary field at Struga, about seventy kilometres east of Tirana, where the Crni Drim river emptied into the north shore of Lake Ohrit: Macedonia, glad to be flying in the clean air above the flies and mosquitoes. I was the fighter escort for *Fliegerdetachement Kessler*, seconded from my recent temporary attachment to *Fliegerkompanie* (Flik) 6F with the acting rank of Leutnant despite my lack of school matriculation, as a special duties officer (*Offizier zur besonderen Verwendung*). I was in company with a two seater UFAG-Brandenburg C.1 of *Fernaufklärung* (F-Flik), one out of a complement of five aeroplanes, normally based in southern Montenegro. The C.1 was flown by my old friend Lt. Kessler, now in command of this detachment, with whom I'd previously lost touch following my complicated postings. In the rear seat was a Leutnant observer/photographer. I reflected that my fate seemed frequently to be tied up with Kessler's own. The aeroplane I was flying had originally been assigned to Kessler and he'd lost no time in having his personal challenge painted across the elevators: *Mein Handschuh, Dein Gesicht!* My gauntlet, your face!

But he knew the terrain so was detailed as photographic pilot. I just had to follow carefully in the KD D.1 and shoot down any enemy machine that tried to interfere with Brigade orders.

~-~

I didn't particularly like the KD. Few did.

Following the heavy and prolonged fighting around the garrison of Prezmysl where I had flown two-seat Brandenburgs and Aviatiks on reconnaissance and bombing duties I'd been given a fortnight's leave.

With the fearfully accurate flak and the threat of a million Russians on the Carpathian Heights now gratefully behind me, I'd accompanied an injured Kessler to Berlin. But after three days, when I was just starting to relax, my leave was cut short. A telegram from the *Kommandant der Jagdeschwader* at *Luftfahrtruppe* Command, delivered to the Kessler residence, ordered me to proceed to the nearest railway station and make my way to the aerodrome at Fischamend, near Vienna: a grinding railway journey via Dresden, Prague and Brno of some five hundred kilometres.

As I packed I cursed the perversion of the military, bade farewell to Ernst and his insatiable 'bedchamber maids' and after an exhausting day's travelling, reported at the main gate. I found myself with a group of serving pilots of varying experience. We'd been assembled as an 'average cross-section' to sample some new Austrian types which were in the process of evaluation by *Flars*, the *Fliegerarsenal*. These included the very first Austrian-built Albatros D.IIIs, beautifully-finished, shark-like machines with improved climb and level speed by comparison with the D.II and an improved cockpit view - especially if compared with some of the other types which needed a damned periscope to see ahead! The D.III was a revelation, but no sooner had I filed my positive report than I was sent to a fighter Flik on the Italian Front, being posted back to Galicia in the early spring of 1917.

The fighting had raged on, and I eventually got to fly a superannuated, German-built Albatros D.II. Although not as good as the new D.III, like any sensible fighter it was fitted with twin Spandaus and I felt totally at home, scoring two aerial victories in quick succession, an Anade, whose rear gunner gave me a lot of trouble and a Russian Nieuport 11. Another black-tailed Nieuport bearing skull and cross-bones had been all over me, shooting bits off my poor Albatros from every direction until I dived away in panic. I learned later it might have been the formidable Russian ace, Kozakov, and I considered myself lucky to be able to tell the tale.

To my chagrin I was then re-posted like some orphan parcel to the south-eastern front with no explanation. I'd said goodbye to my Flik, and at the end of May, with two other pilots, I had arrived by truck at an airfield near Kraljevo on the Ibar River in occupied Serbia, where we familiarised ourselves with the aircraft which had been assembled there: three of the few available *Phönix*-built KD *(Kampf-Doppeldecker)* D.1s, rather quaint single seaters which had been released for service on this ramshackle front. In my case though it was a re-familiarisation flight and I swallowed my deep disappointment that they weren't Albatros D.IIs or even Halberstadts.

~-~

I'd flown a KD before in Austria and it hadn't impressed me.

Although quick and sturdy, it was loose directionally with a tendency to fall into spins if climbing turns weren't smoothly balanced by careful rudder input. It had already gained a bad reputation when pilots, training on the first machines at Matyasföld and elsewhere, had suffered fatalities following accidental spins. These became steep and fast and the small rudder had been reportedly ineffective. As a result the fighter was feared and detested in some quarters, being nicknamed *Sarg (Coffin)*. This was thoroughly bad for morale considering it was the premier front line fighter aeroplane of Austro-Hungary, at least until more Albatrosse and improved Phönix types could be delivered. Even so there were few enough of them. So I had mixed feelings when detailed to fly this morning's escort.

~-~

Existing maps being unreliable we are charged with making a detailed photo strip map of central Albania which it was hoped would also identify some partisan strongholds. Moreover with Greece's capitulation under diplomatic pressure from the Entente she was now in the enemy camp and we were looking for signs of troop movements whether French, Italian or Greek. Kessler is on his first operational flight since his last bout of malaria. Most of the other pilots and observers were down with or still recovering from its debilitating effects or from dysentery or both. So it was the Greek situation that had prompted my posting from Galicia with some other crews drawn from that hard-pressed Front. Compared with Galicia the posting was regarded as an 'easy billet' but the biting flies, the clouds of mosquitoes, culex and malarial anopheles, as well as other blood suckers made life hellish. Kessler would get so mad he'd try to shoot the bigger ones with a Luger and anyone in the vicinity was forced to take immediate cover.

~-~

The approaching sun-dappled hills of Elbasan-Berat appeared like a rumpled quilt, diffuse in faded hues of blue and ochre: like a flung robe upon the earth, where, according to the *Poet*, 'man lives like lice among its folds'.

Three years before the Serbs had thrown themselves with heroic abandon at the invading Austro-Hungarians and thrust them back in the early stages, gaining much valuable equipment. Our troops had sustained heavy losses but the Serbs had fought two earlier Balkan campaigns and were nearing exhaustion. The unrelenting winter of 1914 had played havoc with Serbian supplies and by December the Austrian advance saw Belgrade taken. By a tremendous effort the Serbs had smashed through the Austrian lines, but their ranks depleted and suffering the ravages of typhus, they'd been unable to press the advantage. Both sides had suffered enormous losses, including over half of Serbia's crack troops and stalemate prevailed for months.

By 1916, the Albanian mountains had witnessed a ragged Serbian retreat, a defeated army moving through rugged, snowy terrain. From Kosovo across Albania towards the Adriatic ports they'd trailed like slow brown caterpillars, taking with them hundreds of Austrian prisoners. Taking too their precious reliquary: the catafalque of Stefan Nemanje, first crowned king of the medieval Serb dynasty, borne by determined toiling men up the rocky trail to the chapel of St. Basil in Montenegro. Many Serbs had been evacuated by the French and Italian navies while the Austrians were transported into captivity abroad.

We turned south when we saw the wide loops of the Semani River and the photographer released his escapement. It was important to fly steadily and accurately from this point into the Pindus Mountains. It looked peaceful enough from 4000 metres with drifting cumulus that thickened as the morning wore on, but the purple clefts in the hillsides were dangerous places. Despite the latent Serbian collapse Austro-Hungary was no nearer controlling this wild countryside, particularly the mountains. This was a land of feuds and vendettas, haunt of brigand and terrorist. The *malisores*, the fiercely patriotic mountain dwellers had driven out a powerful Turkish army intent on suppressing them in 1910, expelling the invaders from Kosovo and securing Skopje.

They'd never been disarmed nor would be. Besides that the Serbs were re-grouping.

~-~

I am replying to questions from Browne, who asks me about my war service. By this he means the war which ended on November eleventh 1918, even though it hadn't in many places, not least in Eastern and Central Europe.

I considered that there are those for whom war is a gift. There are others to whom it falls whose generalship must predict and account for losses beforehand, who weigh the outcomes heavily. Others revel in war and profess to know nothing else, yet still show their humanity and these we sometimes lean to for our strength. Such a man was Ernst Kessler. Of robust constitution and possessed initially of a keen sense of humour which made difficult times bearable, he would change after his first period of captivity. He was increasingly capable, I thought, of a sort of corrosive cruelty, corrosive to the self though directed as much to some of his colleagues on the Flik as to the enemy. It made him fearless in combat and so a danger not only to the enemy but to himself.

I served with him through our basic training, and he was instrumental in my escaping the hellish circumstance and victimisation that would have seen me tried for murder if I'd not made my getaway, else suffered the fate of some other young cadets. Rumours of suicides at Helmsburg, (or at any rate unexplained deaths) embraced the fate of 'Dragunavicius' which had suited my purpose in the most pragmatic fashion, though I'd wished it otherwise.

'There are those,' I tell Hawkeye/Browne, 'Who use war to mask their appetites, to cover their crimes – aberrants without conscience - laying waste of innocence. It makes me think that evil exists as a force independent of man and wars for his soul: the price he pays for free will.' Parsifal Wöbbe was an aberration, one that emerged all too readily using the power conferred by rank for self gratification and plunder. Ernst fell into the camp of the adventurer that professes to know naught else. A good man to have alongside in a tight spot. A winged knight.

Kessler had informed me that the cruelty of the Turks had re-enforced in the Albanians an implacable hatred of invaders and stiffened a tough and vigorous people into a deadly foe against all comers. War for them had been a way of life for decades. Even the children were excellent marksmen in whom fear was an alien concept. While many of our troops were contemptuous of them, considering them in-bred mountain men, Kessler admired them in principle - from a distance. Their country was no place for a forced landing.

Strange where one's mind drifts when flying over mysterious landscapes. Sometimes, on a long lonely flight, a pilot might fancy that he is alone in the entire world and will return to earth when his petrol runs out to find that there is no-one else alive; as if he'd flown through time to the end of the world for mankind. Or crash-landed on the dark side of Mercury. Flying at this height the misty earth passes slowly, mesmerically. It would be easy to daydream: reminisce on blissful idylls, riding the grassy plains or with two well-born girls on my arms walk in paradise beside a wooded lake. But these were dangerous skies. The spring offensive by the British against the strongly defended Bulgarian line from the Voras Oros Mountains, the Vardar River to the Dorian Lake had all but petered out with heavy losses. Icy rain and northerly winds had made the campaign more difficult with unseasonably bad weather. The fine days we now enjoyed were a welcome break.

Like my comrades a hundred metres away I am wrapped up in woollens, wear fleece-lined boots, heavy flying clothing and a helmet. A scarf is wound around my face under my high leather collar but there are two patches of cheek beneath my goggles that are flayed by the wind despite an application of grease. Now they are merely numb. I'm strapped firmly in my seat with broad webbing and so swaddled that I find it difficult to move. Flying the biplane straight and level does not require any effort other than concentration but the air gets bumpier as the sun warms the mountain slopes.

I push the KD's rudder bar left and right occasionally, to keep my limbs from stiffening as much as to see directly ahead - even though it means falling back a little in formation. In spite of the shapely scalloping of the upper fuselage cross-section, the view beyond the big-six Austro-Daimler, past struts and the exhaust stack is poor. In time I suppose one would get accustomed to it, but another blind spot is the upper wing itself with the 'baby coffin': the streamlined aluminium fairing encasing the single machine gun that fires over the disk of the propeller. It is fixed so far above that when the gun jams (and Austrian cartridges frequently achieved this) it will be quite inaccessible. I might get the riggers to knock together a raised seat to improve my view, but that would expose me to more of the icy slipstream. It could use a bigger celluloid windscreen for sure. Not to mention a fixed fin and bigger rudder. In truth the whole damn thing needed a re-think! Phönix Flugzeugwerke *had* brought out an improved model with fin, but 'my' machine was the original version.

Subsequently I discover that Offizierstelvertreter Julius Arigi of Fluggeschwader 1 had experimented with a fixed fin modification which Phönix later formally adopted, while other KDs were equipped with angled guns. Josef Kiss actually had a synchronised Schwarzlose fitted.

I was slapped out of my reverie by an invisible hand and our formation bucked - turbulence from wind over the hills or thermal activity. Recently, at the Aspern test centre, I'd heard tell of newer Austrian fighters under construction at Phönix and Aviatik, the latter having a very thin 'reflexed' wing, designed to absorb gusts. Those in the know said it would be steadier and more stable. To my ear that sounded weak and flimsy. However, we had started equipping with KDs in 1916 and were stuck with it for the present and if there was one consolation I had to admit it was rugged. It had been designed by the German engineer, Heinkel and it was powerful and certainly better than the obsolescent Fokker D.IIs and the E.III monoplane - in spite of its spinning tendency. But the biggest drawback of the KD as far as I was concerned was its single unsynchronised Schwarzlose. If indeed the KD had been designed to an official specification, that specification was seriously out-dated.

I craved an Albatros with twin synchronised Spandaus! I even dreamed about it. As far as I was concerned, the sleek D.III represented the flower of German single-seater fighter design. Manufacture of the type was now proceeding in Austria. The Germans were already flying them in Macedonia where Lt. Fieseler, 'Tiger of Macedonia', was creating a name for himself: but it was unlikely that we 'Austrians' would be equipped with something so relatively advanced in this backwater. I thought that my best chance of renewing my acquaintance with one of those sharks was to get transferred to the Isonzo River, Caporetto and the Italian Front!

Meanwhile it's my lot to be flying the KD. Clamped to the struts between the left wings spins the Morrell anemometer whose dial informs me that airspeed is 135 kph: a respectable cruising speed at this height. Between the right pair, the ears of my tattered *Steiff* bear mascot flutter in the breeze, tightly tied upon his star-strut perch. Dipl. Ing. Heinkel's most unusual star-strut system of wire-less wing bracing gave rise to another nickname, *'Spinne'* (*spider*): 'double pyramids' of streamlined struts joined at their apices mid-way between the wings that gives the wing structure considerable strength and its angled struts a likeness to a menacing arachnid. And I've never liked spiders.

We drone south, cocooned in the lazy rumble of our motors. It is a beautiful day and visibility is unlimited as the haze has burned off. Though I stare to the southwest past the narrow, low-lying coastal belt, I cannot yet detect a smudge beyond that might be the Italian Adriatic coast. We'd have to be a few thousand metres higher to get a glimpse I supposed.

From time to time I consult my own map to check our position although the primary navigation is left to Kessler. I note Berat on the Osum River. I am keeping a constant lookout for British aeroplanes operating from lower Macedonia or Italian aircraft crossing the Straits. Macchi-Lohner seaplanes might be aloft from what they called Valona, the Italian expeditionary base at the port of Vlore. Kessler in the bigger

Brandenburg is directed by his observer who concentrates on the terrain and his large *Reihenbildner* strip camera mounted on the gunner's floor, the shutter exposed through a ventral hatch. I glance at my instrument needles shivering in their brass bezels: water temperature, oil pressure, engine revolutions. But my eyes are constantly scanning the horizon. I see Ernst's leather-clad head turning as well.

After twenty-five minutes on a southerly heading Kessler rocks his wings. Motioning with his arm he begins a turn through ninety degrees in order to take pictures through the lower boundary of the section to be mapped. We'd do another twenty minutes on this leg with the wind on our starboard quarter and then turn north past the looming prominence of Mt. Ostrovice avoiding the autonomous province of Koritza or Korce, to run off the remaining film before cloud cover increases. Beyond the next valley where the Osuma River flowed lay the Greek border and the provinces of Kastoria and Florian. Korce was currently occupied by the French. It had been the scene of a Turkish massacre of teachers at the first Albanian girls' school at the end of the last century. Fanatics opposed to the education of women.

Talk in the mess at Struga had been of strange alliances. Germany and Austro-Hungary were allied to a newly self-confident, self-styled 'modern' Turkey under Enver Pasha whose Young Turks had been fanatically pro-German for years. Now basking in the glory of Gallipoli where the ANZACs had suffered over 100,000 casualties, Turkey, German-armed, supplied via the captured Berlin-Baghdad railway and its naval blockade, was keeping pressure on the Allies in Lower Macedonia. The vast Allied encampment at Salonika, pressed between German-occupied Macedonia, Bulgaria and Turkey with the British then reluctant to push Greek neutrality too hard, was referred to jeeringly as the self-imposed 'Great Allied Internment Camp' or 'The Birdcage'. However, pro-German King Constantine had finally been forced to abdicate and this would doubtless change the stalemate situation on the ground. The Allies had re-taken the Serbian town of Bitolye (Monastir) which had been severely damaged the previous year. It was only 60 kilometres and two mountain ranges away so we were very conscious that our temporary landing ground was vulnerable to raids.

When the Balkan League had driven the Ottomans out of Europe, Turkey had turned again, taking advantage of the rivalry among the League members to regain a European foothold. Although an arch enemy of Turkey, an ailing and disgruntled Bulgaria had accepted a German loan and sided with the Central Powers in the present war in the hope of regaining territory ceded to Rumania at the end of the earlier conflicts. The hapless populations of the war-torn Balkan states had suffered endlessly. From Montenegro to Greece, Christians had met murderous savagery under the Ottomans, but inevitably the members had turned in on themselves in the aftermath.

The one and a half million dispossessed Armenian, Christians and Jews between the Black and the Caspian Seas had suffered worst of all, Natasha. The massacres began in the previous century: Turkey, jealous of their industry and success within that largely Islamic autocracy, in a world distracted by war, had initiated a final solution by 1915. With numbers already reduced by slaughter, emigration or forced conversion to Islam, where children were reportedly injected with typhus-infected blood, women and children gassed or burned in their own churches, girls raped and butchered except those deemed pretty enough for the harem, the remnants were driven into the desert, and left to die of thirst and sunstroke. A nation had disappeared into history as if they'd never been.

Pilots like Steiger were at best amateur historians and pundits with no power to decide with whom they were allied, but wondered what might be the outcome for these devastated lands when the final picture emerged, the war lost or won. It was troubling to the mind.

~.~

Rolf's narrative continues:
I look down at an abandoned trench system zig-zagging away east. A line of anti-aircraft fire pocks the sky further to the south. White AA bursts. Italian or British! They are too far away to affect us. Perhaps they are firing to drive off a reconnaissance machine or Halberstadt fighters operating from German-occupied upper Macedonia, Drama or somewhere. Or they could be a signal to an Italian patrol from Vlore on the coast or even a British patrol from lower Macedonia. Thanks Allied gunners, I thought. The whole country was a crazy mix of Bulgarian, Serbian, Rumanian, Austro-Hungarian and Allied camps with mountain redoubts, trench systems and communicating valleys, confusing fronts and skirmish lines. These skies were dangerous and forewarned is forearmed.

Eighteenth century reports, Kessler had informed me, referred to the local practice of exhuming bodies and 'killing' the *undead* with stakes hereabouts, based upon whether a white (or in some cases a black) horse had shied at a grave. Suicides were still buried with wrists bound, stones wedged between their jaws and heavy stones laid over their coffins.

380

'Otherwise they'll chew through their shrouds and burrow out of their graves,' he'd said. 'Feed on their fellow corpses then move on to the living! Don't forget to sleep with one eye open and a sharpened stake at the ready, young Rolf!' Delivered with a mischievous grin despite his suffering.

For me the shredded victims of mechanised warfare spoke more eloquently of horror than did lemures. Or vampirism's red-headed *strigoi* with two hearts, however gruesome that myth.

'Snap out of it!' I order myself, thrusting away Kessler's tales of superstitious nonsense 'Day dreaming idiot!'

~-~

I renew my vigilance, searching in deep field for any tell-tale dots or flecks of light above or below the horizon that would reveal enemy aircraft. We are flying north again but based on the anti-aircraft bursts being a signal, an attack may be expected from the south, from our rear.

I fly in a series of gentle sweeps, 'S-turning' to provide a clear view left and right of my tail while still following the track of the C.1. Suddenly I see sunlight glinting on wings three kilometres to the southwest about a thousand metres below. I open my throttle wide and overhaul Kessler, pointing urgently and giving him the signal for maximum speed. Kessler banks and looks down to the southwest, then waves to me and pushes his nose down, dark smoke emerging from his exhaust pipes. I see from their slightly swept wings that the climbing formation is made up of Nieuports, French-manufactured and widely used by many Allied combatants. Italians from Otranto given the direction of their approach. Or British, based in Lower Macedonia. So far the English types had been rather obsolescent, apart from the two-seat Sopwith 1-1/2 Strutters and some fast Vickers scouts. I'd heard they also used wireless-equipped Armstrong Whitworths for army co-operation and gun ranging: tough adversaries, as well as DH.2s and the staid B.E.12, 'fighter', wireless-equipped with long trailing aerials; an easy machine to bring down. Whoever these Nieuports may belong to, they are more formidable fighters, light and nimble, powered by 80 hp. Gnome rotaries, though slower than the KD.

I would be alone facing five enemy aeroplanes. But they'd lost the advantage of surprise and I had the height. Although they could match the retreating C.1, Ernst has the advantage of height and is using it to make speed by descending under power. I cover his tail by gaining even more height and circling where they could see me. I knew that they wouldn't pursue him with me above, ready to dive on their unprotected rears. They might of course split their formation but I'd have to wait and see.

I spare a glance for the Brandenburg photo ship disappearing rapidly northwards. What was Kessler's motto? 'Live fast. Love hard. Die young!' How he hated flying two seaters.

I prepare myself. I am keyed up but I need to be calm. Icy. Coolness will see me through, not an unplanned charge. A 'little bull in a china shop', Katya had called me about a hundred years ago it seemed. The odds are one to five. I am waiting to see what the Nieuports will do. They are still climbing, seeming to hang in the sky like storks, details gradually emerging. It occurs to me that this could be a set piece. A trap. I rapidly scan the sky above me, looking for other intruders who may be trying to ambush me, turning the KD and still climbing, flying by instinct and 'feel' so that its treacherous stall-spin doesn't ambush me too. I see no upper threat; only a beautiful sky with some feathery 'mares tails'. I can concentrate on the threat below.

The Nieuports seem to have abandoned any intention they might have had to chase the two-seater. I am to be the sole focus of their ambition. I knew each would want to claim a victory over my Brandenburg.

They are getting close, splitting up to avoid a bunched target group and giving themselves space to manoeuvre. I admire their elegant lines, their rakish wings with the big green white red Italian cockades clearly visible. Lightweight designs with a spinning gyroscope of the rotary engine in front and a narrow bottom wing to provide the best downward view for attack – they are technically *sesquiplanes* and the antithesis of the KD with its massive stationary engine, broad wings and blind spots.

They are climbing fast. I have to lean far out into the slipstream as I turn to keep the formation in sight behind my lower trailing edge. Three hundred metres below I can see five pilots' leather-helmeted heads staring up at me behind their Lewis guns mounted on their upper wings. Just like the gun on my KD, but without the clumsy fairing. No wait! There are six heads. One is a two-seater, a Nieuport 10 by the looks of it. The other *chasseurs* seem to be single-seat 11s. I would have to look out for a flexible rear gun on the 10.

Their other advantage over the KD is that the Italian single seaters have an over-wing gun rail: I can see the sun glinting on its curve. They can slide the weapon down to clear jams or fit a fresh ammunition drum. They can also fire upwards without risking a stall by raising their noses, raking a target from underneath - if they were allowed to get close enough. Altogether superior in design terms to my relatively new, *archaic* KD!

They are still climbing and closing. By slowly orbiting above and gaining height myself I can at least hold their attention and give the more vulnerable photographic machine a good start.

As the Nieuports approach I see that the odds are further altered. Two of the single seaters aren't 11s, although one is equipped with an over-wing gun. I see they have fully circular engine cowlings unlike the 'horseshoe' fronted cowl of the Type 11. These are thus the newer and much more formidable type 17s powered by 110 hp. Le Rhones and reputedly as fast or faster than the KD. They are variously armed with a synchronized Vickers gun and an over-wing Lewis, or even *twin* Vickers. These two were already out-climbing the remainder of the gaggle. Out-numbered, out-gunned: discretion would now seem the sensible option.

I considered making a fast shallow dive to follow the Brandenburg C.1, now almost invisible against the mountains, but I dearly wanted to have a shot at the intruders. In a moment I'd made up my mind, and rolled-off into a steep dive, straight into the middle of the now scattering formation. 'Live fast, love hard….'

I'd selected my target, a juicy Nieu 17, one of the two most formidable scouts. My revolutions are 1800. I dive like a peregrine on a flock of pigeons with the wind shrieking through the struts. I see the 17 skid sideways and then roll away as I bank in concert and pull to keep him in sight. The undersides of his narrow lower wings are painted red to port, green to starboard with silver in between: the colours of the Italian flag. My ailerons are stiff at this speed and the roll is slow, vision dimming as I pull hard. I flash through their formation, whirling silver-grey, red/green Nieuports all around me, but the one I was hunting is nowhere to be seen. He must be hidden by my top wing – there's danger of collision but I continue my dive, not daring to flatten out. They'd be ready to pounce if I give them a chance.

I dive with teeth clenched, the airflow battering at me, but we do not collide. I risk a glance over my right shoulder. There is no-one behind. I pull hard into a climbing turn which regains some of my lost altitude, the rudder lightening as the speed washes off. There's the gaggle of Nieuports above and below my own level. A delicate situation which demands instant action. I climb at full throttle for the higher, more dangerous pair and open fire. Curse it! I have forgotten to cock my machine gun! I quickly pull the cocking cable and fire a snap-burst ahead of a 17 which is jinking violently away up and to the right. I follow in a rising curve, but he easily out-climbs me and I do not dare pull the nose higher for fear of stalling. I hear a brief rattle of a gunfire from below. I am now pulling hard in the turn but the other Nieuport is out-turning my *Kurvenkampf* and still above. I catch sight of another diving Nieuport from my right and I drop the nose and turn sharply in, under him.

Suddenly it's getting out of hand. I cannot see more than two Nieuports at any moment. I am twisting in the cockpit like a marionette in an effort to see everywhere at once, horribly vulnerable to assault from various blind spots. I rock my wings to assess the situation and I'm greeted by loud hammering in my right ear. Slits appear in my right lower wing with strikes on the star-strut complex. Not good! A fight is no place for pretty flying so I shove the stick forward and over with too much rudder, swerving in a wild skid. The KD plays her ace and flicks into a belly-up oscillatory spin, motor spluttering, starved of petrol from the gravity feed - an unintended manoeuvre, born of desperation.

A hurricane is blowing through the cockpit and I can hardly breathe. My goggles have flown off and are battering me about the head held by their elastic. All I can see through my slit-eyes are the clouded hills gyrating through a haze of spraying petrol as the nose whirls round with the horizon pitching about somewhere above my flailing boots, the shadow of the wings passing over and over through my consciousness and a blizzard of rainbow shards streams from the sun. I jam my feet back on the rudder bar and slam the throttle shut, pulling back on the stick at the same time. I centralise the ailerons with both hands and push hard on the rudder bar which has the most resistance. The spin and the banshee winds increase. The aircraft is separating, but it's debris, dead flies and grass stalks flying around my face. I look up to see the vortex of inverted hills spinning closer. Hell did I get into this? I could have just flown away! I knew how manoeuvrable Nieuports were.

'*Die young!*' Kessler's mocking voice echoes in my mind.

The spin slows, responding to the little rudder, then stops and I'm diving in the last quarter of a loop. Thank God the propeller is still revolving against the rising purple hills. At last the horizon emerges. My eyes are streaming from the raw benzene. Gravity pins me in the seat as I recover. I open the throttle and the Austro Daimler backfires then gives a lusty bellow just as something warns me to roll right. I react instinctively as a machine gun hammers away. A silvery Nieu 17 with a daubed slogan on its fuselage has followed under full control and narrowly misses me in recovery. Cramming my goggles back onto my head I look around for the sun remembering Boelcke's *Diktat*, making skidding turns to put the enemy off his aim, praying I won't spin again. We've lost a few thousand metres, me and the KD , and we're now at the cloud layer, playing hide and seek amongst broken fair weather cumulus.

I fly north, but two Nieuports appear above, blocking my escape. To fly under them would be suicide so I turn away east, inland, hoping that they won't follow and risk getting too low on fuel. They turn after me, closing, using their superior height to head me off. The other three are also above but some distance away. I circle to the south. By careful flying I am just able to out-distance the pursuing Nieuports. One is faster, so I assume it's one of the 17s.

The other three are attempting to cut me off so I risk a climb, which gives advantage to the two higher Nieuports, but it's a balancing act, a deadly waltz; a game of chess with me turning gently away avoiding the closing jaws of their pincer. It's working, but they are getting closer all the time. I seize my chance and make a diving break to the west as they come together, but their agility enables them quickly to take up a stern chase. Gradually I bring my nose around to the north. The closer Nieuports are the slower 80 hp. 11s and the 10 with its rear seat observer/gunner. Suddenly there is machine gun fire ripping into the bottom of my fighter tearing long slivers out of the plywood floor. A 17 has closed the gap and is firing from below with his Lewis gun elevated. A split appears below the rudder bar and the renewed smell of petrol tells me that my tank is holed. Break right, breathing fast. Thank God it wasn't an incendiary. I'm deliberately flying erratically, apparently unconcerned with the risk of collision, hoping to unnerve my combatants: convince them they are confronting a desperado or madman. They'd not be far off the mark, but in truth I am careful not to unbalance the KD too much, ever watchful for the sudden pitching cartwheel which heralds a spin - with less room for recovery now as the hills are rising higher.

Suddenly a white rocket rises above the battle. It's from the flare pistol of the leader. Reluctantly the Nieuports fall back. I imagine they're at the limit of their range and need to return now or risk running out of fuel. Nearest to me is the Nieuport 10. Standing up in the gunner's cockpit the observer is levelling something at me. Instinctively I break away to the left, diving and turning. I look up as the Nieuport turns away to follow the others and take my last opportunity to re-engage. I open fire from underneath closing to within 30 metres and my gun jams, curse it! I break away. But I am losing fuel from the holed tank and would have had to disengage anyway or risk a crash landing if I failed to gain my base at

Struga.

I head north for the distant blue lake snatching a quick look behind. The Nieuport is spiralling down into the Albanian hills apparently out of control or making an excellent job of faking it. I memorise its approximate position just as I discover that my cockpit is drenched with petrol. For the first time I appreciate the remote position of my Schwarzlose machine gun. Enemy action apart, firing a synchronised, fuselage-mounted gun could have ignited the lot!

Fifteen minutes later, thankful for a tailwind, I make out the mosques and spires of Struga beyond the blue lake, a beautiful sight for a returning hunter. My height seems good but I am descending downwind as confirmed by the sock. Kessler is down and already parked near the canvas hangars and a few other aircraft are visible, Rumplers and Brandenburgs. I need to make a turn to position for the best approach to the field and start to open the throttle when the engine coughs and cuts and my propeller slows and stops. A flock of startled pelicans lifts from the lake shore. The area ahead is reasonably level but I am now committed to coming straight in on the glide over the multi-barrelled anti-aircraft wagon. I hope the gunners will recognise me if they're awake. My airspeed combined with a tailwind is too high for an elegant landing and I'm too low to risk a turn

I am whistling over the grass but there's plenty of room ahead of me so no need to 'fish-tail' to kill speed. I ease the stick back, losing all forward view. The slipstream dies away and then I'm down, bumping merrily along faster than usual, observing the passing scenery from academic interest. I have no further control over proceedings now that the engine has stopped. I remember to knock off the ignition switches and am almost relaxed.

Without warning the Brandenburg swings to the right. I jam on full left rudder but it's as effective as a postage stamp without propeller slipstream. The KD waltzes in a half circle, the left lower wing dragging the grass. I guess a shock chord has been shot through. We are moving quite slowly but just when I think we are about to stop, the wheels encounter a patch of soft ground and cease revolving. There is enough residual energy to lift the tail and the heavy engine carries us beyond the point of equilibrium. I have a slow motion view of the world turning over as the KD with me firmly strapped-in stands on its propeller. I am instinctively trying to draw the stick through my stomach and into my spine, a hopeless attempt to lift the nose. For a moment I think it might just stay there, balanced on its propeller boss and me suspended in the cockpit metres above the ground. That moment passes and it gradually topples onto its back, the machine gun casing taking the first impact, crushing under the weight as it crunches onto its top wing, wheels in the air, collapsed like a drunk on roller skates.

The KD stood on its nose.

I hang there, with my head above the grass trying to undo my lap belt. The engine tinkles as it cools. At least the fuel has drained away so it shouldn't burn. The lap strap is wedged under my diaphragm and I cannot undo it. I realise that if I do manage to release it I will drop some distance head first before I can get my arms above me to break my fall. I see a battered upside down staff car speeding towards me in my new upside down world and decide rather to wait ignominiously for help than risk a broken neck. Kessler is the first to arrive at the cockpit. He goes down on one knee, offering me the coup de grace.

'What have you done to my beautiful fighter?' he asks in mock horror. 'What a Goddamn lady's landing!' A grin splits his upside down face. 'You *are* a natural pilot, Rolf!'

'Don't!' I say, trying not to laugh as the belt is painfully constricting my diaphragm.

'Your work here is done!' he chokes, helpless with laughter. 'Maybe they'll give me an Albatros now!'

'Ernst,' I gasp, addressing his boots. 'Just help me out!'

'First tell me whose side you're on.'

I ignore the jibe.

'Lt. Kessler,' I say, collecting myself. 'Let me state for the record that there are only two kinds of KD pilot. Those who've landed like this: and

387

those who have *yet* to! Now help me get out of this bloody thing!'

Kessler reminds me that last year the 'Chief', our mercurial 'hands-on' Oberst Emil Uzelac, commander of the LFT at the Army High Command, had been hospitalised after putting a new Brandenburg heavily on its back. So I was in good company.

I stand next to the inverted machine for photographs and further ribaldry while the mechanics plan how best to get it back on its wheels using ropes and a ladder lashed upright to the back of a truck. I tell Kessler how I'd 'resorted to dangerous flying' to unnerve the enemy, but didn't know if it had actually worked. He says, straight–faced, that 'every time I flew it was bloody dangerous until I was safely on the ground'. I didn't know whether he was being unkind about my flying or is genuinely concerned about my well being. Or that of others.

'Five!' says Kessler, milking it. 'You weren't supposed to take on *five* Nieuports single-handed, Rolf. Attempted suicide is punishable as self-inflicted wounding. It's in Army Regulations!'

'Well, I got one anyway. Almost makes up for this.' I indicate the crushed MG fairing and the crumpled wing. The propeller had stopped in the horizontal position and had suffered no damage when the machine went over. Heinkel's rugged strut arrangement has held the wing cellule rigid so there's only superficial damage to some of the upper ribs.

'I hope the strip photographs are worth it.'

I look at the punctures and slashes in the bottom of the fuselage. They've narrowly missed my nether regions. A longeron is split and there are holes in the wings and tail and of course the petrol tank. The aircraft will be out of commission for several days.

The riggers have a rope over a ladder and are pulling the tail down. In a moment it's back on its wheels and looking 'almost normal for a KD', except for the crushed gun canister and the fact that it's sagging to one side. Sure enough the rubber cord suspension has been parted by bullets.

'Oh no!' Kessler moans in apparent distress from the other side of the machine.

'What's up?'

'They've got *Klaus*!'

I walk round to the right wing cellule. I'm going to need a needle and thread and some straw stuffing. *Störtebeker*, Graczy's Steiff bear mascot has been shot clean through the head.

That night I wrote my report and read up on the details of the type I'd brought down. According to LFT intelligence the Macchi-built Nieuport 10 had a range of about 250 kilometres on a good day with no reserve. Which meant if operating from Otranto, the closest point on the Heel of Italy to the coastline of Albania, it would have no more than 30 minutes flying time if he were to return to base with any reserve fuel. Equally it could be from an Italian squadron based on the mainland of Albania. Either way it was just his luck that the formation was called back when he was in a position for me to make one last pass. Before my inaccessible gun jammed on me.

Hitherto, long-range types like the excellent Caproni bombers had ranged as far as key targets in Austria. I considered that from an intelligence point of view it would be a good idea, covertly, to find out where such a short range machine had been operating from. A good excuse in fact to go and look for it. There had been no eyewitness to corroborate my 'kill' so I was unable to claim it officially. I knew I'd be forbidden to explore those dangerous hills so I wouldn't ask permission, and intended to set off at dawn.

I wonder what effect this admission of yet another breach of good order and discipline would have on my Whitehall interrogators. To hell with it, I think. If they're to take me on it would be just the way I am.

~.~

I stood swaying slightly from the exertion. The last person in the world I expected or wished to see was crouched before me like a hyena over my kill, very far from Helmsburg. Two large dun-coloured army horses were tethered next to the wrecked Nieuport, one saddled, the other harnessed to a cart. The Serbs stood in a bunch, the four heavily-bearded prisoners taking a break before continuing with their detail: digging two shallow graves in the stony soil. Wöbbe came erect to his full swaggering height, his brows knitted. The two years between boot camp and this punitive forward echelon duty posting had improved neither his looks nor his temper.

'Who the hell are you?' he growled. I noted the slung carbine and the holster.

I said nothing, my mind spinning with possibilities and dead ends. He stood and examined me at length, eyes still akimbo. One by one, expressions of inquiry, recognition, astonishment and fear scaled the unprepossessing cliff of his face. He stared at me intently, mouth pursing for the question that remained unspoken. But sly triumph now settled, glittering in the little werewolf eyes. It informed me that my means of escape, impersonating the unfortunate Steiger, the victim of his perverted assault, had finally dawned in his brain. It could only be me: no ghost but an imposter in the flesh.

'You!' he smiled evilly. 'You, boy, are in some damn big trouble.'

I said nothing. I glanced out of the corner of my eye at the burial detail. They were taking a keen interest, sharing a cigarette.

'It's you who's in big trouble, you murdering bastard,' I said quietly.

I heard a low moan from one of the bodies. Glancing down I saw the bigger man moving slightly, eyelids fluttering.

'This one's alive,' I said.

'Don't worry. He'll be dead for sure pretty soon,' he said nastily. 'And you'll be facing a court martial.'

'Detail!' I yelled over my shoulder in Russian. 'Get over here and get this man on a stretcher, now. And go easy with him. Use your tunics and break off some branches.'

'What did you say?' shouted Wöbbe. 'Who the hell do you think you are giving orders here? It's you that's under arrest.' He tugged at his holster.

I stepped closer with a hand in my flying coat pocket, careful to stay out of range of his legendary fist.

'Leave that weapon,' I hissed. 'I have a 9 mm trained on you. And I outrank you now, *Feldwebel.* I see you've earned your demotion.'

Wöbbe was practically frothing at the mouth. 'My cavalry patrol will be back here in two minutes and then it's *you* who'll be the prisoner!'

'Detail! Here *now!*' I shouted in my best Russian officer's manner without taking my eyes off Wöbbe.

The Serb soldiers clustered around. One or two threw me curious looks since their hefty captor now stood awkwardly, his bulk half twisted away, an ogre with mountainous shoulders, menacing in the fading light. They hastily complied with my instruction, feeding stout saplings through the armholes and buttoning them together. I took an opportunity to examine the crash, keeping Wöbbe covered. The gunner's cockpit was undamaged. No weapon was mounted on the gun ring. With one eye on Wöbbe I checked the cart. Inside there were tools including shovels and what looked like a strongbox. There were gilded candlesticks and other valuables that I presumed had been looted. Wrapped in a beaded dress was a cine camera. So that was what I'd seen pointed at me before I'd opened fire on the Nieuport.

I turned back to the injured officer. He wore a British uniform under his flying suit that had been undone, presumably by Parsifal Wöbbe when foraging for identification and anything valuable. I reached for his wrist; his uniform cuff revealed a tab with the embroidered words in English, 'War Correspondent'. I felt his pulse and lifted an eyelid. Apart from some blood in his mouth and nostrils and a bruise on his temple he seemed undamaged externally. I imagined he might have suffered some internal injury and was concussed at least. The other man, the pilot, was beyond help.

I had a premonition that the situation was about to change and was ready for Wöbbe to try something drastic and warned him to back away. He knew that he would face interrogation and probably a trial for the murder of young Steiger, whatever charge was levelled at me, something which he was of no doubt aware in the depths of his consciousness. He might have been inebriated when he'd struck the fatal blow, but the information that it was Dragunavicius who'd unexpectedly died in sick bay after a training accident would have taken him by surprise. A ruptured spleen would have been the recorded death of Cadet Rolfus Dragunavicius who was being treated for a few broken ribs. Cadet Gustav Rolf Steiger on the other hand had marched stiffly out of camp with a squad of *Luftfahrtruppe* volunteers early that next morning, before Wöbbe had surfaced. He'd never actually seen Dragunavicius' body. This ghost which now stood before him in the failing light was very much a thing of flesh and blood.

I always heeded premonitions. I remembered how fast Wöbbe moved for a fat man. He'd lost a little weight since I'd last seen him but, I presumed, none of his speed. He probably knew he couldn't un-shoulder and aim his rifle before I had time to shoot, nor could he undo his holster and draw his revolver quickly. Suddenly he flung down the rifle twisting and lunging in my direction, uncoiling like a spring. Swerving to avoid the covering arc of my pocketed pistol he charged head down like a maddened boar. He held a long bayonet in his fist, outstretched like a lance, a compromise weapon for close order fighting.

I scrambled away backwards though his bayonet caught my sleeve as I raised my hand then I kicked out hard as his momentum carried him on, tripping him neatly. He fell sprawling and cursing, trying to rise from a half-dug grave. There was nothing else for it. I stepped close and dropped heavily, one knee on his bulging back. With malice aforethought

I dug the Mauser into the thick neck behind the ear. The safety was 'off' and I curled my trigger finger to the first pressure. Killing him, on balance, seemed the best thing to do.

I was breathing deeply. I hesitated, imagining a neat round hole in the base of his skull welling dark blood as he shuddered in his death throes. I wondered if I would feel emotion beyond relief and a sense of overdue justice performed for an innocent youngster, my unwitting saviour who'd been one victim among many. The Serbs stood back in silence awaiting the conclusion of this 'Balkan act'. Still I hesitated to pull that last travel of the trigger. How swiftly death would come. I would not be able to undo the action of the next second. I note the two wristwatches upon the thick wrist. They are almost synchronised.

~-~

I tell myself that this is no more uncivilized than shooting my enemy in the back in aerial combat. How do you define the one as 'legitimised murder' and this as an assassination? No matter. If I am judge, jury and executioner, it's no more than happens in truth ten thousand times a day in war. And as far as assassinations went, in this country it was the national sport. Just across the Serbian border the very act had been committed that started this whole mess. But I'm still torn. Guilt is a heavy burden, this I know. What then would I become? Wöbbe is struggling beneath me and I shake away these thoughts. Fight injustice my father had said. I will not spare another second with the memory of this living minotaur whose back is arching powerfully like a bull's. My arm is trembling. I take a deep breath. At that moment I hear a commanding voice and the decision is taken out of my hands.

I raise my head. A small army is silhouetted against the sky. My eyes gradually take in the details: about a dozen tough-looking brigands in rakish black silk bandanas, ammunition bandoliers across their shoulders and long daggers in their belts train their fierce eyes and long rifles at me and on the Serbs shrinking back into the pines.

~-~

Returning to Struga and swearing him to secrecy, I confide the full story to a cynical Kessler. The discovery of my downed Nieuport in the foothills and the eventual fate of Parsifal Wöbbe. I'm not sure he believes it and favours me with a wicked smile from within his mosquito net.

'Serves the bastard right anyway,' he'd grinned.

I write a convincing report for the CO which differs appreciably from the truth. I will become adept at this form of subterfuge over time.

~-~

That night it started to rain again, remorselessly, curtailing flying for days. Eventually flying resumed but sorties were fewer and though it wasn't as hot, the humidity soared and the malarial mosquitoes descended with renewed ferocity. So we were short of crews again. Not a day too soon and much to our relief the entire detachment was ordered back to Austria.

Kessler was mollified as he'd said he was heartily sick of Macedonia, its flies and its climate. He was putting in for transfer to the German *Luftstreitkräfte* which he felt, as a bona fide German citizen, he was legally entitled to do, despite his having been *persona non grata* with certain Prussian regiments before the war. He confided that this had been mostly due to insolvency, a low point in his career brought about by hedonistic addictions resulting in his spending time at the Kaiser's pleasure. Now they'd likely take an experienced officer with a good flying record and hopefully overlook his term of imprisonment due to the exigencies of war.

Apart from which it was becoming dangerous on the ground. He was convinced, not without reason, that he was the object of a vendetta with some locals taking shots at him recently. Being confined to the *Krankenstube* with malaria had probably saved his life

'I am a 'marked man' here, Rolf,' he grinned, but I noticed that the smile did not reach his eyes. He poured himself another *slivovitz*. It was said he was trying to get the damned mosquitoes drunk so that they'd lose control, crash and burn. Perhaps we all looked as strained. He told me that the only way he could safely leave the airfield was on wings, and I'd just broken his single seater. I suggested he had a word with Father Joseph.

'Who?' he asked.

'You know. The Franciscan monk who could levitate!'

Kessler didn't smile. He was determined to get some real 'Western Front action' as he put it, on decent equipment, instead of the ridiculous obsolescent types we were operating in this Godless mosquito-ridden mud hole.

'Jesus, Rolf. Even *new* Austrian aeroplanes look like something out of a nineteenth century patent catalogue, devised by lunatics.'

It permeated at every level through the military, he said.

'No wonder Germany describes our alliance, like fighting - *shackled to a corpse.*'

'There are some good designs appearing now,' I said defensively. 'The latest Phönix….'

'Dammit, man. The Austrian-built Albatros D.III is as good as anything in the air. Better. Yet we're stuck out here with these clownish KDs equipped with an inaccessible machine gun. You can't even see where you're going. It's a bloody joke!'

There was no disagreeing and off he'd stomped with his Luger to shoot some more anopheles or keep the locals at bay while I wrote my diary.

~-~

I was forced to remain behind. The airframe of what really was now 'my' KD had been repaired, but when I'd test flown it, the motor refused to give fill revs even though new plugs had been fitted. So I watched the ragged formation of my comrades disappear into the grey murk and the mountains, Kessler leading in a two-seat Brandenburg, wishing I'd gone with them despite the poor weather.

I thought that Kessler was lucky to escape given the jealousies he'd aroused among the locals, associating with certain women un-chaperoned. One stood out. Some sort of minor aristo, able to flout convention to an extent. A servant girl visited the aerodrome the day after the squadron had gone and sought me out, prevailing upon me to carry a letter to Lt. Ernst Kessler on her mistress's behalf. It was sealed with wax bearing the signet ring imprint of a pelican. I was to be sure it was delivered into his hand. I said that I would perform that request.

But no matter. Whatever Man may plan, remorseless Fate already had us in her grip.

~-~

When I returned to Austria I refuelled at Graz and proceeded to a forward airfield to join my old Flik supporting the Austrian positions on the Isonzo River Front. Kessler was nowhere to be seen. I'd learned that he'd been successful in his application to the Western Front. So he'd got his wish and for a while enjoyed flying the best that German ingenuity could create: some of the first, fast-climbing Siemens-Schuckert D.IIIs to be provisionally issued to the Jastas. He'd been making a name for himself, despite seizures and other teething troubles with their complex, geared-rotaries. But then I'd received a letter from him saying that, to his disgust, he'd been despatched north again, attached to a hastily-formed mixed *Schlacht-Kampfgeschwader* (its number censored).

In the Carpathians, Kerensky had been urging his Russians to continue the fight despite the soldiers' councils which were against the continuation of a capitalist war, threatening mutiny or worse. In the air the Imperial Russian Air Force pilots continued to fight valiantly and they had some quite good equipment, mostly French, by late 1917, even though many of the supporting troops were deserting or refusing to co-operate. Kessler, I later heard, had been forced down behind Russian lines where as rough a bunch of vagabond troops that still served the provisional government had taken him prisoner, reported by the shot up crew of the two-seater he'd been escorting. His subsequent fate was unknown to me at that time. But to fall into Russian hands as an enemy and an officer at this time, his life would not have been worth a light.

I feared the worst for Ernst.

Chapter 28. *Homeward and Revenge:*

Latvian border, Autumn 1919

From the Latgale woods I moved south.

Kuznetsowa was close enough to contemplate for a man on foot in two days, but fear of being caught by Streltsi, Bolshevists or Nestor Makhno's Greens made me proceed with caution. That there might be peat bogs in open moorland which could swallow a horse gave me more reason to proceed with care.

I moved by day and night, conscious of my hunger, tightening my belt and slaking my thirst by swift rivulet or more often peaty or brackish water where I found it. Water was the essential to survival by the 'rule of three': three minutes without air, three days without water and three weeks without food: generally all result in death. But I had a will to live that flowed like fire through my veins and it was fierce enough to taste. Though gripped with a fugitive's dread I felt elated to be in my homeland once more. The sense of solitary freedom I'd known as a boy: riding my pony, Flitzer, and running wild with Wolfie, returned with a rush.

I could not estimate quite when I left Latvian territory and entered Lithuania. Just felt it. Several times I encountered Bolshevist or other positions; wooded encampments or roofless and burned occupied villages and was forced to make detours and stay off the roads in daylight. Every hour I'd discover bodies lying unburied, stripped and barefoot beneath trees or in water-filled ditches, pallid and wrinkled: sometimes singly and others in groups where they'd been shot in the back of the head. Remnants of uniform from combat units on all sides: occasional pitiful remains from the previous winter, legs sawn off just below the knee: an expedient way to remove a boot when the victim had been frozen hard. Most were civilian; some in family groups bearing evidence of torture. The road to Utopia is paved with the corpses of the innocent, I thought.

A thick cloud of flies led me to a half-flooded shell crater where five part-decomposed nuns were arranged in a 'mandala', a wheel whose symbolism was beyond me. Carrion crows hopped and tugged at the wretched bodies and a great raven glared up at me, head on one side. I clapped my hands and shouted and they reluctantly flapped off to a nearby tree to remonstrate in raucous protestation. I wrapped my scarf around my mouth and nose to keep off the black flies and to reduce the stink from the pit. Half naked she lay on her side, the Mother Superior; her blackened talons clutched a box or it had been cynically placed there. A reliquary, perhaps a rusted nail from the true cross had once been its preserve. Someone had carved crude lettering, 'ALVB', in the dark, split flesh of her swollen back that crawled with blowfly maggots.

Famine I knew stalked the lands further east and there was talk of cannibalism, finally acknowledged by Lenin whose response was, 'Shoot more priests: the more the better!'. But this evil act was wanton and perverted. Apart from the ministrations of the crows, there was no sign at all that she or the sisters had been de-fleshed. Though from the mass of larvae and beetles gnawing at a wound where her ribs protruded, it looked as though someone had cut out her heart.

As I left, the crows fluttered back to their feasting, like vultures at an old lion kill.

Civil war seemed more vengeful than any other, driven by avarice, hatred; fired by propaganda, religious, class, grudge and tribal conflict at the bottom of which, I also knew, crawled the Semite, lapsed or otherwise. Spurned of the earth. I was filled with foreboding for my parents, apostate though they were.

In the woods by evening I stumbled across half-dug trench workings with a forester's hut nearby. I was ravenous but dared not spend much time foraging for food. Anyway there was precious little to be had across Russia or the Baltic States which the Bolshevists wished to reclaim for the new Soviet Russia. There was evidence of habitation, probably irregulars or partisans. Cooking smells hung about so that my hunger became unbearable. I'd begun a quick search of the open cupboards when I stopped still; my blood running like ice water. Voices called; howls like wild dogs communicating at a distance, some near, some further away. I had to escape from these four walls or risk being trapped by who knew what.

Without a backward glance I fled to the vampyric twilight of the trees, my Mauser in my fist with no illusions of what would happen to me if caught by whatever side. I ran and ran away from the sounds, a crepuscular ghost slipping through the cathedral-grey of the forest. There was enough light to avoid the worst of the snagging underbrush and the crash of bracken and leaves that created a resonant sound image of the

398

fleeing animal I had become. The sounds of my pursuers diminished for a while and then regained their volume, booing and whistling with catcalls and hollering; no words that I could recognise. With barely a hint that the noises emanated from human throats I might have been pursued by a hag o' the mists, hooting apes or yelping dogs.

I ploughed into deep cover and stopped close under the shadowy bole of a fir, aware of my heartbeats, the rasp of my breath that I struggled to quiet. I crouched there for minutes, chest against the trunk, breath held, eyes on stalks, trying to see around the tree into the murky forest, pointing my pistol towards a small glade where a faint evening light filtered because that was the furthest I could see. I realised that the evening chorus had ceased. Apart from the occasional drip of moisture on a leaf, the forest was quiet.

Minutes dragged before I had detected a slight movement fifty metres off, though it was hard to judge due to thick foliage and poor light. I forced my gaze onto that spot where I was convinced I'd seen a hint of motion; a 'flicker' of something. But then there was nothing. No swaying grass or shaking leaf revealed a lurking killer. I was tense and aware that I hadn't eaten for two days. My head ached, my body was weary. Back and thighs hurt relentlessly. I forced myself to concentrate on a piece of vegetation half a metre across as the evening light faded into darkness. This could be a war of nerves. He might be there waiting for me to break cover, aware of my position but not able to see me. A waiting game. He who moves first forfeits life. Each of us doubting that the other is there but neither prepared to move and give away his hiding place. He was probably well fed and relaxed. He could afford to wait; a trained sniper, a hunter who could stay focussed for hours, not moving a muscle. No matter how uncomfortable.

My eyes ached with the strain of staring into darkness. I blinked and re-focussed again on my target area, but no amount of effort could reveal anything in the dark. I heard a soft footfall off to my right and nearly died of fright as a dark shape moved into my field of view. It was a full grown deer with a yearling following quietly behind. They'd not detected me, frozen as I was in darkness. And they'd not caught my scent.

The pair crossed ahead of me through my line of view with the dimly seen 'target area'. They kept moving unconcernedly until they were close to where I'd detected movement. I was telling myself I had glimpsed nothing more than a bird or some wild creature disturbing the leaves when I had a sudden impression of the lead deer halting. She gave a warning 'cough', stamped her foot and suddenly erupted into movement, back in my direction. A dark figure emerged out of the undergrowth, much closer than I had anticipated, and fired a shot after the retreating animals which jinked to one side, the bullet clipping bark from my tree. Without hesitating I fired two shots straight at the gun flash and was rewarded by an agonised scream and the sound of a falling body. I had no idea if he was alone or whether he was in the vanguard of those other pursuers, but I wasn't waiting around to find out. I fled deeper into the forest, falling and stumbling, arms in front of my face to protect my eyes from twigs and branches, running for long minutes and stopping to listen from cover. I spent the night moving as stealthily as possible, adrenaline still pumping, jumping at shadows and the disconcerting impressions of figures crouching amongst the bushes. Eventually, exhausted, I covered myself in leaves and fallen branches and lay still, listening for the sounds of my pursuers, gun in hand.

By morning I had slept and woke, cold and stiff, to a cataract of birdsong. I was haggard and weary and my chest whistled as I breathed. Misty streamers of sunlight invaded the leafy glade in which I'd lain. Despite my discomfort I felt a wellspring of emotion in my chest and gladness for being alive. I had out-waited the sniper, although if not for the intervention of the deer family it could have turned out differently. Whichever way you looked at it, he'd blinked first.

I stepped to the side of the clearing. The trees that last night had been ranged about in stealthy communion were now just the lovely trees I knew from my boyhood. For some reason my eyes were wet. I sucked in a lungful of air and expelled it in great sob of relief. I slapped my arms vigorously to encourage circulation. The birdsong was deafening, though I could identify many species of my Lithuanian birds among their voices. 'Children!' I thought, involuntarily whispering the word. They are the innocent children of the forest, singing and laughing in the misty sunshine, rejoicing in the clean air. Oblivious of this tortured soul who'd emerged from the woods. I stood and listened. I told myself that I had been lucky so far. But I wondered what had happened to all the other innocents; the human children of Lithuania.

A sudden rattle of noise! Woodpeckers or machine pistols in the distance. No time to linger. I pressed on into the day. South by east by compass.

~-~

That afternoon I found the Grunewald Denkmal, shell-torn and leaning. I gathered dry moss and twigs, and stripped some birch bark from a fallen tree. With this oily kindling, I struck a spark from the flint and striker which I'd carried since childhood. Then in the hollow overhang, protected by fir boughs, I built a fire where the *rough as badgers* beaters had built theirs many years before, and was nourished by pine needle tea, boiled in my water bottle cup. Soon I slept sound where nearby I'd dropped Old Kaiser; where I'd been rewarded by the blossoming love of Katarzyna, sweet Kat, and felt guilt for betrayal of my first love, Krysia.

But by early evening I had rested. I'd been chewing roots and bark to lessen my hunger. My stomach was twisted with pain and I was forced to make further holes in my belt to tighten it. I wished I'd had the time to set snares on the obvious game trails, but it was time to move.

That night I feared an hallucination. I recall the image of a ghostly creature, an agile though ill-proportioned changeling that moved like a tightrope walker, arms grotesquely extended that had fled chittering through the underbrush in the twilight woods - when I'd passed the poor blackened figure twisting in the wind on the crossroads gibbet, recognizable by the irregular lengths of its lower limbs – since when, with mounting horror, I'd viewed the burned-out ruin of *Ausautas* and encountered the *Ziburinis:* a wild-eyed madman in the woods who'd twittered and gibbered at me so that I was unnerved and drew my pistol. He had fled, cackling and shrieking into the dark like a spectre, flapping a near fingerless hand, his cries echoed by a distant screech. A starving ape and a crazed old man with cobwebbed hair, a ghost gibbon and a deranged leper, far from his island. They'd seemed well cast to haunt those woods.

Nor was it over. Hours before the iron embrace of the savage trap I had unknowingly drunk from the lake to whose shore Hannah had walked one quiet night, her heavy coat laden with stones, and drowned herself. The terrible knowledge of how each of my parents had died, believing that their only surviving son was by then dead too and the news of the short existence of my two deceased and hitherto unsuspected siblings was monstrous. And now the Graf was promising something *momentous*. What more *momentous* than all this could there be?

~-~

The Graf has a pensive look. He turns and lifts something from the shelf behind him.

'I had the tusks mounted for you.' He says. They are proportional to the size of the animal, crossed like sabres and set on a polished wooden stand. He hands the trophy across the desk for me to see. There is a silver plaque with some engraved lettering.

'In Honour of a Great Marksman. Rolf Dragunavicius. 1912.'

I think, *where were you heading, Rolf, in 1912? What were you, sixteen or so?*

~-~

Kristian's Story

Kuznetsowa Estate,
Autumn 1919

He was painting a picture for me, the Graf as a younger man, tanned, tall and ambitious, who'd roamed the bush with his Askaris tracking lion, buffalo, leopard, every variety of plains game. And of course elephant, for rich clients: 'White Hunter'- licensed, for the ivory trade.

'I was due to leave for home in ten days and this safari was to have been the last contract after many years in Africa.'

But, he said, there was to be one more, for the biggest prize of all.

He'd sold up the sisal plantation in 1894, that he'd bought with the Royal Gift for keeping Germany's Africa possessions safe for a grateful Kaiser, the reward he and fellow officers had received after twelve long years' service, which some used to purchase suitable acreage for a cash crop and a peaceful retirement. Drinks with far flung neighbours or gambling in Dar to relieve the tedium of living on the property, if that's what they chose to do.

'I could have sat on the veranda, Rolf, while the crop ripened. Sipping a drink while the sun went down like the other colonials, listening to the local pride roaring into the night. And I'd have gone out of my mind.' The occasional safaris were just sideshows.

He lit a pipe and was off somewhere else, his eyes fixed on a picture of Sophie. I'd held to a romantic notion of him stepping out of the bush with his Askaris, leopard on a pole and meeting by chance his beloved Princess Sophie like some displaced *niad*. The story of his 'last safari' as

402

sketched loosely for me by Marik.

I let the silence hang until he wanted to return. After a few moments he rummaged in his woollen house jacket. 'Rinderpest had wiped out all the local game in '92, and the native peoples were starving. Even those with filed and pointy teeth in the hinterland.... Malaria, yaws, pneumonia, bilharzia, sleeping-sickness - all were rife. It was hot, hellish and the lowlands were mosquito-ridden. I knew that hunting was over for a year or so, but anyway I had decided there was bigger game to hunt, or at least a bigger dream to follow.' He opened his palm dropping a thimble-sized nugget onto the blotter. 'Up country. The Lupa valley. If it wasn't another Klondyke, there *was* gold worth washing out of the ground. After the thunderstorms of the rainy season newly exposed gravels were just waiting to yield their 'tail of gold in the pan'. Or so I told myself.'

He was convinced that it was just there waiting for him and he was the first European who knew about it thanks to his obsession for ranging widely in his copious free time with rifle, water bottle and a few necessities, like quinine: living off the land. 'Happily, Rolf, I seemed to have a natural immunity to malaria. So did my brother, but in his case it proved unfortunate.' This last comment of his quite baffled me.

He'd soon staked his claim, he told me, sold the plantation at the right time and formed a mining company registered in Dar-es-Salaam.

~-~

The Graf is telling me something of loneliness. That he wakes with a sense of unease that has been his constant bedfellow these last months. He lies a while, listening to the silence of the house as his eyes accustom to the familiar shapes of the room; the tall curtains, the canopy, drapes and pillars of the big four-poster. The furniture and paintings, soft and shadowy in the pre-dawn, a time for reflection before the house begins to stir. His left arm is stretched out. For years he'd woken from dreams in which the woman he'd loved more than any words of his could express still occupied that side of the bed. His later infatuation with Elenja had given him a lovely child in Graczyna; but Elenja, who had loved him more than he felt he'd deserved, and who had lost her life in giving birth, had withheld a dark secret from him.

I now know what that the dark secret was.

Still the caressing hand was for the ghost of Sophie, not Elenja. The recent dreams were more unsettling, and not without cause. His outstretched fingers seek beneath the pillow the re-assuring touch of his revolver; its needful presence become the grim surrogate for tides and times in the affairs of men.

The mention of his late wife, Elenja, reminds me that I have yet to see Katya despite her being 'around the house somewhere', as I am assured. Katya, who had been the special big sister and surrogate mother to Graczy returns to me in memory, and in one particular incident that comes fleetingly as the Graf is speaking.

I am perhaps eleven years old and have been playing a hard combative game with Marik who overpowers me. Wearily I am sitting in a part of the herb and flower garden that is fenced off, in the shade of a clump of hyacinth-blue flowers that gives off a heady perfume. I am drowsy and can see little Katya and her half-sister, baby Graczyna, sitting some distance away under some trees at the edge of the orchard. Katya is grooming Gogol with a fine toothcomb and the cat loves every stroke, rolling on his back in enjoyment from the attention. There is something in the trees that I cannot make out, a shape in the shadows that seems to have a more rounded bulk than just the darkness amongst the foliage. I am finding it difficult to concentrate but I am sure I see an arm stretching out towards Katya's curved back. My head is swimming and suddenly I feel very sick.

Perhaps it is Marik playing some joke. But then I hear Marik's voice, and the responding voice of the Governess, the sounds carrying from the open French windows at the rear of the house. I try to react, attempting to stand, to move towards the threat. I shout but only a croak emerges from my throat. I think I am going to throw up and my head is swirling as I stumble forward, my vision blurring. I am dizzy and about to collapse but I see the arm withdraw into shadow. Katya looks up in alarm in my direction and Gogol streaks for the house. I think I glimpse a face in the tree shadow, and have the distinct impression of a pair of fierce eyes upon me. The shadow moves back into the deeper darkness as I hit the ground, losing all consciousness.

I awake to the alarmed expressions of the Governess, Nina, Katya and Marik. I try to remember what it was that was bothering me before I passed out, to explain but I'm not making any sense for them, and Miss Hammond is convinced I have been hallucinating. The Graf appears and she rounds on him, almost like a wife, vehemently demanding in a low but forceful voice and in a manner that will not be reasoned with, that 'those horrible, dangerous *alien* plants be destroyed at once.' I vaguely remember the upset years before when a pet kid of Krysia's had got into the fenced off area where I'd been sitting and had eaten some of the flowers. It had become sick and very soon afterwards it died. The wooden fence had been heavily re-enforced.

Almost immediately the Graf gave orders to Berg that the flowers were to be destroyed, despite their medicinal value as a powerful anti-arthritic agent, but I know that they had seeded themselves elsewhere, or were deliberately re-seeded, far away from the house and herb garden.

There's a cry of distress from Katya. Someone has cut a lock of hair from the fine blonde head of quietly sleeping Graczyna. The servants with their rural superstitions are wide-eyed and whisper the word *Baubas*. The name of an evil red-eyed creature: the bogey man. The evil spirit that tears hair from human skulls.

~-~

Kristian proceeds with his tale. He tells me that he rises and dons a robe into the pocket of which he thrusts his pistol. He pads barefoot across the floor towards the rear of the house to a narrow Gothic casement whose window overlooks an inner courtyard with its bolted archway door. Beyond the encircling wall are the less formal gardens and greenhouses, the crouching beehives; a small collection of outbuildings and wooden sheds couched nearby. Trees cluster close about once well-trimmed hedges but with cleared spaces to reduce cover to any who would approach the house unobserved. Further off there is the lake, bordered by birch and willow, visible in the morning mist. Sometimes the lake mist glows strangely. Not like the marsh lights of the peat bogs, more diffuse and sometimes the house itself seems almost to vibrate as if a life force trembled within. Across the courtyard to his left the view takes in the stables and the clay tile roof of the coach house, now a motor garage. Doves shuffle on the tiles as he unhooks the window catch, cracking open the narrow casement, disturbing a white owl that glides past like a silent messenger from the Moon.

He recalls the eerie phenomenon that Berg had reported; the other owls. Nina has told me this too. In 1916 they had come, a huge and silent flock of eagle owls in the twilight of a windless day in late October while he, Kristian, had been in Petersburg. Birds like this are solitary and do not ever roost together. The barn owls had fled and these heavy, yellow-eyed speckled owls with their prominent 'ears' had colonized the linden trees;

more than two hundred of them was the estimate. They'd stayed all day and the next night, but were gone as silently as they came by the following morning. Berg had fired a shot to frighten them off during the day, but they'd barely taken any notice. It was considered unlucky to shoot one, even though Berg was tempted. Nina had begged him not to and even Lebedovich had warned against such an action.

Liutas and Tigras had barked furiously and then sat staring and growling at them for an hour before giving up in exasperation. A couple in the lower branches had puffed themselves up, arching their wings, hissing loudly at the dogs like lynxes.

Nina, demonstrating the thin veneer of her Russian Orthodoxy told me she thought they were demons sent as harbingers by the old Lithuanian spirits - indeed several of the servants tended to revert to the old beliefs when under pressure. In Lithuanian mythology *Giltine* is goddess of death whose sacral bird, the owl, is harbinger of disaster. What unspeakable magnitude of disaster might two hundred owls predict?

Giltine has a sister goddess, *Laima*, goddess of darkness and light and of fertility. Her sacred tree is the Linden - the name of this house. For a superstitious staff these omens were terrifying.

Nina's description of the event brought to my mind an engraving by Goya, '*The Sleep of Reason Begets Monsters*', wherein the student philosopher slumbers at his desk: notebook open, pencil fallen from his fingers, while all about the space is invaded by demons in the form of huge-eyed eagle owls that fill his dreaming mind.

~-~

Roskov

Nina's mother had died shortly thereafter, and Kat had then had a terrifying experience one evening, returning from a Chopin piano recital by a young prodigy fresh from Petersburg, Nadia Reisenberg, who was staying on a neighbour's estate. Count Vassilichikov's, Nina tells me. On the road she was nearly abducted by some ragged men, only escaping when she shot the ringleader, 'a wild-eyed wiry figure of lower than average height', as she described him. Shot him point blank in the neck with her muff pistol, then drove back to the safety of Liepus Namas with her injured coachman bleeding by her side.

Hauptmann Kretschmer and his troops had mounted a search for

406

the perpetrators but apart from some bloodstains at the scene, nothing was found. They did not think to look in the little brook where lay the wounded malefactor in a fishing coracle, drifting slowly, troll-like in darkness, listening to the words of the search party, stemming the blood flow from his throat. For sake of symbolism he is the very incarnation of the red-throated Lithuanian spirit *Raudongevklis*, but his vengeful dreams are those of *Der Wassermann*.

Perhaps such owls as they'd seen *were* harbingers.

The Graf at the casement breathes the cool air. Beyond the stables are meadows of wild flowers. Sleek cattle had not grazed there these few years past. He looks to the horizon, across the flowing grassland to the haze of hills and trees. Early in 1918 in a crowded second-floor flat on Pilies Gatve in Vilnius *Old Town*, Kristian had met, among others, Jonas Basanavicius, leader of the National Movement and prime mover behind the Lithuanian Declaration of Independence. For some years he had harboured the same dream of nationhood and even though such a constitution had required provisional German sanction at that time, had been so persuaded by his inspired oratory, patriotism and commitment to Lithuanian self-determinism, he committed to join their ranks. But after a brief respite from years of unremitting war, by late 1918 the Baltic States and its neighbours are under siege on all sides and the Graf has mustered his own militia, attached to the Baltische Landeswehr.

Yet he thinks in pictures of what is represented by that independence, in a morning's reverie, of the beauty that running horses symbolize in this land of horses; and water in this land of lakes: he pictures freedom from war and want, from suffering and oppression. His fingers fall to a favourite bronze, an equine statuette; an image full of vigour. His lips move in silent praise of a beautiful vision in which he moves, with the image of grace beside him, his mystic Sophie, his eternal soulmate; *Lithuania, how precious this land. How free you will be. How like a bride I will dress this house in flags of red, green and gold for your new independence.* For his dead wife who loved it, though it was for her a poison cup, and for his son who, pray God, would finally return from service in the murdered Tsar's army.

Marik's wound was healing when last he'd written, but things were dangerous with more revolution in the air – that was just prior to November 1917. The Graf had not received it until he'd returned home, weeks later. He'd written letter upon letter and tried to pull strings but Petersburg was in chaos and the bureaucracies that had not been dismissed had collapsed under the strain. Worse, there were public executions, the streets reportedly full of dead civilians – counter revolutionaries they said – haunted by a cadaverous, sinister figure: son of Belarus, his own erstwhile neighbour, one Felix Dzerzhinsky driving in triumph in a Rolls-Royce, arresting and putting the fear of God into innocent people.

Again the Graf fumed that had he known in which Vilnius basements he'd skulked, cranking out lies and incendiary propaganda in those early years he'd have emptied his revolver and saved thousands from arrest and execution in the torture chambers of the Lubjanka.

~.~

That Darkest Place in the Heart of Man

To know the soul of another is to enter a dark place. So the saying goes.

Could he see into the heart of one Nikolai Sergeyevich Roskov, Dzerzhinsky's once and future satrap, the drifting *water goblin,* Kristian von Strelitz would have stared into a well of venom. Roskov, creature of the night: an erotomane of jealous rage and blood-curdling savagery; a pit viper at one remove, this 'half-human cipher' coldly plotted violent retribution for the fire of stinging riposte.

Roskov, Elenja's stepbrother, Nikolai was *her* nemesis and would be Kristian's if he failed to act. Thirteen years since Christmas, Katya, who was then but nine, had ridden with her in the carriage, a few versts only from Liepus Namas. Elenja had recognised him riding furiously, wearing signature dark glasses in daylight, raising his whip in an angry gesture; an ironic salute, while the mares reared in their traces.

Later, though she'd not admit it, Elenja, in late pregnancy had been threatened and intimidated; was seen to tear up several letters, one of which young Katya had pieced together. It was *her* dark secret. Stepbrother, Nikolai Sergeyevich, was demanding money or there'd be trouble. Notes arrived frequently by hand, at the gatehouse, so Roskov himself had probably delivered them, making sure that he did so when the Graf was not at home which suggested that he was watching the house. That he was in the vicinity terrified Elenja and she eventually confided in Nina and Baroness Nadia both, that when she was thirteen her father began to fall ill. A long illness. He was thus unable to continue in his position as a town official, nor able to uphold his position as head of the household in their Minsk suburb, being mostly confined to bed. Her Georgian stepmother was engaged in simultaneous affairs and as neither maids nor nurses stayed long, much of the caring obligation had been left with Elenja.

So begins her tale.

Night.

The black river sleeping in frozen darkness; she sees herself, a younger Elenja Roskova picking her way through a snowy Minskoye Gubernii to a house whose dim-lit entrance cannot dispel her sense of foreboding. Three storeys and a round tower of stone and brick that is the Roskov residence on the east bank of the *Svislach* that in summer flows gently through the heart of Minsk. Streets aplenty navigate the capital in anonymity, as yet un-baptised by the civic authorities, but hers bears the name *East Moskovaskaye*. In summertime its tree-lined walk would have a pleasant outlook.

She pulls her none-too-warm winter coat about her shoulders. The horse tram had deposited her four streets distant, off the *Prospekt Masherova* and this evening's praise from her singing teacher, Bukovskiya, for her rendering of Schubert's *'Du Bist…'* has already dimmed.

She pictures her father, isolated in the tower room, neglected by her step mother. His view of burgeoning Belarus, could he struggle from his sickbed, are gloomy outbuildings and an overgrown garden where mad Nikolai prances by moonlight; a shaman in his squirrel cloak. Woods lie to the east and nearby is a small Orthodox graveyard with a Jewish cemetery beyond. Hardly a prospect to cheer the dying for soon enough that is undeniably to be his fate.

From the house there hurries a bundled figure, head down. Elenja calls out and the girl stops, looks at her. Elenja sees tear-stained cheeks and the anger still hot in her eyes.

'*Svetja!* What's happened?' Elenja's restraining mitten on her arm.

The girl stares, shakes free and is away without a word. A pattering of snow drops from the trees.

Elenja sighs. *Rozalina.* What slight or cruelty had been a step or a slap too far? Or had Nikolai Sergeyevich offered up something unspeakable? At the rear are the grim outbuildings where are secreted her step-brother's ugly motivations; his journey to enlightenment' that he sneeringly imparts, of the occult path he's chosen, the darker side that lesser men would shun, quoting Jung: *that mankind cannot understand the world through intellect alone.* But Nikolai is twisted, given to sly torment of the servants. He is physically powerful for such a runt and Elenja detests the sight of him, abhors his sadistic descriptions of experiments on small mammals and resents his malign obsession to convey such gruesome detail which she perceives as psychological abuse. Yet he will drone on; an automaton, relishing to share though most often supercilious and aloof, which is how Elenja prefers it.

Each evening she returns to the venomous bosom or at best the indifference of Rozalina, the red-rimmed snake eyes of Nikolai upon her: the possibility of bereavement and the certainty of turmoil in that rattling house that once felt like home; the songs of her mother a faded memory as she moistens her father's brow or reads to him. Or rocks, lonely in her room, writing letters to the dead in her head.

Nikolai meanwhile, a few years her senior, intelligent: suffering from both photophobia and a severe undefined personality disorder had persecuted her in the family home. He'd called her 'Princess' but crushed her finches and over time disposed of other pets in ingenious ways. He was aroused by newspaper reports on the Chicago murder castle of the notorious surgeon-serial killer, H.H. Holmes, supplier of skeletons for medical research: the greased chutes down which were slid unfortunates, chloroformed young women (he too preferred blondes), who suffered agonising deaths on the 'operating table' in his dungeon.

Nikolai enjoyed the acts of poisoning and skinning. He pursued her with small animal carcasses and entrails, secreted toads or an eyeball among her underwear with confused cryptic notes and tarot cards. Once she woke to her pet cat's face regarding her from the pillow and she reached out her hand. Elena was alarmed when she failed to encounter a warm, furry body. Horror-struck she'd pulled back the sheet. The torso was absent along with the back of the skull.

Her father being more seriously ill, was hospitalised for periods, and with her stepmother's frequent absence, Nikolai gathered about him unsuitable friends; youths and the occasional whore, *lorettes et flaneurs* as her dear mother would have described them in the genteel language of the bourgeoisie, who lounged about, drinking and helping themselves to everything and over whom Nikolai seemed to exercise a mesmeric power. Among the older members of the gang were an ascetic *raskolnik* flagellant, a fugitive from the gendarmerie; a skilled artist drug addict with a face 'like a leering Christ' and an older, half-Mongol gravedigger-mute who supplied Nikolai with choice artefacts for his increasingly grisly tableaux: fetish, chimerical constructions which he believed conferred upon him occult power and had as much in common with voodoo as the

410

pagan talismans of Northern shamans. These, she discovered, he'd nail upon the doors, during nocturnal robbing forays, of those he viewed with malice in the community, but he bore a charmed existence as he was never held for long by the local gendarmerie, over which his mother held some sway.

Nikolai was expert at psychological warfare and control. He saw himself as an artist of the macabre: a sculptor/surgeon of human tragedy, fascinated by the process of death and the corruption of the body. He railed against religious dogma and kept a large inverted crucifix on his black-papered bedroom wall, but was directionless and irrational in most matters. Elenja's teacher had noticed her distraction during lessons and had drawn just part of the story from her. Horrified, she'd threatened to go to the police on her pupil's behalf, but Elena had begged against it because she knew that Nikolai Sergeyevich would out-manoeuvre them, protected by his harpy mother. She felt she would be in even greater danger thereafter.

Latterly, entering her room at night while her sick father lay again upstairs at the far end of the house, he'd horrified her with what she considered must be false tales of his nocturnal visits to the morgue, boasting of the obscene acts of congress he and his friends enjoyed with the recent cadavers. She'd been forced to barricade her door against intrusion as he pushed and scraped at it, protesting his love, howling: an animal in the dark. She became a wreck and could scarce keep food down from mental torture and his repellent touch.

Her outlet was singing, at which she excelled, showing great sensitivity and emotional depth in her rendering of songs by the young Rachmanninov; love songs transcribed from Turgenyev and the classical German repertoire. But his later sexual advances were the worst culminating in a fumbled rape. She'd taken to sleeping with a kitchen knife in her hand and trembling with fear and rage told him, *Nikolai Sergeyevich, you may steal my virtue and you may ruin me. You may even kill me. But you will never own me. You will never break my resolve to escape you. All I will ever give in return for your assault on my honour is my contempt. I despise you as God is my witness, I curse you into the bowels of hell. I hope He condemns your corpse to rot on the windsails of eternity.'*

Perversely this vivid word picture seemed to please and arouse him. He enjoyed her frantic struggles and even when she'd managed to stab him, far from fatally, he'd seemed nourished by the pain. Nevertheless, since that vehement rejection and stabbing he'd been incapable of achieving a full erection, so Elena was spared the final indignity, though he'd hold her blindfold, suckling and biting at her half-naked body in a frenzy of frustrated desire, begging one moment and dribbling formaldehyde or some fluid into her ears; whispering she'd forever be his zombie slave and jabbering his demented incantations. He'd claimed he was a reincarnated werewolf and none of this was his fault.

One night his collaborators had raided a Jewish graveyard, arriving at the house drunk, carrying a head wrapped in a cloth and accompanied by two drug-addicted prostitutes.

This head they installed in the drawing room, cushions and a cloak representing its body, votive candles to each side held by their acolyte whores. Elenja had been forced to drink some concoction which rendered her incapable of resistance. She was stripped and painted with ritual signs and as far as she had been able to recall, was forced to embrace this '*strigoi mort*' in some parody of a religious ceremony: part wedding, part sacrifice to a hellish apparition straight from a book on vampirism after which the gang groped her aggressively and though she didn't remember being raped, did recall her projectile vomit.

Not unnaturally she'd suffered hysterics as she came round. Nikolai and the others had laughed. He'd taunted her that his life's work had just begun. That a great artist is outlived by his art, informed she would be 'branded' with his special motto, once her pitiful father had given up his futile struggle for breath.

All this was reported to Kristian after Elenja's death by Kat, supported by Nadia and Nina's testimony, which both enraged and deeply saddened Kristian: that his wife had not felt able or feared to disclose her ordeals of childhood and early womanhood to her husband, but had invented a fairytale instead. Unable to express his feelings of anger and grief, his later reactive depression was so bad Claudia was worried for his long term health and sanity.

Elenja's father died a lingering and painful death, *poisoned* by then she believed; administered somehow by Roskov. Orpiment: trisulphide of arsenic, acquired by one of his contacts – the Christ-like artist - so she'd gleaned from one of their loose associates.

Although his passing had provided her with a small, far off estate, willed to her despite the fact of her father's marriage, she was terrified that a similar fate would befall her in due course, so wasted no opportunity to escape from Roskov after the funeral, standing apart from her stepmother at the graveside, a stubborn woman who would see no evil in her son. Nikolai, suddenly pale and retiring, seemed shocked that she'd evidently planned to leave. He was suddenly ineffectual, at the last, pledging undying love; that he'd never harm her, but she was armed, organised, packed and ready, fleeing that day with her jewellery, with her father's weak signature on a bankers draft and her papers in order; gone before he could touch her again. Her beautiful soprano voice would become her salvation, away from Belarus. Perhaps her future would be abroad. Perhaps the world.

~-~

Kristian is convinced that Graczyna's premature arrival and Elena's death shortly afterwards was the result of her fright on the road. For the Graf, however illogical, Katya's escape years later from the clutches of the ruffian and his band when she was returning from the piano recital had had all the hallmarks of a Roskov attack. The Graf had been obsessively convinced of it when he'd been told, though there were surely enough villains and murderers on the loose.

He'd heard of the man, ringleader of a gang who'd been sentenced to death years before. A heinous kidnapping had been committed in Moscow where they'd amputated a young violinist's fingers, then left him bound in a locked room to die of thirst after three days following confusion over the handover of ransom. Sentence had been commuted in the interest of psychiatry, to further the aims of Russian psychiatrists led by Professor Orlinsky, whom Kristian knew slightly as a distant colleague of his friend, Augusts. Roskov, he knew, had become a patient at a then recently established department of forensic medicine, where he'd consented to be the subject of research into his toxic paraphilia, his lycanthropic fantasies and the psychology of the criminal mind in general: undergoing various radical therapies including volunteering for electric shock treatment, which at low level produced his first proper erections, the staff noted.

But, as it was told, the patient had been awaiting his chance and had planned his escape for six months, pausing only to say goodbye to Professor Orlinsky, according to terrified witnesses, as later reported to Augusts.

'But, Nikolai Sergeyevich!' Orlinsky had protested, ears and gonads wired to a magneto. 'We were making *such* progress!'

~-~

Gravitating to his old Moscow haunts, Roskov had discovered that his mother had been murdered by one of her boyfriends. So gathering a small band of robbers under his command he decided to try his luck in the south, carry out freelance depredations: expropriations for the 'cause' in Belarus, and pay another visit to his stepsister, Elenja, who'd done so well for herself. He'd left his calling card several years previously when he'd crept into the grounds of the house where he'd tracked her down, but had seen no sign of her then. Just her infant child, so casual enquiries had elicited: his sleeping niece in her perambulator in the shade of the lilacs, from whom he'd cropped a flaxen lock. A harmless family souvenir to be going on with. And a warning.

But it was on this later visit he had made a mistake. He found that contrary to his information the Germans had not yet retreated from the pre-Brest-Litovsk front line, indeed in many areas they had advanced. His crew of cut-throats had fallen or scattered under fire, with Roskov beating a hasty night time retreat on foot, up the Petersburg highway with just one confederate. Trying for an opportune 'soft' target he'd flagged down a landau, while his accomplice 'collapsed' in the road, feigning injury – a sometimes successful trick. The accomplice had fired at the coachman who was incapacitated, as Nikolai Sergeyevich lunged at the female passenger but was then shot in the throat for his trouble. The girl took the reins and they escaped despite a volley of shots. Roskov blundered into the night, dazed, throat numbed, drifting downstream in a fishing coracle, swearing revenge through bloody teeth while German troops beat the bushes about.

Later, following Lenin's enthronement, criminals of every stamp were released and the cells made ready for cramming full of the bourgeoisie. Arbitrary execution of anyone without evidence of manual labour on the palms of their hands, as well as professionals of any sort, were marked for special treatment.

Roskov made a painful recovery but without normal speech. He vowed to hunt down those who'd wronged him. Doctors were particular prey for Comrade Roskov, in his role as a self-styled commissar-executioner, especially any that had served in a Moscow clinic. *From his theatre of perversion: something of which he'd been particularly proud…he and his crew had nailed a family hand and foot at their dining table, wished them* bon appetite *with an appetising meal set before them, tantalisingly beyond reach of their mouths, shutting the door on the children' sobs and their parent's pleas for mercy.* His personal motto, *Ars Longa, Vita Brevis,* was bloodily initialled into their naked backs.

414

As for fateful coincidence, the girl who'd maimed him, whose identity he'd established, and those dear to her included *his* niece; Katarzyna and Graczyna were the very daughters of the ruling class personified, of Von Strelitz, widower. Husband of the late Elenja, the half-sister plaything, betrayer, who, in his deluded mind had loved him in his youth. This Graf, most hated member of the most despised class, had stolen her. And dishonour must be assiduously avenged.

Roskov, the fanatical Bolshevist adherent, enthralled by the ideology that legitimised his passions, saw Graczyna as his surrogate property. Yet, *by her own involuntary existence*, a betrayer of the proletarian roots *he* now falsely claimed. An ironic Nietzschean demon incarnate, cunning, unversed in scholarship living beyond moral and social constraint: de Sade's own bloodhound, he trailed by instinct *his* Graczyna, the daughter he would have had by *his* Elenja, now beyond his reach but not beyond the limits of his imagination where he tormented her still.

Striding alone, with limitless capacity for hatred, clinging to the dark and the Russian winter, figuratively, petal, by petal he tore apart the white rose he would have held to his lips: Elena. Vowing now a greater hurt than dear Kat could imagine. This hybrid daughter/niece would serve; be possessed, worshipped or punished as *he* saw fit: *purged* for her mother's betrayal of class in the Revolutionary Age he so zealously espoused: he would revenge her mother's wilful spurning of his heart - a peculiarly Georgian take on the Madonna/Whore Syndrome, Bolshevist style. Like the *Wassermann* in the fairy tale, he *would* hurl the headless corpse of his perceived human child at the feet of her mother surrogate. Figuratively or otherwise.

The deviant Nikolai Sergeyevich possessed in full measure the schizophrenic thinking so useful in an apparatchik commissar, Cheka agent, torturer and executioner.

~-~

Oblivious of this, Kristian lights a candle and pads painfully down the corridor, his leg wound sending sharp tugs of agony through his buttocks, burning still, like hot lead in his inner thigh. He pauses for a moment to listen for the breathing of his precious daughters in their adjacent rooms, but the heavy doors defeat him. He'd dearly wished he could go to Petersburg, correction *Petrograd*, and demand that someone take responsibility for the fate of loyal soldiers now incarcerated, many of whom, he'd read in reports, could not afford to eat, the Reds having abrogated all interest in their welfare and what food was available was anyway unfit for consumption. Typhus was rife and Spanish 'Flu was spreading like wildfire. Hundreds of thousands were infected and dying. But the level of local insurrection was also dangerously high and he had to remain for his girls. It wasn't safe to send them south and the Gulf was mined apart from a narrow channel. Only with the greatest of difficulty and using all his persuasiveness, tact and organizational skills had he eventually managed to get Claudia out together with the ailing Baroness Nadia. This was achieved with the help of the eccentric Colonel Howard Alexander, a young Englishman who had been appointed to lead the Baltische Landeswehr as a security measure for seven months following the split with von der Goltz's Freikorps.

He tells me that he'd thought about me too. He stirs uncomfortably in his chair and I imagine that his wound is bothering him. His looks sick, his eyes taking on the mottled appearance of some aged sea creature.

'Rolf, tell me true, you had nothing to do with the death of that young man, Welikowsky's youngest boy, did you?' His eyes plead that I had not.

I feel the heat of blood at my cheeks again but my reply is cooler.

'Sir. I explained this before. It was only my idea to teach him a lesson after what he'd done to me. After what he'd accused me of. I could have died under that lash. He was a bully and a coward but I didn't wish him dead and I didn't kill him. I've met others since who were worse.' I choose not to elaborate.

The Graf seemed satisfied at this. I was hurt that he'd had to ask me again about the murder, but I could see it from his viewpoint. It had come out that I'd been assaulted and mercilessly whipped – ostensibly for having poached a prize stag from the neighbouring estate although I knew that the reason was jealousy; my easy-going acquaintance with the Countesses, the daughters of von Strelitz, which branded me an *upstart parvenu*.

But in good time Fate had turned upon the culmination of my months of plotting. Count Mikhail Welikowsky had been at the gambling tables. He was making his way home worse for wear after his friends had peeled off to their respective houses. His horse had trotted on its familiar way in the dark, when a rope net had taughtened between two trees and he'd spilled out of the saddle and onto the road cursing and struggling to sit up, nursing a jarred elbow. Petras and Tomus, my confederate disciples and fishers of men dragged him to his feet and I gagged him with a rag and wrapped a blindfold around his eyes, while Vladi retrieved

416

the horse lest its return to the family seat cause premature suspicion.

Mikhail-Antonovich fought and struggled in vain: naked and roped to a tree, he roared and cursed us roundly when I removed the gag, then beseeched us by turn, promising no repercussions and offering the world if he were to remain unharmed. I let him rage on and in time he grew quiet, listening and apprehensive in his blindfold.

'If you've quite finished we will proceed,' I said.

'You!' he roared. 'I knew it. You will hang for this!'

I was at his side with my hands tightly around his throat. 'Shut your damn mouth, Mikhail,' I'd hissed in his ear. 'Believe me, this could be a *lot* worse for you, I swear. A whole lot!'

We let him hang, pale like a fish in the crepuscular light, while we openly discussed the ingenious possibilities for his brief, certainly miserable future. He was shivering uncontrollably by now, from the cold but equally from considering the probable outcome; the culmination of his short and hedonistic life.

I took the revolver from Vlad and spun the chamber for Welikowsky to hear.

'Let's play an old Russian game, my friend.' I placed the muzzle on his lower lip and cocked the weapon. I waited while Welikowsky breathed fast the sweat breaking on his cheeks despite the cold. The 'click' seemed deafening as the hammer fell on an empty chamber.

'There was a gasp from Welikowsky, chest heaving as he re-emerged, still in the land of the living.

'Your Excellency has one chance in six every time, those are the statistics if you believe in that sort of thing. Or are you more the reckless gambling man, Mikhail? Are the odds good for you or would you like me to shorten them?' My confederates laughed nastily.

Welikowsky shook his head mutely.

'Click!'

'Lucky again, Mikhail. Let's see, shall we place bets on the next one, comrades.'

'Ten roubles says he gets it next time,' said Vladi.

I set the chamber spinning again.

'This'll get you better odds, your Excellence,' I said, and cocked the gun.

'Click'

'You have the luck of the Devil, Mikhail.'

I spun the chamber again.

'This time I feel sure, don't you?'

The lads were silent, expectant. This time I squeezed his nose so that he opened his mouth for air and I shoved the barrel all the way into his mouth, scoring the soft pallet and making him gag. I knew somewhere in my heart with faint disgust that I could be a torturer.

'Click!'

Welikowsky's stomach heaved and I drew back as he threw up, causing merriment and jeering among the lads. They were bright-eyed now in the darkness, waiting for the conclusion, but we were all aware that we risked death ourselves if we continued with this charade too long.

'He's pissed himself, too! said Petras. 'And the other!' Vladimir and Tomus were chuckling, dragging furiously on Welikoswky's excellent cigarettes.

I stood in front of the Count and took aim as if at a target. He heard me cock the pistol again and made a soft whimpering sound as if he knew this time, irrevocably, this was going to be it. The hammer fell again and again on an empty chamber and the prisoner jerked in time with the sounds, until he realised that no gunshot would issue, no bullet tear into his flesh as his lash had torn into mine.

The tension fell away from me completely. If they expected me to shoot him this was not my way. And anyway not with an unloaded gun. It was enough that Mikhail-Antonovich had been thoroughly humiliated.

'I will let you live,' I said to him. 'You have learned your lesson, I think.'

My revolutionaries crowded about me.

'Are you mad, Rolf?' Tomus whispered in agitation. 'He can identify us all'

'His blindfold protects you. He knows *me* only, by sight and by my voice,' I replied quietly. 'And tomorrow I will be far away, courtesy of my Graf. Gone. Do as I have asked you, conceal him for two days until I am out of the country and then release him unharmed somewhere, in naked humiliation on his estate. You should be able to hide him for that long without fear. He is known often for staying with some whore in town and won't be missed for a while.'

And with that I'd departed.

~-~

Ah, but we know that bad news travels fast. Krysia had already been dispatched to Paris so it was a white and fearful Kat that had ridden to my home, pulling her bay up in a slither of hooves in the courtyard.

418

My father was out attending to a patient and my mother had made a rare solo trip into town to buy some small items for my journey. The Countess found me packing my kit with young Daine in attendance. I dismissed her with my thanks. Kat was twisting with agitation and could barely wait until we were alone to speak.

'Rolf, what in God's name have you done?'

'Done?' I enquired coolly, guessing with a sinking heart that it had to do with my manoeuvres of two nights before.

'Tell me what happened.'

'Kat, calm down. Just tell me what you've heard.'

~-~

The Graf had been visited by his *Falstaffian* Belarus neighbour: the great boyar, in towering anger, full of vodka and vengeance, fur-hatted Count Welikowsky the elder, wrapped in a bearskin cloak, wrathful and grieving, had arrived in a convoy of open cars with a retinue of stocky men, his private security force of hard-eyed *mauserists*. They stood about on the steps, questioned the staff without a 'by your leave' and poked around the grounds while Welikowsky lurched into the hall, a staggering gait replacing his habitual heavy swagger, throwing accusations, echoing right and left about the stairs. What did the Graf know? Did he have any information of insurgents or malcontents? His two older sons were already picking up likely suspects and subjecting them to severe interrogation. The gendarmes were scouring the countryside. Did Kristian, in light of their long friendship as neighbouring landowners, standing square against Bolshevism and insurrection, have any information at all that might lead to an 'arrest'? Finally throwing his heavy beseeching arms around Kristian's shoulders in drunken embrace, he veered from the vengeful to the maudlin and then wept, as Russians do.

Welikowsky's reputation for his free use of the killing knaut, even in recent times, years after that scourge had been outlawed; his cruel indifference to his erstwhile serfs and the casual suffering he'd inflicted on the peasants was well known in the region. Kristian had had an unresolved dispute with him over the diversion of a small river which had caused hardship to some of Kristian's peasant farmers and millers along their common border whose waterwheels no longer turned and he thus did not recognize their acquaintanceship as that of friendship. Indeed, Kasparis, the Graf's solicitor, had mediated most of their business.

The upshot was that his youngest son, Mikhail, had been murdered.

He'd been found, throat cut, the body dumped in a stream outside Valksarnis two versts from the Welikowsky mansion.

~-~

'Tell me it wasn't you, Rolf,' begged Kat. 'Please!'

'Kat, darling, I didn't kill anyone. He was alive and unharmed when I left him, I swear.'

If I was shocked and worried about the consequences of this news, Katya was frantic.

'Kat, you must believe me. I didn't harm him, just frightened. He was OK when I left and I thought he was in safe hands. I gave orders that he was to have been released.'

'You promise Rolf? You didn't …..' she shuddered….. 'slit his throat?'

'Never, Kat. Come here. You're cold as ice.'

I put my arms around her. She was trembling. Suddenly my head was full of her perfume and it felt so good to be holding her. I was missing her big sister and by God she knew it. I was falling into those big green eyes and before I realised it I'd pulled her to me and we were kissing passionately. We moved as one into my bedroom, mouths locked and tongues entwined, breathing hard, her coat falling from her soft shoulders, my fingers exploring her fervently and then she was tugging at my hair pulling me down to kiss her neck, my lips on her naked shoulder and then the soft succulence of her small puffball breasts. I pulled off her riding boots and skirt and she lifted her slender arms for me to remove her blouse and chemise. No confining girdle restrained her beauty. My clothes were dropped in a bundle and we fell into each other's embrace, each glorying in the sensation of firm youthful flesh on the other's skin. I was mightily aroused and she bit my neck and stomach, writhed and climbed all over me as I twisted and forced my tongue into her softness, kissing as she moaned and cried out in ecstasy somewhere above me, arching her back in a half dozen violent spasms. I lifted my head and her grimace of pleasure urged me to enter her, gently at first, then with a mounting tempo of powerful thrusts that drew further moans of delight from her parted lips, her eyes shut in total bliss.

~-~

Her father had managed to shield Dr. Dragunavicius from the

onslaught by Welikowsky but the police had been tireless in seeking the murderer and had already made several arrests among my feral friends including one of the co-conspirators, Vladimir Zverov, who'd kept his lips sealed despite hard interrogation.

'It was '05 all over again,' said the Graf. Vlad was later brought to trial although the case eventually collapsed through lack of evidence. Rolf Dragunavicius, now officially suspect, was long gone by then thanks to the timely intervention of Graf Kristian in placing him with a regiment in Austria. But my disappearance had branded me with the mark of Cain. The name *Rolfus Dragunavicius,* tearaway and n'er-do-well had been whispered about as perpetrator. Murderer! Guilty as sin, *in absentia.*

But then had come the news, via circuitous means in time of war, eventually by telegraph from Vilnius, under German occupation, that *Rolf had been reported dead.* Augusts' and Hanna's late lamented boy. Marik's best friend outside the Tsar's army, those two who'd ridden, played and shot together since Rolf was about nine years old. One wounded and the other dead, though Kristian did not discover this until he'd returned from Petersburg. And whose fault was it? Thank God Krysia was safe in Paris – he'd tried to make her understand that in 1914 that the Sorbonne was a reasonable compromise for an intelligent girl. There *was* no Hanse merchant on the Baltic littoral, Rolf, only unsuitable suitors, and even if some could have provided a wealthy partnership in a marriage of equals, to expand the estate - Stolypin's reforms would no doubt have put paid to that.

Since then the young men of well-to-do families had been cut down like grass on both sides along with the conscript armies, and he believed it would take at least a generation to rebuild the economy and two to restore the population.

~-~

The Graf moves to the main staircase landing, hoists the candle to the red-haired beauty whose eyes meet his as they always do, and with such candour that no oil painting should convey at that hour, what with the shadows jumping. And that part of him that he thought had died with her, remorselessly gripping his heart. His throat constricts the same way as it did those years ago, such power there is in her timeless serenity; she seeming to stoop, to raise in him memories of her grace and kindness.

He tears his gaze from her and descends the staircase. Below the landing is affixed a mighty Teuton double-handed sword, a symbolic weapon truth to tell; for Tannenberg, for which it is engraved, and a symbol of defiance of the Golden Horde, that had finally run out of energy in its terrible conquest of all the Russias on the borders of Greater Lithuania, centuries before. Nevertheless it remained a powerful symbol of a country so long ruled by and defended by the sword. The Graf reflects that although the Mongols could not press further, the bacillus they carried with them continued its deadly work westwards and to the south, where their own plague-ravaged victims were catapulted over city walls, at Graz, to spur the Black Death on through Europe; to conquer where they could not in their depleted state; a last, vengeful blow of such alien callousness that it chilled the blood - even in this new terrible age when chemical weapons had emerged and germ warfare was again a threat.

A dim shape moves silently across the floor towards him, the grey ghost of an ice bear in an Arctic winter: *Tigras*, the great white-coated beardog, identical and inseparable twin to Liutas who'd died gulping, jaws bloody and frothing, eyes bulging a month since, struggling to breathe, choking on the stony stable floor with a distraught Graf and Berg trying to make him vomit the poison. The spiteful attack was just one symptom of the present troubles; mindless, vindictive, jealous and cruel.

The dog moves silently to Kristian's side and he reaches down to pat the noble head. The dog had looked for his twin for three weeks and then stopped. Meanwhile his doting gaze would fall mournfully, pleadingly upon his master, seeming to question fate while conveying empathy for a deep human loss.

Chapter 29. *Fragile Gifts*

We are back in the study.

The Graf it seems has staked all on that nugget from the alluvial plain below the Lupa Hills. It was to be the biggest he'd find in his African travails. He'd engaged engineers and invested in expensive equipment and good security. For nothing. In a year and a half of frustration and false leads, watching the temporary flooding through the rills and cuts, anticipating the gold appearing in the newly exposed gravels as thunderstorms broke down the terraces, but the serious pay streaks eluded him. His company, the Dar-registered *HANSA Ostafrikanische Handels und Auslandsexplorations AG* was wound up with debts due to the *Deutsch-Russische Bank* of Petersburg. The crew was paid off what he could afford and the machinery that was serviceable sold at rock bottom prices. His safaris now became his employment, and he thanked his stars that his natural immunity to malaria gave him access to areas forbidden to most whites. He lived off the bush and charged by the day the rich Americans, Germans and others who whored after a piece of feral Africa and the thrill of danger, under his protective field craft by day and within Askari-constructed *bomas* at night, safe in their tents under their mosquito nets, picking off their jigger fleas around the smoky campfires.

A romantic image had been conjured by his words, but his next statement is as pensive as it is resolute, that though restless young men crave adventure, seeking wealth, glory, fame and love, as we mature we perceive the follies of our youth and the hurt we've done to which we bear testimony in our hearts to a secret shame that injures the spirit. Man was unique in the guilt he bears. Happiness and joy are transient at best.

'St. Thomas Aquinas gave us seven proofs for the existence of God. We must admit the truth at the end: at a certain age all that is left us is to seek redemption.' His eye seemed again to implore understanding from me, Rolf. The doctor's boy.

'Rolf, you know, the things we truly love can seldom belong to us. We change them by our 'ownership' if we think of them in that way. Sometimes we are privileged to share moments of great happiness in the company of those we love. But they always leave us in the end, or are taken from us, and that can be hard. Some, like old Count Kuznetsow had grace enough to set free that which he most loved, and whom I most desired. But now I am twice widowed, which is perhaps my punishment. But thank God I have two lovely daughters who are the image of my beautiful Princess, and another delight in my Graczyna despite the tragedy of her birth. My boy, Marik, I hope and pray still lives.'

The Graf's eyes fill with tears which he wipes away angrily with the palm of his hand.

'But all these gifts are fragile and in these times most precious, more precious than my old bones. I would happily die for them if it meant their survival.'

I did not doubt his words.

'Promise me Rolf, that if it is in your power, you will help them, should I fail. My heart is no longer strong. Can you find a way, with God's help, to get them out, Katya and Graczy?'

~-~

The Graf continues to unburden to me.

I visualize him leaning at ease, all crumpled white duck and a soft hat, like Peter's, on an azure afternoon, when the bolt of desire strikes: consumes his heart entire within his chest.

She radiates luminosity, an angel, Rolf, in a wide-brimmed hat. He is dazzled. She fills his senses, floating through sunbeams in the raised dust of the bazaar, a beauty who speaks wordlessly to his mind of sadness. Her Somali servant with part-drawn sword and belted pistol keeps close and an Askari boy carrying behind a red-tailed grey parrot in winding entourage. Her travelling skirt sways gently as she walks tall and straight, eyes now upon him. Beyond, an elderly man in white dismounts, stiff-backed from the carriage in an eddy of child beggars. All slides into focus among the gold sellers, the silk merchants, the snake charmers, the dealers in spice, vice and slavery. He steps forward, bows and removes his hat: presents his card and offers his felicitous services to the Count whom he has heard is hiring, and to the Princess by whom he is already enslaved and now secretly worships with his eyes.

His words transport me from the fleshpots of Zanzibar to German East Africa, whence the party encamps upon the shores of a fly-swarming lake, the Graf von Strelitz, Count Kuznetsow and Princess Sophie Kuznetsowa under their nets. The old count is on his swansong zoological quest, his wife now the focus of the infatuated Kristian. He speaks of strong passions when the insects have subsided and the moon has sucked the heat out of the world and before dawn they decide they cannot live, one without the other. Night moves to that moment in the way of things, when the Count asks for an explanation and Christian feels

424

his life hangs upon the answer in this desolate place. Only the bearers about the fire and Joshua, a silent servant, whose devotion to Sophie is absolute, exist upon the darkened planet and his eyes of jet follow her every movement: have followed her to his tent.

The old count carries a loaded rifle and joins Kristian at dark water's edge where hippos grunt their nasal guffaw. It's dangerous to move about in the night when they come ashore to graze their verdant salient, says Kristian.

The old man reveals to Strelitz the wanderlust of his youth, the need for adventure and a thirst for a knowledge of the Earth's open spaces. He'd joined some early Russian expeditions in the 1860s: explorations on horseback, like a modern Marco Polo, one with Fedchenko to the Pamirs seeking the *Almasty*, a strange, hirsute man-like biped, that reportedly roamed the valleys. They never found it but there was tantalising evidence; footprints, and at night unidentifiable screams and whistles electrified their camp. Once, briefly, in the flaming torchlight, red eyes had surveyed them from the darkness, its gaze higher than that of a man's. He'd travelled as assistant cartographer, artist and then photographer, with a geodesist, topographer and a chronicler of natural history in a great expedition with Peter Semyenov, an aristo like Kuznetsow. Both had enjoyed a traditional military upbringing and been educated at the University of Petersburg. With full military back-up they'd reached the waters of lake Karakul and were the first Europeans to have seen this spectacle in modern times. They'd climbed to fifteen thousand feet and suffered altitude sickness, many of the men bleeding from the nose. Kuznetsow's final expedition was to the Celestial Mountains, but without the younger man's stamina he had been repatriated from the expedition in failing health. He had married but had divorced and, late in life, had re-married: Sophie, the youngest daughter of a family, of noble blood and straightened circumstance.

This African adventure was by way of treating a bored twenty-nine year-old wife, to a little of her husband's erstwhile passion for exotic travel: exploration in less arduous form, although the humidity and mosquitoes made it an ordeal near water.

The Count demonstrates the dexterity of his trigger finger and shares the secret of his recovery from arthritis: the boiled residue of the Issyk-Kul root. From Kirghizia, haunt of exotic snow leopard, and of tiger. There, east of the Caspian Sea, *Berkut*, the half-tame steppe eagle riding on his arm, the half-wild horseman hunts the plains. Named for the lake, Issyk-Kul is now cultivated and growing happily on his estate on the Lithuanian-Belarus border. It is fenced off from young animals to which it is poisonous. He told the Graf that the dried root in concentration was deadly and that in Turkestan, unfaithful or otherwise inconvenient husbands were dispatched by the expedient of soaking their shirts in an infusion of that root. Ironed and dried, a shirt would be given to the unfortunate victim after he had bathed and the pores of his skin were open to the venom. He would sicken and die in a month or two in a very natural manner. And nobody the wiser in those regions.

'The message seemed clear, Rolf. The tragic death of a minor European nobleman on safari along the shores of a remote lake in German East Africa, a hippo victim perhaps, the body then devoured by lions and hyenas. It could be easily explained even if the unfortunate was an experienced hunter.'

Whether a faithless princess might meet a similar fate had crossed Kristian's mind. His heart seemed to stop. The old count's trigger finger remained un-flexed. The rifle remained lowered. The tension ebbed away.

'In the end it was all very civilised, Rolf. We even had his blessing at the last and he bestowed the Kuznetsow Estate on his beloved wife in a settlement when they divorced. Released. Childless for him: although Marik was conceived that first night in what is now Tanganyika. Released in the way that some wild things must be released, even if truly loved. They must be set free, Rolf, or they just die.'

Perhaps what befell her was ordained. Her lingering guilt at the way she'd treated her first husband for whom she'd had affection might have found expression in the selfless, almost reckless way she'd organised and assisted in the nursing of those villagers who were suffering from cholera in Lithuania, and the concern she had shown towards the lepers who were among her inheritance on that estate. These acts guaranteed her 'sainthood' and later the erection of the white obelisk in the town to her memory.

~-~

Venus Betrayed

Though I'd not seen them until this day, the photographs in the album the Graf was proffering were familiar. Their subject a languid sophisticate, a study in nonchalance lounging on a ship's rail in well-cut boating jacket and panama had been very well drawn for me. Or else I'd

426

have guessed his identity. If not from the black tie and dinner jacket with a 'full-on' cigar and a 'poker face', or the lovely arms draped about his neck at blackjack or roulette table, then from the expression in the dark eyes above the Burma cheroot, eloquent of his weariness with the playgrounds of the World.

'My beloved elder brother,' said the Graf. 'The late Peter Rudolf Heinrich Graf von Strelitz, in his element, raising his game one last time.' Much as Marik had described him. When he'd done everything that there was to do and just got bored with life, famously stepping off the taffrail into those seas where Tambora blew, or Krakatoa, which had changed the World's weather for decades: sunset spectaculars for artists like Turner. A Prussian *roué* who'd gone swimming with the banded sea craites and flashlight fish, as the legend went, among the active volcanoes and the gem light reefs about the Island of Fear. And kept his last assignation with his final lover, *Ratukidul,* Mermaid Queen, goddess of the South Seas. Drowner of men.

So goes the family fable.

Peter von Strelitz's last cruise had been aboard the German iron screw-steamer, the ex-*Königin von Preussen,* the '*SS Ennui*' of his ironic letters – then operated by a Djakarta freight company; a two-hundred foot rusting tub with white-painted upperworks festooned with sun awnings, a crew complement of mostly Lascars and Filipinos.

Strelitz's diaries and tattered sketchbooks overflowed with freely executed drawings of deck hands and serangs, the shipping off Rangoon, all the rigs of the South Seas; exquisite water colours of dolphins and their blue marlin *sword brothers* that leaped joyfully between the text describing their wave-hurdling plunges into phosphorescence, pale green nebulae in the deep ultramarine. His rapid hand arched to capture them, seeming to stroke them with his brush as if he'd ached to join them at play in synchronized flying arcs of clean-cut energy, zig-zagging across a bow wave; hyacinth blue and indigo-black torpedoes with their creamy-white 'boot-topping' and smiling beaks lead cut-water and 'dolphin-striker' by centimetres – reference to his time under sail; before the mast aboard barque and clipper - the young adventurer eschewing his Hanseatic commerce roots and his commitment to the old Graf for a hard life at sea. A romantic role model; once a younger Rolf bethought his own life might mirror as a child, when the boy that I'd been had ridden to the call of the wild and climbed tall gantries among the chuckling gulls, pulled by the restless tide.

Too soon from the blessing of the dying Karl, the newly-anointed

Graf Peter, rake, romantic, gambler, *black sheep* and spendthrift with an entourage of amusing titled cash-poor leeches and a concubine or two, as Kristian himself put it, toured the hashhouses and gambling dens of Paris and Monte Carlo, Jamaica and the Indonesian Islands, drawn to his haunts of old and the call of the sea; now a smooth-handed dilettante artist/writer, emerging as a lonely figure, finances from the Kreuzhof Estate dwindling and his fair-weather companions drifting away.

An Island Casanova, he'd picked up the spirochete *Treponima Pallidum* who knew where? The symptoms and soreness had retreated and he'd had treatment following the Wasserman blood test in Paris. He'd gone through the secondary stage, glandular enlargement, headaches sore throat and the Ehrlich arsenical drug *Salvarsan* had proved the final cure for him, he believed, and was asymptomatic for some years, carrying on with his habitual lifestyle and had fathered a child.

But he wasn't clear. The *Venus Betrayer* was still at work.

The truth was that he'd travelled south one last time, below the equator, to try the old desperate remedy of catching malaria to burn out the syphilis before it reached the third and final stage. The supreme irony was, like his brother, Kristian, his immune system prevented him from catching the disease, even though he slept naked each night without mosquito nets and was bitten repeatedly.

The third and chronic stage can affect the skin, skeleton, heart, liver and nervous system, emerging in the latter case as the General Paralysis of the Insane in which the brain and the mind are affected as well as the spinal chord: an horrific end to contemplate.

'And you are telling me all this, because….?' I asked, leaving the question open. I was having trouble breathing such was the sense of dread I now felt.

'Because, Rolf. Because……,' the Graf was still hesitating. 'You must know, Rolf, in your heart. He was your father.'

~.~

So the pox-ridden Peter von Strelitz had gone over the stern rail of a steamer somewhere in the green Java Sea, complete with Burma cheroot and Panama according to Marik, all except the bit about the pox. 'Just got tired of living. Terminal *ennui*.' Marik had told me in so many words, when we were children.

And now the twice-widowed Graf, hero of his own tale, White Hunter, wife stealer, Peter's younger brother, chaser after *fools' gold* who had to make a name for himself, to be worthy of his father's love, which was showered *not* on him, but the prodigal Peter, was my *uncle*! What then had Dr. Augusts Dragunavicius to do with all this, a cuckold for my fretful mother? A sick woman who was invested with herbal remedies that never worked until it was too late: when the good and valiant doctor that I'd always called my father, whom I'd loved, was dead and never saw the success of his great effort. *Peter von Strelitz,* damn him, *and Hannah*? I was trying unsuccessfully to imagine them as lovers.

So Peter Graf von Strelitz, my wastrel of a father gone overboard to avoid the awful nemesis of the tertiary stage of syphilis. I wasn't sure at that moment how I felt. Disoriented, yes. Anger. Amazement, none of those words adequately described my state of mind.

'You're family, Rolf,' said the Graf softly.

So my best childhood friend, Marik was my cousin. My God! My *lover*, Krysia, was my cousin too, and Kat and Graczy. Cousins. My head was swimming. I had two dead siblings, also Peter von Strelitz's children by Hannah?

'So. Let me get this quite straight. You are my *uncle*. You had to kill any romantic relationship between myself and Krysia or Katya (there, I'd admitted it), not because it would have been a 'morganatic' association, but because of our *blood* relationship.'

'Of course! And not only that, you might have been a *carrier*. Congenitally syphilitic. As soon as we knew we did the Wasserman test. You were about five years old and without symptoms but for a whole variety of reasons there could be no relationship later on, between you and the girls. Obviously.'

'Obviously.' I repeated somewhat sardonically. I remembered being wakened by the clatter of hooves as the nightriders arrived at Ausautas when I was very young, the whispered conversations and the mention of Djakarta, of Java. Later I'd been examined carefully and blood was taken. I'd forgotten that 'til now.

And so, when my adolescent attachment to Krysia and she to me could not be ignored, I'd been sent far away and wound up on the 'wrong' side in the 'war to end all wars'. Perhaps the Strelitz immunity had protected me in Macedonia when many of my comrades had succumbed to malaria. Like everyone else, I had been roundly bitten by the mosquitoes that spread the fever from the 'Allied' Struma marshes to the Struga lake and had suffered very little effects.

'But that, of course, is only half the story, Rolf.'

~-~

As anyone knows, two is the minimum requirement for a tango.

The next shock I was to receive was the returned letters from Norfolk which the Governess, Claudia Hammond had sent to her family who, it seemed, had disowned her. They contained photographs of a young boy and even drawings; small quick pen or crayon portraits of a child at play, quite recognizable as my younger self. Her technique was excellent and professional as befitted a former student of the Slade where she'd sat in overcoat and scarf at her drawing classes in the freezing studios. She'd abandoned her studies to join an artists' commune on the Left Bank of the Seine in '96, and had been trawled in the *Pays Latin* by the elegant Graf Peter and added to his *Schmetterling* collection. But she was different, or thought she was. She was also pregnant by the following year, which is when Peter tired of and abandoned her. For him she was one among many. For her he was the love of her life.

I read some of the letters. She wrote, 'The tennis courts are being laid down to the excitement of the children who cannot wait to play. Temporarily they set up nets on the lawns which are now cut by petroleum-driven lawn mowers rather than hand-hauled cutters and rollers. Horses cannot be used unless their hooves are wrapped and padded.

'Rolf is growing quite tall now. He is a handsome boy, given to quiet moments. He catches me looking at him sometimes and I have to check myself. Sometimes I cannot speak for the pain of it, but I would have it no other way. Not to see him at all would be unbearable and the Doctor and Hannah are such good people and do not live far off. Rolf lacks for nothing and is stimulated by everything new. The Doctor is a great reader and so is Rolf. I understand they are to go to Lüneburg as there is a medical conference in Berlin, and Rolf is to go with him and will visit the great Heath on their return, where there is to be an event with man-carrying balloons and flying machines. Such nonsense, but they are both so interested in the science of it all.

'The Sinovskys came to dinner last evening. Such *travelled* people you never met! They had an epidiascope with slides of their Egyptian tour and their recent visit to Central America…

'Rolf and Marik are the best of friends although Marik is nearly three years older. They play happily together and Rolf will follow him everywhere. Such a blessing to have him near, but sometimes it breaks my heart so that I cannot hold him.'

She had borne her child at her family home, Cheriton Cottage, on the Norfolk farm estate of her stepfather, but had been pressured into having the child adopted or face social exclusion, bringing shame on the

430

family. With me at three months of age she'd scraped together enough money to take passage from Harwich bound for Esbjerg aboard the *SS Riberhuus*, an aging Danish paddle vessel of *Det Forenede Dampskips-Selskab A/S*, the passenger ticket from which she'd glued as a momento into her diary, which was here among the effects still at Liepus Namas. She made her tortuous way with her tiny child, via Kiel, Lübeck and Rostock, by rail, coach and ferry to Danzig and then by rail again to Silute, inside the Curonian Spit and thence by farm cart to the old Hanseatic mansion on the Kreuzhof estate where lay her unanswered letters to Peter. She'd arrived exhausted and destitute to beg acknowledgement of her child, only to be told that Graf Peter had left that same week for Jamaica with no date for his return.

Hermann Berg, estate manager at Kreuzhof was in the process of closing the house, having already dismissed the servants. He wired from Silute to Kristian von Strelitz advising him of the unexpected arrivals and their pitiful condition. Berg was ordered to provide them with sustenance and accommodation for the next few days and stay put until he himself could make his way to the Baltic coast to review the situation personally.

Kristian had offered her the funds to return to Norfolk, but she was adamant that she wanted to stay, to confront Peter himself however long it might take. In the end Kristian, Berg, Claudia and her baby travelled to Kuznetsowa, to the Linden House, where Princess Sophie graciously welcomed the distraught young Englishwoman and offered her the hospitality of the house. Kristian had been hatching a plan on the journey, which he put to Miss Hammond. Although they had a nanny and tutors were yet to be required, it was decided that there would shortly be the need of a governess for Marik, who was but three years old, and eventually for baby Krystina. Princess Sophie was pregnant with her third child and in due course such a position would have to be filled. Miss Hammond had several accomplishments and spoke English, fluent French and quite good German. She was naturally good at languages and felt she could pick up Russian and even Lithuanian in time although that was still a banned language, spoken only by the servants.

So both my biological parents were artists, which explained my inherited skill. And my name too, Rolf, was a diminutive of Rudolf, Peter von Strelitz's second name. The Strelitz's friends and near neighbours, the Dragunavicius's two sons had succumbed to diphtheria. Placing me as their adopted child had filled a great emptiness in their lives and enabled my natural mother to keep a relatively close eye on my upbringing, which was the best she could expect in the circumstances. As

I grew older and became a constant guest at the house, a firm friend of Marik's, Claudia's pain was lessened by my closeness, innocent as I was of the beating of her maternal heart.

But who the hell was I now?

I'd left Lithuania as *Dragunavicius* and returned as *Steiger.* Now I find that my father was a *von Strelitz* and my mother is a *Hammond.* So I'm not a native Lithuanian, but half -Baltic German and half-English which I've heard is a *very* mongrel breed.

Hell, I thought. I'll stick with Steiger. It has a certain 'ring' and I am feeling little love for the name *Strelitz* right now. Besides, the 'vons' were a bit out of fashion nowadays, back in Germany as elsewhere!

~-~

'She wept for your loss, Rolf. How she wept!' The Graf was well into the vodka, drinking to subdue the pain of the bullet wound. His Landeswehr had carried him back to Kuznetsowa last year *with a hole in my upper thigh you could put your fist into, Rolf.* It was yet to heal properly and a poor diet didn't help. Claudia had been inconsolable.

'I wouldn't have blamed you if you *had* cut that bastard's throat. And to hell with redemption'

~-~

He'd meant Welikowsky. I'd intended to execute Wöbbe. What was the difference? As a child I'd punched a boy on the nose for insulting the Tsarina. I'd attacked the Gollub for amputating a young schoolboy's fingers. So vengeance would be mine, *one bullet at a time.* My mind is now so mixed up, perhaps it *was* me who'd cut Welikowsky's throat. I'd killed men and felt no compunction, men doing the same job I did on the enemy's side, sanctioned by act of war. What did that make me?

It could be argued that I'd been fighting on the wrong side anyway. Frankly I no longer cared about the morality of what I had done or had been accused of doing. My soul was probably damned anyway. I just wanted to find Krysia and the killing to stop.

Chapter 30. *Kat*

I woke again to the sound of chopping wood. I rose and made my painful way out onto the patio. The air was cool. I stopped to watch the woodcutter. A slight leather-jacketed figure was swinging the long axe expertly, changing the grip to render each stroke with the maximum economic force, deftly splitting each log exactly in two, stooping to position for next the blow, all in a continuous motion. Like a machine.

'Hello, Kat,' I said in Lithuanian.

The pause was imperceptible. The next log was neatly placed and cleaved and then the next. I was about to speak again thinking that she hadn't heard when she straightened up and turned to face me. Her hair was cut short: convenience I expect.

Her face was without expression as far as I could tell. Her eyes had something of the look I'd observed on the night of my arrival. No welcome, little recognition just a coldness as if she was viewing something inanimate and not very interesting. Never had I seen such a change in the appearance of an individual who was not either already dead or dying. *Sweet little Kat. Clever, beautiful Kat, with humour to match her looks.*

She stood hard and straight with the axe level, balanced in her hands.

'Why did you come back?' she asked at last. Her voice was clear but 'flat' and toneless in the cold air.

'Why?' I retorted. 'For my family. For my friends. My country. For you….'

'She's not here any more, Rolf. Katarzyna went away. She doesn't live here now. Just me. Instead. Take it or leave it.' Her voice was icy.

'Kat…….I know what happened.'

'What happened…,' she repeated without emphasis.

'To you.'

'Oh, that. It doesn't matter.'

'It matters very much to everyone, Kat. To Kristian. To Graczy. And to me.'

'It's *war*, Rolf. It's what happens. You cease to be a person. Just a thing. For you, a number. For me….' She broke off with a small helpless gesture that was something other than the front she'd presented to the world with until now I felt sure.

She turned away and looked northwards, out beyond the charred roof of the stable to the hills that were just visible beyond the trees.

'God lives within Man and Nature, Rolf. Isn't that what Nietzsche says.'

I made no reply.

'Except God is dead isn't he? Nietzsche claims that too, doesn't he!'

'Please look at me, Kat,'

'So if the death of God is true then God is also dead in Man. Man's capacity for evil and good is coeval since we have free will, but in the absence of morality the idea of God's wrath and judgment is removed. Where then is the constraint to do good? Does it matter whether we do good or ill when all is permissible?'

'Please Kat.'

'So rape, like mass murder, is a legitimate weapon of the class war.'

'I beseech you. Look at me. We all love you Kat. You are safe now.' Though this last was a lie. *A comparative lie concerning comparative safety.*

'Love? What is that? We are born and if we are lucky it will be into a family where we are indoctrinated that life is pleasurable. And for some it is, it's smooth and easy and soft and luxurious and privileged. And then it suddenly isn't. It's vicious and stinking and bloody and brutal and agonising and that's the way it is for most people now. For the greater good that is *Bolshevism.* I see no end to it.'

'Listen to me Kat. To strive for good is harder than to destroy. Bolshevism first seeks the destruction of institutions which it sees as corrupt, and these include the cultural institutions of a people. These include the family unit. To control and level an imperialist tyranny will seek to destroy a culture by removing trace of heritage whether in stone or from the libraries of a nation; it will make an assault on literature, music, re-write history and even ban a language. That's what *Imperial* Russia did to Lithuania.'

Katya continued to stare out at her distant hills.

'*We* are the new Lithuania. We can stand and fight for that or we can capitulate to this other monstrous thing that has emerged in Russia. If we do that we are doomed as a nation to more oppression and bloodshed. Germany will soon be powerless to help us and even if that were not the case it would only do so in furtherance of its own imperialistic ambitions.'

I move nearer to her, painfully, leaning on my stick.

'But for now we must be practical. It is dangerous for you to move around as well you must know. This place must be better defended.'

No matter what treaties were in place the Bolshies were still skirmishing and crossing from Belarus and Latgale in large numbers.

Kat turned full towards me. In the brittle morning sunlight the scar above her eye was clear now, puckered diagonally into her hairline. She'd been very lucky to survive. But her manner told me that she didn't think so.

'Kat, for Graczy's sake….'

'Are you a priest, Rolf? No? Then you can't help me.'

'Kat…..'

'What good am I now, Rolf?' Katya interrupted. 'I can't feel anything any more. I'm all hollowed-out inside. I don't want anyone to love me, not even Graczy. I can't love them back, not now. Love means you only hurt again afterwards. Love makes you weak.'

'Kat. You're bigger than this. You're a survivor. Graczy needs you, she's hurting for you and so is your father. You were always her little mother surrogate right from the beginning. You adopted her as your own, you know you did in spite of Nina and the others all of whom were older and whose duty was to serve the Family. She was special to you and you to her and that will never change as long as you both live.'

'Why should you care, Rolf. You're not even family.'

If that was designed to wound it did, but it made me realise the depths of her pain.

'You are the only family I've got here now. And I am family, so I've just discovered.'

'Oh yes. So you are. The family skeleton returned from the grave. My father told me after you'd been 'killed'. Uncle Peter's shameful little secret. So hello, *cousin.*'

'Kat….' I stepped awkwardly forward and reached for her, my natural urge to comfort and embrace her overriding the warnings she'd been giving me.

She backed away her eyes widening the axe raised defensively across her breast

'No Rolf! Don't touch me. I can't… ' she left it unsaid. I stood there feeling wretched, futile and stupid.

'Kat. Use the hate. Hatred makes you strong for a while. By all means use it to help you get through. But love endures. Love is stronger. Love is strength itself.'

'What are you now Rolf? A lay preacher? Or my incestuous lover?' She raised the axe and slammed it into a log then stooping she picked up some of the split logs and put them into a sack which she shouldered.

'Kat,' I smiled. 'You have enough logs in the music room to last two winters.'

'It's not about the logs,' she said. 'It's about me. I see his face each time I swing that axe.'

~-~

'So,' says Browne, 'What did you make of the *Strelitz's*? Were they typical?'

'Of what?' I ask.

'Imperialists. Landowning German gentry. Squires of all they surveyed. Grinders of the faces of the poor. Has not your sojourn with the *Bolshies* polarized your thinking? How did you fit into all this?'

The questions are delivered without any emphasis, although with what seemed *relish*, and I found myself wondering what species of political animal was this Home Office warrior. Given the rough and tumble there'd been on the streets, the gathering socialist momentum right here in London, was the ship of state veering? I had an unlikely and momentary vision of bloody Fenian or Leftist hands opening the sea cocks, tugging at the wheel; Browne pretending sympathy for the mutineers, applauding their passion in Hyde Park while shadowy men took photographs. Were agents provocateur recruiting in Whitehall or was this a dispassionate enquiry couched in populist terms?

I think for a moment. In the corner the stenographer flexes her cramped fingers.

I had unquestioningly steered my little ship's natural middle course through the shallows of childhood, navigating the shoals, borne upon both the high and low tides of society. I felt I'd naturally and unconsciously embodied the egalitarianism and cross-cultural acceptance of the good Doctor who'd dealt even-handedly with rich and poor; ministering within the Pale of Settlement. Perhaps not so generally representative of polyglot Lithuanian society even at its cosmopolitan best, his demeanour squared superficially with the public attitude of the middle class. In the cultural meld of Russo-Lithuanian, Polish, Belarus, and Latvian peoples, as with their religions, Catholic, Lutheran, Russian Orthodox, Tartar or Jew, often with Orthodoxy and Judaism each divided against themselves, there tended to be a general acceptance of cultural difference when times were good. Though anti-Semitism swam beneath the surface it was also true that many resented more the German land-owning elite – though it provided a livelihood for the artisan

436

working class.

Among the landowners, even in my little experience of the German variety, there was nonetheless some Slavophile history. A Christian liberalism held sway, locally modifying the absolutism of the monarchist tradition which co-existed with the devout Orthodoxy that would, with a willingness to improve the peasants' lot, have enabled Old Russia to move into the modern age, which in truth it was gradually doing up to the Revolution. There had even been hope that things would turn out for the better under Kerensky: an *Augean* cleansing of corruption and intrigue at court after the Tsar's abdication. The elimination of the *Rasputin camarilla*, the in-camera minister-courtier cell with a direct conduit to Germany: that is until the *Praetorian Guard*, one hundred Lett riflemen escorted Gorbunov's *Antichrist* Express, straight as an arrow, its virus hermetically sealed-in, from Switzerland to Finland Station; a germ-laden hypodermic that was Lenin, injected deep into the nerve centre of revolt.

Nevertheless, the old class surface-tension strained by the growing friendship that Krysia and I had enjoyed, when it had claimed the attention of the Graf became a matter of grave concern. The subsequent dreaded informal conference between Kristian and Dr. Dragunavicius, his good friend, *Katya observed,* would sorely impact on us both, as much upon her sister as myself. The raised voices she reported to me: the 'Iron Countess' Charlotte berating the Graf... 'Are you quite mad, Kristian? Have you not seen the way that...boy looks at Krystina, and she at him when she thinks she's not observed.'

I'd accepted that the passionate Krysia would inherit wealth and surely marry well, and for self-preservation I'd felt I had to distance myself from her towards the end, though my heart ached. Such reality in one so young and in love. It almost seemed that I was able to split myself in half, the ardent lover, hot-headed and heedless of danger, and a coolly dispassionate observer, watching himself in time's mirror. Heine's *Doppelgänger,* wringing his hands at the portal of fate.

I cling to images of better times. A younger Krysia smiling wryly at me as we walk the shore, when our love was yet unexpressed and tentative. Klammersdorf had been instructing her and Kat on the philosophers. 'But Rolf, why do I need Kant and Hegel? I have my Chopin, and he can tell me about love and passion. I am a country girl after all.' She laughs, and ruffles my tousled hair. 'You don't understand do you, passion?' I blush and cannot answer her. I want to tell her I love her more passionately than anyone.

Other suitors had already presented their cards. Importantly they were the scions of the landed and wealthy. But upon this convention Krysia, in turmoil, expressed herself in furious rides alone, secretly, and at unpredictable times. The *Grand Tour* that Krysia was hurriedly embarked on with the governess, as a distraction, was even more hurriedly curtailed when in Switzerland she'd practically thrown herself at her skiing instructor, and in Paris, had fought so ferociously with her middle-aged fencing master, she'd been asked to leave the premises and not return.

Within a year, with such military influence as the Graf wielded, I found myself with a cavalry regiment as a Helmsburg cadet, thanks, it turned out, to Claudia, who had interceded with the Graf when his intention had been aired to send me to a German regiment. Fearing the growing tension between England and Germany she had begged Kristian to think again; said she couldn't bear the thought of me being the victim of such a conflict. Fate decreed that Austria's response to Sarajevo was war with Serbia and Russia, in the first instance, while I was about to suffer under perhaps the ugliest man in the Austrian army; reflecting that the name you bear can shape your life. Krysia was by then in Paris, studying at the Sorbonne, medicine I think, under Madame Curie. We'd had a night of passion before she'd left. She'd flung an epée at me and fought me to a standstill in the stables before demanding her forfeit while Buran thudded and whinnied in his stall.

~-~

Big Ben struck the hour.

I looked at Browne and Colonel Rose without expression. 'What difference does it make what I think?' In many ways the family Strelitz *was* typical: in others very atypical. He, Kristian, had accepted German help when it was offered, which I suppose made him a 'collaborator', but then in extremis he'd also sought assistance from roving members of the Expeditionary Force.

'He was doing his best for his children in the hardest of times, with his hands tied behind his back, so to speak. In Bolshevist eyes he was an aristo and therefore automatically condemned. But in the end he was a survivor. A Lithuanian patriot. Like me.'

We broke for lunch, Browne and Hawkeye excusing themselves with my being put in the care of a fresh-faced young Home Office type, one Lindsay-Langton, who provided congenial enough company but who was unable to shed any light on what it was that Browne and Co. wanted with me, although I could hazard a pretty good guess. It seemed, at first glance

438

preposterous that with the collapse of Germany, the Kaiser in exile in Holland, Allied armies of occupation with military intelligences in place on German soil and the Versailles Treaty dictates and reparations beginning to bite, that HMG would need to insert a 'specialist', a secret agent of some stripe into the matrix when all avenues for reporting back were perforce covered. And were likely to be so for the foreseeable. In peacetime what in fact were legations and embassies for? Business always provided a discretionary ear and I was sure Whitehall had its amateur informants as well as others who were 'on the books'.

'Secret Agent' had a sort of nineteenth century ring to it. Intelligence Officer is the position that I'm officially seeking I remind myself. It covered a broad spectrum of possible covers from an eclectic church of skills and career experience. But I presumed with my linguistic capabilities, experience of Russian captivity, service within Austro-Hungary/Germany and in the emergent Baltic States, my ability to move within various strata, I might be useful in some long-term strategy when things had 'normalised'. Who knows what sort of Germany would emerge from the current torment, with Silesia and Westphalia in uproar and strife, and Red units still embattled in Berlin and Munich, by all accounts, despite the growing power of the Freikorps in backing the provisional government.

Wherever they might choose to place me, *if* I agreed, I surmised it would be somewhere in northern Prussia, Berlin or further northeast I was sure. The situation was volatile still and of what possible use could I be? Perhaps a perceived and direct Bolshevist threat *were* presented to the United Kingdom though surely none more than that represented by the Fenian menace over the Irish Sea, though it seemed to many that the two may be linked. In Northern Ireland murder, kidnapping, bombings and violent confrontations flared.

A few months back the papers had been full of the savage murder in London of Sir Henry Wilson. The recent Chief of the Imperial General Staff, who'd been elected MP for an Ulster constituency, had been shot to death at three in the afternoon by Fenian assassins on his own doorstep in Eaton Place. Though the murderers had fled, they had been bravely apprehended by an angry crowd, despite being fired on by the assassins. In Russian cities such shocking crimes had been repeated twenty thousand times over.

But to do *what* was a more vexing question. It seemed very farsighted of someone to wish to 'plant' me, a recovering amnesic, a *mental* case, recorded in my new British medical notes as an 'autistic savant', unless of course that *was* now the kernel of the idea.

Perhaps my obsessive, newly found ability since my brain injury had made me a perfect recording machine. The total recall I was capable of astounded no one more than myself. They, previously Saunders and co, Browne, especially the mesmeric Rose only had to ask a simple question and I was away chapter and verse, citing details I'd completely forgotten before the accident. The minutiae of daily *Lietuvo-Germanic* life, regurgitated from the depths of my mind, amazed even me. When first I'd struggled to recall as much as my own name I was terrified that I'd be trapped forever in a void of half-remembered imagery, mind's eye recollections viewed through gauze. But it was almost as frightening what was now resurfacing. As if I was on some truth drug that compelled me to tell all. Like the two-way unburdening and confessional I'd had with the Graf before the collapse of Liepus Namas. Before the fall of the House of Strelitz.

~.~

Unexpectedly the afternoon's planned question and answer session was postponed and I was furnished with funds for my return to Norfolk by Lindsay-Langton. My temporary passport, which I'd surrendered on arrival, was retained and I was asked to stay at my seaside lodgings for the time being and await further communication.

I was no closer to making a decision on whatever employment if any I might be asked to agree to since no offer had been made. I was certain that a bigger meeting was now in process and my case was being discussed with higher beings, furnished with the stenographer's notes from her fair aching hand. But that they were still interested I was certain and I had my own half-formed reasons for wanting to return to North Germany and the Baltic. That the estate there might conceivably become my own inheritance in a free Lithuania had not then occurred to me, not while the Graf's family was still unaccounted for. I was still searching my mind for glimpses of those bits of memory that eluded me, for completion of my own story to date. I worried that those gaps concealed passages in my life wherein I had acted in a way that I was sure was, if not reprehensible, then at the least had been severely traumatic in some way.

After my evacuation through the port of Rostov, aided by the gallant pilots of the British Royal Air Force's Expeditionary Force, for whose assistance I would be forever grateful, I'd spent time in a military hospital sharing wards with those severely wounded in both the recent war, Ulster, and the continuing war in Europe, Ukraine and Russia.

Though suffering from broken bones and a slight fracture of the skull the physical trauma was uncomplicated. What still worried me were the implications of the brain injury that I'd received. I still had headaches almost every day, but more particularly I wondered what long-term effects might yet be waiting in ambush for me.

~-~

I am the only vertical in the picture. Like the monk on the shore at Rügen, I am suddenly part of the *German Romantic Movement*. The cloud, like Friedrich's cloud, is diffuse. The sea is dark. No sound save the gentle lapping of the waves intrudes here. Like Friedrich I am only too aware of the smallness of man. The original was a bold picture, for 1809. That was before that Corsican egotist, Napoleon, besieged Moscow. Now I would besiege it myself to prick out the incumbent whelk if I had an army strong enough.

I am on Great Yarmouth harbour wall. I glance out to sea briefly at the steam drifters with their tall 'Woodbine' funnels and a gathering of Hewett's 'Short Blue' trawler fleet returning with their catches. I view the little fishing boats, the herring smacks and dinghies moored within and sitting upon the shelving beach, seen dimly in the crepuscular light. All told the vessels number thirty-seven. I re-count them slowly. Still thirty-seven. The first glance took maybe two seconds, the re-count about ten. It seems old Dr. Campbell was right. I have a new gift since the crash. I might be quite an asset to them it would seem. A linguist who could move easily through society's strata. A pilot with military experience. An eidetic memory: the man with total recall, except that is for a little repository of remaindered information hidden in his aching brain.

There is still no indication that the locked door in my mind will creak upon its hinges, let me glimpse the remainder of my missing past. I look anxiously at my palms. No sign of stigmata yet by the cold light of a rising moon: a dead ghost's spoiled face peering through the cloud. Do you too furtively draw your heat from the world, as they say of the stars, enigmatic succubus to the Earth?

I stare out at the dark lapping sea, east, towards the invisible Baltic shores. They say no one can remember anything that happened before their second or third year. Yet somewhere I can recall a sea journey at night and being held in gentle arms, shining eyes looking into mine, feeling such contentment and happiness. The smell of her. And lights upon the water, like diamonds. Were they the lights of Danzig? I wonder if it was real.

I considered the musing of Sir Isaac Newton himself, the scientist beachcomber upon the shore, prefiguring both Friedrich's monk and Nietzsche's *Joyous Science*: 'swooping upon each new pretty pebble or seashell of discovery with childlike delight, while right at hand and unsuspected the great Ocean of Truth lies undiscovered before him.'

~.~

From my silent soliloquy I return to a solidifying world. In the darkness something darker moves inshore: something that my newly found talents cannot assist my discerning. If it's a boat it has no lights. Maybe it's a vessel adrift but the shape seems wrong to me. I descend to the strand to get a closer look but the moon is suddenly obscured by cloud. The night is thickening. The blob seems to be stationary in the water with the tide perhaps on the turn. I'm pretty sure it's a drifting buoy. So why do I see an eidolon: picturing a horned-head in my mind, black like the devil? One of the manifestations of my condition I suppose. I am feeling tired and think it will keep until the morning to inform the harbourmaster if that should prove necessary.

At my digs, my landlady's stew and dumplings filling my belly and a bottle of ale or two in the snug, sharing the jestful companionship of some grog-blossomed mariners, I sleep the sleep of the just. Or the ignorant.

Chapter 31. *Death of Klammersdorf*

Upon our moonlit way a thing of rags and tatters hangs. Beckoning fingers implore us. *Wait!*

I gently lower him from the scaffold where long ago I had been horsewhipped, standing upon the *telezhki* while Kat holds steady the reins, the horse restive and wide-eyed like Arkadi by her side. Sunblacked, crow-pecked, he grins eye-lessly, ivory teeth white in the fleshless jaw. I hear his voice.

'Rolf,' he had said. 'You were right. It's only the grave will cure me.'

I had found his clownish horse grazing contentedly and heard the cocking of his Russian Colt: turned to see him sitting against the bole of a tree, wrapped in his greatcoat, an empty vodka bottle at his side.

'Ach, it's you Rolf.' He'd indicated the bottle.

'I am afraid I cannot offer you a drink - sadly it's empty. Not so the revolver!'

Whatever he'd intended I had interrupted things. I collected his horse and helped him with some difficulty into the saddle. If he'd seemed heavy then it was because I was but a youth. I had led him back to the Linden House and into Nina's care.

In the dripping night he's no easer to lift. Though aided by Arkadi, carrying him is a struggle and I feel the blood seeping from my wound. I lay the Jewish cripple beneath the trees. We have no time to bury him, nor shovels. *Alas.* Our lives are at stake, but I could not have left him hanging to rot, displayed as a grim trophy to cruelty and unreason. Scholar and polymath, victim of a brutal levelling, annihilation of class and culture by proclamation and mobdom. I wonder again, when will this horror end?

He lies there in the dark wetness, sockets staring emptily, facing his abyss: polished dentures of *Loxodonta africanus* grinning lop-sided at the moon. *They'd never fitted well in life, 'clicking' his way distractingly through the classics, to the barely stifled amusement of the K sisters.* We scatter leaves upon his body and I bow my head a moment. I manage a smile for Arkadi then turn my eyes to the scudding clouds. Above the firs, like apparitions, moonlit wraiths swirl their way from Petrograd, carrying a hint of winter. A painting by Chagal. I remember the two fleeing ghosts: that '*white changeling*', the albino gibbon keening, chittering, *alas, alas.* The innocent old leper, maddened by solitude. And words form in my mind.

Alas, Poor Gibeon.

Pale clouds do scurry,
'Cross a gibbous and unhealthy moon,
And sails the black gibbet,
Where swings poor eyeless Gibeon.
And gestures a figure,
In long cobwebbed hair,
All a gibber, eyes a-glitter,
In wild de-lirium....
And snow-white gibbon grimaces,
At gibbet's foot and rocks,
And rocks and rocks and rocks,
And rocks,
 In silent woe.

'Moonlit wraiths swirl their way from Petrograd...'

We are moving as fast as Arkadi's miserable horse will allow along roads that cut through woods where in a moment might be revealed any of a dozen enemy bands: partisans, insurrectionists, brigands. Bolshevists of every stamp.

Before we'd left Liepus Namas an incident had occurred which confirmed the present danger that persisted in eastern Lithuania. A window had smashed in the east wing of the house. Berg had taken one look into the room and slammed the door when he saw a British Mills bomb rolling across the floor of the reception room. It failed to explode immediately, saving his life. When the grenade detonated, it blew the door off its hinges, with Berg underneath.

Kristian yelled for Joshua to bring his hunting rifle and limped upstairs like a wounded crab, forcing open the doors to the veranda above the main entrance. Going down on one knee, the barrel resting on the rail, he took aim at a fleeing figure and dropped him with a single shot.

The Graf ordered Berg and Joshua to retrieve the corpse for possible identification, covering them with his hunting rifle as they wheeled out a handcart to haul it back along the carriageway, like a trophy stag. It was a 'Kaiser' shot, right though the heart at over two hundred meters.

'Not lost your touch, Kristian,' said Berg breezily. 'Going to have him mounted?'

The Graf was looking intently at the terrorist's face. In death it had not relaxed its sneer. A face 'like a leering Christ', Elena had described it. It could apply to any wild-haired, bearded Bolshevist with a murderous streak I supposed, but Kristian stated grimly that it was evidence enough that Roskov was nearby.

They buried the man in a shallow grave under the trees by the lake. Kristian said he'd be disinterred and the body collected when things were calmer. The Graf didn't want the man on his land one minute longer than absolutely necessary.

~-~

We leave the road and enter woodland by paths scarce wide enough for the small cart, some little more than game trails: steering by my compass and a boyhood's knowledge of the terrain and Kat's own instinct for terrestrial navigation. The cart's axles are heavily greased whilst the creak of the harness and the clumping of hooves hopefully do not carry far through the underbrush on a windy night. The going is soft after rain which deadens sound of our progress although we become stuck occasionally and have to alight and assist the horse, pushing on the wheel-spokes to free the vehicle from the mud. It's a light cart, piled with some of last year's hay which conceals the lift pump and a drum of precious aviation spirit that had been cached at *Heinrich*.

My argument had persuaded Kat to assist in the plan to gain arms for Liepus Namas by helping me to salvage the Ju, assuming no-one else had discovered it the meanwhile. I carried with me the slender crank handle from the Sizaire. Just the tool I thought to pull the flattened wingtip into an approximate aerofoil shape, which is where my mind is when three armed figures step out of the trees across our path.

A voice speaks in Latvian. 'Stop! Identify yourselves.'

I am gripped as if by an icy hand. After all we've been through our plans are now in jeopardy. I rack my brains for a reply that will defuse the situation. If they find our aviation spirit it can hardly be explained away.

'I know these,' whispers Kat, her face tense in the moonlight. '*Lacplecis. Bear Slayers!*'

To my surprise Kat speaks up firmly. 'I will identify myself when I know upon whose authority you are asking.'

'What!' one exclaims. 'Dismount now, woman, or suffer the consequences.'

I can see no alternative. Rifles are trained on us. Arkadi is rigid at my side.

Kat removes her bonnet. 'I am the Countess Katarzyna Aleksandra von Strelitz.' Oh, I think inconsequentially, I didn't know her middle name was 'Aleksandra'. 'My father is the Graf. We are acting in the interests of democracy, political freedom and independence for all Baltic States.'

A moment's hesitation among the trio and a brief discussion.

'What way are you *acting*?' sneers the spokesman.

'I am not prepared to discuss matters of state. Who is your commanding officer?'

'This is Latvia, *your majesty*.' A change of tone I note, but in mockery, not deference nor concession made to her rank. 'If the *tsarina* would get down from her 'carriage' and present her papers……if you are who you say then you will be taken for questioning along with your 'footman' and 'page'!' This causes a titter from the other two. I can't decide whether these are quasi-military, deserters or just highwaymen.

'You first!' The spokesman indicates me with the point of a pistol. 'Get down and lie face down on the ground, arms outstretched.'

I hand the reins to Arkadi and get to my feet. I feel the weight of my Mauser in my flying coat pocket. The idea of drawing it and perhaps holding their leader hostage is dismissed as soon as it arises. It would not work with their weapons already trained on Kat and Arkadi, even assuming they held their commander's health dear.

Their leader steps up to me. He strikes a match and holds it to my face studying it carefully. 'Why, it's the little 'Doctor's Boy'!' he announces. 'Hey, Karlis, this one shot the biggest boar in the Baltic some years back. Small world, eh Rolfie?'

I recognise him as one of the 'rough badgers', whom Gorbunov had called *Timotei*. In that case, I reasoned, he'd have recognised Kat by her title and the name *Strelitz* and if he'd meant us no harm would have offered due deference. The other Bear Slayers close in for a better look, rifles loosely levelled.

'Aha! From that scar I think this hard-mouthed little mare is same countess who sleeps with *Wolves*!' said one; passable Lithuanian, grinning. 'Didn't you have a nice wolf cub, then?'

I realise in an instant that Kat is gripping her pistol under her coat. Suddenly she stands up and looks over the shoulders of the two facing her. With an exclamation of surprise and apparent recognition she calls out, 'Marik, thank God!'

The two *Lacplesis* militiamen turn their heads instinctively moving their rifles slightly off target, which is enough for Katya to throw Arkadi into the well of the cart as she jumps to the ground. The *Bear Slayers* are too close to the horse to re-align their rifles quickly. Timotei shouts and raises his pistol but I slam my elbow into his solar plexus. I hear three shots: two from the Steyr by its bark and the crack of a carbine. The pony rears in the traces and Timotei has doubled up but is staggering erect and I hear the Steyr speak again as Katya makes sure of one of the others. Timotei is swinging the pistol back to me so I jab the Mauser in his face and grab his gun hand, twisting the pistol away from me. He's as strong as an ox and my weakened leg is giving out. He knocks my gun hand away and my Mauser discharges harmlessly into the air but Kat appears at my side and digs the Steyr into his ribs. Timotei ceases to struggle and lets fall his pistol. His two confederates lie where Katya has dropped them. Arkadi has calmed the horse and is picking up the weapons. Timotei is even paler now by moonlight.

'That was well done, Kat,' I say. Kat's face is impassive, her breathing controlled. She'd proven that her shooting skills had not diminished, as attested by the Graf.

'There was no other choice,' she says simply. She'd pulled an old trick, but her performance was convincing enough that for an instant it had succeeded, and that was all she'd needed.

'We now have a fine dilemma,' I say in French.

She looked at me with cool judgement.

'I mean, what do we do with him? He's a liability if we take him with us and we can't just shoot him.'

'Can't we?' asks Kat. She'd not even bothered to look at her two victims. If we were to tie him up and leave him for his other friends to find him our lives will be under threat for sure, sooner or later. Other *Bear Slayers* or their allies may be on their way here even now if those shots were heard.

We use him to haul the two militiamen into the trees before tying his hands with baling cord, gagging him with a soft cap and putting him in the back of the wagon. He will be our prisoner: at least until we get to the Ju. Their rifles will add to our collection.

So we proceed quietly, on compass heading, armed to the teeth: more tense and watchful than ever.

~-~

In the Norwood night James Delcroix is talking about Harry's experiences as a slave at Fili as told to him twenty years before in Frankfurt.

'Harry was a born survivor, John. But the things he had to do to survive, aged ten, would make your flesh creep. Apparently he was picked up by a train which was transporting much needed workers for the war economy: repairs, construction, all sorts. In Harry's case it was to the big plant at Fili: the building site for the poison gasworks. He said some of the prisoners were in an agony of despair at being parted from their families. They'd not even been given the opportunity to say goodbye: were simply picked off the streets, bundled into trucks and delivered to the station in whatever they were wearing: some with business suits, wearing soft shoes. Two decided to escape by enlarging the hole in the cattle truck floor, used as a toilet. The train was going quite slowly. It had a snowplough on the front so maybe it was clearing its own passage, although the snow on the railway line didn't appear too deep.'

'Those that didn't escape were put to work in sub-zero conditions immediately, men, women, children - using bare hands to pull rusty cables. No gloves, so their fingers were in shreds in no time. No protection from biting wind. No shelter during the day, no heating in the wooden huts. No bedding. No toilet or washing facilities. Little food and of poor quality. Later on they died in their tens of thousands, John, Harry told me, when the first 'Five Year Plans' got going. *Five in Four!* was the slogan of the *Stakhanovites*. And there was always a supply. The Cheka just arrested more on the streets of Moscow, Leningrad, Minsk, and the '*stans* or wherever. These people weren't criminals or even politicals. Just conscript workers. Unpaid slaves of no intrinsic worth.'

'Train stopped to bury bodies at one place,' Harry had said, 'I was glad then I had not tried to escape through the toilet hole in cattle truck floor. At back of the train, under guard's van, was welded two heavy scythes. Blades extended within inches of the track, very bloodstained.'

'Those two gentlemen didn't make it home after all, James.'

~.~

Flotsam

I awake to sunshine and the cries of gulls. I love that sound, as I know the sea is not far away. Praise be! I don't have a headache. My alarm clock has not wakened me so I rise and draw open the curtains of my attic room. It's a beautiful day but something's afoot. A crowd has gathered along the sea wall and some activity is apparent on the beach the details of which I cannot make out from my lofty but oblique vantage point.

I pull on my trousers, boots and a seaman's sweater and I am quickly downstairs. Breakfast had been laid for an hour and I thank Mrs. Hewson but I'll just have some buttered toast and eat it on the way to the quayside. She's already heard about the mine.

I join the gathering at the wall. A policeman has ordered the crowd further back but they keep drawing closer for a better view. The tide is out. The big mine sits on its dark reflection on the wet sand, like a mechanical sea urchin. I knew I'd briefly seen its black devil's head by moonlight's glow, about three hundred metres out. Two army lorries are parked against the sea wall and a sapper is carefully examining the object. Wet footprints indicate that the distance to the sea wall has been paced out. A dozen men are filling bags with sand and building a v-shaped revetment to landward.

I spy the 'sea captain' and work my way over to his side. I have inquired and discovered that he lives at the seamen's mission and has done these last few years. He recognises me and returns my greeting.

Some fishermen from last night at the *Waterside* give me grudging acknowledgement. Somebody says it's a type H-11.

I tell him that I'd reported my observation in the pub last night but the gnarled salts had just chuckled in their beers, said it was a rowing boat adrift.

'The evil flotsam of war is what it is. Filthy inventions.' He has the local accent.

'I wonder how many more of them are out there.'

'One more is too many,' he says, gruffly.

Ironic, I think that the Royal Navy had done such a good job in clearing the Red Channel off the Baltic coast, yet the North Sea still gives up its dark secrets and probably would for some time to come. British mines too, untethered from their moorings due to poor quality chains would wander at whim of wind and tide.

'Better they wash ashore than menace shipping.'

'One took my ship,' he says so softly that I scarce hear him. 'This month, three year ago.'

My heart seems to stumble in my chest. This too I'd heard. 'Not the *Artemis* by chance?'

Named for the Moon Goddess. A stab in the dark. Of the more than eight hundred and fifty Allied and neutral ships reported lost to mines, the Lloyd's Losses are burned into my brain for that month, 1918. The only other was a British warship, both to drifting mines in the North Sea.

He looks at me for a long moment. 'The same,' he says and looks back at the activity. Gulls wheel and scream overhead. The crowd is animated and chatting excitedly, as if waiting for an entertainment.

'Were there many survivors?' I ask him after a while.

'Fourteen,' he says at last. 'Seven crew, seven passengers.'

That was all out of forty-nine. One of the two lifeboats was blown to bits in its davits. Captain McCann was the last to leave. It was pitch dark and people were in the water. They'd fired flares and dropped lifebelts and floats but it was a filthy night with an ugly, breaking sea. Lots of white water everywhere and freezing cold. They'd salvaged a lantern and though they looked for survivors for hours before help arrived they found only bodies. My mother, Claudia Hammond, had not been among them. So if it was coincidence that my gaze had met the old captain's on those morning constitutionals it was also fate. A bitter link with the life of Claudia, my lost and broken-hearted mother. Somehow I'd known his presence would be connected both to the indifferent sea and to my storm-tossed, benighted life.

'The sea giveth,' Dr. Campbell had said. Yea, and it taketh away. McCann's livelihood on the point of retirement and my soul's closest blood-tie this side of Heaven at the point of salvation from civil war. Baroness Nadia had survived, a while at least: but my mother, thinking her only child was four years dead, had gone down with the *Artemis*, a ship named for the Goddess Moon and with cruel irony for the sanctuary Temple of Ephesus.

I'd wandered that same shoreline on other nights and thought bitterly of those awful deaths by drowning. Hanna, my mother as I'd known her in Lithuania, deliberately, in a lake. My real father, Peter, another suicide, in the Banda Sea. And then Claudia, my real mother and I never knew it. My surrogate father, Augusts, though had died by fire. All but Peter's as the result of war. He might have sold his birthright, but he hadn't witnessed the wholesale destruction of the society he'd eschewed for the fleshpots of the South Seas: the cataclysm of a world at war, bloody revolution and suffering prophesied by young Marik and old Gorbunov, both in their own way: Morlocks eat Eloi and the Antichrist that would strike the match to the powder keg. I found myself near tears, looking out again to sea; Kristian's words about redemption being the last path we all must tread echoing in my mind.

Chapter 32. *Death of Dragunavicius*

I'd been summoned again to No 2. Whitehall Court. Browne is in his customary chair. Hawkeye-Rose is absent. In his place is a Squadron Leader Frankland in the smart new uniform of the Royal Air Force. His breast bears RAF wings and two ribbons: blue and red and purple and white. *I recall that these had been worn by MacIntyre, confirmed via 'cover' documents provided me by Saunders in support of my legend as ex-RFC, that these are the DSO and DFC.* Frankland suggests courteously that I now describe my flying experiences from the beginning, starting with how I came to join the Austrian Air Service.

~.~

I am transported in vivid memory to the hospital ward at the regimental barracks, Helmsburg Fortress near Angerfurt where I am trying to sleep which is the only possible escape from the pain of my cracked ribs. I am alone on the ward as the medical orderly has gone off duty this Saturday evening. The MO is on leave and his replacement is not due until Monday. The orderly reckons I won't be needing any assistance tonight so it's safe to slip into town to see his girlfriend. It had been confirmed that my lung was not punctured and there's no treatment for busted ribs other than to lie still and wait for them to heal, so for the orderly it's worth the risk. He's quite candidly told me what he's up to, after all a cadet who has no likelihood of becoming an officer is not about to grass-up an orderly corporal.

My injuries are the result of a mishandled telegraph pole during a team building exercise. Wöbbe's corporals dragged the cadets to their feet from the tangle of bodies lying under the pole after it had been dropped at one end and bounced, shivering and slamming me in the ribs, scattering my fellow cadets like chaff. From the bottom of the heap I'm pulled roughly to my feet, in agony down my left side. I am driven to continue with the exercise but the pain incapacitates me and to Wöbbe's fury he is obliged to have me escorted to sick bay.

Later, in the half-waking drowsiness and semi-dark of the lonely ward, I am aware of Wöbbe. He fails to see me. He is groping about in a cupboard in a side room, where the medicines are locked. I have no idea what he might be doing and keep very still. After a while, without a glance in my direction he leaves. I hear an outer door bang shut. I must have dozed. How long I slept I have no idea but I am awakened by the sound of heavy breathing and a dragging, shuffling sound. I open one eye and can see two NCOs, two of the *Wise Monkeys*, half-carrying a limp figure which they dump onto a nearby bed.

'He'll be OK,' says one. 'The orderly will sort him out in the morning.'

Then they were gone. After a while I see the figure draw up its knees.

'Hello?' My voice betrays my nervousness. There's no reply.

I lever myself up on one elbow. An agonising pain racks my side. I grit my teeth and force myself into a sitting position. 'Are you all right?' I ask fatuously. There's no response from the other. Wearily I pull myself upright, ignoring the pain, and pad across to my anonymous companion. It's Steiger, eyes closed, his face tight. Gently I touch his shoulder. 'Steiger, what's the matter? What happened?'

He seems almost delerious. Eventually he half opens one eye.

'Rolf?' he asks weakly.

'Yes, it's me. What's the matter?'

Steiger's mouth is clamped, controlling the pain he must be experiencing. He breathes in, seems to hold his breath and then expels it slowly. He does this several times.

'Shall I get someone?'

He shakes his head. 'I'll be alright,' he whispers.

'What happened to you?'

He breathes slowly a few more times, controlling the pain.

'Wöbbe,' he says at last.

I feel impotent anger boiling in my chest.

'What did he do?'

Steiger seems to be lapsing into unconsciousness.

'Steiger. Gustav, listen to me. What happened? I'll try to get some help.'

Steiger opens his eyes wide and looks at me as if for the first time.

'There's no help in this place, Rolf. It is a death camp. They do what they like.'

'What do you mean? What happened to you?'

'Wöbbe tried to…' Steiger has difficulty continuing.

'What? Tried to what, Gustav?'

Steiger raises his slender hand. It is a gesture of peace and resignation, almost I think of farewell. *'Like the hand of a girl.'* Wöbbe had said. Suddenly I get the full revolting picture - those notches on his swagger stick. I even have a flash of understanding about the shadowy presence of Wöbbe hunting about in the drugs room, to which he has a key. My father had used muscle relaxants on horses. Amyl nitrate. Damn that orderly going off duty. I need to raise the alarm.

'It's alright. I will be OK when I've been able to sleep. The pain is easing off......'

'Did he....?'

'No, Rolf. I fought the bastard off. But he punched me hard.' He indicates his stomach.

Wöbbe's boast was that he could knock out a horse with one punch, and he had proven it when drunk in Angerfurt.

'Rolf.'

'Yes.'

'I'm going to be a pilot tomorrow!'

'Sure you are,' I said. 'Wish I was going with you. Now you hang on, I'm going to get some help.'

~.~

We had been on parade, drilling in the morning sunshine. It was a lovely day with a gentle breeze that barely raised the wings of the double-headed eagle on his pole. We'd felt the usual rasp of Wöbbe's tongue and a few of us were already on charges for sloppiness or for uniform irregularities, invisible to all but Wöbbe and the *Wise Monkeys*. The previous week I suffered verbal dismemberment and found myself on hands and knees weeding the parade ground in blazing heat for having an untidy locker, my soap tin being five millimetres off-centre.

At around mid-morning we'd heard an unfamiliar sound, an aero engine. A few cadets looked skyward only to be screamed at by Wöbbe for lack of parade ground discipline.

Slowly the sound grew louder, a thrilling powerful note, symbolic to me of man's greatest achievement this century: to rise up on wings, like Ikarus. I risked a look upwards, moving my eyes only as the aeroplane droned overhead. Since Hans Grade at Lüneburg Heath I'd not seen anything so majestic and wonderful. Right overhead the parade square at Helmsburg, as if to mock our miserable, lowly existence, sailed the most beautiful aeroplane. I knew at once it was a Taube. It was even more bird-like than Grade's machine, bigger with an elegant curve and sweep to the wings and a long dove-like *fleche* of a tailplane. Sunlight diffused through the fabric covering so that the details of the ribs and bracing stood out like the veins in a butterfly wing. Its undercarriage seemed dainty, with thin, spoked wheels on a Blériot-type chassis. The letters *ETR* were painted in black beneath one wing and *ICH* beneath the other. It flew, skidding slightly sideways against a lovely sky of soft fair-weather cumulus with a heavenly blue between. It was the last epiphany.

'*Etrich Taube!*' said Kessler out of the corner of his mouth.

'Stand still!' screamed Wöbbe. '*Richt euch!*'

Gradually the aeroplane forged out of sight, disappearing over the turret roofs and the fortress walls. Wöbbe deigned to watch its passage. As its motor faded he turned his attention back to us.

'If any of you skivers have got the idea that you're going to escape your duty to the Crown by joining that lot, you can think again. That pathetic contraption will never replace the horse.'

But only a week later a dramatic poster had been tacked up in our billets, showing a sleek monoplane emblazoned with eagles attacking a

456

Serbian observation balloon, the aeroplane passenger aiming what looked like an elephant gun at the flaming target whose crew were falling to their deaths. Below it was a notice, signed by Uzelac, asking for volunteers to join the growing *Luftfahrtruppe*: young men, physically fit with a sense of adventure to crew the new aerial ships that would bring confusion to the enemy and scout far behind his lines. There had been a rush to submit applications but many were rejected at the first hurdle, being the office of the Wachtmeister, whose duty was to vet applicants and weed out the hopeless cases before they were sent for further aptitude tests and assessment. Kessler, Steiger, Hecht and others were successful, but Wöbbe was moved to call me to the guardroom where he to tore up my application in front of me without a word, except to dismiss me.

I burned with fury and frustration. Next day it must have shown in my sullen expression as the inspecting officer asked in an audible aside of Wöbbe. 'This one has a sour *störrisch* insolence about him. Does he have a problem?'

'Yes sir. He is a Lithuanian pigdog intellectual Jew, sir! But we'll beat that out of him.

'Very good, Wachtmeister. Carry on.'

I half-understand the psychology of being broken in spirit so that one becomes a dumb machine with an unthinking hair-trigger response to orders. But I don't agree with it. I will continue to think for myself.

I am placed in the charge of some of the older stablemen and ordered to look after the sickest horses, infected and lousy. It is laborious and foul duty, but I am able to offer my experience of working with animals learned from my father who was also a vet, and I am gratified by the good recovery some of the animals begin to make. After some weeks of this exhausting work, sleeping at the stables since I am kept apart from the other cadets from the lousy condition to which I have descended, Wöbbe appears and inspects the survivors. He seems actually impressed but informs me with spiteful satisfaction that they are now ready 'for the glue factory'. Not only have my efforts been entirely wasted but I have grown attached to these beasts. I protest that the horses are now fit and healthy, which gains me some latrine cleaning and additional guard duty. I am at my wits' end, sweating with controlled fury one moment then totally drained, depressed and half dead from exhaustion.

~-~

After a week, having done what I considered to be my duty under most odious circumstances, thinking that perhaps I'd proven my worth in the stables, I'd dared to present myself again before Wöbbe with a written request for transfer to the *Luftfahrtruppe*. That night I am ordered to the guardroom where Wöbbe says he has a test which I must perform to prove I have the natural balance required of an airman. I arrive full of suppressed excitement, immaculately turned out, buttons and boots polished to perfection. Nothing has been overlooked that might jeopardise my chances.

In an anteroom, I am ordered to strip to underwear and socks, watched unnervingly by Wöbbe who stares at me through slit eyes. Suddenly I am seized by the *Wise Monkeys* who pull me back over a heavy wooden rod, like a very thick broom handle, which has been jammed behind my knees. Despite my exertions they fold me down and force my forearms under the rod, lashing my wrists together at my knees with the insides of my elbows forced painfully under the 'broomstick' and my ankles tied together.

Compressed into this agonising bundle I can scarcely breathe but I am lifted so that the broomstick ends sit on the backs of two wooden chairs set parallel back-to-back and straddled by two of the NCOs. The broomstick is free to roll back-and-fore along the chair backs and this how I am 'tested'. Wöbbe removes his belt. I am whipped, kicked and punched between Wöbbe and the third NCO, Feldwebel Dzykowski, so that I spin sickeningly about a tight-radius with forward and backward somersaults. I am violently sick and stung by the pain of the blows to my unprotected body less than by the humiliation, the jeering laughs and comments of the perpetrators who add new weals to my scarred torso.

Eventually, tiring of the entertainment, one of the seated NCOs rises so that the chair tips over and I drop nearly a metre, into blackness.

I wake up in sick bay with a severely bruised shoulder blade, a vicious headache and a twisted back, not to mention much of the rest of my body being sorely bruised. Officially I've been involved in a fight with persons unknown, then tripped descending the guardroom steps. I gather I'm lucky not to be on a charge of being drunk and disorderly.

The message was clear. I did not have what it took to be an airman; an ignoble calling in Parsifal Wöbbe's personal view, and I would not be recommended for transfer under the aegis of the Wachtmeister's office in this regiment. Moreover, my persistence in this matter would probably result in further and ever more extreme punishments. I began to think that Wöbbe was determined to keep me here for his own sadistic pleasure. There will be no point in my reporting this abuse to a senior officer; the only witnesses are the guilty. My future looked bleak and I burned inside with murderous rage at the man and the situation.

~-~

Recovered, I am standing with Kessler and a few other cadets outside the billet in the early evening. We watch a DFW Mars biplane rumble overhead: grand and sedate, identifiable by its banana-like wings a huge engine and its four-wheeled chassis, accompanied by what I think might be an elegant Albatros BII trainer. Curvate black 'Maltese' crosses emblazon their wings with the red-white-red stripes of Austria at the tips. *Wunderschön!* I must escape this existence. I must! At least I've been able to shower, plaster myself with de-lousing powder and return to the barrack block.

Kessler jokes that if I *really* wanted to fly I should apply to an order of Franciscan monks and learn how to levitate. The philosopher/mathematician Liebnitz had testified that a certain Father Joseph could soar to the height of a church steeple and travel considerable horizontal distances. His physician had testified that, upon his death in 1663, the monk was seen to levitate above his bed, the doctor passing is hands beneath the dead or dying monk to demonstrate that there was no trickery. His feats were proclaimed miracles and Joseph was sainted by the Pope four years later. He says that with practice and determination I am sure to be able to soar over the garrison walls.

I'd read about an English Bishop, Geoffrey of Monmouth, who'd leaped from his church tower on wings similar to those I'd made myself as a boy. His leap of faith had made him the first accident victim of heavier-than-air flight since Ikarus. Anyway I am in no mood for Kessler's humour. He and a few other cadets had been accepted for pilot training. Other things crowded in on my mind and I was missing Krysia, and indeed Kat, more than I cared to admit.

Next day we are to perform a 'gun limber' exercise involving telegraph poles or something.

~-~

I have made my way to the hated guardroom, nursing my side. One of the monkey corporals, Dzykowski, is doing duty as corporal of the guard. *I have a fleeting memory of Dzykowski lacing Wöbbe into a corset in a corridor back of the guard room one evening when I'd nervously reported for 'sentry go'.*

A grotesque 'unicorned' minotaur; longjohns and a 'German issue' Pickelhaube! I'd carefully averted my eyes. He demands to know what I'm doing out of my billet and improperly dressed. I smell beer on his breath. I try to explain about Steiger. He snarls that if I don't want to be on another charge I should make myself scarce, *on the double.* Again I say that Steiger is in trouble.

'It's you who'll be in trouble in a minute!' he says. 'I am counting. You have ten seconds to be out of my sight. One…'

'But…'

'Two, three…'

It's hopeless. I turn and walk away.

'Move it!' he yells, but I ignore him. My ribs hurt too much to run.

I enter our billet and find Kessler's bunk. I explain the situation and we stealthily make our way to the hospital building.

~-~

In the discreet lighting of the ward Steiger looks very peaceful. I lightly place my fingers on his wrist. No pulse. I feel again at the throat. Nothing. I look at Kessler with a hopeless expression.

'What was it do you think?' he asks.

'I'm guessing his spleen was ruptured. He didn't last long after that bastard…'

I place my hand on his chest in a faint hope that there'll be a heartbeat and find his *Soldbuch* in the breast pocket. Slowly I withdraw it. My eyes meet Kessler's.

'I know what you're thinking,' he says after a moment.

'In this man's army you are whoever your paybook says you are,' I say quietly.

'Do you think it will work? We are… that is Steiger and me. We were leaving in the morning with Werner Hecht, Volker Häfflinger and Wick.'

'Well we don't have to take leave of the CO.'

Wöbbe might be a problem but he'd be sleeping one off and would be unlikely to be around to kiss the section goodbye when they embarked for the station. Not at 0600 hours, or whatever time they're due to leave camp. The only other difficulty might be the orderly when he comes back on duty. But he's not likely to make a fuss and draw attention to the fact that he hadn't been on duty the previous night.

The medical orderly's own replacement would arrive in the morning and as far as he would be concerned a certain cadet Dragunavicius has died in the night from complications following his injury suffered on the previous day's exercise as written in the *Krankenbuch*. If the first orderly wasn't there to hand over the shift, that was something for the two of them to account between themselves, I was sure. Fortune favours the brave, as some fool once said.

'You'll need his travel warrant.' says Kessler, locating it in the other breast pocket. By rail: *Helmsburg~Graz-Thalerhof.* Austria's second city.

I look down at the still body of Steiger. I think to myself 'Sorry, lad. But thanks for providing my escape route from hell. If I could find a way ...' But I leave it unsaid.

'What about your ribs?' asks Kessler.

'They hurt like a bitch, but nothing will stop me walking out of that gate tomorrow morning as Kadett Gustav Rolfus Steiger. Known also as *Rolf*, was he not?'

I take out my own paybook and slip it into Steiger's breast pocket.

'Ernst,' I speak softly. 'Say my name.'

'What?'

'Say my name. Get used to it.'

'Rolf,' he says. 'Rolf *Steiger.* Actually it suits you better than the other one!'

Rolf Steiger. The name has a whole new meaning for me. It means I have a future. And more than that, it will be in the *Luftfahrtruppe*.

'Goodbye, Rolfs Dragunavicius. *Requiescat in Pace.*'

~-~

Five of us left the camp next morning with our movement orders; stepping smartly and presenting travel warrants and pay books at the gate. Our faces were probably known to the bored corporal on duty but he may not have been able to match them to names. The guardroom door remained closed. Of Wöbbe, *murderer*, there was no sign. The relief medical orderly would not be on duty for another hour. I had at least an hour's head start and the railway station was only fifteen minutes march away. My nerves were at breaking point and the effect of the tablets I'd looted was beginning to wear off. As I waited at the station, my imagination filled with expectations of the arrival of the military police every second that passed. I reviewed all the precautions that I'd taken to swap identities, exchanging my personal effects for Steiger's in our respective lockers, all except my photographs of Krysia and Kat. And a small Steiff bear.

I racked my brains for whatever it was I might have overlooked that would find me out. So it was with enormous relief that the train arrived. Kessler took my kitbag and threw it onto the rack and I collapsed painfully onto the seat, anxiety gnawing my insides: until, with a hoot, slowly and maddeningly the train chuffed out.

~-~

Dramatic mountain scenery with lush Alpine meadows dominated our view that afternoon as the base car collected us from the Graz depot. The training field was dotted with white-winged biplanes, some with red fuselage and wing tip striping, all with black 'Maltese' crosses: Lohners, Albatrosse and Phönix-Brandenburgs, we learned.

On arrival we were provided with an escort to experience the sights, sounds and smells of the repair hangars, where damaged airframes were undergoing renovation; breathed the heady fume-filled atmosphere around freshly-doped wings: toured the wood working shops to see spars being glued and the engineering shop where millers and lathes rumbled, running from overhead belts to the smell of cutting oil. We looked in on the classrooms where we'd attend ground school, studying theory of flight, navigation and rudimentary meteorology; blackboards and chalk dust, redolent of school days. We familiarised ourselves with the messing facilities, the parade square and the shooting range. Here we would shoot 'clays' and also targets from a sort of dog cart, like a medieval tilting cart, rattling down a narrow-gauge rail track with a free-pivoted Parabellum and ancient ammunition that jammed in the breech.

On our second day we were roused at first light by an NCO banging on a suspended exhaust pipe. Following a hurried breakfast, we paraded on the airfield for the first time, in a state of controlled excitement. Two biplanes were already on their backs with no-one much hurt; one concussed cadet stretchered-off to sick bay, the other a 'walking casualty' holding a scarf to his bloody nose. A typical training day I was to discover.

I was at once awestruck and dismayed when, in critical close-up, I viewed my first real aeroplane in its natural state - apart that is from the little Grade monoplane of my starry-eyed youthful visit to the Lüneburg Heide.

They sat on the grass in long straight lines, like rows of arrow-winged mantids. With their cambered and swept *Doppeldecker* wings, a dozen or more struts and myriad piano wires and strainers they were at once elegant and clumsy: vivacious and draggy. Their slender fuselages were like rowing skiffs. Most had small pointed spinners on the propeller hubs and were equipped with upright six-cylinder engines; 120 hp. Austro-Daimlers whose water jackets and radiators towered overhead. The blades of the brass-bound propellers were like twisted paddles. Each mantis held its puny 'turnover skid' ahead of the open-spoked wheels, supported on a tubular truss: like a varnished wooden caterpillar held in the pincers of a monstrous winged insect. Still, I felt it was me that might soon be devoured.

We walked respectfully around these rakish paradoxes while our chief instructor delivered his analysis of the Lohner *Pfeilflieger* design. It was, he said, slow but safe. We would fly a variety of types here, but this was to be our primary trainer.

He paused, directing us to watch one approaching at some distance, descending dragonfly-like, shining prettily in the morning sunshine. It sank, hit firmly and shuddered, rearing up as if to paw the air in panic before the whole assembly dropped again. The wings collapsed accompanied by appropriate sound effects, spars splintering, wires twanging; paddles proceeding to flagellate themselves to matchwood, throwing a shower of debris on the turf. The creature finally subsided, ruptured radiator hissing like a steam boiler, its remaining wings pointing accusingly skyward.

There followed an awed silence that was broken by Kessler.

'So *that's* how it's done,' he said in mock wonder.

Shrill on the alpine air, the instructor's voice could be heard, colourfully expressing his opinion of his pupil's intelligence, parentage; of Lohners, cabbages and *Königen* and the world in general. We were startled, relieved and amused by this event, but it was salutary, a point underscored by the CFI.

'Expensive lesson number one: for your benefit entirely, *gentlemen*.'

A white-painted ambulance was pounding towards the wreckage, bells trilling.

'That is what happens when you let your speed fall too low on the descent. Near the ground that can be fatal. Observe, reflect, avoid.'

Next morning I carried out the pre-flight inspection of the machine I was to fly, another Lohner *'Arrow'*. Under the watchful eye of *Offizierstellvertreter* Greiner I itemised as secure all aspects of the craft, speaking tersely to hide the pain that I was suffering from my strapped-up ribs. On the walk-around we halted next to at a rounded, black-painted aluminium casting, topped by a horizontal anemometer apparatus that was bolted to an interplane strut. Its glass dial faced the cockpits.

'This,' said Greiner, 'Is a *Morrell* airspeed indicator. Pay attention to it, especially at low level and don't let the needle fall below that red line. When you're an old, experienced pilot, you'll be able to fly an aeroplane by reference to the 'feel' of the controls and the song of the wires. In the meantime remember…. *Death* is just Nature's way of reminding you to watch your airspeed!'

Came the old ritual of, 'Switch off, fuel on!' from somewhere ahead, repeated by the pilot.

Then, after the propeller had been turned about six times, 'Contact!'

The switches were flipped on and thrillingly the engine started with an eager roar.

My initial air experience was a mass of unforgettable sensations, noise, battering slipstream, motion in the 'lumpy' mountain air and vertiginous views of the earth. I forgot my pain as Greiner allowed me on that very occasion to handle the machine - at a safe height. *You have good hands, boy.'* Bracing words for a pupil on his first flight.

Takeoffs were mostly sedate, dreamlike affairs, head to wind, but could be challenging if the nose wasn't pointing straight into it. We eventually practiced 'out of wind' too, building up our handling skills. The aeroplane would veer on its soft undercarriage, swerving away left or right 'til the rudder decided to bite, the pupil dragging it sideways off the grass, teeth welded together, not taking a breath until he'd reached a height of 200 metres above the field - keeping his eye out for other trainees who might be bearing down on him, oblivious to each other's lumbering existence, though peering intently between the bulk of engine cylinders, radiators and other clutter. Near misses were inevitable. Learning to spot other aeroplanes was as important as spotting landmarks and navigating our way around the Austrian landscape.

Landing approaches were easy as long as you monitored your airspeed. 80 km/h. was safe. The Loh could be kept flying until it settled in a gentle wash of air, like gossamer, though the view ahead was obscured as the machine adopted its landing attitude. Slipping-in carefully with opposite rudder provided a better view until the last moment, but getting too slow with 'crossed controls' could be fatal, as the aeroplane was sluggish to react to corrective action. Before you knew it you'd be falling, not flying; on the verge of a deadly 'spin' from which it had demonstrated a slow recovery at a safer altitude.

464

But that same week after a few hour's instruction, I'd flown solo: a milestone in life for any pilot, which changes him - forever. I remember how the aeroplane climbed better with only myself on board. The sense of wonder and freedom, gradually becoming used to the ravishing Austrian scenery, so different from home; lush meadows with sleek grazing cattle, scenes which radiated peace as we prepared for war, framed arrestingly between ribbed biplane wings and wires. Enveloped in the sound of the engine and the tumbling funnel of air, wings flexing gently in the turbulence off the mountain slopes midst the rushing slipstream, the happy singing of the wires, I felt much as a captain might at the helm of a stately yacht, flying through the spindrift of the Great Southern Ocean. I imagined albatrosses sailing alongside, thundering down *The Roaring Forties*, instead of choughs above the Alpine passes, witnesses to my lone passage.

~-~

A first flight on a single-seater was another marker; a pretty little single-bay Fokker biplane with a balanced rudder but no fin. In its open-bottomed cowling the B.II had an 80 hp. *Oberursel* rotary which required as much attention as the flying itself. It had no compensating carburettor, instead, an ignition cut-out button on top of the stick. Greiner made sure I knew where the various air and petrol lever adjustments were set to enable the engine to run sweetly at different revolutions.

I sat at minimum idle, both air and fuel levers set lean as possible. His voice, torn by the slipstream, told me again to avoid getting it over-rich on take off, the daily aphorism shouted through a cupped hand over the buzzing rotary:

'Remember, *Junge*, speed is life but altitude is life *insurance!*'

As a fighter it was entirely mediocre, but stripped of its *Schwarzlose* machine gun it was a reasonable aerobatic trainer, despite the old wing-warping lateral control.

In spite of Greiner's careful tutoring the first take off was a heart-stopping affair. I realised immediately how sensitive was the rudder and performed a zig-zag take-off before I'd got things sorted, losing concentration on the mixture and suffering a 'rich cut' less than three hundred metres over a wood. Shuddering on the edge of a stall I stuffed the nose right down and turned off the petrol fine-adjustment lever, as the wires whistled; nervously counting off the seconds as advised before trying to re-start the wind-milling rotary. The trees tops loomed perilously but I was successful in re-starting it, though it stuttered a while as a plug had oiled.

But I got the hang of things and recalled my joy at throwing it around the sky, flirting with clouds, diving into my own head-on silhouette, a cloud-spectre ringed with rainbows. I blinked involuntarily as I slammed into the grey vapour - a shock-less impact, emerging in brilliant sunshine to a blue horizon of lovely Alps: shouting in wild ecstasy though I scarce could hear my voice above the rotary's thrum and the exhilarating rush of air! With my limited experience I thought it a great little aeroplane and for a moment I was riding on Flitzer's back, arms outstretched like raptor wings, Vilkie running by my side through cloudy chasms, darting though sunlit glades of moisture, as if their aerial spirits shared my joy - and perhaps they did.

Through the torn cloud, here and there, peep tiny fields and toy villages perched on verdant hillsides a thousand metres below. I dive low over the Mur, back towards Graz, looking down at the Cathedral. I buzz the battlements of the castle that dominates the city and once had been the seat of the Habsburgian Court. I fly over the Opera House then Prinz Eggerberg's Palace to the west of the city. My winged image flits over the walls of the beautiful Stift Rein Monastery, like the shadow of the Black Death - to frighten the Cistercians: then it's away again to open countryside and suddenly I'm in a mock-fight with Kessler flying a 100 hp. Fokker M-17, a bigger two-bay version of my B.II; whirling round and round, getting on each other's tails in a dizzying whirligig, jockeying for position tight-in, using the 'blip-switch'. It's a no-holds barred, undisciplined fight in which we try not to collide, pulling invisible triggers on non-existent guns, whooping our war cries and grinning across the invisible diameter of our turning circle.

For these moments I knew I'd been born! I'd found my high and beautiful retreat.

~-~

Soon, I tell the Whitehall inquisitors, I was posted to a reconnaissance *Flek* in Galicia: then it was back to the misery of a training school for a while as an instructor. Thankfully, after six months I was posted to a fighter *Flik:* single-seat Halberstadt Ds: then Brandenburg KDs in Albania, 1917. Later I'd been sent to evaluate new German equipment at Adlershof, then served a month with a Prussian Jagdstaffel; finally being posted to the Italian Front before war's end.

466

There I'd had my wish, serving with a unit operating the excellent Albatros fighter. I recalled the flight in my *Tagebuch* following a short leave, collecting these machines and later flying in formation to the Isonzo or Piave front lines. I'd lain on my bunk and written my impressions of the delivery flight.

Memories… Flecks of light. I must had been in a reflective mood, viewing things through a hazed memory of mist and cloud in the mountains; that 'particulate infusoria' of my reverie, recounted for Frankland.

'…floating in a shaft of sunlight, twinkling like a shoal of little fish.'

~-~

They were floating in a shaft of sunlight, twinkling like a shoal of little fish, invading the cold desert of the mind. A strange diaspora. A four-dimensional menagerie in unstructured choreography: three hundred metres below our formation and closing, the little armada had swum into focus.

Brandenburg variations! KD Star-Strutters, no two exactly alike. At range the mind fills-in details that the eye cannot yet detect. Habsburgian anomalies. Anachronistic, obsolete at birth, three…no five in loose cavalry formation, neither echelon nor vic, rising and shining in sunlight against the Alpine snows, their Austro-Daimlers coping valiantly with the altitude.

The distance closes revealing the deep-bellied baby they are nursemaiding; a UFAG C1 reconnaissance machine with a tall exhaust stack, like a winged rhinoceros: its half-seen observer huddled below the gun ring of his Parabellum, swaddled to the gills in leather and fur.

We waggle our wings in salute, conscious of the impact our new high-flying D.llls with their high-compression engines will have on the Brandenburgs which many of us ex-Flik 55j pilots, including me, flew until recently. We receive a half-hearted wing-wag from a couple of Star-Strutters as our formations draw apart. The UFAG gunner remains immobile; too cold I suppose to bother with a gesture.

Brothers-in-arms, each of us bound to our destinies. We flew southwards into a smoking landscape of mud, scrub, trenches, dead men and horses.

I reflected, particularly for the benefit of Rose and Browne, upon the prosaic footnote to the diary entry I'd afterwards made in the *Jasta* log, in my capacity of acting adjutant. It contained the official line, for examination purposes of course, to ensure that no Leftist leanings, politically dangerous ideology or defeatist attitudes were expressed in the diary of a fighting unit. Perhaps I did then still believe, naively, in some of the received information passed down from the official channels of the *Oberkommando des Heeres*, but precious little was accepted without a sneer of derision, or at least some cynical comment from the aircrews.

We passed over a flock of Brandenburg D.1s in the mountains. There could be no greater contrast between them and the sleek new Albatros D.III we now fly, such is the pace of technology in war. With such equipment as we now have, Germany and the Austro-Hungarian alliance must prevail.

The (February) revolution in Russia is indicative of the dissention within the aggressor's ranks, that and the common people's revolt against their own government. Soon we may see this in France and Italy, where protests against the war are reportedly on the increase. Britain may soon be isolated and sue for peace.

For good measure, recalling my springtime visit to Berlin in 1917 I wrote: A greater Austro-German alliance will emerge, united against oppression and the Red Menace from the east, which may yet be staunched by calmer voices within the opposition. As long as the Home Front holds fast, ignoring words of defeatism, our gallant womenfolk will sustain hope, keep the fires burning until their husbands, brothers and sons return triumphant, in final and glorious victory.

That should do for the Brass. Drafted for those braided-pheasants, full of spin and hubris. The truth was that the Dual Monarchy was collapsing and it was Germany that held it up. It would break asunder if Russia rallied and the Allied onslaught began in earnest.

468

We enter into an Italian amphitheatre. The lower strata of cloud lies like smooth, grey stones in a rock pool over which swim the gladiatorial combatants, silver minnows above the smoke on the Isonzo River Front.

In Whitehall I am relating these flying experiences at the express wish of my inquisitors.

This is the twelfth battle on the Isonzo and this time we have the advantage of German divisions to stiffen our lines, protecting the soft belly of the Dual Monarchy. Our side fields 35 divisions facing 41 on the Italian side. But our forces, commanded by General Arz von Straussberg, drive through under a devastating barrage of heavy artillery at the weakest point in the lines. Our troops are breaking through concealed by smoke shells. Gas is released and *Flammenwerfer* used to deadly effect.

Above the battle I note Italian fighters and light bombers descending to attack our advancing troops. I signal for a dive and note Uffz. Oskar Schertzer is with me; I see his gentle motion in the corner of my right eye, the round, white-painted spinner of his Albatros's propeller whirling six metres from my tailplane. Hermann Vogel is trailing. As we dive the details sharpen. Before me appears a shark: an obsolete Roland two-seater, one of the supporting German *Schlacht* machines. Its engine cowling of a sudden bursts upwards, haemorrhaging thick, dark smoke, the colour of blood pumping deep under water. The *Haifisch* falls away, mortally wounded, and I see his killer: light flashes briefly on the straight, thin wings of an Italian SPAD as he turns to view his falling victim.

My heart beats furiously. The SPAD has vanished against the dappled fracto-cumulus, the ramparts fissured by impenetrable clefts; purple darkness on sun-bright cliffs of cloud. The cloud bases descend to darker shades of ochre, merging with the tarry smoke of the barrage. To seek him there would blind me to the other dangers.

High relative motion – I jerk my head up quickly in time to see a gaggle of Hanriots against high, bright cumulus, chasing a black-tailed Albatros V-strutter from one of the German Jastas trying to out-dive its pursuers. I am turning and pulling when I see the Albatros's right lower wing shudder and twist violently away in a shower of fragments and flailing wire. The D.III rolls rapidly, half-throwing the pilot from the cockpit before entering an ever-steepening dive, the upper plane shuddering and flapping. It folds and falls, a stricken gamebird, dropping through the lower depths to drifting yellow gas clouds where guns flash and massive explosions pulverise the ground, churning the brown river of floating bodies like a vision of hell. *Ein Massengrab.*

Schertzer and Vogel are covering. I am hard into the three Hanriots, using the speed of my dive to bring the nose steeply up and the guns to bear on the leading fighter.

Spandaus cocked, I train the bead two aeroplane lengths ahead of the leader, who is himself turning towards our *Kette*, followed closely by his wingmen. This will be three on three. The distance rapidly closes and the deflection angle narrows. My breathing is rapid under my scarf. I modify my attack, waiting until the last second to open fire on the manoeuvrable Italian fighter whose Vickers gun is already winking, his angle of bank increasing. My Albatros vibrates as the Spandaus open up and in the fraction of a second before I slam the stick hard over left, the propeller of the leading Hanriot disintegrates and the whole rotary engine leaps bodily out of the airframe: the tangled mass of the forward fuselage and overstressed, collapsing wing structure tearing past me with a sound like an express locomotive. I brace against the 'g' as I haul back on the stick, and rudder hard into the tight turning Hanriot pair, Spandaus hammering like my heart.

A fighter appears rolling into stark planform, frighteningly close in a vertical turn. The pilot's eyes look into mine. I pull furiously, the 'g' rising, feel the impact as my wheels graze his top wing. I am startled to see a ragged line of bullet holes in my own upper wing with no idea who is shooting. Coolant is escaping from my wing radiator, a trail of steam pouring past the cockpit – I side-slip to avoid a scalding and crane my head to try to spot my attacker. Vogel is gone but the steadfast Schertzer is still covering my tail. I see Vogel lower down with a SPAD on his tail, and with a quick glance around, roll into a diving pursuit. Oskar is sticking like glue. A Pomilio two-seater suddenly appears flying in a series of swoops with its pilot dead at the controls, the gunner grimly hanging on while trying, vainly, to reach past him to the stick. The third Hanriot is far off, flying south trailing smoke. Probably hit by Schertzer. Other aircraft are engaged in individual fights at different levels.

I close rapidly on the SPAD who suddenly turns away from Vogel, and dives vertically for the ground swathed in drifting smoke and misty stratus five hundred metres below. I decide not to chase it and pull up alongside Vogel who gives me a wave. He looks relieved and smiles wanly beneath his goggles. Flak is bursting nearby. Grimly I reflect that this is a

470

large aerial engagement for the Italian Front, matching the savagery below.

For an instant right in front I see a massive shell at the top of its ballistic curve. It seems to hover on my level for a moment before falling away to explode in the depths among the struggling bodies advancing, clashing or retreating through curtains of smoke, gas and dust. I realise with horror that we've been fighting our aerial battle within of the arc of shellfire from the heavy Austrian guns brought up to bombard the Italian artillery positions.

A strip of fabric is flapping from my top wing and my engine smells hot. Steam is still escaping. I point to the stream of vapour and indicate that I'm turning for home. Schertzer and Vogel take up positions on each side and slightly back, a close vic. This is not the best formation I consider for flexibility in defence, since both pilots are looking inwards at the leader. I signal them to open out, widening the formation which enables them to relax and scan more of the sky. Not perfect, but it will have to do.

Our *Kette* has proved again, if it was necessary to do so, that flown very aggressively the Albatros would manoeuvre with most of the available enemy machines, except perhaps for the latest Sopwiths and Hanriots, height and speed being my best friends always. The fate of the stricken Albatros we'd just witnessed however, makes for an unnaturally cautious approach to air-fighting. This does not sit well with the German *Fliegers*: an intrinsic weakness in the design of the vee-strutter - partly overcome by field modification in the German *Fliegertruppe* though not in *Blacktail's* case evidently. I reflect though, in *Luftfahrtruppe* service, the Austrian-built machines are much superior.

But this is a detail. The battle went well. The Italian line is broken. They lose 300,000 casualties, killed or captured and will take four days for their survivors to retreat across the river.

I make it back with a near-seized engine. With radiator replaced it will fight another day.

Offizierstellvertreter Rolf Steiger in an Albatros D.II

Chapter 33.

Berlin, Swinemunde and the VI Reserve Armeekorps

I have related that combat as one fight that stands in my memory. Frankland has asked me about my aerial fighting experience and I had chosen this, almost my last combat in Austria. It provided a flavour of what it was like when numerous combatants shared briefly the same few cubic kilometres of sky. His interest seems more professional than germane to the line of earlier questioning.

But experienced though we were, I tell him, however good our equipment was becoming technically, it was all for nothing. In 1918 came the decisive battle of Vittoria (later *Vittoria Veneto*) on the Piave River; the Italians, backed by the Allies, eventually pushed through and the overstretched Austrian lines collapsed and a continuous fighting retreat saw the Austro-Hungarians thrust deeply back. The Tyrol was occupied including the capital, Innsbruck. That was when war ended, November 3rd 1918, one week before the Armistice was signed in the West. The Fliks were ordered to bases well within Austrian territory.

No-one seemed to know what to do when we arrived. It seemed these were the last days of their lives. In certain regiments, discipline still obtained and daily orders were carried out punctiliously and in the finest tradition of the Austrian Army. But elsewhere, including in my Flik, people hung about or drifted away and standards of discipline fell sharply along with morale.

There were soldiers' councils in Austria too, the Bolshevist influence had spread across the Carpathians via pamphlets like a plague on the wind. Home-grown propaganda leaflets were everywhere, blowing in the streets. Town council meetings were loud and often violent. People were frustrated and hungry. Many were destitute because of the war. The mood of the returning troops, demoralised and suffering, fuelled the feelings of anger and futility. I had a gnawing ache in my heart to return to Lithuania as fast as possible. I felt no loyalty to the teetering Austrian crown, only to my comrades in arms who were already talking about picking up what might be left of their civilian lives. Meanwhile the Empire was fissuring along the old fault lines. There seemed no future whatsoever in the military unless it was the old guard versus new socialism, meaning that civil war was on the horizon. In any event we were all heartily sick of it as the year wound down to a Christmas celebrated at best with mixed emotions and precious little fare.

Duty was a dusty, jaded concept. We felt a sense of betrayal and loss and more than most I felt I was the outsider with no place here. I thought that were I to fade out of sight I'd not be missed, and once that was decided the sooner I could stitch an escape plan together the better.

At Aspern aerodrome orders were to render the aircraft un-flyable by draining the petrol tanks, removing spark plugs and even propellers. These actions were carried out at best half-heartedly. There had been an immediate ban on the export of war materials from Austria, especially aeroplanes - soon to be ratified by the St. Germain Treaty. But there were rumours of fighter aircraft already being flown out to continuing war fronts in the battles for emergent independent nationhood to staunch the flow of Bolshevism. I was sure machines such as our powerful and beloved 253-series Albatros types and the later Phönixes would be in demand. These were already being flown in ones and twos into the old Hungarian part of Empire where fighting between various factions raged; the old guard, the Reds and some others in between.

Quite suddenly, the belated news that under the terms of the Austrian-Italian Armistice, all German troops were to be expelled from Austrian territory *within fifteen days* or face internment arrived with a regiment of Italian troops, stopping and searching anyone in the street who appeared to be of military age. My papers identified me as 'Steiger' and 100% German, so I decided to make myself scarce.

Without much of a plan other than to get the hell out, one bitter evening in early February 1919, under cover of darkness, I stealthily collected petrol from the tanks of parked or partly dismantled aeroplanes whose fuel hadn't already been siphoned or stolen. Dodging the bored Italian guards, who mostly hung around the braziers trying to stay warm, I made ten wearying trips and by midnight I'd brim-filled the tank of the most airworthy-looking Albatros on the field. I had no idea what the situation was in Lithuania so decided to make for Germany, for Berlin, which I figured would be big enough to lose myself in and take it from there. Early next morning, grabbing a few maps and some personal effects I strode purposefully to the machine in flying kit. No one tried to stop me. I'd bribed a mechanic to help me start the D.III's Austro-Daimler and made a *Kavalierstart* before the guards had woken up, heading north above misty Alpine passes, landing at Munich where I obtained fuel and got away again before anyone thought to impound the machine or arrest me. I made a nerve-racking flight across southern Germany where I thought I saw Allied fighters on two or three occasions but managed to outdistance them. After two hours, low on fuel, on a grey, blustery afternoon I'd gratefully thumped it down on the grass of Staaken aerodrome.

I abandoned the D.III near two gigantic Zeppelin sheds, close to some battered and forlorn Fokkers and Hannover C-Types. Rain was falling and I slipped away in the evening light before anyone could ask awkward questions. I ate the remains of a hunting sausage as I walked, then managed to hitch a ride as far as Charlottenburg. Berlin seemed to be in revolt with grim-faced people either queuing for non-existent bread or rioting, many with firearms. It seemed easier to get yourself killed here than at the fronts I thought, ducking for cover from sporadic machine gun or rifle fire at the end of a wide boulevard. Spartakists wearing odds and ends of military uniforms tore about in open cars or wagons with red flags and machine guns. Revolutionary banners proclaiming *Victory for German Workers and Soldiers!* and *'Arm-in-Arm with our Red Brothers we will Overcome!'* festooned street lamps and hung from windows of patrician houses along with posters of Marx, Lenin and Rosa Luxembourg. Another asking *'Who has the Prettiest Legs in Berlin?'* draped incongruously above a partly-wrecked hosiers. Smashed shop fronts spoke of looting but things had been so bad on the Home Front that pickings must have been pretty meagre. A large poster that screamed *Berlin, Your Dancing Partner is Death!* bore a macabre grinning skeleton waltzing with an expensively-attired young woman, the message drawing on the classical literary theme of *Der Tod und das Mädchen,* (Death and the Maiden) was clear as was the phrase, crudely daubed on street corners, *ANARCHIE IST ORDNUNG!*

'He who possesses Berlin controls Europe,' Karl Marx had written. God help Europe then, I thought.

Several streets away from the present trouble I joined a soup queue while I thought about what to do. Hansoms clattered about with students handing out pamphlets. Motorcycles tore through the streets with riflemen on the pillions. Two blocks away street fighting continued. A troop of steel-helmeted cavalry clattered down the wet street. I watched from a doorway as mounted policemen supported by Freikorps with rifles and cavalry sabres charged a crowd, ending with several dead and injured among the strikers and rioters, but a sniper brought down a horse and the mounted police took off at speed. There was an attempt to contain a crowd by some militia but tempers were running high and fights broke out without warning like sparks in dry tinder. I moved on, skirting a road block of furniture and a burned-out lorry. A camouflaged armoured car controlled a road junction. Around the next corner I was forced to shield my head and run from a fusillade of pebbles. A flag-bedecked barricade manned by hard-faced youths wearing steel helmets a size too big, armed with lethal catapults, had forced my retreat. Why, I asked myself, had I picked Berlin?

But I had a clear idea by then where I was heading. My destination was a fine house on a leafy boulevard on the far side of the Spree, where I'd spent a week or more enjoying the sights of a sunnier city. That was my goal if I made it through the zone of class warfare.

~-~

Almost two years previously I'd been detailed to escort Leutnant Kessler: from Brno via Dresden to Berlin. I'd volunteered to accompany him on his rail journey. Ernst was on crutches after he'd suffered an ankle injury falling off a wing.

We'd both been due leave simultaneously, anyway I had nowhere else to go - except to the *Snapdragon*: Graf's *Iron Aunt,* Charlotte von Rosen's Vienna mansion. But she had probably been informed of my reported death. I could imagine the vapours if she discovered I was alive having fraudulently served for two years in the assumed identity of a deceased comrade.

The mood among Berliners had been very different then, quietly confident of eventual victory under their Kaiser. The Spring Offensive was underway with the Battle of Arras and the fast new Albatros fighters with their twin forward-firing machine guns were cleaving outstanding victories through the enemy scout patrols along the Western Front: a 'Bloody April' for the RFC.

Kessler had telephoned from a railway station *en route* and his uncle had a car waiting for us at Berlin Central. We'd hoped to spend ten days there at least, in the Spring of 1917.

Young women as well as children commonly collected pictures, *Sanke Karten* of Boelcke, Almenröder, Voss and Richthofen. Kessler had printed a few dozen photographs of himself in uniform in heroic pose and it didn't take long for us to put plan 'A' into operation.

Next morning, after breakfast on fine china with real coffee, we wheeled cheerily along in the balmy weather: the handsome, wounded hero flier in bath chair and his faithful comrade, mingling with the

Sunday throng at the park like two gay boulevardiers. Pretty girls, amusing and un-chaperoned, fluttered down lakeside, begging autographed pictures with the Kessler's telephone number on the back.

'War is art,' said Kessler the previous evening, paraphrasing Clausewitz. 'It makes the very highest demands upon the individual character. New situations provide a challenge and opportunity; their variety is limitless. Their influences must be quickly assessed and evaluated to achieve the desired end. The fortunes of war may dictate the tactics in the field but clear thinking and foresight can turn a bad situation to advantage. An officer is, in all disciplines, a leader and educator. So watch and learn, Rolf.'

Responses numbered close to what we'd optimistically anticipated considering that military uniforms were to be seen everywhere and the senior types had more spending money. Evenings were spent at restaurant, *Bierkeller* and dancehall, where Ernst's war-wound was milked shamelessly. Introductions and assignations were effected, though formal requests to well-born young ladies were unforthcoming despite Ernst's alleged status and connections and his distributing visiting cards like confetti. Perhaps Ernst's notoriety in Berlin society had not been forgotten.

'I've been a bad boy, Rolf,' he grinned. 'That's why I joined up in Austria. I was almost penniless by then and no regiment in Germany would have me!'

~-~

On the third morning a haggard Ernst had opened his door to my knock, tightly entwined with a *fille de joie*. From a nearby couch a blonde pouted in her layered underwear. Another sprawled in voluptuous splendour on a magnificently wrecked feather bed. Wine glasses, plates and the remains of a hock of ham littered the room. Champagne bottles lay on the carpet like the dead men they represented.

'Rolf, come in. Join us!' he enthused. 'This is Francoise, and over there, that's Irma. On the bed and feeling no pain is Annelise. Francoise is from Paris, trapped here for the duration! I think she is a spy, come to test the stamina of innocent young pilots on leave!'

I bowed slightly, suppressed a heel-click and said I was enchanted. I'd escorted my own date home the previous evening, receiving a chaste kiss on the cheek and no promises. Perhaps I was giving out signals that my thoughts had been elsewhere. Francoise reached around Kessler's neck, took my hand and smiled sweetly.

'Bonjour, cherie! Come and have a *leettle* drink.' she said. 'Or maybe, a *beeg* one!' Her eyelids drooped suggestively, or perhaps she was just sleepy. She seemed to have lost the knack of standing unaided and Kessler, who was trying not to put weight on his injured ankle, waved me in, placed her in a chair and drew me to the window.

'War is hell, *nicht wahr*!' he grinned. 'Please take your pick. Two if you want.'

'I didn't know the *Folies* was in town,' I smiled. 'But it's rather early in the day, I think.'

'C'mon. Help me out here, Rolf. This was *our* plan. I've been going all night and they're still up for more. My prayers to *Priapus* are falling on deaf ears.'

'Come again?'

Ernst gave me a wry, slightly pitying look.

'Well that's just it, isn't it! That's the problem right there......'

'Oh,' I said lamely.

The one on the bed began snoring loudly. Irma lit a cigarette. I explained that I'd just received orders to make my way to Vienna, Fischamend Aerodrome. Immediate. Sorry.

There was a knock at the door and I opened it for the cadaverous butler, Haglund, to inform master Ernst that two young ladies had called and were waiting for him downstairs. Should he send them up?

'Dammit, Rolf,' he'd murmured. 'Never mind the ankle. If this keeps up I'll have to return to the Front just to give my manhood a rest.'

~-~

Count Harry Kessler's Berlin residence was an impressive, welcoming mansion set back from the street where mature trees and elegant street lamps alternated. I couldn't remember the address but I was sure I could find it again. I just hoped it was still occupied and that he would remember me as he'd been busy with matters of state on the previous occasion and we'd not seen much of him then.

Two hours later, with the sun firmly set, having avoided further skirmishes I rang the bell of the Kessler house. Haglund answered the door, an ancient horse pistol stuffed in his cummerbund. He recognised me at once. I asked for the Count but was informed that, regrettably, his Excellency was not at home. However, to my relief I was invited in and he limped ahead of me to a large downstairs room with heavily draped windows and a warm fire. A bed had been made up and a figure was propped upon the pillows. Both feet thickly bandaged, hollow-eyed but still the old insolent smile tugging at the corners of the mouth, half-reclining in the Count's silken bed jacket; Ernst Kessler, and almost alive by the look.

'Rolf Steiger, *gottverdammt*! How did you get here?' he asked weakly.

'My God, Ernst. It's me that should be asking *you* that!'

~-~

I continued my story in Whitehall.

Veterans, the great majority, came out of the Great War sick of the slaughter and sick of the smell, the waste, obdurate commanders and the brutality of the NCOs. Weary and disillusioned, cynical, angry with a post-war society that thought it could carry on as normal and ignore the wounds or thought it could. Others would carry on with the war on the streets, destroying the old institutions before thinking through what they would erect in its place. Others had a very clear idea and it would not include the bourgeoisie or the ruling élite.

Most didn't want to talk about the war. The few that did hadn't *really* been there or basked in the glory of dead heroes, from whom they stole their bravery. There were exceptions who'd had a 'good war' of course and after a period of reflection some of these would launch into print for a younger generation, eager for tales of glory. They stimulated the insatiable imaginations of young romantics, oft combined with post-bellum propaganda: political demagogueries for socio-economic advance and the elevation of the Germanic race.

But who with a mind who'd seen them, the street theatre of the grotesque; the deaf-blind and armless man, placard round his neck: *Loyal Servant of Kaiser and Fatherland*, helmet inverted between his knees would speak again of glory? A midget too, with half a jaw, rump set upon wooden wheels for want of legs, licking his earlobe with blue-bulging tongue and swallowing his glass eye for *Pfennige* to the sound of a churring barrel organ. The man with the thousand metre stare who stands trembling beside them, waiting to escort his comrades to their shelter from the winter's night. Would they praise sacrifice *pro patria*? Still there were those who would force political agendas by means undemocratic, who'd find a rich recruitment amongst the angry veterans, the vengeful and among the fresh flowering fields of willing youth, their hearts beating to a distant and deceitful drum.

We joined the queue at the Königsplatz to drive a symbolic nail into the wooden effigy of General Oberst Paul von Hindenburg, Chief of the General Staff and future statesman, tossing our *Pfennige* into the pail for the soldiers' charity. It was a magnanimous gesture for the officer class remained loyal and Hindenburg was well regarded. He negotiated hard to get our boys back from the scattered fronts, returning undefeated in spirit with their heads held high for the most part. And so did Count Harry Kessler. But there was anger aplenty and a feeling of betrayal in Germany that winter of 1918.

And there were addicts like Kessler and me. No permanent home to go to, knew only how to fight and fly, hooked on both. It was the flying really, always was since that first hour aloft. The fighting took on a very personal edge after Brest-Litovsk for Ernst, but it was not for glory that I yearned for my Baltic land.

Kessler's capture and rough handling was followed by prison camp where he witnessed cruel indifference to typhus and starvation, endured some creative brutality and half-hearted attempts at political indoctrination. Escalation to random murder of the officer class by the Red Guards was followed by his unexpected release. To his own devices. Before it was anywhere *near* officially over on the other fronts.

For me I'd mis-appropriated the property of his Apostolic and Very Imperial Majesty, screw him: just took an aeroplane and flew to Berlin. For Ernst it had been a long shuffle, coiling south, spat upon, jostled, beaten, starving in a dead man's boots. It was confusing and disorienting to say the least, wandering back to a Germany that was hostile and unrecognisable, sundered by civil unrest in which the Spartakists seemed to be gaining the high ground and any man in uniform might be beaten insensible in an alley.

Those who believed they'd been stabbed in the back and forced into a humiliating surrender formed disciplined corps and fought pitched street battles while we recuperated at Uncle Harry's and watched from the wings. Through Ernst, Count Kessler in absentia had kindly extended his hospitality once more, including excellent cognac, cigars and hot baths. A lucky break for me in Berlin, given my lack of papers and no means of support.

~-~

By April, Ernst considered, perhaps unwisely, that he had made a sufficient recovery to consider what to do next. Berlin was still in turmoil, going Bolshevist was the common view. But almost as soon as he could walk he was keen to get back to flying. We'd already jotted down details from the new recruiting posters which abounded, exhorting ex-officers, NCOs, and men from the ranks of the disenchanted to join the 100,000 strong Border Defence Force: defend the Fatherland and our fellow Germans in the Baltic States against the Red Horde. News reports of gratuitous killing, torture and rape were rife and I was by now determined to return home, impelled by a desperate anxiety for which there was no cure.

We heard rumours that the *Inter-Allied Military Control Commission* was planning systematically to destroy 'our' aircraft. This was on top of all other strident demands for punitive reparations that were surfacing among the victorious powers. Astonishingly, Siemens-Schuckert fighters have been exempted, part of an allowable *Luftpolizei* arm, while most other types were being confiscated as reparations or piled high for burning. *Staffels* of SSW D. IVs, the latest variant of these fast climbing interceptors, had remained in production at Siemenstaadt, Berlin and were now said to be arriving on station in Lithuania with the Border Defence Volunteer Force!

Kessler was really excited by this news and we immediately applied to join the *Freiwilligen Grenzschutz Ost: XVII Armeekorps,* which was based in the Baltic, reporting to their Friedrichstrasse recruiting office. As veteran war pilots we expected to be welcomed with open arms. But to our bitter disappointment we were turned down. On medical grounds, C.3 at best: Ernst as he'd still not fully recovered from his Russian internment and long march: and me due to recurrent deafness in my left ear, following my injury at Conrad von Hippel and later exposure to loud aero-engines without ear protection. There was the possibility of a damaged eardrum.

Protests also fell on deaf ears. With the forced contraction of the Army and Navy there were more than enough pilots volunteering, they said. If we wanted to join the ranks of the foot soldiers we were welcome to apply. But we weren't hard enough or fit enough for the *Stosstruppen,* the shock troops; *never would be* was the parting shot.

Fuming and downhearted, we left to consider what we should do next. Ernst heard on the grapevine that money could be made ferrying aircraft to neutrals, the Netherlands in particular. Tony Fokker was paying well for D.VIIs to be flown across the Dutch border before they could be surrendered to the Military Control Commission. We'd heard the decree, *'In Erste alles Fokker D.VII Apparate'* issued as part of the reparations: for confiscation by the Entente, such was the esteem in which that excellent fighter was held.

But Staaken aerodrome was a depressing scene. We'd parked Count Harry's car in *Gaswerk-Strasse* and followed the smoke trail to the wire. The Allies had already confiscated many of the more advanced German aircraft which remained under guard. It was unclear if there was an actual ban on flying *per se* since small air taxi services were starting up elsewhere in Germany using converted C-Type machines, or so we'd heard, with one or two passenger seats hastily fitted; typically Rumplers, Hannovers and LVGs. But dozens of single seaters, the Albatros I'd stolen among them, had been pushed together in heaps here and prematurely burned. Their shrivelled and blackened carcases still smouldered. The newspapers were full of French demands in particular for massive reparations for her war losses. The nearby Spandau machine gun factory and arsenal had been occupied and weapons were leaving by the wagon load. I wondered what was in store for a pariah, vanquished Germany with her ceded territories, sandwiched between emergent states with the occupation of the Ruhr; the Polish Corridor to the sea and the new de-militarised zones forming their cordon sanitaire. Would the new Weimar Democratic Assembly be able to negotiate solutions to overwhelming international and domestic pressures?

Personal survival drove us to 'casual enquires' about flying jobs, specifically ferry-flying. But we'd received only blank looks, or worse, angry invective at Staaken, departing none the wiser.

But in the shadowy depths of the *Zeppelin Werfthalle*, we glimpsed the *Monstrum*, as Ernst exclaimed: the part-constructed, all-metal Staaken E4/20 prototype. Four big Maybach Zeppelin engines were sitting in wooden crates awaiting installation on the thick, cantilever wing and the hangar rang to the sound of tools as workmen laboured on the elevated platforms. A magnificent yet forlorn behemoth, everyone said that this airliner was the shape of things to come. But the Sword of Damocles hung over the world's most technologically advanced aeroplane. The cutting torch was waiting and the uncertainty was palpable. For the moment work continued, but its probable fate seemed to us to be an act of premeditated spite.

Asking around Berlin, meanwhile we'd heard rumours of Fokkers, in particular, being smuggled out by barge, railway flatcar, on backs of lorries - fuselages, engines and spares hidden in horse-drawn hay carts moving undercover of night before the roving soldiers of the military commission discovered their whereabouts. Kessler said he knew where to find people in the know, but secret meetings in cheap hotel rooms and upstairs ante-rooms yielded nothing except dubious leads for which shady characters demanded outrageous advance commissions. It was exhausting and dangerous traipsing around the shooting gallery of Berlin in worn civvies, caps pulled over our eyes, blending inconspicuously with activists and idlers. Ernst was remorseless but still looked ill, as did many of the general population; thin, tired, grey of face and miserable. Soldiers' and Workers' Councils still met, mostly noisily, and monopolised the *Bierhallen*.

There was no theoretical shortage of pilots to fly the remaining machines across the border, but many airframes had been vandalised or were incomplete it was safer to transport them by surface than to make ferry-flights. Assuming that petrol was available. Remaining aircraft were likely to be widely distributed. Travel was expensive and difficult. Surveys of the condition of reported fighters were rushed and unreliable given the circumstances with 'surveyors' liable to arrest, interested only in collecting their fees and disappearing ahead of the Military Control Commission.

At one seedy *Händler* we left suitable pseudonyms and a contact address of a hotel a ten-minute tram ride from the Kessler residence and set about trying to find other sources of flying work. Since air traffic movements had been banned for the present, except in special circumstances, this was proving fruitless.

However, early in May 1919 we had a message to call a number. The voice at the other end said that if we were keen to deliver some 'pigeons' to be at a *Bierkeller* address for a rendezvous that evening. It turned out to be a popular *Hofbräuhaus* and there was a political party rally going on. It was hard to hear for the noise and bustle, but a serious, thin-faced man informed us that three Fokker D.VIIs were sitting in an open-ended barn on a small farm near Magdeburg, about 100 kilometres west of Berlin. Occupying troops had been in the area poking about, looking into farm buildings but had missed these, secreted we guessed by some stalwarts for the day near at hand when the German Eagle-Phönix would rise again and drive out the occupiers. It was probably only a matter of time before they were discovered and either destroyed or confiscated. They were apparently still armed, with fuel in their tanks. However it would be considered prudent to drain the system and add fresh petrol in case of contamination.

We were required to pay a 'bond' of one hundred marks per aircraft against which we were provided with enough to buy sufficient black market petrol for two of the D.VIIs. The third aeroplane would be collected by another pilot. Arrangements were made to collect some carboys of water and glycol, assuming the radiators had been drained over winter. It was up to us to establish whether the fighters were airworthy, that no-one had stolen the wheels, hack-sawn through the longerons or put sand in the fuel tanks: that the retaining bolts were still in the wing strut fittings, etc. It was a shady deal. Nobody asked who the aircraft 'belonged to'. All military aircraft were forfeit in any case. The big idea was to fly out 'before sparrows' in the morning and make for the Dutch border at medium level, maximum cruising speed, hoping we wouldn't be intercepted by a 'police patrol' of fast SE5s or the new Sopwith Snipes, squadrons of which were distributed across many ex-Imperial air bases.

From Magdeburg, say to Eindhoven, would be about two hours flying, probably at maximum range for a D.VII, but it would get us across the Dutch border on a single tank of fuel. We'd have the rising sun behind us so we'd be poor target for anything coming head-on and it would be a quick fighter that would catch us from behind. We said we'd do it, providing someone would be at Eindhoven to refuel us if we had to go on to Rotterdam or wherever Tony Fokker wanted them delivered. We'd heard there was a squadron of RAF Snipe fighters based at Beckendorf or Butzweilerhof and we wanted to keep well to the north of Cologne to steer clear of those. We asked about the other pilot, since it made more sense to go in a *Kette* of three rather than a *Rotte*, to provide a better lookout while the formation leader navigated. Besides if one or two aircraft were spotted taking off, an investigation of the field would reveal the third Fokker.

Payment would be on delivery, allegedly seventy five US dollars per machine based on their condition when delivered. Transport to Magdeburg would be by a small building contractor's lorry, driver provided, to carry the fuel and the other pilot. Two would have to travel in the back. We would be disguised as workmen and have travel papers and evidence of the job we were travelling to or from should we be stopped and searched. The fuel would have to be explained somehow and with a flourishing black market a good explanation would be necessary. In any event we had to move fast.

~-~

Kessler and I pitched up at Magdeburg mid-morning in a condition of nervous excitement; delivered by lorry along with a cheery young aristo, Albert Hugo Dreystunck-Ulzburg, a Leutnant in der Reserve, of the 1st *Grossherzoglich-Mecklenburgisches Dragoner Regiment Nr. 17* as he proudly informs us. Our third pilot. He's brought a small dog with him. He explained that he couldn't leave Mikki behind as he had belonged to his girl. He didn't elaborate on what had happened to her. Like Ernst, when he'd briefly transferred to the *Fliegertruppe*, Hugo had flown the Fokker D.VII and also the Siemens-Schuckert D.III fighter with Jagdstaffel IV then under the command of the famed Oberleutnant Udet, *Staffelführer*. This was the aeroplane which Kessler had been raving about, with a phenomenal climb rate.

All of us are dressed as labourers with our flying kit stowed in haversacks; carrying tool bags, wire, some linen fabric, dope, brushes and so forth. It took the rest of the day to completely drain and refuel the Fokkers, all of which we were pleased to discover had the 185 hp. BMW III engines; to fill the radiators, check for leaks, check the oil and to meticulously examine the aircraft, the three of us crawling over and under them one machine at a time to be thorough. We'd made some small repairs and adjustments and felt sure nothing critical had been overlooked by the time darkness had fallen. We were ready for take off at dawn next day.

The hay bale 'wall' which had protected the fighters from the eyes of the Control Commission had been breached enough to enable a D.Vll to pass through and the gap temporarily covered by a roped tarpaulin. We camped comfortably enough in the barn overnight rather than draw attention to ourselves in the town. Besides, now that we'd checked them over we felt happier sleeping near 'our' fighters.

Next morning we were up and raring to go. The weather looked dreary with a low cloud base but visibility was adequate. Dreystunck-Ulzburg insisted on shaving and being well turned-out as befitted an officer, a gentleman and a Prussian, so we felt obliged to follow suit. We borrowed his razor and did the best we could. Then just as we were finishing breakfast a car appeared on the field. This didn't look good, but there was nowhere to hide and it was coming at speed towards the barn, bouncing over the grass.

To our surprise it was our thin-faced contact, 'Felix'. He was relieved to see us, having driven hard from Berlin overnight, hoping we hadn't already left. There was a change of plan. He wanted the three fighters delivered to Swinemunde, on the Baltic coast, a shorter distance than to Eindhoven at any rate. We were to hand them over to an agent who would meet us on the airfield. That's when we'd get paid. That's all he would tell us, apart from a rumour that Mexican gold dollars were circulating due to the instability of some other currencies. It raised a forlorn hope we'd be paid in that coinage rather than American, or some other forgeable notes. Anything but Marks. We discussed this new development, but we had no choice other than to agree or forfeit payment. We spread our maps and plotted our new course. We'd assess the wind aloft for drift. The distance being slightly less than to Eindhoven improved our fuel situation and even the wind appeared to be in our favour.

We fired-up the D.VIIs, one a bit reluctant, but eventually we had all three running smoothly. We lost no time in taxiing out in case the sound had been heard by inquisitive ears in the still morning air. As I lined-up I saw an old boy in a Nineteenth Century soldier's tunic standing at the gate. He solemnly threw a smart military salute as we turned and roared overhead.

Kessler led. For me, the flight began in a state of mild anxiety in case we had caught the attention of someone on the ground who might have alerted the authorities. However, as we settled into loose *Kette* and the countryside flowed past, I fell into the usual pilot's attitude of relaxed awareness.

I recalled my first flight in a prototype D.VII at Adlershof, January '18. Just as in '17, I'd been sent to the fighter competition representing an 'average' Jasta pilot to asses the newest German equipment, comparing them with what fighters Austro-Hungary had to offer. My report, along with others', was enthusiastic and Austria was to begin production of the type, though nothing much came of it before war's end. Later examples like this, it was said, handled better at height than did the early models with the 160 Mercedes engine. It felt good to be flying one again, especially with the powerful BMW.

~-~

Our *Kette* was holding to the west of Berlin when suddenly I spotted a formation of aeroplanes approaching from our left, same level, about two kilometres distant: four of five in a loose gaggle. Their large wing dihedral identified them as British SE5s. I opened my throttle and pulled alongside Kessler in the lead, pointing in the direction of the SEs. He nodded and opened up to full power. I'd heard these SEs were fast but today we just had the edge over them and gradually pulled away, continuing to keep our wary eyes in their direction and everywhere else.

After another ninety minutes I made out the Stettiner Haff and Swinemunde beyond. We'd completed the flight without any further heart-stopping moments and landed to find a number of aircraft assembled on the grass; a motley collection of fighters and reconnaissance types and a few big twin-engined types, Gothas or Friedrichshafens. We reported to the pilots' office on the aerodrome to find that no one knew anything about our flight or knew anyone to whom we should hand over, let alone receive payment. We sent Hugo and Mikki back in charge of the D.VIIs while we tried telephoning Berlin at the contact number, but were unable to get through. Eventually the operator told us that lines to Berlin were down or disconnected.

Asking around the airfield we learned from assorted personnel that the aircraft were intended to be flown to Latvia via East Prussia and 'the newly independent Baltic State of Lithuania'. It meant crossing the still disputed territory of the Polish Corridor so held an element of danger; but Poland was engaged in furious clashes with Bolshevists on their eastern and northern borders as well as having Bolshevik elements to deal with at home, so slipping through before dawn for the short hop to Königsberg seemed a reasonable risk to take.

The aircraft were part of a reinforcing element for the hard-fighting forces of General von der Goltz and the regiments of the volunteer force we'd been hearing so much about; the *Baltische Freikorps* which was aggressively confronting the enemy in the North East. My ears pricked up at the mention of Lithuania and there and then I determined to join this force if only to get back home. As far as I was concerned the Fokkers were ours until such time as we were reimbursed for our ferry flight. Dreystunck-Ulzburg and Kessler felt the same. These two musketeers were actually hoping that they'd not be paid off, but could join this armada which would consist of eleven aircraft for this trip: our Fokkers plus four others and an Albatros D.III (Austrian) fitted with cameras, flown by a fresh-faced young Lt. Johann von Moritz, and a couple of Halberstadts. The leader was a piratical-looking Major Max Ritter who would navigate on a Halberstadt CL.IV, complete with an *Unteroffizier* observer/gunner.

We duly signed up to embark on this aerial adventure as temporary Freikorps pilots, attached to the flight for the purposes of ferrying. We had to sign a chit to absolve the Freikorps of any liability for our deaths or injury, which we in our youthful innocence and desire to fly gladly did. For details of my next of kin I wrote 'none'. That we soon might face a bitter and implacable foe scarce concerned us. I was determined to return to Lithuania by fair means or foul and that was my imperative. If that meant one Rolf Steiger joining what was known as the VI Reserve Armeekorps then I'd do so most willingly, and with a short ceremony and the swearing of an oath, we were all 'in'.

Chapter 34. *Kampfgruppe Wiking:*

The Kameradschaft of the Jasta

I am walking by the North Sea shoreline but as ever my mind is elsewhere.

I hear again the voice of my interviewer and I'm suddenly transported from Swinemunde where my thoughts had been dwelling, onwards to Latvia, to a time several months later. I recalled Big Ben chiming as he spoke. Time for tiffin someone murmurs.

~-~

'So what happened to you in Latgale. I mean after your encounter with the *Bear Slayers?*'

This was from Browne at my Whitehall Court interrogation. He was taking me back over territory I thought we'd covered, but he wanted the fine detail. I was answering questions out of sequence and my mind was all over the place. Perhaps this was the idea, to try to trip me up on dates and places.

I forced my mind back to the Latgale woods. I told them about our return to the Junkers in the pre-dawn and tying a rope to the tailskid. The effort of lifting the rear fuselage with the aid of Timotei while Arkadi coaxed his horse to pull a rope that we'd attached to the skid, dragging its weight out from under the trees, whilst Katya covered our prisoner with her Steyr. We cleared the runway of fallen branches and I'd checked over the engine and then used the *Sizaire* starter crank to roughly pull out the dent in the wing tip. Timotei morosely pumped fuel under the threatening eye of Katya's automatic.

Start-up and take-off went without fuss. Katya left Timotei tied to a tree. She told me she would find a detachment of Lieutenant Colonel Harold Alexander's *Landeswehr* and report to them. Alexander, an ex-Guards officer and an outstanding wartime soldier was a friend of the Graf's and had rendered assistance to her father after he'd been wounded. The British military mission in the Baltic, led by General Sir Hubert Gough had placed Alexander in command of three battalions of German troops who were entirely loyal to him. Meanwhile, in October

Bermondt-Avalov's army, still advised and effectively controlled by von der Goltz had attacked Riga but were driven back by the Letts with support from the British fleet. Yudennich's assault on Petrograd failed, in part due to the sabotage of the six British tanks that had succeeded in driving through the Bolshevist positions: sabotaged by *Tsarists*. Sand in the gearboxes, put there by spiteful hands of a few, unhappy at the idea of a British–style democracy breaking out in Russia. By such small random acts do campaigns fail: the fate of millions and the history of the world is changed forever.

Some months later, Baltic peace treaties were signed with the Soviets allowing them to concentrate on Denikin's and Kolchak's White armies in the south and far east. By then I was in the Ukraine.

But I go back to a time before we were forced to withdraw from the Baltic: where still it snows upon the childhood in my mind.

~-~

Peterfeld and Alt-Auts,
Lithuania.
Early Winter 1919

I have been dreaming again about those days. Blizzard dreams or soft snowflake dreams, consciously recalling too, balmy summer's days, riding free on half-wild horses. When we played and swam in lakes, chased coruscating carp with our dogs, made undying friendships and fell hopelessly in love with unreachable young girls. Or so it seemed.

But when I think of Lithuania in absentia it snows. It blows. It howls and rages.

I wake to find that the snow has stopped. The reluctant dawn is a banded sky of pink and grey, with a high overcast. It's bitingly cold; cold like a witch's tit, Kessler says. Freezing fog shrouds some low, distant hills, smudged with the darker brownish-grey of conifers. No wind yet. The *Wetterfrosch's* guess is as good as ours I think. I flinch at a rifle shot, but it's ice cracking on the river beyond the birches. We are all a little tense.

Snow scrunches loudly underfoot as we walk, like over-stuffed *Steiff* bears to our 'Tin Donkeys'. The sound carries on the frigid air. The mechanics are stamping about to keep warm. They've stripped the icicles off the leading and trailing edges, brushed the wings and tailplanes clear of their dusting of snow. They've already warmed the engines, so starting again should be straightforward. My machine is the further of the two, recognizable at a distance due to the painted medieval knight, in red and white; the Lithuanian hero *Vytautus* upon his steed, brandishing his sword, that I myself emblazoned on the corrugated sides using prepared paper stencils. My emblem needs no explanation since my allegiance is well known. Kessler stops at the port wing root of his aeroplane and grasps the coaming of the cockpit that reaches above head height, swinging his right flying boot onto the steel footstep. There is a black pelican on a yellow shield painted beneath his cockpit. He's never actually told me why and I refuse to ask him. It's an unspoken battle of nerves, though I suspect it has to do with a minor aristocratic beauty he'd known in Struga. He pauses at my approach, my gloved hand slightly raised to indicate caution.

Junkers D.1s in Latvia before a Schlacht mission. Kessler's machine is in the foreground.

Sotto voce, in his ear, so that the muffle-eared mechanics at the propeller will not hear my words.

'You know where I must go?' Actually it is a statement.

Kessler merely looks at me, clouds in his eyes. He's put on a little more weight these few months but signs of strain still show around the eyes. Through them understanding, reproach, resignation, maybe a little fearfulness for my well-being, journey in succession.

'You'll cover for me?' Again, a statement put as a question.

~-~

Leutnant Kessler and myself, *Quadratkarten* stuffed into the big map pockets of our leather flying coats, fasten our broad lap and shoulder straps in the cockpits of our two D.1s. I feel more than a little cramped in the cockpit this morning. The old two hundred times ritual commences. 'Switches on!' comes from somewhere ahead of the twinned

491

Spandaus. If the *charge* is right, winding the cockpit *Hand-Zündapparat*, the hand-wound magneto, with motor magnetos retarded on the cockpit lever, *perhaps* the BMW straight six will fire on compression without further hand-propping, or maybe with just a *slight* swing on the big mahogany propeller from the ground crew. A little exercise might help them keep warm but it could be a real struggle trying to start these engines in cold weather and I'd rather be flying the things than pushing them about. Or trying to maintain them – draining the oil while hot and keeping it warm all night in big perforated-top cans set on grills and open fires - padded engine covers and hot air generators not yet having arrived. But indeed these new 'tin' ships were easier to look after than fabric-covered biplanes with the many wires needing adjusting all the time for the cold weather, especially in conditions such as these. Metal airframes only needed the snow brushing off and they were ready to go. As long as there was no build-up of ice. Wing tarps and sheets draped over fuselages help when available.

I pump the long-handled brass primer until a fitter tells me fuel is draining from the carburettor overflow, then wind the starting magneto vigorously, creating a series of sparks on all twelve plugs, though several combustion chambers will be redundant for starting. Neither I nor Kessler are wearing breastplate armour on this sortie, nor steel flak helmets and visors. The stick is gripped firmly between my knees to keep the elevator 'up' and both hands free.

Eventually both the big BMW engines are running with their distinctive, 'hollow' blattering rumble. The two fighters with grey smoke issuing from their saxophone exhaust manifolds waddle, like tin tractors, across the snowy expanse on thin wheels, leaving deep ruts and a third skid trail between, oil and petrol stains where they'd been refuelled.

Kessler, once the *Happy Bavarian* leads off. We go back a long way, I am thinking, as we line up in echelon. Right from boot camp and all that had entailed, until he'd wangled a transfer from Macedonia to the Western Front, ostensibly to 'see more action', before finding himself in Galicia and a prisoner of the Russians. In truth he'd already seen plenty 'off-limits', such was his 'vincibility' with the opposite sex, which meant several heavily-moustached relatives taking umbrage and beating a path to the airfield, seeking forfeits. His famously liberated Circassian silver samovar might soon have contained his own forfeits had the Flik not been transferred. Ah, but those handsome Monte Negran women apart, the refugee Circassian women were of unsurpassed beauty and Ernst frequently demonstrated just how much he admired them. I saluted his

492

stamina back then, between his bouts of malaria.

But yes, we were still young; it's just that sometimes we *felt* very old. I'd followed the Flik's departure a few days later in my repaired KD, the Brandenburg D.1, only to be transferred to fly my wished-for Albatros fighters on the Italian Front; D.IIs, and later on, 253-series D.IIIs.

I'd enjoyed Count Harry Kessler's hospitality for the second time following my desertion from the Austrian Air Corps during which time Ernst had escaped from Russian captivity. Now we find ourselves serving with the Freikorps, to fly this time against Bolshevism, though for different reasons. For me it was to regain my homeland from its hateful grip, and to see my family and friends again. For Ernst, well he just liked fighting, and Bolshevism, after the rough handling he'd received, was a cause worth fighting against. For others like Ritter it was a Nordic crusade. For Balticum. But he too had lost an estate in Estonia, and God knows what family.

~-~

The squat, grey shape ahead of me heads northwards. We maintain 1500 metres altitude in comfortable starboard echelon, each of us cocooned in our droning bubble of noise, able to communicate only by pre-arranged hand signals. My Ju had lifted off after a longish take-off run and it had taken a while for me to catch up with Lt. Kessler. Hunched in our cockpits, trying to hide from the sub-zero slipstream thundering around the bluff contours of radiator and gun breeches, we are temporarily absorbed in our own thoughts. Kessler's workload is higher, since he is map reading. That is as far as is possible in this white wilderness, and given the inaccuracy of the maps of the region.

The briefing is 'armed reconnaissance'. Essentially trying to find the 'lines', such as they are, on a fluid front where skirmish and raiding, burning and retreating, is the order of the day, with less than a cohesive action plan evident for most of the time. But when the Reds attack it is usually in force, with troops of all calibres. Gun batteries and especially armoured trains are to be reported on, so that the bigger CL.1s could be brought up with their higher bombing capability. They, or the remaining Friedrichshafens and Gothas that are still on muster somewhere — if they'd managed to be ferried to East Prussia out of the reach of the Occupying Forces which had of course cancelled all German flying, officially, so German aircraft found airborne within their remit was liable to be attacked without warning. Although we were well outside the Allied Zone of Occupation, we were still regarded as hostiles by Red and Interventionist Forces alike, not to mention those of national self-determinism in the Baltic region, with whose aspirational sentiments I personally agreed.

Usually when formation flying I am relaxed at the controls, religiously scanning the horizon and keeping Kessler's aeroplane within my scan, so as not to get too close nor let my leader draw away. This loose *Rotte*-formation pair is safe, and allows both pilots to watch for the enemy. Deep down, however, I am tense and pre-occupied. If I allow my thoughts to drift too much away from the act of flying I become unsettled and will begin to lose concentration. Outwardly I'm flying with care and remain watchful. Inwardly I am already fighting another war.

And whenever I recall Lithuania now it is snowing.

~·~

It snows in my dreams, despite the lush pasture, the grazing cattle on the flat, *glacially* – flat land, the shade of trees and the wind off the Baltic of my youth that I make the effort to recall, where I ride fast, forward over the neck of my mount, my head to his head, standing in the stirrup – racing my friends. Or galloping loose in the saddle under a baking sun, one bare arm and shoulder free, bathed in a glorious cool airflow, like a Tibetan horseman in Sven Hedin's saga of exploration. Except sometimes when *she* rides nearby. Then I will sit tall: a young *Uhlan*, straining to be manlier and more impressive than my then thirteen years.

I examine the angular creature that rises and falls gently ahead and to the left of my machine. Ugly? Well Professor Hugo Junker's thick-winged D.1 is certainly no beauty. But it is an impressive advanced weapon and quite unlike anything flying anywhere else on the planet in 1919. It is brutally functional in its severity of line and its only purpose need not be guessed at. With none of the shark-like elegance associated with the flower of German aircraft design from that 'War of Wars'; it has a crude efficiency that stamps it as thoroughly for mass-production as any steel helmet or bayonet and is as distinctive in its singular application.

The cockpit view is unprecedentedly excellent for a fighter of that time. Beyond the gun *mantels*, bestriding the long crankcase; beyond the prominent radiator filler-cap lies the almost featureless, grim white northern Lithuanian landscape, which continues to roll slowly backwards, map-like, beneath our wings.

I find myself again analysing the D.1, a self-censoring activity, which at least stops the mind wandering into forbidden territory. Its lines are supremely logical given the construction which is maybe a generation ahead of anything else that was at the Front a few months ago, before the Armistice.

'Ernst, didn't they tell you? The War is over!' I shout in my mind. Except it *isn't*, not here anyway, and may never be for myself. Nor, for all I know will it be for Kessler either, who relishes hard fighting. Neither of us has illusions of immortality, and just because one may die for a cause, does not *per se* make that cause right.

Kessler is not now as other men. He doesn't smoke now, rarely drinks. His humour is dry. Apolitical, he accepts that his attitude is mercenary with a shrug. All his energy is given to the challenge of the fight and is sometimes listless on the ground, and at others seems to war against himself, restless and volatile and is best left alone at those moments. I think somewhere he has lost his way, lives only for the adrenaline of combat and burns to get at the enemy. He hates the Bolshies as much as I do. I have strong personal reasons. For him it is something to fight against which he needs like a drug. His only vice had been the fair sex, on which he'd overdosed earlier in the big war.

For him the lines might have been written, 'I serve war: its holy spirit is my very oxygen.' For us, aeroplane types are divided between fighters and targets and we fly the fighters. All else is fair game if it doesn't bear the cross. But here we are usually kept busy with *ground* targets, most often locomotives. These are almost always armoured so our machine gun bullets will not penetrate the boilers. Sometimes on the un-armoured locomotives, to make sure we will be less inclined to shoot, human shields are roped all over the engines, tied firmly to the boiler plate, men, women and children. Lightly clad, as if by 'come as you are' invitation, they'd die from exposure anyway after a while: how quickly depending on the air temperature and the average speed of the train. It does not diminish our aggressiveness.

'I think we'll all be going to hell, Ernst,' I said
'I think it's all around us,' he said, and on that we all agreed.

We ourselves are armoured to a degree: breastplates with back armour, terrifying facemasks with images of death upon them. We sit strapped tightly into our cockpits, seated on thinly cushioned frying pans to protect our future prospects; sliding in crab-wise to the rail track at nought feet, the Jus themselves flying as if on rails, snub-nosed and menacing. We see the locomotive wheels sparking from the brakes and the muzzle flashes of weapons aimed at us from the tender and carriages. We tell ourselves we are doing those miserable wretches a service, dispatching them with bullets. In our airy judgment we deem this preferable to their slow, agonizing death from freezing. I allow myself no feelings about this sort of action. Such victims are far enough away, their faces gone in an instant, that the agony is impersonal. But what horrors they must have endured before death or terrible wounding, even if the boiler failed to blow.

All of us have volunteered for this most right wing *Gruppe* of the parent *Geschwader,* based variously in East Prussia, Poland, Lithuania and Kurland, with General von der Goltz, we endeavour to hold the line from Belarus, keeping civilization safe from the Red Horde just as the distant forefathers did with that other Horde, of *Gold.* We live a gypsy life, but mobility is our protection in this skirmishing war whose savagery knows no bounds.

But men are injured and dying: my comrades. I help lift a dead observer from the wreckage of a C-type Albatros that's made it back to crash-land, its injured pilot in a state of shock. The padre says some words that don't penetrate my consciousness. Though my reservoir of courage remains undepleted, I know enough about the randomness of war. I harbour no youthful illusion of immortality.

~-~

I recall that Teuton double-handed *souvenir sword* of Tannenberg, or Grunewald, on the firebreast at the Linden Haus: the only weapon, according to my cousin, Marik (I cannot get used to the idea that I am related to my best childhood friend, let alone to Krysia and Kat) among the artefacts and documents that Kristian had removed from the Hanse Haus. After the evacuation of the *Kreuzhof, the late Peter's crumbling estate I've never seen, that now might in part be mine if distaff primogeniture inheritance from the wrong side of the bed held any legal precedence.* That sword, symbolic vanquisher of the Teuton knights and Kristian's allegiance to the independent new way was displayed with due ceremony in the large hall, one of two immediately visible phenomena: the sword on the firebreast and the portrait on the landing, seen at once upon entering from the flight of steps at the end of a sweeping linden-lined drive. Except many of those

496

trees were now gone. But Sargent's *Lady in White* remained steadfast. Her radiance outshone all.

But the D.1 is *our* new 'rigorous sword' against Bolshevism, Sachsenburg had said. 'If we had more of these superb machines we would be *invincible*. The enemy in the air would be powerless to stop us.' However, I'd had trouble accepting the cantilever *biplane* wings of the good old Fokker D.Vll when first I saw one, that ubiquitous fighter called for to be *specifically* surrendered under the terms of the Armistice itself, mentioned by name, '*In Erste alles Fokker D.VII Apparate*,' even as Kessler, Hugo and myself had circumvented that edict on behalf of designer and entrepreneur Tony Fokker under the nose of the Military Control Commission. Reason for a little personal satisfaction.

However, the Junkers D.1 was something else.

~-~

A few months previously, a rain-swept, colourless April day in East Prussia, I'd negotiated slippery duckboards laid over grey mud, to join the little knot of pilots in a canvas hangar belonging to the *Marine Feldflieger Abteilung und Flugpark Nord.* We are to surrender our beloved Fokkers to less experienced pilots and so we join those clustered eagerly around our first D.1. It is an impressive if unusual sight. With its tall car-type radiator it stands high and mighty, its body mass and thick wing incongruously set on a slender steel tube undercarriage and narrow wheels. These other pilots look so young. They gaze at the new technology wide-eyed, with awe and not a little trepidation. It's so different from what they've known. There are questions on range, speed, rate of climb and manoeuvrability. However most of them will be flying escort in the D.VIIs and Albatrosse.

The rain on the canvas roof creates a din which is strangely comforting, but means we raise our voices. This includes the cheery Leutnant who is briefing us on the technical aspects of the Junkers D.1 in a deliberately affected Prussian nasal tone.

Kessler's scarce regained his health after Russian hospitality. His long trek to Germany means he now finds standing for long periods wearying. Cold, damp weather makes my joints ache too. This I must not reveal for fear of being passed unfit for the coming campaign and the longed-for return to my homeland.

We examine the deep-section aluminium-skinned wing. Rectangular in plan, leavened only by the apparent afterthought of a curved wingtip –

and that only at the leading edge, although the outer aileron has a pleasing curve ending in a sharp tip. The entire skin has corrugations, adding to the considerable stiffness. These are of course aligned with the airflow and organised to minimize drag. The brute is painted a grey-green, in irregular markings, although later, for the winter, the riggers will add splotches of white distemper, which will render these aircraft all but invisible on a snowy aerodrome, and quite hard to see in the air. Their pale blue-grey under surfaces will render them equally well-camouflaged against a wintry sky, but the big, black straight-edged crosses on wings and fuselage compromise that effect. It will give the Bolshevist anti-aircraft gunners something to aim at. The white-painted rudder, in contrast to everything else, is small, looks ineffectual, but *isn't* and this is also decorated with the simple, heroic black cross of the German national identity.

'Gentlemen, I welcome you all to this new unit, the *Kampfgruppe Wiking*, in which we have the honour to be under the command of *Hauptmann Maximillian Ritter von Sternberg!* To give him his full and correct name.' He might have added ... *under the command of the mercurial self-styled warlord Max Ritter, (forseeably) while this vicious campaign endures.*

The rain has increased and is roaring on the hangar roof, trying to drown his sales pitch.

'And *this* is what many of you lucky boys will be flying,' says the *Technische-Komische Offizier.* 'Built by the Junkers Flugzeug-Werke A.G., Dessau: I present the Junkers D.1!'

'So where's its top wing?' asks Kessler laconically.

'Quite, yes. 'D' is for *Doppeldecker.* Like the Leutnant here most of you will have noticed, *prima facie*, this aeroplane has a bloody big, fat, *single* mainplane, a low positioned monoplane wing, ergo a *Tiefdecker.* However, in the tidy little minds of the High Command, fighters are decreed to be *biplanes*, per se. Therefore, if this is a *fighter, ipso facto* it is a *biplane.* Logical? Of course not! But then this is still the Army!

'So this is your *Blechesel,* gentlemen,' he continues. Amusingly nicknamed – a Tin Donkey.

'Hardly an epithet to convey a sense of grim efficiency or to strike dread into the enemy in combat. Yet I present to you the most potent and superlative killing machine ever fielded by the *Fliegertruppe!*' He talked like a snake oil salesman. 'These aircraft are now under the control of the autonomous detachment of the Imperial Naval Flying Regiment, the *Kampfgeschwader Sachsenburg* in its *Iron Ring,* for armed reconnaissance and *Schlacht,* that is strafing with machine guns and close-support with bombs,

498

for which these machines have been specially adapted. We also have the bigger Junkers CL.1, which is a two-seater obviously, with an additional flexible machine gun and greater bomb-carrying capability.

'They were just too late for the Western front, I'm sorry to say, and we only have limited numbers, so we must please try not to break them. Lt. Sachsenburg and Hauptmann Ritter would *not* be best pleased. These aeroplanes are 'sub-let' to our motley little *Schlachtjagdgruppe*, as of now, that is you, me and about fifty other ranks, mechanics, doctors, orderlies, cooks, clerks, batmen, dogs, camp followers and so on. Its flying complement comprises mostly ex-*Fliegertruppe* pilots. But that you already know, since that's what you are unless they've sent me the wrong *gottverdammts* personnel!' This last is perhaps his final attempt at a joke. Nobody laughs.

Someone asks how many of these wonderplanes are on strength. We are told that we have twenty altogether between the main force and *Wiking* plus about the same number of the bigger, two-seater CL.1 *Schlacht* versions. Of those we have six D.1s and only two CL.1s available to us on *Kampfgruppe Wiking* as well as several good Fokker D.Vlls and an Albatros D.lll *Foto*, high-speed photo-reconnaissance machine. We also have some older two-seat reconnaissance types as well as one of the latest, very powerful Albatros C-Type two-seaters, a Halberstadt and wagonloads of spares. The D.1s are all new and our complement would be flown north from the rear to the most forward Baltic airbase in the next few days, depending on weather. In the meantime we were to familiarise ourselves with these aircraft on the ground. I take a look outside. Apart from this one in the small hangar, the others are all parked outside in the rain with canvas covers and oilskin sheets protecting the cockpits and engines. Rainwater is running off the corrugated trailing edges as if from tin-roofed shanties.

Later I find Kessler deep in thought standing next to the D.1 in the dim lit, fume-filled hangar. The rain has stopped and the younger pilots are having some kind of noisy premature Valhalla celebration in the mess tent. Two mechanics, one holding a lead light connected to a raucous diesel generator, are busying themselves with the engine. The rudimentary corrugated cowlings are leaning against the undercarriage. Kessler clambers noisily onto the wing root with the aid of the exposed, steel-tube crash pylon and swings easily into the cockpit, moving the controls. He looks around, trying to assess the field of view in a tail down position, and has to admit it's better than any biplane he's flown, except for the view straight downwards beneath the broad wing.

'So what d'you think? Is this the shape of the future?' I ask him.

'Looks like a cross between a tractor and a damned tin chicken shed to me!' he growled.

'Say what you really think,' I encourage him.

'Well, if it's fast and can stand punishment, doesn't handle like a bear, and the fuel endurance is OK and everything works like it's *gottverdammt* well supposed to, then, maybe. But I'd rather have a biplane: preferably a Siemens-Schuckert.'

Conservative, like most pilots.

~-~

Next day the pilots assembled early, arriving in ones and twos, some rubbing the sleep from their eyes after their nocturnal insanity: for whatever reason the young had to celebrate for going to war. We wore a variegated selection of insignias on our naval and army uniform blouses, jackets and flying kit. Most carried their flying jackets or one-piece overalls, their leather over-trousers, fleece-lined boots and helmets so as not to overheat in the confines of the crowded briefing office with its woodstove.

Conversation was desultory; no one was especially voluble at this ungodly hour with the sun still below the southeastern horizon of fir trees. There were the inevitable jokes from the irrepressible Brühning, but Kessler for one was unusually taciturn. There was a certain tension, though nothing untoward, each to their own thoughts about the coming flight northeast. Equipment and such personal effects as were needed had gone forward by train or with the field kitchens and motor convoy, efficiently organised by our quartermasters and supply officers. Supplies included complete engines and all conceivable spares on the engineering side, with aviation spirit and oil carried in well-separated rail cars in case of accident or ambush by Lithuanian *Savanoris, Latvian Streltsi* or affiliated Bolshevists. It was unclear how much opposition they'd face crossing Polish-held territory.

But we weren't nearly a *Gruppe* in terms of strength. More an extended mixed *Staffel,* a heterogeneous collection of aircraft types, able to perform diverse roles; many suitable for more than one. But while that made us abundantly capable of a wide variety of combat, close support, armed reconnaissance, high and low level missions, it formidably increased our maintenance and supply problems.

We'd waited impatiently for orders to mobilize and here it was. We

500

regarded ourselves as veterans, Kessler, myself and a few others. We'd confronted the enemy in the air before. But the Bolshevists were a new force on the ground *and* in the air to an extent. We were to stem their incursions to assist in the assault on Riga and drive a wedge between the Red armies from Latgale to the sea; mop up those contained within the Klepaida-Vilnius pocket or throw them back across the Belarus border, back into the Ukraine and let the remaining regular German forces or the Ukrainian separatists deal with them as they would.

For several of us it was the first time we were formally to meet Hauptmann Max Ritter, commander of *Kampfgruppe Wiking*, the Old Man, who made himself understood with his first uncompromising statement, delivered forcefully in a clipped manner.

'*Leute*,' he said. 'I've flown sorties up here, with Sachsenburg, and believe me this will be no picnic, even for some of you 'old hands'. So let's get it straight from the start. *Wiking* doesn't need gentlemen sporting pilots. Some of you are veterans but for the young and starry-eyed, *chivalry*,' he sneered emphatically, '*If* it ever existed in the air, died and was buried in the first full year of the last war. With black candles, incense and all funerary rites. Amen!'

Ritter paused only briefly.

'We are in the aerial artillery business. I don't need fancy fliers and I don't want self-obsessed aces either. If you think potting ancient Ivan 'lattice-tails' will gain you medals to impress some whore back in Hamburg you're in the wrong company. I want men who are not afraid to get in among the trees and strafe the enemy *on the ground*. I want pilots who shoot straight but can hold their fire 'til they see the whites of their subhuman eyes; who'll fly up a Bolshie trench in the teeth of machine gun fire and press home the attack; in a firestorm. I need bomber pilots who can hit ground targets, defended bridges and armed vessels with precision then go back and do it again despite the *Flak*. I want men who will go immediately to the aid of a fellow pilot even if it puts them in mortal danger. I need killers who are not afraid of death! Exterminators! If any of you are not of this mettle you can catch the next transport back to Germany, *now*.'

Wiking, he told us, was to operate on the right flank as a free-roving *Schlachtgruppe*, attacking identified targets gleaned from high-flying *Aufklärer* and by low-level, high-speed photo-reconnaissance types, such as the two Albatros OAW 253 series *Foto* machines. Their oblique cameras could capture images lost to high level reconnoitring, such as Red cavalry encampments lodged within thin woodland or copses, using light cover to conceal their night bivouacs. Pre-dawn sorties by the *Albatros* would give an 'edge' to such operations.

'Men, when flying *Schlacht*, face and body armour is uncomfortable and is optional. But I'll be wearing mine. And I'll be sitting on a frying pan.'

That rings true at least.

Our attention had long been on the large scale map of East Prussia, Poland, the Baltic States and Belarus tacked along one wall. It extended north up the Gulf of Bothnia, and Finland, with the cities of Petrograd and Moscow, both ringed in red. Red ribbons radiated in salient peninsulas and marked theoretical forward lines, though the old hands guessed correctly that these were outdated and fluid.

'The *Freiwilligen Grenzschutz Ost* will be stationed on our southern flank. They are briefed to prevent any south-western Bolshevist incursions, but not to support our north-eastern strikes. That's to be our job exclusively. However, with notional Lithuanian independence, in due course these will be held in reserve and may be moved back from the frontier. When we know where that will be.'

Mention of the *Grenzschutz Ost* caught Kessler's attention. We'd heard they'd been equipped with the very latest versions of the Siemens-Schuckert fighter. The D.IV, the high-aspect ratio-winged variant of that fast-climbing interceptor Kessler said could reach 7000 metres. '*In under 15 minutes with a full war load, Rolf.*' On our way to Königsberg, Kessler had briefly broken formation in his D.VII shortly after we'd left the *Pommersche Bucht* littoral to make a low pass over some lines of parked aircraft on the airfield at Kolberg. On arrival at Königsberg he'd confirmed that Siemens-Schuckerts were among them. Rumour had it that these were brand new aeroplanes which had remained in production until now. While all other German warplanes were being confiscated or destroyed under the watchful eye of the Inter-Allied Control Commission – part of the surrender terms of the Versailles Treaty, certain types had been legally exempted, for use in limited police actions, to secure the German borders and theoretically to render protection to colonial German interests in the Baltic States.

With the official status of a 'free' Lithuania these were to be used in a 'passive role' assisting the nascent Lithuanian government forces if called upon. We hoped that a looser interpretation of that protocol would be enacted. Top cover provided by the 'best fighter aircraft available on the planet', according to Ernst, would be most welcome if we were forced to engage with a large force of enemy fighters when flying low-level missions. But it seemed a dim possibility at best.

~-~

Despite his early rhetoric, Ritter proved to be an inspiring and charismatic leader of men. No clip-winged eagle, despite an artificial leg that we'd not suspected at Swinemunde.

Story was it had been almost shot off by Flak while trench-strafing with a *Haifisch* on the Western Front and his gunner had been badly wounded. He'd tied his scarf around his thigh to stem the bleeding but the shattered leg had interfered with the rudder bar. Held on by a flap of skin, he'd cut it off and thrown it at the enemy, a derisory if futile gesture, and turned for home, making a tolerable landing with a faltering engine. He'd arranged for his gunner to be stretchered away and insisted on making his report before finally passing out in the cockpit. The gunner, Becker, flew with him still.

~-~

In Whitehall, Frankland had cleared his throat and demurred, drumming his fingers on the ribbon of his DFC while Browne stared at me icily and with evident disbelief.

'I rather think that story belongs to the RFC,' he said, stiffly.

I repeated that it was simply the tale as I'd heard it in East Prussia. I was in no position to confirm whether or no it was apocryphal; though having met Ritter I could believe it true.

~-~

Ritter had stomped about in front of the map with a cane, which he used as a pointer, not for support, reminding me greatly of Uzelac and thought, not for the first time, that a parrot would not look out of place on his shoulder. He would lead many operations personally and robustly encouraged initiative in his pilots. He said that creative measures and tactical improvisations would provide us with the advantage in this unprecedented type of warfare. New methods of attack to suit the situation as it unfolded might need to be evolved. Close liaison with our troops on the ground was the order of the day. Despite our black crosses we should also expect to be shot at by everyone on the ground: partisans, Freikorps even. Everyone was nervous of low flying aircraft so ferry flights should always be at medium level: 2,500 metres.

The talents and weaknesses of his little air arm and the best *mode d'emploi* of his equipment would be found in the coming days. Above all daily intelligence gleaned from aerial reconnaissance followed by a rapid close-support response were key to tactical victories. The supply situation once our armada had moved off was unclear. Meanwhile we could not afford to waste a drop of petrol or a single cartridge.

Most of our Junkers D.1s had the 160 hp. Mercedes, but Kessler and I had grabbed the only two 185 hp.BMW-engined machines. No time to air-test our fighters: the controls were the same even if the handling was a little different, and we'd all flown behind reliable BMW engines before. As for the D.1s we'd learn to fly them en route to Latvia! Our track lay though the skies of a notionally independent southern and western Lithuania providing an opportunity to top up our tanks in what might yet be German-held territory, for a while, before flying to the front.

'Go and get some breakfast. *Abfahrt* 0800 hrs.'

~-~

We were given a further briefing in the mess tent. Kessler as an acting flight commander provided some additional words of wisdom aimed at the freshmen, specifically formation positions and separation and the need for constant lookout. He stressed that the fighters will fly on the flanks slightly to the rear of the reconnaissance and *Schlacht* machines and 600 meters higher, in left and right echelon, the four Junkers D.1s on the left and the Fokker D.Vlls on the right so that the high performance fighter element will be better placed when manoeuvring as units with the advantage of offering better protection from interception. The *Foto* Albatros and the other reconnaissance machines will fly in the central 'vic' behind the lead Ju CL.1 aircraft.

We crashed to attention when Ritter stumped in, wearing full leather kit, fleece and fur-lined for winter flying.

'Gentlemen!' Ritter's voice was firm and confident. 'The sun is up. Your engines have been warmed. You have your maps with your tracks and drift lines plotted. You know your formation positions. Loose formation please for those unused to how we fly in or near to enemy territory.' This aimed at the younger contingent which might be inclined to demonstrate its prowess at tight formation flying, as raised earlier by Kessler.

'It's not an exhibition. We fly 'battle formation', at least ten wingspans apart so everybody can use their eyes and not worry about

504

colliding with their wingmen. To recap we will fly in a broad 'arrow'. I will be navigating and leading in a CL.1. You will recognize it by the white letter 'R' on the fuselage and starboard wing. Are there any questions?'

'Sir. What if we see the enemy? Do we draw attention to the formation leader by flare pistol, or by a formation break to draw the Hauptmann's attention to the appropriate quarter?' This from Laumann.

'*Unteroffizier* Becker will be watching my rear so he'll see any formation break and will in any case be the first to note the appearance of hostile aircraft. He has the eye of an eagle, *nicht wahr*, Becker?' He nodded at his observer/gunner who smiled proudly.

'But in the unlikely event that the Bolshevists have any effective aerial strength this far southwest, the procedure will be for a section of single seaters on the flank to break formation and investigate the nationality of the unknowns. If they prove hostile they will be engaged. A second section will climb to provide top cover for the engagement and watch for a trap. It will be entirely possible that the first enemy aircraft you see will be a diversionary target - a stalking horse to enable a few Red D.Vlls to 'bounce' you out of cloud. They have some good pilots among them. Some old German *Kämpfer* who've gone over to Bolshevism either as mercenaries or because they've decided they'll be on the winning side this time. They are wrong! But we are more likely to encounter Latvians.'

'Sir?'

'The Lithuanian fighter force: *Lietuvos Karo Aviacija*. It's almost non-existent although equipping with the *Albatros*. Some refurbished leftovers from our equipment. They're also equipping with some D.VIIs. But we should have no trouble from them, for the time being. They're busy squaring-up to the Bolshies invading from Belarussia and having desultory engagements with the Poles.

'Latvian fighters may be a problem but might equally give us a wide berth. After all we're all fighting the Bolshevists. Our Intelligence says that the Bolshevist 1st Aviation Division has withdrawn from their Latvian base at Spilve. However there *are* Red Latvian patrols on the ground and we would not want to fall into their hands any more than we would the Bolshevists. Our latest intelligence on the Red Latvian *air* arm indicates that they have three detachments commanded by Rudolf Stukalis: two reconnaissance detachments comprising various types based partly in western Lithuania. Their sole fighter unit comprises Nieuport 17s. These are still useful fighters although naturally the D.VII out-performs them. If you see a fighter with red stars we *will* engage. If however we see *ungkrusts*, that is their red *swastika,* we will refrain from engagement unless attacked. The Latvian Nationalists have some Sopwiths, we understand, so they are potentially very dangerous. There may also be experienced combat pilots, among them. Englishmen. Don't forget, it's not just the quality of the enemy aircraft you will encounter that matters. It is the quality and determination of the pilot in its cockpit. Any more questions?'

'What about engine failure?' From young Leutnant Hugo Dreystunck-Ulzburg. He wears the collar facings of his Mecklenburg dragoner regiment on his field grey uniform that he'd carried together with his dog in his D.VII from Magdeburg.

'Don't let that happen! If that's all then let's get going. There's a long trip ahead and we are flying at maximum range for most of us, so put your trust in God and the mighty *Bayerische Motoren Werke.*'

I reflected that we were still a young air arm despite the veteran status of some pilots. It would not be for us to re-write the rules of air combat or ground attack straight off but we would no doubt experiment with those in due course given the versatility of the D.1. But the hard won experience of the recent war must not be allowed to atrophy. It was only five years since any aeroplane in any air force had carried a mounted weapon let alone a pair of synchronized forward-firing machine guns or a useful bomb load. Once deployed and settled-in, ideas on search and destroy, flying for range, and problems of accurate low-level navigation using imprecise maps, especially later, over snowy terrain, if the campaign lasted that long, would need addressing. When winter arrived there would be many challenges to overcome. Kessler and I were considered veterans, but we were innocents as far as the war we were about to embark on was concerned.

We trooped out into the light of a fine Baltic morning with Mikki marshalling us like sheep and barking excitedly.

'Boarding for the Riga Express,' called Kessler affecting a Berlin accent, as if we were off on some harmless jaunt.

'Wunderbar,' said Hugo breathing the air joyously. *'Kaiserwetter!'*

'There'll be no talk of Kaiserwetter!' growled Ritter. 'Not while that hound skulks in the Hague! It's *Jägerwetter* from now on: no more, no less! Start those engines! *Abflug'*

~-~

Our flight to Latvia was uneventful. The wide sweep of the Neman

506

River appeared on time, its coils gleaming to the east in the bright sunshine and then we were into Lithuanian 'airspace', the Neman widening and draining into the Curonian lagoon with its long slender spit. I still called it the Neman, but most of the Staffel would know it as the Memel. Some words of a famous poem returned from my childhood:

'...*kur Nemunas teka Tai musu tevyne, grazi Lietuva.*'

'...where the Neman flows. That's our homeland, beautiful Lithuania.'

My eyes roved around the formation; the Ju's brutish and efficient; the Albatrosse rising and falling slightly, gleaming like sliver sharks in the sun; the bluff-nosed Fokkers higher, a protecting flight on our right flank. In the distance a series of castles stood out in the mist along the bright loops of the Neman, an ancient defence line against marauding Teuton knights. Below lay the great medieval fortress of Memelburg and to westward, off the port wing of the *Staffel,* appeared the coastal town of Klaipeda. Smoke rose from many chimneys. I assumed it was from chimneys.

Since the armistice a red wave had flowed over the landscape leaving as much misery in its wake as four years of war. Regular German soldiers in the northern Baltic, with their sense of grievance and betrayal, had abandoned their arms to Bolshevism in 1918 or joined in its onslaught. By early 1919 the Freikorps had swarmed into the Baltic in their thousands to stem this tide and the main Bolshevist thrust had been halted and reversed in southern and western Lithuania We were part of a renewed aerial support against powerful Bolshevist forces still invading Latvia. How effective we would be was yet to be determined.

Evidence of more recent war was clear at our altitude. Crop fields were still blackened and villages appeared empty. Buildings were burned out and roofless and many small towns seemed deserted. Here and there factory chimneys stood amid the wreckage of their surrounding buildings, like blasted tree trunks after a forest fire. Heavy guns and transport lay wrecked along the roads or heaved into ditches; trenches scarred the fields. 'What a waste!' was the thought that came frequently to mind.

Some transport was evident, occasionally identifiable as German trucks or horse-drawn vehicles and columns of men were marching south. Little rebuilding was evident, but some pale, straw-like rafters stood out, fresh symbols of hope in adversity. I hoped it was no false dawn. There were small boats on the Neman and barges, which were moving from their wakes, although they seemed stationary from our height. Far out to sea dark smudges that were somebody's warships lay at anchor. British or German? Most likely they were British. The Royal Navy had denied von der Goltz an easy maritime supply route but even-handedly had destroyed or captured Bolshevist ships which would have threatened Estonian and Latvian ports. For the moment it was stalemate insofar as direct intervention on the ground was concerned.

~-~

The weather deteriorated and over our shoulders cloud had obscured the sun. But before long our landing field at Alt-Auts emerged though the stratus with a few aircraft visible, parked near the brown Bessoneau hangars. A distinctive river wound nearby, tributary to the Western Dvina. To the North hung the smoke of battle. Ritter began to lose height, the main formation strung out now in a wide, stepped-echelon, letting down into wind over the mud brown-grey landscape. The helmet-studded perimeter defences, *Feldschanze* and communicating trenches were evident and beyond them the tank traps, above which the fighters circled like buzzards, waiting their turn to land.

This then was a front line airfield, if front there was.

Face armour worn on Schlacht missions, to frighten the Bolshevist gunners.

Almost from the moment we'd arrived we were in the thick of it.

The D.1's metal skin was at once its salvation and the reason we Junkers pilots were exposed to the greatest danger. We spearheaded our infantry pushes in the wake of artillery barrages at ultra-low level, strafing Bolshevist dugouts and wreaking carnage in back areas and assembly points. High level reconnaissance provided us with the intelligence which enabled us to make our way at moderately low level to troop concentration points with the advantage of surprise, to make devastating firing passes along trench lines ahead of our own shock troops' breathtaking advance.

For *Schlacht*, Ritter and his gunner wore breastplate armour from the start as well as 1916 pattern steel helmets with the deeper visor. Each had a full-face clip-on steel visor with slits for the eyes, painted like tribal war or death masks; not only to deflect small arms fire and shrapnel, but to frighten the shit out of Russian peasants who for the most part made up the Red conscript army. Their deep superstition could be relied upon to gave way to terror when confronted by seemingly unstoppable winged monsters of 'iron' flown by ghoulish spectres; immortal spirits, spitting fire and death into their gun pits and horse lines from twin forward-firing Spandaus; and with the CL.1, a flexible Parabellum gun enfilading from the rear cockpit.

The theory was they'd abandon their positions and flee in terror from these *tchorts*: these winged devils incarnate. Indeed it seemed to have such an effect. Before long *Kampfgeschwader Wiking's* armourers were spending every spare moment beating out steel breast plates and visors for all the low-level attack pilots, the eyeholes burned out by oxy-acetylene torch.

Kessler and I had two of the first and painted them to look quite terrifying, Kessler's was black, decorated with a white swastika each side and a wicked red grin. Mine was a simple death's head, also with grinning teeth. They seemed both ancient and symbolic, like African tribal helmets, though we lacked the cowrie shells. Perhaps the ancient content of the collective unconscious is archetypal, from our fearsome cannibal-warrior origins. For practicality they were fleece-lined, both for warmth and improved comfort.

Before the War one's close support military intelligence horizon had been limited by how far an Uhlan could see, standing tall with binoculars, balancing on his horse's saddle. Such was our paradox, we contributed advanced technological warfare with shameless voodoo: the fetish-mask element of the occult!

Now high speed low-level photo reconnaissance revealed pockets of the enemy's dug-in positions; ambushers along the roads ahead of our advancing field grey; though the real heroes and shock troops of this conflict as we viewed them were the tough *Freiwilligen* Regiments of Rohrbach, Fischer, Kettner and Hess. Bischoff's *Eiserne Division* and Fletcher's *Baltische Landeswehr.*

We soon discovered that despite our technical advantage we could in turn be ambushed. A *Judas Goat* would be rolled out. A locomotive making steam to attract our roaming fighters a short distance behind the lines, or a railway balloon company would raise a decoy gas bag. We would be lured into a strafing attack only to become the focus of concentrated fire from concealed positions. We were lucky if we avoided casualties on such occasions but the assault aircraft invariably returned peppered with holes and leaking fuel. We learned quickly to cross the lines out of sight and attack the locomotives from the rear, outwitting the gun crews.

Sometimes Red cavalry would circle in the dust to raise a cloud to attract a patrolling Halberstadt or Ju CL.1 *Schlachtbomber.* Again we would be subject to ambush and learned a bitter lesson with injured crew and damaged aircraft; Lts. Betz and Pohlmann lost and Lt. Schnell lifted from the cockpit of his shot-up Albatros, more dead than alive.

While the myth that the corrugated metal fighters were armour-plated and impregnable prevailed, nervous machine gun crews were persuaded to abandon their positions, fleeing our determined attacks. We'd heard from prisoner interrogation that these derelict gun crews were summarily dispatched by their commissars for cowardice in the face of the enemy, but it would only take one Ju to be brought down to dismiss the misconception. It went without saying that any *Freikorps* pilot unlucky enough to be brought down alive and faced with inevitable capture in Bolshevist territory should avoid falling into the enemy's hands *at all costs.* In extremis he was to use his side arm on himself. Death would be easier by his own hand. This was the most bitter conflict against an enemy that did not abide by conventions and the alternative was not to be contemplated.

We gained daily experience of the fluid front with its shifting warfare of cavalry and armoured trains. Covered by our Albatros and Fokker D.VII fighters, we circled and dived on enemy positions, getting right on the deck, flying on the same eye-line as a mounted cavalryman. We sprayed field kitchens and motor transport alike with tracer, shot the train crews and rolling stock, strafed mobile workshops, buildings, balloon companies and armoured cars with 'fanatical leather-coated commissars' firing revolvers at us as we tore past. Mostly the Red aeroplanes we saw were crashed or wingless on rail flat cars and we destroyed those with great prejudice. Better on the ground than in the air! In the air we engaged Red Sopwith Strutters and Nieuports, generally getting the better of them despite their manoeuvrability. They stood no chance against the Fokkers and even we *Schlacht* pilots could handle them.

We hit ammunition dumps and fuel trucks, glorying in the blossoming flowers of orange and black, braving the hail of lead from furious machine gunners; firing on running men, merciless in our winged vengeance, adrenaline pumping in dangerous low flying: attacking bridges and hitting transport in congested narrow roads. Kessler and Bachmann backing up my lead, slashing in from left and right so that the Bolshevists in the rubble of nameless villages or defending Kurlandian railheads had no respite. They were hardly able to draw bead on a low flying D.1 before they'd be attacked from the beam by a steel-clad knight with a grinning face of iron, by 'armoured aeroplanes' piloted by the 'undead', their terrifying skulls or red fetish masks, daubed like Red Indian faces; all flying in pre-planned, simultaneous figure eights over railway sidings, over ruined factory or town, woodland or farm.

Von Ritter and a Kette of the bigger CL.1s flew in and dropped their bombs into hell on earth from low altitude, their gunners spraying anti-aircraft positions as they broke away. Top cover was provided by Fokkers and Albatrosse. That flown by the flamboyant von Moritz was by now *very* distinctive. His *Bayerische Wappenschild*, Bavarian-blue-and-white diamond fuselage be-flagged Austrian-built D.III flew alongside the drab-painted fighters of Klein, Laumann, Dreystunck-Ulzburg, Stausebach and the other Jasta members - good men all. They patrolled above, watching our tails, diving and twisting though the smoke, firing on any targets we may have missed as our own ammunition ran low and we headed for base. Rarely it seemed were we to encounter aerial opposition. We were the lords of the sky: Teutonic eagles and one secret Lithuanian falcon, each claiming their contested domain.

But Hugo said it: 'Yesterday, gentlemen, we were just boys, climbing trees like monkeys, running and playing children's games. Today we are masters of all that we survey, vengeful gods; relentless in punishing, bringing fear and retribution to the ungodly of the earth. Tomorrow we'll be lucky if we can beg a job cleaning public toilets.'

Worse. Overall, we were losing.

To continue day after day like this would have been suicidal. All our aeroplanes had suffered hits from ground fire. Betz and Pohlmann had been shot down and killed in the first week. Then Altmann and Lindner. I'd been hit in the face by a round that caromed off the induction manifold, saved from injury by my 'death visor'. We had lost the advantage of surprise and the enemy had become more wary of us, moving more often in darkness. We mounted some night patrols along railway lines and landed by light of flares. But after some initial successes bad weather began to hamper us. Our funeral parades increased and our 'mess' parties became wilder and more desperate.

Altogether it was not a good time to go AWOL.

~.~

From notes abstracted from Tagebuch Kessler written after the Civil War
'Listen!'

Kessler, head cocked, motioned the little group of pilots to silence. The murmur of voices quieted. Faintly they heard it, the distant growl of an approaching aero-engine, rising and falling on the wind, becoming gradually louder. The pilots exchanged brief glances then followed Kessler's lead through the door of the pilot's room and out onto the duckboards surrounding the tarred and lagged hut on the advanced landing field. The wind torn sky was shades of grey and the air was chill. Outside it was more difficult to identify the direction of the sound, masked by the flapping of the ragged windsock and the gusting wind itself.

'Look, there. It's a Ju!' Hartmuth was pointing.

At once they saw a white flare rise into the overcast and the dark, blunt shape of a Junkers diving towards the field. They heard the shout, '*Alarm!*' And the air raid claxon's tinny squawking in the wind.

Estonian and Latvian forces had captured several German aircraft in the recent retreats, including Halberstadts, CL.1s and possibly a D.1 or two. This could be an attack. At the northern perimeter crews were manning pairs of swivelling *Spandaus* strapped to cartwheel gun mountings, axles stuck upright in the ground. They provided makeshift anti-aircraft weapons, effective against surprise low-level aerial attack. A captured, immobilized Bolshevik Isotta-Fraschini armoured car was positioned inside the perimeter under camouflage nets, which is exactly what it looked like from the air. But it had a heavy machine gun in a rotatable turret and its crew was alert.

They heard the motor throttle back. This was no raid! Could it be…..? The word went around. '*Steiger?*'

The Junkers whistled overhead showing its black crosses. The engine opened up again in the familiar, full-throated and viscerally-thrilling basso roar as it banked around, revealing the red/white Lithuanian Knight emblem on its fuselage. Light rippled on the dirty grey-green camouflaged wings as it turned to dive again towards the assembled pilots.

'*Leute*!' yelled Steinhauler, orderly officer. 'We don't know it's him! Take cover. Now!'

The men broke and took cover positions behind the wooden building as Steiger's Junkers dived to make a fast pass across the field, the deep drone of the full throttle BMW alternately echoing from the trees or muted by the huts and canvas hangars. The muffled pilot figure looked sideways, waving to the stragglers as the machine banked, then pulled up sharply over the conifers on the eastern perimeter.

'It's Steiger!' Kessler shouted, already running onto the field to intercept the fighter as it broke into a slipping turn, engine popping and burbling happily, the sound torn by the gusts.

The Junkers touched down, bumped and lurched across the rough grass of the temporary aerodrome on its 'perambulator' wheels: an ugly, lovely, battered, heroic tin box of a thing with its big straight-six engine. Breathing heavily, Kessler made it to the cockpit following his head start, twenty yards in front of the other pilots. He landed with a clang on the wing root, just as Steiger switched off.

'Gottverdammt, what happened to you, man?' Kessler gasped.

Steiger screwed up his eyes and lifted the flap of his helmet to hear: the engine's roar still ringing in his ears.

'Listen!' Kessler spoke loudly, directly into Steiger's ear. 'I reported that we'd become separated in cloud at the Latvian border, over Latgale, south of the Western Dvina twenty K west of Daugavpils. That's all. Stick to that for Christ's sake or we're both in the *Scheiße*!'

The other pilots were jogging up and within earshot. Ritter's car swept around the wing with the gangling figure of *Oberenginieur* Schneer, Chief Engineering NCO at the wheel, the adjutant and the Major in the back seats.

The Major, standing before the car came to a halt, climbed awkwardly out. 'Leutnant Steiger!' he roared. 'Good God, man! Where the hell have you been?'

The pilot unbuckled his harness and lifted his leg over the cockpit rim. He pulled off his helmet and stood unsteadily on the wing, clutching the turnover pylon and grinning at the Jasta which noisily clustered around, Laumann and Bachmann clicking away with their Leicas as if at some strange fauna or exhibit. Ritter pushed forward through the throng.

Steiger drew himself up and saluted. 'Leutnant Steiger reporting, sir,' he announced.

'You've been gone six days. How do you account for yourself?' The question was very serious, but some relief was evident in Ritter's tone.

'Came in for the attention of some light flak, Major. My leg is strapped up.'

'Leutnant Kessler, please assist this officer down.'

Kessler gripped Steiger's arm and helped him down from the wing.

Schneer was winding his two-metre skeleton out from under the right wing. 'Took some ground fire, eh?' he mused: announced to no one in particular with his usual informality. 'Small calibre. Just missed the aileron cables. *Lucky!*'

'The vital ones entered the cockpit,' said Steiger wryly, reaching firm ground.

The major looked at the bloodstained and lacerated flying trouser leg.

'Get yourself examined by the MO and get your dressing changed. Have something to eat and then write me a full report. On my desk in two hours. *Ohne Verzögerung!*'

'Yes, sir.'

'Meanwhile consider yourself under arrest and surrender your side arm to Lt. Kessler.'

'Sir.'

'And Rolf.'

'Yes'

'Welcome back.'

Rolf shuddered at the Major's retreating back.

There was sure to be a party in the mess tonight. Celebration of a Jasta victory or in this case Rolf's safe return, would mean the invocation of the Staffel's very own tradition: each pilot to imbibe a 'leg of ale', quaffed by turns from the Major's tin prosthesis. His spare, we hoped.

'Ach, Rolf,' lamented Hugo wryly. 'We Germans have ceased to be a nation of poets and dreamers. We have succumbed to the cult of brute power; seduced by Nietzsche's *Supermen*. We are fallen among ogres and tin-legged Vikings.'

~-~

Steiger's official report described how he and Kessler, flying as in *Rotte*, had been looking for targets of opportunity along the

Latvian/Lithuanian border: Bauska-Rokiskis as briefed. They were nearing their critical endurance point, for a safe return to Alt-Auts on remaining fuel, when Steiger's BMW had begun running rough. He'd fallen behind Kessler's D.1 and had started losing height with the motor misfiring badly. Orographic cloud had formed in the hills, clinging to the trees and obscuring the lead aircraft as he descended.

At that moment ground fire had penetrated the cockpit floor, injuring him in the left lower leg. He hadn't seen where it had come from. Steiger turned away from the locality suffering nausea and losing blood. The engine was still running, just, so he'd turned south looking for somewhere to dump it. He managed to put it down in a firebreak, stemmed the blood flow and walked several painful kilometres, stopping frequently to apply a tourniquet to his calf.

In a state of near collapse he knocked at the door of a *Försterei*, a forest ranger's cottage. It was the home of a Lithuanian family, which was good luck for the Flieger Leutnant, who placed himself at their mercy. Their hospitality and care was unfailing despite the risks they ran should Lett militia or Red soldiery have discovered his hiding place in the attic space. They shared what little food they had with him and undoubtedly saved his life. The forester had gone out the next day to find and camouflage the abandoned Junkers with netting and tree branches.

Basic first aid had been performed on his wounds, a bullet was removed from his calf muscle and the wound cleaned and stitched by the very practical forester's wife. The forester had driven him back to his aircraft by cart as soon as he'd felt confident to fly it back or die in the attempt. He'd determined that a main magneto lead had become detached and some of the plugs had become oiled. Enough tools were carried to establish this and spare plugs were fitted, after which the engine was cranked into life. It delivered full static revs, wheels chocked against some logs.

Steiger had flown southwest until he found a German supply column in bivouac and landed in a field nearby to scrounge some petrol. The *Nachschub Kommandeur* provided the information that *Kampfgruppe Wiking* was still operating from Alts-Auts as far as he knew.

He'd considered that he was very lucky to have avoided being discovered by enemy troops, deserters or wandering bandits.

It was a totally convincing fabrication, he thought. Except for the 'bullet wound'.

In the lazarett *Oberarzt* Major Brandt commented to Steiger that he seen many odd things in his career but Steiger's 'bullet wound' was perhaps the oddest.

'How do you explain it yourself?'

'I don't explain it other than to admit I was very glad of the first aid. I was unable to walk far and had to have some days to recover before attempting to fly back. Do we have to say more than that?'

Brandt gave Steiger an old fashioned look. 'As far as I am concerned the wound was very professionally dealt with. Clean, and expertly stitched. Quite the seamstress I'd say.'

'Yes she is. A loyal and trusted servant of an old and well-loved family.'

'Hmmm. Well I'm entering it on the *Wundzettel* as a healing wound to the left calf and lower left shin. There's no need to enter the word 'bullet'. I'll fudge that. I'll have the orderly apply a new dressing. There's a stick you can use for the time being. Do I need to mention that you're off flying for two weeks at least?'

'Thanks, Doc,' said Steiger, and meant it.

~-~

Rolf had stooped to examine the repairs being effected by Oberinginieur Schneer. The chief mechanic unwound from beneath the fuselage and looked him in the eye. 'You must have been damn low to collect those wounds, Herr Leutnant.' he joked, brushing forefinger and thumb together in an unambiguous gesture. The gunfire residue; black powder burns around the holes were still evident. Rolf's expression was enigmatic: good enough for Fabian Schneer.

~-~

But Ritter was not easily impressed by the detail of the report. He'd carpeted him in his office with the adjutant present and demanded to know where the supply *Kolonne* had been located and who was commanding it. Steiger admitted he hadn't ascertained the name of the column commander and was vague as to its position. Ritter suggested in no uncertain terms that Steiger was lying and that if the column commander had provided such information he should face a court martial since Steiger was carrying no identification and the Ju could have been a captured aircraft flown by a Bolshevik spy. In fact, he intimated, the whole event was highly suspicious and he, Steiger, was lucky not to be facing a court martial: indeed perhaps he'd gone over to the Bolsheviks and was now himself a double agent.

Steiger could think of no further explanation to offer, and was forced to stick to his story, if only for Kessler's sake.

Ritter gave him a withering look and told him that if he was going to lie he'd be advised to take lessons, to do it better in the future. He said he knew about Steiger's motivation and the pain he must have been going through, Ritter having lost a Baltic estate of his own and numerous family members, dearly missed. But divided loyalties had no place in Army Group VI and even less in *Wiking*. If pilots were derelict in their duty things would fall apart even quicker than they were doing already. He fined Rolf a month's pay and confined him to camp like a junior cadet, although he would continue to fly operationally.

Though chastened, Rolf had already made his next implacable decision. After all, as he saw it, he was fighting more than one war. If the Freikorps could not effectively protect German Balt families on their northeast border with Belarus, then he would have to help them to help themselves.

Their fate couldn't be left in the hands of a merciful God; not for an apostate. Not here.

Chapter 35. *Return to Liepus Namas*
Tagebuch Steiger

I find I am thinking of a warm summer's day, murmurous with insects droning among the long tasselled grass. Two horses graze contentedly nearby. Their riders lie on their backs in the grass and tell each other secret, fanciful dreams of adolescence - she the more mature, he the gauche youngster, hopelessly in thrall, both slipping tentatively into the uncharted waters of first love. They gaze up into the hot blue sky with its pretty, puffy cumulus. He wishes more than anything that he could fly up there, above the land where they lived, voyage far upon the winds to see all the lands of the earth, like a great eagle or albatross responding to the pull of the sea, free-flying under the great dome of the sky. She likes the idea of an albatross, sailing on the wind for weeks at a time.

'Then I will be an albatross too, and fly with you always,' he says. 'You know that they pair for life?' It is the boldest declaration of love yet, and he blushes when she turns and looks deep into his eyes. He feels he could look into those eyes forever. The choice of birds is prophetic in a way that neither one could know. This is the occasion that they share their first kiss. It too is tentative, exploratory, shy and awkward.

Much later they will share such a moment again, more passionately. And then, because the young learn quickly they are soon expert, and believe that no one, in all literature or life, love as they do.

But when I think of Lithuania now, it is not of sunny pastures. It is with melancholy, and it snows upon the childhood of my memory.

~-~

I sit fifty metres off Kessler's starboard wing as he gently rises and falls, turning his head slightly this way or that as he tries to identify woods and frozen rivers. I should be leading because I know this territory, or at least I am approaching an area that should soon become familiar. Yet it all looks so different under snow. Beautiful and enchanting, but difficult for navigation, especially with fog in the shallow valleys.

My D.1 is trailing a little, indeed I am using more power to maintain height and have been ever since I joined up with Kessler on this sortie. It had of course to do with what I'd loaded the night before, cramming boxes of 7.62, 9.0 mm *Kernmunition* and other calibre rounds into every cranny in the cockpit, under the seat and even in the rear fuselage. I'd also secreted small arms aboard so that the aircraft was dangerously over laden with the centre-of-gravity as far aft I dared move it. It is for that reason I am not encumbered by my body armour and steel helmet. I had looped the bungee over the stick immediately after take-off to pull it forward and take the load off for flying it so far out of trim – and getting worse by the minute as fuel was burned off. I had convinced myself that no one other than Kessler knew what I was doing. The general collapse and our rearguard efforts at stemming the Red advance meant that much equipment had had to be abandoned. Trucks were set on fire if they couldn't be moved and our troops were moving back in an orderly fashion - so went the official line. *Kampfgruppe Wiking* was one unit that was still operating with some success, but were now bowing to the inevitable. Provisions were scarce but accounting for every box of ammunition had gone by the board. Some regiments had broken up and begun the trek home in small vulnerable groups. A bad idea. Regrettably our own Freikorps had succumbed to the vice of looting.

Identifying the railway junction at Spogi we turned northeast, half-heartedly looking for armoured trains. Telltale steam was visible for twenty miles or more on a clear day, but now all was grey and foggy. It was rumoured that that loose cannon Count Bermondt-Avalov had amassed an armada of nearly 150 aircraft. But it almost seemed he couldn't make up his mind which side he was on, if any, and we'd never seen his air force in the air. The Reds had increasing numbers however and they were occasionally skirmished with. But mostly our targets were locomotives, horse-drawn wagon trains, motorised convoys or troop positions. In the event of a forced landing near Bolshevist lines the order of the day was to put a bullet through your own head. I'd not be engaging the enemy at all as my machine was too heavily laden and on this occasion both Kessler I would make the southern detour to Advance Landing Ground *Heinrich*, the once manicured lawns at Liepus Namas. I was looking for the landmark lakes near the village of Kuznetsowa and the town of Aleksandras where we'd land and unload the cargo of weaponry and ammunition.

This time Kessler would stick with me and was planning to either land after me, if the going looked reasonable, or stay in the vicinity to provide aerial cover. That was if the situation looked safe. If the snow proved too deep I'd be in trouble. But that was another matter. Things were so desperate that if I had to stay and fight on the ground, then so be it. Ernst could not help much, other than to keep the enemy's head down until his D.1 ran out of ammunition or got low on gas. If all was clear we'd both be able to refuel from the fuel dump, if it was still intact. If not… well that was war.

We fly on, and after a while the sun appears, casting long shadows across the milky pools of the shallow, fogged-in valleys. The fields are radiating moisture as the air warms and I know that the visibility will most likely worsen before there is any possibility of improvement.

Gradually familiar landmarks begin to appear, and away to the north the shadowed hillside with its obelisk becomes visible, the Grunewald Denkmal hanging clear of the misty river valley with its memories of Katya and the great boar shoot. We are a little north of track, so I open up to take the lead, dark smoke issuing from my saxophone exhaust. I waggle my wings while turning right, about 30 degrees to the southeast. Kessler banks and follows.

Soon we approach the low-lying wooded hills and little cluster of lakes with the one-time leper colony island that identified the north westerly border of the expansive Kuznetsowa Folwark. I fly overhead to look for signs if life. It has been many long weeks since my autumnal aerial visit: delayed by forces beyond my control.

From 500 metres altitude Liepus Namas under snow stands as proudly now as ever. Only the high eastern gable shows evidence of fire damage, snow having drifted inside the roof space. With the BMW throttled I enter a shallow curving glide, circling the house and stables, the angular shadow of the D.1 flitting briefly across the inner courtyard and the formal gardens the hint of pilaster and gateway casting pale shadows in the weak winter sunshine. Any hope that the house has been spared is extinguished by the total lack of glazing in any of a half a hundred windows. Away to the north, from the stand of trees clustered about the lake ice a sudden movement against the snow causes me to lift my gaze, my gauntlet instinctively opening the throttle wider.

A dark shape is plunging through the crust of drifted snow, a fine black stallion, blazing with energy fleeing from the sound of the engine which must be bouncing from the trees. The stallion galloping now across iron hard fields, heading west to the purple shadow of more distant woodland and the well remembered water meadows of a sometime idyllic youth. *Buran?* That same tempestuous black horse I'd tended, still living and vital? I drop the nose in pursuit, a little unnerved, almost willing there to be a rider on its back; but the horse is running in terror from the pursuing monster and runs alone.

Pulling up over the trees, heart pounding in empathy, I swing away to the south. The scale is wrong. The poor beast is barely the ghost of a Buran – a frightened *Panje* pony, its emaciation visible at low level… probably riddled with parasites. I abandon the creature at the edge of a thin cover of birch, to recover or die.

Circling low I am reluctant to break the spell of the house, but the loftier illusion of a veil of calm has been drawn back forever in my mind. At low-level, in brooding close-up, the dark-streaked façade is testament to strife. With a dread that makes me physically tremble and a sick feeling in my stomach, I throttle down again, breathing deeply under the muffler that protects my nose and mouth from the freezing air. I make my final turn towards the right hand of the two once-manicured lawns and back into what little wind there may be.

My imagination now in check, subconsciously steeling my muscles, I make a careful approach to land. Dispassionately I note that more of the mature lime trees that had lined the two-carriage width formal drive have been felled.

I touch down surprisingly gently: the snow-camouflaged assault monoplane rolling softly to a halt in snow that is no more than 50 mm deep. I switch off and sit looking at the house for a time, the engine tinkling as it cools. I release my straps, climb out heavily in my multi-layered clothing onto the corrugated wing, and drop to the ground at *Heinrich*.

My ears are ringing with residual noise but in the distance I think I hear Kessler's engine still. I cannot identify the direction but the sound seems to be receding. That was not in the plan! My ears are still buzzing and at first I don't really hear the word *Rittmeister*, until it's repeated. I turn to see a little boy, maybe ten years of age. It is he who's promoted me from Leutnant to cavalry captain! He has a pinched white face and his cheeks and nose are red from the cold.

'Rittmeister,' he repeats louder. 'Excellency, I saw your flags, sir!'

Part Four

Chapter 36. *Frankfurter Hof Memories*

At Norwood Hill James is recounting young Arkadi's stumbling story of the assault upon the Linden House verbatim: told with much effort in the comfort of Harry's Frankfurterhof suite. James recalls it clearly, though it is two decades since that first meeting at the Frankfurt *Buchmesse*.

'You know, James?' says Harry. 'Furtherance of Bolshevist ideology was prosecuted by any and all means. One example, to destroy and defile, eradicate a class and a culture with malice aforethought using savage measures against all owners of property written into bloody manifesto.'

By now Harry's use of both the definite and indefinite articles is arbitrary.

'They legitimised suffering for the hated bourgeoisie, allowing 'Soldiers of the Revolution' to enjoy unbridled spree of lawless excess against families of stature; women and children who might hitherto have been unspoken objects of fascination and desire - they were at the mercy of this *affliction*. Gripped in the terrible jaws of mass predation, standing helpless before a beast inflamed by unholy and perverted lust.'

After he was shot and injured by Fanny Kaplan Lenin's fury was boundless, his thirst for revenge without limits. He is more paranoid than ever, seeing enemies everywhere and 'bays like hound' for blood, so gives *carte blanche* to act in the most brutal fashion, allowing the Revolutionary masses to slake all carnal desires, gives power by decree for the seizure of any person and all property; power of arrest, transport, and to commit murder at the same time. *Dead: believed interrogated*, was a common cynical comment. Lenin has lifted all taboos concerning how ruling or middle classes are handled. He is like the Saracen invader, releasing torture, murder and looting on an Old Testament scale, for an ideology. He knows it is uncontrollable and allows them their heads, knowing that like children they will tire in time, sated; but by then will have done what he could not do in months or even years of ordinance and legislation; to erase a whole strata. Then, after this, the *first phase*, he could reel in the loose cannon, his barbarian children, imprisoning or liquidating, or otherwise promoting them, depending on his mood.

Considering how drunk they were for much of the time it's amazing they achieved what they did. Revolutionary zeal among the most forceful leaders was matched by their indiscriminate use of murder and rape as a 'political' tool. The demonstrators along with the Revolutionary Guards were drinking fine wine from Nicholas II's cellars, the bottles smashed in the gutters of the Winter Palace Square, 'lapping it like dogs and fornicating with women in the streets'. Successive guards and armoured divisions and finally the Petrograd fire brigade were called in to try to restore order, but all succumbed to the bacchanal.

It was farcical but has been thoroughly re-scripted in the official accounts and heroically immortalized in Eisenstein's subsequent film. Like everything in Russia since, airbrushed, revised, slavishly contorted to the Party's view of History, right through the Great Patriotic War and beyond. How an empire could be built out of this and all the 'mistakes' that were made later is astonishing, and it is down to the strong backs of the Russian people and the will and determination of one man, who would bury anyone who questioned him. Once rolling, the apparatus of the state terror organization and its tiers of bureaucracy was unstoppable. It became necessary to hold two diametrically-opposed viewpoints in one's head at same time. One was Party Line on everything and the other might approximate to the unspoken truth.

'What more is needed for proof of evil at the dark heart of Bolshevism? Seeing widows of murdered officers first selling their jewellery, dressed in rags to hide their breeding and beauty, then selling their bodies to feed their starving children is a great satisfaction to the most zealous of commissars, who are already living in their expropriated houses, wearing their finery. Smirking and jeering as the loveliest of women become debased syphilitic suicidal wretches that even they, hard-hearted venereal transmitters as they are, would not deign to further rape. Is this final triumph of their acts of perversion for the revolution? No, there was plenty more to come: enslavement and death for millions.'

Harry had handed him a yellowed pamphlet, the faded print declaiming 'Bolshevist Press Message – 30th. August 1919' Pinned to it was a more recent English translation.

It outlined that:

'......in compliance with the decisions of the *Soviet of Peasants Soldiers and Workers Deputies of Kronstadt,* the 'private possession of women' had been abolished, social inequalities and legitimate marriage having been an instrument in the hands of the Bourgeoisie thanks to which all the *'best species of beautiful women'* have remained the 'property of the Bourgeoisie'

…means by which 'proper continuation of the human race' have been presented have induced this organization to issue the present decree.'

Proto-communist polemic. Long-winded and typically pompous, even in poor translation, James thought.

It continued:

'From March 1st, the right to possess women of the ages 17 to 32 is abolished. The age of women shall be determined by birth certificate and passport. Failing to produce such documents the age will be determined by Committee which shall be judged according to appearance.
'Former husbands may retain the right to continue using their wives but resistance to the above decree will result in the husband forfeiting his right under the first paragraph. All women according to this decree are liberated from private ownership and are proclaimed to be the property of the whole nation. The distribution and management of appropriated women in compliance with the decision of the aforesaid organization are transferred to a Special Committee. All women detailed by it for use by the whole nation are obliged to present themselves to a given representative and to supply the required information.
'Any citizen noticing any woman not submitting herself to the address under the decree must make the fact known giving name of woman.
'Men citizens have the right to use one woman 3 times a week for 3 hours observing rules specified below.
'Every man wishing to 'use a piece of public property' should be bearer of certificate from Authoritative Committee of Workmen, Soldiers' and Peasants' Council certifying he belongs to a working class family.
'Women, when they become pregnant, are released for three months before and one month after childbirth.'
'Children born are given to an institution for training after they are one month old where they are to be trained and educated until they are 17 at the cost of Public Funds.
'In case of birth of twins a mother is to receive a cash prize (£20 equivalent at 1919 rates).
'All citizens are obliged to watch themselves carefully and those who are found guilty of spreading venereal disease will be held responsible and severely punished.*('Death Penalty' had been written here).*

'Women who have lost their health may apply to the Soviet for a pension.'

There was much more in this vein.

'What's that garbage?' James was annoyed and playing devil's advocate. 'Forced prostitution of an entire class by *decree*? Are you asking me to believe it's any more than the clumsiest piece of demonising propaganda? It's the sort of despicable nonsense the *Anarchists* would have trotted out, from what I've read?'

Harry looked at him sadly.

'So what have you read? Anarchists had mostly been *liquidated* by Cheka in 1917. It is accurate, *literal* translation from original taken from proclamations pasted up around Kronstadt and Petersburg. It is not particularly well phrased, in fact primitive. As is *spirit* of document itself. I offer it as *one example* of official attitude. Not just so that whole section of society in class war would be exterminated, intellectuals and bourgeoisie, but to grind last particle of humanity, decency and compassion from society. Legality granted to animal lust: to degrade in most punishing and vile manner women deemed guilty of belonging to higher class.'

This was Bolshevism according to Harry with its hyenas unleashed, and who could question his passionate denunciation of its vilest horrors, given his experiences at so young an age? Despite the avowed idealism of its leading lights for the emancipation of the proletariat. It was not as if he were describing collateral damage. Such perverted cruelties were deliberately inflicted by zealots and criminals roused to a pogrom of unrestrained savagery in which they could delight with no consequence for the morrow. Worse even than the Ottomans, he said.

As with all Harry revealed, it rolled out sometimes unexpectedly taut, often eloquent and dramatic, *slow-burning* through each cycle of events, but not necessarily in true chronology. The freezing gulags, slave camps. Punishment camps for women. The horrors of 're-enforced interrogation'.

'Eyes gouged, tongues ripped out, women's breasts, fingers cut off. Men's beards torn out. Castration, rape: all was done. For what? Thousands of people tortured for months, years even, by the State. So very many 'Enemies of the People'. There were always queues of snakes ready to denounce their neighbours. Some even received medals for it. The *Black Ravens* were worked overtime. It typified waste in soviet society: waste of potential. Waste of *human flesh*!' Harry is scathing. 'What a feast for the unfortunate cannibals in the worst of camps. No wonder

KGB chief Dzerzhinsky needed those expensive foreign rest cures! It must have been exhausting to preside over all this horror.'

The lime pits were filled all night long, the vans in convoy. They had to work faster in the summer months with so much daylight. To fill the quotas. To achieve the minimums.

'The cult of the personality achieved perfection at that time, James. I remember when I had been pardoned for the crime of being homeless Polish orphan. I had been released after surviving nearly nine years as slave labourer. Anniversary of the Revolution parade in Red Square. I had been transported by railway wagon, given a hair cut and clean vest and trousers to march with hundreds of others before being 'deported' or whatever was to have been my fate - I was too cynical even then to believe they thought we'd work for Comintern. There we were tens of thousands, along with the foreign press to spread the word of Russia's economic miracle and her military might. There were garlanded maidens dancing and marching with the workers with their picks, sickles, shovels and sledgehammers. Floats with red and gold banners, lorries laden with sacks of sawdust masquerading as grain, a groaning cornucopia of plenty defended by tanks and aircraft. No hint of hideous famine.'

'There was the usual sycophantic Soviet poster art. Stalin smiling in his snow-white uniform, bigger than the skies of Russia, straddling - like Kolossus - the bountiful wheat fields of Ukraine, kindly father to his happy people. The land was overflowing with milk and honey. *We are heading towards prosperity!*' Smiling tractor drivers and grateful children. *Thank you, our beloved Stalin for our happy childhood!*' When he died, years later, siren mouths and factory hooters howled all day. People were mad with grief and fear. The monster had gone leaving a monstrous hollow, an abyss, with nothing there to fill it. As if only his will and vision had held it all together. They thought Russia would implode, the sky would fall.'

'In portraits his arms were painted as if they were same length, like court portraits of Kaiser Wilhelm, who also had a withered arm. Moreover those purged from his circle were painted-out of official portraits and photographs, airbrushed, like Stalin's pock-marked skin. Artists and photographic re-touchers were kept at it full time, painting-out the latest non-personages who'd been liquidated, who'd disappeared without trace along with their families into the misery of the slave ship cages, the camps, the torture cells. Or were busy adding Stalin's prominent figure to depictions of important historical events around the revolution, when he'd perhaps been too cautious, or too *minor*, to have actually been present. It was politically advantageous to create pictorial evidence for each up-to-the-minute historical revision and an opportunity for endless retrospective creativity.

For in the USSR you never could tell what might happen yesterday!

~.~

Many towns and cities bore the name of 'Stalin'. Gigantic banners trucked through Red Square testified to the vogue which elevated the personality. They were indeed monstrous. Phalanxes, profiles of Marx and Engels. Stalin shoulder to shoulder with Lenin in infamy. Then Stalin alone, mighty, omnipresent, indefatigable. Despotic.

Later on, the most gigantic aeroplane of all. Propaganda machine *Maxim Gorky*, flew over Moscow - *that is until it crashed after a collision with a stunting fighter.* And the most gigantic flag of all fluttered over Red Square, towed behind a *troika* of PO-2 biplanes with their fighter escort. Slowly, majestically it trailed the massive head, its nine metre black Georgian moustache on a red background; the sky illuminating the whites of the eyes. A malevolent hovering demon. Big Brother watching us from the skies. Orwell captured it perfectly.

Natashka, Russia is still in denial about its past. The Cult of Personality has been revived. Stalin is being widely rehabilitated. Lenin has never been interred.

The official history of the USSR and the Great Patriotic War, written in the spirit of Putin's view of 'Positive History', now claims that the West appeased Hitler until grudgingly it entered on the Soviet side, 'once we could see which way the wind was blowing' no doubt! So obviously the Battle of the Atlantic, the Battle of Britain never happened. This grotesque lie is then compounded by glossing over the treacherous non-aggression pact between the USSR and Nazi Germany which divided a prostrate Poland between them in 1939 and was our very reason for going to war. Britain and the Commonwealth alone until 1941.

So what about the brave British convoys, attacked en route by the Luftwaffe from Norway; convoys in which Britons died providing Stalin with precious munitions and

528

materiel via Archangel? Was this given more than a short paragraph in some revised Cold War Official Histories: still less that Bomber Command's offensive was the de facto Second front demanded of us by Uncle Joe?

And so we again zoom-in, from macro view to micro.

~-~

It was obvious that Harry's childhood experiences were still hard for him to articulate. The psychological wounding was very deep. It was both depressing and agonising to pick off the scabs and examine their lividity, to disinter such memories after all this time. After the scar tissue had formed.

He describes the scene in the white bedroom: the young Arkadiusz struggling to break free from the powerful grip that holds him, that forces him down upon the soiled and tender flesh of the prostrate young woman who arches and jerks against her bonds, trying to spit, but with no saliva because her mouth is dry.

'Her throat is raw from screaming and she only makes a whimper. A sort of piteous mewling, like a drowning kitten.

"You know what!" one says sagely, "He cannot get it up yet. He is not yet developed. The *soldier* is too tiny!"

Wit of such profundity that all of the assembly rolls helpless on the floor.

Harry's thinking quickly, that *he* might yet escape this. He swiftly dons his breeches and tries to make an exit, when a hard arm blocks his progress, and a voice close by says softly. "Oh, no! Ye cannot go yet. Stay. Enjoy the party. *We* stand upon tradition, and thou hast not been *blooded.*"

Harry turns then from the window and stares me in the eyeballs. "James, someone took a hunting knife and thrust it deep inside her. Then her screams were awful — and still I hear them faintly. And so they came back to me, and held me very tightly, marking my young body with red stain of her lifeblood. For my initiation, as member of their *wolf pack.*"

The madman speaks through Harry, his voice becoming husky. "Now you are as one *with* us. Cub of *Roskov's Wolf Pack!* And the drunkards start their howling, opening their mouths: throwing up their faces and baying at the ceiling."'

I sit transfixed by what I perceive as the throbbing metre of James's delivery, as much as by the message. If Delcroix had felt the perspiration tickling his collar despite the cool night breezes and the sweet scents from the *Haschmarkt* then here in Norwood my brow is damp too, from that gruesome re-telling, like a deranged parody of the *Song of Hiawatha*. I sink another can.

The young Harry, crying and sobbing, had somehow found his voice. Shaking like a leaf he'd had the strength to curse them shrilly all to hell. He said that the Count would make all of them pay in blood for what terrible deeds they'd done. That they'd never be forgiven by God for this crime. Then the one with the quiet voice and mad eyes had come close. "Didn't they tell you, little soldier, there is no God?' he'd whispered. 'Official. Banished. Exiled to Siberia. Replaced by the Central Committee. God is no more and we *can*, and *will*, do *exactly* as we please."

'It's not true. Damn you for a pigdog. God hears you, shit of the devil. He will punish you. The Count...'

The hard little man stares with what seems like excitement in his eyes.

'What Count?'

'The Count....' Harry's bottom lip trembles.

'Oh, *that* Count. You want to tell *that* Count.' The man smiles mirthlessly. 'Come then. Let us tell him.'

'He drags me, James, down a corridor to a long dining room. The silver is stacked on one side ready for transporting. Everything else is smashed or desecrated in some way. There are turds, shit everywhere, James. On the tables and chairs. I am sorry if I am indelicate, but grim actions and dreadful deeds deny delicacy in the telling. There is a heavy stench and what I take to be the carcass of a boar upon the long table with smashed crockery, bloody garments and gore. It takes me some seconds to realise what it is. He has been skinned alive, James. Still breathing though mercifully unconscious, I believe. In shock but dying I think.'

'"Tell him about his beautiful daughter!"'

'*Graczyna* means beautiful in Lithuanian, James. Graceful. And so she was, in life.'

'"He can hear you, I'm sure," says my tormentor. "He will be interested to hear how many times we fuck his little girl, and how she howls like wolf and loves it so much we naturally feel obliged, every one of us, to do it again, over and over."'

'They bring me next to the body of this man, a nobleman who has always treated his servants and workers well, truly felt the obligation of nobility, paid for medical attention for the poor, laid on feasts at Christmas, Easter, Forefathers' Eve – *Dziady* - and saints' days. A man who loved life and had done well for himself, not just sat back and enjoyed inherited wealth like some: and I am told. "Here is the scum of the earth. He and his class would be liquidated to a man when the Popular Revolution moved onwards beyond Belarus, through central Lithuania now that we had gained passage, Prussia, Germany, Europe, England. Yes even to America. The common man would inherit the earth and all privilege would be eradicated along with the ruling class. We are the 'clean up squads' of the Revolution, preparing the way for the United Soviet of the Earth!"'

'The Madman whispers in my ear. "Tell him about his precious daughter, boy. What a whore she was in the end like all women. Like his dead whore of a wife, Elenja. Like that other whore, his dead White Russian princess, Sophie, the *'Saint'*, whose painting I have much improved, don't you agree? *Whores!*"'

'He thrusts me close to the battered face of Graf Kristian. "He might hear you boy, if you speak up. But he might find talking difficult, I think."'

'There is a juvenile snigger at this, James. Then I understand the stink of cauterised flesh, realise in stomach-wrenching horror what it is protrudes from the Graf's bloody lips. Was common form of mutilation at that time, James, and not the worst that was done to the class enemy by Bolshevist rabble.'

Harry seems wearied by these last terrible revelations, which I believe he had successfully buried for a long time. He turns from the window, the firm jaw relaxing just a little, and sits carefully in an armchair opposite me.

'He held me close to the dying Graf, James, and put a long knife against my throat. "Tell him boy,' he hissed. 'Speak up and don't be frightened! Tell him the *Wassermann* has visited. Presented his calling card of vengeance and will do now with his youngest harlot what it is the Water Goblin does best."'

'I went into shock, James. For maybe a half-hour, several minutes at least, because when I was aware again I was alone lying downstairs in a corridor.'

Harry said that his throat had been burning from retching bile. Some commotion was going on in the hall. He must have automatically put on his boots, so he was at least physically ready for the last attempt to escape from Hell.

'I was terrified, sickened, but managed to sufficiently collect myself to search feverishly for an exit on the lower level. But all doors I'd tried to the outside were barred and locked. The bars I could lift, but there were no keys in the locks nor near at hand.'

They were on a drunken 'bender'. Before they left, the 'commissar' had told the surviving staff that they were not to touch the house. It was to be left with its bloody hammers and sickles daubed, and the bodies left to rot. Not to be removed on pain of death as a warning to others, like dogs or wolves that had marked their territory. But it was not practical and ate into the souls of devout and good people, so when they were gone, those same servants and the village people came in piety and assisted with the burying of the bodies with great reverence in a special plot atop the village cemetery.

But a while later the Wolf returned, or some of his rabid pack, perhaps to loot some more as if they'd not been able to carry enough the first time. They checked the village cemetery and found disturbed earth and freshly laid stone slabs with new crosses and the hated names inscribed with affection. So they desecrated the graves and took revenge on the people, hanging six villagers, four of them women, some of whom they'd identified as servants, others for good measure. These were dragged to the House, stripped, beaten, strung upside down like sows from the stable beams, among them Nina. And they were still suspended there, hacked, bloody and stinking to heaven when Krysia returned.

~.~

The Apple Barrel of the Hispaniola

But back again in Liepus Namas the terror is not over. A commotion in the hall had caused young Harry to tip-toe to the doorway and peer round from his dark retreat to see what might be in store and to look frantically for some other avenue of escape.

The mood in the house now differs sharply. There is a palpable change of atmosphere and no more the sound of drunken excess. Even though some of the men stand stupefied, at least most are now on their feet. Harry's nerves are in shreds, but he is keyed-up, his senses heightened, body tensed to the emergency, looking for any chink in the defences that might signal an opportunity for a last ditch escape, so he is keenly aware of the mix of visceral excitement and anticipation among the Wolves.

It seems that someone had arrived with an armed retinue and the noisy arrival had carried afar to some ragged village boys, wakeful from

532

hunger, as Harry would discover later.

The armoured locomotive *Victory to the Revolution* and its tender, pulling a boxcar studded with machine gun turrets and a flat railcar, had come hurtling out of the night on the main Petersburg railway line. It had squealed to a standstill in a shower of sparks at the nearest point to the Kuznetsowa estate near the village and two little urchins had tumbled out of their long ransacked, half-burned home and made their way to the railway line, shivering, hiding in the trees, huddling together for warmth. Looking for a chance to beg food or steal something to eat, if there should be an unguarded moment.

A piquet was mounted along the track, which was seen and avoided, but it proved too dangerous to approach the train. On the flatcar two armoured cars, *broneviki, Arkadi, bristling with Maxim guns*, had been cranked into life. They drove down heavy box-section ramps to disappear into the dark. Then the dazzle-painted locomotive had pulled back some distance, into a cutting, where it hid among the trees, a telltale plume still drifting from its stack. Steam was kept up 'til the armoured cars re-appeared, and once re-loaded on the flatcar, the train had reversed northwards at speed, the way that it had come, back into the frosty night. When it was quiet, the two starvelings had run back to their cheerless home, climbed into their beds and tried their best to get warm, unaware that a few miles away the marauding cruelty and terror visited late upon many a household, including Arkadi's, had now at last befallen those at the Big House.

~.~

In the Frankfurt night Harry sits with James in the darkness of his memory. Two decades later, in the genteel Home Counties, James sits before me: the cool of the evening made ominously darker by the ghastly tale by proxy, that Harry unfolds. As though we are at a séance and Harry is coming through with all the gory detail, such is the spirit of the age and the menace of time and place that James re-invokes with all of Harry's mannerisms.

'Do you know Stevenson, James?'

James answers are unfailingly wrong. 'Builder of the second steam locomotive, after Watt?'

'Robert Louis Stevenson, James. Master of adventure and suspense.'

'Go on.'

'I am the cabin boy on the *Hispaniola*.'

This literary reference is not immediately clear.

Like Kristian with Rolf, Harry dances around the mystery that he wishes to unveil, building tension, creating powerful mental images, like an illusionist, to drive home the story at first by allegory, to focus, to educate, make the listener's mind work for the reward.

For the truth.

Both were reluctant to reveal the secrets held captive in their hearts: the late Graf through shame that he did not acknowledge his own blood, and then had to break the awful news of the savage passing of those Rolf his entire life had known *in loco parentis*. Harry, plainly due to traumas in his childhood that were deeply painful to regurgitate, but also for a reason that was harder to fathom, James thought. Not merely for release, an unburdening of the soul, but hinted of something else more tangible, both dangerous and seductive, even after such a long time: and so would it prove to be for all time in the affairs of men.

'There are shouts and challenges from without,' Harry says. The sound of powerful motors draws near. The word *Koba* is spoken, apprehensively. One or two of the bandits toss back more vodka and at this the Madman rounds on them savagely. 'Koba', for it is after all just a man and his armed bodyguard, makes a stage entrance. 'Like something out of *Don Giovanni*, James' he stands there in the doorway, backlit by electric headlamps and wraithed in swirling mist. He has narrow eyes and a wide dark moustache, wears a military greatcoat and a cap with a red star, a furashka. He is little taller than the Madman whom he faces down with a yellow, unblinking stare. He sniffs.

'God's bowels, Nikolai Sergeyevich, it *stinks* in here. Like Armenian whorehouse.' The voice is low, guttural; foreign to my parochial ear.

His armed henchmen are similarly clad, some with ear-flapped papakhas. Most are over a head taller than he and of military bearing. Many have rifles. The obvious commissars have drawn revolvers. He walks slowly, looks about suspiciously, surveys all with icy stare: moves in unhurried silence through the ruin and destruction. Silence pervades the gathering broken only by the crunch of his boots upon the tiles, on chandelier crystals, heading for the dining hall, drawn thither by the stink of cauterised human tissue. The smell of blood hangs heavy in the air, both dog and human, and those rank odours of excrement and urine. The horses had by now been led outside but their droppings at least smelled sweet.

All this Harry observed from his hiding place as he vainly watched the doorway in case it might be unattended for a few moments. But

534

though it remained ajar, more guards could be seen hovering outside, smoking, rifles slung.

Harry hears the footsteps moving to the dining hall, where they stop. He knows that the man of stature, Koba, a general perhaps must be looking at the raw, flayed cadaver that was Graf Kristian von Strelitz. There is a long silence. Perhaps he is shocked. Perhaps gloating. Perhaps neither. He returns to face the Madman.

'You've been having a party,' he smiles coldly, crinkling the narrow eyes that disappear into slits. It is a terrible grimace in a pocked face: a soundless snarl from an uncaged tiger. 'Get that shit out of here,' he grates. 'I want a word with you, somewhere quiet.'

The '*Madman*', I later discover is one *Roskov*. He hisses some sharp commands in his theatrical whisper. The table is upended and only then does Harry see that he's been skinned from his shoulders to his hips. All he lacks is a crown of thorns. The Graf has been crucified upon the boards.

The table pitches sharply and like a china doll's, the Graf's eyes both open and he utters a dreadful moan. Harry, who'd thought the Graf was dead, nearly faints away at this, but stiffens to the action, viewed through hinge and doorjamb.

The big doors now open to a scene lit by ethereal light where the struggling Wolves grapple with the tabletop, manhandling the dying Graf's rude catafalque in the doorway. The image is almost heroic in its brutal irony: a grotesque parody that a king, fallen in battle, is borne reverentially to his rest. A sudden wind invades the house. Candles and oil lamps gutter and mist wraiths swirl about the entrance. It seemed to Arkadi that a pale wrack swept up the staircase to that place where the painting had hung. 'I believe that was when the Graf passed.' He says. Some of the Wolves 'eye' each other surreptitiously, even make the sign of the cross – *Old* style: a final irony perhaps.

'Before I know it, Nikolai Sergeyevich Roskov, a name I have now branded on my brain, and 'General Koba', Battlefront Commissar, are coming my way. I have no chance to escape and so must precede them down the corridor. I discover a room that like the others has been torn apart with dresses and linen scattered about and I throw myself in. In the gloom I find a laundry hamper and hide within, pulling down the lid and a sheet over my head as the voices draw nearer. Further along the corridor I can hear the muffled sobbing of women.'

'The footsteps go by the doorway and then stop. "Who is that?" I hear the Georgian accent for what it is. And Roskov's reply. "Just the servant girls and women. They are locked up. For now.'"

Hidden in the laundry hamper, through the thick woven cane, I observe two shadows looming in the dim halo that marks the doorway.'

The Georgian 'general' speaks. "In here, then. We don't need light. Time is short."

To Harry's increasing terror the two men enter the room. A match is struck, and by its red flare Koba's pocked face becomes the Devil's: *Ryaboi – the pock marked one,* a mask of evil in the mind of Harry who is staring wide-eyed through the lattice weave of the basket, trying to quiet the beating of his heart. *He will see these sinister eyes again. They will haunt him, staring out of posters and on statues. Glaring down from gigantic banners, fluttering above Red Square, towed by aeroplanes.......*

'So, Nikolai Sergeyevitch, you are well, I take it?' Koba lights his pipe and studies the man narrowly in the light to which all eyes are by now accustomed. The affable platitude, incongruous in the circumstances, is the sole preamble to the matter at hand. Roskov replies hesitantly, as though he has been wrong-footed. Harry thinks, that maybe the Madman wondered how Koba came to be there, how it was the 'general' tracked him.

The Wolves could have been anywhere, but avoided locations where the Landeswehr patrolled in force. Bolshevist reconnaissance units were theoretically under military discipline but others followed their own inclinations, path of least resistance. These predating and skirmishing Bolshevist gangs, especially the autonomous 'irregulars' were just bands of criminals and not controlled or monitored at higher level.

'Brigands, James. Disorganised. Barely affiliated with the Red Army. Of course I did not know this at the time, but have learned much since of the malice, lies and distortions that fanned the flames in those bitter years, and the instruments of evil. And at ten years old I was exposed to the full horror of it and the greater duplicity of the plotters among whom the majority would cut their mothers' throats for power and advantage, or a fortune in gold.

Harry is holding his breath in sudden terror as Koba walks purposefully towards his hiding place and pauses. Harry feels the crush and hears the air whistle out of the basket as the man sits heavily on the lid. Squashed, Harry scarce now dares to breathe at all in the deeper foetid darkness. He lies rigid, listening to the low-tone urgency of the business at hand, which proceeds in a swift exchange of Russian.

'He was *Jim* in the 'apple barrel of the *Hispaniola*, the ship in

536

Stevenson's *Treasure Island*, listening with baited breath as John Silver plotted mutiny with Israel Hands and the crew. That's how he described it to me, John.'

He closes his eyes and fights against panic, struggles to breathe. With the memory of his family and their probable end he is fighting back the sobs and reaction. *His* fate is now that of a fatherless child's, perhaps motherless too in a world that's insane, who'd seen hell already. Perhaps Harry was hallucinating as his oxygen supply dwindles, the boy suffocating beneath the sheet. Under the heavy spread of 'General Koba's' unbuttoned greatcoat upon the hamper lid, breathing in the heavy tobacco smoke he tries to hold to consciousness, concentrating on the forceful orders issued in that Georgian accent.

The stressed and overloaded brain creates survival endorphins. They mercifully switched off the demons as the boy drifted away.

Later there came the little bliss of self-awareness, that dream state before the mind fills in the detail, though it lingered only briefly and the memories returned to re-invade his mind with horror. He was suffering from cramp, but through the door the sun was shining and at least the house was calm and quiet.

~-~

Meanwhile, last night upon the misty lake in his little coracle, the emaciated wild-eyed creature that is *Cobweb* had rowed the trembling, soaking figure of Katya to his island whence he himself had secretly returned to live in even deeper mad seclusion since he was so wronged by undeserved accusation: of molesting baby Graczyna and young Kat years before. He silently paddled them beyond the faint glow of the mist, away into the darkness to the only safe place he knew, leaning back and pulling, a surprising strength there is in his mostly fingerless palms.

~-~

It all seems strangely still. Despite everything Harry has fallen into a long, exhausted sleep in the cramped confines of the basket. Light is streaming through the door. After listening a long while he slowly pulls away the sheet that had concealed him and raises his head. Rubbing his cramped joints he puts a tentative foot on the floor and nearly falls. 'Pins and needles' in his foot have to be massaged away first.

Creeping from the room he listens for any sounds that might betray the presence of the enemy, the *Wolves of Latgale,* or of the soldiers who'd come with their menacing commander of the night before.

All is still. He tiptoes along the corridor to the room where the sobbing had been heard and finds the door open. There is no sign of the servants. A welcoming fresh breeze with the scent of linden helps diffuse the rank odours of the night. He moves to the hall. Stains mark the floor tiles and crude slogans are daubed upon the walls in what he assumes is blood. There is a sudden piercing scream, like a demon from hell, a whirr and flutter from down the hall. Another inhuman shriek and he recoils in fright, heart thudding madly but it is no demonic vampire bird, only old Gagool, trailing her silver chain, flapping weakly at the French windows of the music room.

With trepidation he climbs the wide stairs to the white bedroom of the four-poster. There is no young defiled body upon the sheets; just the still red testimony to her violation, the wrappings of a martyred saint and the accusing imprint of her agony.

Outside the sun is shining. The Graf's body is nowhere to be seen. Gone too are the other corpses, the Estate Manager, the dead Wolves and the carcass of the beardog. The stained dining tabletop lies on the portal steps. The nails that held fast the hands and feet of Kristian still remain, driven in deeply as they were. He feels the autumn sun upon his face, the gentle wind that blows through the lindens: far off a skylark's farewell to a Russian summer.

Steeling himself he re-enters the house and snatches up some bread and a small slab of sausage from the filthy dining room and runs out again quickly. Again the parrot screams from somewhere deep in the interior, in apparent terror it seems to Harry. He wonders whether he should return and release it to the outside, but thinks better of it. It would not survive. With a still thumping heart he begins to walk towards the village, ready to flee across the fields or into the trees at first sight of danger, taking a more difficult path, cutting across the Estate. He eventually intercepts the road on a bend and drops behind a thicket to observe. There is a rider approaching from the direction of Liepus Namas: Jonnas, who was invalided from the war minus one leg. He has a rifle slung over his shoulder and there is a horse-drawn wagon following behind. Next to the driver is a woman, Kat! The daughter of the Graf, the Countess Katarzyna, with a few older village lads and hands. They have shovels and some are armed with ancient rifles. All are grim-faced, none more so than her Ladyship. A relieved Harry stumbles out of cover with his arms high and three rifles are suddenly on him as Jonnas reins in his mount and halts the plodding caravan.

Identified, Harry is hauled aboard and sits carefully, respectfully in the back, next to some bundles where old Cobweb rides, a weaponless observer to the rear. The hard-eyed countess addresses Harry with but a single question. Had he seen the Lady Graczyna? He shakes his head dumbly. It is too terrible to tell. No one else speaks. Of the dead marauders there is no sign and had Harry given it any thought at all assumes that they have been carried off or dumped by their comrades in murder. And so the burial party returns to the blackened village of Kuznetsowa from whence these volunteers had been drawn early that morning.

But Arkadi had forgotten that the mark of Cain was on him, from the savage ceremony of blooding and that it did not go unnoticed. Arkadi's worst fears were confirmed, that he had been orphaned, and his sisters had been abducted by stray elements of Roskov's pack of killers. Grief and vengeance flamed in his heart, though he was but a boy.

Kat, too was moving through a vale of grief. She was twenty-two and strong as only those who survive against a colossus of hurt and injustice can be truly strong. She'd not allow it in, to crush her, now or ever. The panic and horror she'd felt on the evening of the attack, when she had been outside and unarmed, so escaped by a hairsbreadth, she disguised with a mask of cold determination from which no tears would fall. It allowed her to cope with the immediate burials and the release from imprisonment at Liepus Namas of the young female staff, among them Nina, who greatly aided Katya, carrying too the larger burden of her grief, who'd tried to comfort her.

But Kat had already turned from weeping and from sorrow. She had decided to avenge her father and in the absence of Graczyna's body there was the slight possibility that her half-sister might still live and she swore that she would find her even if it meant sacrificing her own life. She closely questioned Arkadi, who tearfully gave a full account of what had happened, and felt guilt that he could not have saved Graczyna. Kat had stood in silence, a tower of ice before him as he sobbed out the whole story. Then Katarzyna kissed him, and the first time for a long while, she embraced another tightly.

He trailed her back to Liepus Namas where she'd gone to the gazebo, reaching down beneath the flooring to retrieve her Mongol bow and quiver: returning quickly to the study for the hidden automatic. She took tubers from the garden that had borne the purple blossom, the heavy perfumed flowers, and in the kitchen boiled them. Then to Arkadi's fascination, dipped the arrowheads in solution, and dried them in the sunshine.

Roskov's men were all on horseback but too drunk to travel quickly. 'Wish me well, I'm going hunting,' were her last words to Arkadi.

~-~

Kitting herself with warm drab-coloured clothes, boots and a knapsack of provisions, Arkadi told me, she'd shouldered the quiver and pocketed her Steyr. I wanted to go with her, for the sake of my sisters, but she gently forbade me, saying I should stay with my cousin, Daine. 'She gave me a strange look for a moment, then kissed me again lightly on the cheek before turning without a word and walking off.'

It was mid afternoon and the sky had a high thin autumnal overcast with mare's tails as she loped eastwards to Belarus and Braslav, a slight figure, disappearing into the trees with her little ram's horn bow.

~-~

Piecing together the diaries and notebooks Rolf re-enters that place of many memories in the winter of 1919.

At first he doesn't really hear the word *Rittmeister*, until it's repeated twice more. Lt. Steiger's been promoted and nobody's told him. He's hearing voices in the clamorous ringing of his ears. He turns and sees a boy maybe ten years of age, wearing heavy padded clothes and a woollen Lapp-style hat. He has a pinched, white face and his nose is red from the cold.

'Rittmeister,' he repeats, louder. 'I saw your flags.' He gestures to the full-chord black crosses on the Junkers' wings, which on the pale sky-coloured undersurfaces are clear and sharp. He holds a bundle of kindling. Nearby there's a sledge.

'That was my horse, Excellency.' He says simply. The boy has a steady gaze and a firm chin. He speaks Polish-Lithuanian. He is thinner that Rolf remembered, but he recognises Arkadiusz at last.

~-~

Steiger walks slowly towards the house. There is scarce a breath of wind.

540

The house still smells of ammonia with dried horse droppings evident. The downstairs rooms and the dining hall are ravaged. The boy tells him something of what befell Liepus Namas but the place is its own testimony to massacre. Arkadi tells him that Katya had survived and how she'd arranged the burials before going north by east, pitifully armed. And that he had learned that the other lady, her sister, the Countess Krystina had arrived a week or so later and there were more bodies then to bury, including Nina who was well loved in the region. He says that there are still people living in the village who might be able to give him more information regarding the fate of the family, and only at that he averts his eyes.

Steiger explores, sickened at the devastation, pain grabbing his chest like the jaws of some nameless animal. He climbs the left hand staircase now free from any carpeting. The ornate banister has been smashed and hacked to pieces. He feels the anger pounding in his head, like poltergeist footsteps tracking him *forzando* across the landing. His mind arranges this as a dim unbidden diversionary memory, by *Schnittke* perhaps, sombre, like a slow movement from *The Fairytale of the Wanderings,* whose dolorous footfalls follow his own, room to room. He looks from the upstairs window of the master bedroom at the sweep of the carriageway under snow, the gaps in the lindens, the stumps like rotten teeth. He sees the beauty of light beyond the low hills, dreaming, drifting cloud fragments of Naples Yellow, soft-edged and lilac, pale wintry blue between. And indoors, this unnatural yellow radiance. Like light filtered through a jaundiced membrane.

The sheets have been removed from the *Himmelbett,* but the stain of the crime will remain if this sundered house stands five hundred years. Here is loss beyond crying and the rending of clothes. Here sobs will echo, eye will chase eye in dark mirrors, hollow and anguished. I am just a ghost here of someone else's future, he thinks, a ghost alone in a room, dissolving in a cracked mirror. *And Krysia. His hellster Stern von allen. He knew that she had gone away, across the galaxy, on the void behind the mind. Far to a high bright star he'd never find. Confined too close, together yet apart, lovers in innocence they were, but now might meet as strangers. No more, he thought, were we those children, hand in hand and long ago.*

Beyond the broken windows: behind the trees, purple cloud stretches out to sleep in a lake of yellow dusk. Steiger suddenly clutches his stomach and retches. He needs to get out of this sickly internal light, this fearful hollowed-out house with its smell of death, and set course for the spear of cloud, pointing westwards, over the horizon. Where he can fly into the glory of the setting sun, west towards the eternal light until he runs out of fuel, away from the madness and blind cruelty of Russia. And not have to think.

Downstairs books have been burned in a fireplace, hundreds of them. He recognises a spine from *Schellendorff* on Natural History. Another on astronomy: on philosophy. The blaze has caused a greater conflagration that had partially destroyed the upper floors and a section of roof; the damage he'd seen from the air. Anything that could not be easily carried away had been smashed, burned, slashed. Eradicating learning and a whole culture is thirsty work, as the empty bottles testify.

And here is the broken frame of the painting by Sargent.

Are these your shards, the reliquary of your sainthood Princes Sophie? Does Kristian's candle still pause in nightly ritual upon the stair, where the patch of pale plaster bears witness to your being? You were both human, Kristian and you, his Princess, with human foibles and needs. But your life ended serving the sick and needy and you were suspended in perpetual hagiolatry in this house of martyrs. Sophie, Graczyna, Kristian and the others who died with him on that night: martyrs, witnessed by a half-mad Arkadi, or if he's not he should be.

There is a rustle of movement at the entrance. The last subject of his reverie stands breathless on the step 'Excellency. People come!' Steiger moves swiftly to the door, the automatic in his hand.

Ragged wraiths emerge black and silent from around the looted mansion and fall it seems suppliant in the snow. An old woman of maybe forty-five years climbs the steps, grasps Rolf's hand in her thin fingers and kisses it, beseeching, in the old and formal way, 'Good Sir Knight, pray come you to deliver us from the *Bolshevists*?' the voice is thin and her breathing laboured, but the last word rising from somewhere deep within her chest is a curse, sibilant and clear. One by one they recognize Rolf and a keening threnody rises on the icy air, a traditional lament that expresses inextinguishable sorrow. Some of the women, Stenja of the secret chickens among them, touch and kiss the painting of their patron saint and folk hero, Vytautas, on the corrugated Junkers fuselage, as if it were an icon, which in truth it is.

One comes forward. She is Daine, little *'Song'*, now grown to a pale slender beauty, with bruised darkness about her eyes. She cannot believe I am alive. She has lost her nearest brother to a Bolshevist bayonet and her father to a bullet. First Tsarist deserters had come for food and anything they could steal and then Bolshevists had arrived, accusing them of collaborating with enemies of the State. They tore through their home and found her grandfather's campaign medals including the Order of St.

542

George and confiscated 'these trashy baubles' which they now claimed were worthless and void. When her father had protested they shot him dead. Her brother had attacked them with an old pistol that mis-fired, so they bayoneted him and left him to die too.

It was here upon the staircase, she tells him, that the young Countess Krystina was witnessed to have fallen upon her return, sobbing and retching, clutching her aching sides before she cut off her hair and became 'a knife'. Became a soldier, a hard-face, implacable, like her sister. Then her only other action was to see that the mutilated corpses of the servants were cut down in the stables and properly buried, assisted by a few willing and able-bodied men, returned soldiers perhaps from neighbouring families. Those who still harboured respect for the family and honoured Princess Sophie's memory, despite the fear of reprisal or betrayal by a spite-ridden perpetual underclass that sought gain: parroting the doctrine that 'property was theft'. No one knows where she went, but she was mounted on a good horse.

Steiger has a sudden thought. The gazebo! To the garden behind the house where he scrabbles around in the snow beneath, and there in the secret letterbox he finds a letter in a leather pouch, addressed to 'Rolf'. It reveals the stark horror of what had happened in matter-of-fact terms, and expressed the hope that Rolf was alive and would return to find this message. It was simply signed 'K'. He assumes it to be from Kat, who was as familiar with their method of communication as were Krysia and Rolf himself. Krysia he imagines presumed him dead, unless Kat had left a message for her under the gazebo too, but in that case he would have expected any note from Krysia would have been secreted there as well.

He was still far from certain which of the two had left it.

Chapter 37. *Act of Mercy*

The short afternoon of the northern latitudes is moving to its close. Time enough to take leave of this cursed and bloody house of Agamemnon.

Harry's description of the departure began with Steiger handing out the weapons and ammunition. If there was no longer any hope for Liepus Namas or its erstwhile tragic occupants, he could perhaps provide these women with a means of defending themselves against further attack in their homes. Though they might in the end succumb to a trained and determined force, they would at least now have the option. Almost all of them had been violated and their men taken away or murdered. Many had small children, some of whom were sick. Many had had influenza and it seemed all had lost family members to that epidemic, particularly the elderly and the young. All are malnourished and especially vulnerable.

They say that this whole area is now occupied by the Reds. The line has moved, bringing the second echelon killers into the back areas again. *There's been sacrifice on Sophie's obelisk, the Babushkas say. Or else it's a miracle, pure whiteness running red with an immovable stain, stigmata in stone, or a bloody omen for the Civil War. Red trumps White. Old Belarus superstition? I will have to take the villagers' word for it.*

Some refuse arms, saying if they are caught with weapons they will surely be executed. But Steiger cannot take off with the extra weight of guns and ammunition in this snow and he needs to refuel, quickly.

With the help of the women he raises a sunken drum of aviation gasoline from the camouflaged *Luftstreitkraft* cache aided by shear legs, a pulley and crank and with the pony harnessed to its sled drags the drum a half-kilometre to the Junkers. Meanwhile Daine is unloading the weapons and cartridge boxes and passing them out to the babushkas. He will have to find time to instruct those who desire to learn, the technique of loading and clearing the automatics and the four rifles.

With the drum he collects the long-handled lift pump and a flexible tube which goes to the bottom of the drum. A half-litre of fuel is delivered with each smooth stroke.

Steiger turns over the propeller and climbs into the cockpit. He has briefed Daine on the starting procedure. The engine is not completely cold, at least not yet as cold as the ambient air. Primed with fuel and throttle cracked with the motor just before TDC it should fire on the hand-starting magneto. If not, he'll switch off, re-set and follow the procedure again. At worst Daine would have to swing the propeller gently, stepping back clear of the blades, as he's shown her.

The good old BMW fires immediately and settles to its reassuring throaty rumble, blue smoke pumping out of the 'saxophone'. He straps in as he warms it up. Opening up he turns the aeroplane around with bursts of throttle against rudder to taxi back some distance to gain the longest available take-off run. The snow-covered surface would drag at the wheels and the nil-wind conditions would lengthen the take-off. He'd be lucky if he would clear the trees on the far side of the grounds by much of a margin. Daine and Arkadi run along with him at the wing tips, as directed, to help him to turn around in the difficult conditions.

At the extreme tree-line edging the nearer side of the enclosed grounds he slows the big Junkers and slews it around in a flurry of snowflakes with Daine hanging on to the left hand wing and digging her heels in, dragging for all she's worth while Arkadi runs as fast as his small legs will carry him, pulling on the other wing, whose tip he can just about reach, to pivot the machine through 180 degrees.

'Was heavy plane to push around, James; snow compressing underneath the tyres.'

He makes his final instrument and controls 'full-and-free' checks, noting that the control surfaces waggle obediently in all the right directions and scans the sky. He raises his right hand to bid the two a solemn farewell when a bullet clips his mitten and whacks into the exhaust manifold with a very audible clang, followed by spurts in the snow ahead of the wings. There isn't a second to lose. Steiger pulls down his muffler and yells. 'Arkadi, jump in quickly. Daine, grab the crash pylon! *Quick!*

With no clear idea of what he's going to do, Steiger advances the throttle slowly. Arkadi appears on the right wing and hauls himself up the fuselage side, throwing himself on top of Steiger, settling onto his lap and squirming against his throttle arm to allow Steiger enough movement of the control column with his right hand. He vaguely notices the hand is bleeding. Daine has clambered onto the left wing root and is standing grasping the tall crash pylon behind Steiger's head. Her left had grips the leather cockpit coaming. Steiger opens up fully, engine bellowing, the valve gear dissolving into a blur of motion, feeling the aeroplane accelerate sluggishly from the additional weight and the depth of snow. Drag will be enormously increased as the speed rises, however and he's not even sure if he'll be able to handle the machine like this, with restricted movement of the controls.

It seems to take an age for the tail to rise and the view ahead to improve. He is aiming between gaps in the linden tree drive for the take off, and the trees are already nearer than he'd have liked at this stage. Daine's bonnet has blown off and her hair is streaming like golden fire on his left. He is faintly aware of the occasional click as bullets hit the airframe and that Daine flinches.

Steiger has a vague plan that he might be able to fly for a few minutes and put the pair down on a remote field away from present danger. It was obvious that Daine would not be able to hold on for long like that, exposed to the brutal blast of the slipstream in the freezing air. Wind chill is bringing the effective temperature down, probably to −30C. He notes she's wearing gloves − un-gloved, her hand would freeze instantly on the steel crash pylon. The Junkers is running lighter, tail up, over the snow-laden grass but Steiger sees running figures emerging from the trees at extreme left, peripheral view, trying to intercept the roaring monoplane, raising their rifles.

With a bump the Junkers is flying though the handling is dire.

Whether Daine realises that the drag and weight of her frail body is prolonging the take-off or whether she can no longer hold fast to the steel pylon Arkadi and Steiger could not know. If she has sacrificed herself or if she has been hit makes no difference; the effect is the same. She lets go at about two metres off the ground, passing just under the tailplane, and is stunned by the fall.

Steiger is instinctively hunched in the cockpit as bullets click and snap into the metal skin, keeping the machine low, grimly, desperately making distance between themselves and their assailants. Relieved of its additional burden the Junkers roars over the carriage drive though the gap in the linden trees, the light façade of the house going by in the corner of his eye and they climb safely over the firs on the perimeter and bank away from Liepus Namas.

Daine's sacrifice, however she'd played it in her mind, that valiant act, has enabled Steiger and Arkadi to escape. Another martyr for the Linden House.

But the boy is craning back, and suddenly screaming, 'Ne!' above the deep bellow of the full throttle BMW, screaming at what he sees is happening below.

Climbing and turning Steiger looks back, sees troops running to the spot where the girl has fallen. She is moving, rising, stumbling and then starts to run just as two soldiers reach her. She doubles up violently as one of them swings a rifle butt. Other soldiers are still shooting at the Junkers but they've no hope of hitting it at that range and Steiger pays them no attention. But he is horrified to see that they are pulling the tattered coat from the girl's limp body, tearing at her dress. Stripping her. She lies motionless on the snow. Rape and possible gratuitous mutilation, will be followed by a begged-for death at the hands of merciless killers who are likely to prolong her suffering for fiendish amusement.

Arkadi knows it too and cannot bear to see what is happening to his only living kin and comfort, who has loved and cared for him. Hysterically he screams above the engine, 'Shoot. Shoot, kill them. Kill them *all.* You must do it. Please do it now, Rittmeister. Pleeease!'

Steiger turns away, pointing the aircraft at the dying winter sun, red in the pale sky. He twists, looking back over his shoulder. Details are diminishing in the fading light but he notes that out-flanking soldiery have joined the party, some stragglers running up, not to miss the fun. Arkadi's face is a pale mask of horror, fixed on the shrinking tableau. They fly on for a further minute, still climbing. He cannot leave her to this. Praying that she remains mercifully unconscious, he cocks the guns, throttles-back gradually, asks forgiveness of a God he refuses to acknowledge; then, silently, wheels and dives.

He places the dark knot of figures exactly above the radiator cap, perfectly silhouetted on the pale blush of the snow. They are intent on their prey, probably shouting, urging each other on. The first rounds arrive before they hear the snarl of the now full-throttle engine, the shriek of the avenger; banshee vortices streaming off the corrugations. The soldier-bandits begin to scatter almost not believing what they are seeing. One holds her legs in the crook of his arms and another lifts her armpits. They drop her, but are hacked down. Silently screaming, dark figures writhe calligraphically, like in an animated Japanese print; black and red upon the purity of the snow.

'*Atsiprasau*, Daine. I'm sorry.'

Steiger swoops, engine roaring, over the steep roof of the house, dropping behind cover, to make a second pass from the northwest, turning, coming in obliquely, on the deck, slanting dangerously through the trees making the aeroplane a difficult target.

He uses the element of shock from his first diving attack. The troops are unnerved by this metal monster with its spitting Spandaus. Steiger is depending on speed, manoeuvrability and the deep, exuberant bellow of the BMW to unman the scurrying enemy who fail to 'lead' their

548

target before they run for cover.

He shoots. They fall.

The scene is timeless, like a monochrome vignette or woodcut in the border of a medieval treatise on the art of war. Against the snow they throw only their pale shadows in the cold afterglow, like a fabled hunting scene in a painting by Pieter Breugel. Hunters hunted. 'Like some fearful terror from a German Expressionist film, James.'

Three are running towards the Linden House, one holding his arm. Another, half-crawling in the snow, heads for that sanctuary Arkadi never found.

Steiger makes a hard turn feeling Arkadi's body crush against his own under the 'g-force' as he banks and pulls, conscious of the danger of losing control at such low level with the lad's body obstructing full movement. The rudder pedals are unobstructed and so the turn is at least co-ordinated. Steiger keeps the horizon in view. It would be so easy to fly into the ground in this light with no shadows to aid depth perception and provide an indication of height. He flies by feel alone and cannot risk even a glance at the few instruments to confirm airspeed and RPM.

Targets are as rapidly acquired as lost as men jink between the tree trunks or race towards the house. The machine guns hammer deafeningly. Short accurate bursts. Arkadi's head is down in the cockpit out of the wind and the whirling scenery, so close to Steiger's hand sharply moving the stick, that his face is struck violently more than once by Steiger's forearm. There is a tang of cordite, the stink of oil and petrol fumes in the cockpit. Cartridge belts rattle in their troughs as spent cartridges and links patter through the collector chutes. The boy feels sick from the relentless, savage motion, the sickly oil smell and the awful din. Sideways glimpses reveal sky and trees, then snow, with a snapshot of fleeting figures and a brief impression of the Big House going by at a crazy angle, then the 'g' rises hard, forcing him back into Steiger's chest and he retches bile. He gasps for air and briefly, as the horizon tilts again, sees above the wing leading edge the torn red figure of Daine, a rag doll between the corpses of her assailants as they bank tightly round. He shrinks from the horror eyes tight shut. Steiger makes sure all suffering is at an end.

A final hard turn and Arkadi briefly swoons, coming to as they barrel-in fast towards the house again only for Steiger to curse that they're out of ammunition. But near the house there are more corpses. The wounded irregulars have been met with fire from the *babushkas* who now move among the fallen with their little knives. They wave in farewell to the aeroplane.

Steiger rocks wings and sets course, aware that some of the men have escaped and more trouble will doubtless befall the tormented community. Deeply upset by the death of Daine, though he rationalises what needed to be done. She'd made the choice to help Steiger and Arkadi and at least her sacrifice had been in some measure avenged, even if some had got away. He remained an executioner, but of the innocent along with the supremely guilty. No choice then for him.

And now he had a new responsibility, Arkadi Piotrkowski, orphan.

~.~

Steiger sets course, flying southwest into the lowering winter sun.

It is just after 2 in the pm. The boy shivers uncontrollably behind the inadequate coaming and tiny windshield. Steiger has tightened the throttle friction, reaching behind him and dragging the folded cockpit tarpaulin forward to act as a shield for the boy. He holds it around him with his warm flying mitten, deflecting some of the freezing slipstream. Gradually he stops shivering. But Steiger fears that it is not because he has gained warmth, rather that he is near to death. His small frame and thin body will not retain its vital core temperature much longer. But Steiger can do no more than press on at maximum cruise for the next forty-five minutes.

A red sun in a purple mist limns the tree-lined horizon as they approach the landing ground Steiger throttles-back. He has some difficulty in manipulating the throttle and mixture because of the boy's slight but stiff body.

At 400 metres, turning into the field, Steiger identifies Kessler's aeroplane by the black pelican on its yellow shield, sitting on its long blue shadow in the tinted snow. It is there amongst the other Junkers and Albatros machines scattered about the perimeter. To his surprise and relief, Steiger hears a faint voice above the quieter throb of the idling engine, the *swoosh* of the propeller. 'Are we there now?' Steiger thinks he hears the question; the boy's cracked lips have difficulty forming the words. To Steiger's relief Arkadi turns his frozen, tear-stained face to look the pilot in the eye. The face has a bloodless caste, the lips cracked. Steiger nods. His own mouth, he is certain, is a dark slit in a frozen mask of ice around his muffler. They've commenced a gentle turn to starboard and Steiger is concentrating on the approach to land.

'Keep fighting, my Rittmeister,' Arkadi cries, and with a supreme effort launches his near-frozen body stiffly onto the cockpit coaming for the long drop to oblivion, upon the frozen ground of his Lithuania; freedom forever from unimaginable agony of mind.

~.~

In Norwood Hill I sit spellbound by James's recounting of Harry's tale. Outside the night is thick and the leylandii hedge hides Reigate's sodium glow. Few cars have passed in the last hour, their passage marked beyond the trees by the swish of tyres and a swerve of headlights blazing across the 'blackout curtain'.

James gets up stiffly, and paces to the window, looking out into the night. There is nothing to see, but his agitation is evident.

'I'll be leaving here soon, John,' he says quietly, but where his destination might be he does not elaborate.

'Among the notes and letters, in the diaries and wild jottings you may have already read, if you've pieced any of it together, you may know that Steiger made it back from Liepus Namas, both he and his passenger intact. Steiger's arm had enough strength to prevent the frozen child in his weakened state from making that long final leap into the snows of Peterfeld. He struggled to keep him on board though the boy fought like a wildcat to escape the reality that was then too much for him to bear. That Steiger managed to do that and land the Junkers monoplane safely in semi-darkness says a lot for his piloting skills, I think. That the near-dead, frozen Arkadi was able to move at all demonstrates his toughness.'

~.~

'James. It was Steiger saved my miserable soul, a long time ago in Lithuania.' Harry tells Delcroix in the dark Frankfurt night.

'I was, for practical purposes, dead from cold and fatigue. I was in an agony of mind – *balance of mind disturbed*, as a lawyer would say. My parents and sisters murdered, my cousin's family wiped out too. Only Daine had remained and I had begged Steiger to kill her, so that her suffering was not prolonged. She'd wanted to be a doctor, James, but her last wish, a survivor of massacre, was to join a *Womens' White Death Battalion* to fight the Bolshevists and avenge our family and all those families who'd been destroyed without pity in that great terror.

'Imagine all that I'd lost, James, can you? I was ten years old, no more than a child. So I tried to end my suffering by jumping from the open cockpit of that aeroplane.'

Harry had to stop for a while. Then to James' distress he began to weep, huge tears rolling uncontrollably from those piercing blue eyes, rolling down his lined cheeks, running from his hard jaw, and he sobbed openly for a full minute, rocking in the chair, head bent low so that James stood up and went to him with a comforting hand. But Harry didn't seem to notice.

After a while he composed himself. He apologised briefly and said that he hadn't wept like that since he was a boy, not since the night he was lifted from the cockpit by Steiger's comrades and taken to the pilots' hut and had his circulation slowly restored before their stove. Eventually he tore at the food, bread and sausage offered him but he'd retched immediately. So he was given a thin soup, to prevent his stomach from rejecting the nourishment.

At Alt-Auts, Peterfeld and other bases as they moved north, Harry was adopted as the Gruppe mascot. Steiger fiercely defended Harry's position as the smallest *Wiking* volunteer, complete with paybook. He'd had the Jewish tailor create a smart uniform for him, identical in style to the tunics and breeches that most of the fliers wore.

For his duties Harry learned to be quick off the mark running any errand that the men asked of him, becoming indispensable as a supernumery batman and a 'gofer'. In the hangar wearing a small, cut-down overall, he learned about engines and airframe maintenance, fetched tools and assisted with aircraft rigging. He saved the mechanics much bending and stiffness, Harry running about picking up fallen items, passing up wrenches and being generally helpful, draining the engine oil and heating it over stoves through the colder nights. And Harry loved it. He had a sunny disposition and an infectious laugh and was a favourite with officers and men, and saved his deep sorrows for the night, sleeping fitfully in a bunk in Steiger's quarters where he confided in the pilot who'd saved his life, for whom he now had a closeness that bordered on filial love. A purely survival viewpoint demanded that he would form such allegiance. He was at once fiercely proud of Steiger and thought him the best pilot in *Wiking*, being hero, big brother and best friend rolled into one, with others like Kessler, von Moritz, Bachmann, Hugo and Henschel all favourite uncles in one big surrogate family of fighting men who informally adopted him into the Jasta in loco parentis.

'Arkadi Piotrkowsky, honorary *Flieger*, junior Freikorps frontline mechanic and messenger boy, and proud of it, James.'

When sorties were flown Harry, wrapped in woollens and a fur hat

552

like a little Russian doll, would be at the end of the flight line watching the Junkers D-Types and C-Type two-seaters taking off. He was always there when they came back no matter how cold. He would watch von Moritz in his sleek Albatros 253 *Foto* off on dawn missions, well before the winter sun was over the horizon, and would help the mechanics aiding the frozen pilot down from the cockpit, releasing the biplane's camera hatch, even in the darkroom hut assisting with the developing, to see where the Bolsheviks had advanced or retreated, helping to drag the bomb carts - or the sleds when it snowed. He'd wave solemnly at Kessler who'd wave solemnly back from the cockpit of the *Black Pelican*. But above all he was there for Steiger, waving him off in *Vytautus*, and jumping up and down excitedly when he came back rocking his wings to declare a locomotive strike or a successful strafe on troop positions. Even an occasional air-combat, though the Junkers were not best suited to one-on-one dog fighting, the original design aim. But as a trench-strafer and ground assault monoplane it almost equalled its 'big brother' Junkers CL.1.

Harry though is still a very disturbed young boy whose nights are full of horrible dreams, and bloodcurdling memories of the fate of the young Lady Graczyna and the Graf flash up unexpectedly at all times of the day. These moments Steiger thinks of as 'absences', transient, like small epileptic events. He can often see them coming and is sometimes able to intercept them, distracting him, bringing Harry out before he goes too deeply into himself, into the blackness and misery that resides within. But at night he fights the terrors alone.

'Why did they do it?' Harry asks pitiably and more than once.

Steiger shakes his head. 'I don't know, Arkadi. Because they could, because they were looking for revenge on a class that they had learned to hate. Because they were drunk. Because they were evil and led by evil and were able to gratify their lusts without fear of chastisement. Because Revolutionary leadership told them they could and should do it.'

Because as Dostoevsky said, if you believe in nothing anything is permissible. It was as Katya had said. If as Nietzsche has claimed the death of God was true, then God is also dead in man. Man's capacity for evil and good is coeval, since we have free will. But in the absence of morality, the idea of God's wrath and judgment removed, where is the constraint to do good?

Does it not then matter whether we do good or ill? To strive for good is harder than to destroy, whether we seek the destruction of institutions or the cultural traditions of a civilization. So to control and level, a conqueror, an imperialist tyranny may seek to destroy culture by removing trace of heritage, whether in stone or from the libraries of a nation; will make an assault on literature, music, re-write history and even ban a language. So with totalitarian regimes. The evil that men do lives on after their death; the good is interred with their bones.

Russian nihilism among the leisured elite contributed to the unpreparedness of society to change for the better, despite the efforts of some at court. The cauldron of revolution within a society that was, we were informed, mad for change, from the bombardment of agitation, was stirred with malicious intent. Malignant narcissism dines on power.

'But, James,' Harry spoke softly into the gloom of the Frankfurt apartment. It was easier to speak into the concealing dark than to meet the eye, even of a comparative stranger. So too as James related it to me in the Norwood night, passing the cup. 'I have asked myself that question later, in slavery, and knew even then that there were both political and strategic answers that are entirely pragmatic. The more terror you instil, the more feared and powerful you become so that the last bastions will negotiate or surrender to avoid the ultimatum of remorseless annihilation. For where there is no God all is permitted or you *become* God, like Ivan the Terrible, then all is permitted by your decree. Even the lowest *zek* knew it, in his misery, and so too the *muzhik*. Though he may worship his 'Little Father' he knew that his plea for justice would not be heard. But nor would they under Bolshevism. Under that the family was a weapon used against itself. Because in those regimes the *State* was your father and your mother too!'

Harry paused for a moment and looked again out of the window 'Remember under Naziism, that propaganda movie, *Quex*….where a child in the *Hitler Jugend* informs on his family for uttering seditious 'communistic' comments …. is rewarded by the grateful State? So with Bolshevists. They even erected statue to one of those little shits, in a Moscow park for denouncing his father for 'hoarding' grain from what had been their own farm. The father was sent to gulag in Siberia. It's said the boy was then murdered by his own grandfather, or at least that's what the old man confessed to under torture by Cheka, though he failed to stick to his script in court. The shot him anyway along with three other 'conspirators'. The witchfinder commissars zealously sought out enemies of the people and often framed people for murders that the Cheka or NKVD had themselves committed; victims they could represent to the proletariat as martyrs for the State, but who were eliminated for other reasons altogether. But it was claimed they'd died for Communism and for Stalin. More people rounded up, more show trials and publicity, more

554

fear; warnings to be on guard against the eternal enemy, internal and external.'

Harry seemed to be rambling.

'Neither Kamo nor Roskov would have asked, "Is rape legitimate weapon of the class war?" But Stalin would have answered, "Don't ask if a weapon is legitimate or illegitimate. A weapon is a weapon, whether it be truth, half truth or lie, the best of which contain *some* half truths. Asking about legitimacy of a weapon is bourgeois indulgence. Use the weaknesses of the 'soft society' against itself and the more horror you instil the more powerful you become. Each forced confession, and concession obtained through the revulsion of our methods, proves our indomitability and drives our wedge deeper, opens the way wider, until the bourgeoisie cringe within the collapsing structures of their doomed legislature, fleeing to the borders of their misconceived reality, 'til they have nowhere left to hide, not even inside their heads. And nothing left to give except their lives and these they give up in secret, without honour.

'You can break a man in many ways, James. You can kill hope. You can extract all humanity by degradation, by making him eat shit. The final reduction/refinement of entire process of stripping away all layers ends in *'Man Without Qualities'*, soviet-style *non-sapiens*. Not book by Thomas Mann. The camps did it, with the help of dead-eyed time servers and the trusty *Urkas* who ran them. What they had in common was bone crushingly hard labour and the threat of reduction of meagre rations for not fulfilling work norm. Also the cold. It was most effective weapon by itself. Most camps had 'end product'; crushed stone, minerals, timber…. for others end product was destruction of intellect. These were mostly reserved for the 'intelligentsia', the writers, the poets. The 'thinkers'. Urkas didn't work, they terrorized: scientists and professors driven insane by state perverts. Kremlin would have taken satisfaction in that but Stalin was perhaps too busy to gloat much, busy adding his signature to the endless lists.

'No matter how heinous the crime, finally you can always lie about it to the world, bluff it out, barefaced. You control the media. Remember the Armenians who were massacred by the Turks? Only now among the thin Armenian diaspora….. As Hitler said: 'A lie that's told often enough becomes the truth!

'What is truth anyway. Is it what historians write? What governments tell you? You are just blotting paper unless you research and subvert. You must decide what's right and stick until death, though society, brain-washed and indifferent, mocks you as delusional.'

Harry is sleeping in his bunk below an exhausted Steiger, with Ernst Kessler and Johannes von Moritz snoring in their bunks on the far side of the hut. A hint of the scented tobacco smoke from Von Moritz' extinguished pipe lingers in the air. Harry is half awake, he thinks, waking from a confused dream of suffocation, trying to throw himself out of an aeroplane at the same time. He is struggling to breathe but dares not cry out. Some horror weighing him down…. a creature with demonic face, narrow-eyed, illuminated redly from below. The pocked face of the devil in a melodrama staring down at him, filling the sky. He wakes fully with a start and cries out, throws himself out of that cockpit again and lands on the floor of the hut, body convulsing with the effort to draw a full breath.

Steiger sits up in his bunk, half awake; tells the boy gently to get back into his bed and try to sleep. But Harry is shaking with the memory of an event that until this moment had not fully revealed itself to his conscious mind. He begins to tell the sleepy and at first reluctant Steiger about Commissar General Koba and Roskov.

He tells Steiger how he'd been biting the bed sheet in the stuffy linen basket to stifle any involuntary sound he might make, though it seemed his heartbeats themselves would be audible through the wicker sides.

Roskov, in his throaty whisper, had asked the General how he had managed to locate him here, out beyond the Belarus border. Koba smiled. Arkadi could hear it in his voice.

'Nikolai Sergeyevich, you should know that Felix Edmundovich always keeps an eye on talent.' He said.

Koba, as far as Harry had been able to understand the orders, had told Roskov that he must accompany him east on the armoured train *Victory to the Revolution* that was waiting a few versts distant. That there was a special mission that he had to carry out immediately that was vital to the success of the Red Army in the civil war, and that he would be a great hero when it was all over. He was to pick his best men to follow later, for whom road transport would be provided at the town of Braslav in Belarus, but no more than ten, he said. Others would join them later. In Moscow, Roskov would go to a certain address and collect uniforms for the insurgents as well as official orders and passes issued to the Red Guards. He was then to go to a particular church, a Roman Catholic church, where worship still continued for the present. Here he would attend the confessional and would obtain his orders regarding his group's assignment to an armoured train, the interception of which would be carried out at a location to be revealed verbally.

At that location the railway line would be cut and simultaneously the accompanying soldiers and guards, all except the locomotive crew, engineer and fireman, would be disposed of. The train would then be driven north on a branch line east of the Urals and special arrangements would be set in place for its cargo to be unloaded onto a barge. The tonnage was great, Koba indicated. Only a barge would carry the load securely.

'Only one map is to be made of the final location of the cargo. After successfully secreting the bullion the remaining personnel are to be liquidated. Understand. Only you and the comrade surveyor who will make the map are to survive and report to me at Kazan or Perm where I am supposed to be even now, conducting this bloody war, or Petrograd if you hear otherwise. You realise of course that neither am I here now. From the moment you are transported to Moscow you are to speak to no one about any of this. No telephones, nothing written you understand? And you will get your orders only from the confessional box.'

As an aside Koba revealed one more thing.

'Nikolai, you must understand. We have incontrovertible intelligence that Vladimir Ilyich is planning the movement of a large amount of bullion. He's losing his nerve, comrade. He is attempting to transport a vast amount of our remaining gold reserves out of Russia at a critical time, just when the tide is turning in our favour. Already we have lost a gargantuan fortune to the criminal Kolchak and the Interventionist thieves. This reserve belongs to the Revolution. To the People. You must not fail. Iron Felix has commended you to me for this vitally important, this heroic mission. I am assured that you have the resourcefulness to carry this off. My train-robbing days are long gone. There are other things at stake now. I have important work elsewhere where I have to be *seen*. I cannot be anywhere near it, you understand?'

'I will not fail you, Soso,' said Roskov huskily.

James, this was one of Stalin's pet names, short form of Josef or Osip, used only by intimates.

'Of course you won't,' said General Koba softly. 'Or in an eye blink comrade *Kamo* would serve me up your still-beating heart.'

~·~

'This, James, was synopsis of what I told Steiger. I don't know if the others heard me. Everyone was tired out and slept like logs undisturbed even by artillery fire, although as soon as the murmur of an aero-engine was heard they awoke, ready for action. Flying almost every day, the combat, the cold, struggling to keep equipment serviced and running: the strained supply situation in a region occupied by Germany for much of the War was now threatened by the Polish independence movement. Food was scarce anyway with famine across Russia. It was great strain and that makes for fatigue among men many of whom had been fighting for five years. Morale, however, was still the highest and all this was 'just business as usual' at the front line.'

~.~

'"I think I have remembered it all correctly, Rittmeister." I said.'

'Steiger turned his face to me. I could see the signs of strain around his eyes, the grey pallor of fatigue even in the soft lamplight. He was thoughtful for a long time. He listened to the others sleeping, and then he told me to go back to sleep and to never tell anyone about what I'd heard. He said, quietly but firmly that it was a deadly secret and anyone who spoke about it would be at risk for his life. I was so relieved to unburden myself of this and of what had happened at Liepus Namas. His sincerity and seriousness impressed me very much and I never did speak of it again until now.'

~.~

'Jesus, James! I thought that about the worst things that could happen to a boy had already happened to me by the time that Steiger rescued me. My family had owned three horses and six cows as well as chickens, ducks and a pig. We were self-sufficient and could sell milk. That made us capitalists. All livestock except for one cow and a horse were confiscated by Bolsheviks. Then our cow was to be shared by several families in a collective. One cow. After, my father was murdered and my older brother. I don't know what happened to my mother and sisters except, I was informed later, that they were defiled as required by Lenin.

'Steiger had row with Hauptmann von Ritter that time when he'd brought me back from Kuznetsowa, near dead from cold, prepared - even wanting to die. I was so miserable and broken-hearted after my cousin, my last relative, was mercy-killed. On my own appeal, James, to save her from terrible fate. Steiger fought to allow me to stay with the Staffel. I just wanted to die and said so.

558

'Steiger called Ritter, in his polished breastplate, a 'latter day Cortez', who cared nothing for the displaced nationalities and the suffering refugees of this once Russian littoral: the ordinary people, who, after half a decade of unremitting war could see no end to the suffering. Ritter had expropriated a fine house for the Staffel, in which the family was still allowed quarters. Ritter who was all for sending me to live with a peasant family was persuaded to consider the publicity advantage of a small 'native' Freikorps mascot, orphaned, heir to the ancient Baltic fiefdom, whose 'freedom' the German volunteers claimed they upheld, adopted by the Staffel. Good copy for the papers back in Germany. Except they didn't fight for a free Baltic, James. Their aim was still Pan German expansionism. Except for Rolf. He stood for liberation but realised that first the Bolshevists had to be defeated. Steiger breached all military discipline to ensure my safety and for that too I thank him.'

Major Ritter had told him that he was lucky not to be facing a court martial (there wasn't time by now for such conventions) for dereliction of duty in landing his Junkers on a private estate, probably not for the first time (although it had been used as a landing ground in the war) but as an example he, Steiger, would forfeit all awards. Steiger said that he didn't have any except those he'd won in Galicia and as far as he was concerned, the Major was welcome to them. Ritter said that in that case he'd not be considered for field promotion. Steiger said he didn't care how many pips he had as long as he could carry on killing Bolshevists. 'In any case,' he told the Major, 'The fewer pips you had the fewer nails would be driven into your shoulders were you unlucky enough to be caught by the Reds.' This well-known punishment for officers matched the number of rank stars on your shoulder boards with that of the long nails they would hammer home; such tortures being enough incentive to remain non-commissioned it might be thought. The discussion ended there with Ritter satisfied that the Junkers was back and repairable.

For his part Kessler had been forced to return during that bitter episode at Liepus Namas. He'd seen two Red Latvian Nieuports approaching *Heinrich* after Steiger had landed and driven them off south east, one having been forced down under control to land near a wood, but he was then compelled to return west, direct to Alt-Auts low on fuel, leaving Rolf to his fate, unaware of the impending ambush by a Bolshevist murder squad.

'But, James, with Ritter's approval, I had joined Freikorps! Ten years old!'

Harry's eyes shine again with the memory.

'The following weeks were about happiest of my life. I had family again. They were my older brothers I never had, my surrogate uncles and my heroes.

'I soon learned how army worked; how it suffered, how it bled. How it shared all, how it ate. How it starved and to *hurry up and wait*. How it swore, how it fought and how it smelled. How teams worked, how to belong and to give something my total loyalty.'

He thought later that Steiger might have deserted. After all his mission to reconnect with his and with the Strelitz family had succeeded as far as it went, although the truth of what he'd discovered was more bitter than he could ever have imagined. But he fought on with total abandon it seemed to Harry, from what the other pilots themselves admitted. Each in their way shook their heads. Steiger, and Kessler too, took fatalistic, excessive risks. They ought not fly so low, turn so violently at low level just to hit more targets. 'I can never forget those low-level manoeuvres in that last fight against the *Wolves* at the Big House. Was unrestrained and at the same time consummate flying without thought of danger.'

Harry looked very old all of a sudden.

'But nothing good lasts. We were in untenable position. Our supply line broken. Political action undermined what support we had at home – I mean occupied Germany where the Allied Control Commission's remit demanded disbanding of all Freikorps. But still we continued to fight.'

They had just beaten off a small band of Latvian freedom fighters when they'd came under attack by Soviets troops, a surprise assault on the northern and eastern perimeters. Harry was one of the first to raise the alarm.

'Next morning snipers were in tree line, their bullets slashing through the canvas hangars. I crawled through communication ditches with ammunition bandoliers for aerodrome defence company as bullets hissed overhead. They suffered many losses, standing and fighting up to knees in ice water.

'Fabian Schneer was shot in his spine while running for ammunition and was evacuated by truck, surviving an operation to remove a bullet from close to his spinal cord. No chloroform. Biting on pistol. Airfield was under attack on north east side from Russian mortars.'

The attack escalated as from over the horizon came the crack of howitzers, artillery shells bursting in the trees and showering the hangars with bark and shrapnel, getting the range. Pilots managed swerving takeoffs in Jus and D.Vlls, avoiding shell craters. They were back in what seemed like minutes to re-arm, flying many sorties that day and the next. Troops fought close contact right on perimeter while less than a kilometre away, crews refuelled and rearmed the assault planes, to strafe and bomb the Bolshevik gun positions.

'Kessler's Fokker blew a tyre on landing so he picks up rifle and charges the trees! Woods are full of Bolsheviks keeping up constant rifle fire. Kessler trips and falls, which probably saved his life. The decision was taken to evacuate. We had held the aerodrome long enough to fly out some aircraft under fire, even damaged ones. But others had to be left behind. Abandoned machines were booby-trapped, wires attached to pins so that if the controls were moved they would automatically explode the grenades.

'Then, as we began to move south, Freikorps re-inforcements arrived from the German-Polish border on foot! In defiance of Reichswehr prohibition: tough fighters of 37 Jaeger Battalion marching 1000 km, but they were just in time to assist with evacuation, holding back Lett and Lithuanian partisans who skirmished on our flanks just when we were trying our best to defend those countries from Bolshevism. Lt. Gottshard Sachsenberg's Freikops Kampfgeschwader was also withdrawing. It was a much bigger outfit than Ritter's, with famous German fighter aces like Joseph Jacobs, Theo Osterkamp and of course Sachsenberg himself.

'Somewhere in my child's mind the agenda had changed. It was a landslide and we were fighting for our lives.

'Then came worst day at emergency field. Last five Junkers aeroplanes had gone out. Three returned, one smoking and damaged beyond repair with the facilities that were left. The Ju's of Steiger and Kessler was the pair that failed to return.

'The new airfield was attacked in force. The order came, *Feuer frei!* I had a rifle that was bigger than me, but I lay flat and killed some of the attackers. I was a good shot. They charged across open ground straight into our fire…we had camouflaged machine gun nests with crossing fire, but these they outflanked. In the end it was hopeless. We made a fighting withdrawal through mud and slush. Then it got colder and snowed heavily which concealed our retreat south to rendezvous at some earlier Freikorps aerodrome. We'd managed a temporary escape without further loss, though we travelled with heavy hearts.

'Next few weeks were jumble of activity, planned dereliction, rearguard actions: divisions drifting southwards. Ammunition and heavy weapons disabled and abandoned, huts, stores, aircraft and motor transport torched. Discipline was now declining and soon it was every man for himself. I lost contact with the pilots. Last I remember was Leutnant von Moritz flying south, disappearing in a snow flurry in our remaining CL.1 - with a trophy: woman 'gunner', wrapped in bear cloak: goggles worn over fine sable hat. Fabian Schneer said Johann had won her from Latvian warlord: poker game in some shell-blasted *Gottlosen* town involving drunken gunfight. I don't know what truth was, only that my guardian, Leutnant 'Rittmeister' Rolf had left me and Leutnant Kessler also.'

Harry was silent for a while and pensive.

'Soon I was advised to 'lose' my uniform,' he continued. 'This upset me because I was proud to be youngest *Gefreiter* in Freikorps, a *Wiking* soldier. But it was out of my hands. I was relieved of tunic, belt and cap and given woollen sweater some sizes too big and civilian jacket that had been found somewhere. And a dirty hat. I must have looked like scarecrow. It was for my own safety of course. We were in eastern Poland then I believe. Poles were fighting here and down in Ukraine – big war. Conditions were harsh. Food was very scarce again. I was growing boy and I was ravenous.

'One night our truck came to schoolhouse with part of roof missing. There were many children there, some very young. All quiet. It was run by nuns and was actually temporary orphanage. They had little food for additional mouth, but they took me in. Truck drove off before I realised that I had been forgotten by *Gruppe*. I felt desolate and miserable. Some of the smaller children seemed very sick and thin, even dying. It was sad place and there was little warmth although I'm sure sisters were doing their best. But I no longer considered myself a child. I had seen too much death and violence and I considered myself a soldier. I could not bring myself to believe 'my' Freikorps, even in retreat, had abandoned me. I made up my mind to steal some food and leave, which I did early next morning.

'I began to walk in what I thought was southerly direction. It was snowing again. I think I had vague hope of catching up with my Freikorps. Maybe reach Germany. I had idea that it was a place of learning, of science and culture but not slightest idea which way I should go.

'Sometime later I was stumbling along a country pathway, enveloped in a salvaged and bloodstained Russian greatcoat that trailed in the snow. Suddenly I stopped. I'd smelled a wood fire and the next thing I was hailed from some trees by two filthy-looking individuals.

"Boy, here come," shouted one gaunt, bow-legged figure in Russian. "You hungry? Eat. Here come !"

'I was starving but caution made me take to my heels, throwing off the hindering coat. I'd seen quite a few dismembered corpses by now and knew that a tender young boy would be better fare than carrion.

'Another day of trudging and hiding. I found myself following railway line because the tracks were recently cleared of snow. It was windy day. I was freezing, weak from hunger and walking in a trance and didn't hear train which appeared from behind, very silent: gliding before squealing to halt. There was no escape for me. I thought it might be going to Germany, but I was wrong. It seems I was in Ukraine.'

Harry looks at James as though he realised the impossibility of conveying what happened next. Harry decides to be brief.

'Ukrainian People's Republic was fighting for independence and train was full of prisoners of Bolsheviks, all nationalities. There followed nearly nine years of slavery in Russia. The USSR granted most favoured trading nation status with defeated Germany, James, just like in Tsarist times, and about first thing they imported was most deadly war technology. 'Phosgene gas manufacturing facility, some of it prefabricated. I was to spend years at Fili building factories and foundations for storage tanks and later on railways, track laying and repair. In all that time I never had enough to eat and sometimes had to fight for food.

'On that first train journey, James, we were jammed in cattle trucks without proper ventilation, only hole in floor for toilet. Men were crammed in, some young boys too. I don't remember women. We had no food and no water for two days, moving slowly first east then north I think. At one place we stopped and were ordered out at gunpoint. Three boys and an old man were already dead, James, and by God we were glad for fresh air. We were given rusty water to drink from locomotive supply tank on tower: just a few sucks from pipe for each man. Then put to work. We were marched through railway sidings with armed guards, about hundred of us. We were ordered to bury body parts. Amputated limbs of White troops, surfacing and rotting after spring thaw - I think from evacuation of nearby hospital. We had first to dig communal trench for this purpose, working hard soil virtually with bare hands, sticks, only improvised tool. Like prehistoric man with reindeer horn: cursed and punched by guards.

'Nearby there is open air mass, huge gathering of people standing silent. Very impressive bearded priest, tall, black-robed, no vestments. No sacerdotal adornments. He stands in front. Like patriarch. I am Roman Catholic, however, I am much moved by deeply intoned basso profundo litany of Russian Orthodox Church ritual. It resonates effortlessly from his chest, has deeply moving effect. I stop digging and feel tears rolling down my cheeks. My fingers and nails are bleeding. I am exhausted and emotional. His voice rises in thrilling, soaring hymn of such power that fills the blue dome of the sky entire. Up to throne of God himself, sending his soul and his flock to their Maker.'

With a breaking voice, Harry describes how in a callous act, a commissar steps up and shoots the priest in the back of the head. Harry sees his eyes turn up and with arms outstretched in parody of the crucifixion he tumbles forward into a pit. The commissar had snarled, 'Enough of this cultish claptrap. Long live the Revolution!' Another piped up, 'Long live Comrade Lenin!' A wail of anguish rose from the assembly, the signal for the kill-frenzy to begin. The machine gunners open up.

The unfortunates from the train are forced to bury those victims too.

'James, later on, not only did Bolshevists steal entire food crop, even stole seed corn from the population of Ukraine, so that maybe ten million died of starvation – nobody was reporting it except some brave individuals and they were soon liquidated. Bolshevists accused Church of not 'providing vessels necessary for cooking and drinking' meaning priceless holy vessels and these were forcibly taken from the Church. Even though many more alternative vessels *were* provided by Orthodox Church as well as money, by massive public donation, to provide such. The offers were ignored and the Church leaders including the Metropolitan were scapegoated: arrested, defrocked, paraded and sentenced for "causing the people to starve."

'Lenin's response was. "It is fault of Church. Shoot more priests." In other words *Christianos ad leones!* Christians to lions! But it was not a sacrifice to the gods of misfortune, but calculated and cynical pogrom of murder to rid state of ecclesiastical dissent and succour to which the people could turn. No Church, no turning! No going back.

'USA provided a colossal amount of direct aid, over sixty million dollars for American Relief Association directed aid. Lenin was furious that Hoover's terms to grant this aid included it's being distributed by US troops. At least this ensured that most of it went to the starving. Of course we never knew about it until years later. But US Army's ranks were infiltrated by Cheka spies. Any Soviet citizen who spoke too much, smiled, showed too much gratitude was marked out for arrest. Indeed even members of *POMGOL*, independent licensed organisation which had drawn international attention to the plight of the millions of starving were arrested.

'*All-Russian Famine Relief Committee* was then formed under the banner of Maxim Gorky. Some fifty non-Bolshevik 'refugee' intellectuals were summoned back from oblivion, James, to lend their expertise to distribute aid and alleviate suffering: usual 'bourgeois filth', physicians, writers, agronomists, some surviving nobility - apart from Maxim Gorky, a convenient proletarian figurehead. Cheka made sure Gorky and their 'plants' were absent when they arrested the committee at gunpoint and threw them into Lubjanka. Alexandra, Count Tolstoy's daughter was among those summarily sentenced to death. Perhaps 10,000 Soviet citizens who'd worked alongside foreign relief personnel were arrested, exiled to special isolated camps, the beginning of the Gulag system, James. Even then Lenin ordered that starving citizens must *not* be allowed to eat 'food tainted by capitalist contagion', only ideologically correct food may be eaten, and was precious little of that. Plenty for Politbüro of course.

'Archbishop was shot without full trial and the information buried. One hundred thousand starving White soldiers living in terrible hunger behind wire were also forgotten and just allowed to die. Lenin's way of dealing with surviving five thousand of the twenty-thousand he used to charge German and White machine guns, soaking-up the lead 'til gun barrels melted, was to have them all executed, James. Most aid went to cities while peasants starved. 'Agrarian experts', Kulaks, were hanged or shot – very people who could have managed the farms, as collectivisation failed miserably. Meanwhile aid money was used to buy arms and grain was actually sold for agricultural equipment - which included tanks of course - while Lenin plotted more revolution and conducted savage terror against class enemies. People were burned alive, like under Ivan the Terrible: hacked to death. Worked to death. Starved, raped, buried alive, mutilated on gargantuan scale. By brutalised thugs, brainwashed and merciless. Under the Red Star. This was bloody *twentieth century!*'

And of the historical record from that time of breathless revolution; there is the official literature with its air-brushed *origin* mythology. Eisenstein's iconic jump-cut heroics. Propaganda films with their spirit of endless, collective optimism; works of Socialist Realism on public display.

No Russian Holocaust. No injustices. Just the greater good and the prevailing common will to build a workers' paradise within the safe borders of the state.

'James, there is total amnesia now in Russia about these truths.

Chapter 38. *Rolf's Story*

I tread the Norfolk shoreline again, lost in my thoughts. In the blur of memories that invade my mind I can see, perhaps by virtue of my new 'savantism', pages, columns of notes that reveal the last days of Baltic combat in the air: of ground attack, the lost logs that I try to call to mind to explain the final events. Whatever came later was on a different front, a different time and place.

I have slept badly and my dreams did not flee instantly with the dawn. In my urge to remember things it seems I'd been transported from my attic - down the coast a way.

I recalled lying helpless as the creature next to me finishes strangling a girl. Another lies lifeless. The creature turns to me. I am next, he tells me; the words registering in my mind though his lips do not move except to smile his evil smile.

I have entered that dark place inhabited by the mind of another. I ask, '*Who am I?*' The answer is that *you are the ghost of another reality and that what* you *might perceive as truth matters not, for it will never be told.* I feel waves slapping against the hull as the memory fades.....

I stare out to sea, eyes barely registering the soft vertical, a stack of square sails - foremast of a barquentine rig that breaks the grey horizon; the coasters or the 'Woodbine' funnels of the 'Short Blue' fishing fleet that lift upon the tide. I sit on the sand in the shelter of a grassy hummock and close my eyes. My head hurts again. I think the headaches are getting worse. The door to the past is still firmly locked though I doggedly tread the path to that portal from this or another direction. I am still in the maze but I have established where some of the dead ends and returns now lie. I shiver suddenly. The great 'Spanish' influenza epidemic is far from over and I've been lucky so far. I feel depressed and lost. Perhaps it would be a blessing to succumb to something so consumingly powerful that would take all worry away. But it is a horrible way to die and I feel I have much to accomplish: that the struggle is far from over.

I force myself to think back. Not just for Whitehall but to patch my own ragged recall.

Dates and take-off times are vague, but individual sorties stand out from my remembered logs. Type: Junkers D.1. Serial: such and such. Take off from *Bertha*, the code name for our field during the retreat.

Strafe Red Lett troop positions. Damage recorded, wagons left burning. Afternoon: Locomotive assault. Flatcars with ammunition set ablaze. Slight damage to a/c from MG return fire. Formation: *Kette*, Dreystunck-Ulzburg, Kessler, self leading in vic. Encounter with Lett Nieuports and Sopwiths. (Sopwiths dangerous and very manoeuvrable - *Camels*). No result. Attack on ground targets - unspecified. Attack on supply convoy. Airfield defence patrol flying Fokker D.VII with Laumann and Moritz.

Fokker D.VII: Airfield defence responding to alarm. Hurried take-off (in sleet) with Kessler as wingman, also in a D.VII. Engaged Bolshevist fighters north of field, including Fokker D.VII which made friendly identification difficult in the heat of combat. One enemy shot down. Moritz sick. Photo sortie in Albatros 253 low level. Red cavalry spotted. Horses spooked by low flying. Managed to shoot a few cavalrymen before breaking off. Chased by two enemy Fokkers, narrowly escaping. Ju D.1 *Rotte*: with Kessler. Attacked Red armoured car patrol approaching *Bertha* in snowstorm. Many enemy ground troops identified. Stopped snowing: Bolshevist night assault. Staffel hurriedly moved to *Dora.*

We were forced to leave the bodies of our comrades behind, those who'd fallen defending our shrinking perimeter before we beat back the last but one, the final attacking wave. We dragged their bodies through the snow to the old cemetery. They stayed there, under tarpaulins, lying conveniently alongside the aerodrome, weighted with stones to keep them from the wolves. Soon they would be frozen as hard as the ground itself. We weren't able to bury them, nor could we spare the benzine for cremation.

An unexpected thaw on top of which it rained. And rained. The roads and landing grounds turned to slush and cloying mud. Officers and men alike struggled to extricate aeroplanes that were bogged down. Engines roared, men heaved and were sprayed with freezing water. Mud coated everything. The Junkers were like great grey hogs or hippos at a wallow, flanks and wheels caked in mud from which there emerged human bones and artefacts more than a century old; rib-cages, muskets and materiel of the Napoleonic War.

I remember a raven sat atop an ancient musket someone had stuck upright in the mud. I sensed its bright eye as I floundered in the muck, heaving a Ju by the wing along with Schneer and the others. *The ominous bird seemed to contemplate my fate with corvine humour. We were far from Borodino but the skirmishers had harried Napoleon's wretched and depleted army this far and further south in the winter of 1812.*

Any aircraft previously fitted with fabric wheel covers had had these removed weeks since, torn and soaked as the aeroplanes were taxied or pulled along duck boards by slithering men and horses. Wagons stalled in the mire. Everything took on the same tone as our sodden greatcoats. A sky of lead with clouds of putty: the landing field, the same monotonous dull grey. To walk was exhausting. Everything froze again in a week and we were digging aeroplanes and trucks out of iron hard clay with picks in threadbare gloves. The same men would be guarding the new perimeter at night in stiff greatcoats, the bone-chilling cold kept at bay by bowls of soup, iron discipline and shared comradeship. We all stank the same and could not remember the last time we'd seen a bath company or slept between sheets. I remember snatches of conversation.....

'My God this war stinks!' I said. We struggled in the rain and wind, me and the crew, jacking-up *Vytautus* on a duckboard in the sticky clay so we could change a wheel.

'All wars stink the same,' said Schneer. 'It just depends on where you're standing.'

Schneer's long body, bent like a ploughman's, pushing, hauling, indefatigable, encouraging with his humour, as we dragged the aircraft free and prepared them again before he was dropped by a sniper from across the river.

I remember the Geschwader reports. Junkers D & C-types, Halberstadt CL.IV: Bombing operations against troop concentrations, all available a/c. Heavy return fire: as someone sagely remarked in our dugout, 'there are no atheists under a sustained barrage'. Aircraft damaged. Limited operations due to bad weather and thick cloud. Riggers and mechanics work like automata; robotniks in a state of permanent fatigue.

Kessler lands his Ju and sits hunched in the cockpit, engine ticking over. We rush to his aid. He is fast asleep.

Strong winds and no flying for a week brought no respite due to the constant anxiety of attacks on the perimeter. Later operations hit by maintenance problems. Moving south. Serious equipment losses in the planned withdrawal. Red aircraft increasing in numbers, mostly Nieuports but also SPADs and SE5s. Note: Despite everything, Junkers D & C-types still best a/c by a long way for winter ops.

~-~

We are shivering and weary, standing in the shelter of a canvas hangar, munching sausage out of the sleet and freezing rain. It is reported that a young sentry has died of exposure the previous night. Visibility is limited to five hundred metres. The '*Staffel*', which is what it's become, is down to about six operational aircraft. The Jus are among them. I ask Kessler if he thinks we're doing any good.

'I don't know whether we are,' he says tersely. 'We have a finite amount of ammunition and they keep coming. I'll keep slaughtering them until I'm down to the last round, then it's every man for himself. We have to make sure we have enough fuel to fly south, Rolf. I can't be captured by them again.'

We have much in common, including that neither of us would ever receive a letter from home. Discipline is good but you can see the strain in the eyes of the men. They are exhausted and edgy. No one gives a thought to what will happen after the war. There is no 'after the war' for a Freikorps fighter pilot says Kessler and I think now, for perhaps the first time, that I may not survive this.

Food is always in short supply and we are draining the unserviceable machines for every last drop of petrol until the promised supply column arrives, if ever it does. Then terrible news. Wiking's doctor, Major Brandt, has been found murdered, throat cut and the body stripped and left in the Azuolas woods. He'd gone to attend a woman in labour at the request of a local villager and he and his guard had never returned. We couldn't find the man who'd made the request but a *Jägerkommando Sonderstaffel* entered the village and executed ten men, then burned it to the ground. There was no proof that the man had been from that village and I felt very uncomfortable about the action. I am haunted by the arbitrary injustices and suffering of war.

Then nothing.

To be honest with myself I think this war is over. I am tired to the bone. But there is to be one last mission with what's left of our bombs and remaining fuel, leaving just enough at base to refuel and fly south. A last mission anyway flown by Kessler and myself and not recorded in the Jasta log or in any logbook anywhere that I know of.

I go over the events even though it's painful to record. The motorized snow plough, driven askew between two powerful half-tracks, had cleared a wide swathe at dawn; gaunt men had re-filled the engines with hot oil and warmed them at half-hour intervals; busied themselves with wooden scrapers, knocking icicles from the wing corrugations, brushing them off the trailing edges into little tinkling piles in the snow.

We were airborne early, or as early as it's possible to get aloft in winter in those latitudes which was about 08.45 hrs. Even though the

CL.1s were light bombers, equipped with a fixed forward and a flexible machine gun, our D.1s had been adapted to carry two light bombs as well, born of necessity in our *Schlachtbomber* role in addition to our two forward-firing Spandaus.

Based on a high-level dawn reconnaissance report, Kessler, Laumann and myself were hauling two 50 Kg bombs, one under each wing on lash-up mounts bolted to the truss ribs at the spars, the skin patched over. Externally-routed release cables ran through fairleads from cockpit loop-pulls. Ritter and Moritz were flying their battered CL.1s, Ritter leading. We were heading for a Bolshevist division that had reportedly outflanked Bermondt-Avalov's 15,000-strong army and was moving south parallel to the Petrograd railway line north of Daugavpils, near Lake Razna. Along with our two remaining D.VIIs we have two Siemens-Schuckert D.IVs flying top cover from a *Freiwilligen* detachment which Kessler greatly envies. Everything seems loose now anyway and these two are attached to *Wiking* in these closing days. The problem is we have very little castor oil, essential for the lubrication of a rotary engine, although supplies have been promised from somewhere.

The weather was increasingly overcast but with good horizontal visibility at our low formation height. I adjusted my 'death mask' and happened to glance down. A solitary figure in a long coat stood in a snowfield, staring as we droned overhead. Something about its stillness made me look back. I sensed a female spirit presence, but no sooner had I felt this than I experienced a strange sensation; as if I were out of my own body, seeing our battle formation though *her* eyes, yet with a peculiar omniscience; that we were misguided and insignificant fools, simultaneously a part of the vast cosmic continuum to which we'd yet to earn a right to glimpse even its lowest level of attainment. The figure remained motionless as long as I twisted my neck to look at it, until I was forced to return my attention to the formation. I'd also had a momentary recollection of twisting round for a farewell glimpse of my parents as passenger in the Graf's *Torpedo* and the memory of my mother's face as she waved her last goodbye.

Perhaps though I had just seen a scarecrow. Or the ghost of one.

The railway line was clearly visible with a cluster of lakes beyond the trees. Our target. A thin plume of steam identified a supply train, stationary, in an open area with a hundred or so troops alongside unloading equipment. A field kitchen was set up on the western side of the tracks, clear against the white background. The train was armoured and equipped with anti-aircraft weapons of the usual calibres. If it was supposed to be a decoy I couldn't see where the threat would becoming from, except from the AA guns themselves, and we were going in too low for those to be really effective.

Ritter and Moritz went straight in from a shallow dive, hoping to gain the advantage of surprise. They planted their bigger bombs across the target, the explosions straddling the train and killing many of the enemy, blasting one rail car off the track and effectively trapping the front section of the train with its locomotive in Latgale, within range of further sorties assuming we'd be able to return and re-arm before they cleared the wreckage. On the ground soldiers hid in or under the train or could be seen running for the sparse cover of the woods, plunging awkwardly in the drifts. Meanwhile our three D.1s got to work aiming for the locomotive to ensure incapacitation or destruction although our light bombs were ineffective and we failed to score direct hits. Ritter and Moritz circled at low level shooting up anything that moved.

Down on the deck in our more manoeuvrable single seaters, turning at low level to provide the most difficult targets, we roared in fast from behind and between the fir trees, using them as cover until the last moment. I clearly saw a commissar with a pistol, turning men around who'd failed to stand to face our attack and shoot two in the head before taking aim at me. We concentrated our fire on the largest masses of troops but saved a few bursts for anyone who looked vaguely as if he was in charge, our targets sharply defined, dark against the snow. Some heroes stood and took pot shots but by then most were running confusedly. I was breathing hard, moving my head around to gain a better peripheral view at low level due to the limitations of the visor. I felt consumed with hatred for all Bolshevist killers and rapists, which is how I classed them, even the conscripts, and flew into harm's way more than once. This was a personal war and Vytautas seemed invincible: but then the heavy machine guns and 76.2 mm AA cannon started, and I suffered big hits in wings and fuselage as I pulled up at the end of a low level strafe and something tore a piece of leather from my coat collar and clanged on my iron cheek. I felt the aircraft shake as strips of corrugated metal were torn away and a section began buzzing and fluttering in the airflow, risking the handling. To the east I could see a flight of Russian SPADs being engaged by our top cover men. If this was the Bolshevik 'ambush flight' they'd arrived too late. Thank heaven for our escort or we'd have been in trouble; a premature thought as it turned out.

Had I not just run out of ammunition I think I'd still have backed off in my headlong vengeance. A one man crusade against the killers of the house of Strelitz would not return my Krysia, or Kat. Nor would it recompense for the deaths of Hannah and Daine, the murders of Augusts, Graczyna, the Graf, Berg, Nina, the servants. What would be accomplished were I to die in this futile way?

Close to our fuel limit for returning to *Dora*, Ritter and Moritz turned away west, followed by Laumann. Kessler and myself bringing up the rear. We'd both unclipped our visors and I'd just replaced my goggles when I noticed a thin trail behind Kessler's D.1. It was dark and might have been a smudge of hot oil and smoke combined as it began to thicken rapidly. A jet of steam had then begun to pour from the radiator and the fighter was slowing noticeably, Kessler side-slipping slightly to see ahead and avoid the plume of steam. The other three assault aircraft drew away westwards covered by our fighters, all now low on fuel.

We'd made less than seven kilometres and were short of the town of Preiji, according to my map, when Kessler's propeller stopped as the motor seized solid. I flew alongside and looked at his face. It was set with a look of grim determination. He'd raised his goggles and was peering through slits of eyes into an icy 100 kph wind; two flesh-toned circles where his goggles had been. The whole front of the aeroplane glistened with oil which had coated the windscreen and Kessler himself. Snow landings are difficult at the best of times, when there is no defining feature to give scale or depth of field on a landing approach. Under the poor light of an overcast there is little effective contrast to aid a pilot. The area was flat as far as could be judged, but the snow would be at least 20 cm deep. No great problem for landing but a take-off would be fraught with danger, if not impossible. Not that Kessler would be planning to take off.

I would, however.

I would have to prepare for a landing alongside my comrade and try to extricate him by carrying him aboard as a passenger as I'd done with Arkadi. I had come to that conclusion when I'd seen a detachment of soldiers on the road from Preiji. Who they might be I couldn't say. Lett freedom fighters, Red Letts, Baltische Landeswehr from Col. Howard's divisions or straightforward Bolshies, part of the army corps we'd just shot up, it was just impossible to know. The chances were they were hostile. Given our recent raid I would not have bet a kopek on Ernst's future.

I concentrated on the D.1 ahead. He was descending into the large snow-covered area while I flew above and to his left. I had no remaining ammunition to keep a hostile force at bay while Kessler made off, and had no illusions about how far he'd be able to get, assuming he was uninjured.

He looked well positioned to land within the available distance, a good five hundred metres, I estimated. He touched down about seventy metres in from the boundary marked by low trees and a snow-filled ditch and what was possibly a lane at the downwind end. At least he was landing away from the approaching troops. Whether he'd noticed them I wasn't sure - not that he could do other than he was: concentrate on making the arrival survivable.

The wheels touched leaving two streaks in the snow and then the skid was down and breaking through the surface, decelerating as I overtook to follow him in, circling round to the left. Out of the corner of my eye I saw the Junkers shudder as it hit some snow-covered obstruction. Looking back as I completed my turn I could see that the Ju's undercarriage and one propeller blade had completely sheared off and the aircraft was at rest on its belly. Kessler was standing in the cockpit which suggested that he was unhurt.

I glanced towards the detachment as I hauled around to line up on Kessler, making sure I was well off to the left. I didn't know what he'd hit but if it was a ridge of some sort it might extend across the field. I wouldn't know until I touched down. It was all very tight. Some of the soldiers were running awkwardly, dark silhouettes stumbling through the snow in the direction of the crash-landed Junkers, rifles un-slung. I couldn't tell what colour were their greatcoats, didn't really have time to take it in. I was keyed-up and concentrating on pulling this off. The familiar transition from a flying creature invaded my perspective. I was reverting to that heavy terrestrial organism to which we are doomed to return after each escape to freedom. Even in war, the beauty and miracle of flight cannot be denied.

I was down quicker than I thought: before I was ready, before I'd brought the stick right back the Junkers was thudding and bounding across snowy tufts and bone-jarring shallow ridges, motor cutting briefly as the fuel aerated. This was a rough field indeed, masked by it's camouflage blanket of white, but I was thankfully down and turning the Junkers as hard as I dared to taxi back to where Kessler was now jogging towards me. I swung the Ju vigorously back into wind using forward stick to unload the skid and Ernst jumped onto the heavy-ribbed wing root. He'd abandoned his steel helmet. But his breast armour and leather coat were slippery with engine oil and he looked like a greased pig.

'Get in behind me!' I yelled hoarsely into the exhaust fumes, gesturing with my thumb.

I released my shoulder and lap straps and threw the seat cushion and frying pan overboard, leaning forward as he clambered hurriedly into the cockpit. I sat down on his knees, my head now somewhat higher than the windscreen. The view over the Spandaus and cylinders was quite different and I experimented with how far I would be able to pull the stick back, which wasn't very far with me leaning back against Kessler's metal chest.

'All set?' I yelled.

There was no time to bother with straps: Kessler merely slapped me on the shoulder as I opened wide the throttle. This is *déjà vu*, I thought, easing the stick forward.

The Ju gathered ground. Unfortunately it was also gathering snow ahead of the wheels, like before at *Heinrich*, Liepus Namas. I got the tail up and it slowly accelerated, banging and shuddering into the frozen grass tummocks. It didn't help that we were two-up, but I'd used all the ammo, half the fuel and dropped two bombs as well, so theoretically we should be light enough to make this plan work. In any event it was the only one I had.

It was almost a carbon copy of my earlier escape, taking off with rounds cracking past our ears. The section of starboard wing skin that had been torn up by artillery fire was vibrating and buzzing, spoiling lift and we needed all we could get for this enterprise. I found I was using a lot of left stick to keep the aircraft level in ground effect. I eased back too soon and sank back into the snow. The hedge was coming up studded with low trees with a small farmhouse beyond - which I hadn't noticed -

straight ahead of us in the next field. I yawed slightly to ensure that I'd miss it and prepared, like some weighty percheron, to leap the fence.

We almost made it. We were flying and out of ground-effect when we hit the top of the hedge with the wheels. I don't remember a thing after that until I woke up with a sense of unreality, being stripped of my flying clothing, my nose and mouth streaming blood and my ears ringing with more than residual engine noise. My Junkers was minus its undercarriage and propeller, like Kessler's while Ernst himself was in the snow being kicked in the face and ribs in turns by two soldiers in greatcoats with red and white armbands and stars. With my puffy eyes it was hard to distinguish between my friend's blood and the engine oil. I was roughly turned over and felt my shirt being ripped off. Kessler was already naked from the waist up and bruised. Someone stood on his chest while another pulled off his fleece-lined boots. A couple of soldiers were fixing bayonets. It didn't look good.

Then one noticed my scarring. There was a hiatus and a babble of voices. I seized the initiative.

'Comrades!' I cried passionately, my voice thick with the blood. 'We are conscripts. Only mechanics forced to fly reconnaissance for the German capitalist adventurers. I am Lithuanian, an ordinary worker, mechanic. See how I have been treated, whipped and abused by feudal landowners? With freedom of choice I would gladly join with my Bolshevist brothers. Long live the Revolution!'

They looked disbelievingly at me, but there was some hesitancy. At least my Lithuanian and part-Latvian/Russo protestations seemed to have been understood.

They pointed then at Kessler. '*Kalpotajs!*' They shouted. 'Officer!

'No, no! He is my own brother. *Muy brat!* We were conscripted together and we have always looked out for each other. Right through war. We worked as mechanics until forced to fly because Germans were desperate for pilots!' This was shamelessly intended to make the Red Letts feel better about the military situation.

'Long live Comrade Lenin. Long live Red Latvia!'

I noticed one sharp-looking individual tracing the mounted 'Vytis knight' on my fuselage with his finger. It attested to the desire for an independent statehood for Lithuania. Not a soviet statehood. He walked over to me and smiled. He was holding my bullet-scarred iron death mask. He slammed it into my face and I drifted away somewhere where pain and consequences did not figure.

Later I blurrily recognised a snow-camouflaged B2 Russo-Balt armoured car approaching. It bore the slogan '*Death to the Enemies of the Revolution*' in red on the sides of the turret. It halted and a leather-coated commissar stepped out. I was freezing, shivering uncontrollably. I could barely recognise Kessler through my swollen eyes. He was stripped and bloody, slumped opposite me against the thick wing of the Junkers resting flat on the snow. He looked blue with cold and stone dead. The commissar seemed extremely interested in the aircraft and looked at the two of us. He then seemed to give very explicit instruction to the Lett guards. My head was ringing so much I couldn't hear what was being said and soon after that I passed out again.

~-~

I was behind barbed wire in the open air, me, Kessler and about fifty thousand others: a great, grey slowly-revolving mass of human misery at some shit-hole called Kozhukov near Moscow, or so I had been told by a prisoner. I have some recollection of an uncomfortable rail journey jammed into a stinking cattle truck. Our horizon was marked by trees and the chimneys of an abandoned factory from which no smoke issued. To the east the spires of a church signalled that man had once believed in God. Smoke *had* appeared from that direction for a while. Apart from our beatings we had been fit and reasonably well-fed when we'd arrived but most here were already starving and had been here for weeks. To begin with the prisoners had been fed a thin gruel, black bread and 'soup' in the afternoon, but feeding so many with failure of the harvests was an impossible task. Now food was scarce or non-existent but a little bread was thrown over the wire and that was fought over; the strongest managing to grab a fistful which was immediately consumed. Apathy set in with the cold.

Some of those incarcerated were Tsarist or White Army officers, but many other ranks of all armies and ethnic types who had fought against Bolshevism were represented. That the Bolsheviks used arbitrary methods to select immediately those deemed unfit to exist was evident. Red Guards had marched off a section of some one hundred 'class enemies', 'politicals' and 'Tsarists', among whom were conscripts of various nationalities: Tartars, Kazaks, Don Cossacks. Some Austro-Hungarian POWs and Whites meanwhile were left behind. The prisoners were formed–up and marched away from the compound, heads high, in perfect order, despite their miserable physical condition. Prolonged firing in the distance testified to their liquidation. This happened at intervals of every few days until the typhus appeared. We considered perhaps that they had been the lucky ones.

We'd been interrogated by their technical people, the usual hard-eyed commissars sitting in, about the Junkers all metal monoplanes in which the Russians, to whom we'd been handed over, were extremely interested. No doubt they would have salvaged the two D.1s. They were certainly repairable. Kessler couldn't help them much due to his injuries, but I told them all I knew about its handling, performance, endurance, payload, serviceability, etc. There was nothing to be gained from holding back and nothing to be lost either. The war was practically over in the Baltic. The Soviets were honouring the independence of Lithuania, Latvia and Estonia, I was informed by another prisoner who appeared mysteriously to know what was going on, and it was rumoured that Petlyura had secured the Ukraine and lost it again, depending on which newcomers' versions seemed more recent.

But the Polish war was brewing. I suspected that the Baltic truce was only contingent on the present military commitment of the USSR on other fronts and that Russia wasn't about to give up its Baltic ports and lush agricultural lands that easily. But world events held little interest for us now as our horizon was reduced to one of personal survival in the most extreme circumstance. After our technical information had been extracted, we were deemed of no further use, and thrown into this vast concentration camp with no facilities and no food, forgotten and living mostly in the open in freezing conditions, only the crush of men providing some warmth in the first days.

I was delivered to the compound a few days after Kessler. It was a dismal morning, foggy and ice cold. He was watching the new arrivals and waved when he saw me. That is he raised his hand in a furtive gesture which brought me to his side.

'Welcome to my world.' He said. He looked sick, head cocked on one side, like a bird, trying to focus one eye. He was unshaven and ragged.

I looked around. Everything seemed to be in the usual shades of grey. The clay-plastered wooden huts had open windows without glass. Glass could be used to make stabbing weapons. Hut occupants defended their billets with some force. There were deaths by night and day, and for a while the willing able-bodied had dragged the dead to the far edge of the compound away from where most congregated. At first the bodies were removed every few days under guard in hand carts or sleds, but as the numbers rose, they were stacked instead, piled high like logs, each

578

row alternating, heads and feet. Those frozen in awkward postures had to be straightened out, a very difficult and exhausting process.

Three weeks without food takes its toll of the healthiest and those men were at their lowest ebb, chewing scraps of leather, risking death by scraping ice off the watchtower stanchions in the morning, breaking icicles off the wire to suck. Meanwhile a trickle of new prisoners continued to arrive, looking starved already. All now face, with such fortitude as could be mustered, the apocalyptic riders that prance in triumph halucogenically, about our huddled masses....

Some of us foraged about the wooden huts at night, tearing boards from the walls and splitting them into firewood. Fires were started with some difficulty using friction. Thin rags were lit which kept a few fires going around the compound. The guards apparently had orders to put these out, confiscating the timber, but we managed to keep some smouldering rags and re-lit them when they'd gone. They too were apathetic and after a while they let us be. The miserable warmth was keeping us alive a little longer, but I began to fear for Kessler. He'd hardly spoken a coherent sentence since the beating he'd received. We were dressed in layers of rags picked from the corpses and wrapped yards of old uniform around our heads to minimise the heat loss, if heat could even be used as a relative term for our body temperatures: still a fog lay above the men, which proved at least that we were breathing. And we breathed the stench of open latrines – our misfortune that the wind was in the East although most of the stench was contained under the frozen yellow crust. This then was *that world ruled by zealots where good men turned to clay.*

We were all infected with lice, but embraced each other in slow *dumkas* of two hundred or so prisoners and beat at our arms and legs to get some circulation going, jigging for hours at a time on snow that compressed into ice until we lost the battle to exhaustion. At night began the earnest shuffle known as the 'dance of death'. We were packed so tight for body warmth under the watchtower lights that men would be held upright even in death. Our slow gyration exposed each by turn to the outside of the crush. Only then would they topple and fall, and all the while we were tormented by our savage hunger and frostbitten feet. We could no longer feel anything below our blackened shins.

As for Ernst, his facial swelling had gone down but he plainly couldn't see well and his swollen lips were badly split. He told me mine were too. They felt numb and it made talking difficult. I think he looks terrible. He tells me I look terrible too. I hadn't realised I'd spoken aloud. Typhus and the bitter cold had killed hundreds by our second week and we couldn't see ourselves lasting through a third. How long before Spanish Flu would arrive, I wondered.

We all had severe headaches. Rat armies were more active at night, scurrying through the compound with high pitched-squeaks. At first we recoiled from them as they rushed upon the corpses. Almost immediately they in turn were preyed upon, pursued avidly as sportsmen address the choicest game: using coats as nets or sharpened sticks as spears. The huntsmen were themselves emaciated and corpse-like, swaying marionettes controlled by drunken puppeteers.

Soon enough, uncollected bodies were cannibalised. Factions or tribes seemed to be forming in the camp; men reverting to beasts, tearing at cadavers in the dark with teeth loosened by starvation or pellagra, hunched about corpses, mangy lions and hyenas, reduced to bloodily ripping out tongues from the newly dead. At least the freezing conditions kept the meat reasonably fresh. Others managed to cook the flesh: tongues, rumps and thighs that still were partly fleshy, jealously guarding their fires. The guards still threw over the occasional crust of bread, just to watch desperate men exhaustedly trying to kill each other with their bare hands for a morsel of sustaining food, falling under a crush of bodies. This was a form of entertainment which they seemed to enjoy.

Prisoners prayed aloud for death as much as for salvation until their tongues had thickened, or they hallucinated that they were somewhere else. One climbed the watchtower with what little strength he possessed and tried to jump over the wire. He was shot for his trouble and left hanging on the barbs for a day and a night, perhaps as a 'warning' to others. If so they'd completely misread the psychology. Death, including suicide, was such a close companion that his proximity had no effect. Indeed he was becoming a close friend. That's another poor bastard who's no longer suffering would have been the common feeling expressed, but wordlessly, through our eyes since commentary took effort. On reflection he was probably left due to the characteristic apathy that infected the camp, inside and outside the wire. Inside, once valiant men were giving up hope. Outside, as the sun went down, they couldn't have cared less. Our silent prayers and incantations fell upon a deaf universe.

~-~

It was afternoon. I had survived another night and was sitting shivering, back to back with Ernst for mutual support on a rag pile in an agony of cramp suffering a vicious headache, lousy and scratching, when I saw a car pull up on the other side of the wire. It looked like a Rolls *Silver Ghost* so it had to belong to some high ranking commissar bastard, though of course 'property was theft'. I'd tried appealing to the guards from time to time to obtain some food, but I had nothing to bargain with save for obscure promises of reward of some kind when the 'bureaucratic mistake was recognised' and I'd be 'finally released'. They simply shrugged their shoulders and warned against approaching the wire with a threat show, shoving a rifle muzzle and bayonet through the wire, snarling some traditional Bolshevist greeting such as, '*Fuck your mother, capitalist lackey!*'

The one ray of hope I had was in conversation with a Belarus cavalryman who'd been captured in Ukraine. He told me that he had encountered a White cavalry brigade which had joined forces with them for a while led by an able commander, about the most fanatical fighter against Bolshevism he'd ever met. Called the 'White Vengeance Brigade' they wore blue tunics and their commander was known only as 'Madamoiselle X'. What most caught my attention however was her reported hair colour. Red as flame!

As ever, even in our greatest apathy, something different happening would draw the most jaundiced eye. The sight of a spare, great-coated figure striding along the edge of the wire stirred something in my memory. Suddenly I scrambled to my feet, nearly falling with giddiness and causing Ernst to collapse painfully on his thin back, which at least woke him up.

In my mind I was running to the wire, although an observer would describe it objectively as a crab-like stagger, skirting dozens of inert and ragged bundles with snow upon their shoulders, like my own.

I gripped the wire oblivious to the barbs and to the Red Guards running towards me with their bayonets fixed. I was focussed on the man; thinner, sallower, taller than I remembered but for certain it was him. I would know Marik anywhere.

~-~

I was calling his name. There was a dull murmur of voices and the constant hacking and coughing from the compound but my voice I felt sure was audible above it, although the reality was a croak. The two accompanying soldiers turned their heads to look at me as I struggled along inside the wire.

'Marik, Godammit. I know it's you. For God's sake, it's me, Rolf!

Damn you, stop. Look at me, will you?'

The tall figure strode on, straight-backed, looking only ahead.

'Marik! If it's you for God's sake tell me. You've got to get me out of here. I'm dying.

I was having difficulty keeping up with them, in my weakened state and having to negotiate prostrate or huddled figures, standing singly and in groups.

'Marik! Don't you want to know what happened to the Graf. To Graf Kristian. To the girls. To Graczy? For God's sake man! What sort of traitor turns his back on his entire family?'

Guards were running towards me inside the compound, rifles held like clubs. He marched stolidly on with his escort and no hint of an acknowledgement. I remember the first blow only; saw the lightning flash and entered a black void with Marik's name and a curse on my lips.

~-~

I'd had a beautiful dream.….lying in a meadow with Krysia, looking at a summer sky. She was telling me not to worry, her eyes brimming with tears. I am overwhelmed with love for her but have a sense of dread, of impending separation.

My eyes gain focus and I am still lying on my back with a fading memory of her kiss. The cold bites in and I'm looking at a charnel sky, the smell of smoke from our miserable fires in my nostrils. A calm acceptance of what I presume is impending death is creeping upon me. I try to resist, calling upon all my anger at the injustice in the world, holding to my memories of Krysia and Kat, building now on my hatred of Marik for his treachery. But I don't have the strength to rally. I feel a weakness that is almost euphoric along with the desire to fall back into that dream, to seek out Krysia on that grassy bank. *She is speaking to me but I can't hear the words. There are clouds drifting in her blue-green eyes. A noise stops me from hearing. There's something I must do, but I'm gripped by a restraining torpor. I should do something urgently, to save her, but I cannot act. Her hands are reaching for me and mine for hers as the dream dissolves.*

Ernst is supporting my shoulders. He has drawn a greatcoat over my thin body as a last defence against the cold. I assume that means that others have died. I notice that his left eye has returned almost to normal though his right is still closed and puffy. From time to time he turns his head and coughs. My head aches mercilessly, not just from the bruising I'd suffered from the Red Guards, but something profoundly worse. My stomach has shrunk but still it grinds for food. For some reason I thought it would soon be Christmas and we'd all be released.......

Two flesh-eaters shuffle slowly past. There is a special gleam in the eyes of these anthropophagous zeks. It's a mixture of triumphalism, shamelessness and something else. It says, 'Judge not, for we have crossed our *Rubicon*. We will surely survive you unless you join in our nightly cabaret'. For all we know we are their next meal. *Yob tvoio mat!* Much may it profit them. We have maybe days. When we are gone they'll be fighting to eat each other. Perhaps we'll be waiting for them beyond the *Styx*.

'Liebnitz believed a monk could fly, Rolf.' Ernst's voice comes from some fragile husk, from far away.

'You told me.'

'Levitation through starvation.' The words are faint but clear. 'Transportation through flagellation; ascetic meditation to canonical corroboration......finally posthumous Papal sanctification, by Pope Benedict XIV in 1667. But I can't now remember the name of that monk. Why is that do you suppose?' He looks at me quizzically, hawk-like.

'We must both be getting old, Ernst.'

'Do you think if they starved us enough and beat us enough we too might reach that state of lightness, of Hindu-like transcendental grace. That we might just..... float ....over the wire?'

I managed a smile. 'I think the only way out of here will be on wings. Always put your faith in wings, Ernst. Wings and airspeed.'

Grimly I thought; yes, we'll be lifted by angels wings. That's the only way our souls would escape this hell on earth and our frozen bodies would lie until Spring, until they couldn't stand the stink. Merry Christmas you bastards!

Meanwhile the ankle I'd fractured as a boy, believing I *could* fly on cloth wings, feels as though I broke it yesterday and the scars on my back burn as if I'd been whipped this morning. I drift in and out of consciousness. I wonder where it resides, *consciousness*. I presume I'm awake but my viewpoint is elevated, 'bird's eye' in fact. I seem suspended above the compound looking down on myself in Kessler's arms. I am not alone. I am aware of other souls looking down with me, in a sort of collective consciousness. The impression lasts perhaps a minute before I re-inhabit my old crust; my shell of pain, and feel again the coldness. Now wounds from my encounter with 'Old Kaiser' and those from my training days at Helmsburg are throbbing too: ribs and the backs of my hands. Livid, like stigmata. I feel a bitter ending is nigh.

Later it's dark. I have been dreaming, watching Hanna collect stones for her drowning. I stand by her lake like a miserable child, uncomprehending. I wake gasping in the freezing air as if experiencing her last moments. I think that stars are moving above me but when I close my eyes the show goes on. I am back at Helmsburg, washing at a freezing ablutions trough in the open air, for 'toughening up' while a band plays, ironically in my head - given our present circumstance, the *Marsch des Russischen Grenadier*. I face the charge of a giant boar; hear Wöbbe's terrified screams as the Graf lifts me up and asks if I'm a good little soldier. I see Greiner's gold incisor in the Loh's rear view mirror. I wonder which is real and which is an hallucinatory figment, until I remember they're all dead now. Nearby a gaunt figure stares at me through spectacles of shiny skin.

Ernst says, 'Stay with me, Rolf. Don't you leave me.'

I am dimly aware of movement nearby, the impression of heavy figures with ear-flapped *papakhas*: guards moving among the pitiful bundles and *quasimodos*, pushing and questioning in harsh tones. Ernst is shivering uncontrollably next to me, thin arms wrapped around me. An hour ago he was retching but had nothing to vomit. I think we are both in the last stages. Someone calls out near at hand. An old name. Dragun? Dragunovich? *Dragunavicius.*

'Dragun? Dragunovich? Dragunavicius!'

I'd been able to keep some soup down at the second try, and a slice of black bread, the sole diner at a scrubbed wooden table in the luxury of a warm canteen. Bolshevist flags and the banners of the Revolution festooned the walls, colourful exhortations to destroy the Capitalists, smash the Interventionists, dramatic images with bold Cyrillic calligraphy.

Two Red Guards watched me eat and then marched me to the office of Colonel V.N. Krasov as the name on the door had announced. Krasov's dark eyes observed me from behind a wide desk. He sat straight, his hands resting lightly on a blotter. On the wall behind his emaciated Christ-like head blazed a plaster *bas relief* gold star with hammer and sickle, like a gilded halo. Above was hung an heroic portrait of Lenin staring into the future. Like Lenin he'd grown a small moustache and goatee beard since I'd known him. I sit and watch him. With an iron discipline I have dredged from somewhere I refrain from scratching my body and arms. He'd dismissed the guards and a silence hung between us, each waiting on the other.

He began, as if we were back in our philosophers' tree, continuing a discussion we'd been having in our adolescence.

'You see, Rolf…. you must understand, how decadent we were. The old regime was last century. It was discredited and corrupt and had been for hundreds of years. The Duma was a toothless talking shop. Change was inevitable. The elevation of the common man, the unleashing of his whole human potential, that's now! That's modern, twentieth century! World revolution, that's inevitable too. We are unstoppable now!'

'We?' I hold back my revulsion.

'Yes, we. I am committed. It's the only way. You can save yourself too, Rolf.'

'I won't ask you how you became *Colonel Krasov*. I imagine it was much as I became Lt. Steiger. But can you sit there in that uniform when I tell you how your father was crucified, how Kat was raped and nearly killed and is missing, believed dead? How Krysia carries on the fight? How Graczy…. ?' I was momentarily overcome, struggling with my anger. 'I can hardly speak of it.'

Krasov's expression betrayed no emotion. I could see how he'd survived. I believed he was an exceptional actor and had convinced himself that survival demanded he adopt the most extreme mantle of disguise, had talked himself into the person of 'Krasov', whoever he'd been, some dead soul, like in Gogol: revolutionary apparatchik, jailer and executive officer of Lenin's apparatus of liquidation. In this case by doing nothing, by having the iron will to stand in the wings while fifty thousand men, his erstwhile allies, slowly died: taking others out for summary execution on some cold order of Dzerzhinsky's at the Kremlin, from the nerve centre of the Central Committee.

'So, you are no longer with Voltaire!' I sneered.

Christ, no, I thought. You are the ascetic monk, treading your secret shoreline, torn between land and sea.

'You'd always managed to hold simultaneous, diametrically-opposed views didn't you?' I said scathingly. 'And now you hide from the Bolshevist Inquisition, right here at the heart of their murder camp, burning ants under glass on your journey to Utopia.'

'In case you think you can judge me, I will tell you I did not choose this path. Choice is a luxury but Fate always has the last word.'

'Whether we have choice or not, we live in the 'now'. Will breeding out if an infant son is brought up as poor doctor's child? What's to be my fate, cousin?'

He raised his eyebrow.

'Don't tell me you didn't know. About Uncle Peter?'

A range of expressions wove their way across his solemn face.

'You really didn't know, did you? That Peter was my father. Claudia Hammond, your dear governess, my mother - now safe in England by the way. Oh, and yes, the parental substitutes that I knew and loved for the first seventeen years of my life, they are dead too. Augusts, murdered by your Bolsheviks in the bonfire of his hospital while saving patients' lives: Hanna's suicide the result.'

His already hollow face seemed suddenly to cave in.

'My God,' he said. 'Oh my God, my God.' As if the reported deaths of his father and the horrors of his sisters' fates had touched him no more than by a feather's caress. Had been as unreal as his own make believe identity, something he'd armed himself against, shut off in a remote chamber of his consciousness. But face-to-face the revelation of the simple fact of our blood relationship seemed to bring the entire house of cards down about his head. He placed his elbows on the desk, looked down and drew his hands through his hair and across his face: clawing at his cheeks in a down-dragging motion which suggested a soul in the torment of despair, his eyes dark sturgeon pools beyond the lattice of his fingers. A low groan escaped his chest. He shuddered and then seemed to gulp for air, head in hands, his body convulsed with uncontrollable sobs.

Boots clumped outside and there was a sharp knock at the door. A guard's voice called out. Krasov stopped instantly, snapping upright in his chair, the whites of his eyes visible, encircling the pupils. 'It's alright,' he called, his voice thick. 'The prisoner is just a little overcome. Relax, Comrade.'

After a slight pause, the boots retreated.

Krasov turned to me. 'I will get you away from here,' he said with a great sigh. 'It is the one chance for you, to be re-educated. Become part of the Revolution. You are a pilot, yes?'

'Yes.'

'The Revolution needs pilots. Comrade Trotsky, Commissar for National Defence has ordered that suitably vetted candidates, including former officers, can be re-educated and placed at the disposal of the Army as instructors for the *Workers' and Peasants' Red Military Air Fleet*. I have the authority to direct the Committee, to recommend you for vetting. Under the command of Comrade General Sergeev we are in the process of building the greatest air arm the world has seen.'

'Is that for the Cheka listeners with their ears against the wall?'

Krasov gave me a direct look. 'That's what we *are* building, Rolf. A powerful nation armed with the most modern defences, an impregnable fortress with the vast natural resources of the USSR and its indefatigable manpower. A wealthy, peaceful, powerful Soviet Russia, self-sustaining, equal to or greater than the decadent capitalist empires of the planet, built on equality. A fair society protected from intervention where we can rebuild this great country in security. There is no escaping it now.'

'Do you honestly believe that? You can't even feed your people, Marik. You are in the grip of famine and your only reaction is mass murder. Your prisoners die in agony of starvation but indeed you *cannot* feed them any more than you *will* not feed them, by edict of Lenin. Those you gun down can count themselves lucky.'

'Take it or leave it, Rolf. Attend the re-education programme, *Comrade*, and eat. Stay here and you'll die in a few days along with all the others. To Lenin you are already dead.'

I was silent for a long moment.

'I have a condition.'

'*You* have a condition! Rolf, I only have to raise my voice.....'

'I have a friend. A pilot. He's hungry for re-education too.'

Chapter 39. *Culturing the Bacillus*

We were taken to a fine old Tsarist military hospital near Moscow, snappily re-titled, Bolshevist style, *The Sanatorium of the Red Heroes of the October Revolution*, where we remained under guard. Here we were treated with professionalism by a wary and taciturn medical staff. Our wounds and frostbitten feet, our hands and ears were treated. Gangrenous slices were cut from my earlobes but I kept all my fingers. The food was poor but we were young and gradually regained our strength. Momentously a specialist doctor informed Ernst that, though it now looked fairly normal, he would most probably lose the sight of his right eye. It streamed as a result of frost damage to the tear duct, but the more serious injury was the result of the savage handling he'd received during capture. This put our hopes of his gaining a post as an instructor with the Red Air Fleet in serious jeopardy, given that his grasp of Russian was limited, although I coached him constantly. He seemed distant and failed to concentrate, dwelling instead on hopeless, whispered plans of how we might escape.

Once deemed fit we embarked for another camp. Behind barbed wire again, though this time in hutted accommodation, we began our re-education period in the grounds of an air academy which had its own special classes for 'thought reform'. Ernst had managed to bluff his way through his medical by swapping hands, covering his right orbit on *both* occasions when reading from the eye chart. His greatest difficulty had been in identifying and pronouncing the Cyrillic, which distracted and annoyed the medic. Thankfully the comrade nurse was unaware of the ophthalmologist's pronouncements at the *October Revolution*.

We were assembled in classrooms where we were expected to complete tests on our knowledge of navigation, internal combustion engines and theory of flight, but much more attention was placed on political theory which permeated every lesson. Kessler and myself were seated with about twenty ex-Tsarist pilots including a few officers who'd managed to avoid the firing squads. Like us, they were 'paroled' for screening and indoctrination. Perhaps for no other reason than my bandaged ears made me stand out, I was chosen for the honour of igniting the pyre at a ritual burning of works deemed counter-revolutionary and corrupting. The titles, some of which were familiar to me, represented some of the greatest works of literature in Russian as well as English and other languages, text books and religious works, including hand-written copies of the Bible in Cyrillic, the Koran and Talmud. Beautifully illustrated and of some antiquity they had been singled out for the foulest defilement before being torn to shreds. I hobbled forward on my recovering feet and did this without a flicker, my features impassive as the flames licked at the bindings. I became an obedient apparatchik for the *New Inquisition* which deemed that the heresy of literary expression was a plague, not on the soul but on the state. I was closely observed by the narrow-faced commissar educator for any deviant sign of political insecurity or moral backsliding. A suspected Cheka *agent provocateur*, an individual rendered obvious by his pretence of familiarity and a garrulous manner, also watched from within our ranks, ready to pounce.

Part of our rehabilitation was to write a weekly polemic criticising a selected author for professing heretical ideologies, for perceived capitalist or counter-revolutionary propaganda in their *Index Librorum Prohibitorum*. Of course I secretly wrote Ernst's as well, as it had to be rendered in reasonable Russian. But soon they seemed to tire of these charades and fifteen of us, those not *ex-communicated*, were sent by train chivvied by our political watchdogs, to the recently established 1st.*Vysshaya Shkola Voennykh Letchikov*: Podolsk Military Pilot's School of the RKKVF, south of Moscow's industrial area. We were now wearing the standard forage cap, blouson, loden jacket, belt and jackboots (which were agony to wear at first) of the Red Army. We'd been issued with identity papers and pay books, but were yet to receive pay. In any case party activists ensured that a percentage of our wage was already earmarked for an emergency war loan for the government, which no one dared deny. The irony was not lost to me that my assumed identity was now officially acknowledged by what would become the mighty Soviet State.

But we'd succeeded in the first part of the plan. We were still standing! We were on our way, you bastards. State laboratory technicians: part of the apparatus that would culture its bacillus, multiply and spread the *Communistic Pandemic*, by giving it wings!

~·~

It is early 1920 and winter's dead hand grips the very air around the snow-covered flying field of Moscow's *Podolsk Shkola Voennykh Letchikov*. There is a high overcast and some wisps of grey stratus, estimated at around 750 metres. A mix of types is based on the field, Avro, Farman,

590

Voisin and Nieuports, types 10 and 12. Morane-Saulnier parasol trainers as well as Albatros B-Types: slow or very slow machines of mostly limited range. For single-seat advanced training there are various petite Nieuports from 11s through to the 24 and a couple of Spads, all Russian *Duks*-built. These latter types are perforce RKKVF front-line equipment although mostly their designs are at least four years out of date. Some of the fighters are still equipped with guns, sans their MG cocking levers; nor is ammunition issued in case someone had insurrection in mind.

Ernst has been assisting with basic training, although his grasp of Russian is still meagre. His initial technique is to let the eager young cadet pilots under his tuition make every possible mistake in the air before demonstrating appropriate recovery. It's a good system which I have adopted myself and the trainees learn faster when allowed to experience loss of control, learning not to be fearful once they've acquired the skills to regain control quickly. I help Ernst write up his pupil pilots' records and comments on their flying ability or unsuitability as the case may be. In every way we are exemplary Bolshevist NCOs carrying out the frenetic training programme alongside our Red brethren, with whom we mostly get on well. After all we are all comrades now, pulling together for the same victorious outcome under Trotsky's increasingly well-organised War Programme.

Considering that failure to get sufficient pupils through the courses is seen as sabotage, an arrestable crime, punishable by firing squad, we make every effort to fulfil the quotas, even when some of the initial material would have been considered to have been below acceptable quality in Austro-Germany. However, persevering frequently pays off and most trainees have succeeded in obtaining their brevets without too many broken propellers and undercarriages. It is exhausting work but such is the demand at the Fronts that we do not let up for the winter weather unless it is extreme.

I have a serious black mark against me however. I am charged with writing a report on how one of my better pupils managed to kill himself whilst engaging in low aerobatics yesterday. The Nieuport had spun out of an improperly executed stall turn, a manoeuvre which I'd demonstrated but which was not in the novice pilots' curriculum. It had little value as a combat manoeuvre, the machine making a stationary target at the top of the figure.

Kessler and I had witnessed the event; the Nieuport 17 recovering too sharply and stalling-in from low altitude, impacting vertically on the frozen aerodrome.

'That's gonna hurt in the morning,' Kessler murmured cynically. 'An extremely painful way of impressing *absolutely no-one!*'

Later Ernst managed to salvage the dead cadet's boots. 'Luckily he was my size,' he says pragmatically. The pair the quartermaster NCO given him previously had been too tight. Ernst is convinced it was deliberate act of malice.

~-~

It was still dark when I took off from the hard-as-iron field at 0630 hrs.

I'm detailed for a meteorological flight on the sole Fokker D.VII that is based here. *(Probably a captured example, Natasha. The Soviets did not officially receive any D.VIIs until fifty were purchased from Fokker in early 1922, despite Steiger's identifying them as enemy types in Latvia.)* It's more advanced than the other fighter biplanes on strength and equipped with a supercharged 185 hp. BMW. I am enjoying renewing my acquaintance with this machine since flying the type briefly in the air war over Latvia - along with the 'tin' D.1. Rumour has it that the Red Air Fleet is likely to equip with the D.VII in the short term, being one of the best fighters extant. It's also in great demand throughout Europe to re-equip many smaller air arms so there'll be few enough for Russia. We aren't allowed to discuss such things of course and our every word and action is reported on.

The official attitude is that the engineers of the new socialist republic are unequalled and soon we would have the greatest, most advanced fighter and bomber force on the planet. I maintain a low profile. I have almost enough to eat, given the war economy- it's not safe to mention famine - and work as an assistant instructor at the school, billeted alongside fourteen other pilot instructors. The 'watch dog' political commissars are forever snooping and behave like jailers. The only 'freedom' we feel is when airborne. As now. Petrol is strictly rationed in case we try to defect, although we would not get far on the modest fuel endurance of any of the school aircraft. Our maps too are cropped to show just the local area, within 80 km of base. A wanderlust deterrent.

Yesterday the germ of a plan had seeded in my mind with the arrival of a high-ranking commissar, a wingless colonel in the RKK, travelling in some style as a passenger in a converted Halberstadt CL.IV powered by a 160 hp. Mercedes engine. Its black crosses had been over-painted with red stars like all other captured aircraft. The colonel had a roving commission from the aviation inspectorate and a signed requisition from Sergeev for the aircraft to be immediately refuelled wherever it landed.

The aircraft retained its forward-firing machine gun but the free Parabellum had been removed from the gunner's cockpit. Instead the gun ring of this excellent ex-German *Schlachtbomber* has been in-filled with plywood, lined internally and fitted with a padded armchair. There was even a light desk and a small typewriter so that reports could be prepared en route, as well as a Morse key and a wind-up aerial on a drum wheel. A cabin top had been added and there was celluloid glazing each side. A speaking tube was fitted for communicating between the passenger and his pilot/chauffeur. Altogether it was a superbly converted, comfortable, fast, aerial-taxicab, communications-aircraft and office!

I'd been admiring the aeroplane, the standard military version of which both Kessler and I were familiar with from the war in Latvia, until warned away by Commissar Pokrowsky, a persistently annoying Chekist weasel who snooped and reported any action he viewed as suspicious, which was just about *everything*. I knew my time here was limited and I was sure to face arrest by Comrade Andrei Ambruszov's resident Cheka office once we had provided enough trained pilots. Next stop Siberia - if I was 'lucky'. I walked away, but I'd already climbed onto the port wing and had seen the map case in the pilot's cockpit; a security lapse that allowed me to confirm that it contained uncut maps of European Russia and Northern Ukraine, unlike our training maps which were limited in the extreme.

I recalled that the top speed of the Halberstadt is 165 kph, about 60 kph faster than the old Albatros trainers. Although the Fokker is faster still, at 186 kph, and some of the other fighters almost as fast, they are all single-seaters with less than two hours endurance when fully-fuelled. With maximum fuel and two-up the Halberstadt could *cruise* at 145 kph. for three hours!

We'd made the Halberstadt pilot very welcome; a German mercenary, name of Hermann Rowehl. Feigning gradual inebriation on nothing more potent than tap water, we succeeded in getting a rather bemused quartermaster sergeant and Rowehl stupefied on cheap vodka that evening, *no, Rowehl – not wood alcohol. This is good stuff. Yes the camp is supposed to be 'dry', but we are on the 'ways and means' committee.*....swapping war stories. *Rolf, tell friend Rowehl about that time you were gang-banged by five Nieuports in Albania and landed 'deadstick' upside down...*singing bawdy squadron songs, sharing sentimental reveries and improbable tales of heroism and endurance with the opposite sex. Naturally we toasted the political vision of our great leader, comrade Lenin, in both the German and Russian languages, careful lest our sentiments be taken for irony; and Trotsky's tireless military genius. The snoopers had invaded our party's periphery, listening to our ribaldry but nothing we said could have been misconstrued as a political comment or a jibe against Communist idealism. As we drank to Battlefield Commissar Stalin's courageous leadership, they'd retired, bored.

We left the sergeant in a chair feeling no pain and locked Rowehl in the equipment store, tucked up under thick woollen blankets to sleep the sleep of the dead. His colonel had slept the night in Moscow where he'd delivered a report to Trotsky who seemed *never* to sleep. His Halberstadt slumbered with canvas covers over motor and cockpit, an armed guard patrolling.

It is due to fly out again at 10.00 hrs this morning. Weather permitting.

~-~

I am experiencing a rare peace. This morning thick stratus lies some distance to the south west, apparently moving or forming in our direction. I climb to determine the height and thickness of the upper layers to make some sort of prediction. Perhaps the weak winter sun may burn some holes in it. If the weather thickens we'd be restricted to flying circuits. Planned navigation exercises would have to be postponed. If my report is negative, the training schedule is deferred and the sun subsequently appears I will probably be accused of sabotage. However, I will phrase my weather report with ardent revolutionary optimism.

I'd checked the aeroplane meticulously before starting the engine and also the meteorological equipment we carry, a psychrometer of German origin and a large sensitive altimeter, also German made. The Cheka is not above sabotage by slackening a critical bolt or some other deadly interference, to cause an accident that they can blame on pilot error or lack of care in a pre-flight examination that will demonstrate our unreliability or their revolutionary vigilance. I am hated by them for my background despite my following the party line. Any slip could result in my arrest and probable torture before facing a firing squad. Kessler is considered even more the foreigner and so is more at risk I fear, damn their godless souls. We are useful, for now.

I bask in the familiar deep growl of the slow-revving BMW, relax in the steady beat and the sussuration of the slipstream. I open the throttle more as the stratus layer approaches, noting its altitude: lifting the nose and feeling the good old D.VII steepen her climb, rising steadily on those thick, cambered wings. I note the altimeter winding up and look down at the dark wing with the silky lozenge fabric; strut shadows moving on the muted ochres, blue-greys and indigos. I still cannot get used to the absence of bracing wires on this cantilever *biplane*, even though I flew the Junkers monoplane for six months.

I steepen the climb. The Morrell 'windmill' informs me that 'we' are only doing 60 kph at full throttle and the climb rate is lessening. Ease forward to improve cooling. 80 kph. More like it. Climb rate has increased and the big *Axial* propeller is biting better. I am supposed to level off at every 50 millibars on the big altimeter. At each stage I'm to record the temperatures on the twin thermometers, the 'wet' bulb of one, wrapped in wetted muslin, is of course already frozen into a ball of ice. Just holding a pencil in thick gloves to make a mark against a graph is more effort than it takes to control the aeroplane, so I determine to fudge it before I report in.

Despite the temperature I am lost in fond reverie. I frequently use the plural form when referring to an aeroplane I enjoy, as if the machine shares my pleasure in flight as I almost believe it does. Aeroplanes, like locomotives, have a heart and a soul. They rise above the pettiness and politics of the national symbol they are forced to bear on their wings.

It was cold enough on take off but now I'm quite frozen. *Gott im Himmel*, 4,500 metres altitude already and colder than Lenin's heart. I can see the smudge of Tula to the south. Time to ease off. Conserve fuel, get my bearings. The air's thin but I can lean-off, get the revs back for an economical clip. How nicely she handles on aileron and rudder. Elevators a *little* heavy. But they're big elevators on a long lever arm and she reacts well. No point in having elevators which are so light you can't hold your bead on an enemy in the rough and tumble of a fight.

I make a clearing-turn out of habit, scanning the sky for conflicting aircraft, though none are likely early on a winter's morning. Then over with the stick to the left, a little left rudder to initiate the turn and full power. Top rudder, keep the nose on the horizon. The Fokker DVII sails around the steep turn: stick hard back, the 'g' rising. Rock solid, engine bellowing. This 'feels' like a fighter! I am grinning under my scarf, happy to be back at the controls of a good German aeroplane again. Easy to fly, not like a Camel or even a Spad, both of which I've flown since my capture and re-education. Far less still the super-manoeuvrable Fokker Dr.1. But a workmanlike machine ....made fighter pilots out of novices.

Let 'em live long enough to learn; and aces out of experienced pilots if flown to best advantage.

I reverse the turn. Changeover is steady, predicable: ailerons are excellent – far better than a Camel's. A Sopwith can win on sheer manoeuvrability due to its *in*stability, though, utilising the dynamic rotating mass of the engine's gyroscopics that a skilled pilot with a sensitive hand can use to his advantage on the turn and in the climb.

Until tamed, the vicious little Camel could easily kill its novice pilot. Not so the D.VII.

Far off, in the distant landscape I think I can make out the site of my erstwhile internment camp, lagerya Kozhukhov, the stink of which lingers in my memory. I resist any thought of overflying it to see if any of its miserable prisoners remain.

I let the nose fall, roll to the inverted, pulling through to the rising note of the engine, slipstream screaming over the inverted pyramid of tubes securing upper wing to fuselage. Drag is holding the speed below 250 kph. She stands on her nose with the grey-white aerodrome seeming stationary at this altitude. Stick forward, right arm stiff, forcing her beyond the negative lift angle. Throttle back: engine noise dies, propeller is now a rotary airbrake. The airflow seems almost solid; buffeting around the fretted gun *Mantels* like surf on a rocky shore. At this speed the sensation of progressing through a thick fluid medium is elemental. I have to duck my head into the cockpit to catch my breath. The small, oil-stained windscreen between the guns breeches is a poor deflector. There's no more protection from the icy wind than in a Ju.

The air is thicker at lower level so we aren't going any faster. At 2500 metres indicated I take the pressure off the stick and ease out of the dive. As the nose passes through the horizon I apply full power. At 230 kph the D.VII soars like a gull up a cliff face. The nose is nearly vertical, over 70 degrees anyway, lift being generated from the deeply-rounded Fokker airfoil - even the small axle wing contributes. Up she goes, the speed falling now until at 85 kph she hangs like a claw in the sky, engine bellowing, nose up at 45 degrees, ruddering against the helical slipstream to keep the nose steady. If there was an enemy in my sights now I could hover; raking his undersides at my leisure. If the guns were armed.... This is one of the D.VII's great attributes, the ability to prop-hang and to regain height fast.

The nose drops in a spiral; try the ailerons again in a roll. She's agile for a big aeroplane – compared with a Nieuport say. A double-roll to the right, a short dive and then a big open loop….a little reduction in back-pressure to round it off; some deft footwork inverted to keep it straight. The old familiar rise in engine note and slipstream on recovery. A half-roll and pull through, combined manoeuvres tumbling one after the other down the sky to the airfield where the Comrade Captain Instructor awaits my meteorological report.

A Soviet Fokker D.VII performing aerobatics, mid-1920s.

I make a low pass and a fighter-break around the hangars for the hell of it. I am elated to be flying this good bird. I commend the perspicacity of our Bolshevist comrade leaders in their choice of this fighter as interim equipment for the Workers and Peasants' front line squadrons: until our glorious revolutionary designers can provide us with even better machines, of course.

I make a slipping turn onto my final approach….the dark trees blurring off to the left as I pull up and around into what little wind there is. By its limpness the windsock would seem to lack revolutionary ardour. It occurs to me that it might be frozen like me. The throttle is right back and the D.VII is *sighing* through the air, propeller swishing. *Don't get too slow here on the turn. She's docile but will bite if pushed into a corner. She's curving round nicely, balanced, answering immediately to rudder…add some slip…keep it going a bit longer, now a last look! Straighten and flare, sinking, hanging on to the last whisper of slipstream…..and then she's down; a thumping racket of the wheels on the frozen ruts.*

Rudder control is lost as speed dissipates, blanked by the big, triangular 'unstallable' tailplane. I re-open the throttle to taxy only when the energy has diminished enough to avoid an embarrassing swerve!

Some muffled-up figures are approaching to catch the wings, Kessler among them, to lead me back to the hangar and out of the cold. I pull my scarf down. I am trying to grin but my face is numb. I know he thinks my cracked smile is enjoyment at flying this old *Kämpfer* again. It is of course. But it's more than that. The weather is breaking and I think our desperate, last chance plan may actually succeed.

Chapter 40. *It wasn't personal ...*

In Whitehall I had prepared a list of the types that were in service at Podolsk and described the training regime there. Squadron Leader Frankland had been making his own notes while the stenographer jotted on her shorthand pad. He'd called a halt when I began to describe my escape plan. He spoke very quietly to Browne but I was just able to catch the words.

'Mr. Reilly should hear this, don't you think?' he said.

Browne agreed. The interview was adjourned for an hour during which time I was not free to leave the building but was entertained by the smooth young civil servant who'd been my companion on the earlier occasion. When I was invited to return to the room overlooking Horse Guards, there was Hawkeye-Rose seated alongside Frankland and Browne. He greeted me with some warmth this time and enquired of my health. I told him my wounds were healing and my stamina was increasing daily. He asked me to go back over my escape plan from Podolsk. In detail.

I described the situation on the ground. I was scheduled as leader in a formation practice later that morning on Nieuport 24s but I had yet to eat breakfast. Later that morning I was to brief the Nieuport pilots, but before that I was to take a near-solo student on a forced landing exercise on an Albatros B.2.

After breakfast I splashed some water on my face. Tightening my jaw, I told the chief instructor that I had a severe stomach ache and said I'd have to defer the force landing exercise and might have to postpone the fighter briefing. I was told to report sick and saw the MO at 08.30 hrs. Meanwhile Ernst had paid a visit to the equipment store to top up Rowehl's vodka level though this had proved unnecessary as he'd been comatose. Ernst stepped into the breach on the force-landing exercise and sent for my student. They'd departed at 09.30 hrs. into a lightening sky.

At 10.00 hrs. the wind had increased slightly. The fuelled-up Halberstadt was ticking over as the commissar colonel's car arrived. He climbed aboard behind the muffled-up pilot who turned to ensure that the cabin top was properly latched before strapping-in himself. The planned flight was to Orel which had been re-taken by the Bolshevists;

information which had been imparted by the inebriated Rowehl the previous evening. The *gosporti* earpieces were then connected from their helmets to the common speaking tube.

'Everything in order, Rowehl?' The commissar's voice vibrated in the pilot's ears over the rumble of the Mercedes.

'*Da*, Comrade Colonel.' The pilot's reply was muffled by the scarf which covered the lower part of his face. He mimicked Rowehl in that his Russian replies were broken and Bavarian accented. 'Flying time should be two hours, more if this westerly wind increases.'

'Good.'

The motor was 'braked' against the chocks, the whole airframe vibrating in harmony with the bellowing straight six. The pilot waved away the chocks and the wing walkers assisted in his taxying out onto the grass and pointing the aircraft into wind. The pilot looked twenty metres to his left to where a marshal was holding two flags; the red flag was erect while he watched the sky for a landing aeroplane that might be in conflict with the one about to take off. Satisfied he lowered the red flag and flourished the green. The pilot's helmeted head dipped in acknowledgement and the engine opened to full throttle, the Halberstadt accelerating across the snow, tailskid lifting, curved rudder wagging to keep straight as the tail rose.

The deep growl of the motor faded - I describe the scene from a watcher's point of view.

Soon enough the shouts of an angry German mercenary pilot would be heard coming from the equipment store and a sergeant quartermaster would be desperately looking for his keys. Then the body of commissar Pokrowsky would be discovered, jammed under a barrack room bed.

'I assume you killed Pokrowsky?' This from Reilly.

'It proved necessary,' I said.

'Why?'

'Because he would have blown the whistle on the plan which we'd very hurriedly arranged. He'd searched my locker and discovered Rowehl's flying kit and documents. It didn't take a genius to work out that I'd planned to assume Rowehl's identity. Kessler was in jeopardy too, he'd gone ahead and should be waiting for me in a field about 20 kilometres to the south on an agreed compass bearing.'

'So... what happened exactly?'

'I entered the barrack room. My locker was open and Pokrowsky was laying out Rowehl's kit on my bunk like a valet. The other pilots were finishing breakfast, or about to brief their students on the day's exercises.

I'd been to the barrack block with 'stomach ache' so was excused flying. I only had 20 minutes to present myself as 'Rowehl'.'

I paused, not enjoying the memory I was about to share.

'Go on.' That was Browne.

I cleared my throat. 'It didn't amount to much really,' I lied. 'Pokrowsky was the sort of rat-faced sneak so beloved of the Cheka. An informer who'd denounce you for talking in your sleep or turn you in as an 'enemy of the people' so his sister could have your apartment. However, this time he had the best evidence possible of treason, espionage, desertion, defection, and another half dozen crimes against Bolshevism that I hadn't even bothered to think about. He was also armed. I was not.

'You dirty spy!' he shouted. 'I *knew* you are spy! Traitor! Pig! Dog!'

'He was gloating, taking pleasure in describing the grisly fate that awaited me in the torture cells of the Lubjanka.

'He'd drawn his pistol, a small calibre automatic, motioning me to turn around so he could march me to the guardroom. I did as I was bid and was told to stand in the middle of the room. I looked to my left and caught sight of his reflection in the mirror on an open locker door. He was fumbling for his whistle intending to raise the alarm so that he would not have to escort me single-handed. In case I tried anything clever. He really wanted to deliver me alive.

'He was momentarily concentrating on the whistle, pulling it by the lanyard from his tunic. I measured the distance to the barrack room door with my eye, wondering if I was far enough away from him that he'd not be able to hit me with the first shot were I to make a break for it. Outside, across the aerodrome, I heard aeroplane engines starting up.

'It was a desperate situation. I threw myself sideways and slid under a bunk. I heard his shout and several shots, then jackboots clattering down the aisle between the beds. He'd dropped the whistle and was running forward with the pistol raised.'

I explained how I'd desperately squirmed around and propelled myself forwards, catching the nearest boot in both hands, yanking him off his feet and twisting the foot violently. He fired twice more, one bullet through the straw mattress past my shoulder, the other clipping the toe of my flying boot. He fell backwards with a curse as I climbed from under the bed for more leverage savagely wrenching the boot all the way around so that he turned involuntarily, screaming and trying to grab the whistle with his free hand and level the pistol at me at the same time. I just kept winding that foot until the knee creaked and he was on his stomach, half-gasping, half-yelling and trying to kick with his other leg.

This was not a *Wöbbe* moment. This time I had no compunction. I didn't know if the shots had been heard but I had to ignore that possibility for the moment. I saw his trigger finger whiten with the gun at floor level and stamped hard on his wrist, grinding down with my foot. He was panting hard and talking excitedly. His leg was bent up behind his back and he screamed again as I continued to rotate the foot with all my strength. The joints were creaking and he was begging by then, unable to move and in a lot of pain. Holding his boot now with one hand at an unnatural angle I reached back, almost overbalancing as I dragged the nearest pillow from the bed. I dropped his leg and he gave a momentary cry of relief. I fell heavily on one knee in the middle of his back, driving the air from his lungs while I clawed the automatic from his hand.

Quickly I rammed the pillow over his head, buried the gun barrel in it and pulled the trigger twice. The clip was empty. Pokrowsky was struggling furiously. He was still wearing his cap. I wrenched it off and I hit him hard with the gun butt over and over until blood was flowing and he'd ceased to fight. I checked his pulse. It was still there and he was breathing gently.

I looked straight at Reilly.

'I took the lanyard around his throat and used the empty clip of the automatic as a handle, as a *Spanish Windlass*. I wound it as tight as I could, until he stopped breathing.'

'How did you feel about that?' asked Reilly.

'I felt nothing at the time. The flow of adrenaline kept me going and I was focussed on escape.'

'And now. How do you feel about that killing?'

I have a sudden flashback of the lanyard cord embedded deep in the flesh of the thin neck of the Chekist. The empurpling of the features. He was probably little more than twenty. The smell as the body relaxed. Breathing hard through my mouth. My heart racing. My stomach churning in revulsion.

'I feel nothing.'

'Do you think of yourself as a murderer.'

'No. I did what was necessary. I took no pleasure in it. I don't think about it.'

'And in the War. You took life then as well.'

'I am not interested in analysing it. War is war. Kill or be killed. It wasn't personal.'

'So you have killed successfully both at a distance and up close.'

'Yes. But I'm no assassin. If that's what you're looking for then look somewhere else.'

Reilly smiled darkly.

'Tell us what happened next. At Podolsk.'

I said that happily there were no other snoopers nearby. Most activity was on the field and around the hangars. I hoped that Pokrowsky's pistol shots had been masked by the sound of revving aero-engines: trainers and fighter-trainers straining against their chocks.

There was no time for reaction. I had to act. Had to get to the Halberstadt in Rowehl's flying kit and muffler and get it started. I pushed the body under a bunk and dressed quickly, hampered by trembling hands, in a very nervous state. My pulse was racing. I didn't tell them that in some way I was afraid I might have enjoyed it. Killing him….the 'rush'. Or the fact that I'd put all the anger and hatred for the odious, torturing regime of murder and defilement that was Bolshevism into that single act of revenge and self-preservation. And that in retrospect it still wasn't enough.

Lenin said. *Peace and Pacifism is for Philistines and clergymen. The slogan of the proletariat is 'Civil War'. For the soviet patriot that means endless revolution and class war.*

If he wants a war, I thought, I'm in it!

~-~

'We flew south towards Orel. After ten minutes or so I began to manipulate the ignition switches to create the impression that we were experiencing engine trouble. My passenger's voice sounded concerned in my earphones. I told him that it was probably dirty fuel and that it should clear soon, but that I'd circle over some suitable fields to be safe. I'd seen Kessler's old Albatros rising from the practice force-landing field we'd used on training sorties. His pupil would have made some approaches and overshoots before Kessler had taken over, landed and switched off to discuss emergency landing methods. Given his broken Russian, he'd explained to the enthusiastic pupil pilot, it was difficult to cover the finer points of forced landing technique whilst actually in the air. All the time he was listening for the approach of the CL.IV.

When the faint sound of the Mercedes was heard Kessler had climbed into the rear cockpit and the student obliged by swinging the propeller. Kessler opened up and waved the astonished youngster an ironic farewell as the Halberstadt flew overhead. The last the student would have seen of Kessler and the Albatros they were climbing away in the same direction as the CL.IV.

I described how I'd landed the Halberstadt in a flat, frozen stubble field 2 km. further south, having created some realistic effects with ignition and throttle. The Commissar had been much relieved that we'd got down safely but cursed the delay that this forced landing would mean for his inspection tour of airfields.

I'd climbed onto the wheel and reached up to fiddle with the plug leads. I muttered something about magnetos as I prodded and pulled at the ignition cables, keeping away from the hot exhaust manifold sweeping up under the upper right wing. Out of the corner of my eye I saw the Commissar was watching me with interest through the small celluloid window in the front section of the cabin. In a moment he'd unlatched the cabin roof and was standing up. I kept my head averted, busy at my work.

'Rowehl?' he asked hesitantly. He'd climbed down off the wing root and I heard his boots crunching around the port wingtip. I could also hear the sound of an approaching 100 hp. Mercedes.

I carried on fiddling with the plug leads.

'Rowehl!' The hesitancy was gone. The voice was of command.

'Ja!' I said distractedly, half turning. I still wore my goggles and the muffler was a legitimate disguise as the day was very chill.

'Would you get down for a moment?' Polite.

The Albatros engine was now clearly audible to both of us but he was looking only at me.

I climbed unsteadily down from the tyre and turned to face him. He stepped forward. He was a well-built man in his mid-forties I guessed, slightly taller and a lot heavier than me. With no more ado he reached out and pulled my muffler down below the chin.

'Hah!' He smiled grimly and his right hand dropped to his gun holster.

'Hold it, comrade,' I said. 'You are surrounded and outnumbered.' My eyes flicked towards the throttled Albatros side-slipping into the field.

His eyes were unwavering as he unlatched his holster. Moving as fast as I could in my heavy flying clothing I grabbed his gun arm with my left hand and punched him hard in the face. He reeled from the blow and I pressed my advantage, deflecting his attempt to strike me with his left fist. He was still trying to release his pistol but the holster belt was worn high and he didn't have much leverage. He was strong and quite agile despite the heavy leather coat and evaded or parried my right-handed blows as we rocked back and forth in a savage embrace. I slammed him against the wooden fuselage which resonated like a drum. He kicked out at me. I pulled him sideways, trying to trip him, pushing him backwards so that we both fell in the snow as Kessler came running up and threw himself on top of him. I stood up with the liberated automatic levelled at the colonel. He lay on his back in the snow. We were all breathing heavily and the tension had yet to bleed away.

'What now?' Kessler asked.

'I'm thinking.'

'Don't think. Just kill the bastard.'

I hesitated. Despite my desperate act back at Podolsk and my thirst for vengeance I couldn't just shoot someone in cold blood.

'Rolf, we have to get going. All hell's going to break out back there.'

Kessler was right. By now Rowehl's yelling would have drawn attention to the quartermaster's stores. Probably they'd have searched the barrack block and found Pokrowsky's corpse. Armed fighter aircraft would be on their way at full throttle, searching the skies for the Halberstadt and the kidnapped colonel commissar. They'd probably spot the Albatros in the field, dark against the snow, and investigate. If we burned it we'd leave a black column of smoke hundreds of metres high, drawing Bolshevik aeroplanes like flies. We had to leave without delay. The comrade colonel would be another unfortunate casualty of this civil war.

I looked into the commissar's eyes. He stared at me with hostility and contempt. Courage and defiance in the face of death among the

Bolshevist clan.

'Get up,' I said. I just couldn't shoot a defenceless man. Pokrowsky was different. It was him or me.

'What's your name?' I had heard Rowehl mention the name *Koroshnikov*.

'I am Colonel Vassily Koroshnikov.'

Koroshnikov climbed heavily to his feet.

'What are you crazy rebel bastards attempting to do? Denikin, Kolchak are retreating. The White armies are finished. The Interventionists are withdrawing. You are hundreds of versts behind the lines. Give yourself up. Surrender to me now before the fighters of the RKKVF arrive. I will see that both of you get a fair court martial.'

'Oh yes?' said Kessler. 'We've witnessed the fairness of your system and the quality of Bolshevik justice all over this blood-drenched country. Kill him, Rolf!'

'Just hang on a minute,' I said. I opened Koroshnikov's greatcoat and removed various documents, Cheka passes and a signed order of requisition for fuel.

'Rolf, we have to move. Shoot him. Let's go.'

Still I hesitated. Kessler lost patience.

'Give me the gun,' he said, holding out his hand.

I relinquished the weapon, feeling ashamed that I was unable to commit this final act, but was prepared for Kessler to carry it out.

'Comrades…. I am a simple soldier. I have three children.'

'We've seen what simple Bolshevist soldiers do to children,' spat Kessler. 'Turn around and walk.' He roughly spun the colonel round and dug the pistol in his back

Koroshnikov moved off slowly.

'Look,' he said. 'Just let me walk away. I can't stop you. Just go. I'll not be able to tell anyone which way you flew. There's no sun. I don't know which way is which.'

'Except there's a compass in the Albatros. Nice try, Colonel.'

'Ernst, we can smash that compass,' I called out. 'Just let the bastard go.'

'OK, Rolf. Whatever you say. I'll just make sure he keeps walking.'

I climbed up into the Halberstadt cockpit and strapped in, puffing with the exertion. I thought I heard a report and then Kessler was running up. He stood at the propeller.'

'Ready?'

'Contact!'

He gave the big airscrew a good swing and the still warm Mercedes rumbled into life.

Kessler scrambled into the rear cabin without looking at me and latched the roof. I opened the throttle. The Halberstadt moved forward gaining speed and lifting off with room to spare at the upwind end of the field.

We climbed away on a southerly course. We were heading for the Ukraine with no particular destination in mind, just keen to cross the front line, steering away from Orel, birthplace of Turgenev. Pilgrimages would have to wait. We had the fuel requisition and they were expecting Koroshnikov so we might have bluffed it out. But I felt sure they'd have already been alerted by telephone. We would fly as far as our fuel supply lasted and hopefully we would land near some White Russian stronghold or Allied Expeditionary airfield where we'd throw ourselves upon the mercy of combatants who, we hoped, would accept our story.

I'd heard she was fighting in the Ukraine. If she was alive I was determined to find Krysia. Then maybe we could all get out of this bloody war.

Reilly was looking more hawk-like than ever. He, Frankland and Browne were observing me closely. Browne spoke.

'You tell a grimly elaborate and fascinating tale, Steiger. I wonder, sifting through the political rhetoric, the homespun Baltic philosophy and reminiscences, how much of it is actually true.'

I feel my jaw tightening. I try to conceal an involuntary tensioning in my fingers that were trying to ball into fists.

'I tell it as I remember it,' I reply slowly. 'It's what I do nowadays…. Remember, or try to. Instead of living.'

'We know your history following your meeting with the Royal Air Force Expeditionary Force. But there are parts you've not told us yet….about your crash. What was your motive for fighting what amounted to an independent war?'

'My motive must surely be clear to you from what I've already said.'

'But you're surely not suggesting that you were trying to fight a one-man campaign in Southern Russia……. just to find a girl.'

'Not "just to find a girl". An heroic woman. Someone who was very important to me, who believed in taking the war to a ruthless enemy, putting her life in extreme danger for a principle. And to avenge her family.'

Frankland joined in. 'There were free Russians flying with the Royal Air Force. Ex-Imperial Russian Air Service pilots. Why didn't you just apply to join with them – once you'd been vetted? Co-ordinated effort would have been more effective. What could you possibly hope to achieve as an irregular force of four or five captured aeroplanes?'

'It was virtually out of my hands. I was lucky to avoid being slung into a White jail or worse: shot! The RAF was running short of aircraft and equipment. They weren't about to just let me join up! A German Balt! Although I am half English – and that's the only thing that secured my evacuation, afterwards.'

'So, how did you come by the means to fight your own 'campaign'? Ammunition, spares, aviation fuel?' asked Frankland.

'There were several abandoned or captured Ukrainian aeroplanes, German types scattered about the British airfields. Hannovers, Halberstadts, many of them damaged or wrecked. Remnants of Symon Petlura's air arm adorned with the golden trident. Some were being used for spare parts, but apart from instruments, turnbuckles and things, little was compatible. But there were some Austrian-built *Albatrosse* potentially very useful - formidable even, which were flyable, or could be made flyable with some work. The Poles were flying this type aircraft too, in some numbers; in Ukraine extending into Southern Russia. Obtaining tools, spares, tracer ammunition, fuel, Bessoneau hangars: these were more difficult. The machine guns of course had been removed. I managed to obtain replacements for these from….various sources.'

Reilly's eyes were smiling.

Suddenly another part of my fractured memory returned. I remembered with an electric shock where I'd seen Reilly before. It was in southern Russia. The Poles were fighting a successful guerrilla war behind the Bolshevist lines. The Social-Revolutionary leader Boris Savinkov and Reilly had arrived from Warsaw and appeared with a Colonel Bahalovich on the airfield to liaise with the British. Bahalovich led a large guerrilla force of mostly 'broad church' White Russians and cut-throats. Reilly and Savinkov along with another British agent had been supplying funds and arms to supplement those which Bahalovich's raiders had managed to steal in attacks. Reilly and Savinkov had toured the divisions exhorting the troops to keep up the struggle to smash the Bolshevists.

Reilly had had a valuable contact in an SIS agent who was an ex-merchant navy man, a buccaneering figure name of McLaren, who was raising and supplying a small 'guerrilla air force' based in the Ukraine. This would be manned by some White Russians, Poles and other odds and ends, even vagabond German pilots (Kessler was one after all), operating close to the Bolshevist front, between the Polish Army in the west and the RAF Expeditionary Force in south-central Ukraine: a flexible unit to add an air component to Bahalovich's irregular infantry and cavalry troops. We immediately applied to join and were warmly accepted.

The RAF was hard-pressed although very successful in aerial engagements but reluctant on security grounds to offer an irregular force control of a sector which *they* had hitherto patrolled. I for one was itching to get back into the air. I'd have flown anything with a machine gun. But I'd suffered a broken collar bone on my arrival so I spent my time organising the refurbishment of available aircraft, securing stores and spares and poring over maps. These provided alleged updates of the fast-moving military situation which the RAF at first reluctantly shared with us along with their messing facilities. However Squadron Leader MacIntyre, the commanding officer was pragmatic and perhaps glad of the assistance, although we had yet to prove our value. We would be flying a heterogeneous collection of patched-up machines, which we'd called *McLaren's Marauders* for want of a better name. For the most part they proved effective, but were only maintained airworthy from cannibalising others of dubious worth. Now I realised how the offer had come about. Reilly had been pulling strings in the background.

Browne said, 'Your most irregular activities were reported on. I am interested, however, in what you *haven't* said yet.'

'I've told you. My memory is still patchy with regard to the latter days of my time in Russia. Up to when I regained consciousness.'

'I can assure you we are in a good position to check your 'remarkable' story.'

'I venture to say, Mr. Browne, that if you are in a position to have checked my story in its entirety then your Intelligence Service is obviously the best in the world. And…'

'Yes?'

'And if it's that good, which I doubt, why would you need an amateur like me on board?'

'We all start as amateurs, Rolf,' said Reilly. There was a twinkle in his eye and perhaps the glint of caution.

'*Rolf* remains out there, in the past. I thought it was imperative to maintain cover.'

'Indeed. You have potential, Mr. Stygers.'

No one spoke for a while. 'Has our Mr. Saunders been showing you around London?' Browne asked finally, changing the subject.

'Yes. He's been very good at getting me assimilated.'

'Stygers, we are convinced that you have many qualities that we could use. In fact we believe that your recruitment into the Firm would be of great benefit to the security of the country at this time. However, you have yet to fully recover from your injuries. We think a job could be found for you in the future, somewhere where your experience, expertise and linguistic skills could be put to best advantage: subject to *Control's* blessing, naturally.'

'I hope I can be of service,' I said

'Is there anything else that you need to tell us in making our assessment of your background and potential?'

'I don't know.'

Reilly raised an eyebrow.

I didn't know whether Reilly had had British sanction to fund and assist in the creation of an independent 'air force' in Russia so I'd refrained from bringing it up at Whitehall Court. Feigning memory loss seemed the discretionary best alternative. I was not to know that he'd had the support of the Minister for War, Winston Churchill, against the general mood of the Government, growing socialist sympathies amongst the populace and a *de facto* Parliamentary recognition of the Soviet Government: all this following the terrible suffering that the War had brought.

'I mean…. there are still bits missing,' I said. 'There is something I've yet to work out.'

'Well when you've worked it out to your satisfaction we'll talk again,' said Browne, rather superciliously. 'Meanwhile there's someone I want you to meet.'

Browne turned to the female secretary. 'Ask him to come in now, please?'

Chapter 41. *Fighting - with Flares*

January 1920,
Northern Ukraine

We'd flown south for over an hour when we saw the fighters. They were a mixture of Nieuports and Spads approximately on our level; tricky enough opponents for a Halberstadt with a single fixed forward-firing machine gun and no means of rear defence. Probably up from Orel which we were skirting. They were strung out in a line, patrolling back and forth, silhouetted against the cloudy sky and obviously on the lookout for something. I was right. Orel had been forewarned by telephone.

'...a mixture of Nieuports and SPADs.'

I turned slightly east to keep my distance in the faint hope they'd not spotted me. It was to no avail. Soon two, then three Nieuports wheeled in pursuit, then the whole flight of six aircraft joined in, line-astern. I put the Halberstadt's nose down to gain some speed, opened the throttle wide and cocked the machine gun. The airspeed climbed to over 200 kph in the shallow dive. We seemed to be gaining on the fighters although a Spad was now leading the field and out-distancing the Nieuport 24s. I noticed that its nose was painted red and that it had red streamers fluttering from the struts. It was most likely a Spad VII so would have a single Maxim-Vickers gun firing through the propeller. Not as heavily armed but quicker than the Nieuports. However it would only take one bullet in the right place for it to be 'game over' for us.

I held the dive. We were down to about 500 metres and the Spad hung on grimly, a greyhound chasing a hare. Below I saw the signs of battle. Thousands of men were marching or camped along the roads. Ahead there was something on fire. I saw howitzers being pulled by teams of horses through snowy roads. One had slithered into a ditch and men and animals were straining to drag it out. I partly felt, partly heard the familiar strike of small arms fire on the aircraft. It seemed as though I had blundered into an advance.

I strained to see where the Spad was only to hear the rat-tat-tat of close machine gun fire. Kessler's voice was suddenly in my ears yelling for me to break right. He could see behind better than I could so I didn't hesitate to comply, feeling the 'g' rise as I banked steeply, pulling until the long-winged bird shuddered and buffeted in protest. I looked back but couldn't see the Spad, just two Nieuports closing in on my tail. I continued to turn into them as the only option. To turn away would present myself as a sitting duck. I didn't know what the Spad was doing but I knew he couldn't match my turning circle. The Nieuports banked and pulled but their speed was too high and they sailed past overhead.

'Where's that bloody Spad?' I yelled into the *gosporti*.

A muffled reply from Kessler, then, 'Break left, NOW!'

I rolled the Halberstadt through 180 degrees from a steep right to a steep left turn as the Spad roared past underneath, spitting fire. I looked up to see the two Nieuports at the top of a zoom climb, stall-turning like synchronised dolphins to reverse their flight paths and dive on me again. I pulled the nose up opening fire head-on as their tracer fire concentrated around me.

Suddenly there are two more Nieuports and another Spad joining in, taking snap shots as I dive away in a curve. I can smell their cordite. Below there is an army of Red Cossacks, hundreds and hundreds of armed men on horseback watching the spectacle of six fighters with red stars on their wings shooting at a two seater - also with red stars. It probably didn't make much sense, but then we'd already been shot at from the ground and the red stars had been no protection hitherto. I briefly see rifles raised then I am assailed by a Nieuport at point blank range, bullets smacking into the cockpit, wood splintering: a scar on a cabane strut, an instrument glass shatters. I hear Kessler shouting something. I turn violently at low level. Horsemen are swerving, their mounts rearing and panicking as I roar overhead. The fighters cannot shoot me now without coming down to my level which is no more than a raised sabre arm above a mounted man's head. The horse army seems to extend to the southern horizon, thousands of them. For now they are my protection from attack from the air.

I see movement to my right. A Spad is pacing me no more than two wingspans away. It's the formation leader. To my left the other Spad has now caught up. My engine is at full throttle and smells hot. I am trapped. We are approaching the vanguard of Budyonny's Horse Army from the rear. When we pass the leaders I will be vulnerable to attack once again. I hear Kessler say, 'Keep her steady, Rolf.' I have no idea what he's up to but I do as he says. There is a slight change in slipstream noise as a panel pops out in the rear cockpit and then a bang and a flash. A vivid red signal flare arcs out, just missing the right hand Halberstadt interplane strut and flies a curved path, straight into the cockpit of the Red squadron leader.

The Spad's nose pitches violently as the missile strikes. The pilot's arms flail in wild paroxysm. I watch in fascination as livid flame burns deeply into his neck, spitting a fiery trail along the fuselage. The nose drops and the aircraft rolls over, falling, cartwheeling in a pool of fire amongst writhing horses and flying riders. Then the image is gone and so is the Cossack mounted army. A flutter of red flags in the vanguard and then it's the open rolling country of the Ukraine as far as the eye can see.

The Spad to my left has zoomed high and intends to dive on my tail. Behind me Ernst is breaking the celluloid glazing of the cabin to give himself a wider field of fire.

'Weave left, Rolf.' His voice is strong and vigorous in the earphones, the hint of victory there above the engine's roar. I pull left. 'Now right!' he says. I follow his instruction, rolling the Halberstadt to evade an unseen enemy. I hear the report of another flare from behind and see a Spad roll sharply away from the arcing red fire. The sound of machine guns is close again as two Nieuports close in for a kill. How well we could have fought this battle had Ernst been armed with a Parabellum.

Ernst continues to shout instructions. I am tiring from heaving the two-seater about at low level but I push fatigue aside as the grim battle continues. I don't know how many flares are stored in the cabin but I assume it's no more than six. He's fired at least three so far. I crane my neck left and right trying to glimpse my pursuers. I need to engage with my forward-firing gun to give us more chance of survival. I see a flanking Nieuport off to my left. I assume it's trying to get ahead in order to cut off our escape. The Halberstadt has the edge of speed if I can keep flying straight but the running combat has so far prevented this.

I risk cutting the throttle momentarily which puts the Nieu 24 ahead. I rudder the Halberstadt onto its tail. I give it full throttle and snap shoot just ahead of the cowling. The grey biplane flies into the swarm of tracer and falls away smoking. Two out of six, so far, I think grimly.

At full throttle still I maintain my low level flight. Ernst is making encouraging noises from the rear regarding our out-distancing of the pursuers. Except for the second Spad that's rejoined the chase and is closing in again. I hear the flare pistol's report and a curse in my 'phones as Kessler misses. There's a low hill ahead with a copse of trees on top. I fly at it, descending gradually to make best speed. The good old Mercedes is smoking a bit and I see steam pouring back from the wing surface radiator. I don't think I can keep up this pressure on the engine much longer. I'll have to throttle back and let it cool or face the possibility of a forced landing and capture or being strafed by the fighters. But the situation won't allow it. I have to press on at full speed. I glance at the fuel gauge. It's getting low. Damn, I think. So close to a successful escape with our ramshackle plan in which luck has played a big part; before it turned against us.

Here it goes then. I bank steeply around the hillock as the sun comes out and bathes the hillside in light. A flock of birds erupts from the trees in panic. I look back at the round radiator of the Spad. What a neat little aeroplane I think distractedly. I see the gun winking at me. I pull harder and feel the buffet. Surely the Spad can't turn as hard. He is committed now to *combat en cirque* as the French describe it. If he breaks away or reduces his angle of bank he will present me with an advantage; bringing my gun to bear as I close the gap. I can't pull much harder myself or I'll risk stalling and flick-rolling. I am slowly sinking towards the grassy hillside anyway since the wings cannot sustain lift at this angle. The Spad's short narrow wings, suited to an interceptor, mean that his wing loading is higher so his turning circle is wider. The much greater wing area of the CL.IV means a lower wing loading despite the higher weight. Gradually our positions are reversing. The Halberstadt starts shuddering. The Spad pilot is pulling tighter and suddenly it's over. Before I get close enough to fire a shot he's over-pulled and flicked into the ground, shedding wings and bits, crumpling in a cloud of debris and entrails. Three.

The last combat has allowed the remaining Nieuports to close in. These people are determined, I have to say. I am fatalistic. I will invest them head on with my fixed Spandau, like a knight: eye pressed to the gunsight. Kessler I know will be watching from behind. He is silent. Only the three fighters remain. I can see two.

I open fire on the right hand of the Nieuport pair. Bits fly off the propeller and the fighter gyrates out of view. I transfer my fire point blank to the left hand machine. He pulls up and rolls over my top wing. I look up into the pilot's eyes as he passes overhead. I almost think I can see what colour they are.

Where's the third Nieuport? We've been fighting against extreme odds, effectively with one hand tied behind our backs. Two-seater manoeuvrability generally doesn't match that of the best single-seaters, but they usually have the advantage of a rearwards firing flexible gun. An experienced two-seater crew can create a lot of trouble for single-seaters if flown well. Indeed a pair of two-seaters which fly co-ordinated manoeuvres can constantly bring guns to bear on an attacker, which makes them dangerous adversaries. But we had none of that. Just a commissar's aerial carriage with a single, fixed forward gun and Kessler in the back with a typewriter and a flare pistol!

We turn south again. The Mercedes is running rough. Something's been hit. Suddenly a Nieuport is diving in from the left.

Kessler says, 'Look out, right!'

I glimpse the flash of another Nieuport close to my right side and turn that way to close the angle. The left hand Nieuport will probably get me, I think, as I dive and turn, trying to make myself very small in the cockpit. A silver biplane with red stars hurtles past trailing smoke, flames curling around the engine cowling. The first Nieuport! The lower Nieuport which I've just turned towards breaks away below me with a strange dark biplane on its tail, firing. Another dark-painted machine zooms past me. It's a Sopwith. I see the cockades. British! I recognise them as Camels. We are now in even more trouble. Pilots who fly Camels *have* to be *Experten*. I hear twin machine guns very close and the stick bucks in my hand and the rudder bar kicks and I fear that the Halberstadt's empennage may have disintegrated in the hail of machine gun fire because we are out of control.

Chapter 42. *Albanian Justice*

In Whitehall we have more tea and biscuits. All very relaxed. Reilly, Browne and Frankland back in their places with an empty chair next to Browne. A discreet door in the oak panelling opens and a big man walks in. Wing Commander Frankland stands as he enters. I have the impression this is good manners rather than an issue of rank. Reilly remains seated. Browne swivels in his chair.

'Ah, Thomas. You know our friend, I believe.'

'Indeed so.' Peregrine-Thomas moves around to my side of the desk, hand extended. He's grown an impressive moustache above his wide grin since first I'd seen him; lying on a bed of pine needles in the Elbasan-Barat.

I move to greet him, my mind reeling. He's out of context and uniform. Then, 'Gott vor dam. You!' I exclaim with a smile. 'How are you now?'

'Absolutely in the pink, Old Boy! What about you? Been in the 'wars', I gather.'

'You might say. But I'm mending alright.'

'I don't think I thanked you sufficiently for what you did for me. I have no doubt I'd have been buried with my pilot if you hadn't turned up and taken me to a German field hospital.'

'We were entirely in Shiroka's hands as I remember.'

'Just as well he had his Austrian plaything to distract him; entertain the clan. Grim times, Leutnant Steiger.'

'Didn't *Reuters* work out, then?'

'Still with 'em, Dear Boy. Best cover there is for mucho travelling. Income's useful too!'

Browne interrupted with a prim cough. 'For the present our friend is here under the pseudonym Lt. Ralph Stygers, RFC retired. Recovering from wounds.'

'Jolly good. *Stygers* it is then.'

Browne turned to me. 'Mr. Peregrine-Thomas will be your mentor for now. You're officially on board for training purposes. But we've more de-briefing to complete for the present.'

Reilly stood up.

'Welcome to the Firm, Ralph,' he said quietly. 'I'd like you on my team but you still need to achieve full health. I'm afraid I won't be around for a while, but I'll be glad to continue our conversation in the near future.'

'I look forward to it, Mr. Reilly.'

'Gentlemen,' Reilly said with a glance at all of us. I detected a slight shadow that flitted across his eyes. He stretched out his hand to me and shook it firmly. He did the same with each of us, last of all with Caradoc Peregrine-Thomas. Did the last handclasp linger just a moment too long or was the look in the eye a little uncomfortable? I could not be sure, but I was to reflect on it later. With that he left and the meeting broke up for the time being. CPT collected a stout walking cane and took me under his wing for a stroll in the sunshine, away from ears, or so I'd assumed.

'Rolf, what a coup!' he said smiling. 'You handled yourself well back in '17 with the Albanians.'

In truth it had been a dangerous situation and our lives were in the balance.

'I think Shiroka may have had a sneaking regard for his Britannic Majesty. He was anti-everyone else, that's for certain. I don't think I would have survived without you're being there,' I said.

'Nor I without your intervention with that bastard of an Austrian NCO.'

'*Wöbbe*. It was Kismet. We went back a long way and there was a debt to pay.'

~·~

My mind races back four years to that Albanian hillside.

I am about to pull the trigger on Wöbbe. Or am I? Unlike the challenge of air fighting, facing an opponent in mortal combat, this cool decision to take a human life, however odious and worthless I judged that life to be, would be an irrevocable turning point. That the world would be a better place without his existence I have no doubt and the physical act involves only the slightest increase in trigger pressure. But my instincts and reason warred with my sense of morality against such a cold-blooded act to terminate life.

But the decision has been lifted from my shoulders. The war party that suddenly controls the situation have us under their guns.

Their leader, swarthy and unshaven with a huge black moustache, strides forward with his rifle at the ready. His leather waistcoat is stuffed with cartridges. 'Le tei shkojei!' he growls. Albanian; but the meaning is obvious. 'Ndalem!'

I stand aside and point my pistol barrel downwards. A little brigand with a jutting beard and moustaches circles behind and disarms me, retrieving the Mannlicher from where Wöbbe had thrown it. Wöbbe rolls over in the grave with an oath, the colour draining from his face as he takes in the situation. The bayonet droops in his grip. The leader gives another command and two men move closer, pointing their rifles in Wöbbe's face. The leader speaks to me again, in Serbian this time, a gruff bark. I get the drift and reply in Russian.

'Acting Lt. Steiger, k.u.k. Luftfahrtruppe. Whom do I have the honour of addressing?'

I am quivering inside but I show an outward calm, formal and respectful. I knew that to show fear would ensure that what remained of my future would be spectacularly uncomfortable. Wöbbe is disarmed and silent, his pistol and bayonet stuffed into Albanian belts. One of them roughly removes a ring from Wöbbe's little finger and hands it to their leader who studies it a moment.

He approaches me, stands very close and stares. He is broad and looks as hard as nails: a national stereotype. I hold my ground. I have the impression of looking into the face of a king cobra with its hood inflated, into the hot black eyes of another species; an alien. I reconsider. It is me who's the alien, intruding on *his* land and I can feel the hate.

He calls forward one of his soldiers as translator. Through him we have the following conversation.

'You have special honour of addressing Colonel Essad Shiroka, *Bajraktar*, clan leader.' he states imperiously, his voice strong and clear. 'How DARE you to be in my country?'

The translator's voice is different, but quite as growly.

'I am a soldier in the service of my adoptive country. I go where I'm ordered.'

'Adoptive? What do you mean?'

'I am from Lithuania.'

'Ah, Lithuania. It is a long way, this Lithuania?'

'It is. A very long way.'

'So you fight for Austrian crown!' His hot eyes are probing into mine.

'Yes.'

'So, you are fighting against Italy?'

'Yes.'

'Hmm. Italy thinks it owns Albania. Gabrielle D'Annuzio, *pah*! They dare use my flag. So too the French. Austrians have Tirana. They too use my flag.'

He holds up the ring for me to see. It is a gold signet ring with an enamelled setting, a red oval upon which a black double spread eagle is depicted. Its expressions are as fierce as Shiroka's.

'So, does Lithuania also seek my flag? To own Albania?'

'No.'

'Do you think yours or any country will invade and hold Albania, we who drove out cursed Ottoman?'

'I'm sure they won't.'

'You're sure? You had better be damn sure, Lithuanian,' he says, pushing the ring onto his own finger.

The war correspondent had been watching, fully awake. His head is turned towards us, eyes wide and comprehending, taking in the prostrate body of Wöbbe, the Albanian rifles - the twin graves.

'And who is this?' The colonel indicates the injured observer.

'He is an English war correspondent. He was hurt in the crash.'

'Hmmm. English. Saint George! Does England wish to invade Albania?'

The man finds his voice, speaking slowly and with difficulty, but in good Russian. 'Colonel, I come only to report the war to the outside world. I wear a uniform because it is required. I would tell the story of what is happening to Albania.'

'Then tell this to great outside world, *English*. Albania will be free!' Shiroka was suddenly passionate. 'I, Essad Shiroka, colonel, army of Bajram Curri under black eagle of my flag — in my veins flows red blood of Albania - I Shiroka: *Shi-ro-Ka*, swear it! That Albania will be free! Remember!' I reel in shock as he suddenly strikes me hard across the face with the back of his hand. 'So you will not forget.' He looks from me to the Englishman.

That blow is also a tradition in Russia, so that a younger man will forever remember the day he had met a knight. My cheek is bleeding from contact with the signet ring. But it gives me hope.

'I would tell them,' says the war correspondent softly.

'So. What was happening here?' Shiroka indicates the prostrate form of Wöbbe. 'Why do you want to kill him?'

'This man is a criminal,' I say. 'Understand?'

Shiroka eyes me suspiciously. 'So, you are judge and executioner in my country?'

He spoke rapidly to the partisans. One relieved Wöbbe of the wristwatches, going quickly through his pockets. He handed a British paybook and wallet to Shiroka. The light was failing. It is apparent that Lt. Caradoc Peregrine-Thomas, as his paybook identifies him, can sit up unaided but can barely stand, let alone walk. He is also in need of urgent medical attention.

Shiroka is speaking again. 'This is what will happen,' says our translator.

He orders the burial party to complete their grave-digging and the broken body of the pilot is interred without ceremony. He orders that Peregrine-Thomas be carried by the four prisoners on the makeshift stretcher using the long shovels instead of the more flexible boughs, the tunics buttoned together. I am to ride the cavalry horse and take the carbine as protection. A soft rain is falling.

'So, you're letting us go?'

'I am letting 'St. George' - English war correspondent go. You go to look after him.'

'Where are you hurt?' I ask Thomas in English. 'Do you think you can stand?'

'My chest,' he says, with a vague gesture. 'And… my head. Yow! And my damned ankle. I don't know what happened.'

'I shot you down, yesterday. My apologies.'

He gave me a strange look. We lift him carefully onto the stretcher.

~-~

'What about him?' I indicate the visibly quivering body of Wöbbe.

'Ah, pig of a devil dog. That bastard, he is mine.'

He sees my questioning look and speaks rapidly to the translator.

'For your satisfaction I will explain. Serbs were my guests. Hostages, you understand. For ransom. But we are not barbarians. I myself was raised by Jesuits for while. I know about forgiveness and redemption. But since then have rejected both concepts, especially in this case.'

'What case?'

'Dog of a raider who burns houses. Filthy coward who kills women, rapes children. Nails baby to tree!'

Wöbbe has been watching this activity from the open grave and gives me an imploring look, eyes still akimbo - though more rabbit than *bufo*. 'Dragunavicius, what's happening? Don't leave me here, I implore you.'

Shiroka's dark eyes watch me as I mount up, the Mannlicher crooked in my arm.

'Wöbbe told me that his mounted patrol is due back soon,' I say.

'Don't need to worry.' Shiroka smiles a gold-toothed smile for the first time when his aide conveys this information. 'All are ready for crows. Only horses survive, good animals.'

He hands me my Mauser and slaps my horse in farewell. As we leave I hear him call out in Albanian. A small boy is brought forward carrying a blade. *We are not barbarians.*

I hear some chatter in Albanian and a short laugh. One of the Serbs looks round with a horrified expression.

~-~

We wend our way down in the semi-dark for several minutes. The rain has stopped. A night wind is rising that carries a sound, like a hog makes in terror for its life. It follows our departure, growing fainter as we descend the mountain path, fading only with the distance. We stop within a half-kilometre of my waiting car.

'Men,' I say speaking Russian. 'Ten kilometres to the south is the road to Cerrik. I suggest you head southwest to the port of Vlore. The Italians will look after you. Keep to the trees for the first few kilometres and good luck.'

I have them dismantle the stretcher and retrieve their coats. One shakes my hand, my right covering them with the Mauser. I ask them in Russian what had been said by the Albanians as we were leaving. They look at each and one speaks in broken Russian.

'Sir, I think he said, " Cut off shutters first!"'

'Shutters?'

'I do not know word in Russian, 'covers' for eyes. So that he must watch.'

Seldom, I thought, had justice been so well administered, better than I could have done despite my torturing of young Count Welikowsky, which had been psychological. I hand them a pack of cigarettes. They nod their thanks and leave without a further sound.

I wished them success, but I'd deliberately not said how far away the Italian lines were, nor offered advice on how they should make their way safely through. It was not my problem. Nor would be the eventual discovery of two mountain graves and the wreckage of the Nieuport. It would be assumed that Wöbbe had been overpowered and killed by brigands in the pursuit of his duty. A dead hero. I would be careful not to give my real name when I delivered the survivor into the custody of the field hospital staff.

I waited until they'd gone before assisting Thomas into a sitting position against a tree. Telling him to stay quiet I unsaddled the horse and released its bridle. Giving him a slap on the rump I watched as he cantered off into the darkness. I made my way down to the road, throwing the rifle and saddle into the bushes on the way. I told my driver a quite different version of events. I'd failed to find the crash but had come across the survivor of my 'aerial victory' and had managed to help him walk nearly as far as the road, but that he was now in a state of collapse. *I tell him this with Wöbbe's porcine squeals ringing in my mind.* Between us we managed to get Thomas into the car. He was a big man. When satisfied that he was comfortable we drove through the night to the ancient, semi-ruined Ottoman fort which served as a field hospital.

'Leutnant,' said Thomas as we passed through the gates. 'Your name please.'

He spoke again in English though he had understood Russian and German from what little information we'd shared. I told him: *Steiger.*

'Thank you,' he said. 'I must say you think fast and handle yourself well. I will not forget your assistance to me. The rest will remain secret.'

My driver spoke only German. Fortunately.

~-~

We left Whitehall Court through Horseguards Parade where CPT had flourished a small ivory card at the two mounted troopers who saluted him through the archway.

'Privilege of rank,' he smiled. 'That pass allows direct access through St. James's Park, past Buck House.'

We progressed to Green Park, chatting about everything but my recent interview then stopping for a while on a bench on the green to rest my leg. He'd needed a halt too. I'd noticed his heavy stick with its large rubber tip and prominent lip that was hardly a gentleman's fashion accessory. Noting my gaze he smiled lightly, lifting the cane like a rifle, sighting on a pigeon.

'Sometimes in our line of work a stout stick can come in handy, eh Rolf?' His voice lowered slightly. 'So now you'll be joining the Firm! Have you any idea what you're in for?'

'I need to do something,' I said, also lowering my voice. 'I don't know what I'm good at except that I've learned to dissimulate and stay alive in tricky situations. I know the Baltic region and speak some useful languages. I have a good technical grasp of aviation and a bit of flying experience. I thought I might prove useful and so did Saunders. And I think I went down alright with the Wing Commander, Frankland. Not sure about Browne. Reilly seems a confident type though. I liked him.'

'Our Mr. *Rosenbluhm* alias Sidney Reilly. A man of many talents.' Thomas saw my furtive glances and grinned. 'Don't look so worried. No one's in earshot.'

Not if you ignore a flock of nannies pushing perambulators, I thought.

'He's SIS's top agent without exception,' he continued. ' Fortunately when Russia closed down a number of our people managed to escape. But we lost many of our contacts: arrested, compromised, liquidated or turned. Some may now be double agents. Many a brave lad died under torture, women too. Who knows who or what they gave away, or who gave them away? ST-1 was able to escape and rumour has it he's been over since, more than once. A few years back he'd seemed to pop up everywhere with offices in New York and Tokyo, making and losing fortunes, brokering war matèriel for huge commissions; cartridges, rifles, gunpowder, shells: but leaving a trail of bad debts. Broken hearts and promises! Spread rumours and confusion in his wake and still came up smelling of roses.'

We recommenced our walk, crossing to Hyde Park, turning right along Broad Walk inside the gate. I was walking in a trance, finding it difficult to believe what I'd just heard. I'd been quite shocked at the broadcast of super-sensitive details *en clair* with people passing by. The principles of 'need to know', 'between these four walls', 'for your eyes only' seemed to have been lightly tossed aside. Thomas, I thought, was dangerously garrulous for a ranking secret serviceman. '*Boltun nakhodka dlya shpiona.*' as Saunders would say. '*A chatterbox is a gift for a spy.*"

There now seemed to be some sort of commotion ahead and almost before I realised it we'd joined a throng at Speakers' Corner. Before the War Karl Marx had held forth here and Lenin. The general mood of the general public following the Armistice was Socialist, with open support for Bolshevism. Revolution was preached in Hyde Park and the soap box orators were not even apologists for Lenin, since they refuted criticism of him or his Party. Hecklers were shouted down with anti-Capitalist epithets that could have emerged from the throat of any guttersnipe

624

commissar. I found it easy to believe that Cheka agents were in the crowd and the loose-talking sortie with CPT had left me feeling deeply uncomfortable about the security, the professionalism of the Service.

Thomas seemed to have read my mind.

'Two years ago the Firm was run by a bunch of amateurs. Actors, bullies, cardsharps and confidence tricksters. It's a little better now. At the sharp end we have some sound chaps. But with *Mr. Punch...*'

'Who?'

'*Punchinello. Control. 'C'* as he signs himself. Captain Sir George Smith-Mansfield Cumming to give him his full title. The original enthusiast. A monocled Mr. Toad. An eccentric amateur is what he is. Your fate will be in his hands, God help you.'

'I thought that the English Secret Service was the best in the world.'

Thomas laughed loudly. 'If so I'd hate to see the worst!' he said. 'As I said, our operatives are first class and reliable. It's more than can be said of their Whitehall bosses. Talk about *Tweedledum* and *Tweedledee.*'

I understood the reference but not the present context.

'MI5 and MI6,' he said. 'Or to be more specific Kell and Cumming.'

'What do you mean?' I was talking in what I thought was just above a stage whisper and *that* seemed too loud. But the crowd seemed transfixed by a middle-aged man in a dirty mackintosh who was telling them what should be done with the King, shouting through a tin speaking tube. A big policeman stood on the periphery looking stern.

'Vernon Kell, head of MI5 is sharp, multi-lingual, young, and has many fine attributes. Naturally they put him in charge of domestic security. Cumming speaks only English and a smattering of French. Naturally Whitehall gives him rest of world. Another own goal; departments shot in both feet before they're even up and running. Typical military-style thinking, always cocking things up. Lenin would have shot the lot them. So of course it's been the cause of much jealousy and animosity over time. Came to fisticuffs and worse with Cumming beating Kell over the head with his own wooden leg in the corridor a while back.'

I looked at him disbelievingly.

'Wait 'til you meet him,' he said. 'You'll see.'

~-~

Peregrine-Thomas told me something of his background. Llanelly-born, on the coast of South Wales he'd started life as a cub reporter before Cambridge where he joined the *Conversazione Society*. 'Met some interesting people *as well as some absolute rotters, dear boy.*' With degrees in modern languages he joined a daily newspaper, a junior foreign correspondent on politics and defence matters. On outbreak of hostilities he was commissioned as a war correspondent and had seen close action in several theatres and engagements until I'd shot down his Italian Nieuport over the Albanian mountains. Recurrent pain from his badly broken ankle was the long term result of that meeting.

'In this cold weather it feels like it was broken only yesterday,' he said, rubbing it vigorously.

He'd been repatriated unfit and after his recovery was summoned to Whitehall for a debriefing on his time in captivity. Since then he'd carried out numerous intelligence assessments and sat in on interviews of foreign nationals, prisoners and suspected enemy agents, among them Fenians, Russians, Baltic separatists, Ingrians, Jews, Germans, Georgians, Ossetians, Chechens and all sorts of mostly European refugees and suspected Bolshevist insurgents. He hinted at other activities but unlike his previous demeanour he seemed suddenly coy.

Probably noticing our quality overcoats and egged-on by megaphone man, a few among the crowd started muttering about 'toffs', and there was some jostling before the policeman intervened. He respectfully suggested that we might like to move along for our own welfare. We returned to Whitehall by taxicab, each of us now lost in our thoughts, arriving at the appointed time for my meeting with 'C'.

'Y'know, Rolf,' said CPT, the two of us alone in the lift, 'With your language skills and experience, you'd be a damned good asset to SIS. It's what makes ST-1 so valuable, that and his utter ruthlessess. The Firm's original blue-eyed boy, even if his are as black as his heart. We can both learn a lot from Reilly.'

The lift shuddered to a halt and we had to climb the steep, narrow staircase from the upper landing, CPT puffing ahead of me with obvious difficulty.

'Don't get too close to him, Rolf. *Reilly*, I mean. People close to him get burned.'

'How exactly?'

He'd paused on the staircase to let me catch up and for the second time only he'd lowered his voice.

'He's a scoundrel and a deceiver,' he breathed. 'A charming

'mountebank', clever and without scruples. Consorts with riffraff, pimps, prostitutes - racketeers of all sorts. Sups with the Devil and swims with the sharks – of course that's the secret of success in murky waters. His identities are many; Russian Jew, Greek businessman, a naturalised British Subject of course, an American Citizen, a *maharaja* if required and he moves easily through all societies. Forgery is his strongpoint; knows how to play one side aganst the other like nobody else. Arms manufacturers, shipbuilders and governments alike, he's provided his services to all: made millions in commissions in the War, largely through corrupt officals in Russian arms procurement - lost most of it too. Credible disinformation is his stock in trade, even sabotage. I've tried to warn Cumming to be careful but he won't hear any it and trusts the man. Cumming is a 'chancer' - though he does have his reservations. Of course Reilly's very useful meanwhile with what's going on in Russia. As I said, we can learn a lot from him – but by arm's length observation. Just watching the ripples.'

CPT made to proceed but stopped still and spoke again very quietly, head inclined towards the shadowed upper staircase.

'You know, Rolf. We Welsh too are a naturally dissimulating race.' I could hear that he smiled. 'Comes from years of bloody servitude to the English. We know how to smile when we kill, eh what!'
I assumed he spoke figuratively.
'Makes us bloody good spies.'
Bloody talkative ones, I thought to myself as we climbed. Unless that was also part of his cover.

~.~

Real stories, not romantic adventure novels by George Henty or John Buchan, rarely have neat 'endings', Natasha. Life always has loose ends. What is left but the unravelling of lives when the fire has gone out, after the limbo of pretence that a once lovely summer can ever be recaptured. What is left? When a love affair is over forever. When there is no hope that passion will ever thump you in the midriff and get your aching heart violently beating again under your ribs…….. When my Angelika's taped rendering of 'Surabaya Johnny' she'd left at our flat faded to a faint memory. What is there? Succumbing gracefully to middle age? Do we become self-caricaturing, half-mad old war-horses in later years, with a too-often told tale at the fireside of our local.

'Old so-and-so is off again. Buy the old Major a drink if you're bored and he'll talk your head off: a tale told by a legend in his own mind, full of sound and fury, valorous deeds and tactical cunning.'

But not those who've seen too much reality, eh Rolf? Not your *civil war* veterans. The memories are too brutal to give them tongue. Compete against the hubbub at the crowded bar off the Staines Road after the hooter's gone? Never. Not old spooks, neither. Natural agents. Live sources. People who know how to listen and remember, not gossip and shoot their mouths off, know what I mean, bruv? *"Boltun nakhodka dlya shpiona, nye', Tovarich?"*

The voice in Rolf's mind is Douglas Saunders, Staff Sergeant, Royal Artillery, Rtd. Doug, a meticulous de-briefer for HMG visiting him in hospital with his temporary passport, befriending him after his leaving, courtesy of Bell & Co. Showing him the ropes, how to survive the Peace, if you like. And showing him London. Of course, as a professional talent spotter for His Majesty's *Infinitely Deniable Service*, he was grooming him.

He is quite different from CPT (who seems very full of himself I think). A 'natural'; a ranker, no degree, salt of the earth but with sudden depth that caught you unawares. Like his grasp of *Russian*. Sort of man you felt you'd like to have on your side in a scrap. Like Kessler. Watching for any latent talent that 'Ralph Stygers', as I am henceforth to be known, may possess. Watching too the bright young things coming and going in the pubs of Cambridge, seeking talent in his usual stamping ground. Watching to see which other talent spotters prowled, poaching for the other team in the watering holes where undergrads congregated and with whom: observing the unguarded and covert acts of the *Apostles*.

As for Reilly, perhaps I was a little under his spell, but he seemed straight, astute and darkly charming. I thought I'd play it safe, though, and took on board what CPT had said. But I was quite unnerved by his volubility on what was after all our short acquaintance, despite that he clearly felt we were now bosom pals after my having rescued him from certain death. Did I imagine it though, as an agent on His Majesty's Secret Service, that he'd hinted at a personally divisive attitude to a *united* Britain?

I reflect that my first contact with the British at home seemed to confirm my naïve preconceptions of them as a polyglot race, though I've found it increasingly difficult to define them since: especially the Celts.

628

Despite CPT's character assassination, Reilly had seemed to me to be a relatively 'straight bat', as the English would say. I would postpone my opinion on that for the time being and make my own mind up about Mansfield Cumming. As head of British Intelligence he had to be a pretty shrewd customer, whatever his idiosyncracies.

But my story of adventure and escape, with all its loose ends, is far from over for my audience in Whitehall.

Chapter 43. *How to Crash!*

January 1920
Southern Russia, the Ukranian Border.

I am struggling with the controls of the Halberstadt. The engine is misfiring at full revs, but when I throttle back the nose drops alarmingly and it does not respond quickly to elevator. Only adding throttle brings the nose up, very slowly. We've lost quite a bit of precious height, down to about 300 metres. A burst of gunfire from behind. I look back to see a Camel pulling alongside to investigate us. He's possibly wondering why the other Bolshevist fighters had been attacking us so he's not about to dispatch us yet. After a long, slow look the pilot, whose face is muffled like my own points at our machine and then indicates that he wants me to turn left.

I make a compliant hand gesture and begin to bank away. I hear another short burst and cringe involuntarily. I look behind. He's dropped back a bit on the outside of the turn. Kessler's voice in my earphones informs me that the pilot is indicating that I should slow down. I tell him if I throttle back the nose will start to drop uncontrollably and at this height there may not be enough room to recover, even with full power. In fact we can't slow down enough to land, which I presume is what they want.

There is another burst of gunfire from our left, attracting our attention. I crane my neck to glimpse another Camel cutting-in on the inside of our turn. Ernst tells me that the second Camel pilot is indicating that we should now fly straight ahead. Both Camels are having difficulty in matching our speed. I have throttled back as much as I dare, but it should be obvious to our British escort that I am holding the stick almost right back and that the elevator, as reported by Ernst, is shot to bits.

Ahead I can see a snow-covered airfield with what appear to be British aeroplanes lined up in front of canvas hangars. The left hand Camel seems a little quicker than the first and draws alongside pointing downwards, directing us to land. He also points to his Vickers gun and makes a finger wagging gesture with his mit, pointing downwards again.

The rudder seems effective if lethargic as I commence a gentle turn over the field for a proper look. The Camels fan-out, covering us. They've now been joined by another three or four Camels, all watching our progress.

'I'm holding the stick back but the elevator's shot to bits...'

I have an idea. I shout to Kessler on the *gosporti*. Making my words as clear and unambiguous as possible.

'Ernst, can you un-strap and move back as far in the cockpit as you can? Face backwards as it will enable you to withstand the landing better. I need you to almost climb into the rear fuselage if you can, but be careful of the control cables!'

'*Nyet prablema.*' He replies in his peculiar Russian. His morale seems good anyway considering we are likely to die in a few minutes.

I can sense him via the controls moving about in the rear cabin and then I feel the thump as he kicks out a plywood frame. Suddenly the stick load reduces a little and the aeroplane is climbing gently. Kessler's done it. He's altered the centre-of-gravity enough to allow me to throttle back some more, pushing his feet as far as possible in the direction of the tailplane, chest touching the rear of the cockpit padding. I wonder if it's enough to raise the nose to 'flare' the aeroplane for landing. Otherwise it's a fast wheel landing with every chance we'll do a forward somersault and crash upside-down at speed.

I experiment with an increase in power trying to bring the nose up watching the ASI needle and applying full power to raise the nose higher still. If I were to overdo it and stall then the aeroplane would probably

632

spin. Either way there's not enough elevator to recover. It's still much too fast for a landing I decide. In addition the engine is misfiring even worse and it sounds as if it will quit at any moment. I note that the water temperature is also very high. I enrich the mixture but the banging and back-firing is worse. The situation seems grim.

Suddenly I make my decision. There is tree-line around part of the airfield's southern perimeter, raised on a mound with a drainage ditch on the other side. I circle to the North, tense in case the Camels infer this as an attempted break out. I waggle my wings to reassure them. When I've judged that we are far enough away I make a gentle turn to line up broadside to the southern perimeter and slowly throttle back, being careful not to drop the nose too far and mindful that the engine could die at a crucial moment.

'Hang on tight to anything you can, Ernst,' I shout.

I don't notice if he replies. I am concentrating very hard on this landing. Just as I did at Struga and in the Latgale forest when my engine was out of fuel. Ironically this time it will be at high speed due to *too much* engine and precious little elevator control.

I settle the aeroplane into a fast glide, descending with enough power to keep the nose from falling too far while keeping the airspeed as low as possible. It's *way* too fast for a 'wheel' landing so there's only one chance. I aim straight at the tree line, descending to within one metre of the ground. The elevators are sluggish yet require precise movements to keep the nose attitude. At one point I feel the wheels touch and the aeroplane starts to balloon. I catch it with throttle and accompanied by some more bangs and pops I hold it level. There is a brisk crosswind from the East, possibly with some tailwind as well just to make matters worse, so I am having to crab slightly with rudder and a little aileron to make the aiming point which is exactly between two tough-looking birch trees that I estimate are about three metres apart.

'Hang on!' I yell one last time to Kessler, even though I know he will be holding on for dear life as he's no longer strapped into his seat. At least he won't see the crash, I think, and switch off the ignition as we pass between the trees.

Part Five

Chapter 44. *Paranoia and Parallel Histories*

Mill Farm, Suffolk:
Spring 2008

I see Natasha sitting bolt upright in a shaft of moonlight. She's had a sudden premonition that Lilia and Tania had died. The dream was intense and had not immediately fled mockingly, in tatters, into the shadowed corners of the bedroom, the way that dreams are wont to do.

It was three weeks since the post woman's discovery of the bodies of Clarissa and Chrissie Blundell. She'd arrived in her van at Mill Farm, hammering on the door until Natasha had let her in. She was incoherent and in shock. Emma had just left for school.

'I telephoned the police,' she'd explained at the interview, before ringing the school to find that the bus had not yet arrived, then puttering off in her ridiculous 2CV, leaving the postie to make herself a cup of tea.

~-~

She'd continued in her own journal:

I was roundly remonstrated for contaminating the scene. I'd thought I'd been careful not to touch anything, although I admitted that I probably did touch the Land Rover door. I'd needed to know that Emma was safely on the bus. There was no-one at the stop so I'd continued first to Grimstone. I had to find out for myself what had happened to my neighbours. I didn't think about danger, just followed the smell of burning.

I had been questioned again. It appears that the PM results showed that Chrissie had died from a stab wound to the heart, one of many such wounds on her body, some of which would have soon resulted in death from blood loss. For a while it seemed likely that Clarissa had killed her long term lover. A kitchen knife bearing her fingerprints and covered in Chrissie's blood was found near the Land Rover and Clarissa's body had a good deal of blood, Chrissies's blood, on the front of her coat. Clarissa was seventy-three. Evidence was still suggesting that it was a sort of suicide pact. But there were the dead dogs and the unexplained marks on Clarissa's wrists…

'Forensics' armed with dusting powder, Luminol and white lights on tripods had by then swarmed over Grimstone House and the burned-out caravan like masked maggots; wearing white plastic overalls, hoods and blue latex gloves. And the thing they'd turned up that rather blew the murder-suicide theory had been a bloody part-hand print on a door jamb with what looked like six fingers.

I told them that I knew, whatever Clarissa might have done with her own *Black Dog* at her throat, and Chrissie's cancer back, I didn't believe they would have hurt their beloved Border Collies.

~.~

I lie in bed listening to the house. I'd given up trying to sleep with Shostakovich and Sibelius as the CD player was using up batteries at a serious rate.

I've dreamed again of Iron Vikings. My avatar rooted in some distant dimension; a solitary ghost, wingless, dreaming at REM Stage 1, still as a birch tree midst the northern snowfields. They'd droned overhead, emblazoned with the cross. I know them now for what they are. Or rather were. Soldiers of ill-fortune. Crusaders. Proto-Nazis from my father's own cryptic journal, hunting: death masks searching over gun mantels for living things. Valkyries that bear the spirits of the dead on their wings.

The full moon, like an empty ghost peers mindlessly through my window. Shut up, I think. The moon doesn't mean anything. She is no succubus. It is there as a magnetic counterbalance to stabilise the earth that rocks upon its axis, controlling the seasons, enabling life and civilisation. God is a philanthropic physicist.

I dream of owls. But they are not harbingers. They don't mean anything either. Unless the white face of the moon and the face of the barn owl are manifestations of the same dread thing. Some sort of screen memory. I wonder, what is a ghost but an electro-chemically induced retinal image? A memory; a file drawn from the synaptic reference library, no more than a recording from the theatre of the mind. Not a 'grounded spirit'. My head seems full of chatter. I wonder if Emma is still hearing voices. Has Kelvin's lamenting spirit visited her here; or something else?

But I have a chilling idea. My father's strange theory that we 'reincarnate in clusters' might make a fearful sense. Or else it's more co-incidence, the trigger of fate and a hint that I live in a looking-glass world; have kissed the cold lips of my old schizoid self. Am I suffering paranoid delusions? Do I need a psychiatrist? Is this 'conspiracy theory' or evidence that we influence the outcomes of those things we obsess about.

Facts: as they are presented from the bloody history of Baltic Russia. The massacre at the House of Linden: rapine and butchery. *The Terror* in microcosm…..

Liepus Namas: Two women, seek vengeance and disappear into the maelstrom of civil war, two red-haired Lithuanian beauties who might *almost* have been twins. The remainder of the household dies horribly. The youngest girl, Graczyna's fate is unknown, but her suffering in life was equally terrible.

Grimstone House: Two girls, from across the Lithuanian border in Belarus disappear into thin air in Suffolk, beauties who *are* identical twins. The two elderly members of that household die violently and mysteriously.

Mill Farm: Emma is suffering her own special hell. Self-harming still. 'Things' have been seen around the farm house. A suicide had taken place in my kitchen.

Steiger spent half his sanity across the border in Norfolk walking the shore, tearing at the veil that was spun across the labyrinths of his memory. I too am trying to get a grip on events. My father may have been the grandson of a German Freikorps veteran who Russified his name for 'showbiz', *or it was Russified for him by Mara, wrapped in a bearskin fleeing as a passenger in the Junkers: the love of his life that he allegedly won in a poker game. Or a gunfight.* Had he anglicised it again later? So is that my real name? *Von Moritz?* If I buy into this stuff.

From my father's chronicles the psychopath, Roskov, the one I've *christened*: one of the many perverted sadists that Lenin, Stalin, Dzerzhinsky and their ilk used as their special executives, had been responsible for the depravity and horror at the Linden House and elsewhere. He had suffered earlier at Katya's hand when she'd defended herself on the road but he'd then exacted his terrible revenge. Since my return from that same Baltic manor house things have been seen here in Suffolk that suggest that I am watched and pursued: a figure who clutches at his throat. *Raudongevklis?* Red Throat. Is that paranoia? Emma's pony is slashed. That's real. I have taken to sleeping with a carving knife under my pillow, like Elena in Lithuania before me, sleepless, dreading the sound of Nikolai's fingernails scratching at her door.

Fact: A local newspaper reports a fierce house fire in Upper Thurston, a small village near Bury St. Edmunds. Two children burned to death and the mother horribly injured, but alive, suffering from smoke inhalation. The fire service is investigating the cause of what the paper termed 'an inferno'. But what rivets my attention in the picture of their fire-blackened home is the car in the driveway. The registration plate is not in view but there is a clearly visible dent in the driver's door of the old Volvo.

~.~

Willis is a prowling menace. I feel him slowly spiralling in on me the way that the 'Elf King' spiralled in on Kristian, in the form of the jealous Wassermann, the Goblin of German Myth, who flings a headless corpse, his half-human child at the feet of his disobedient human wife — who sings to the moon. Or so it's said.

I have spared Emma the knowledge that Polish Fred had confided; that he'd found poor Quantum's corpse, and buried him. A road kill? Possibly, but he did tell me, when pressed, that the little cat was missing his head.

I wondered what it was that stalked the Fens.

So must Lilia's fate mimic Krystina's? Does Tatiana's life mirror Katarzyna's? Does this paranoia play out on every level 'til Nirvana, when all will be forgiven and explained? Does Roskov's undead corpse, cursed by Elena Roskova still turn upon the windmills of eternity, malign and vengeful, its spirit spitting venom, dimension to dimension? Or had it climbed down from its sail, found it's way like

~-~

My father had written of the emotional journey of that night's meeting in Surrey, at the safe house at Norwood Hill, where the story unfolded. There the spirit of Harry in all its vitality and fortitude had been invoked by James, who tells the tale sympathetically, without recourse to notes. In his safe house was revealed that bloody thing that swam through the dark like the *Water Goblin*, tracking Harry's past even in Frankfurt: given tongue to speak the unspeakable in its foul quest; a voodoo curse with the name *Strelitz* in its lamprey mouth.

'James, I have to tell you the last I hear of Countess Katarzyna…. was from boy, himself dying little by little each day, alongside me at Fili – chemical exposure. He was from village close to mine and knew family Strelitz, and Countesses by sight. He had been in railyard gang, loading wagons with material and he swore to God that he'd seen her in railway wagon, chained to floor, half naked and filthy like some dog with mad eyes. He'd heard rumours that had spread after her return to Kuznetsowa, remembered her scarred forehead and colour of hair, matted though it was. He said *Wolves* had taken her again.'

Had she by then seen Graczyna's corpse?

John had told James Delcroix that he was beginning to wonder how much horror he could take in one night. James said Harry's was a story of triumph and survival, but that the collateral loss and suffering was … extreme.

Chapter 45.
Wolfgang, Zubr and the 'Little Prince'.

James seemed more agitated as night became early morning. Despite the best efforts of the single electric filament the room had become cold and I'd gone out to the car to put on my leather flying jacket. The night air was moist and Reigate's glow was dimmed by advancing rain. I automatically glanced towards the road. All was quiet but I was aware of a car sitting some distance away that hadn't been parked there when I'd arrived. The lights weren't lit and it was hard to tell but I thought that there was something in its interior that looked to be more than just shadows. *Lovers* was not my first thought. From the muscular shape and the chromed mascot I'd have guessed it was an XK150 with a hard top; a very dark shade, black or midnight blue. Significantly the 'safe house' was detached and fairly isolated. In other words the car wasn't just parked outside 'another' address, but discreetly distant from James' hideout. If I hadn't gone for my jacket the occupant could have approached the house undetected, if that was his intention. I pulled back into the shadow of the leylandii and kept watch for a minute. It occurred to me that James would be wondering what I was up to; if I'd suddenly got cold feet and left.

I had used my initiative. On my return from Hannover, instead of taking the briefcase to the Guildford Estate Agent as Alexa had ordered, I had secreted the briefcase. I had brought some identification and after he'd made a few telephone calls I had been directed here instead, *sotto voce* by 'Victor', who'd ensured I had fully memorised the address. The briefcase was currently in a St. Albans basement, in the *salon de refuses* of a portrait painter in the Inkerman Road, among his rags, brushes and turpentine, buried under a pile of unfinished canvases. James had not asked for it and I was beginning to think that he didn't really want to be associated with it any more, even though it contained the answers to the innocent research he'd initiated - into an obscure aeroplane's history that so determinedly he'd sought to unravel. But it contained much besides, and would seem to have been worth a lot to someone. He seemed to me distracted. From what he'd implied he was ready to be rid of it all. That included the *Tigerfalk* and Unity Valkyrie Mitford's 'celebrity list' with its remaining member of the House of Lords.

Through a gap in the trees I saw a glint as the driver's door opened. A broad-shouldered figure loomed there, briefly illuminated by the interior light. A second, slighter figure emerged from the passenger's side. They closed the doors silently and began to move towards the house, splitting up; the smaller one heading for the rear.

I shrank back into the darkened porch. I had to warn James but was afraid we'd both be trapped in the house if they encircled us. But there was nothing for it. Moving quietly and as quickly as I dared I entered the house and locked the front door. I found James had not moved. He was sitting, staring at the glow of the electric fire.

'Quick. On your feet. We have visitors!' I hissed.

He looked at me with growing alarm. 'Where?' he asked, gaining his feet.

'Front and rear. How many exits? Do we play dead or run?'

He peered out of the lounge window between the 'blackout' curtains.

'Just the two doors. Let's try to get out of the back, there's a big bastard coming down the path.'

'What d'you think?' I asked feebly. 'Neo-Nazi or KGB?'

'I suggest we don't wait to find out. Come on,' he whispered.

We moved rapidly through the kitchen to the rear of the house. James silently opened the back door and looked out. Past his shoulders I could make out fruit bushes and an overgrown garden; a path ran down the centre with a clothes line while trees created a barrier to either side. The carport under which I'd rolled the Escort lay alongside out of view.

Two sheds crouched against the fence running along the back of the property. In the darkness behind lay fields with the solid shapes of trees beyond them.

We crept out onto the concrete path and I indicated that we should make our way along the tree line which seemed to provide best cover, given the direction from which I'd seen the smaller figure approaching. Cloud now obscured what starlight there had been. A thin drizzle was falling. I had a bad feeling about this. The two intruders were almost certain to be armed. We'd be conspicuous fleeing across the fields even if we made it over the fence without being intercepted. Our only hope was that they'd investigate the house first, including the upstairs, and give us a head start. At least they'd lost the element of surprise - on which they'd have been counting.

We reached the fence at the bottom of the garden and climbed out between the sheds. The brambles considered, we managed it without too much noise. I risked a backward glance. No-one skulked in the trees that I could see or was coming around the back of the house. Mr. Big would be at the front by now, perhaps peering through the window. Mr. Small? Where he was I had no idea.

We made our way at a fast jog through the muddy field which muffled our footfalls, heading for trees at the far corner two-hundred yards away. We were both wearing dark garments so that helped somewhat. I wondered how long they'd hang around the house to ransack it or if they would decamp: whether they'd disable the car to prevent my using it or hotwire and take it. The keys were in my pocket. I was puffing with the exertion thinking how unfit I was for this kind of thing and that the loss of the car would be a blow to any wider plan of improvised escape and evasion.

We gained the trees, breathing hard. It took a minute for each of us to recover and find the breath to whisper our thoughts regarding the next move. In two hours it would be daylight, enough for the 'enemy' to discover us if we hung about. But the thought of the car was a powerful attractor for a rapid exit to somewhere else.

~-~

We hid among the trees in a state of indecision as the minutes passed. If we could be certain they had left we might safely return and retrieve the Escort. Apart from the glaring evidence of the car itself James had left clothes and personal effects behind and it would be obvious to the intruders that we'd taken off in a hurry and might be close at hand. But we had no clear idea of where we might be heading if we were to strike across country onto other peoples' property where we might be apprehended, or raise a hue and cry if a dog were to catch our scent. We'd probably be reported to the police and that could start a whole new round of explanations and revelations from which we might not be able to extricate ourselves. Either an unbreakable cover story would be necessary or we had to stay put to watch what transpired.

'How did you make your way to the hideout?' I asked James. 'Do you have transport nearby?'

James didn't. A taxi had dropped him off at the end of the road with a suitcase and the keys to the property that his estate agent friend had given him. Instructions were to lock up and leave them inside when he vacated. A 'phone call would tell Victor that the place was empty again and in due course he'd send someone along to re-erect the vendor sign and cut the grass. James' place in Bristol had been burgled and some odd characters had been seen hanging about. He'd received a message to meet Peter at Ramstein but had been spooked by a hooded prowler who'd accosted him one night and told him to 'leave off his researches if he knew what was good for him'. Two plainclothes 'policemen' had then called at his flat and flashed a warrant on the pretext that a neighbour had complained about 'noise'.

'There was no 'noise', John. I didn't even play music loud and since when does CID get involved in complaints of that sort? It was a warning. They were very cold and threatening. Came in without invitation or a search warrant and looked around. Searched through all my books and cupboards. I'm not sure they were looking for anything in particular. Just trying to make a point. I went to make a telephone call to complain to the station but they prevented me from doing so. I don't believe they were real, or if they were they weren't local. Of course if they were 'real' I am dealing with something at such a level that I cannot put up a fight against. What would I do, get a civil rights lawyer involved? I have a list of names – you'd never believe whose name was included there - that could see me dragged out of a canal as easy as buying a paper. And there's a clue to something even bigger contained in that briefcase involving a hoard of Russian gold. Its whereabouts were known to Peter, perhaps, and it's somehow buried in a story from the past. Peter was fond of writing in riddles. He used to devise elaborate *Haikus*. Stripped-down poems which contained a world of expression and experience of life in just seventeen syllables. Maybe it's in one of those!'

We huddled there getting colder by the half hour. I was for reconnoitering the house to see if they'd gone, but James' had evidently been thoroughly frightened recently and seemed reluctant. He argued that we'd have seen their headlights if they'd driven off.

'That's if they'd used them,' I retorted.

The first hint of a muddy dawn seemed to be lightening the sky in the east. No 'sultan's tower caught in the hunter's noose of light': rather the suggestion of a lesser darkness and an increase in precipitation. I was wet, hungry and fed up. This was no way for two adults to carry on. Discomfort was overriding my natural caution.

'I'm going down to have a look,' I said. 'You can come with me or not.'

James looked grim but resolute.

'Oscar Wilde said you should try everything once. Except incest and morris dancing'

~-~

We crept up on the house from the rear. It remained drab and inscrutable and in darkness. We trailed around the high tree hedge and the tangled undergrowth at the side of the garden, moving stealthily and staying low. The idea was to reconnoitre the road where they'd left the Jaguar before returning to investigate the house. Although we'd hidden far enough away to have avoided detection in the night, the lightly falling rain could have masked the sound of a car driving away. Perhaps with just sidelights illuminated we mightn't have witnessed its departure behind the thick roadside hedges from our hiding place under the trees. This was all ludicrous and uncivilised I thought. But James' real worries were contagious and the story he'd unburdened to me had made a deep impression, random details of which had been confirmed by my cursory investigation of the briefcase in Hannover.

We hung back in the field alongside the house above where I thought I'd seen the XK.

Slowly we advanced bent nearly double behind the hedge. At once I saw it. Still there, with Mr. Small back in the passenger's seat. So where was Mr. Big? Just then I heard the sound of another car. Dipped headlights were approaching from the direction of Reigate. Mr. Small shrank down in the seat so that he was invisible to view.

A grey Vauxhall Cavalier saloon rounded the bend, the headlights extinguishing as it drifted to a halt about a hundred yards from the property. The occupants remained motionless for a while: James and I could see them watching the Jaguar and the house. Nothing moved. Mr Small might not have existed. The only sound was a wren prematurely heralding the sunrise.

After five minutes two figures in black roll-neck sweaters emerged from the Vauxhall, closed the doors softly and moved quickly towards the house. There seemed to be no-one left in the car.

My eyes were well adapted to the light and one thing was apparent. Both men were armed with hand guns. And the guns had long silencers. To anyone who'd read a spy novel or seen a James Bond film the implication was that this was a killer squad.

From the behaviour of Mr. Small it was clear that these two pairs were not aligned. The men slipped into the garden of the house and vanished behind the leylandii. As soon as they'd disappeared from view Mr. Small evacuated the Jaguar and ran towards the house. He too carried a pistol.

James and I stood together, very aware of the danger of approaching the house ourselves, completely unarmed as we were, neither of us trained in covert operations and unarmed combat. The rain was slackening off but we were cold and soaked-through anyway. We held a brief discussion. Getting the police involved was off the agenda. There was no public phone box for miles and too many questions would be asked. Incriminating evidence remained, namely James' personal effects that might hold clues to his identity. My hired Ford was too dangerous to try to retrieve and contained a copy of the rental agreement in the glove compartment with my signature. Besides, if the police were involved at some level - and with a vast fortune at stake everyone would have their price - putting ourselves in their hands might be equally fatal. So far we were witnesses to a crime that had yet to be committed and with the sun due at any moment our exposure would soon see us complicit, one way or another.

One alternative was to hot-wire one of the cars and make a break for it. North of London perhaps to that other 'safe house' and my Inkerman Road artist friend.

We approached the Jaguar cautiously. It was indeed a powerful XK150. The passenger door was unlocked. I leaned inside. The automatic interior light illuminated a bulky cell-phone installation on the forward gearbox tunnel, but no keys in the ignition nor spares in the glove box. It was worth checking if the Cavalier keys remained in place. I ran quietly across the road to peer into the front. Yes! Amazingly the ignition key was there and the doors weren't locked. Perhaps the hit squad were convinced by the seclusion of the house and wanted to be sure of making a quick getaway. I climbed in behind the wheel and motioned to James to join me. I spoke urgently. *'M.25 First stop – St. Albans!'*

I was about to turn the key when a sound caused me to freeze. James and I looked at each other in astonishment. The thumping from the boot and a muffled voice told us that we had a passenger.

We were primed for escape with no time to investigate so I turned the key and the engine fired. Simultaneously there was a flurry of movement in the garden. A man ran into the road towards us. He looked momentarily taken aback and then pointed his long handgun at the windscreen. I felt he had me cold so I'd raised my hands from the wheel when there was a double flash from the garden. I dimly registered both reports as the gunman crumpled against the bonnet, still holding his silenced pistol. Mr. Small walked out of the darkness and coolly shot him again, in the head. The body of the gunman slid bloodily out of sight. Mr. Small made a 'key-turning' gesture indicating that I should cut the engine. In a state of shocked fascination I found the action of raising my hand to the ignition and turning the key supremely difficult. But I'd clearly had no choice.

With a cursory glance at his victim, Mr. Small walked round to my side of the car, his pistol trained on us.

'Hände hoch!' he ordered and waited till we'd raised them before approaching more closely and peering into the back of the car.

'Raus!'

We both did as we were bidden. The occupant of the boot remained silent.

He ordered us in German to pick up the body and carry it to the house.

'Machen Sie, schnell,' he growled, indicating with his pistol that we should precede him. He retrieved the pistol and silencer from where the dead man had dropped it and picked up a spent cartridge. But the road was not free from evidence of strife. Both the Vauxhall and the road were heavily bloodstained.

James and I struggled with the body, my head whirling with scenarios and rejecting all possibilities of escape for the moment. We stumped into the dim-lit living room where James had regaled me through the night with the story of Harry, the beginning of the quest for the Romanov Treasure and the 'Valkyrie' list. Just who these two warring factions were I wasn't sure, but given that the KGB and the Neo-Nazis were both involved, I was fearful that falling captive to either would be the beginning of a short career.

~-~

The scene in the house was one of calm following a very evident storm. The lounge was lit by the dim bulb which swung pendulously from the ceiling, throwing shadows that made me feel queasy after my exertion. Mr. Big seemed to fill the room. He stood over the kneeling form of the black-clad survivor of the two-man 'hit squad'. The man's own silenced pistol was trained on him. Big had sustained a gunshot wound himself to the lower arm. It bled but did not seem to bother him. His eyes were lion-like, grey crystals of ice flecked with yellow. He wore a straggling beard and moustache and his whole presence reminded me of a portrait I'd once seen of Leo Tolstoy. He spoke in English to our captor.

'Have them put him on the sofa, Wolf,' he said. 'And then tell these two to stand facing the wall. Arms raised.' His voice was deep and sonorous.

I started to speak but was silenced by 'Wolf' who barked out Tolstoy's commands in German. We complied.

'Cover this one,' he said, presumably meaning the one on the floor. I then felt a hard arm jerk me bodily backwards and I was thrust forwards so that I leaned against the wall on outstretched hands. Balanced against the wall, there was no possibility of my making any movement without attracting attention. The same performance was effected with James to my left. Out of the corner of my eye I saw the other gunman hauled to his feet and deposited on my right. So we all leaned in a reluctant stooping line, like a trio of military prisoners.

'Now,' said Tolstoy. 'Let's start with who we all are. Check 'em Wolfgang. I have them covered.'

Wolfgang went though our pockets and tapped us down for hidden weapons. I saw him out of the corner of my eye remove and pocket a flick knife he'd found strapped to the gunman's ankle. He then searched the dead man and deposited various collected items and cash on a side table.

'No passports,' reported Wolf.

'You!' Tolstoy tapped the gunman. 'Do you speak English?'

'Yes,' he replied huskily.

'What is your name?' Tolstoy's speech had a slight intonation, identifiably foreign. I could not see him but from my brief assessment he was well over six feet in height and very broad with a deep chest. Fit-looking, possibly no older than forty. Leo Tolstoy in his prime in fact.

The gunman made no reply.

'I will ask you again and then it will get rough!'

'Unger,' he croaked. 'Claus Unger.'

Unger seemed no more than in his early 'twenties.

'Where are you from, Unger?'

'Hamburg.'

'And your business here?'

Unger remained silent.

'If I have to remind you again not to fool with me you will be sorry.' The voice was not raised but the steel was evident. 'For those who are hostile and un-cooperative, we don't wear kid gloves.'

'What type of car did you come in? Answer without hesitation or suffer.'

'A… er …*Opel*-Vauxhall Cavalier.'

'What type of gun is it you carried?'

'Walther… P-38.'

'What colour is your car?'

'Grau…'

'And what is your business here?' Tolstoy continued in the same tone and pace, disallowing any thinking time.

'We are an investigation team……' Once he'd started he found he couldn't stop. 'We were ordered to find an Englishman.'

'What *particular* Englishman?'

'We were to look for John Morris and his associate, James Delcroix.'

'And who sent you on this errand? Don't *think*, just answer and remember I am serious.'

'Mein *Sturmbann*… my Group Leader.'

'Your *Sturmbannführer*? What are you playing at, boy? Are you supposed to be an example of the *Neue SS*?'

'I am a soldier of the NPD.'

'Dear God. Are you telling us that the *Nationaldemokratische Partei Deutschlands* has a military wing? *Heaven forfend!* And they recruit *schoolboys* as their *'V-Manner'*. It's just like 1945, Wolf! They've already built their bunker.' Tolstoy is withering. 'What's next? The ovens?'

Unger allowed himself a faint smile. 'That myth!'

Tolstoy took a long breath.

'Watch your tongue, Unger, or risk losing it. What is your day job, assuming you are not a full-time SS man in the new *NSDAP?*'

'Travelling representative.'

'For whom?'

'For a cement company.'

'And your mission, once you'd located Morris and Delcroix?'

'To interrogate them, of course.'

'About what?'

Unger was silent. There was a movement from behind and Wolfgang's gun barrel sliced viciously across Unger's cheek. Unger cried out and his knees buckled as he raised his hand protectively from the wall. Instantly the barrel slashed across the opposite cheek and a hand chopped hard into his lower back, forcing him back into position. In the corner of my eye I saw his left cheek. A deep graze with blood gathering.

'We were to ask him about….' The voice was shaky.

'Yes?'

'About a briefcase.'

'And did you find these three? Morris, Delcroix and the briefcase?'

'Nein.'

'What was the name of your Sturmbannführer?'

Unger hesitated for a split second and Wolf's automatic dug into his skull.

'Sturmbannführer Karl Promnitz, *mein Herr.*' He said, in a rush.

'And what does he do – besides?'

'He is a lawyer.'

'Where does he practice?'

'Bremen.'

'And what was special about this briefcase?'

'It…. was possibly burned….'

'Yes, and?'

'That was how we should recognise it.'

'What was to have stopped Morris or Delcroix from having transferred the contents elsewhere?'

'Nothing….. that's why we were to interrogate them.'

'And what do you know of the contents?'

'We were not informed with regard to detail. Except that the enclosures were likely to be typed and written notes. Lists. Note books. Articles. Possibly film or tapes…..it was not really specified.'

'And the general subject matter? There must have been some clue to identify it within certain parameters?'

'No, none.'

'So why were you supposed to retrieve this briefcase? Why was it so important?'

'We weren't told.'

'Oh come on, Unger. You had to be motivated. They must have given you some clue to keep you keen. Make you heroes realise how important this secret task of yours was.'

'We didn't ask. We were told it was very important. That's all. We were just obeying orders.'

'Oh, of course. *Befehl ist Befehl.* The oldest cop-out in the German Army Manual.'

Unger was silent.

'So how did you find this place?'

'We had directions.'

'Who gave you those directions?'

If Unger intended to remain silent, Wolfgang's automatic grinding into his neck changed his mind for him.

'Victor.'

'Victor?'

'Victor.'

'Victor who?'

'Just Victor. That's how he was identified.'

'Where did you meet Victor?'

'We called the estate agent office. We enquired about properties for sale. Guildford area.'

'And?'

'He met us. I asked especially to see him. I said *Stephanie* wanted to retire in Surrey.'

'And what did Victor say?'

'He gave us this address.'

'Just like that.'

Unger was silent.

'Where is Victor now?'

No reply.

'Claus, where is Victor?'

'Dead.'

'Some sort of accident, eh Claus?'

'Thomas did it.'

'Of course. Thomas would be the dead piece of shit on the sofa, right?'

'Ja. That's right.'

'Thank you, Unger. Your Nuremburg will come later.'

He moved to me. 'You! *Sprechen Sie englisch?*'

There was no escape from this rapid interrogation. Neither James nor myself would be able to invent a cover story that would hold up for more than ten seconds. James seemed to have gone rigid. I wondered how well he'd known 'Victor', who'd provided this shelter for him. This no longer safe house.

'John Morris,' I said. 'And who the hell are you?'

'I am the man with the gun,' he said. So I am the one who asks the questions.

'And you are?' He asked of James. James identified himself. There was no fall back story or alternative identity for either of us.

'Very well, Mr. Morris. Your car rental agreement document would seem to confirm that. So you're not part of this Nazi plot? Turn round and let me see you. Both of you. Wolfgang has a nervous trigger finger. Be warned!'

'We've seen it in action,' I replied grimly.

Tolstoy remained standing. He told us to sit opposite him and stared at us unblinkingly.

'Secure that one, Wolf,' He said without shifting his gaze. 'Put him in the kitchen.'

Wolfgang snatched up a small table lamp pulling the wires out of the plug in the socket then deftly snapped the electrical flex out of the base of the lamp. Unger was spun round then laid face-down on the carpet and his hands firmly tied with the flex, very professionally I thought. Though little taller than Wolfgang, the flaxen Unger had a 'central casting' Aryan-killer hauteur, heightened by his black roll-neck sweater and black gloves. He might have been cloned from his blond dead twin Thomas on the sofa in some *Mengele*-style laboratory experiment; his NPD handler's double *wet dream*, I suspected. Wolfgang led the 'New SS' man out of the room. He returned and gently helped his boss out of his bloodstained tweed, rolled up the red shirtsleeve and examined the bullet wound. The flesh of the forearm was torn below the elbow and the exit wound was apparent. The forearm was pale and the blood was flowing freely, not yet clotting in the body's rapid response to trauma. Wolfgang beckoned me to approach.

'Put your bleedin' finger there and press,' he ordered, indicating a point above the elbow. He disappeared and returned with a bowl from the kitchen and washed the injury while the big man stood there holding the 9-mm casually in his left hand pointing at my midriff. I noticed that he was swaying very slightly and there was a tremor in the gun hand. I hoped the safety was 'on'.

'So tell me, Mr. Morris,' he said conversationally. 'Is it safe?'

There was no point in asking what.

'Safe enough,' I said.

'And would it be close?'

'It depends on your definition of "close",' I said.

'Don't fence with me,' he grated, the steel never far away.

'Apart from the fact that you have a gun,' I retorted, 'What gives you a right to it?'

'Good question, John. If I may call you that.'

'You might, if I had been granted the benefit of an introduction.'

'For now you can call me *Zubr*.'

In the background James grunted involuntarily. Recognition I assumed.

Zubr was perspiring but I didn't think it was pain. His tiger eyes surveyed me calmly. He was as imposing a human being that ever I'd met: self-controlled as a knight might be standing comfortably before his own fireplace. Yet my impression was that this man *may* be an alcoholic.

'You have the fuckin' honour to meet a nobleman of the fuckin' royal blood,' interrupted Wolfgang. 'My Count is a *hospodar*, descended from a family of knights what rode beside the Jagiellonian Kings a thousand years ago. His descendents fuckin' died at Katyn at the hands of the bastard NKVD. Now my Count is the last and rightful heir to the bleedin' Polish throne!'

'Wolfgang. Don't overdo it on short acquaintance.'

'The sooner they know what's at fuckin' stake the better. That's my advice for worrit's worth,' he said. 'Unless we're going to torture the crap out of them.'

Wolfgang seemed to be a sort of cold-eyed cockney-German 'Sancho Panza'.

'So what is at stake?' I asked, impressed by my own *cajonas*.

There was a sudden fire in the flinty eyes. 'At stake!' The Count's voice rose only slightly. 'At stake is a nation that has suffered the repression of the cruellest regime on the planet since 1945. After they were betrayed in 1939, fought two enemies, were murdered by the tens of thousands, escaped and fought like eagles, like lions to help the Allied victory. And then were denied the right to march to the Cenotaph alongside the British and the Czechs, the Norwegians, the Commonwealth troops, the Gurkhas, the Free French, the WAAFs, the

Home Guard, even bloody *ENSA*! But not the Poles, who were the bravest of the brave: so as not to offend that bastard dwarf Stalin and his puppet Polish government. That vile thug. Worst murdering Bolshevist psychopath that ever drew breath! That is what is at bloody stake!'

Count Zubr's' diatribe was no temperamental outburst. He was still under perfect control. Just expressing in forthright terms, for those of us who might need re-educating, the parlous position of his country and the fate of his courageous countrymen in yoke to the oppressor.

Wolfgang had the Count remove his tie to tighten around the upper arm to stem the bleeding which was somehow managed without compromising his armed status. My gaze was drawn to the small embroidered logo on the dark blue material; a Polish flag, a white-over-red banner whose flagstaff formed the second upright of a capital letter 'N'. Iconic graffiti, *Solidarnosc*. Gdansk dock worker Lech Walesa's protest movement which was confronting the Jaruzelski Government, organising strikes throughout Poland and was the prime force for change in Eastern Europe. I recognised it immediately, though not the additional green banner underneath. With the word *Cymru* in white capitals.

Solidarity, he volunteered, was a home-grown, socialist solution: so what then was the position of the expatriates? What of the scattered shards of those noble houses? They were powerless to do other than to accept that if it meant a first step on the rung to a long denied autonomy they too would support it, grasping it with both hands. His assurance was delivered with a smooth urbanity. For the Poles, who'd suffered enslavement by two murderous fascisms in 1939, releasing them from the grind of the disasterous Communist experiment and the depressed economy they'd endured since the War was the only consideration. Hopefully Walesa would triumph. Wider restitution would wait.

Dawn arrived and Zubr was looking through the lounge door at the front doormat that was piled with unopened circulars.

'Wolfgang,' he said. 'Would you take a cloth and a bucket to wash the blood and brains off that Vauxhall radiator grill; before the bloody Royal Mail makes an appearance?'

James and I spoke at once: what we'd forgotten until that moment. About the passenger in the Vauxhall's boot.

~-~

Still covered by Wolfgang's automatic, James and I made our way into the road. We checked for the sound of approaching traffic. All was silent. We quickly approached the car and unlocked the boot.

A young woman was tied with duct tape at the ankles, her wrists secured behind her. A rectangle of tape was stuck across her mouth. She was dressed in jeans and a denim jacket. A mass of blonde hair fell across her face and her grey eyes were more furious than fearful. She looked about the same age as my own daughter.

'Good God, Amelia!' James exclaimed. 'It's my youngest!'

James gently removed the tape from his daughter's mouth. I felt I was living some sort of black farce with me a hapless Brian Rix.

'Daddy!' she gasped. 'What the fuck's been going on?'

The ankle restraints proved more difficult but Wolfgang solved the problem with Unger's flick-knife. Amelia in an agony of cramp was helped to the house. Wolfgang stayed to remove the traces of violence from the front end, before the traffic began.

Though spooked by the body on the sofa, Amelia had calmed down a little after she'd made herself comfortable and her ankles had been massaged. Zubr was very concerned for her and became courtesy itself. We rapidly transferred Thomas's body to the kitchen to join Unger.

~_~

Our *V-Männer* had encountered a 'slightly stoned' Amelia Delcroix as she'd paid off the taxi in Lower Bristol Road. Re-interrogated, Unger confessed that her mother had been dead drunk when they'd arrived an hour before. Neither a cold shower nor any amount of coffee poured between her lips had sobered her up. From Bath they'd driven to Surrey, following up their other lead with Amelia in the boot. Evidently they intended to use her as a bargaining chip. They could hardly have left her behind. They'd turned the place over but considered that Audrey would probably remain unaware they'd ever been to the house. Given that they were otherwise quite ruthless, Amelia's eventual chance of survival seemed limited. When James and I had tried to steal the Cavalier she'd heard me speaking English and had tried to attract our attention, only to hear shots as Wolfgang terminated Thomas; then further commands in German. She'd remained silent - in fear for her life until we'd opened the boot thirty minutes later.

~_~

Zubr took me to one side and asked about the briefcase. We were hostages however you looked at it and Amelia's safety was now another concern. Zubr seemed civilised but Wolfgang had killed a man in cold blood in front of our eyes. Nobody had mentioned the police, and James' recent experience fuelled the 'paranoia' that we were the victims of a conspiracy both here and in Germany. Indeed the only real accident that was incidental, indeed seminal to the situation had been Peter's death at Ramstein. It seemed I had no real choice in the matter and like James I was ready to turn over the whole thing to our present 'captors' for an assurance that we'd be left in one piece, whatever else was at stake. I had nothing else to negotiate with.

Zubr checked the landline connection before going outside to use the car cell-phone. He'd returned having failed to obtain a signal and spoke in low tones to Wolfgang. Zubr told us he'd be back. I heard the throaty boom of the Jaguar starting and the sound of it making a three-point turn before Zubr drove off towards Reigate.

The outside doors were locked. We sat in the lounge as the sun came up, James and his daughter on the bloodstained sofa now discreetly covered by a bedspread. I sat with my back to the window while Zubr's *mauserist* guarded us, monitoring Unger, covering him languidly with what might have been homoerotic interest from the toilet doorway when nature called. I decided it wouldn't hurt to strike up a conversation with Wolfgang, hoping that he wasn't a fully paid-up psychopath and that 'normal' people might find it more difficult to execute captives with whom they'd formed a relationship, however thin. Talking might also be a useful distraction - to *what* I dared hardly imagine. A variation on *Stockholm Syndrome* was probably becoming a factor, witting or otherwise.

Wolfgang seemed uninterested in talking at first. He was more wary now that Zubr had left and his 'equaliser' was hardly out of his hand. He seemed interested only in the contents of the kitchen cupboard and the small fridge which was still working. He made himself a Marmite sandwich. James had stocked up on a couple of loaves and tinned food.

Any plan I might have been trying to hatch was stillborn and I could see that James was tense, quietly trying to comfort his daughter whose expression appeared more agitated with the daylight.

I persevered, asking Wolfgang how he'd met Zubr. He chewed on a Scotch egg and looked at me as if he was re-assessing me and my motives. He was physically small, about five feet three I estimated. Wiry. His head was shaven. He looked like a skinhead's kid brother, but he'd demonstrated his ruthlessness. I briefly wondered if anyone had actually taken any notice of him before he'd thrown in with his *quixotic* Count.

Had he been a petty criminal or a milkman? He could have been anything I suppose. A handyman. A fitness instructor. It was the shaven skull and the coldness in his gaze that arrested one. And the Polish Army automatic he fondled.

But he'd provided more than I'd expected, seeming almost relieved to tell his story. As if validating afresh who he was: hearing his own legend animated and spoken aloud…an only child from an Army marriage, father an absentee drunkard and an immigrant mother, a barmaid from BFPO Rhineland who'd spoken little English when first she'd met her Tommy. His schooling was flimsy and largely 'reform'. He'd truanted and soon joined an East End gang, getting his kicks from beating up Asians and rent boys, an authentic half-German member of *Combat 18*: Nazi skinheads. He said that terrorising the manor, vandalism, theft, gratuitous Nazi graffiti - organising running fights with rival gangs at 'footie matches' – were the limits of the unit's endeavour. But he'd craved more. Much more than conventional criminality as an outlet for his energies.

He found it on New Year's Eve, the night he and some of his 'crew' had rolled a 'heavy drunk' who was leaving their local. They'd put him on the ground and administered a vicious kicking. Wolfgang recalled his astonishment as the 'drunk' climbed out from under their 'bovver boots', throwing one of the attackers bodily through a glass shop front. Two others were gripped, each by the throat and their skulls banged together with such a crack he felt sure they'd been fractured. The remaining thugs had taken to their heels but he'd found himself in an ally with no escape and the giant closing in on him.

Wolfgang had attempted to use his Stanley knife but wound up gasping for breath, nursing a broken wrist. He remembered staring up into a 'face of granite with eyes like a tiger's' as blue lights and sirens converged on the battle-zone. Next thing he was lifted bodily, carried a distance and thrown into the back of a sealed cab Land Rover. He was driven westwards for hours, across a long suspension bridge, on and on into rolling countryside as the sun rose behind them. He was held for a week in a farmhouse, his broken wrist set and plastered by someone with medical knowledge. He went on to describe, with a sort of fervour, the intensive 'thought re-programming' by an enclave of activists that held to higher ideals than trouble for its own sake: that Poland should rise again. It was the 'trumpet call' he'd been awaiting all his short and brutal life: a role he'd been rehearsing since adolescence. His mother had not reported him missing. A month later he'd moved out and returned as Zubr's full-time lieutenant operating from a seedy flat in the Welsh capital. This was the first career advancement for Wolfgang Warden.

Wolf's rootless Nazism had made way for a passionate struggle for a new Free Europe, starting with Poland which had been one of Nazi Germany's first victims. A 'reformed whore', swept up by the 'cause' he was embraced as 'new blood' by a second generation Celtic-Polish enclave aggregated about aging warhorses and hard-drinking veterans, inspired by the oratory and determination of Zubr - now the focus for their movement. They dreamed wistfully of returning 'one day' in triumph to a Poland that no longer existed, nor would exist again. The 9-mm. Radom automatic was a token of their acceptance with a promise that 'direct action' might be necessary - some day, for which he prayed as fervently as any. *'Na Nowy Rok, przybywa dnia na kurzy krok!'* Little by little, like the steps of a 'little chick' from Wolfgang's painful New Year epiphany, that day might come.

Between these spoken lines I seemed to detect Zubr's own controlled anguish. In secret dreams he'd perhaps held too long the deluded image of that triumphant journey home at the wheel of an American jeep, his people wearing their campaign medals, heads bared in homage. *Ecstatic multitudes 'neath Baltic skies welcoming their liege. Bread, salt, garlands and kisses: roses and rosaries lining the route to Warszawa.* Perhaps that's why he drank, though the Poles were famous for their stainless gullets.

Wolfgang was his untutored mouthpiece, a quick-draw, foul-mouthed *Captain Flint*, perched on Zubr's broad piratical shoulder. He'd lowered the automatic so that it no longer directly threatened. I happened to notice Wolf's unsurprising wrist tattoo, a crude swastika.

A decade later, Natasha, anti-Semitism would erupt again in Poland. Ironically the swastika would re-appear as Nazi skinheads fought in the streets and at football matches signalling their frustration that the collapse of Communism had delivered them another disappointment in the failure of the new free market economy. In truth the old hatreds had swum always close beneath the surface of the Baltic States and in Russia too, after the fall. In the cemeteries, in the rusting mills and industrial towns swastikas are scraped on the iron. Daubed upon the walls. 'Nazis Rule': in Russian, German, English too, for the benefit of tourists? Young men, high on bootleg hooch: a cocktail of cleaning fluid and industrial waste, go mad or blind in derelict factories: in stinking stairwell or dripping underpass, where they hang themselves. It's no longer a state secret. How like Britain now, I gather, viewed from my Baltic eyrie.

Harry's, Arkadi Pietrokowski's roots were Polish despite his Lithuanian upbringing. He'd been a frequent visitor in the 'seventies and 'eighties to this cadre of expatriates, amongst others, rather than its stalwart. Feeling its pulse. Zubr's father had been his very close friend before and during World War Two. Zubr senior had been a cavalryman with a squadron that had halted a Panzer assault on Kutno, so Wolfgang related; riding down the tanks with *Molotov Cocktails* and routing them - before a *Stuka Geschwader* had blasted them to bits. The Count had survived, had been lucky not to have been executed at Katyn. Only *Operation Barbarossa*, the German invasion of the USSR saw both his and Harry's release, near to death, from the Soviet slave camps by order of Stalin who'd intended to use them as cannon fodder. Simply abandoned alongside railway tracks they were jeeringly invited to 'walk out of Russia' if they wanted to fight Fascism. Many died on the way but Harry and thousands of others had eventually found themselves re-grouped in Persia under General Anders with the British, receiving medical treatment and proper food, re-building the strengths that enabled them to fight valiantly alongside the Allies.

Despite my misgivings, the fact that I was buying 'goodwill' and information - and possibly *time*, I felt myself being drawn into all this. James was listening too, holding Amelia's hand. The atmosphere seemed a little more relaxed with this tale and its telling, regardless of the grim detail. But it occurred to me that now it was in our possession, our knowledge of these clandestine para-militaries, however loosely organised or amateur they might be, put us in an unenviable position of being complicit. At worst it had sealed our fate. The data had been freely gifted. So did this mean that our futures had been already decided - in that brief *sotto voce* discourse between Wolfgang and Zubr? Before he had driven away in the XK?

The sound of the now returning Jaguar most likely heralded those answers.

~.~

At Norwood Hill, Zubr had returned. Whether this was a good thing I hardly dared consider. I knew it meant that a decision of some sort would now be made regarding our futures, if we had any. Zubr drew Wolf aside and spoke quietly. Wolf left immediately in the Jaguar and we settled to waiting again. Zubr was concerned, he said, for Amelia's comfort and was at pains to ensure that she was not to worry about hers or her father's safety: that no harm would come to them. He didn't attempt to reassure me however.

It was a good hour before Wolfgang returned. He was in a rush, running up the path holding a small package. It turned out to be a Polaroid camera.

'Were you followed?' Zubr asked.

'No boss. I'd have shaken 'em anyway, *tossers*.'

Zubr walked casually into the kitchen and released Unger from the plumbing. He pushed him forward into the kitchen and into the light from the bay window. Unger's hands were still secured behind his back.

Wolfgang took six exposures then sped off again in the Jaguar. Unger was returned to the kitchen. Wolf was back within the hour and reported to Zubr, sotto voce. The Count's expression didn't change. He stood up and returned to the kitchen to collect Unger.

Unger was visibly trembling.

'So your cover story about being a para-military was true. All except the organisation you work for. And your actual name. Your name is Claus *Auer*. Your *Sturmbannführer* is Promnitz of *Promnitz, Strauss und Weissgerber: Actuaries and Commissioners of Oaths* with offices in Bremen and Bonn. Your party boss isn't Adolf von Thadden or his successor, what's his name, *Mussgnug*? You're not NPD, you're not even German League are you? Nor the *Deutsches Liga für Volk und Heimat*? Apparently, according to our sources, you are a hit man for something called the ELA, the *Eiserne Legion Ausland*. Your organisation is a far right outfit of dubious heritage, drawn from holocaust deniers and unreconstructed Nazis. Dept.VI SS killers who've remained at large in Germany and elsewhere in Europe. But especially from South America. What do you have to say?'

Auer had nothing to say.

~-~

It seemed that we were all to proceed to St. Albans, James driving the Vauxhall with Amelia and Wolfgang as passengers. Wolfgang of course with his 9-mm. I would have the privilege of driving the XK, since I knew exactly where I'd be going, with Zubr as passenger, resting his arm injury, Auer's Walther P-38 to hand. Claus Auer would be trussed up in the cramped Jaguar boot. Thomas' corpse would take Amelia's place in the boot of the Cavalier.

It was now late morning. Wolfgang reversed my rented car into the road. I noted in passing that the driver's window had been forced. The Cavalier was then backed under the carport enabling James and myself to load Thomas into the boot under a blanket. The occasional car and van was now passing in the road. With the Escort back in place the convoy set off through the lanes for Dorking and Leatherhead, joining the traffic crawling towards London.

My artist friend was unlikely to be at home in his mezzanine studio. He was not a full-time painter and was most probably at his desk at Building Research, Garston. Zubr had not indicated that I should telephone him to warn of our visit. Possibly he thought I might send him a coded message.

The car phone buzzed and Zubr engaged in a prolonged and vehement telephone call, partly in Polish with several words in English, including street names and addresses. To my surprise Zubr directed me to turn right onto the A25 and head for Dartford. It seemed he'd been thinking through a plan for our car boot cargoes.

Outside Dartford we pulled into a back lot behind a garage in a run down industrial area. A parked Jaguar Mk. 2 saloon flashed its lights and drove off at speed. Zubr told me to follow and we drove through a maze of back streets towards the Thames. We ended up in a lorry yard with trailers parked around and a loading bay at rear, its metal shutters half-raised. The Jaguar doors opened and three heavy-looking men emerged. Two more in overalls dropped like apes from the roller shutters. Zubr motioned me out as the Cavalier drew up behind. The metal gates to the yard closed behind us. It was raining again.

Auer was noticeably shaking as he was dragged unceremoniously out of the XK boot. Thomas's body was lifted from the Cavalier and carried towards a lorry trailer. Zubr turned to Wolfgang.

'Your automatic, Wolf,' he said. 'And your spent cartridge cases.'

Wolfgang hesitated for a microsecond before handing over the Radom, rummaging in his pockets for the cases. One of the heavies pulled on latex gloves. Zubr handed him the weapon. The man ejected the remaining cartridges into his gloved palm and pocketed them and then proceeded unhurriedly and thoroughly to clean the pistol with a rag. Auer watched in terror. Holding the Radom with the cloth the man advanced on Auer who was being held by two of the men. Gripping his right arm the pistol grip was forced into his palm and his index finger curled firmly around the trigger. I saw Auer taken, handcuffed by his left arm to the inside of the trailer frame and the gun tossed inside out of his reach next to Thomas's body. Auer cringed as Thomas's silenced Walther was discharged in the trailer near his head. This weapon too was cleaned and placed in Thomas's cold hand before the trailer door was slammed shut. A lorry tractor started up and reversed towards the trailer and hooked on. The gates were opened and the combination roared away.

Zubr turned to me. 'See? We're not cold-blooded killers.'

'There's not enough blood,' I said. Most of it had been over the Vauxhall radiator and the sofa!

The lorry trailer had once contained tobacco. It had been hijacked, re-painted and plated. It would be dumped in a lay-by somewhere and the police informed in a day or so.

'A forensics blood-spatter expert will see through it in a moment. The police will *never* buy into that scenario.'

'You're perfectly right,' he said. 'But how will *Auer* explain it?'

~-~

Perhaps, Natasha, societies when emerging from tyranny, are forced into a period of degrading hopelessness for many of the young and disenfranchised, before democracy matures, or before their governments abandon the experiment like they reluctantly abandoned that other one: to reclaim the nationalism and pride that was there at the beginning of the Twentieth Century. Can we thus explain Russia's resorting to jingoism in the Twenty-first? Gathering up all that pride and re-vivifying their armed forces. It's a dangerous world, my dear. Never more so than the present.

It was the early evening when we'd arrived at Inkerman Road. *Sebastopol Towers* was a looming grey house standing aloof at the end of a street of tall Victorian semis.

'I'm sorry, Louen,' I said. He'd answered my rap on the brass wolf's head doorknocker wearing his painter's smock - all barrel-chested three feet six of him. A founder member of 'Dwarf Power' and a damn fine portrait painter.

We followed him inside to his softly-lit living room, cluttered with books on artists, sci-fi and aviation that overflowed from their shelves and littered the low table. Kropotkin, his anarchist ginger cat hissed and made himself scarce at the intrusion, squeezing through a gap in the French windows into the walled Zen garden. A two foot statue of Anubis stared enigmatically from the fireplace. A Great Western Railway clock ticked over the mantle.

'This is 'Count Zubr' and back there is his minder, Wolfgang.' My gesture indicated my companions. Zubr bowed and offered his hand. James and Amelia were squeezing though the door. Behind them Wolfgang just stared.

'And this is James Delcroix and his daughter, Amelia. My good friend, Louen Richard Henry Jones, Prince of Brecon'

'How do you do. Please sit down if you can find somewhere,' Louen said unflappably. 'Drinks anyone?'

'I am sorry to land on you like this. I wasn't able to warn you. I should point out that Wolf is armed.'

'Oh, really,' said the dwarf. 'Nothing *too* deadly, I hope.'

Wolfgang glowered. Zubr smiled. 'Excuse our intruding,' he said. 'We merely wish to collect the briefcase.'

Louen gave me a penetrating look. 'It's OK,' I said slowly. 'I'm handing it over. There's been enough…. Well, I want to avoid any trouble.'

Louen rose and made his way into the kitchen and opened a heavy door. The sunken-cheeked death mask of a previous occupant hung from the handle. This portal I knew gave access to the basement, his personal *Salon de Refuses*.

'Do you want to give me a hand?' he asked, looking at me through the living room door.

'Sure, if it's alright.'

I looked at Zubr.

'No, no. Wolf will assist you.' Firm but obliging. 'Give Mr. Jones a hand, Wolf.'

Louen clicked on the basement light and descended the steps. Wolfgang followed with the Walther in his pocket, confident I was sure that the dwarf would be no trouble. Louen, I reflected, had a sharp mind and a great sense of humour. He had been known to arrange 'happenings' in an earlier time, such as fifteen 'little people' in boiler suits lugging a fibreglass Firestreak air-to-air missile around the Metropolitan Line, freaking out London commuters.

A minute later Wolfgang re-appeared with a heavy brown paper package in his arms which he carried into the living room. He was followed by Louen whose eyes were fixed on my own. His hands were behind his back. All other eyes were on the package.

Suddenly we heard the loud, unmistakable 'click-click' of some 'big mother' being double-cocked. Wolf stood pale and rigid in the middle of the room with the briefcase while Louen calmly described just what it was that Wolf could feel pressed hard into the base of his spine.

I stepped forward and withdrew the P-38 from his coat pocket.

Louen had planted his *Gebruder Mauser Rakete Pistole* firmly against Wolfgang's lower back, just above the coccyx. James relieved him of the briefcase being careful not to stand in front of him. Louen had described how the 25-mm projectile would pass clean through Wolfgang if something upset him and the second trigger pressure was accidentally pulled. Zubr sat silently where he was, eyeing the scene inscrutably. Only Louen and I knew that not only was there no flare projectile in that old collectable but the firing pin had been filed down fifty years ago.

I ordered Wolfgang to kneel on the floor while James knelt across his legs and tied his hands and feet with string which Amelia had obligingly found in the kitchen. It was not at all that I considered Zubr any less dangerous, but it improved the odds, and I had some doubts whether he'd stand for such an indignity and might be moved to call our bluff. But I had James carefully disarm Zubr as I covered him lightly with the automatic, making sure he'd seen the safety released. The dwarf had lowered the muzzle of his pyrotechnic cannon to everyone's apparent relief.

'So, gentlemen,' I said. 'This puts us into a *slightly* different negotiating position.' I tried not to sound too smug. 'And brilliant work, Dick, by the way.'

'Well I knew I had to do something dramatic with the clues you gave me. I hoped that I was reading it right. Reversing my name order….and you've never in your life called me Louen. You know how much I *hate* it.'

I faced Zubr. 'This cursed briefcase has already cost lives; Peter's, Victor's and nearly mine. I don't exclude the recent Thomas. I do not intend that it should cost any more. Neither do I feel inclined to just hand it over without a good argument. So you'd better tell me what you know. I should warn you that if you do try anything clever I *will* shoot. I am no expert with a handgun so I can't be certain where my bullet will hit. I can however guarantee that it will hurt. But first you can start by telling me who you really are.'

~-~

The Count sat back in his chair.

'Relax, Wolf,' he said with an ironic smile. 'I think John, James, Amelia….. perhaps even the *Prince of Brecon* can be trusted with my identity.'

He looked at me with his yellow-flecked eyes. A thousand-yard stare: that top predator gaze, as if he were surveying his own Serengeti menu. It said: *I could take you if I wanted to, even with a bullet hole in my arm and you wouldn't stand a chance, my friend.*

'Yes,' I said, holding the Walther out of his reach. 'Let's all be civilised for the sake of the children.'

'I am Josef Count Wieniawa-Klimaszinksi, but you can call me 'Klim'. I would say 'at your service' but for the circumstances.'

'So what's this all about... Klim?'

'What it's all about.......it's all about the restoration of the autonomy of Polish statehood. If that takes the form of a returning regent as pro-tem head of state then so be it. But more than that. We believe that the great Litho-Polish pan-Slavic state, a buffer of Christian democracy, decency and freedom against the might of the Soviet Bloc will soon be a possibility for the first time in recent history. After centuries of Russian domination.'

Wieniawa-Klimaszinski's face seemed to glow with ardour, his eyes lit with fervid patriotism.

'Do you think that a country that fought against a million bastard Reds with their bare hands and teeth should have laid down for a mob of Huns? What was this German masquerade, this 'master race' *thing*, harbouring a fantastic delusion of world domination as birthright, sanctified through their pure fucking Aryan bloodline? By what perverted political contortion was any credibility afforded such mendacious documents as they signed?'

He breathed deeply. It was as if he had to keep repeating this history lesson to people who really weren't interested, were even ignorant of their own rich history. He seemed to be having trouble controlling his anger.

'We were told by the Alliance, "Do not mobilise. Don't give them the excuse to invade. Don't rock the boat." Then Heydrich trumped up a border incident with fresh cadavers in Polish uniforms at the Glewitz radio station. We had trusted in the Alliance and were caught between two monstrosities. The rest is history.'

I knew this. When the surviving Poles were freed and allowed to fight they fought brilliantly for their freedom and for ours.

'Apart from that breathing space between two wars, very soon now for the first time in centuries, John, Poland will be free. After the massacres at Katyn. The rising, and the massacres of the Warsaw Ghetto while the bloody Red Army waited for the SS to do its murder. At a moment when the USSR will be at its weakest, its most demoralised and rotting from the Kremlin downwards, we will make our move. Poland will be free again. Walesa's socialist revolution may well be the first step, but we don't believe he can sustain power even if he grasps it. He is a welder not a statesman.'

'Who's 'we'? The *Royal* 'we', is it?'

'My organisation.'

'Does it have a name, this organisation?'

'It has a name, but shall be nameless.'

'Come, come, Klim. Why be shy? After all, it must be *some* organisation to be able to contemplate such a coup. Polish Government in exile and all that, is it? Is there a Lithuanian counterpart? Or are you taking that as read?'

'There are elements of such a body of course. They have been consulted.'

'Yes, but what do you call yourselves? It is a legal or an illegal association. Do you operate above or below the line, or both?'

'You can call it the Henryk Joszewski Co-operative Society if you like.'

'Wasn't he the character who tried to unify Poland and the Ukraine?' This from James.

Klim's hooded eyes widened. 'My, my,' he said. 'A European historian in our midst.'

'It was something Harry had said, that's all.'

Klim's eyes narrowed again sharply.

'So what is it you need?' I asked. 'What is it you are searching for so fervently? The Holy Grail?'

'This is too big a matter to be discussed openly.'

'I should have thought the re-unification of Lithuania and Poland was *itself* too great a matter, and you've already provided chapter and verse on that.'

'Revolutions, coups d'etat, all need to be bankrolled.'

'And you want to know where the money is?'

'I think *you* may know, John.'

'Let me see, does that make me feel powerful, or vulnerable?'

'You tell me.'

'Not powerful, Klim. Not at all. That's why I'm holding Auer's little equaliser.'

'So do you know where it is?'

'I don't even know *what* it is.'

'Should I believe you?'

'Look, I have had only the most cursory rummage through this burned and battered case. So if that's where the clue is secreted, I have no

666

idea what it is or what form it takes.'

'So, of which *Harry* are we talking?' Klim was looking at James. James looked startled. 'Oh, just an acquaintance.' Covering up. 'Drinks anyone?' asked the dwarf.

Chapter 46.
Farnborough: Late Summer 1988

Saturday morning, bright with a fresh breeze and puffy cumulus. I make my way through the crowds below the grassy rise and the familiar blue and white-striped exhibition tents, SBAC banners flying. I walk between the shiny rows of aircraft: light planes, feeder-liners, combat trainers, turboprops, advanced mock-ups and helicopters. There's the rank smell of jet fuel, the roar of something making a low pass; flurried motion among the long lenses, the whirr of shutter motors. Dominating all is the mighty An 24 transport, twice the size of a 747, its huge nose cargo door hinged upwards, like a cross–channel ferry. It really is Russian Week at Farnborough.

There's a sense of excitement that will keep me coming back to events like these. It's a public display day. Normally I would attend the Show for the press days, interviewing representatives of British Aerospace, CASA, Aerospatiale, General Dynamics, McDonnell-Douglas, and a few dozen other aerospace companies for my magazine: making new contacts, meeting old friends and greeting familiar faces on the Rolls-Royce and Pratt & Whitney stands; taking pictures and gathering material for freelance articles I'd sell to the aviation press.

Brian Thomas, the swashbuckling CEO of BAeS, Prestwick hails me jovially from the door of an incongruously camouflaged BA 146.

'What do you think of my 'bomber'?' he asks with a piratical laugh.

I smile and wave. This time I am going straight ahead as directed, past the multi-bladed MD-81 Un-Ducted Fan Demonstrator, ignoring a Swedish Air Force *Metroliner* III with a massive AEW antenna pack over the fuselage. I'm walking towards the two Mikoyan MiG 29s, the first ever to have been seen in the United Kingdom.

These formidable state-of-the-art Soviet fighters are impressive and lethally beautiful, like hooded cobras. I approach them closely, almost cautiously, as if they might strike. A single-seat MiG stands alongside a two-seater, each with its huge square under-slung jet intakes, high-set, clear-vision canopies, sharp radar noses. But it's not these grey-green supersonic fighters that I am focussed on. Parked nearby, alongside the 'heavy metal', in glossy-red paint, is a twin-engined propeller-driven aeroplane. It has a long tapering nose, pointed wings and a framed canopy for the tandem crew. Beautiful in a very different way from the MiGs. It is the sole surviving De Havilland DH.88 Comet, winner of the 1934 MacRobertson Air Race: Britain-to-Australia, which had seen three Comets participate. The famous registration, G-ACSS is emblazoned in white on fuselage and wings. The nose bears the sponsor's name, *Grosvenor House*. For the hotel.

I look at my watch. At nine minutes past eleven precisely, her trademark appointed time, she is there.

She is wearing wrap-around sunglasses but I'd recognise her anyway, looking as she had in the Sophienfriedhof-Kirche, Berlin; much younger than her years. Stephanie…Alexa.

She wears a white blouse with a thread of gold at her smooth neck. A grey knee-length skirt matches her leather shoulder bag. She carries a cream jacket. Stylish, ageless, she moves from the static display area indicating I should follow. Walking unhurriedly we head for the refreshment tent. I have a sudden feeling of nausea and almost stumble as I recall Ramstein and Peter Neumann. I'm tasting burning oil and I smell the scorched flesh that stayed in my nostrils for weeks. I touch the crown of my head involuntarily. The hair has re-grown although it's shorter than I'm used to wearing it.

She sits in a cafeteria chair and I get us drinks from the bar.

'Good to see you… Stephanie.'

'You too, Johann.' Her voice is even huskier than I remember. Deepened by age perhaps. She's removed her sunglasses. The Nordic goddess eyes perhaps a little more set back, but I have to think she's sixty-seven at least. Her body is that of a much younger woman. Her hair has grown a little, looks softer, giving her a more youthful appearance. I realise for the first time, with a little shock, that she reminds me of my long dead Angelika. I wonder if she too can sing *Surabaya Johnny*. Probably, if cover demanded it, I think.

'Johann, back there where we met. The MiGs. You know I picked that rendezvous particularly.' She half smiles but her eyes are intense.

I was thinking she was being a little melodramatic or about to make a Teutonic quip. Something about *glasnost* invasion tactics; the first time that MiGs had been displayed in Britain. The elephant in the room, thin end of a 'Trojan wedge' or some other half-serious Prussian warning. *At every stage in this saga, Natasha, I am forced to consider that nothing is ever what it seems.*

'Johann, darling. That pretty De Havilland aeroplane. The racer.

Komet.' She pronounces it with the accent on the second syllable. 'It very nearly played the key role in what might have changed history at the time of the invasion of France. But for a technical 'cock-up' Johann, the war would have taken a completely different course. Either it would have stopped in its tracks, or Hitler could not have lost. Either way it would have been very different for Europe and the world. Pressure would have been off Britain at the crucial time. Dunkirk might not have happened or at least the evacuation would have been less costly for the Brits. Maybe the *Sitzkrieg,* as you called it, would have gone on for longer…. Either way a lot of lives might have been saved.'

I look at her in disbelief.

'That little wooden racer?' I say.

It had been the forerunner of the phenomenal De Havilland Mosquito of course, so it was a gallant predecessor, but really…..Mosquitoes would have been hard pressed to have changed history had a whole *bomber wing* been available in 1940: at a time when the yellow paint was barely dry on the prototype.

'Never mind, that's not what I want to talk to you about. *That* story will keep, but it's connected with the German Underground movement, to one man in particular. It would have meant a one-way ticket to Dachau at least for anyone remotely involved. I myself was in Norway, on the opposite side, *Liebling,* aged 19. Transmitting my virgin observations for the Abwehr. I was a believer then. I would have gone to hell for the Führer. Unfortunately many of us did, including all my brothers. *Ein gutes Nazi-Mädchen!* That was me, I'm sorry to say.'

She'd once told me she was never a Nazi. Reconstructed or otherwise. Maybe this was a day for unvarnished truth.

She's paused and looks very pensive for a moment, and quite sad. For a Prussian.

'Please darling, get me another drink.'

~-~

She begins to unravel some more recent history. But before she can unpick it, she must first weave her own tapestry, spinning the legend as she's imagined it, Natasha. Good spooks know how to tell a tale, to fill in the detail. Keeping it real.

Imagine an elderly man, shrunken now with age and the thing that will kill him. Once he had been a hale fellow. What you'd call the 'muscular jocular' type, she tells me. Gets on with everybody, or so he thinks, *nicht wahr?*

Her own tradecraft dates from before the war, so she knows about these meetings: but much has to be surmise. I see him as she describes in Morozov Park by Moscow's autumnal light. In the middle distance gold, white pearl and lapis lazuli gleam soft among the clustered spires; a gilded two-barred cross declaims Christ risen above the misty tree tops. The red star also shines there: an uneasy partnering. *I know it well, Johann*, Krasnaya Presnya District, two kilometres west of Moscow. A stooped babushka sweeps the dry leaves that husk about the pathways and benches. Wrapped against the chill, lovers walk by slowly like lovers everywhere. Cold to be sitting out-of-doors especially at his age.

After a while a middle-aged man, well-padded in a dark overcoat and fur cap comes by, sits next to the older man. He rummages in his overcoat, lights a cigarette.

'Imagine if we could have eavesdropped on their conversation. I could have scripted several versions myself of how it might have played, Johann. But I didn't need to. Somebody, it could have been me, tossed a matchbox near to the bench while brushing around and tidying the grass verge. Wouldn't that have been clever of me darling, at my age. Tracking down 'Merlin' after all that time. Gaining a visa under an old workname with a communist background attached to it – I do have some useful passports and a Cuban identity that works well for me still. I wouldn't have used any of my official identities this time, BND forged passport or my *Staatssicherheit* ID. This would have been personal and I didn't want any security loopholes.'

Stephanie reaches into her bag and withdraws a matchbox-sized receiver/recorder.

'It's Japanese, darling. Made by a subsidiary of one of the big companies, Akigusa KK. Dinky, don't you think? With glue or a magnet it becomes a 'limpet'. Here, put this small earpiece in your ear. The tape has been re-recorded and extended to include my translation, so the third voice you will hear is my own, to explain all.'

Stephanie places the other earpiece in her own ear.

An elderly voice is speaking Russian.

'Bewailing wistfully that he'd never *actually* met *Wittgenstein*,' Stephanie says on the tape.

The other voice repeats the other's observation, turned around with what sounds like only mild indifference.

'Lytton Strachey I knew. And Bell. Later of course, Guy Burgess. Maclean. All of the Cambridge Persuasion. But Wittgenstein was a little before my time.'

'Embroidery, darling!' Stephanie murmurs over the top.

The first voice continued, listing methodically how Yuri or his department had run Blunt of course. And Philby.

'Maclean, Burgess…… Gone now mostly, except Blunt who's been 'defrocked'. Kim Philby's as much of a tragedy as Burgess ever was at the end. They'd embraced their inevitable alcoholism like true Russians. I don't see Philby much longer for this world. Rufine Ivanovna looks sick with worry herself - according to our mutual friend.'

'Actually, darling, Philby died in May,' Stephanie murmurs. 'Two months after this recording. Final release from his sixth floor Moscow birdcage; a minor state burial and a volley over his grave. The headstone's pretty basic though, just his name and the dates. In a few years no-one will know who the fuck he was.'

There's a pause on the tape as footsteps pass by.

'You would have run me I'm sure if I'd been ten or fifteen years younger. I'd pretended to let Orlov recruit me, to provide an additional veneer of legitimacy. But in fact I'd already made my own arrangements years ago; worked both sides of the street and down the middle my whole career. Anywhere there was traffic.'

There is the hint of a Russian smile on the tape.

Yuri says nothing. Whatever it is that Sergei wants to tell him he will tell him in his own good time. Yuri didn't get to be the best controller of KGB agents within MI5 and the Establishment by being too eager, *by talking when he should be listening, darling.* He's just sitting, observing, though he's not once looked at Sergei Kamov since he'd seated himself. He crosses his legs and sits forwards, shielding his cigarette in his palm.

'I have a tumour, you know,' Sergei states matter-of-factly.

'Secrets and lies,' says Stephanie - not on the tape, almost to herself, 'They eat you up inside. And guilt is a *canker* on the soul.'

About the tumour. Yuri didn't know.

'Sorry,' *says the other voice.* 'Is it operable?'

'No.'

Stephanie snorts in derision here.

The silence resumes.

'Did you ever know of my part in *Alberich?*'

This is it then, the golden kernel of this meeting. Yuri is silent for a while. 'No, Sergei.'

Stephanie stops the tape for a moment to explain.

'To admit he'd not even heard of *Alberich* would be to lose face, Johann. But information always has some value even if it's out of date because one never knows what might have influenced events. Learning about that is to learn from a secret history. Knowing what part this old agent had played in some unheard of operation was perhaps no less important. Consider; it is sometimes more important to know what your enemy knows, not just to know something you think your enemy doesn't.'

Stephanie's finger hovers over the switch.

'*Liebling*, Sergei-Merlin had been pensioned-off years ago and had not been operational since just after Kim Philby's defection in '63. He was a mysterious and complex character for an Englishman, Philby I mean,' says Stephanie and makes a wry face at my look.

'Yes *some* of them are clever, Johann, but really most are not. I was as good a female agent as any in my day. I could do *anything* a man could do, backwards and in high heels!' she smiled. 'Enemy agents! I could run rings around most of them. The dangerous ones, like those who caught me in 1942 were resourceful. Some may be incredibly devious and Philby was certainly one of those. But he was extremely vain; probably spied on himself in hotel rooms!'

In her opinion his acts of betrayal seemed to be as much a *raison d'etre* as his contempt for the British Establishment. 'Sergei's' attitude to the bourgeois social conventions of the British seemed rather to mimic Philby's, she'd said. Both had sneered at the sentimentality of the *duraki*, the hoi polloi that'd failed to seize the initiative after two world wars. Both had felt that they belonged to an élite with a moral right to decide the fate of the workers, lay waste a whole country if needs be: bring on ruin and misery if it undermined rule by capitalism and class with all its extravagant hypocrisy. But their treachery was narcissistic, driven by their vanity and delusions of grandeur. Their cells had damaged Britain's intelligence services and by association those of NATO.

'It seemed that to outwit MI5 in the nineteen sixties you only had to utter a denial of being an enemy agent, Johann. On newsreels no-one could fail to note Philby's averted eye; that *thing* he did with his mouth each time he denied his treachery, a rolling jaw motion. *Very* strange.'

That the faith the United States security service placed in the 'special relationship' was strained to breaking point could in truth be laid at both their doors. Not that she gave a damn.

'I don't give a damn because like your own MI5, stuffed with Soviet agents, the BND was totally infiltrated with Stasi. It was a bloody joke Johann! That's why I used my private issue Cuban passport when I went over.'

She fixed me with her Nordic stare.

'The KGB is totally efficient and ruthless most of the time. Just sometimes when they put together an operation with the Stasi, their most faithful adherents, they tend to 'over-egg' the pudding, if you know what I mean. Each committee has its little power struggle, each department needs to be seen to contribute something of inestimable value to the operation: get itself noticed, warm congratulations from above when it all goes well. Dangerous though if it all crumbles to dust. Even more dangerous for the plan or the individual if they have differing agendas. Or someone is working for himself out of the long shadow of Brezhnev, or in the new nervous uncertainty of Gorbachev's vision.'

For a moment I am almost beginning to get an inkling of what she meant.

'Philby and *Kamov* were 'Angels'. She told me, going back to the meeting. 'That is fully-evolved members of the elitist undergraduate association that grew out of the *Conversazione Society* at Cambridge: drawn from St. John's, Trinity and King's Colleges and known more commonly as the *Cambridge Apostles*.'

Anthony Blunt, now stripped of his knighthood and the late Guy Burgess were among that self-regarding élite.

I am still trying to make sense of all this. Perhaps I don't have the intellectual wattage but something doesn't seem right with this scenario and I was more confused than ever. As I was learning, nothing is ever as it seems. And the *Acts of the Apostles*, covered by Official Secrets, were still emerging over the years. They'd betrayed us from the start.

~-~

From my retrospective Baltic retreat, Natasha, I wouldn't have questioned an old spook's need for absolution. A lonely, perhaps embittered man facing his own mortality would call on the nearest thing to a father confessor, his controller, a handler, who sometimes had to be a hand-holder; those who've controlled agents from George Blake to Anthony Blunt, who understand men's frailties, the way Sergei did too. Still he whispered it – it's difficult to hear on the tape but Stephanie's had a go at re-interpreting it:

'Yuri. Why do we do what we do? Because we can't help ourselves? Because we are mischief makers? Because we are insurrectionist? Perhaps all of those things, yet at heart we are idealistic.'

Stephanie completes the line, 'Because we see the utopian ideal always besmirched by the grubby-fingered imperialistic speculators, international financiers, the bankers, the capitalist war mongers. Usual Marxist diatribe, Johann, but always with a hardy kernel of undeniable truth yet faked on this tape for the benefit of gullible Western ears.'

The tape continues with Yuri's reply.

'Sergei. I respect you for your work, but I didn't come to sit in park to get sentimental listening to an old man's maudlin regrets for betraying his own. You want redemption, go to a priest. You want to talk about old times, sure. Who knows what will turn up? You could have made appointment; come to my office, drink vodka, but ok, I need the exercise and Morozov is pleasant walk from Kremlin, not too far. You have pension. Stay retired. Like you did fifteen years ago. Enjoy what you can. You have hero's medals from grateful USSR. Evidence of your success in chosen profession. I am sorry for your illness......'

Then, quieter…'Yuri, can I trust you? Well don't answer. It doesn't matter if I can or I can't. But I sure don't trust your 'office furniture' or, heaven forbid, the telephone. My life will be over soon. But there is something that I'd like to finish. Too many of my schemes went off course or were compromised. But then I recall that they were all for short term advantage, all about myself gaining power, running my own Joes. Like you, I invented many of them, not only to disguise my sources, but for the payroll. My *Creatures of Prometheus* someone once called them.'

~-~

Natasha, you may think as I did that there is just too much information to have been recorded on a tape boldly dropped to eavesdrop on this top secret conversation. Unsurprisingly so did Alexa. It was packed full of chronological story-telling, every blank filled-in, every tee crossed. So over-egged it wasn't true.

'Johann. They had tried to bloody set me up, Stasi, KGB. They wanted this information to get out so the whole thing was scripted. The telephone call transcripts setting up the meeting, passed to my department at BND, all contrived. Even gave me four day's notice to organise my flight and visa! How very convenient! Do you think they would have sat there on that bench while Merlin recited *Pasternak* or *Mayerkowsky*. No they'd have passed the time of day and some vitally important coded matter of state and then be gone, or have walked about a bit if they wanted to be more secure.'

'So what is it about? Why entrap you and then not hold you?'

'Because they wanted me to *do* something I suppose. Cast-off. Having made me feel clever that I'd managed to record this deep secret.

676

So that I should react in some way. They'd cast the lure and were reeling me in. Which means they are watching me.'

'But they could just have arrested you in the park. I imagine that most of those 'strolling lovers' were KGB as well.' I was warming to this version of her story, although the thought that *we* might be under surveillance right now was unsettling.

'They didn't want *me*, Johann. They could have picked me up any time if they wanted to. The Stasi knew I worked for the BND, it was one of my best qualifications. Markus Wolf, HVA Chief - *Stasi* to you Johann - he had so many people working at BND offices it was necessary to have some reciprocity! They got so close to Willy Brandt, remember, it forced his resignation. It is considered that something like one in five East German civilians is an *Inoffizielle Mitarbeiter,* a Stasi informant or works for them directly.'

'They could have arrested and tortured me, or just tied me up and forced me to appear in one of their top secret pornographic movies: made for the sordid consumption of Stasi officers and Party members. Compromising me both sides of the wire if then distributed.'

The tape continued, recounting how 'Kamov' had supped with a long spoon at many tables. Here in Moscow, with Beria and his coterie, *and survived.* Thirty years ago, he'd bragged to Yuri. And before that others of the inner circle. In the War he'd handled material from the *Red Orchestra* and sent it both ways, although London of course had passed it straight back to Moscow Centre.

'Happily they didn't know it was from me,' he'd smiled for the tape.

'The *Rote Kapelle,* the Red Orchestra was a very effective Soviet espionage organisation in Germany, Johann. Bormann was feeding them everything. Gestapo Chief Müller was also dealing traitorously, both bastards hedging their bets. Both knew which way the wind was blowing in 1943 and it was from the East. Poor old Canaris did his best to scupper Hitler's plans too, but not for personal gain; early on behind the scenes, playing a very deadly game. Dr. Otto John was another member of Rote Kappelle and he transmitted key information to the Allies through Madrid on the significance of Peenemünde. Soon enough it was bombed all to hell. Six hundred scientists, technicians and workers killed and, for a while anyway, the V2 rocket programme, and so much other advanced weapons research destroyed.'

She gave a wintry smile,

'Godammit, no wonder we lost the bloody War!'

The information on Peenemünde originating through Madrid was news to me, but I recalled *Operation Crossbow* and the key role played by the RAF Photo Reconnaissance units with their long-range, camera-equipped Spitfires along with the Photographic Interpretation department in verifying the data. Also their work in identifying both fixed and mobile cruise and ballistic missile sites in Germany.

'Anyway, Johann; KGB, they give out all this verifiable information and some new stuff - or new to me, to make their final pitch irresistible,' said Stephanie. 'You'll see.'

On the tape Sergei pauses.

'Probably looking at the tree-lined horizon, observing the old woman moving away with her brush and wheeled dustbin,' says Stephanie. 'Walking towards the Morozov memorial'

The Young Pioneer, Pavlik Morozov, had been murdered in the early 1930s, *allegedly*, by his grandfather for the boy's denunciation of his own father for the crime of hoarding grain.

'It's covered in *Taubenscheiße* now, Johann. I take that as a hopeful sign.'

I smile at the ironic thought of pigeons crapping all over a statue to betrayal at the heart of the nuclear family, idealised as communist martyrdom; the very spirit of Dzerzhinsky.

Mayerkowsky was the true martyr. Denounced by the Writers' Council, he'd shot himself.

Sergei says to Yuri, 'I'm being frank with you because it doesn't matter now. In 1941, I was a top V-Mann. Possibly the very top. In Gestapo Müller's confidence, although I think he was always suspicious of me. Of course he was probably a spy himself, ironically. I'd already met Heydrich in the Spring of 1940. In fact I nearly stitched him up in my magnum opus, and he never knew I'd planned it…but that's for another time: if I am spared……But through him I was able to penetrate to Himmler's circle.'

'I supplied some good information and some top-rate British intelligence, which the NKVD sent via diplomatic pouch to a Promethean agent in Turkey, and so I was able to place myself in good standing at Prinz Abrecht Strasse and the ministries, and of course I was engaged in reciprocal trade. I even gave some quite high grade stuff to the British on occasions just to keep myself in good odour there, suspicions being smoothed over by our people inside SIS. But you know all this. I stayed shy of the Americans though. I was introduced around but as I wasn't sure how they worked I was keen not to compromise my cover. If I'd realised how vulnerable they were in the early days I might have tried my luck. But there's no point regretting that now. In some ways keeping my distance there probably ensured my own survival when others

were exposed.'

'In any event, it was on Himmler's direct order that I was sent to Southern Ireland. A reconnaissance.'

Stephanie stops the tape there and tells me the rest, as she learned it, partly confirmed by the tape, but also from another, more poignant source, which led her to the conclusion that the main thrust of the story was quite genuine.

It involved her youngest brother.

~-~

'Johann, where were you for one week in February 1986?'

Stephanie catches me off guard. Before I can speak she answers her own question.

'I'll tell you where you were. Dubai!'

She is absolutely right. I was there for the First Arab Air Fair and I still have an insipid blue tie with the logo to prove it. After the rustling cockroaches and other delights of Madame Kara's '*Go vay!*' Hammersmith emporium I'd wearily boarded the British Airways 747 as part of the Sahara Group Publishing team - a sort of *ad hoc* aviation correspondent. We'd flown via Kuwait, descending with engines idling and lights out, reducing out IR signature to avoid SAMs on the way in.

'And somebody met you there? At Dubai?'

I'd rubbed shoulders with scores of people at the Air Fair. But I understood what she'd meant.

'Omar?'

'Exactly!'

I recalled an air-conned exhibition hall, Bedouin-style. Lines of well turned-out Europeans and Americans respectfully watching the procession move regally among the stands. The official opening and speeches. The Sheikh and his robed entourage, brothers and cousins, ministers and security stopping to inspect the latest flight simulator, admire a showroom model of a sleek bizzjet; his Highness gracing us with a nod and a smile, occasional handshakes for the favoured. In their wake a flock of also-rans, seagulls trailing the plough. Including Omar.

'Hello, sir.'

I'd looked round to see a small-boned, olive-skinned man in his mid-twenties wearing a silk shirt and a beaming smile. Dapper, round-faced with a fine moustache he could have been from anywhere east of Tripoli. His snake-hipped movement suggested a Siamese ballroom dancer. In fact he was an Iranian student of aerodynamics and part-time carpet salesman. If he'd combined the two careers he'd have made fortune at the Palladium.

'Have I the honour in encountering the esteemed Mr. John-Johannes Morris?'

My Germanised *Ersatz* patronymic narrowed the field in establishing mutual acquaintances. Abed, handing out free back numbers of the Anglo-Arab magazine arched a quizzical eyebrow.

'I am Morris,' I replied in slight puzzlement.

'I am delighted to meet you, sir. I have read many times your articles. Your treatise on predicted spin characteristics of tailless pushers. Tailless is my own specialism if I may make so bold. It was of seminal import in my design of small, prototype UAVs.'

'Well I'm happy it found an appreciative readership.' It had in truth been no more than three pages with some diagrams in a minor aviation magazine.

Omar elaborated on his 'specialism' at length and I realised as we chatted that he had some advanced ideas on thermoplastics and composite aircraft construction and design that could some day revolutionise light aircraft development, manned or otherwise.

'If I could broach a matter with which I have been entrusted, sir,' he said with his beaming smile after the pleasantries. 'I have a request to make which I hope you will not find burdensome.'

I gave a non-committal smile.

'It is the matter of this volume, sir.' He promoted a polythene bag from *stage left* on his forearm to *stage front*, and unravelled a maroon book of thick proportions and some antiquity. It bore the unmistakeable signature of the Bard, gilded and embossed.

'This is the 1923 edition of the *Complete Works*, sir. Acquired especially and with much difficulty. Published by *British Books Limited: London* containing coloured prints of Shakespearian actors of great merit, by painters of note: including John Sargent, Alma-Tadema, Landseer, Millais and Holman Hunt.'

I was rendered speechless which didn't matter because Omar rattled-on.

'I have deliberately left it unwrapped, so that you can see that it is not hollowed-out to contain illegal substances, nor is anything inserted between the leaves, as you will see if I shake it, thus.'

He tilted the book, decorative spine uppermost. The gilded floriation suggested William Morris. He carefully riffled the pages and what looked like a dead moth fell out. But that was all. *Theatre in the Round*.

'What I am asking, sir, is that you would very kindly carry this volume to Herr Hans-Peter Neumann in Berlin, the next time you travel there.'

I refrained from asking how he knew that I was acquainted with Peter. Peter knew a lot of people from all over the place. And he knew I'd be at the Air Fair.

'Why not just post it?' I suggested.

'Ah, because it is a very special gift. I would wish it only to be delivered directly into his hands. No courier. Just friend to friend.'

My bullshit antennae were twitching overtime.

'So what's in it? Microdots?'

'I can assure you sir, it came straight from the collection of a noted antiquarian. Untouched and uncontaminated by military intelligence implants, concealment devices or systems. Furthermore it does nor harbour any virulent contagious disease, evidenced by my freely handing it."

'You seem very familiar with the terminology for a carpet salesman, Omar.'

'It's the company I keep, sir,' he said with a grin.

~-~

Stephanie was looking at me with an enigmatic smile.

'You see Johann. You'd already been vetted and recruited in Hannover and you didn't know it. I am sorry if you feel we'd used you, but it was better that you knew *absolutely* nothing. And after all it was only a collectable book. Not a concealment device or anything more sinister.'

'So what was it then, apart from the works of Shakespeare?'

'A codebook.'

I'd already guessed that. And to think I'd left it in my room at the Metropolitan for three days; shuttling back-and-fore to the Show in ten *dirham* taxis.

'So how did it work?'

'It was both very elaborate and simple. Above all it was completely uncrackable.'

'I thought all codes were crackable. Alan Turing and the Bletchley Park code-breakers proved that didn't they?

'They had help, darling. They had captured Enigma machines.'

~-~

'So how did it work, this Shakespeare code?'

'Well, we weren't certain it was the correct Shakespeare until you delivered the book. Only the courier knew and he'd been briefed to purchase it in an antiquarian bookshop by our agent in the Levant. It was Harry's special area. His man had spent a month tracking down that particular edition. Harry, Hans-Peter and me, we couldn't take the risk that it would be lost in the post. Nor could it be entrusted to just any courier.'

In the way of researchers and the old spooks network these three had been drawn together in Hannover and Berlin and found they had colleagues and 'agents' in common and were able to assist in putting individuals and families back together from the blind diaspora of war. Which had become their individual humanitarian aims in life in 'retirement', if I could swallow that for the present, as much as spooks ever retire. But when it came to security matters they knew the value of a cut-out.

In any event, Alexa told me, she had not retired. Recruited 1946 in occupied Germany by a top US Army Intelligence Officer with a very German name serving with the Strategic Services Unit (later to become the CIA). With her looks and sharp mind she had been transferred to the Gehlen Organisation for counter espionage, part of a team tasked with detecting and reporting on Communist agents infiltrating the US Sector of Berlin. General Reinhard Gehlen who'd been with German wartime intelligence in the *Heer Ost* was a specialist with knowledge of Soviet military intelligence and had much experience in interrogating Russian prisoners. The Gehlen Organisation itself employed hundreds of ex-SS personnel, including war criminals who were protected for their importance as experienced intelligence officers, perhaps most notorious being Klaus Barbie.

'You've heard of him?'

'The Butcher of Lyon. Naturally.'

'Exactly. But even some lower grade—muscle came from the SS ranks.'

The de-Nazification programme and non-fraternisation rules of the Allied Occupation were cynically side-stepped when it suited the intelligence organisations in the zones of occupation.

'And when it suited *Project Paperclip* – you've heard of that, *natürlich*?'

'*Natürlich*,' I agreed ironically, remembering professor Winter's *Zaunkönig*.

Paperclip was the frantic gathering together of advanced German technology by the occupying troops in '45 and '46 - particularly the long range A4 missile programme, rockets and jet engines. Jet fighters like the 262s which were flown to the West. It included other advanced materiel, blueprints, all sorts of equipment, technicians, scientists like Werhner von Braun, who was laundered whiter than white despite the slaves who laboured in the SS-run caves at Nordenhausen, building his V2s - before things could be destroyed or the Russians could get hold of them. Although they got their share.

'Not only that, Johann. Chemical weapons, nerve gas and other experimental weapons were captured. Medical experimental data was also avidly seized along with some of the scientists involved. The West was delighted to use this material even where they intended prosecuting those who'd carried out inhuman experiments on human subjects. So were the Soviets of course. Some of these experiments were in the area of mind control. You might say that J.C. Lilly's later experimental work helping psychiatric patients through sensory deprivation owed something to that earlier research, though intended for benign purposes, *natürlich*.'

~-~

Stephanie informed me that her organisation, regardless of its legitimate and humanitarian basis was under surveillance by the BND and that Stasi agents were watching to see with whom she made contact. In addition the word had gone out to the Neo-Nazis including the *Eiserne Ausland* division: the 'Iron Legion' goons from Brazil. It was likely that KGB, freewheeling Spetsnaz operatives, loosed from their moorings were also sniffing the wind.

'So who's suddenly been spreading the word that your outfit has a hoard of Russian gold in its sights?'

'Darling, KGB of course. It would have been Yuri's department, hoping we'll show our hand so they could step in with a carefully co-ordinated sting to scoop the pot. Probably told them we'd located the *Amber Room* for good measure. Maybe it's unofficial. Perhaps Yuri and a small team and some close-to-his-chest Stasi confederates. Outside the Kremlin remit.'

'And what's to stop them just kidnapping everyone, tickling you 'til you cry 'uncle!'?'

'Well that takes organisation too, and if it's unofficial and goes tits up, darling, they'll have some explaining to do to their line managers. *None* of us has the complete answer to the riddle.'

Evidently Peter had been trying to dispose of the briefcase into James's safekeeping. It contained all the research notes for James: the *Steiger Saga*, which apart from it's an epic and tracks the story of the Romanov hoard itself, contained the original *Verity List* which is still dynamite forty-three years after the war. Certain Establishment figures would pay a lot to see that disappear for ever. So could there be a British player in this that we don't know about? Somebody with influence at the very top? And anyone with knowledge of that list could be very vulnerable. There's a lot to play for.'

It would explain James Delcroix' fearfulness; the intimidation he'd received from 'the police'.

'So what's Harry's angle?'

'Harry was 'Jim', the original Cabin Boy. Like in *Treasure Island* – hiding in the laundry basket. He was right there at the beginning, unwitting party to the original plot hatched by Stalin and Dzerzhinsky to rob the Bolshevist coffers. It all went wrong and after the hijacking only Roskov and his deranged captive knew its whereabouts.'

'Deranged captive….?'

'Never mind. Ancient history now, darling. We have to have a plan.'

'I plan to try to stay alive, Steph.'

'Better to be alive and rich, though, *Liebchen*.'

'I'm not sure I could handle even a modest share of that kind of money, Stephanie.'

'But you should be reimbursed for your contribution, Johann. Poor Peter had no beneficiaries. His death was a pure accident. Even the KGB couldn't have staged *Ramstein*! He passed the briefcase out of the flames into your safekeeping after all.'

'So if I have the *codebook*, who has the key? And where did it come from?'

Stephanie looked very serious.

'It came from my brother. Arthur, who was dead and then alive. And now is dead again, Johann.'

I waited for this new mystery to be revealed.

'I think you should hear more of the tape,' she said

~.~

The tape continued.

'It's still there, Yuri.'

Sergei was claiming to be the only person alive who knows its exact location. That he could sail into that bay tomorrow and point to the drainage outlet with the rock fall that seals the chamber.

He'd thought about mounting an operation to recover it for years. But it was not feasible to just dump millions of dollars in gold bars onto the bullion market, and to bank it you must have an explanation, provenance. And who could he trust? He didn't even know how or *if* it was stamped. A quarter of a century had passed, some of that as a retired Muscovite.

'My position on the periphery of Intelligence was coming under scrutiny by the late 'sixties, Yuri. I jumped ship a few months after Philby. In Britain, for a long time, no one seemed to notice! I collected my gong, a Moscow flat and a Soviet pension and apart from a couple of unsatisfactory affairs the rest is history.'

~-~

At Farnborough I listen, almost convinced by Stephanie's continuing saga.

'Johann,' Stephanie confided quietly. 'You understand, darling. Much of this information is speculative, but the identity of *Sergei Kamov* was well known to Harry through intelligence gathering by the West which has found eager purchase among the Polish-Lithuanian community in exile. They have rather an unstable 'direct-action' para-military cadre which is busy plotting an alternative future for the region. Different from that archived at the Kremlin, you follow. You've already met *Zubr* of course.'

'How are you tied into all this, Alexa?'

'Let's stick to *Stephanie* if it's alright with you, darling,' she said. 'Until circumstances dictate otherwise.' Basic tradecraft of course.

She puts away the matchbox, looks searchingly towards the opening of the refreshment marquee. 'You know, sometimes I would see my brothers. In crowds, in taxis. In the background shots of TV interviews on sidewalks... they never age you know. Only *I* have aged. I know how most of them died. Almost all of them. But my youngest brother, a year younger than myself, was second-in-command to a successful U-Boat commander.'

That Nordic look again.

'His death was contrived, connived by that son-of-a-bitch, Himmler.

He was hauled off his boat at Kiel and thrown into a Gestapo prison for months. Not ill-treated by the low standards of the time, just neglected and half-starved. Then they let him out, put him into a private's uniform and sent him to the Eastern Front – Summer 1943. Just in time for *Zitadelle*. The Battle of Kursk. He was posted missing, believed killed in action within the week. It was a very confused time.

'John,' she uses my correct name for the first time. 'We made many mistakes in both wars and between them too. Hitler was one of course and we didn't see that coming until it was too late. I was brainwashed from an early age like most of my generation. But if Hitler hadn't been so arrogant he'd have listened to Canaris and to his experienced generals. Like with Stalin, no one dared to speak up for fear of encountering his fearful rage or worse.

'It's too late to turn back the clock. But when Hans-Peter put two and two together and made five, he was excited that here at last was a forgotten fortune almost within reach, confirmed by the coded message which was readable in one of the great Shakespearean plays.'

'If the story is true,' I say.

'*Natürlich*, if true. But it *is* true, John. My brother's arrest is evidence for that. He and the entire crew sent to the Eastern front. Their death's weren't *absolute* guaranteed. The Battle of Stalingrad was already lost. If only von Paulus had been allowed to withdraw in time…but for that *bastard* Hitler's narcissism again. Ninety thousand survived Stalingrad: only a few percent survived Soviet captivity. It was typical of the situation in the East.'

She continued. 'It's possible that there are other surviving witnesses among those sent out later but unlikely. There were a million German prisoners in the USSR, most repatriated a few years after the war. By 1950 some 23,000 remained, classed as war criminals. There were several amnesties between 1950 and 1956. Stasi was 'involved' in their re-integration into society. Those who returned to West Germany were greeted as heroes, even those the Soviets had accused of war crimes. Chancellor Adenauer kept up diplomatic pressure to have all released, and succeeded. Even if it meant that some would serve the remainder of their sentences in Germany. It was not the same in the East.

'The gold is still there, I'm sure. Harry sent a member of the organisation to the Irish Republic some years ago. He reported that the locals still remembered 'Bannion's' wartime visit, the sailing trips around the bays and inlets and out into the Atlantic, or so it had seemed. Old Padraic found his boat later, beached, with little damage. Abandoned

686

during a storm was the story. Of Bannion/Brendan/Merlin/ Prometheus/Peregrine-Thomas there was no sign from that day. He'd been a convincing double agent and probably a triple throughout World War 2 and after. Possibly before, Johann.' *Reverting to the German form again.*

'But he didn't fool those fishermen and crofters down at the *Crooked Billet*. They thought he was a British spy. They were right, of course, it's just at that time he was working for the Germans. Well to be precise for the Reichsführer who was securing his personal pension or an SS-Fighting Fund: a war chest for a *Wehrwolf* counter-offensive or however the hell he'd intended it.

'Harry's agent tried to stir up a few memories about Bannion's activities and especially any later events associated with Sheep's Head; if strange goings-on has been observed. They hadn't. And neither were the locals living in conspicuous wealth.'

'Do we have any idea what it's worth now, Stephanie? Assuming it exists.'

Stephanie looked around, checking perhaps to see if an SBAC babushka or bar staff had dropped a match box in the vicinity.

'About five billion dollars at today's gold prices.

But of course it was not fine, she'd told me. It was rings, teeth, personal memorabilia, gold plate and the occasional looted palace in ingot form.

'Pity we didn't do this in '76 when it was $800 per ounce,' she said wistfully.

I was silent for a moment.

'That's still a lot of money,' I say eventually.

'You're not wrong, darling,' she says with something approaching a smile.

~-~

Harry Piotrkowski, Hans-Peter Neumann, and Alexa were an unlikely alliance. Two had been in the camp of the fascist aggressor at the beginning of the War. Harry had already suffered under Bolshevism as much as any surviving Pole or Balt. Many of the latter became ardent Nazi collaborators or served in the ranks of the Ausland SS. This was as a direct result of their treatment by the Soviets when Stalin had held their countries captive again during the *Molotov-Ribbentrop Non-Aggression Pact*. Many of them fled the country at the end of WW2 rather than face post-war incorporation of the Baltic States into the USSR.

Prior to the surrender Alexa had taken the Admiral's advice, driving across the border into Switzerland accompanied by an infatuated junior finance minister from whom she'd soon disentangled herself. So she avoided the fate of many of her contemporaries who'd suffered the horrors of the Soviet occupation. No ashes in the hair for her. No pallid make up of face powder and cigarette ash, blackened teeth; walking with a stick to add forty years…and still they were raped… two million of her sisters. One in ten died as a result, the majority by suicide.

But the money was running out and she'd felt the pull of homeland. She returned to find that her mother had died two months before.

And they'd all lost family, Natasha. Peter had no-one. Alexa had lost all her brothers and was alone. Harry had lost more as a child than anyone could imagine including his innocence. The trio was drawn together by a mutual desire to 'right some wrongs', to use their extensive reach and contacts to collate information on people for the 'altruistic purpose of re-uniting lost souls' displaced by conflict, to make up for not having family of their own, perhaps. Harry had dipped into the Polish War Veterans' organisations but he was restless and increasingly found companionship with Hans-Peter and Alexa and a few old and staunch friends, like the old Count Wieniawu-Klimaszinski, whose legacy to his son was the old dream of glory: restoration of Polish autonomy at the very least. Another poison chalice.

Alexa's duties early on with the BND included the interrogation of displaced persons and those seeking to settle in Germany and covertly penetrating organisations dedicated to tracking down missing persons: believed prisoners of war, still held by the Russians. Ironic, given the complexion of BND staff that these lists might include: those wanted for war crimes – but good cover for searching for further recruits, which was her real job: building a large intelligence organisation rivalled only by the Stasi with its massive complex at Berlin-Lichtenberg; within which a department also provided finance for terrorist gangs such as the PLO and later the *Rote Armee Fraktion* and such lesser-known groups as *Der Rote Pfad; The Red Path*. This was a Maoist cell with an extreme agenda to kidnap and murder successful businessmen, bomb the 'Banks of Zion' and stage an all-out assault on Capitalism by every means including suicide bombers or unwitting 'expendables', *impatient with Marx's claim that it would devour itself in time, Natasha.*

When Hans-Peter had been researching James Delcroix' Norfolk discovery of the *Tigerfalk*, he'd re-opened contact with some of his one-time colleagues. This was normal for him in his particular field of aviation-related research, but went beyond his selected number. It seemed that Steiger had been associated with more than one of the ministries and wartime intelligence organisations, though in the main, the *Luftwaffenamt*. So Neumann had widened his net.

He had related a small piece of the jigsaw as he'd recalled it as a younger man, Natasha. Passed on to me by James at my 'briefing' at Norwood Hill, describing how a normally even-tempered Rhinelander had been substantially ruffled by a Prussian, back in 1940.

~-~

'Bloody jumped-up SS *Sturmbannführer*. Our bloody crash. *Our* bloody investigation!'

Oberleutnant Horst Edelmann overseeing a *Luftwaffen Absturzunterschungsabteilung*, a crash investigating department, had slammed into the Berlin office in a towering rage, flinging his gloves into his in-tray.

Hans-Peter had raised an eyebrow. As a comparatively junior intelligence officer only peripheral to the investigation he knew better than to ask. Edelmann would elucidate in his own time. The accident was thought to be weather-related and had involved a Focke-Wulf 44 biplane trainer which had come down in the *Rangsdorfer See* two nights before, in full view of the *Rangsdorf Seebadkasino* where a party was in full swing. A female guest taking a breath of air had witnessed a distress flare arcing into the overcast. She'd raised the alarm. The *Stieglitz* had been seen falling, spinning like a sycamore seed to the lake's surface, impacting with an audible splash as the music died; turning, sinking like a broken moth.

Engines had burst into life along the mooring boom. Manned by Luftwaffe and Bücker Factory *Werkpiloten,* the boat crews had spent two hours with spotlights searching the black waters of the lake for survivors. When they finally abandoned the search in the increasingly misty rain, they'd found nothing but a seat cushion and part of a wing.

The second day of the resumed search saw the Luftwaffe-organised dredging operation interrupted by carloads of Gestapo with orders from their chief, Müller, to halt operations and hand over to a team headed by SS that rolled up in *Kübelwagen* with frogmen suits and breathing apparatus. The officer in charge of the SS investigation unit had been abrupt and arrogant in his dealing with Edelmann, but his warrant to take command had been signed by none other than Reinhard Heydrich. Edelmann had no option other than to comply. That SS *Sturmbannführer's* name had been Auer. The missing *Stieglitz* pilot was one Oberleutnant Rolf Steiger, also of Luftwaffe Intel. and a Dept VI Abwehr liaison officer maintaining his night flying proficiency it seems. Flying solo. Why a desk-bound officer in his forties needed to maintain flying proficiency and just why the SS were so interested neither Hans-Peter nor Edelmann knew. 'But there were rumours later, John,' Delcroix had told me.

Hans-Peter had made some sort of naïve comment to the effect that after all, in matters of state security, we were confronting a common enemy.

'Yes, Neumann,' Edelmann had replied with asperity. 'We do indeed face a common enemy. The Gestapo and the bloody SS. Us against them and them against us!'

Neumann told James that he had later discovered that an associate of Steiger's had been run to earth and interrogated. When he'd been broken he'd bought Steiger two days. But by then the fugitive had disappeared beneath the skirts of the Kurfurstendam where the trail had gone cold.

~-~

So, in the early '70s Hans-Peter, exercising caution, in the pursuit of his enquiries had made indirect contact with ex-SS Intelligence Officer, *Sturmbannfüher* Karl-Klemenz Auer, then in a senior placement with the BND. Perhaps that was the only error he'd made.

Auer had worked for Gehlen from 1946. But as of April Fool's Day 1956, that organisation had become the *Bundesnachrichtendienst*, BND, Federal Intelligence Service. Alexa was in what had become East Berlin, working in a secretarial position. A plant for the BND and a minor double agent for the Stasi, a very dangerous occupation in which her loyalty to either side might be called into question. If things got difficult.

Stephanie believed that *Kamov; Sergei*, alias Peregrine-Thomas was dead. He'd died of the cancer that the actor/agent who'd played the part for the tape had pretended to. But Kamov had succumbed *four or five months previously*, as far as she had been able to determine, piecing little bits of information together. Meantime the story they'd been able to tease out of surviving SS records in the hands of the GRU confirmed that von Dönhoff had been navigation officer aboard the U-Boat whose crew had been arrested at Kiel in 1943 and that subsequently he'd been sent to the Russian Front along with the others. He was the sole survivor of that crew.

The truth about *Unternehmen Alberich* was that until Arthur von Dönhoff had returned to Germany, it had been buried; effectively due to

Himmler's ruthless suppression of all participants and a lucky strike by Coastal Command. Klemenz Auer however had a long memory and had been linked to it, insofar as he'd been on the staff of Prinz Christoph von Hesse, a senior SS officer and a close aide to Heinrich Himmler himself. He had heard rumours about the general direction taken by the Romanov gold, but did not have enough information to work on. In fact *Merlin-Kamov-Thomas*, (Stephanie now refers to MKT for short) *had* apparently confided in Yuri some months previously, but he was by then 90 years of age, suffering not just from cancer but possibly dementia as well.

Alexa's version said that the details of MKT's seminal involvement in the secret operation had come out haphazardly in the West, via conduits like Alexa's. But in the East it had invoked passion and had a momentum despite his lapses. Yuri's trained ear heard pattern and purpose in the narrative of what became a virtual deathbed confession. He also knew about hijacked gold trains in the wake of the 1917 Revolution. It was the first time he'd heard the name *Alberich* associated with it however. The Nazis had managed to shred a vast amount of secret data before Germany surrendered in '45. The SS were very efficient at this. Before they could be stopped, Russian soldiery had burned a deal more.

Kept secret from Hitler, Himmler's *Alberich*, had been, however, overwhelmingly superseded by Martin Bormann's much greater vision for a post-war commercial campaign - to re-float the German economy, while secretly perpetuating the aims of Nazism behind future boardroom doors. This was to be initiated through the mass outflow of patents, gold bullion, stocks, bonds and funds abroad. The operation was termed *Aktion Adlerflug*: Operation Eagle Flight.

With the Führer's mental disintegration imminent, the realistic view by many in the upper Nazi hierarchy of the certainty of losing of the war, Bormann, the second most powerful man in the Reich, with the SS, aided by powerful allies like the Deutsche Bank and the I.G. Farben combine, created some 750 world-wide front corporations. In this they were substantially aided by foreign banks and businesses, nominally in the Allied camp, who'd hedged their bets and secretly traded, if indirectly, with Germany. An American corporation, for example, had supplied communications and war material, including 50,000 artillery fuses per month to Germany until 1944. Small wonder that *Alberich* had been lost to view in the shadow of *Adlerflug!*

Alexa, through her job, saw intelligence transcripts emanating from the East and almost simultaneously with Auer had made her momentous discovery. Of several DPs and German POW returnees, some having survived more than twenty years in the Gulag, a name had caught her eye; one of those who'd been released on the fifteenth anniversary of Stalin's death. He'd been repatriated to East Berlin and was held, as normal, for further interrogation by the Stasi. Her own surname had been buried several identities ago, but Arthur von Dönhoff still bore it. With trembling hands she'd read the transcript of the list of names smuggled by a double agent at Berlin-Lichtenberg. Amazement and delight. Her youngest brother had survived as a POW and eighteen years as a 'zek' in logging camps. She'd been distressed to learn that he had been repatriated but had then been held at length in the East for his own protection due to poor mental health.

A committee had been in session at the BND, several floors above Alexa's level. Its secret membership, all ex-Gehlen SS. She guessed, of course, that they knew that she was von Dönhoff's sister. SS files had placed him as an operative in *Alberich* who would know the location of the Romanov millions. As navigation officer aboard the Type VII in the Spring of 1943 he'd also been interrogated by the Stasi following his repatriation. Details pertaining to the mission and the location of the workings were limited to what little they had in their own files. But Arthur had forgotten everything that had happened to him before about 1947, he'd replied, despite the most powerful influences to remember, chemical and physical. *Everybody talks.* That was their boast. *Everybody. You. Me. Your mother.* But his mind had gone to Swiss cheese apparently and doctors and psychiatrists had failed to determine otherwise.

Truth drugs and threats of a miserable and indefinite incarceration had not shaken his story. He seemed listless and dull, reportedly a very different human being from the once smart young navigation officer in the *Unterseeboote-Dienst* of the *Kriegsmarine*. Especially once they'd done their worst. But perhaps they hadn't done their *worst.* Weren't convinced by the whole story and were half-hearted at best. Though the intelligence came from Auer, from the opposition, the BND's SS-men and the Stasi's SS-men were brothers in arms, woven of the same cloth. So perhaps they'd taken the claim seriously at first; pressed Dönhoff so far and only relented when they felt it was unproductive. Dönhoff had been wrung out, so they said, and there was less to him than met the eye. He was once again expendable.

'I was determined to visit him, Johann, but for all I knew he was held for the present - and for how long was anyone's guess - in a Stasi cell somewhere. Possibly the sprawling HQ at Lichtenberg.'

Yuri's research data meanwhile provided the basis for his department to provide certain agencies, from South America to West Germany with clues to the existence of the Romanov hoard, codenamed *Anastasia* by their cell. The Controller then sat back to see what would happen. Stephanie's 'discovery' of the planned meeting in a Moscow park was one piece of bait taken, bread scattered upon the unruffled waters: Yuri waiting for what might break the meniscus from beneath

For the first time Alexa looked uncomfortable.

'Johnn, there is something else, something you should know.'

Her gaze was directed now towards the crowd, following the demonstration of some new airliner peforming a slow, quiet flyby.

'Back then, before I was officially retired from the BND – pension and everything, Johann – I was deeply involved in the shutting down of some lingering subversives, those of the Baader-Meinhof persuasion. West Berlin terror cells actually: Chinese, Iranian, Palestinian, some affiliated, some simply anti-Western and funded by all sorts, including Stasi with whom I'd burned my bridges by then anyway - as much as one ever can. Some were just criminal but with high flown over-arching political agendas, driven by just one or two sociopathic, embittered and malignant narcissists, extreme Left Wing and anti-capitalist – often a male/female unit. *Just you and me, Bubi, against the World.* Plus a string of mauserist disciples, *natürlich*.

'*Rote Pfad* was one of these and it had its own initiation, like the Masons, its own training and methods of coercion and brainwashing which they recorded on tape and sometines cine film. Including the violent rape submission of drugged subjects, part of the breaking down of the personality; team-bonding via 'Stockholm Syndrome'. Along with sensory deprivation, meditation, chanting , like some native spirit tribal rituals– you name it.

'We managed to salvage some of the data although they'd destroyed much of it before we raided them – tipped-off as usual....Johann, there's something you need to know… about your daughter.'

Chapter 47. *Unternehmen Alberich*

Imagine this, Natasha. Towards the end of 1942, for those among the Nazi hierarchy who were less deluded than others, it seemed probable that the War could be lost. Canaris, head of the Abwehr, the German Secret Intelligence Service knew this of course. So did the chief of the Reichshauptsicherheitsamt: State Security, however much he tried to bury himself in obscure books and the occult.

The Nazis had really shot themselves in the foot before the War, sending hundreds of Jews abroad, including some very clever scientists. One of these, Karl-Heinz Liepschutz, made it safely to Britain. But his patented U-Plane submersible and deep sea salvage design equipment drawings were left behind for B &V to develop, which they did — at least to working prototype status.

From the deep seabed off the North Cape of Norway the difficult operation to lift the cargo of an old shipwreck had been undertaken by a special flotilla of the *Kriegsmarine* and a team from the Blohm und Voss Company using prototype submersibles and *U-Träger*, specialised flotation and lifting apparatus. Operational security had been tight, overseen by a crack unit under the direct and most secret orders of the Reichsführer of SS, Heinrich Himmler.

Peter Neumann's research notes have described this operation in some detail. It was called *Unternehmen Alberich*: typically fanciful and Wagnerian - although the sinister dwarf, Alberich, had his precious Rhine Gold stolen didn't he, and here was Himmler doing it himself. His choice of code name wasn't even original: Ludendorff had used it for his strategic 'scorched earth' withdrawal from the Arras-Noyon sector to the Hindenberg line in the Great War.

The Reichsführer had scoured all available maps of Europe in an effort to find a safe haven for the cargo of the sunken icebreaker, *Eisbär*. Switzerland, the traditional place to stockpile precious metal in underground vaults, was ruled out. Stealthy *Nacht und Nebel* movement of Jews by rail to Auschwitz was one thing. The logistics of organising the clandestine shipment of a fortune in gold from North Norway and transferring it by rail across the Swiss border, without raising suspicions or risking its loss, was proving difficult for the Reichsführer, even given the almost unlimited power that the SS Chief enjoyed. Because it had to remain his own special secret, those involved had been hand-picked.

Ultra-ultra secret, *Reich* security. No one breathed a word. But all the same, an under-sea voyage to a friendly country within range of a submarine seemed more likely to succeed and remain secret. And these were increasingly desperate times.

~-~

Well-built, they'd said. A fit-looking tweedy man in plus fours with a wide-brimmed hat. He'd photographed the high dolmens and standing stones and walked the green trail from St. Finbar's sixth century monastery. He'd climbed Hungry Hill, big binoculars about his neck and roomed at the tavern, a 'hail-fellow and well-met Irishman', Natasha, with a ready smile and a fake Dublin accent and an equally fake Irish name. But a fine raconteur for all that with a head full of stories and swift with his round. An anthropologist from Dublin University, they said. Or an industrial archaeologist with an interest in the old copper workings, equipped with rope and other tackle. Or perhaps a speculator given the munitions industry's voracious appetite for copper.

Whatever: a man in the prime of life with a twinkle in his eye; striding the misty mountains and inlets, walking the islands of Roaring Water Bay. He'd hired a fishing boat from Schull though his own small crew of seamen had arrived by charabanc from Cork, the locals had remarked. If Padraic O'Malley had been worried about his old boat he'd not shown it and spent a merry fortnight on the fee. Even twenty-five years later some of those old crofters and fisher folk remembered the man; before Irish tourism would cloud their memories of strangers. The year had been 1942, around September time, and though they drank with him some thought for sure he was an English spy.

Especially when two local men, some said they were IRA, had gone missing, or so they'd told Harry's emissary after the war.

The truth was somewhat darker.

~-~

He'd been observed huddled in the snug one windy night with some increasingly rowdy locals, each with a tall tale to tell for a drink. Suspicions were that his interests lay beyond access to copper ore, or even the rich gold that had been illicitly mined in the gossans deep in the endless galleries of the copper workings. Some hard local lads had met later with the 'loose mouted eejets' who'd spoken out of turn, boys who had a good thing going with the visiting U-Boats that came nosing into the coves on moonless nights in search of fresh water and supplies.

Those fine young men met still later with our mutual friend, sure that the middle aged 'Englishman' with an awkward gait who leaned on a stick from time to time for assistance would be no bother at all. Gripping his arms, they led him to an ancient van while the gale whipped about them. When they ran out of road they continued by sheep trail, then on foot to old roofless stone buildings, his escorts making allowance for his limping progress, their words clipped by the wind. Here lay shafts that revealed their great depths when one lad dropped in a stone, listening with mock anxiety, vainly to hear the splash, or clatter of its rocky destiny.

'People can disappear around here, my fake friend,' he shouted. 'And no-one ever, *ever* finds them. Not ever.'

How true that was. How true though that people are not always what they seem.

In the darkness, our man's toecap had eased the rubber stopper from the bottom of his stick. Moving quickly, he released its hidden trigger and dispatched the speaker with a .410 shotgun blast to the throat. Twisting the handle revealed a stiletto. Though the blade flashed in sudden moonlight there was hardly a moment to savour the look of horror on the second victim's face or hear his scream, torn by the gale.

The two bodies followed the passage of the stone. The van was discovered smashed at the bottom of a steep cliff the following day.

~-~

So, in the February of 1943, a uniquely-modified Type XlV U-Boat left the Norwegian coast and made its submerged passage to Cape Wrath. It was one of only ten built as tankers for the submarine fleet and known appropriately as a *Milch Cow* by the Allies. It had sailed on through the Minches, surfaced briefly off Barra where starshots would have been taken then continued south to Malin Head, west by south, to navigate the Atlantic coast of Ireland. From the Bull Light off the coast of Kerry it rounded the promontory of Ceann Baoi, steering for the rugged coastline of Bantry Bay and Bear Island. It is not clear where landfall was made, but the plan was that assistance was to be provided by agent, 'Brendan', aboard a fishing boat, flashing a coded message by signal lamp off the desolate Sheep's Head peninsula. The U-Boat was to follow at periscope depth, nosing into the little-populated inlet of Cuan Dhun Manais or some nearby fjord.

Some weeks earlier the fishing boat had sailed into that same inlet, reconnoitering the rocky shoreline, concentrating on a couple of likely adits above sea level. These were among scores of drainage outlets in the rough rock face below a sheep trail, once the well-trodden route to extensive copper workings between which lay the frosted furrows of long gone potato fields, destroyed by the blight.

The workings had been expanded greatly during the American Civil War when the demand for brass cartridges was at its height. *For the Gatling gun, Natasha.* It was to be the temporary home to a team of Slav miners who would be landed by submarine a few nights hence.

The SS men scaled the cliff and hauled the miners aloft. The overseers encamped above, in the corbel-roofed ruin of a ninth century hovel. The miners were ordered to cut a gallery into the side of the adit running under the shoulder of the mountain. It was tough going, especially as the prisoners were not used to hard rock mining. The job took longer than intended, increasing the chance they would be discovered. The final task was to install a diesel winch, cable spools, a section of miniature rail track and trolley. After more than a week of back breaking effort the miners were taken off by the submarine under a curtain of sleet, according to my source.

Later some were to be washed ashore on the coast of Wales.

~-~

The cargo capacity of the Milch Cow was fifty tons of heavy fuel oil. Despite the supply tanks being drained the loading crew had had to struggle with breathing apparatus to carefully distribute and secure the cargo, working through two manhole covers either side of the main hull. The remaining cargo was laden aboard a second stripped-out submarine. Maintaining balance throughout these operations was critical.

Undercover of darkness and in foggy weather – Himmler's favoured *Nacht und Nebel* - the load would be further manhandled via rowing boats deployed from the fishing boat over a period of three nights, hauled inshore by the crew and SS men. The U-boats stayed submerged each day until the next evening's efforts. The fishing boat hid around the promontory beyond view of the meagre habitation. With pickets mounted and shielded lanterns to assist it took scores of ferry trips,

698

shipping water at the gunwhales, to and from the cliffs: well over a hundred tons of the stuff - exhausting even for a team of very fit young men. But they did it.

As the U-Boats departed, the Irish agent had sunk the rowing boats, beached the trawler two miles from Schull Harbour and gone to ground. The small fishing boat crew, *SS* to a man, had sailed with the submarines. As planned the second submarine was to be scuttled and the crew transferred to the Type IV for the return voyage. This information could only have come from Merlin himself and was repeated on the tape.

As was so often the case, only one or two individuals knew the exact whereabouts of the fortune at any time. Himmler was one, although the precise co-ordinates remained unknown to him. He took a cyanide capsule and the secret was interred with his body in 1945. The other was 'Brendan', 'CPT' or Alexa's 'MKT' who'd had no knowledge that the U-Boat had been sunk for another week.

At a Dublin 'safe house' he had transmitted a single word: *'Shamrock'*. Mission accomplished! Berlin had eventually replied at a specified time and date. The news was not good. The submarine was missing, believed lost. After the War it was revealed that it had been heading for La Rochelle when it had been surprised on the surface by a Liberator of RAF Coastal Command, bracketed by depth charges and sunk. Just one among one-hundred and fifty U-Boats sunk in the first six months of 1943 – *which showed how far the tide had turned against Germany at sea, Natasha. No survivors had been reported.*

~.~

So the word had gone out. Von Dönhoff had returned and his sister had taken the bait. But Alexa was a vixen. She'd taken a step back from the river's edge. That the hook might have been baited by Klemenz Auer, following meetings of go-betweens and agents acting for his East German opposite number, might not have occurred to her precisely. But her natural instinct was caution. She knew the system, that her Stasi *V-Mann* position was illusory. They pretended to trust her and she pretended loyalty, passing them information while reporting to her BDM boss, Auer, who had scarcely made the pretence of trusting her - until recently when he'd become ominously and uncharacteristically affable. Alexa implies that I may have guessed that one of *Central Casting's* two goons from the ELA had been a relative of Auer's: his nephew. It had crossed my mind.

~-~

Doctor Uwe Meinecke, with the rank of Major, possessing all the relevant identification and authority had called at the clinic where it was confirmed that Dönhoff was now receiving treatment. She had only limited time on this occasion, she'd told the East German staff, but there were a few patients on her list that had been referred to her by the regular psychiatrist who was currently on leave (she'd established) so why wasn't it noted that she would be arriving? She was shown into a side ward where most of the inmates were sleeping.

Had she imagined that she would have recognised the husk? The personality shrinking under the crust of fatigue and change that a twenty-year incarceration with hard labour in freezing wilderness would wreak? That and withdrawal from normal society... if so she was misled. She'd looked for clues under the grizzled beard, the sun-damaged skin, whose pigment had long faded in subsequent institutions when he'd languished in the East, fading like the erosion of self. The sentence for 'fighting an aggressive war' having served in U-Boats had imprinted its bitter injustice on his soul. His mental health had broken like so many of the institutionalised, spending his time staring into space or writing rambling letters to the imaginary, or the dead. She wondered what they'd used on him. Pentathol or LSD to disinter hidden truths or alter his mind. He seemed oblivious of her presence for a short while then expressed what Alexa thought was intense fear *I was not even wearing a white coat, Johann,* and broke into a mixture of German and Russian babble, suffering such clammy rigor that a nurse swept in with a tray and a hypodermic. For a while peace seemed to have descended. When at last he focussed on Alexa he was smiling faintly, eyes wrinkling.

'Don't you know me, Arthur?' she'd whispered, her heart thumping in her breast.

He'd lifted his head from the pillow and looked at her for a long time; whispered that he did. That he'd always believed she was alive and that she'd come to him. He talked about their Schwerin childhood in a thin trembling voice, as if it was yesterday and pressed his 'favourite pen' upon her, the only gift at his disposal, telling her to guard it well and whispered so faintly that she could barely hear it, the title of the old book she must acquire, by diligent searching. And only *that* edition. That it held a great secret.

'Promise you have memorised these things,' he begged her. She did.

700

'*Macbeth*!' It was the last time he spoke with a smile, lying still. Lost in the eye of a treacherous calm round whose orb there raged within, a storm; like that on Jupiter.

~-~

A saving grace of the remote *gulag*, were that phrase not too obscene in context, was the *zek* library system. Books were the most precious commodity and increased a little during the false thaw of Khrushchev. One that remained untarnished by capitalist slur was the acknowledged masterwork: *The Complete Works of William Shakespeare*. In the logging camp library there resided a well-preserved copy of a 1923 English edition by British Books. It had fine leaves that Arthur's thick calloused hands had turned with infinite care and ran to thirteen hundred pages or more, twenty-six of which comprised the *Scottish Play*.

On his way to Kursk he'd learned the fate of the Type XIV, lost with all hands. Although he had memorised the exact lat-long of the Irish mine workings, Arthur obsessed that some sort of key might possibly be smuggled out to the West that would enable the Romanov treasure to be retrieved and put to good use. He'd hoped that his sister had survived the war but had little proof. He dreamed mad dreams that he might some day find her, that they both might benefit from Himmler's deception to which he could now be heir. If it was still hidden there.

'Perhaps, Johann,' Stephanie was telling me what Hans-Peter had postulated. 'A fellow prisoner, perhaps an intelligence officer from the Great Patriotic War who'd been careless enough to get himself captured and had then bravely escaped. Given a further fifteen years for his trouble by Stalin as happened to so many. Perhaps he had told him of a foolproof method of recording secret information. Perhaps Arthur worked it out for himself. He'd had plenty of time.'

At any rate Hans-Peter was well familiar with the method. It involved cutting a sheet of paper to the exact size of a book page and then puncturing it to reveal particular patterns or letters to spell out a message. It was an effective one-time code. All you had know was the page number and the exact edition of that particular book. A modification of this was a zig-zag cut paper which when the straight edge of the sheet was tucked into the inner margin you read-off the letters or figures on the indents. The zig-zag method was preferable as it looked less like a paper stencil if discovered and more like a scrap of randomly torn paper.

Arthur had retained that little dagger of knowledge dangling in his brain. The scene from *Macbeth* and the page numbers of the portal that would be unlocked by those paper keys he'd internalised.

The key's 'transmitter' was the humble *biro* which had made its way into the camps by the long dark teatime of Brezhnev. Rolled inside a shortened piece of plastic pen barrel, the *Kugelschreiber* was plugged with tallow that it might stay safe through the full body examination of his release.

~-~

Harry had arranged that the appropriate book should be sourced outside of Germany to avoid possible security breaches and to be delivered by hand, casually, when next Johann was in town.

Natasha, as Stephanie had already stated: in the Great Game it is sometimes better to know what your enemy knows than to know something trivial he doesn't. He is more likely to act on something he knows or move to obtain information, if prompted, revealing the extent of his intelligence, enabling your countermove. Or you can pretend knowledge and imply that some imminent action might be taken so that he will overreact; be stampeded into action, showing you his hand. Else he's playing a longer game and pretending ignorance. You never know You can never be certain. And you can never completely trust. It spoils you as a human being, to be an effective spy. Paranoia can frequently result.

'But this is what we *thought* Yuri was hoping we'd do. By creating the anxiety that MKT might have provided the KGB with the whole story, including co-ordinates, setting the ELA and the Polish activists on our backs to add authenticity and pressure us with the threat of danger and the need for speed, shaking our tree; hoping we'd make mistakes. They may not have known about the paper keys, but no matter what they'd done to his mind, Arthur had not revealed the name of the only lock that they would fit.'

Stephanie's eyes glowed like blue lasers.

'And then came Ramstein and you were suddenly in the loop, Johann, instead of poor Peter. You must have surprised Moscow Centre as they hardly knew you existed up 'til then. The ELA were on to you and the German police, that is someone masquerading as *Kriminalpolizei*, most likely a covert BND team directed by Auer. Either they or the Stasi burgled your Hannover hotel room and failed to find the briefcase. Peter had been trying to get the briefcase out of Germany, into James's hands. The most important thing in that briefcase, Johann, was that rare 1923 edition 'Shakespeare Codebook', which you yourself had 'couriered' from Dubai! We could have sourced another one, but time was not on our side.'

'So what happened to your brother, Steph?'

I might have dropped a dinner gong by the expression on her face. It seemed to me that any family feeling, sympathy for her brother's suffering over more than forty years had been shed like a snake's skin. That he was now out of the picture and the focus was, and always had been, on *Anastasia*. For a member of a small team allegedly interested in re-uniting families separated by war she seemed to retain little sympathy for her near-demented brother. But perhaps I was being too hard on her.

She'd recovered well enough. 'He'd been reasonably well treated. What could I do? If we'd had the money, the resource, anything would have been possible. It should have been able to get him out, into a hospital in the West. With enough pressure from Western politicians…..'

In the event he had reportedly died the month before. She had no idea where he'd been buried or cremated. She gave me a rather shamefaced look.

'Johann, we can only do what we can do. Such an amount of money can be used for good or ill. If the KGB acquires it there's no question of how it would be used. We have to stay real and how do you say, 'hang tough'?'

There was no doubting the truth of that statement.

'Well that's what the Americans say, Steph.'

'So, darling, I have to ask you again. Is it safe?'

Chapter 48. *With the RAF Expeditionary Force*

Royal Air Force forward landing ground,
British Expeditionary Force on the Donets River.
Twenty miles south west of Kharkov, Ukraine.
January 1920.

For Squadron Leader Duncan Stewart MacIntyre DSO, DFC serving in with the BEF this was his second winter in Southern Russia.

Wrapped up in the cold cockpit of his dark camouflaged Sopwith Camel he flew across the airfield at a steady five hundred feet. Fifty feet to his left, beyond Mac's own red flight leader's banner that fluttered from an interplane strut, flew Flight Lieutenant Jamie Merriwether, his Camel rising and falling gently against the white horizon. Semi-silhouetted; cowlings dented and scratched, fuselage streaked and shining with castor oil-stains, mud-splattered and war-weary like his own.

Behind them, four more straggling Camels made up the complements of A and B Flights, of what was whimsically now known as '*Snargasher*' squadron instead of its official number, to avoid Lloyd George's blushes if things went awry. They were slotting into a controllable formation, most low on ammunition after strafing a Red Cossack patrol. The brief firefight with a collection of Bolshevik Nieuports and Spads, operating at perhaps the limit of their range, had all but emptied their ammunition belts, but they'd had the satisfaction of destroying two, definitely, or perhaps three of the enemy.

Having shot up the *Bolshie* Halberstadt which belatedly they'd realised was *itself* coming under attack from a gaggle of enemy fighters they'd refrained from administering the *coup de gras*. It seemed it had no rear-firing weapon and was doomed to crash due to the shattered elevator, half of which had torn away and was flapping in the slipstream, providing little or no control. It also had a strange enclosed cabin, like the top of a hansom cab with neat windows where the open gunner's cockpit was usually fitted.

Although he'd seen many things in two-and-a-half years as an RFC pilot in France, and even more in the year he'd been in Russia, he'd never seen a performance like the one he'd witnessed a minute before. He and Merriwether had flown each side of the Halberstadt and alerted it with short bursts of their remaining tracer to pay attention: turn or fly straight by reference to hand signals. Or be shot down.

The pilot had complied but it was evident that he could not reduce speed to land as directed because of the damage to the elevator and tailplane. Instead he'd made a wide turn and approached low and fast, under control but at much too great a speed to land; across the aerodrome, out of wind.

The squadron log describes the Halberstadt aiming determinedly between two stout birches a few yards apart. Despite a moderate crosswind the aircraft passed exactly mid-way between the trees, just above the ground at not far short of a hundred miles per hour, disintegrating the propeller, amputating both wings near the roots and shearing off the remains of the tailplane.

Shorn of wings, the sturdy plywood-skinned fuselage had bounced off the dyke, tearing away the undercarriage, careened and slid for about a hundred yards through the snowy outfield, digging its engine into a hummock, standing on its nose and falling over sideways. Circling overhead Mac could see no signs of movement from the wreck.

~·~

At the end of the debris trail Rolf regained consciousness and realised he was sitting in an aeroplane. From the pain in his left shoulder he guessed correctly he'd suffered a broken left collar bone when his harness had given way. His right shoulder felt as if it had been dislocated, almost certainly by Kessler's protective helmet as he'd slid violently forward from the first decelerating impact with the trees. As planned this had robbed the speeding aeroplane of much of its energy. The progressive break up of the machine left the plywood crash-cell of the fuselage with its heavy engine to absorb the remaining energy and had saved their skins, albeit they'd suffered some injury. Ernst seemed to be unconscious. Despite searing pain Rolf checked for a pulse in his friend's neck. To his immense relief it was evident and strong.

After a few moments Kessler opened his good eye, looking up groggily, his head under Rolf's right elbow.

'I take it we're still alive.' he said.

The typewriter had been torn from its mounting in the crash. Rolf almost smiled at the irony of its manufacturer's name: a *Monarch*. How very pragmatic of them.

Running figures were visible, dark against the snow. Whatever was now to befall them, at least they weren't in the clutches of the Bolshevists. More than that, snowdrops were pushing their leaves out of the snow all around the crash. The Ukrainian winter was releasing its grip.

~-~

The subsequent interview by Squadron Leader MacIntyre starts with the presumption that the papers I'm carrying relating to a Comrade Colonel Koroshnikov means that I am he.

I politely correct this case of mistaken identity while my left arm is placed in a sling and I explain the circumstances of our escape. I'm glad to be practising my English. Happily my right shoulder blade is merely bruised. Apart from a headache and some cuts and bruising himself, Kessler is perfectly fine and tells the Squadron Leader that I always land like that. Insolently, I thought, but in passable English that I didn't know Ernst possessed.

We find that we're under arrest for the time being until they can get some sort of ruling from BEF HQ on what to do with us. Turning us loose seems not to be a particularly useful idea as we'd as likely be skinned by Makhno's Greens or shot by *Shkura's Wolves*, the former a roving Ukrainian bandit pack which sounded not unlike Roskov's in the Baltic. Handing us over to the White Army which had withdrawn from the Ukraine doesn't sound as if it would be any more comfortable. In the event it may be that we'll be in for further interrogation if the upper echelons think we can supply some useful intelligence, or they have nothing better to do.

I tell MacIntyre that we are fighter pilots and want nothing more than to fly against the Bolshevists at the earliest opportunity. He looks grave and says that would not be possible and that the present situation is 'very volatile'. They are holding the line but he says that it's not breaching any official secret to say that we might not be remaining in this particular zone for long. They are a very mobile force, he adds.

~-~

The initial interview is concluding and we are about to be shown to some temporary accommodation, no doubt appropriately guarded.

'One thing, Squadron Leader,' I say. 'I wish to ascertain a matter of personal importance regarding a close friend, actually someone from my extended family who has been missing since last year. Have you encountered a lady, a noblewoman. A countess who rides with and commands the cavalry *sotnia*, *White Vengeance*. An expert with the sabre. Very red hair.'

'You must mean Madamoiselle 'X' and her *Bluecoats*,' said MacIntyre.

My heart jumps. 'Have you seen her recently? Do you know where she is?'

'She was with an American Red Cross train here only last week. She was seeing to some of her wounded.'

He said she had been making sure they were treated and sent back from the Front, isolated from the typhus sufferers in the front part of the train..'

'Did you see her?'

'Not personally no. But some of our Russian aides spoke with her at Slavyansk station. She'd been slightly wounded herself.'

'How badly?'

'Slightly, that's all. I don't have any details.'

Alive! She was alive, thank God. Wounded only slightly. I had to find her. Find out what news of Kat. And get her out of this bloody country and this vicious war.

Chapter 49. *Arkadi: War Hero*

Sebastopol Towers,
St. Albans, 1988

Count 'Klim' Wieniawa-Klimaszinski leans back in his chair. I am seated opposite with the Walther automatic. Safety on. Wolfgang is bound and disconsolate on the carpet. Richard, Amelia and James are seated around the room. He is about to deliver a history lesson.

Klim describes the situation in Ukraine in 1918-19. The *Hetmanische Putsch* of 1918 supported by the Germans, had ousted the national government of Simon Petlyura whose own Haydamaka Regiment for a Free Ukraine had driven the Bolshevist Red Guard out of Kiev in 1918. The Germans installed Pavel Skoropadsky, a pro-German aristocrat, as Hetman: supreme chief of the Ukraine.

But with the collapse of Germany and the Armistice of 1918, Petlyura returned as C-in-C with Vladimir Vinnichenko as President. The hoped-for independence of the Ukraine, ratified at Brest-Litovsk did not last. Kiev fell again to the Bolshevists, Vinnichenko left the country and Petlyura as head of state and the Army fought valiantly against the Whites under Denikin, against the Bolshevists and the Rumanians but was forced to withdraw to Poland in December 1919. Again, with Polish assistance, Petlyura's two remaining divisions attacked Kiev in July 1920. After initial success Poland's Marshall Pilsudski and Petlyura were forced back to the Vistula and Warsaw. Then, when all seemed lost, came *The Miracle on the Vistula,* an amazing last ditch victory over the Bolshevists.

But the Red Army under Tukachevsky advanced elsewhere, smashing against the Armed Forces of Southern Russia who withdrew in fighting retreat, including the Don Army into the Don Basin, the port of Rostov and the Sea of Azov: swelling the ranks of Peter Wrangel's Army in the Crimea. Petlyura remained in Polish sanctuary protected by Polish friends and colleagues such as Henryk Jozewski and formed the Ukrainian Government-in-Exile directing affairs from Warsaw until his interment by the Poles in October 1920. Skoropadsky died in Germany during a bombing raid in World War 2, but his émigré movement towards the re-establishment of a monarchist Ukraine continued until the 1980s. Petlyura's forces were decimated in the Ukraine.

'The re-unification of Poland and Lithuania as envisaged by Jozewski could be extended to include Ukraine. There are still in existence structures for change in these countries and governments-in-exile. The time is coming for the new independencies. Poland is showing the way. The people are fearful but sick of Communism, though most now have known nothing else. But I am ready for the challenge. The new future. A new pan-Lithuanian-Polish-Ukrainian tripartite nation, *bastions* of freedom and the Christian religion reborn against the satanic power of the USSR. This is what it's about, ladies and gentlemen. Bulwarks!'

'Indeed! And what part does 'Harry' play in your sweet dream of Empire, Klim.'

'*Arkadiusz* was my father's greatest friend. He will be my advisor, my chancellor. My wise counsel. He deserves to go home the hero after his history. You knew he was awarded the American Silver Star? In Italy? That is about equivalent to your Victoria Cross. To our *Virtuti Militari*.'

'What did he do to merit that?' I asked, not intending it to sound flippant.

Klim took a deep breath.

'He took a German citadel. That's what he did to bloody merit that.'

He fixed me with his level leonine stare.

'Along with Monte Cassino, which I'm sure you've heard of, there were other forts, such as Piedmonte that had to fall along the spine of Italy. Another hill to take, another river. They blocked the advance and controlled the heights. Cassino was levelled by aerial bombardment, but the German defenders continued to fight in the rubble. They still held the high passes. The lesson of the siege of Stalingrad had to be re-learned by the Allies fighting their way into Churchill's 'Soft European Underbelly'. *Softness* is relative I think. Reducing a fortification to rubble does not necessarily reduce the fighting power of its defenders. In fact it provides better natural cover. Cassino left the Allied dead, literally, in tiers until it was taken by those valiant soldiers, who left their dead there too, in the thousands. At the end it was our Polish flag that flew there, victorious.

'Harry was tough, in his prime. But by God he'd suffered to get that tough. Russian captivity had killed many tough cookies, broken their spirit and health in the bloody gulag. He'd made his way to Persia. Some of it on bloody foot! Many died on the way. You know what that terrain is like? To Tehran and with proper food and medical attention he and a hundred-and-more-thousand others formed the new Polish II Corps under General Anders. He was then in his mid-thirties. In his prime. Wiry, hard courageous as only a Pole can be courageous. Oh yes, he was *born* in Lithuania, but of Polish parents. And he's seen a lot of life and a lot of death, believe me, John.'

'So what did he actually do?'

He told me that the citadel had pinned down numerous combined attempts to bring armour and troops up the nearby main road, the only one suitable route for mechanised advance, for supplying the invasion and it was a thorn in the side of the Allied advance

'The fortress was partly encircled by a fast flowing river that had swelled to a flood in the heavy rains. He rounded-up ten oxen. Ten damn great oxen and lashed ten men to each animal, ten tough Polish soldiers on each. On top and surrounding it, all hanging on to ropes. The oxen were also roped together, one behind the other. In the pitch dark, in freezing weather, he rode the lead ox across the torrential river and with his hundred men he scaled the massive walls with grappling hooks. Nearly all the defenders were concentrating their attention on those parts of the fort that were vulnerable to attack. No one expected an assault from across the maelstrom behind them, which they considered *impossible* to ford.'

Klim offered me a wry smile. 'Harry and his men overpowered the few immediate guards then turned their German 88s inwards onto the backs of the defenders whose only option was to surrender. Harry was a bloody overnight hero. He did much more than that, but for the Americans it was enough for a Silver Star. He was still pissed from the celebrations when General Mark Clark pinned it on his chest but he pulled himself to attention for the ceremony. I had a portrait artist paint the scene for Harry about ten years ago. It has a place of honour in my home where he is a frequent guest. It bears a plaque with two words only.

For Valour.

He could see from my expression that I was impressed.

'So don't you think, John, that with a man like that by my side that I could take back Poland?'

Suddenly I felt something blow through me like a wind. I had a vision of a Baltic idyll ravaged by terror, war and murder. A young boy who'd lost his family and served nine years as a slave, then after military service in a free Poland sent again to a Soviet work camp. But with a spirit of such fire that enabled him to triumph over the enemy in war, to be then denied the opportunity, with his valiant comrades, to march with the victorious combatants to the Cenotaph. And to see his homeland occupied by a regime as ruthless and oppressive as any in the history of the planet.

I could see how the Romanov gold would shine like a beacon of hope for these dispossessed of homeland. And if it belonged anywhere, it was among the regions that had made up the Motherland of Old Russia.

Klim took the initiative.

'Perhaps when you've had time to think, John, you might consider the legitimacy of that claim and the illegitimacy of all others.'

Chapter 50. *There is no God!*

In Ukraine: the Last Days

Kessler and I inventoried the remnants of Petlyura's air arm. There was a D.VII and several Albatros fighters in reasonable condition scattered about the field. MacIntyre had told us we were welcome to the lot as long as we didn't get in the damn way and expect the RAF to provide assistance or fuel. The Red Army was massing to the north of Kursk, armoured trains moving towards Kharkov so he had much to concern him. But for the time being we were guests of the Squadron so we had rations and somewhere to stay.

~-~

The Whites had some 40 aeroplanes in the region. A mix of Nieuports and Albatrosse under the command of General Denikin. No doubt they'd commandeer these too if they knew about them, I thought. We spent our time preparing some of the Albatroses and the Fokker, and negotiating with the RAF on how we could conduct our own little guerrilla war; while contriving by any means to obtain petrol. Then, after a week; manna from heaven. Reilly's and Boris Savinkov's' *fixer*, McLaren, arrived with a trainload of General Bahalovich's colourful mercenaries, a cut-throat crew even by the standards of the time. But they brought weapons, tools, spares of all sorts and two wagons with drums of aviation spirit, praise the Lord, paid for with some warlord's looted war chest perhaps. He reported to MacIntyre who introduced me as one of two spare pilots, though temporarily *hors de combat* with a fractured collar bone. I said to hell with my collar bone I could fly alright. Just give me fuel and ammunition belts and I'd be airborne before you could say *na Moskvu!*

~-~

Bahalovich had delivered some Tsarist and Ukrainian Nationalist pilots with a mercenary Austro-German, a half-Danish Estonian and others, some of whom had some mechanical experience: so with Kessler and myself we were a mixed bunch with but a single aim. We'd retained the yellow *tryzub* on its blue field, the trident of the Ukrainian National Republic: there was simply no time then to re-paint it with some other insignia and no-one could decide who we represented other than ourselves. Known unofficially as the *Volunteers*, the air component was informally christened *McLaren's Marauders*. We were united in our vehement anti-Bolshevism and my own sympathies were for free republics everywhere.

Those days were a hectic mix of licking our small air component into shape. A local ataman arrived on day three with a troop of cavalry escorting a motorcar containing a priest in his fine sacerdotal robes. He blessed our aeroplanes with great solemnity before we took off to raid along the Sychevka railway line where a Bolshevik troop train had been reported. But we failed to find it before we were forced to return, low on fuel. Despite the blessing, God had perhaps not been with us that day.

To extend our tactical range beyond the sorties of the RAF expeditionaries, we decided to investigate suitable 'satellite' fields alongside undamaged railway lines in south-central Ukraine, for fuel and ammunition provisioning. Aerial reconnaissance in depth led us to an abandoned airfield which was situated near a small railway station on the Sula river, alongside the Konotop-Kharkov line, which we buzzed at low level in force to check it was unoccupied. A small armoured train with horse-wagons and flatcars was organised which would deliver fuel drums from the station to the field, under a Bahalovich escort.

It was an exposed position in an unprotected salient with known Bolshevik back area troop concentrations some fifty kilometres north and east and maybe straggling south as well. The Poles and their American volunteers had fought valiantly throughout the whole area but had fallen back under weight of numbers, furiously harassing Budyonny's Horse Army from the air in retreat. We were now re-infiltrating *behind* Budyonny's line, and were about to discover the anticipated ravages of his rapacious advance.

Feared as much for their vicious cruelty as that murderous horde of Genghis Kahn, they'd come howling through, screaming and whooping like wild Indians: left bodies unburied in the villages, homes burned and stripped of anything that could be stolen. The devastation and general mess was obvious from the air among those villages that had already been sacked and looted by Nestor Makhno and Shkura's Wolves who'd pillaged them before that. It was rumoured that Shkura had sent a vast fortune in treasure to Swiss banks in three or so years of campaigning.

We lost no time in searching the hangars and made an armed reconnaissance on foot of the field perimeter, placing piquets. A cursory examination of some two-seaters showed them to be elderly, mostly damaged and generally useless.

Always on the lookout for spare parts, Kessler and I moved on to investigate the aircraft dump where some useful bits might be retrieved. This dump was situated in a muddy depression in a corner of the field dominated by a big, twin-engine Ukranian Gotha G.IV bomber that we'd seen from the air. Various dismantled Polish and Russian types, among them two Italian-built Ansaldo *Balilla* fighters, lay in various states of disrepair amongst rusty engines, old motor cars and junk. But we could hardly believe what next we saw.

Nestling on flat tyres in the shadow of the Gotha stood a vivacious single-seater, a Polish red/white 'chess board' painted on its balanced rudder. Equipped with an oil-stained 160 hp. geared, Siemens-Halske rotary engine in which the mass of the engine turned in opposition to the propeller, it was missing its spinner – possibly removed to improve cooling for the slow-revving geared engine - but was still fitted with the huge four-blader and armed with twin Spandaus. A map of the Ukraine lay on the floor of the cockpit, printed in Warsaw.

Apart from a single *gottverdammt!* Kessler was speechless. We'd found an abandoned Polish Siemens-Schuckert D.IV fighter, presumably late of the *Freiwillige* German Border Defence Force, commandeered and a very long way from home!

'All things come to those who wait,' I said.

The two aeroplanes had been used for small arms target practice. The condition of the Gotha was beyond our capabilities to assess. But the damage to the Siemens seemed superficial, with just a few tears in the wings and rudder and a number of holes in the plywood monocoque. The airframe could easily be patched with fabric and it seemed in excellent order otherwise and may have been abandoned simply for lack of availability of castor oil, vital to the operation of rotary engines. We checked, gapped and cleaned the plugs and found there was just enough fuel to start the engine and run it briefly, Kessler in the cockpit and several of us holding down the tail. The windstorm of the propeller slipstream took our collective breaths away as it tried to climb over the chocks!

Kessler decided to fly his Albatros back to the Expeditionary Force for fabric and dope, determined to obtain castor oil, and RAF stocks were nearest.

That night we warmed ourselves by a fire lit in a desecrated church. Some of Budyonny's mounts had been killed in the fairly recent action and were lying around, horribly swollen. The permeating stink from these dead animals was overpowering, and by the next morning, had driven us from our tents on the field. One exploded with a report loud enough to have us running for cover so I led a detail with guards to spike their stomachs.

On the outskirts of the nearby village, filthy emaciated women and children (my first thought was gypsies) swarmed over these animals that buzzed with bluebottles, cutting meat from the legs and haunches, seemingly oblivious of the stench that made us retch in spite of scarves pressed to our faces. Small, near-naked children with horribly swollem bellies, large heads, and bodies like chicken embryos, too weak to walk, wobbled on the periphery. It was hard to stomach, but then they'd probably been living on fine-ground bark and boiled grass hereabouts for weeks. I was struck by the thought that only a few months ago I'd been a starving wretch who'd have regarded such a swollen horse as a banquet. So my half-contemptuous, half-sorrowful reaction to these 'gypsies' was unworthy and hypocritical. I went down to hand them what rations I could spare.

The thin, ragged, brutalised females who'd suffered rape and loss of family members, initially fled our *Volunteers*, hiding in rough sheds or the nearby woods. Then, emboldened, they came close, begging scraps of food. I was moved by their plight and the knowledge that many, among whom were very young girls, were doomed to die, if not miserably from starvation, then horribly from syphilis and all that entailed.

We tried to avoid close contact to reduce the transmission of typhus-carrying fleas but they grasped and kissed our hands in gratitude. That night we were itching and liberally applied flea powder from our med kits. Most of us turned our clothing inside-out, using cigarette lighters to burn out any parasites or their eggs that might be lodged in the seams.

~-~

Within two days castor oil had arrived by truck and the machine was patched and part re-painted white, though the red Polish markings still blushed through, *pink*, as if reluctant to be denied! But Kessler lost no time in air-testing the machine which climbed like a rocket. He power-dived from 2000 metres, zooming into a vertical climbing roll which none of us could perform in a two-aileron Albatros. Kessler looped, rolled around in the Ukrainian sky and generally shot the base up, landing with a triumphant smile on his face. That evening he embellished the fuselage with a stylised 'K' in blue (perhaps he didn't have time to paint a pelican) adding the vainglorious combat challenge, *Mein Handschuh: Dein Gesicht* to the upper surface of the elevator – in the same bold lettering which had decorated those of his archaic Brandenburg KD in Macedonia. Ernst then ceremoniously 'presented' his cast-off Albatros to a delighted Latvian mechanic who was also a pilot, 'itching to fly fighters instead of "just" fixing them', he said.

Kessler's Siemens-Schuckert SSW D.IV fighter with Polish markings still visible.

With its slender wings, huge propeller, aerodynamically perfect fuselage and stylish rudder, the Siemens-Schuckert was a thoroughbred. Standing proud on its tall undercarriage, it was truly the flower of German fighter design, with great emphasis on streamlining and a performance to match. Though vanity is self-deceit and glory the crowning lie of war, Kessler, warrior, who breathed the intoxicating incense of its unholy spirit, seemed happier than ever I'd known him. Godless himself, he would wield his mighty sword to lay waste the foe, he said, and strike down the *Gottlosen* ranks of Bolshevism and saw no irony in the rhetoric.

Deep down, I felt, he must believe in something other than war for its own sake. But I was glad he was on our side.

~-~

My memories of the next weeks are indistinct. I had my crash shortly afterwards which obliterated much. But I do recall many aerial combats of extreme ferocity, scoring successes despite Red numerical superiority. But there was the unstoppable Red advance on the ground, driven on by the zeal of their commanders and Trotsky's political commissars. Lost opportunities and lack of proper co-ordination among the White forces slowly eroded our positions while a weakening of political and moral support of the Triple Entente for the continuing war gradually took its toll, despite the valiant efforts of the troops under fine individual commanders like Peter Wrangel and British 'Interventionist' generals like Maund.

In our aerial engagements at this time I recall a general melée one sunny morning at medium altitude in Ukraine, in the Bolsehvist-controlled Baturyn, Nizhya, Konotop triangle, with individual fights and several machines going down on fire. My engine suddenly ran rough and lost power just as I was singled out for desperate combat with a Bolshevist triplane which out-manoeuvred me at every turn, stitching bullets into my wings and fuselage only for him to be joined by another machine. I fought unequally to gain an advantage and noted that, unusually for a Soviet machine, the *Dreidecker* was a black-painted Fokker Dr.1 with a white 'death's head' on the fuselage. We'd heard tell of a German mercenary ace who flew one of these very rare birds, and now I was at the mercy of *two*, the other being a biplane: a formidable dark green D.VII, possibly 'war spoil' from another front. Bullets were cutting past me as they took it in turns to shred my old Albatros and I was close to accepting that I would surely die, when I saw a brief flash of white; Kessler diving out of nowhere to shoot one down in flames as the other tried to dive away. Before I could roll back onto its tail, Kessler had turned like lighting in the SSW D.IV and despatched the other machine with a short burst at close range and it fell away, smoking.

He zoomed and pulled up past me, arm raised in a pumping action, fist clenched in victory. Not bad for a one-eyed airman! But over a short period we lost several pilots, some to the sharp shooting of Budyonny's *Syphilitic Horse* as we raked their remorseless spearhead aimed at Lvov. There the valiant Poles were again dug in; waiting for them with murder

718

in their hearts.

In a flash, Kessler, in the Siemens-Schuckert, despatched them both.

Eventually reduced to seven fighters, we fell back south in what turned out to be the last stages to our temporary field near Poltava. Here, I remembered, from my rag bag education, that towards the end of the eighteenth century Sweden's warrior king, Charles XII, had lost his campaign in the Great Northern War against Peter the Great; being severely wounded on the field of battle. Had his big toe shot off. I wondered if that was an omen.

~-~

Walking the shore I've been striving to remember the rest. The missing pieces of that last combat in Southern Russia. But now I feel it coming in snatches and flashbacks. Suddenly I am desperately fearful of what it will deliver. The door is yielding and for the first time I dread its fall.

I sit on the strand and pull the creased and faded letter from my pocket and read it for the fiftieth time. It was written in haste and its message is terse.

My Darling Rolf,

I hope you find this. If you do you will have seen what has happened at Liepus Namas. All are dead, murdered by the Bolshevists, by Roskov and his bloody pack of wolves. Nothing, no-one remained undefiled. My father took the Tannenberg sword from the wall in a last valiant act. Some he slew but then he was cut down, mutilated and crucified. I have no news of my sisters except the bitter fact that little Graczyna was not spared their violation. Perhaps you already know this, but I regret also the reported passing of your father. Dr. Dragunavicius was cruelly murdered with his operating staff, all his nurses and patients in Latgale, and I have to report too the suicide death of your mother. I pray that their souls are now at rest. What terrible times, my angel.

I go to my fate swearing endless war against them. I shall die, I know, but I will die with a sword in my hand.

I will pray for you. Long live Lithuania. I love you forever.

K

~-~

My head aches again. Worse this morning than ever. I feel dizzy and have to close my eyes against the bright sea and the light sky that blinds me. Shapes are turning in my mind. I hear the goblin banging at the door, his blows are powerful and splintering, revealing shards of memory which have so far eluded me. I imagine sear arms reaching through the cracks, horny fingers gripping me, roughly pulling me into its cellar of pain and reality. The Baubas, who will reveal to me the mystery I must know. The reality I fear to know.

I picture Reilly's dark mesmeric eyes. I think he has seen into my soul and perhaps planted there a seed of recollection from the time when he and the mercurial Savinkov had rallied the Bahalovich volunteers, the mercenary army of the South Ukraine and raised our little component air arm.

The sea sparkles through the reluctant shutters of my eyes, things moving in the changeling light, shimmering and dancing. I am viewing through a gauze, through a dark glass a scene that I slowly recall. Rolling in waves, five hundred cavalrymen, part of the 6th. Cavalry Division of Budyonny's Horse Army, rifles glinting. They charge the Polish guns, the cavalry splitting their force to encircle before the artillery can react.

My overview is 500 metres above the fray, from the familiar cockpit of my Albatros with my little *Jasta* or *Schwarm*. Kessler on my wing in a

Siemens-Schuckert. Three Albatroses and a D.VII formate behind. Our ammunition is spent from strafing the back areas so we watch helplessly. Defending Polish troops begin to fall back when from a scrub-covered ravine a *sotnia* of blue-coated light cavalry cuts in hard on the attacking flank, turning the Reds with flashing sabre, pistol and rifle fire. Shooting like Apaches from under their speeding mounts they break the charge. As they clash the blues have the advantage. There is a rout upon the steppe with horses wheeling and savage individual sabre fights. The Polish gunners are knocking out the chocks, turning their field guns to their flanks.

The blues hold the high level ground awhile but withdraw in loose skirmishing. The commander's horse falls, kicking violently on its side. I am already descending. I have seen her bonnet rolling in the dust and the hair that flies like fire. Below the rise the Reds are gathering and re-grouping into some sort of order.

I dive like a falcon, wires shrieking. I sense the others behind me. We level above the steppe and charge full-throttle into the throat of the Red cavalry. We hit them with their sabres raised. Smash into them at head-height for a mounted man, controls stiff at 250 kph. from the momentum of our dive. I see their eyes, almost their fear as I slam into them with my undercarriage, the lead horses rearing and plunging, sabres flashing, rifles raised, men falling in the dust while other riders cannon into their rear. It's a riot of confusion; a dust storm in which loose horses and struggling men vanish and re-emerge.

To the flanks Kessler and the others are roaring through the ranks in a shower of blood driving men and horses aside in waves of panic. The Reds turn sideways, turn about and scatter, make off even though we've not fired a shot, such is the terror of the low flying aeroplane, a snarling engine, scything propeller and wheels used like battering rams. I pull up vertically while the others fly on. I stall-turn, cartwheeling back to where she's fallen hardly daring to breathe for what I might find. *Im Ufergrass.*

She's not moving. *Krysia, please hold on. I'm coming.* I turn hard and descend hurriedly, side-slipping, slowing the machine by fish-tailing. I slam it down and without waiting for it to stop I am un-strapped, sliding down the fuselage and running to where she has fallen. I cradle her in my arms and she looks at me with clouds in her eyes.

It is a blue, early summer's day with puffy cumulus and the smoke of battle drifting. Two lovers lie upon a grassy bank oblivious of war whose struggles soften on the breeze to the gentle hum of insects, fading to a murmur: the focus of my life lies before me.

'Krysia, Krysia,' I cannot say anything except her name, tears welling in my eyes.

'Rolf. Look at you – a flier. I prayed you were alive.' Her voice is clear but distant.

She is smiling, her face suddenly wet with tears.

'Let me get you to safety,' I say. But as I lift under her arms her expression stiffens.

'Ach, no, Rolf, it's no good. It's over. My legs, they are numb. My back is broken for sure.' Her breathing now is short. '*Kak zhal*,' she says in Russian. 'What a pity.'

'But I must save you. I can get you to the artillery position….. I can carry you.'

'*Ne*, Rolf. Please, you must do something. Save yourself and find my sister, if she lives.'

'But we must first attend to you.'

She looks sideways, fearfully but not, I think, for herself. 'Rolf they are coming. Please! Quickly, you must go! Help me now, then go!'

She is tugging at my holster. No, I say. No and no. But she is determined. Her strength is failing. I must help her. The Reds are re-grouping. Her sotnia is scattered. The guns have not yet opened up. I can't bear this. Her hands are gripping my automatic, turning it. Please Rolf. I am helping her lift the muzzle to her lips, she is looking at me with eyes of clouded sapphire, her breathing rapid. Ateh! She says.

There is a sound like a rushing wind and a roar of engines. A winged shadow rushes over us like an angel of death. I feel its pressure wave urging us to move. The Staffel is low on fuel. Promise me you'll find her, Rolf! The Reds are coming. Her fate would be under their hooves or unimaginably as their hostage for their sport. If I could get her to the Albatros, engine ticking over nearby. Could she hold on? Could she….?

'Bless you, Rolf,' she says. 'And bless me.

I am not a priest…..

'Rolf, release me. Do it, please. *Now!*'

My finger tenderly encircles her finger in the trigger guard. '*Ateh*.' she says; opens her mouth to the barrel and closes her eyes.

I release her head gently to the blood-soaked grass. I look for her bonnet to rest her head. I am in a daze, barely breathing. Her eyes are half-open, with a searching look, as though attempting to discern something afar off, focussed on some secret vista. A vision of paradise? I search vainly for intelligence there, then I gently close them. I know now there is no God.

Nearby I realise that her brown mare is still screaming, kicking hooves caught in her own bloody entrails. I shoot her through the brain.

722

I find Krysia's bonnet. Gently lifting her head I say my goodbye with a kiss to her lips. Her mouth is full of blood. I lay her down to rest on the steppe.

She could almost be sleeping, though there is no God, her fine hair fanned out: *Raudongalvis*, red-headed spirit of blowing grassland. I find her sabre and fold her hands over the grip. *'I will die with a sword in my hand....'* She is a medieval knight upon her grassy plinth: a gallant, faithful Lithuanian noblewoman; but there is no God. I stand and salute her....*im Ufergras. Ateh*, Krystina, Baroness von Strelitz, my dearest love. May your spirit fly on the wings of an albatross, taking my heart with you. Forever.

Kessler practically knocks me flat with his wing as he dives to alert me to a danger of which I'm well aware.

There is no God. There is no God! Ernst, you bastard. There is no God!

Suddenly I am roaring in pain and anger at the top of my lungs, shouting at Kessler whose D.IV is urgently circling. 'THERE IS NO GOD!' I walk to my fighter with feet of lead, climb aboard without strapping-in, open the throttle wide, holding the swing with rudder and charge the enemy tail-up as their front rank gallops over the rise. 'There is no God!' I scream in anguish, again and again into the wind. I am flying just above them with my left hand, cursing my barren Spandaus and emptying my automatic as I tear through the ranks of the dregs of war, the *Reaper with his scythe*, feeling the slash and thud of their sabres against my tyres, the smack of flesh and bone on my axle beam.

Kessler flies alongside, ploughing his own rapier furrow though the cavalry, slamming his wheels into the riders' heads. I am dimly aware of the blue initial letter 'K' on his fuselage. It now stands for my Krysia, and for her lost sister. And for Kristian, crucified in a parody of Christ. Yet there is no God, only Kessler's God of War!

I am suddenly seeing myself from above, detached from my Albatros with the yellow tryzubs on blue fields upon its wings; the insignia of a free Ukraine. A fighter flown by a pilot who'd once dreamed of a free Lithuania. I turn and dive again. I throw away my empty pistol and take up my big Mauser flare gun, my lone aeroplane ripping through their lines. Gunfire peppers the machine with a hundred hits but I am spared. I fly in a state of grace. Krysia is with me. I am ready to die and would welcome it in that moment.

~.~

I look down on myself, on Steiger, seeing the bursting artillery shells find their mark among the cavalry. There is brief intimation of Pyrrhic victory.

~-~

A Cossack head bounces in the dust. Steiger is dimly aware that it falls from his undercarriage. Horsemen whirl and plunge in terror, with shell bursts among them. He is in harm's way. His heart pounds louder than the carronade. Dirt and shrapnel erupt ahead of the Albatros. Disorientation. Smoke is everywhere, his eyes are dimming. Is he hit? The aircraft feels strange. Has he run out of fuel? The controls feel heavy and then the ground is coming up in a sudden rush. He's pulling back with all his strength but nothing seems to work. The gun breeches are strangely soft and absorb the impact of his cheekbone: tissue consumes steel: bone is an enzyme of gunmetal.

He falls slowly forward into darkness. A Slavic head is grinning. He knows brief terror then 'unknowing'. There are two lanterns in the dark. He remembers the hospital tent before evacuation. His dreams of twin suns viewed from the surface of an alien planet. Bell and the surgeon, forbidding sentinels, turning him back from that final journey. Bell's questions that made no sense because he could not even tell them who he was. The long stop-start journey, days and nights in the hospital train with Bolshevists shooting at the nurses and wounded, aiming at the white bandages through the curtained carriage windows.

His mantra was that not all we perceive is the truth, Natasha. Neither what we read. Not Mr. Dawson's reported discovery, Eonthropus dawsonii from the early Pleistocene, 'deduced' from a skull fragment: an orang's jaw and a chimpanzee's canine at Piltdown, a lie. Not the panacea that Marx foresaw for humankind. Not Nietzsche's belief in the salvation of the species being in the genes, isolated from a gottlosen Kosmos. Neither the ability of the human body to withstand a high speed crash in an Albatros. He recalls Newton on the shores of his 'Great sea of Truth' in which he is swimming…swimming.

He has a new memory, being stretchered aboard an overloaded ship by night, the sky lit by gunfire. A tired-looking Flight Lieutenant Merriwether telling him MacIntyre's been shot, not expected to live. Kessler is missing. No one knows what happened to him. British Tommies are forced to beat off ten thousand refugees who beg, Radi Boga! Pleading for the love of God to be taken aboard, not left to the brutality of the Bolshevists. Someone says they've torched the hospital and burned five thousand patients and the nursing staff. There's total panic. Only British personnel. People and bundles fall from the dock in the crush of bodies. Some shoot themselves first or make futile jumps for the stern rail. Other ships nose into Taganrog and Rostov harbours, making fortunes, demanding scandalous amounts from desperate refugees. Nyet, madam. Not roubles. Steiger, helpless and injured on the well deck, sees the flames reflected by the low clouds; glad of his half-English heritage as the throbbing engines increase their revolutions and slowly they slip out, into the Sea of Azov. They sail SSW, past the evacuating Crimean peninsula, into the Black Sea, SW via Istanbul, Marmara to the Med. Then the long haul; Gibraltar, Biscay, and so to the Islands he'd left as a babe. Then his return voyage had been long on discomfort under a regime of practical nursing and a closeness in suffering to others, some more severely damaged than he. But it was dominated by the struggle to remember, which had made his perpetual headache worse.

~-~

In Norfolk he carefully folds the letter. He buttons it into his shirt pocket, kicks off his shoes and walks determinedly towards the cold, lapping surf. Keeps walking. Soon he is swimming rhythmically in the sun-spangled waters of the North Sea. Towards Lithuania.

Chapter 51. *Hostages to fate*

What bloody man is that? she thinks, unconsciously quoting Macbeth again in the coolness of reflection.

I see her again in my memory. Natasha: fear turned full to anger tearing back the curtain. The floodlights blazing. Her gaze swept the yard. *By the horror in my bones, something frightful…*a dark figure that seemed always to be standing in the penumbra of shadow, a *Schattengeist,* a haunting animus, taunting. Willis, or…..? The terror returned momentarily her body ice cold as she shrank back from the window. But then the rage returned ten fold. She caught up the carving knife and opened the casement. 'Who the hell are you? The fuck d'you want here?' she screamed, letting the blade catch the light. The figure remained immobile. A black eminence in deep shadow.

~-~

The flesh creeps under her robe. The figure slowly raises an arm. Hanging from that arm in the glare of the floodlight is what at first appears to be a football in a netting bag, but it's the blonde head of Emma, a *blondinka* hung by the hair. Natasha screams, at first soundlessly, her chest gripped in an iron band: silently, then chokingly, screaming out her lungs in horror, denial and disbelief at what she sees, before darkness enfolds her.

She dreams the old dream. She is sitting up in bed trembling while the secret police, the terror arm of the authorities, hammer at the door. She holds her infant child, barely a week old in the crook of her left arm. She has managed to drag the dressing table across the bedroom door as a barricade, even though she bled for a while. She points the weapon at the door, waiting for them to break in. She knows that they have come for her, for her child. She is not sick. She is perfectly sane. She will not let them take her alive.

~-~

She awakes with Emma rubbing her ice cold arms. She clings to her daughter as if she'd never let her go. She is in her bed, the floodlights no longer illuminated. Perhaps they never were. What in God's name had she been shown? Emma has rung for an ambulance. Natasha says she doesn't need one. Emma is holding her mother by the shoulders looking concernedly into her eyes. Emma, who's binned her girly bedroom posters for older and angrier Viking images: *Rammstein, Iron Maiden, Black Sabbath, The Ting Tings*, some darker still. Emma with her new tattoo and straight black hair now that she's a Goth - not blonde like the hallucination that Natasha's just experienced, holding her mother with surprising strength. Hell is going on? What does it all mean?

Her daughter explains to the ambulance crew that her mother has been under a lot of strain. Natasha sends them away. Emma thinks that her mother might be a paranoid schizophrenic and is fearful; suddenly vulnerable and alone, missing her father.

Natasha believes that she has somehow seen the other side of an event. One that has been playing in her mind since she's read the narrative.

Der Wassermann. The jealous thing of German myth that flings the corpse of his half-human child from the lake at the feet of his mortal wife, an analogy articulated by her father's symbolic written language was among the last random horrors he'd reported, from Harry's alleged testament. And Steiger's. Written in that moment of rare insight in which fugitive memories of things long hidden are revealed, she believes. That she, like her father had somehow understood Katarzyna's worst torture. That Kat had tracked the Wolves from Liepus Namas, perhaps accounted for some of them with her little poisoned arrows of *Issyk-Kul*. But Roskov's Wolves had caught and delivered her to him: had tossed into her foetid cage her headless half-sister. That is what her father had implied. But where was the real evidence? Was this haunting intended to reveal to her these things? Had his writings played so much on her mind that *nothing* now seemed co-incidental? She felt, not for the first time, that she was losing her grip on reality.

~-~

In those latter chapters of my father's MS much had been compressed. As if time was short.

I'd made a pact with Count Wieniawa-Klimaszinski, Natasha. He needed medical attention. He would leave Inkerman Road along with Wolf and I would arrange to deliver the briefcase to a 'safe house' at a mutually convenient date. We could settle all this then. We all understood the need for caution and security. I felt we could trust each other that far, couldn't we?

I knew I had nowhere I could hide indefinitely and there were other, more deadly forces at work. We might have defused the situation with the 'Ausland' *Iron Legion* but there were more sinister agencies keen to acquire what was concealed in the case. Klim used his car phone to make a call to Harry on an unlisted number and Harry returned the call to *Sebastopol Towers*. He'd suggested that I meet 'Stephanie' at a time and place to be decided soon and meanwhile to stay away from my usual contacts. *He indicated that my own daughter's safety might be in question, Natasha — not from him or their organisation but from others.* If I needed money to go to ground until then it would be provided.

I did not then realise that Klim was needing serious medical attention of another kind entirely. He was dying. His cirrhosis of the liver was already beyond effective treatment. Over the next year he would become increasingly weary, his colour changing to a nut brown, his lion's eyes yellowing the more.

From his bed of misery Klim had raised his leonine head to look past me, to a rain-swept hillside, grey and green: where sheep huddled from the wind in ravines, like maggots sucking at a wound. Above his head an American general pinned a Silver Star on a younger Harry.

'Beyond those hills was born the *Myrddin*: the treacherous spider at the centre of this web.' Klim told me. 'That's the Welsh name, for him, though I can think of others, in Polish!'

Contrary to my first thought he wasn't rambling.

'Caradoc Peregrine-Thomas, code name *Merlin*. A scheming and duplicitous bastard whom you trusted at your peril. Rolf Steiger trusted him completely but by the end would have shot him, like the treacherous hound he was. Steiger did not survive the Second World War - as far as is known. Merlin jumped ship, settled in Moscow alias *Sergei Kamov*. Traitor. HSU. A self-made bitter old man, full of self-loathing, I sincerely hope.'

He'd paused to gather his strength. He was shaking now most of the time. Weak sunlight was trying to penetrate the clouds.

'My land…' he'd said, '….stretches from the railway line to the river, two hundred yards by one hundred of black Welsh soil and bramble bushes.'

'In Poland, viewed from the tallest of my mansions, the borders of my sequestrated estates lay beyond the horizons, with lakes of carp, great fields of rye grass…farms, freshets…fresh flowing brooks and woodland. So my father told me for I never saw them for myself. Nor ever will. I leave this cup with you, my friend. Minister it well.'

Later on, while I was considering the options, he'd slipped into a coma, into the condition known as hepatic encephalopathy from which death swiftly followed. His wife and two young sons were inconsolable. And so was Wolfgang the waif.

~.~

At Farnborough Stephanie was opening up to me.
'You know that Hans-Peter loved me, Johann?'

'It is no surprise to hear that, Steph. May I ask, was it reciprocated?'

'I was fond of him, Johann. But no. I could have had any man when I was younger.'

I didn't doubt that. But did not the aside revealed a stratum of insecurity in the well-preserved Alexa? Am I being tested? Perhaps she thought I needed a prompt. Maybe she would use her still evident charms to try and trap this juicy bug in her web. Suck the contents of that briefcase out of me.

'Johann, Peter had played things very close to his chest. I believe he destroyed the key, those zig-zag bits of paper I'd handed him that fitted three specific pages in Macbeth. If the clue is there, which I think it is, it may be preserved in one of his haikus. We have to look deeper into what was in that case. We are committed to putting this resource to very good use, Johann. For the benefit of the people of Poland and the Baltic States. Perhaps of Belarus. People who have suffered much. The system is crumbling. A fund of this magnitude could be used to help it on its way. If it should fall to crooks and speculators, into the hands of the manipulators or organisations that spread terror and seek to destroy liberty, there's no telling what harm might be done. I've already got my little smelter.' She smiled. 'I, *we*, think you are a good and proper person, Johann.'

It was lunchtime, getting crowded in the marquee. Two men studiously not looking in our direction sat down close to our table.

'Fancy a stroll around the static display?' I asked her.

We walked. A *Rafale* was departing with ribcage-rattling thunder.

'So who are you actually working for now, Alexa?'

'Don't worry darling, I'm officially retired. If I was working for some bad guys you'd already be strapped to a frame selling me your mother. We aren't the Gestapo despite Klim's tendency to employ deadly waifs like Wolfgang.'

'So what's the plan?'

'We introduce it into the bullion market a little at a time.'

She stopped and faced me.

'Let's stop frigging each other, darling. We need that briefcase.'

~-~

April 2008,

The day following my hysterical fit they descended on Mill Farm the way they do in films. Two cars. DI Slater and two male uniformed officers including a sergeant as well as WPC Hamilton and a female civilian. Hamilton, who'd sat mutely at my interview in Ipswich, still heavy on the make up, accompanies a social worker escort for Emma. Early evening. At least it wasn't a dawn raid. They read me my rights and told me I was being arrested on suspicion of involvement in the 'murders' of the Blundell 'sisters'. They'd not bought the suicide angle. They searched and found a carving knife under my pillow and dropped this 'evidence' into a sterile bag, although they had a knife already.

I told them I had kept it upstairs for self-defence, from the monster that stalked me. They advised me that in law it became an offensive weapon if brandished threateningly and that I would be charged if someone were to make a complaint to that effect, even if that person were to be found guilty of the minor offence of 'trespass'. It was a very serious offence, the sergeant said, with the threat of a custodial sentence if proved.

What sort of a twisted society is Britain, I wondered exasperatedly. My protestations were ignored. Emma was frantic. She point-blank refused to leave, shouting about her civil rights. I said that she couldn't stay on her own and so did the police as she was not yet sixteen and anyway she'd be vulnerable alone in a fairly remote farmhouse. She vehemently refused to go and demanded she be allowed to remain. Her pony, she said, would need looking after. Damn, I thought, her exams. I told her not to worry and reassured her that it would only be for a little while as I was sure that this mix-up could be resolved quickly. However things became increasingly heated and before I knew it I was holding on to Emma, who was hysterical, and the social worker struggling to drag her to the car suggested sharply that I should consider seeking psychiatric help. It was only Hamilton's firm restraining grip prevented my fist from making contact with her face, rather reinforcing her point of view

Slater's slight off-centre stare was cool-eyed, thoughtful. Non-committal. I was finally escorted to the first police car and Emma, crying, was carted off in the other.

Apparently they'd been digging into my past and discovered I had been associated with a German revolutionary group while at university, spending more than five weeks underground in West Berlin undergoing some sort of indoctrination. The *Kafka-esque* MI5 file was thin but damning. I didn't have a clue what they were talking about nor what it could possibly have to do with the deaths of my neighbours, however suspicious.

~-~

And then in the cell, the amnesic barrier blurs, dissolving like frosted glass. I began to remember. Painfully, like Steiger had remembered after he'd hunted so long the thing that lurked in his mind, behind the door that suddenly collapsed under his assault. Possibly the dread thing itself had been breaking through from the other side; from which he'd shrunk at the last moment, for the awful memory he'd found there had nearly driven him insane.

They too were insane and disturbing, the horrible things that now churned through my mind. Indeed I had begun to realise that these memories had been leaching out for twenty years and I'd pushed them aside as transient, paranoiac events, fearful as I was of something I did not want to confront. Or I tried to rationalise them as daydreams and nightmares, reluctantly linking them with 'missing time'; aspects and flashbacks from experiments with substances I'd believed I had eschewed: though I *was* a child of the 'seventies after all, Emma. For now I am writing this for you.

~-~

It's later. I've been left to cool my heels, contemplating the eye-level slit in the cell door through which someone peers occasionally. The laces to my trainers have been taken. *Evil Eye Slater* is nowhere to be seen. I've demanded a lawyer firmly and politely. I've demanded a lawyer stridently and angrily. Neither approach has worked.

The door opens and a policeman enters carrying two metal chairs which he sets down facing 'my' bunk and then leaves.

Enter my interrogators who do not identify themselves. I assume they're Special Branch at least. More likely MI5: possibly one each from 5 and 6 if that's how they still define those departments of the SIS. They are in their thirties and forties. Grey suits, low key. One has a briefcase. The other carries a recording device and a notebook. Both are unsmiling. No 'good cop bad cop' routine for me then.

'Natasha Moriszhova.' Forty-something is speaking. Accentless.

'You tell *me*,' I say.

The first interrogator informs me that this could be easy or it could be hard. He quite likes 'hard' he tells me, so if I don't co-operate it's the sort of challenge he relishes. 'Hard' includes, by the way, being sent down for life, whatever 'life' means nowadays he comments wistfully, but not much fun for *me*, even so. My daughter would be at large and we know how vulnerable youngsters are nowadays even *with* parental support. The product of our institutions, by which he means the *care industry*, is not generally good in societal terms.

'Although, Emma's, what fifteen? Pretty girl. I'm sure she'll find work of a sort.'

He pauses briefly to make sure this has sunk in. Don't react, I tell myself.

He then launches into the next *Spiel.* Cards on table. Forensic evidence is compelling and I am placed at the scene. A motive can be pencilled-in without too much trouble. He recalls, unsmilingly, for my edification, the half-joking advice from a senior police officer that the Met never fabricate more evidence than is absolutely necessary to secure a conviction. Given my dossier a case could be made that the CPS would nod through, he assures me. Then it's down to twelve good subjects of Her Majesty's to weigh the evidence, well-spun by a skilled prosecuting counsel you can be sure, Natasha.

So, tell us about the Big City where they created you.

I cast my eyes downwards. A cold hand is gripping my heart. I am remembering again a much younger woman, just eighteen: watching her from above like a guardian angel in a plastic bubble, where the smell of fear cannot penetrate. Our brief only to observe, like the UN.

She'd packed her case, excited to be going to Berlin. *Place of real revolution, Natasha. Where we'll be treading on the heels of famous ghosts,* so 'Che' had said. They'd be meeting some interesting people, friends. Urban revolutionaries. In the Falklands the prelude to 'Thatcher's War', as they'd termed it later, it was just tuning up. Though of course the comrades called them *Las Malvenas.*

At Tempelhof he'd held her passport for safekeeping. On the second day they'd attended a student protest which, not unexpectedly, had turned into a violent confrontation with the riot police. Forced to escape down alleyways with some half dozen people whom Che evidently knew they fetched up, flushed and excited in a coffee house. There she'd quietly observed the group: Wolfram, tall, charismatic, intense, arrogantly good-looking, preoccupied and the undisputed leader, armed with a radically persuasive political philosophy that thrilled and terrified Natasha at the same time. His girlfriend, or so she seemed to be, was the tactile Helga, who'd befriended Natasha at once. Alcohol was consumed in quantity as the evening wore on until by unspoken consent all boarded a VW bus which sped through the Berlin night, she knew not where.

Ushered into a grim, part-boarded building she'd only glimpsed, that might once have been a hotel, she was to meet the others: the angry and unloved of the planet, some students like her, eager to learn at the feet of the new Messiah, become a part of the New Wave: they were already familiar with the words of Mao and had rather sneered at the simplistic message. Good enough for the peasantry: *The Little Red Book* in translation, German, English, Russian, Swedish now here again and required reading. It was chanted like a mantra, like morning prayers until the meanings were lost or took on new abstract forms and only sound pictures remained.

In the Ipswich police cell I view her now, as if watching from somewhere near the ceiling, perhaps in that realm where consciousness lies, when time had allowed the blood to cool.

She found herself, I remember, staring at a point on the wall. Bits of her cryptopsychy filtering down like dust motes in a sunbeam. Her *other* 'arrest' and sectioning fifteen years ago, she recalled, had followed her breakdown after Emma had been born. Her post natal depression had become full blown pueperal psychosis with schizophrenic events and hallucinations. She was convinced that some unnamed agency was determined to take her child from her, or harm her. She'd barricaded the bedroom listening fearfully to the midwife ringing the doorbell and calling from below. She knew it was a ploy to get her to open the door.

At first she'd thought that the threat was from outside, but when she looked into her baby's unfocussed eyes she'd seen things in those dark pupils that revolted her; swarming pools of little goblins swimming there; pouring from the eye sockets in black streams, ejecting their vile mass. To cluster like demonic bats on her baby's face, sucking greedily at her rosebud mouth. She'd been tricked. She saw clearly then that the evil was

734

inside, had been born from her own body, impregnated by a fiend. And now they dropped like roaches from her demon child, crawling upon her shoulder to re-invade her and reclaim her immortal soul! Natasha flung the baby from her in horror just as the fiend broke in and she'd shot him with her Russian automatic. Simeon had gently prised the television remote from her grasp and called for an ambulance while she'd howled in mental agony, chewing her bloodied fingers in distress like a thing possessed.

Strangely, she'd clearly recalled pointing an automatic pistol at Simeon. She wonders if and under what circumstances paranoid schizophrenia can be induced. Or false memories through subconscious eclectic feedback.

He'd tried to joke with her afterwards. When she had fully recovered from the drugs and ECT residual headaches. Asked if it was a *Baikal* or a *Makarov*. No, she thought, it had been an old *Tokarev*. Odd how Simeon seemed to know about such things. Odder still that she herself did. She even remembered later how she'd assembled it from small packets that had arrived randomly in the post; from Berlin and elsewhere. The customs labels had referred to them as machine spares for making jewellery. But back then her short term memory had been affected by the treatment and it had taken her a long while to retrieve it, if indeed she had.

~-~

In Ipswich the moon came to her mind and merged, beaming into the open harlequin face of an owl, or the white face of Alice with her empty teddy bear. She wondered if Alice's particular *Wonderland* came even close to her own.

Her interrogators sit unmoving opposite her. *The Caterpillar* without his pipe. *The Cheshire Cat* without his grin.

'You were told, were you not, that if you were asked any questions about that *ashram*, that polyglot spiritual retreat and the things you'll have learned there, you would remember nothing?'

Another question as a statement of fact.

'Instead you would see, what? The face of the moon or the image of a rocking horse? To rock all your memories away. Confirm?'

The same words are being spoken by Wolfram's spiritual lieutenant, a small man with black burning Cambodian eyes, known only as Ho. All had used aliases, or so she'd assumed. You will see the moon or the face of a white owl that will fly away

735

with your forbidden memories. His feathers are white, my children, as the snow, purged of all thought, pure white, like the petals of a white, white rose.

And somewhere the whirring of a projector with vast close-ups of the Mare Tranquillatis, the Mare Foecunditatis, the crater rays of Copernicus filling the bright screen, morphing into the huge, round, white face of a barn owl.

'What was to be the code, Natasha? How were you to be activated?'

Déjà vu is what exactly? A slip in time between the brain appreciating an event which has just happened? Thus apparently projecting it into the future to be recognised, as some sort of minimal precognition? If that's the conjecture it seems to have sprouted legs. This 'happening' seems to run and run in her mind, in fits and starts, round corners, lying in ambush, a helter-skelter of unrelated events and filmic jump-cuts, scuttling into her mind the way a spider runs: fast, then a dead stop.

She is remembering a totally black, sound-proofed room. She is seated on a chair. There is a faintly luminous violet disc, just a glimmer of phosphorescence on one of the walls, or she assumes it's on the wall. Her eyes are inevitably drawn to it. Over time it seems to grow and then to recede. Sometimes it moves or seems to. She feels her eyes are jumping about to keep it in view. Now - there it pulsates! It's an hallucination, she tells herself, and looks away but after ten minutes or an hour because she cannot tell and she cannot see her luminous watch dial because it too has been taken for safe keeping, like her clothes, it is always there before her. She is feeling the rising panic, haunted by its purple presence which seems to view her with cold malevolence, like the eye of Hal, the computer in Kubrik's 2001: A Space Odyssey.

She is trying to remember things like films she'd seen or friends she'd shared good times with before this first week of indoctrination but the spot drains her spirit of volition and her mind empties as if a stopper has been pulled from a sink. This isn't supposed to be what it was about, coming here with Che. It was cultural, political and perhaps an exciting sexual experiment away from home in an exotic foreign city. A whistle-stop tour of the galleries, the sights, the Brandenburg Gate. Checkpoint Charlie. Not this sensory deprivation, this claustrophobia, not this breaking down of taboos and conventions, folded into a foetal crouch somewhere in a run-down Ku'damm basement. She rails now at her naïvity.

Had she been having LSD flashbacks? Had she indeed suffered drug-induced schizophrenic events? All that she recalled now seemed to have a sort of twisted logic if those missing weeks could be explained by these revelations.

'The code, Natasha. Do you remember?'

~-~

I remember something. I am back, connected by filaments of memory to the mixed-up, over-indulged, spoiled girl in my mind's eye who's floating back to me, returning on the white wings of my Lunar messenger. It is the *Times Obituary Column* which I have read dutifully for years but have now stopped. Emma had begun to notice as she was growing up and made a comment that I must have a morbid interest in the deceased. 'Did I *really* know so many *sunset people* and *crumblies*? Weird!' Ceasing to comply was I'm sure just one among many small subconscious rebellions against that violation of my younger self, building my strong fortress upon the sand. On a conscious level I had no idea I was doing it and would have had no idea what I was looking for until the unique phrase appeared there among the bereavement notices, lamenting those who had shuffled-off. I am sure now that drugs were employed, contrary to my vehement denial that I'd ever indulged, which made me a little old fashioned given the growing number of MPs who'd admitted to trying it - though they'd *never* inhaled at university.

'So, what was your task?' This from Thirty-something? 'What were you targeted at?'

'I don't know.'

'Come now, Natasha. Little girl from a middle class background. Privileged upbringing. Good school. Daddy a journalist for the aerospace industry. Oh sorry, *late* daddy that should be. Put him in a nursing home didn't we, where he died after a couple of weeks. You must feel a *little* bit guilty about that, even for a hard-eyed little Marxist bimbette masquerading under a double-barreled married name. Was that *cover*, Natasha? Marrying your *yuppie*, under orders from your *Rote Pfad Terror Gruppe* puppet master? Pity Stuart-Hedges was a lousy investment banker, with a cocaine habit amongst other things. What was he, a half-assed conduit to an upper strata of society? I mean I don't see much point in using you to pour cyanide into an urban reservoir. Or flood the Underground with *Ricin* when the call to arms is sounded, do you? Not after all the effort they put in to establish you back into society. Pity Simeon blew it for you, eh?'

A burst of memory, seemed violently to tear free from the sediment in my brain. Che had accused me of being a playtime insurrectionist. A 'pamphleteer'. I'd risen to that jibe but then there was a vague, dizzy 'helter skelter' event and the next thing I remembered was the violation immediately I was delivered to them: Helga's white thighs straddling me after Wolfram had finished while the eunuch watched from the shadows. The breaking down of personality and of free will. The forced meditation sessions, the chanting. Role-playing, some of it very violent with a pock-faced emissary of hate helicoptered-in from *Black September* in the part of Leila Khaled's evil twin, snarling at the Muslim girls that they were now *haram*, defiled, outcast from their family and could gain redemption only through martyrdom. Then unarmed combat, the sessions taking place on none too soft exercise mats, with Helga and that humourless white eunuch, as we called him, who knew how to hurt. I said 'we' but it was more 'I'. We labrats were less of a team, more like bee larvae in adjoining honeycomb cells, force-fed their high octane propaganda but not encouraged to talk amongst ourselves - not that all shared a common language. *Trappists.*

I remember certain smells: the sense most evocative to memory. Above all, gun oil. Stripping and clearing of weapons, the automatics: *Tokarev*, old but simple and effective: wartime, robust. *Makarov*, smaller. Effective close range weapon. Russian both. Then the Czech *Skorpion* M61. All stripped and re-assembled blindfold against the clock and punishments if you failed the task. Always naked or just wearing a cotton shift. Always made to feel vulnerable and 'available'. The heady smell of cordite: firing *Kalashnikov* AK 47 and *Heckler* & *Koch* MP5SD2 into the sandbags in a sound-proofed underground cellar where we were delivered in the blacked-out VW Minibus. The ear-splitting noise because of defective ear protection — it was all a little ad-hoc in places, despite the air of superiority and Germanic efficiency our tutors deployed.

'So who was your target, Natasha?'

Had I been ordered to marry Simeon, or someone like him? Had I been brainwashed, hypnotised, drugged. Perhaps I had to answer 'yes' to all three, and more besides. I'd been sexualised, victimised, politicised. I had suffered Stockholm-Syndrome, concentration camp victim 'projection' of power onto my captors, for that is what they were, these self-styled Red Path Maoists with their experimental *Märtyrer Brigade* of which I was just one unwitting guinea pig - any number of whom I could have shredded with my AK47 if I'd turned it sideways in that cellar. But the weird schizoid feeling of impotency and power together, the self-image of a naked girl firing a formidable weapon had the same apparent erotic effect on my hot-eyed Cambodian as it had, I'm ashamed to say, on

738

my own committed-self or even Helga.

What had I become then, Daddy? A ticking time bomb staring into the abyss. Told to despise the consumer-driven *duraki:* the idiot masses of Western culture which should be punished for its crimes and shocked out of its torpor to join in the fight against the multi-national companies, the banking system and individual capitalist entrepreneurs, finishing what Andreas Baader had started.? And at the head of the establishment, those prominent parliamentarians of the Right and later 'New Labour' in Britain both. And the titular head of state, whatever the personal cost to the agent and whatever the collective suffering of the masses in the medium term.

We were told that Britain was finished. That we were just administering the *coup de gras*, giving it a shove to help it on its way. In the end a new society would grow out of the weak, corrupt, incompetent and effete legacy of the Western democratic system. We don't know what shape that will take, they said. What the post-revolutionary world will look like. *We only know it will be better. It will be like nothing we have seen before, without the mistakes of the past to haunt us. A fresh start. The New Way. Your journey along the Red Path, stairway to the stars and the future for the world starts with complete acceptance, Natasha, even if it means certain death for some, which it certainly would. The highway to Utopia, running red with blood.*

My university lecturer had complimented me on my once sharp intellect. Since those days I'd always seemed to be on the back foot mentally and things now crystallised more slowly. I wondered if that perverse Left Wing honey-trap and brainwashing had anything at all to do with it. Yet on occasion I could pull off a coup, such as thwarting Willis's attempted rape of Tatiana or securing a secreted data disk.

'You were a *Sleeper,* Natasha and you've never been de-activated, even though the world has moved on. A wind-up *zombie.* How pathetic is that?' Forty-something was speaking. 'We've had our 9/11 now. We have our Iran and Afghan wars. Islamic Terror is on the agenda, and the collapse of Western morality will fuel crime and feed terrorism.'

'But Mao's followers now run one of the biggest capitalist economies on the planet and at the pace they're growing they'll be on Mars in a decade. The alleged PLO-affiliated *Rote Pfad* Group was Stasi-funded with ambitions for a Western Hemisphere *Year Zero.* What were the Stasi themselves thinking for God's sake? Anyhow, that's now a busted flush so what's the point?'

Each of us needs an ethical justification of own life. Errors, excuses, wrong choices, all must be repudiated else the social and moral redemption in our conscience cannot stand. Urban revolutionaries are as narrow-minded as any, even when their minds actually belong to them.

'I don't know now what the point was,' I said at last. 'I've tried to rebuild since then. That was all 'somewhere else'.'

In my bicameral mind, I supposed, where I'd tried to re-grow a new version of my perceived world from the remains of the old shattered conventions, but here I was impaled, writhing on a stick and trying to deflect the pain.

'There must be a few dozen deeply-embedded *Spetsnaz* agents around the country,' I said in calm desperation, quoting Hans-Peter's own journal. 'Quietly mowing their lawns or attending night school.'

I imagined them, working medium-grade security and going on cross-country runs to keep fit. On paint-balling weekends; 'management' team-building exercises to get their rocks off away from wifey back at home. Keeping their 'eye in' at the same time.

'Why not go after *them* for God's sake?'

It was a spirited riposte I thought, but really only a nervous twitch from the depths. My death throe had already begun, if I was honest. I was caught out. Guilty of treason by virtue of training in a foreign country to carry out an unspecified act of sabotage or assassination, or at least that's the way they'd label it. Of course they'd not need to make that charge stick on its own. They'd be able to provide evidence implicating me of the murder of a political ex-activist and her partner, an ex-GCHQ operative who might or might not have been about to expose me. Case closed.

'So what is it you want? Can't be a conviction, you'd have left that to the police.'

Thirty-something stood up and walked to the door, looking through the slot.

Forty-something spoke, condescendingly. 'We're not interested on who your targets were to have been. That just establishes that you are who you say you are. The 'hit' never happened and *Rote Pfad* is history.'

'Three things,' he said. 'One. We want the list of names I know you have hidden somewhere. And any copies you might have made. Two. We have your father's narrative in printed form and it makes interesting if bizarre reading. We require any copy or disk you might have made of that or anything relating to it. Three. The number of the account in Kloten where the Romanov monies are lodged. This is not negotiable, Natasha. Many people have already lost their lives over this. One or two more don't concern us.'

'Well I'm damned then! I don't have that number. The rest you're welcome to.'

'We are offering you a lifeline here, Natasha. You only have to play ball. Whether it's softball or hardball is all the same to us.'

'No can do. If you've read my father's saga you'll know how cryptic were his messages. You can see how desperate I am to have tried to….'

'Tried to what, Natasha?'

I was going to say 'tried to contact the dead'.

'Perhaps I can jog your memory.' He reached into his briefcase and brought out a mobile phone. It looked like my mobile phone. He handed it to me. Thirty-something still hovered by the eye-line 'letterbox'.

I took the phone and switched it on. I had one 'missed call'.

I pressed the button to hear the message. The words were hurried and breathless, a hoarse whisper but unmistakably Tatiana's!

'Natasha! You must help us, *please*. I beg you this. This phone I have borrowed while he sleeps. Lilia is *very* sick. She has been beaten yes, but is more; she I think has blood cancer, leukaemia. And there is no medicine in this place for anyone who is sick.'

They had to do sex work 24/7. No break, she said. They were exhausted.

'We are sold by Willis to sex traffic gang from Albania or Turkey, to cover big debt, I don't know what.' There were many different guards and pimps of all nations, she said.

'It is *terrible* here. Like Hell of Dante. They have guns. There are many girls from Russian Federation, very young, teenagers. Chinese too. Duped by promise of work abroad and then kidnapped, passports stolen. Many are drugged so they work without trouble. No hope here to escape. Bars on windows. I am telling this while swine who just rape me,' the word was snarled, 'my *client* snores on the bed. I have his mobile phone for maybe two minutes. I remember your mobile number - I have *photo-memory* you know, Natasha. I hope you are well.'

The anxiety and pain in her voice is tangible.

'Natasha, there at house, Chrissie tries to fight them. Willis beats up Chrissie with plaster cast on arm, like club, but he don't kill her. Russian bastard did that. Vicious psycho *demon*. He is madman. He rapes Lilia while I am forced to watch at Grimstone. He ties Clarissa to chair and gags her while this happens, wipes blood on her jacket from blade. Then he part-suffocates her with plastic bag and I see he puts her in 'Jeep' with engine running. Hosepipe is connect to exhaust, into cab, perhaps to look like murder-suicide. I don't know what happens after. Willis hit me and

Lili. Asks us over and over where you live, *bitch with Volvo car.* I tell him I *swear* I don't know. We don't give you up, Natasha. Never. I swear he don't know your address.'

Tania pauses for breath.

'We are thrown into back of van with other girl. Brought here. Maybe a half or three-quarter hour's drive.'

She didn't know what speed they were making. Maybe it was still East Anglia. They could see through one window and from bathroom. Flat landscape, only fields and trees.

'We cannot shout for help in van because of savage dog, rottweiler. If we move or make sound it will attack. If we are now suspected of trying to contact police they say they will kill us. One girl already they have killed for being trouble. So I cannot ring 999 Scotland Yard.'

Her voice is lower now. She is breathing rapidly. It sounds as if she's having a panic attack, almost sobbing, voice cracking.

'*Please* help to find us, Natasha. Lilia, my twin, is *dying.* From *caesium 137* fallout, Chernobyl 1986, when both we are in mama's womb, in Dzerzhinsk. She cannot survive here long now. I could not live if she will die. Maybe I have it too, I too feel sick here. My little brother has had two operations on intestines in Minsk. He too is suffering, Natasha, please. His immune sys….'

The message has ended abruptly. I have a vision of the little glass dome of my childhood: the painted wooden church in the blizzard. Except the pure driven snow turns now to black rain.

I am aflame with emotion, that the girls are alive yet in dire danger and suffering horribly somewhere. Not only that, it gets me off the hook on this double murder charge which only has the forensic detail of my presence at the scene to run with. Here was a full description of events. Or as far as it was possible to pack everything into a secret two minute telephone message from a brothel.

'But this is fantastic!' I exclaimed rising to my feet, burning for action.

This was it. Hard evidence in a desperate plea from the heart from a courageous young woman in terrible danger for her life and sanity not to mention that her sister needs medical attention. I'm sure that they'll both need medical attention and great deal of counselling afterwards if their mental health isn't to *completely* collapse. I knew what it was like to be abused, but this was brutality from another galaxy! And the details clearly indicated that I had nothing to do with the murders. I said so. Emphatically.

Thirty-something stepped forward smartly and shoved me firmly down onto the bunk.

'No it doesn't.' Forty-something spoke again, pocketing the phone. 'What….?'

'It's not proof of anything. You could have had someone fake that message and leave it on your phone for us to find. It's rubbish.'

'For God's sake!' These innocent girls are in fear for their lives and are undergoing the most sadistic sexual torture and defilement every hour of every day for the lusts of perverted men, under two hour's drive away from here. 'You could trace the call easily and…'

'No we couldn't.'

I was dumfounded.

'Our citizens are among the most spied upon with our country dripping with surveillance cameras and more mobile phone and internet bugging than anywhere in Europe. Since before the fall of East Germany and the end of the Stasi. You could pinpoint where that phone call was made from in one minute flat.'

'We could but we won't.'

'For God's sake why not. Sex slavery is one of the vilest crimes imaginable. Even I know from casual reading that about half a million Russian and East European women are trafficked annually.'

'How do we know these two women exist? You've never mentioned them yourself until now. The caravan at Grimstone had plenty of evidence that it had been occupied, but from what I gather these people entered the country illegally and as far as we're concerned they don't officially exist. And *if* we found them we'd deport them irrespective of their physical and mental condition. Perhaps they came here *intending* to work as prostitutes. *If* they exist. Such deportations happen all the time. Home Office policy. We don't treat illegal aliens in our hospitals. Not what the NHS is for.'

I was beside myself with anger.

'What happened to the upholders of right? I thought our secret service was on the side of the angels, for Chrissake!'

'Now what gave you that idea, may I ask, coming from a Marxist-Maoist mole and sleeper who's intent was to disrupt the lives of British subjects, sabotage our economy, our transportation system and destroy our infrastructure? Perhaps commit mass murder or assassinate a prominent person? Even *martyr* herself for a perverted cause? How do you think that should play with us? Is it your intention to hurt our feelings because you're not now capable of anything else?'

'I was brainwashed and hypnotised. Indoctrinated, with something implanted in my mind. Like the bloody *Manchurian Candidate* for all I know.'

In my bicameral mind, the one side hidden from the other, the conscious side. I thought I was going schizophrenic.

'Since the 1990s I've led an exemplary life,' I said. 'And brought my daughter up to be a good citizen.'

'Citizenship is for others to judge. Your family name two generations back was actually Moritz. *Von* Moritz to be exact. Doesn't sound very British now does it?'

'I only knew this after reading my father's story. Even then it was unproven to my personal satisfaction.'

'Be that as it may. You have twenty four hours to come up with a certain Swiss bank account number, after which this telephone message is deleted. Your court appearance will then be guaranteed. Goodnight, Miss Morris.'

'Bastards!' I screamed at the closing cell door. 'Who the hell are you bastards?' A boa-constrictor was slowly crushing my lungs and my legs were turning to jelly. 'Bastards,' I whispered again, to myself.

I felt that I was drowning in that cell and there was no one there to save me. I suddenly missed my father very much. I recalled that last thing he'd written in the Baltic Falcon manuscript. About Steiger's confusion and depression, his apparent suicide attempt in the North Sea. How he'd heard voices faintly calling, perhaps the voices of his mother and Hannah; dead, drowned women whose souls cried out for their departed son to join them….but then there was just a roaring in his ears as he'd sunk beneath the icy water, his muscles rigid with cramp.

Strong hands had pulled him aboard the motor boat, and pumped the water from his lungs. Saving him the way he had saved Arkadi.

'Thought you were a goner, there for a moment, Rolf.' He'd said cheerily. Peregrine-Thomas sitting opposite him with Lindsay-Langton looking green against the gunwhale as the boatman steered them up the Yare estuary. 'Can't have that. You're too valuable to the Service, don't you know?'

Steiger, saved to fight another day, Natasha. To uphold righteousness! If you look for it you'll find the key to his continuing saga.

Steiger had found an unlikely saviour who'd repaid him. Plucked from the certainty of death on that Albanian hillside. Debt fully repaid off the Norfolk coast, eighty-seven years ago.

744

And now I too am drowning, Daddy. I am at sea. I am suspended in the zinc 'Hydro' tank that the Eunuch calls it, or the *Lilly* Tank after its inventor. In a blacked out face mask and earphones and the *Snorkel* bubbling in my ear; Ho's insidious voice whispering inside my brain, *'Precious petal, your sins are washed away now. You are born anew and born to serve. You will remember only the moon and the owl. You will do exactly as we say.'*

Who is there left will save me, Daddy? Who is there left?

Chapter 52. *The Siberian Eagle*

A most unlikely candidate for saviour. DI Slater. My off-centre eyeballed hero.

I had ten minutes to reflect on how I was supposed to come up with a number of a Swiss bank account or lose my alibi and the sole clue to Tatiana and Lilia's whereabouts. Get them to safety and medical attention. I veered between anger and despair.

Slater entered the cell with his silent policeman in tow to collect the chairs.

'You're bailed,' he said without preamble. 'You can collect your personal effects at the desk. I have to confiscate your passport for the time being, I'm afraid, so I can run you home to collect that from you. Save you getting a taxi anyway.'

'Tell me one thing,' I said still reeling from events. 'Who were those shits? They didn't have the good manners to introduce themselves.'

'I have been given to understand that one was what used to be termed HM's 'Totally Deniable Service'. The other was very senior with the Serious and Organised Crime Agency and a ranking with the Border Control Agency. They've provided appropriate credentials and other documentation. Above my pay grade to question it.'

Although he *had* made a puzzled telephone call to his Deputy Chief Constable. He was informed the credentials were above the DCC's pay grade also.

I laced my trainers. Slater spoke to the desk sergeant while I framed my next question.

'Is returning your prisoner in a patrol car part of the service?' I asked, still barely controlling my fury. 'After abducting her from her home and taking her daughter off God knows where? Where is she? When can I see her?'

'Well, I don't think we should disturb her at this time of night. She'll be bedded down by now, with professional foster carers. She's quite safe.'

I glared at him and then looked at the station clock. Christ, eleven thirty. I'd have to take DI Slater up on his lift or face an expensive taxi fare. The local bus service would have finished for the night.

The desk sergeant handed me my purse and wristwatch which I signed for. Slater came from behind flourishing my mobile phone like a conjuror. I breathed an audible sigh of relief, noting again his non-committal gaze.

Slater ushered me outside. It wasn't a patrol car, it was the DI's own conveyance. I wondered if this offer was entirely *kosher* and asked him. He said he was going off duty, the invariable victim of his own fatal good nature, he told me. Besides that, my passport was required without further delay.

But I wasn't finished by a long way.

'I don't understand any of this,' I said, choosing my words. 'First I'm arrested on suspicion of a double murder, for which only circumstantial evidence is offered at best. I am denied legal representation or even a phone call. Then, without seeing a brief, I'm told I'm being 'bailed'. I don't see how that can happen by the way. Ah, but I'm not permitted to leave the country - not that I'd intended to do so. Oh, yes, and then there was that unpleasant little interlude with the two comics from SIS, Special Branch, 'Borders' or wherever.' Even as I said it something didn't seem quite right.

Half-assed. Softball, hardball....? Americanisms of all sorts have infiltrated our language through the media. Those few expressions had clashed on my sensitive ear during the bullying. They just didn't *chime*. Who were these purported SIS who'd learned their English in the USA? I settled into the front passenger seat of Slater's Peugeot where he waggled a cigarette at me and asked if I minded. I said yes, I bloody did. His wry twitch of a smile said I was doing him a favour: muttering that he was trying to kick the habit anyway. The car headlights blazed a trail through the dark. I switched on my phone and was delighted to see the solo 'missed message' flag up. I listened again to the call.

Natasha, your timer is running. We'll be in touch.

I froze, my mind tumbling. Bastards. The original message was being kept on record somewhere I was convinced. Bait. Reprieve if I met their ultimatum. Otherwise, life. Without the option.

'So, you got your missed call?' Slater was looking straight ahead, his rivelled cheeks more deeply gouged in the darkness, eyes concentrating on the unlit road, but for sure he'd detected the mobile against my left ear.

'What is this police state shit?' I snarled. 'What's the big secret that I don't understand. Who is trying to frame me or drive me fucking insane? Can you answer me that, Detective Inspector?'

'I am charged with investigating a possible double murder at a residence only half a mile or so from where you live. You knew the deceased and forensic evidence places you at the scene. Apart from the post woman who discovered the bodies, and who's been eliminated from

748

our enquiry by the way, you are the only likely suspect, not to mention your dubious student past. Running with foreign revolutionaries, bringing yourself to the attention of the Home Office and the Serious and Organised Crime Agency. Something else you didn't bring up when questioned is the existence of the two foreigners, illegals you now admit to knowing. Two very convenient scapegoats for the murders. If they exist, Mrs. Morris.'

'Not for an instant am I trying to blame them for those deaths. They are victims in this whole thing. As much as Chrissie and Clarissa. And they are now undergoing horrible sexual abuse and in terrible danger from their captors and possibly from a radiation-induced cancer.'

'Go on,' he said.

I outlined in brief what had happened to the girls and how I was now being threatened. He said nothing but after another mile or so he swung off the main Stowmarket road.

'What's going on,' I asked, a little alarmed.

He didn't reply but after a minute we entered Upper Thurston. He pulled up in a quiet street. Roofless, grotesquely illuminated by a sodium streetlight, a charnel-house, soot-blackened and agape, the Volvo still in the drive. Once identical neighbouring houses recoiled on either side, their wide-eyed windows expressing horror. I shuddered at the thought of two little kids dying in that 'inferno'. The mother still on oxygen.

'It seems it was a good move of yours, selling them the Volvo. Handy car for children and dogs.'

'I didn't sell it to them. I traded it into a garage for my 2CV. The garage had the bargain, I just wanted to…..'

'What?'

'I just wanted to merge with the background. Camouflage. Take the 'heat' off. But now finding the twins is my only hope; and theirs too!'

'Pity you didn't mention that before. It harms your defence.'

'They were illegals. Nothing to do with me. They were sending money home to Belarus. For their sick brother.'

'Number of times I've heard that one.'

'I am as desperate to find Tatiana and Lilia as I am to see Emma safely home with me.'

Slater stared at the smoke-blackened shell of masonry, his face half in darkness; monk-like in his cowl of deep shadow. We sat in silence for a long five minutes.

'You know what, Natasha,' he said at last. 'I'm beginning to believe you. There's a hell of a lot more to this than meets the eye. They had no known enemies or criminal associations. Just a middle class, one parent family down on its luck. The fire investigation team found traces of accelerant. Neighbours heard the tyre screech of a vehicle driven away at speed at about 2 am. By the time the fire appliance arrived the place was well ablaze.'

He turned and gave me a brief smile, not a 'tick' this time.

'Let's get you back home.'

For the first time since the formal interview I was beginning to like DI Slater.

~-~

As we drove I began to reveal more of what I'd been experiencing, some of which I'd hitherto been reluctant to come forward with, in case it compromised the security of the twins. Until tonight I'd had no idea of their whereabouts. But having failed to 'come clean' at the first interview I'd stuck my head in the sand and since then dug myself in deeper.

I had a sudden thought.

'Can you find out what happened to a Dr. Sheila Grant, GP in the local practice?' I asked him. 'She'd suffered an RTA apparently and was off work about a month ago.'

'Should I know why?'

'It's just a theory I have. I don't know whether you could officially enquire but some details would help.'

Slater was about reply when I shouted a warning. What appeared to be a black 4x4 from its mass had rocketed around a corner with headlights on full beam, swinging wide and nearly forcing us into the ditch.

'Blast him. Couldn't see his number plate,' he cursed.

~-~

Mill Farm was a scene of some chaos. The intruder lights were ablaze when we arrived. The front door was ajar and all the rooms had been turned over, hurriedly by the looks of it. There seemed gratuitous damage everywhere, books ripped apart, the new plasterboard which had been skimmed to create a dry-wall had been hacked into and the boards levered off in places. Some loose internal bricks had been pulled out of the old chimney breast and pots and pans were strewn about. John Morris's illustrated poems had been torn from their frames. In the lounge

750

the sofas and chairs were upended and their bottoms were ripped out. Upstairs bedding was all over the place and the attic ladder had been pulled down. Emma's computer, that is our only computer, had been stolen.

Slater called for a patrol car. The police had searched the house themselves when I had been arrested but they'd left it in a reasonable state. Nor did he think that the Security Service had been involved. I would not have seen evidence of their activities, he'd said. That it might be vandalism for its own sake seemed highly improbable given recent events.

'You need police protection, Mrs Morris,' he said. 'It's late in the night to have to cope with all this. I can find you somewhere to stay for a few days. In any event we need to let 'forensics' loose on this lot. I'm assuming nothing at this stage.'

My protests were overruled and a B&B was found for me in a nearby village, which would also accommodate my daughter for as long as necessary, which was going to be no more than two days, of that I was determined. Meanwhile there was the threat from the 'SIS-duo' to consider. I examined my car which had also been pulled about; driver's door wrenched out of shape, seats cut, but at least it started when I turned the key. So I collected a few personal effects, toiletries and so forth, clothes for Emma and left the key to the house with Slater, to be returned to me when the police had finished their second investigation of my property in 24 hours.

Slater was as good as his word. He and another officer had dropped by at the B&B.

The information he'd uncovered on Sheila Grant, MD was that she was still convalescing at her mother's home in Buckinghamshire. Her small car had been vandalised about a month ago, wing mirror smashed, radio disk player ripped out, headrests stolen, etc. Two mornings later on her way early to work she was rear-ended at a crossroads by what she thought was a black Mitsubishi Shogun. Her recall was good. Though she'd only seen it briefly in the interior mirror she'd had the impression of 'bull bars', steel tubes fitted in front of its radiator. To comply with the law such things had had to be replaced by plastic and then they'd passed out of fashion. She considered that these were far from being 'plastic'. Her head had reflexed back over the driver's seat and her car was pushed into the main road, in the path of an oncoming juggernaut. It braked but still added to her injuries. The 4x4 roared off in the opposite direction. No one managed to take down its details. She'd suffered spinal damage;

cervical three and four as well as a torn kneecap and broken left forearm and would be off work for a long time.

The Practice was under pressure and considered it fortuitous to have someone coincidentally available locally and so well-qualified appear to take on her caseload as locum. However, he'd been with the clinic only a week or so before receiving bad news about a sister who was apparently dying, abroad, he'd said. He'd been around just long enough to be called to give evidence at my father's post mortem and had left quite suddenly, full of apologies, with the ink barely dry on his contract.

~-~

It was Clarissa, or rather the last conversation I'd had with her that put me onto it. I'd bought myself a new laptop and connected via Mrs. Handley's modem at the *Lodge*, and I'd been looking at Russian money laundering operations. The Mafiya had been known just to walk in and take over companies, she'd told me. But more sophisticated ploys were in vogue since the arrival of the Internet including buying into well established legitimate companies and using them as holding companies to transact covert operations.

Returning to Mill Farm and the major clearing-up job, I'd found a card on the mat from the Post Office depot in Bury St. Edmunds. Two large recorded delivery packages awaited collection that they'd not been able to deliver due to my being in custody or at the temporary address. They turned out to be more of my father's final personal effects from Lithuania, sent by road and rail transport from Jankaitis to the barely concealed annoyance of the Abercrombie's in Godalming, from their note, who'd had to re-address them. One was an obviously well-padded guitar case. But I could not believe what I was seeing after I'd dragged in the bigger box from the 2Cv. Among the books was a small package wrapped in brown paper. It contained the missing wooden disk, twin to the oil painting of *The Baltic Falcon*. That sense of déjà vu again.

The ancient paper backing bore the title *The Siberian Eagle*, written in my father's hand before his debilitating stroke. It featured a handsome Steppe Eagle or *Berkut* perched haughtily on a crag. I realised that in my anxiety and distraction in Lithuania - when I'd assumed I'd packed both wooden plaques - that I must have afterwards placed this one in another case, to be shipped later. I had no memory of this I had been mystified that I couldn't find it when I'd begun my recent search for it here in Suffolk. I therefore realised that if my recall could be so at fault it could

752

not be relied on regarding the more bizarre or important things that lurked in my past: hidden by owls, shielded by the inscrutable face of the moon.

The CD it contained was the *second instalment* of Steiger's own saga. Here was more history than I could comprehend at one viewing: a destiny intertwined with Ernst Kessler's. Adventures in America and then the Arctic - I remembered the picture of the old Albatros on skis in Finland, 1922, that was still somewhere in my possession.

Kessler's Albatros L.17 in Finland, 1922. (Archive: Hans-Peter Neumann)

Later, there was a bold attempt to influence political change, regime change in fact, to use a modern term, by direct intervention; but the part that held my attention was my father's own editorial shaping of the work, to provide some terms of reference in the modern age, coincidentally closely following what I'd just been researching: that sometimes charities, largely exempt from close scrutiny where good works were seen to be done, were targeted for distributing funds abroad; into bank accounts that were Mafiya front organisations as much as taking money in from donations.

That this had already happened in the organisation wherein he'd accepted the figurehead position of CEO became increasingly evident. The charity with a strong political agenda, associated with Alexa von Dönhoff, Harry Piotrkowski and the late 'Zubr', poet and dreamer, self-styled descendent of the *Jagiellonians*: of the *Anastasia Bequest* as he'd termed it. A disposable fortune of $5,000,000,000 over time made it a very attractive acquisition evidently, but that was small beer in terms of what was now flowing through its electronic arteries. He'd come to realise that an insidious coup had been staged with many of the advisors and officers of the Trust none the wiser, due to the 'cut outs' that John and Co. had wisely put in place. Some of the Trust employees were trustworthy, Jankaitis he believed was one. I was less certain. But now Alexa and Harry were dead. From natural causes he presumed, and he didn't know when the knife blow would strike through the *arris* that would see him undone, *et tu Polonius*. When the final link with the reality of what the Trust had been would be lost forever.

This for me was the last piece of the mighty jigsaw. My father told me what it was he'd done to thwart the creeping power of the Russian Mafiya. Before his sudden 'stroke' he'd simply changed the password to the vaults at Kloten where not only the *Bequest* funds and the bullion was stored, but vast amounts of Mafiya money paused in transit, roosting there like gilded orioles: and then he coolly destroyed the mother board of his computer. The bronze stallion. Free Lithuanian spirits running through the blowing grasses, all flooded back to me from his *Schloss*, beneath the vault of bright cloud flowing to the infinite horizon. Smell. That most evocative of all the senses. I recalled that tang of burning.

Somewhere he'd secreted that number. The *Caterpillar* and the *Cheshire Cat* who I presumed were ex-SIS mercenaries or even CIA moonlighting for someone, wanted it badly enough to blackmail me with the threat of a life sentence for murder, pressured from some agency or cabal in the Establishment which also wanted the Valkyrie list pretty badly too, unless that was a ploy to muddy the waters further since the war with Hitler had been over a very long time. So here was the *Siberian Eagle*: the Second Saga and further clues to the trove. Were the Neo-Nazis still involved in the chase along with the Russian Mafiya? Pretty goddamn dangerous people to have stalking you, as poor old Hans-Peter himself might have said with his last gasp, warning my father to *trust no one*.

What was I to do? What could be done about the terrible fate of the 'heavenly twins', the most innocent protagonists in this convolute Balkan tale? Assuming that action was still outside Slater's remit as an Ipswich plod. Several increments above his pay grade in fact and nothing to go on except an erased message on my mobile phone to take to his Super.

My father's legacy to me was a poison chalice in a saga full of chalices and no mistake. Run and keep on running I told myself, but I knew I'd never be able to hide successfully faced with the overpowering menace of the multiple threats ranged against me. And then there was Emma. How long would it be before she became a victim or a hostage?

Then what would I do. I had no idea how to go about finding the six or more digit number they all demanded, nor which bank's identity had gone up in flames with my father's computer chip.

I'd never felt more of a hostage myself. To fate.

Chapter 53. *Aktion Direkt*

DI Slater had been moonlighting too, bless him. He'd put his sleuths to asking around the hospitals about males who'd had a right forearm set recently based on an approximate age estimate and came up trumps. The name Steve Wilkins, *Traveller*, had given was false, but significant in that the selected initials had matched those of Shane Willis and the address for the follow-up appointment to be sent to have the cast removed was that of a Suffolk caravan park, confirming something Tania had said. Slater had leaked that information to me to stop me sniffing around on my own and getting into trouble. There were many such sites and he wasn't about to tell me which one. Willis had been hauled-in and asked to give an account of his movements on the night of the murders at Grimstone House.

He had a record of drug dealing and being part of a gang arranging marriages between EU subjects and 'illegals' to gain UK residency. But he had a ready alibi in the form of a barmaid at the park who he'd lived with on and off and with whom he was currently 'on'. Lacking conclusive DNA evidence and without the twins as witnesses no charge of attempted rape or abduction could be brought and Slater wished for me to be kept out of things for the moment; in reserve so to speak as much for my own protection assuming that Willis hadn't already located and ransacked my home. In which case I'd be safer elsewhere for the forseeable while the investigation continued. No hint of where the girls and their fellow prisoners of vice might be held was forthcoming. Attempts to retrieve and therefore to trace the point of origin of the mobile phone message had proved fruitless.

But other concerns were emerging from the secret matrix of my forgotten past that threw everything else into confusion. The Red Path of my youth had disappeared without trace, been rolled up as if it never was or had gone into hibernation. The underground urban salient slumbered deep, mayhap beneath their once and future revolutionary pavements, seeming to release like captive finches the failed experiment of those they'd laboured to turn into remote-controlled zombies. My zealous Marxism which had made me their gift, the entry fee to their academy of mind control had been compromised before ever I stepped lightly with Che amid the echoing arcades, the arcing vastness of Tempelhof's terminal. Or hailed our taxi in which we dumped our backpacks for our cheap café rendezvous. My shapeless desire to save the world by embracing radicalism was a sort of conformity, a student rite of passage that I'd taken too far without understanding where its piper would lead me, but had illuminated me for not only the pipers of the Left but the watchers and talent scouts that I would have then considered sat upon Attila's right hand.

I'd been photographed in Germany at that student demonstration and before that in London carrying a Worker's Revolutionary Party banner. Elsewhere, at an Animal Rights protest I had been dragged swearing into a Black Maria and been fingerprinted for obstruction. Released without further charge I'd been a general nuisance and Greenham Common's Peace Camp seemed like somewhere to rest and regroup after my studies and funds had finally petered out. No doubt my file, however slim at that moment, had been shared with other agencies in case I was to suddenly present myself at an air terminal bound for Cuba or somewhere that might notch me up a further cog for surveillance, security Grade 1. Or just in case I was already persona non-grata in whatever capital I'd set my sights on, though Bonn was eschewed for the older, more colourful capital, long divided.

As the owls and the moons fled the theatre of my mind I recalled snatches of my lonely return to earth, still reeling and in sensory overload. The restraining arm at Heathrow, warrant cards waved and the confinement in a police van with only limited windows as we sped west along the M4 to a *Police Vehicles Only* turn-off among smoky hedges and a substantial steel gate that yielded to a key.

Like many rebels I suppose I yearned in truth for an alternative plateau of conformity upon which I could stand, head high for an honest appraisal of self while the revolutionary within burned itself out like schizophrenia. Perhaps then I could go gently into that dark night knowing I'd done my bit while I was still young and on fire. I never really believed we would change anything with our idealism and little else. Least of all the all-powerful state, brick by brick. So the dalliance with the dangerous Left was no more than that flirtation that my father had accused me of, wasn't it? Or so I'd told them.

I was angry again and this concealed my fear. Not the helpless, drugged fear of my vulnerable self at the bidding of Ho and Wolfram, learning to submit willingly to things that in possession of my free will I'd have shunned like the plague, much as I'd shunned the occult. This was a new reality.

Mine host had begun by offering that, following the Roman evacuation of Britain, the Venerable Bede had upheld his lonely Dark Age crusade, to record the history of these islands in the face of mounting barbarism and book burning, such as had happened within living memory at certain locations east of here. The light of reason and scholarship burned in his abbey window just as the truth would burn brightest here, now. In this room. There was no place here for lies nor was there anywhere to hide. This could be the last place on earth I would see outside a ten-by-eight foot cell if I tried to deceive. The light that burned for the civilisation I took for granted, sought to betray, perhaps do it harm: it had been a distant myth for Bede but would not, repeat not, be allowed to burn out again. Britain was far from finished. Was I clear about that, actually?

Dominic (oh, we were all on first name terms, Emma, though I doubt any were as real as my own); debonair, with a metronomic calm and ordered flow led my new interrogators, whom he disarmingly identified as "a sort of *Global Operations and Security* agency in partnership with *Joint Terrorism Analysis*, Natasha" - for all that I should know if such creations existed back then – steered me relentlessly through my life to date, drawing out my inner being with no room to manoeuvre, to regroup or dissemble for sake of what dignity I might muster. Or if I tried I'd be backtracked, metaphorically side-swiped and set right back on the rails while moving forward chronologically to the point where I'd been trawled and recruited for my political stance at university. Immature though it may have been, based on an emotional hunger and my fear of turning into my chain-smoking mother in net-curtained suburbia; it was probably because my father's love was withheld and he had deserted me, as I tearfully admitted in confessional, aided perhaps by my reading of Freud and what, if anything, they'd put in my tea. Served in a bone china cup with a decorously patriotic thin red line.

The minutiae of my life was ground down, spun away as if by little windmills while the invisible mass of *their* agenda scrolled slowly around my head like a slowly accelerating centrifuge, me at its centre feeling less steady by the minute. I'd never supposed it, that is a co-revolutionary powerhouse in the form of 'Che's' Maoist cell, for whom he was but the courier, would gather itself up and come at me head-on, thrust its poison tongue into my ear and I'd receive that secret so deep within my revolutionary womb, to twist the anatomical metaphor rather; that it would remain firmly concealed by my subconscious even under probing interrogation.

But MI5, or whomever, had recruited mesmerists as skilled as Ho. He'd explored a dismal landscape forbidden to all others, lit by the moon's blank visage and protected by owls. Unlike old Berg he'd persisted until, one by one, Goya's long-eared goblins had flown from their trees and the moon had set blood red.

'So Natasha, how many of you 'silver bullets' were there? Has the BND delivered all the Red Path Zombies to their respective countries of origin, I wonder?'

That I could not answer. Nor could I picture the phrase I would encounter in the *Times Obits*. But I *would* be activated, this much I knew and the pieces of my weapon of choice, travelling as 'metal castings' perhaps - on behalf of some fictitious manufacturing company - would arrive piecemeal. This I'd assemble with gun oil, as I'd been shown and with its ammunition double-wrapped in polythene in a secure box, bury it somewhere, safely out of doors. Then forget it, Wolfram had said. Unless I moved house in the meantime, which I'd done more than a few times over the years.

~-~

For good reasons of their own they, Dominic and co., would return me to my pre-hypnotic state, primed, still ready for Ho's trigger. Or whomever would toggle the switch had Ho been compromised, was at that moment singing his head off in some secret birdcage, or wearing concrete boots, communing with the fish at the bottom of the harbour.

The sinking of the *Belgrano* outside the Falklands Exclusion Zone was being endlessly raked over during *Parliamentary Questions* about the time I'd emerged semi-conscious from the hate factory in Berlin as a primed messenger of death, though just how effective that would have proved God alone knew: but my re-emergence from the clutches of Dominic and co. had an equally visceral tingle in retrospect. I'd been redefined as 'bait' and that had been my unwitting role these twenty-six years, assuming my timer still ticked. Which presupposed something else. Unless the department and its spooks had been shut down at the same time as *Red Pfad* and associated terror organisations had been rolled-up or had gone to ground, I was being watched all that time.

Which raised another point: who was asking me those questions from a shakier perspective after a quarter of a century? Yuri? Not for such a little *rybka*. It was as if whoever it was had read my father's account but had not been cleared to view the complete file, nor been party to the full range of the country's state secrets as they related to Natasha Stuart-Hedges née Morris. Either way the CIA's Caterpillar and the Cheshire Cat, or whoever *they* were, had been operating at half-cock on a 'need to know' and were forced, or cold-bloodedly chose, to use as a lever the lives of two innocent young women. Captive, in dire danger, sick and suffering the tortures of the damned.

~-~

Slater was insisting I move to better temporary accommodation as soon as possible. He didn't want to frighten me, he said, but he felt that whoever was still looking for evidence of the Swiss account would start playing rougher and that Mill Farm was too isolated for my safety. And Emma's.

I couldn't agree more.

~-~

But despite the Cat and Caterpillar there was something I had to do first. If the police wouldn't or couldn't act on behalf of two young women whose existence depended upon my sole evidence and whose whereabouts were unknown, then *I* would have to. And I had only one lead to follow.

I was as nervous as if I were about to set foot on another planet. The caravan park, *trailer park* as our American cousins would term it, with all the sleazy connotations the phrase enjoys, was in semi-darkness. Deep shadows lay between the caravans and statics, thrown by spotlights near the centre of the sprawling camp where there was a barbeque area and *al fresco* drinking venue. Those ranking to the east were better-kept, larger static homes, some with little gardens; miniature picket fences and chain-linked territorial demarcations. The Englishman's home as his caravan, civilised by consensus. A splash of neon identified a bar from which flowed *Country and Western* and the nearby vans were more basic. The vehicles reflected the lifestyles of the residents. Four-by-fours and Transit type vans predominated. This was not just a retirement park.

I'd left my battered 2CV two hundred yards away in a lay-by and prowled around the dark edges of the park, looking for what distinguishing features I could remember of Willis's white Transit among the many parked around the camp. I could part-remember the number and the temporary bung in lieu of a petrol cap, a risky measure in these days of regular fuel price hikes. I felt sure if this was the right park I'd be able to identify it if he was around. Anyway I had nothing other than what Slater had unofficially leaked to go on. Tonight was my final attempt, my fifth caravan park and the last one on my list gleaned from the Internet: those within what appeared to be a reasonable operating distance for Willis's immigrant work gang pick-ups. Tonight I thought in desperation had to be my lucky night; but it was not getting any easier and my nerves were on edge. Of course he might have been living at any one of the other four camps I'd already visited and I may have just been unlucky to have missed him

I wore dark clothing and black gloves and a dark brown woollen hat was pulled over my ears. I'd considered a balaclava but thought that might be going too far should I be spotted by a resident, so instead I had a battered guitar over my shoulder as an alibi, which might work unless someone insisted I play it. It was two am. and the music from the bar had ceased. I kept to the shadows, moving stealthily, hearing people settling down in their trailers. I stood still and took stock, detecting snoring there, low voices here, saw the blue flicker of a TV in the caravan directly ahead. There were the sounds of people emerging from the bar, laughter and loud voices. Someone humming a tune. A woman's voice raised in argument. But I was fixated on a large white caravan in the next row with a scruffy white Transit parked alongside, a plastic bung in place of the original locking petrol cap and a registration plate that looked pretty familiar.

I moved sideways, passing between two vans, stepping carefully around a big liquid gas cylinder, moving quickly into shadow. I peered around a caravan's curtained bay and saw Willis backlit by spotlights on the shiny macadam. Even with the light behind them I recognised him. He was without his cast and leaning on a woman who had one arm around him, the two walking slowly and slightly unsteadily. She had very high heels and seemed to be having trouble steering him home. I hung back in the shadows as they drew level and stopped. He fumbled for his key. They opened the door and I froze as a big rottweiler emerged into the light and sniffed around the caravan before defecating on the grass behind. The dog stood, sniffed the air then looked straight at me, head slightly lowered. Willis re-emerged, opened the back of the Transit and spoke to the dog. The dog continued to stare in my direction, ears cocked. Willis spoke sharply and the dog reluctantly loped over and hopped into the back. Willis disappeared inside the caravan and closed the door. After a while the caravan light went out.

762

I waited for about twenty minutes getting colder by the second. One male walked by, head-down, purposefully heading homeward no doubt. Headlights blazed some rows back and went out. A car door slammed then all was quiet. The camp plunged into darkness as all but one weak lamp over the bar extinguished. My old friend the moon briefly showed herself, a sliver only between dark cloud banks: not tonight the enigmatic shield that hid her secrets from me. Not this night.

I checked up and down the row before moving out, approaching the caravan stealthily and steering clear of the Transit. Carefully I tried the trailer door handle. Unsurprisingly it was locked. I navigated the vague outline of my intentions. I had no actual plan, just the idea that if I could find Willis he might lead me to the twins. Or be persuaded to. I circled the caravan. Again came the sound I'd heard in the field off Stowmarket Road, the rottweiler's deep menacing growl from the back of the Transit. Suddenly the dog's demeanour changed and it hurled its heavy body blindly against the inside of the van with a great deep-throated, tearing snarl, baying and scratching frenziedly, threatening to get me through the metal sides. Telling me it wanted to rip out my throat. A light came on in the caravan and I turned to flee but a leather glove at the end of a hard arm clamped firmly over my mouth while another caught my left wrist in an unbreakable, twisting grasp and I was yanked bodily backwards into the dark, my guitar swinging wildly behind.

~-~

I was nursing a coffee in a caravan interior warmed by little more than body heat it seemed and waiting for DI Slater to appear. And when he did quietly enter after ten minutes I could have written his lines for him, delivered audibly, in a forceful hiss.

'Just what the f-laming hell d'you think you're doing, Natasha?'

I was sitting between two fit-looking men, plain clothes officers I presumed, in a trailer whose interior was lit by dim red bulbs, like a developer's darkroom, two blocks across from the Willis van. Night-viewing binoculars and a camera were mounted on tripods, pointing in that direction through the thick net curtains and some sort of expensive recording and listening equipment was ranged along the opposite wall. Near the door was WPC Hamilton, although I now realised I was out of date and to be politically correct should have dropped the 'W'. She had still not spoken and I was beginning to think she was a mute. She looked like something out of the *Avengers*: as usual perfectly groomed, hair in a ponytail, dressed for action in a black sweater and black tracksuit bottoms tucked into cowboy boots. It was she who'd recognised me and had silently and effectively interrupted my reconnaissance; intercepting and dragging me out of sight just as Willis had plunged down the caravan steps. Half naked. Armed with a baseball bat.

'Do you realise that you might have completely undermined our operation here. Totally compromised us!'

I was told I might have wrecked weeks of surveillance and monitoring of the subject whom they'd had under observation, part of a much larger operation to target Chinese and East European people-trafficking gangs. He continued that I should be ashamed of myself with the trouble they were going to in obtaining a more permanent 'safe house' for Emma and me and didn't I yet realise how dangerous this man and his associates were? Hadn't a double murder at Grimstone in which he was probably implicated got through to me? I would be escorted back to my temporary accommodation and I was to think myself lucky not to be placed in protective custody, this time.

The door opened away from the direction of Willis's caravan aisle so it had been possible for Slater to enter the observation trailer without his being spotted from there and it would be enable me to leave without being observed, under escort, once Willis had re-settled for the night. I was told emphatically that if I returned I would be charged with interfering in police matters, perverting the course of justice, breach of the peace, and anything else they could think of. And this was my final warning.

I considered arguing that it was free country and I'd go where I liked within the law, but thought better of it. I'd been warned off and it was perhaps preferable to have Slater moderately well-disposed than in total enmity and I was sure he could make things very difficult.

Meanwhile Willis had re-entered his caravan and the light had gone out, one of the observers informed. A soft tap at the door then revealed yet another fit-looking type who'd come to make sure I left the site quietly.

I was about to leave when Slater spoke again.

'What was the idea with the guitar, Natasha? You booked for a gig here?'

'An alibi,' I said. 'No one would think twice about a hippy with a guitar, would they?'

'Creeping about dressed in black at this time the morning?' He raised his eyebrow and looked steadily over my shoulder, but this time I thought he might be actually looking at the guitar.

'May I?' He gestured for the instrument. I passed it over without hesitation. He looked it over, balancing it.

'A bit battered,' he commented. He hefted it in both hands. 'Do you play it?'

'No, it's my daughter's. Used to belong to my father. It was among some things that were sent back from Lithuania.'

He looked thoughtful but handed it back without further comment but just as my escorting plain clothes officer reached for the door handle, DI Slater spoke again.

'Stay away, Natasha. I mean it. For your own good.'

'If I'd known you were taking all this seriously perhaps I would have,' I replied.

Slater seemed about to say something else but then waved to two of us away with a dismissive gesture and was reaching for a pair of headphones when he was lost from my view.

~-~

We made our way quietly towards the site perimeter, walking in the direction of my parked 2CV. The escort was briefed to return me home, to the 'safe house'. He would take my car. An unmarked police car would follow with me as passenger. He'd retain my car keys and any spare until a court order could be sought banning me from approaching the caravan site, all explained in detail before I'd left Slater's presence. Exceeding their legal powers I suspected, but what could I do?

We had gone maybe two hundred yards when the night was torn apart by a brilliant flash and a mighty bang. We were hit by a hot pressure wave and bits of shrapnel clattered about the roadway and onto trailer roofs. We turned shielding our eyes from the livid fireball that rose in a small mushroom cloud from the direction of the surveillance caravan. Small pieces were still descending.

My escorting officer yelled for me to run, to get into my car and return home at once. He pulled out a mobile phone and called the emergency services. I stood transfixed watching figures staggering from the inferno. I thought I recognised the female police constable, hair ablaze and immediately made my way forward to see what assistance I could offer.

'Get back!' shouted the policeman again, running forward. People were climbing out of caravans and statics in various stages of attire. I ignored him and continued to run towards the blaze. Nearer it was obvious that a large propane gas cylinder had exploded right next to the caravan. The fire had spread to an adjoining trailer. A plucky resident was already attacking it with a powder extinguisher to no obvious effect. Illuminated by the flames, someone could be seen rolling the policewoman on the grass. She was burned, how badly I could not guess, and in considerable shock but was trying to sit up, presumably to see if her colleagues had escaped. Slater was out, coughing and beating at his clothes. Another very scorched officer lay writhing on the ground amidst bits of electronic equipment. People were milling about asking questions and shouts could be heard from all sides. The fourth surveillance operative was not to be seen. Someone arrived with a container of water to cool the burns. The call went out for more.

Something else caught my eye. Midst the confusion, without lights, Willis's Transit was slipping quietly away into the darkness beyond the reach of the firelight. I could offer no more help than was already being provided for the survivors so I barely hesitated before sprinting back the way I'd come, to the corner of the site nearest the road where I'd left my car.

I made it in under one minute and very out of breath, flinging the guitar in the back. There was no sign of the waiting police car so I assumed it had responded to the blaze. The little flat-twin Citroen fluttered into life. At its most energetic a new *Deux Chevaux* was allegedly capable of 69 mph. Mine would indicate 70 as I'd proven on a motorway, but that could have been downwind with a faulty speedo. Now I needed her to prove it again, on a minor road. I rammed the 'umbrella handle' into first and sped off, lights dimmed.

I drove passed the entrance of the site knowing that the van would have had to pass me if it had turned right out of the park, which meant I was going the right way in pursuit. Just how far ahead it might be was anyone's guess, however. I had to assume it was staying on the main drag towards Lowestoft.

The 2CV rolled alarmingly on the Barmby Bends as a fire engine hurtled past with lights and siren going. There was no other traffic about but I could see the tail lights of one vehicle ahead which might be Willis, though it was still too far away to be sure and I kept losing it on the turns. A flashing blue light revealed an ambulance coming fast towards me in the rain, just a fine drizzle but enough that I needed the wipers that squeaked and clacked. After passing through Oulton Broad, the brake lights flared as it slowed and took a sharp right off the A146. I followed discreetly. I read the street sign: Victoria Road. The streetlamps identified it as a white van, similar to a Transit type.

I followed at a distance. Just our two vehicles alone in the night: via Horn Hill, over the bridge, making a left turn into Commercial Road alongside the dock with a few fishing boats and a moored naval pinnace visible. To my right was a rack of darkened buildings, among them shuttered take-aways, kebab shops and sleazy looking bed-sits, beyond which was the mainline terminal, Lowestoft Railway Station and the fish market that would be opening in just a few hours. It was Monday.

The road petered out into Peto Way. There was no sign of the van and there were any number of side streets he could have taken above Denmark Street or off Battery Green Road. I'd have to retrace my route and see if I could spot where it was parked. Logically it had to be somewhere close as we'd left the main thoroughfare at the bridge. I slowly cruised around the less travelled side of town with its mostly unimproved nineteenth century piles. The ground floor facades now enclosed pound shops, general stores, small foreign marts and take aways. A couple of slummy pubs, a betting shop and some graffiti -smeared lock-ups completed the collective.

There seemed to be some activity and lights reflecting in the damp pavement half way along a long narrow side street, not much more than a wide alleyway really, but I reversed and turned the little car into it, towards some figures.

Cars were ranged down one side. Pink neon behind filthy curtains declared a 24-hr.taxi service, confirmed by a hackney cab parked in a litter of takeaway cartons and paper napkins. Pulled up behind was a kebab vendor's van, still open for business, with just enough room to pass alongside. I slowed to a halt, keeping the little engine running with its peculiar soft, fluttery rhythm. Two girls from the late shift wearing bum-freezer street uniforms and high-heeled boots detached from the group. The taller of the two, in sunglasses, despite the hour, feigned an inviting smile in my dimmed headlights. She clattered over on skinny legs and ducked her head at my window.

'You looking for biz….whoa?' Her expression changed fast when she saw me, whipping off her shades. Afro-Asian. Quite beautiful. 'You not fro' round here, bitch!'

'Yeah, you fuckin' tommin' round here, slag?' Miss scowling anorexia closed in behind. Very blonde and twitchy. The first one was leaning on the car.

I flipped down the window. 'I'm looking for someone. Maybe you can…?'

'If you's looking for yo' man, honey, we fucked him twice tonight already. A done deal. So *do* one.'

'Yeah, and we ain't dykes.'

'Look, I'm not poaching. I want information.'

The second hooker made a gesture at the car. 'You ain't like no pig. What is you, sister? A fuckin' travellin' joke dominatrix? You all too *old* fo' a *ho*!'

'I wanted to know if you'd seen a white Transit come through here and which way it went.' A slim thin-faced black guy in a suit and a dark tee shirt had come out of the taxi office and was looking at me intently. I was beginning to regret coming down here, attracting attention.

'You jokin' me, sister?' The first hooker was looking at me with raised brows.

'I just want to know if you've seen it. Where it went. Do you know who owns it?'

'What yo' game, honey? You asking some shit!'

Where the hell was I? Detroit? There was a bang from the rear door as second hooker kicked in the light door skin.

'You come slummin' down here, bitch, givin' cheapo hand jobs, we gonna mark *you*. Not just yo' tin fuckin' buggy.'

Yep: Detroit!

The sleek 'Somali' was walking purposefully towards us. He reached into his pocket and lifted a mobile phone to his ear.

I raised my eyes to hooker number one. 'Please,' I said. 'It's important. Do you know a tattooed guy with peroxide blonde hair? Drives a white Transit van.'

'Don't dey all, honey?'

'Please.'

'What's it *to* you?'

'He needs some …. urgent advice,' I hear myself say.

'Shit you on, honey?'

The Somali has examined the registration plate and is coming around the back of the car. I see him in the wing mirror, moving towards the driver's side. I freeze.

'Get going!' the Afro hisses through her teeth urgently. I detect anxiety and a warning meant for my own safety this time.

'Oh, oh! *Piggys*!' says Blondie.

In my rearview mirror I see a police car's chequer-boards pass the end of the street and the reflection on wet brick of glowing brake lights.

The car reverses and begins to turn into the street. Although it might be the cavalry I no longer want to be here.

'Hey, girl,' Blondie screeches to the Afro. 'Scoot yo' crack ass over here, *now!*'

'Please….?' I say again.

Afro glances back at the approaching police car. The Somali swiftly returns to the taxi office.

'Shit, honey,' Afro whispers close. 'Down Trafalgar, into Norwich Road, yeah? Then right into Webb's Lane. You asking for some pain if he with Charley fuckin' Manson. He in the Book of Revelations'.

She swung away, her druggie friend with her. I accelerated around the kebab stall and out the other end of the lane. There was just room for the 2CV to pass. Hopefully the police car would find it too tight a squeeze.

~.~

As I drove, I reflected briefly on my earlier periods of confusion and anxiety, when, like Steiger, I had obsessively doodled and written notes to myself. Not in my case drawings of monks in robes of blood, but inscrutable Orientals and round-faced owls. We'd each in our way tried to reveal those hidden things that crouched behind those ciphers. These implanted screen memories: in my case artificial, in Steiger's, perhaps the result of trauma and an unbearable truth. Did we reincarnate in clusters, as my father had surmised? If so, am I Kat, re-running her quest to rescue Graczy with her little ram's horn bow; or Steiger, searching for the remaining sister, Katarzyna herself? Or was I searching for my own identity, as my father had told me I must. Who was Willis? Not the fierce-eyed madman, Roskov. Willis was too pond-life stupid for that identity I was sure. God, listen to me, I thought. This line of thinking itself is madness.

One thing I was sure of. I felt alive and empowered and full of retribution, a cold implacability running through my arteries. If I had no clear idea yet of what I intended to do it was because I'd not yet made a reconnaissance of the target. I felt that eventually there was a chance that Willis would lead me to the location of the twins, if they still lived. That was all. There were a hundred or more arguments to say that such reasoning was flawed. But it was all I had to work with, and that seemed more than the police now had, after the attack on their surveillance trailer. There was no reason to suppose that they were aware or unaware of a nest of villains in Lowestoft or that there may be a brothel around here with East-European girls held in forced prostitution. Perhaps all the key locations were under observation, the Force just biding its time for the bigger fish. But I didn't care about that. There were two innocent girls who were suffering, were sick and needed to be rescued and provided with urgent medical treatment. If not by me then who?

At least I'd now exhumed my old acquaintance from Blaze's earthen stable floor in its stiff polythene: the mechanism smooth and oiled as when it was new. And I had two spare clips of 7.62 mm ammunition which I hoped was still good. Despite that the Tokarev was itself practically fool, water and dirt proof, I saw no reason to risk malfunction and had carefully stripped, cleaned and oiled it again while Emma slept. My only concern from the ordnance point of view was the antiquity of the ammunition.

I wondered what the Afro-Asian hooker had meant. If he (Willis?) was with 'Charley Manson'. Did she mean Charles Manson, of the 'Manson Family' of killers. Murderer of Sharon Tate, her unborn daughter and her friend? That had happened many decades ago, in LA. Manson was still serving several life sentences, as far as I knew, although his girlfriends who'd willingly participated in the bloody massacre were now living free. And what did she mean by the 'Book of Revelations'?

I wondered why a young hooker would even *know* about Manson who'd vowed to provoke a race war, although it had remained in the *Zeitgeist* for years and years like an urban scar on the psyche of the privileged: the *Amfortas* wound that wouldn't heal. That Manson who's notoriety had been a guiding light for the dead-end *Rote Pfad*, the death cult that had given me the skill with weapons and in unarmed combat, so long forgotten. I had to assume that she'd meant that Willis's confederate had shared an attribute of Manson's, apart from the readiness to butcher and kill. The fire-bombing of the house in Upper Thurston and the propane gas tank explosion at the trailer park had been deadly pyrotechnic attacks, not to mention the burned out caravan at Grimstone House - a sure way to destroy evidence. Willis had not detonated the gas tank, I was certain. I'd also had the impression that there had been two occupants of the Transit when it pulled slowly out of the site.

No, the resemblance must be in the *eyes*. The red-eyed madman who burned hospitals to the ground with people inside. The fire-eyed demon leader of the Roskov Wolf Pack. Manson incarnate. Those eyes would be the same. Mad, fanatical, windows on pure evil. The *Wasserkobold*, or

Wassermann: gory tormentor of Elenja, torturer of Kristian Graf von Strelitz and of Kat, chained in her filthy cattle truck as reported to Harry. The jealous Water Goblin of German myth who throws the headless corpse of his half-human child at the feet of his 'disobedient' wife. Endowed with that same cruelty that cuts off a young violinist's fingers. Or those of a schoolboy accused of unpunctuality. The *Erlkönig*. The prowling menace in my garden with the dirty red scarf that 'Plastering Spam' had reported. *The Iron Wolf.* From the time when such men gave themselves fanciful, resonant names, full of power. *Molotov.* The Hammer. *Stalin.* Man of Steel.

I remember Chrissie choking at the séance, clutching her throat. And Kat, Rolf's dear Kat, had shot the goblin in the neck. Sadly, it had not been fatal. And now perhaps, here he was again. *Raudongevklis.* Red Throat. I could hear his heartbeat.

They'd wanted to section me once before but I'd convinced them that I was just suffering from stress and instant coffee. But it wasn't that. I was beginning to believe that my father was right about cluster re-incarnation too.

I was keyed-up but unafraid. Nervous alert. I had 'situational awareness', an expression my father had used about safe flying. He'd also said it was not a good idea to try anything for real without practising it first – at a safe altitude. I didn't have that luxury as I prowled through the mean streets behind the fish market, looking at the darkened buildings, surveying the parked vehicles, the little 2CV purring quietly through the night. In another minute I'd coasted to a halt behind some lock-up garages. A hundred yards on there hulked the dim shape of a light coloured Transit. My next decision depended on this reconnaissance, such as it was. As a general once said, *'Time spent on reconnaissance is seldom wasted.'*

I sat in the car with the driver's window unlatched listening to the faint sounds of the town and the harbour night. I gave it five minutes and then another five before climbing out and moving stealthily towards the Transit, praying that the damned rottweiler wasn't still in the back to raise the alarm. I approached from the side, staying in the shadows and out of the capture angle of the nearside wing mirror. Crouching below the window I used a small make-up compact mirror to check the vacant interior and detected heat from the cooling engine. The occupants were most probably somewhere in one of these darkened houses which backed onto the lane. I froze at a car engine starting, the sound of its engine fading as it drove away from somewhere on the other side of the buildings. Was that late night activity associated with my quarry? I reconsidered my first impulse to deflate a front tyre to deny or at least delay my targets' use of their transportation as without any knowledge of the local situation that might only alert them to enemy activity.

I checked the rear of the seedy-looking two-storey properties. There were no cars parked within fifty feet of the van, so it seemed logical that it would have been left in convenient proximity to the rear. In other words right outside. The other evidence was a dimly-lit window on the upper floor which might be some lonely computer nerd behind his window blind in a cyber-relationship across the ether. Or it could be 'Manson' and Willis. It might also be the brothel where Tania and Lilia were being held, although it scarce looked big enough to house as many girls as Tania had implied worked alongside her.

My mind was reeling. Walking around the front and knocking on the door seemed like a bad idea. Pushing my way in the back was only marginally a less suicidal prospect. No form of entry would be remotely possible or sensible until I knew where the dog was and whether the girls were incarcerated on the property. A six foot wooden gate gave access to the rear. I found the latch and lifted the lever. It was not locked. However, despite my taking care the hinges were noisy. Not noisy enough to disturb whoever was in the house, but noisy enough to waken the rottweiler whose warning growl emerged from the van. I made my decision. Dropping to the pavement I rolled out of sight under the van. The dog barked loudly. From my hiding place I could just see a shadow moving against the blind. The blind rose and the light went out. I could see the dim shape of a head peering out. The casement window creaked open. I was immobile. I could see Willis's peroxide hair and even the hint of a frown. He looked up and down the lane.

'Rocky, shut the fuck up, dog!' The window slammed shut.

I scrambled clear but the dog started barking savagely again, the van rocking with its fury. I heard the house window open again as I fled into the shadows.

'Who's there?' Willis's voice echoed across the lane.

I hid in a lock-up doorway trying to control my breathing, hoping the shadows were deep enough to cover me, my collar up over my face. It's always darker just before dawn I thought. Crouching behind the 2CV I undid my scarf and quietly undid the petrol cap, pushing the scarf deep into the filler pipe sensing the drop in temperature as the petrol soaked into the material.

Willis stared intently across the alley in my direction. I kept very still.

The dog was still barking. Willis's head disappeared suddenly so I knew he'd be on his way down. I had to move fast. The van's filler cap was a plastic bung....

Charged with adrenaline, I ran swiftly to the van extracting a matchbook from my jeans pocket, removed the cap and stuffed the scarf loosely into the filler pipe leaving room for air. I struck a match with trembling fingers and lit the wick. The dog's snarling reached new heights. I doubled away from the vehicle as the petrol vapour ignited with a 'woof' followed immediately by a boom and a crackling roar, counterpoint to the rottweiler's panic-stricken, high pitched screeching which seemed to go on and on. The lane was lit by the livid fire, throwing everything into sharp contrast. Overall the voice of Willis screamed its incoherent litany of rage as Rocky's screams rose in crescendo then ceased abruptly. I considered ringing for the fire brigade and then thought better of it to see what Willis would do next. So much for my reconsideration of deflating a tyre. But then improvisation seemed like it was second nature to me after all, even if the decision was the wrong one. But I'd struck back. The first counter strike in a guerrilla war.

Willis was pacing up and down in what seemed like an agony of indecision, anger and despair, looking about for the arsonist but seemingly reluctant to move more than a few yards from the house. He was glancing over his shoulder every now and then, swearing vengeance and still calling for Rocky; perhaps he'd really been attached to that dog. I hoped so. Then he was on his phone again, speaking low and agitatedly as he strode back to the house.

Someone, probably not Willis I surmised, had called the fire service and an appliance turned up at the same time as a police car. Possibly the one which I'd seen patrolling when I'd been parked in the alley talking to the Afro hooker with the heart of gold. I was back in the 2CV, hiding under a dark car coat, my eye just above the bottom of the window frame keeping the scene under surveillance. People had collected around the blaze, seeming to appear from nowhere, watching while the fire crew sprayed foam on the remains of the van which, so far unknown to any but Willis and myself, contained the blackened carcass of *Rocky*.

One down, I thought. One dangerous member of this gang accounted for. It was fighting fire with fire in my book. They'd started it with plastic explosive and a propane cylinder, murdered one officer and injured two others. I considered that the payback was just beginning and had a half-formed idea that if I shook their tree something might fall out that I could then follow. It was a start.

The police seemed to be making door-to-door enquiries regarding the ownership of the van, knocking at various addresses while I kept hidden in the darkness of the 2CV's front seat.

Dawn came and the policemen had since departed. Soon afterwards I saw movement again in the window of Willis's hideout. I hoped my 2CV looked innocuous parked a hundred yards away camouflaged by some other unremarkable vehicles. A few cars and a van or two passed by as the morning drew on. I drank coffee from a flask and continued my watch. After about an hour a Group 4 Security van turned in from the other end of the street and parked nose-on to what was left of the Transit. A uniformed security guard climbed out and was swiftly lost to view behind the tall gate.

By now the mantra was firmly implanted, that nothing is ever as it seemed. The Group 4 logos could have easily been copied and I was quite prepared to believe either that the van was a 'ringer', or if it was kosher, an employee was 'moonlighting'.

A few minutes later, the 'guard' reappeared and looked quickly up and down the street. He motioned to somcone behind and six small figures, their heads down and hidden by hoods, moved rapidly to the door of the van, followed closely by Willis. The door was slid shut and the van started, moving noisily off, veering close as it passed me by. I had buried myself deep in the foot well of the car before they swept by so I was pretty sure I'd remained out of sight. I waited until the sound of the security van had faded before starting the 2CV, which was cold and took a few attempts with full choke to get it to fire. I slammed it into first and with full lock made off in the same direction. Traffic was still light and I soon caught sight of the van ahead. I kept well back and was happy that another car was situated between to provide cover. Citroen 2CVs were not as common as they once were and I felt already that my battered example made me even more conspicuous than when I'd been driving a Volvo with the dented door. Hopefully Willis had not yet associated me with my present form of transport. If this insurrectionist game of cat and mouse were to continue I felt the need to change it fairly rapidly for something less conspicuous and a lot faster: at least as far as dwindling funds would allow.

Soon we joined the traffic back on the A146 heading for Beccles. We'd gone only a few miles when I saw the van ahead slow and turn off left. I followed at a distance and saw it turn off again, up a leafy lane. I continued driving steadily for half a mile past some houses before pulling into a lay by. The lane had looked more like an entrance to a private property than a side road and I'd made a decision not to follow at that stage and risk finding myself stuck behind it in the entrance to some secluded country house, confronted by a violent and angry Willis and no way of escape.

I had to make a decision about what to do next, and felt that the only safe procedure was to get the hell away from here in daylight, attempt to get back to the 'safe house' in time to get Emma off to school and think things through. I wanted to find out how badly hurt DI Slater and co. were and to tell the police what I'd seen of Willis's movements in company with what were undoubtedly six young females whose ethnicity it was impossible to determine.

My mind was working overtime. Everything seemed clear at once. Location; a harbour on the most easterly point in the whole British Isles, and the nearest port in a direct line to Eastern Europe. In my latest version of events I guessed they'd most probably been delivered to Lowestoft harbour under cover of darkness, possibly by fishing boat which I surmised would have met a fast launch somewhere in the North Sea. Either that or a small power craft had intercepted said fishing boat to further confuse the coastguards and customs people watching our shores; a variation on the containers of illegals shipped out of Esbjerg or the Hoek van Holland into the ports of Felixtowe or Harwich.

I remembered reading about the fifty-eight Chinese found suffocated in the back of a lorry container recently. Evidently losing that amount of an imported commodity was bad for business. But the six girls I'd seen were almost certainly delivered for the sex trade. Given their small number these must be highly prized, probably virgins, all of whom had believed they were being brought to Europe to enjoy a good living in contrast to what they might expect in their countries of origin, Eastern Europe or the Far East. All this was conjecture but my mind was sharp and alive to all possibilities.

I drove as fast as I could, braking only for speed cameras, and made it 'home' to Elmswell by eight thirty, almost out of petrol, in time to find a worried-looking Emma making herself breakfast and watching the road.

'Don't ask,' I said. 'I'll grab some toast and take you to school. I'll pick you up at the café down the road from the school at five o'clock if I can't make the school run in time.'

I ran to the loo, checked myself in the mirror and saw a white-faced blur with dark rings under her eyes. I stuffed money into Emma's fist and told her on no account to return home without me. I didn't want her being alone anywhere quiet, and this hideaway was too isolated by half, even if it was in a small village and not as remote as thoroughly-trashed Mill Farm.

Later that morning I traded-in the 2CV for next to nothing against an anonymous three-year old, high-mileage Vectra with six month's road tax, a twenty-four month repayment deal, full tank and two new tyres. It was a dark grey, commonplace vehicle and fast enough for emergencies. I was conscious that my bank balance had now been severely damaged.

I dropped into Ipswich to the police station to find to my amazement that Slater was on duty, scorched and shaken but determined to carry on working. When the desk sergeant rang through I was told he wanted to see me and the sergeant had evidently been told not to let me out of his sight until the DI arrived.

Slater ushered me into his office and without more ado asked me where I'd gone the previous night after the gas explosion. I told him part of the truth, but not about torching the van and following the Group 4 vehicle. He looked at me disbelievingly in his peculiar way. He was wearing an old sports jacket and a plain black tie. He still smelled of smoke but it was not that of cigarettes; rather singed skin and hair. His temples were scorched and his eyebrows frizzled. His left hand was bandaged. Two of the other officers from last night were still in hospital but were expected to make a full recovery. One officer had died, he said grimly.

'Natasha, you are a one woman guerrilla war and it's got to stop. You are on your second safe house. I take it it's alright, in Elmswell? It's temporary and you may not like it, but if you don't keep your head down, you are going to get yourself killed if I don't arrest you first. Can't you consider your daughter's well-being like a normal mother? I will assign a female officer to ensure that you remain safe. Think of it as protective custody, 'house arrest' if you want to, but I'll not have you sabotaging a major undercover operation involving fifty-five police forces across the country. Do you understand?'

'An operation to do what?'

He looked at me in exasperation. 'I've already told you too much.' He lowered his voice. 'But what the hell. Home Office figures reveal that a handful of British teenage girls are abducted in Britain *every week*. Many of these are from ethnic minorities. Some are not. In either case these girls are sold into prostitution by gangs here in the UK. But just as often they are sold-on, abroad. Many more are imported from Eastern Europe, and from Fujian, the main Chinese people-trafficking centre. The 'Snakehead' Chinese gangs are handling this and they are bloody ruthless.

There are home-grown gangs involved as well as Yardies, Somalis, Albanians, Roma, Turks, you name it. A complex mix, of all nationalities, many living illegally themselves, using false social security identities and drawing millions in benefits. These organised criminals may be at war with one another but on occasions they engage in trade which helps muddy the waters when transporting girls around the world.'

His frankness and volubility was refreshing and as far as I was concerned positively dripping with disclosures. Giving to receive, no doubt.

'As far as we can determine and partly from your own evidence you unwittingly became involved with such an abduction, which perhaps was bungled when the 'illegal' twins of your acquaintance were kidnapped, possibly as a trade to pay off a debt.'

Twins would have a particular value, he said.

'As evidenced from the mobile phone call you allegedly received or possibly for some other reason, the two ladies on whose land they were living in the caravan were murdered. Possibly Chrissie's was accidental, a punishment beating taken too far for her age and frailty. 'Plaster of Paris' residue on her clothing matched her bruising - deflected revenge for the wrist injury you'd caused Willis, but it is a measure of their courage that none of them gave away your address.'

I felt my throat tighten. I'd supposed it hadn't occurred to the killer-kidnappers that I had been living literally a few hundred yards away, down the road and up a darkened farm track. Clarissa had been half-suffocated and then left to die from carbon monoxide in her Land Rover. Jankaitis had only my old Godalming postal address. But perhaps he wasn't part of all this, otherwise Willis and his henchmen would have known where to find me.

Unless......unless there were two factions operating independent of each other. Rivals! Or perhaps these had now joined forces, possibly in a temporary and mutually mistrustful alliance. Like Hitler and Stalin. My mind whirled with possibilities and connections.

But Willis was a smalltime crook, hardly worth blowing up a police surveillance caravan to protect – unless he knew more about this people trafficking than had been realised. And who had tipped the killers off, I wondered? Willis and the pyrotechnics expert. Two grey suits above Slater's paygrade maybe…a mole or two in CID or the Serious Crime Organisation? There was more to this.

'Drugs are involved,' he continued. 'Both in the subjugation of the victims, and to ensure that they become addicted and thus easier to control. Don't forget that they are often brought to Britain in the belief that they'll be getting well paid jobs as domestics, in hotel work, through placement agencies and are subsequently abused. Resistance is punished through violent rape, beatings and threats, but also by drugging. Their captors also bring drugs in with their 'imports'. They are very much into anything and everything, Natasha.'

I remembered my own brutal 'gang initiation' in Berlin. 'Did you know about the 'transit' house in Lowestoft?' I asked.

'No, we have you to thank for locating that for us,' Slater confessed. 'But that doesn't alter the fact that you running around like a caped avenger is in any way acceptable. This operation is costing a fortune. Many chief constables' careers are on the line if it all goes tits up, the crap won't stop above DI level. It will cascade all the way down to those on the beat. Highly-trained CID professionals are on stake-outs nationwide. We can't have anything going off half-cock and alerting the big fish. Two minor victims in this vice web cannot be allowed to jeopardise the op, no matter how pathetic their situation, and that means it's hands-off from you. With or without a restraining order or placing you under arrest.'

'So whose was the caravan you were watching? Willis's ?'

'No, his girlfriend's. We really had no clue to where he was hiding until his van was burned out in Lowestoft.' He was watching me intensely. 'We found drugs in Webb's Lane, by the way. Cocaine. And our sniffer dog found something. Traces of the detection agent, DMDNB. Semtex. And something else.'

He paused to let the 'something else' sink in.

'Well?' I asked impatiently.

'Wrapped up in a cloth at the back of a wardrobe. A mannikin head. Blonde.'

A shudder ran through my whole body as the dark figure returned to me, holding Emma's decapitated head in my tortured imagination. Maybe Willis hadn't known just where to find me, but one arm of this sick den of thieves and pimps certainly had. Maybe a psycho, who worked alone.

I collected myself. 'Are you aware of a Group 4 Security angle in all this?'

Slater looked at me for a long moment and sighed deeply. 'You amaze me, Natasha.'

He told me that illegals end up, when arrested, in Yarl's Wood Immigration Removal Centre in Bedfordshire with all the other undesirables. Group 4 delivers and guards them. However, when security vans have arrived on occasion, to collect inmates for repatriation to point of origin, with all the right paper work in place, they've been known to disappear on their way to Dover. Subsequent examination of CCT video footage of the security vans showed the number plates to be fake.

'These poor women snatched from under our noses, sold and sold again. Those bastards were really taking the piss,' he said. 'So, did you follow the van?'

He'd slipped that one in.

'Which van?'

'Dammit. The Group 4 van.'

'It went past me with six captives aboard, with Willis and the driver. That's all I know. I had to get back for Emma.'

'Then I suggest you think more about Emma and leave policing to those of us who are qualified and paid to do it. Leave urban guerrilla warfare completely alone. That's it. Just go home and bloody stay there! And before you tell me I can't speak to you like that, I just bloody did!'

Chapter 54. *Ninja*

I headed west, back to Elmswell and retrieved the two discs from their hiding place in the house at Station Road. Something had been churning around in my mind for days, ever since I'd examined *The Siberian Eagle* CD in detail. My father's legacy had been our shared love of classical music. I pulled down the blinds and put the second disc, *The Siberian Eagle,* into the laptop. I skipped through the fascinating story; how the gold was retrieved from a sunken barge in the permafrost, east of the Urals, lifted from the River Ob delta - only to be lost off the North Cape for seventeen years. To read again the cryptic message in the last page of the continuing 'Steiger Saga'. They were as convolute as the quatrains of Nostradamus.

My gift to you, Natashka.
First his patriotic masterwork,
An heroic genius who,
Transposed his lady in the play,
That shall not be named.
For you will of course remember,
The great thaw,
Who's own theme resonated,
On a single note encoded;
Next the soft timpanic,
On Ludwig's great,
Reversal: reflective pre-echo,
Of its victorious denouement,

Demonstrated by the didactic Peter.
And at last, the individual numeral,
Of his fair heroine of the Vanity.
On the Marsh;

Chronologically these number,
But one third of that,
Of the Beast itself,
And that's the key.

~-~

I could quite see that someone without the experience of having listened to and loved the music my father had loved and been party to his passions: who had lived in Britain at a particular time and caught a popular TV series he knew I would most probably have seen, would make no sense at all of the above conundrum. Nor would it have helped if they hadn't seen the earlier CD and its description of his conversations with Hans-Peter. But for me, at last, it was beginning to make almost total sense. My once sharp mind would now be put to the test.

I copied the blank verse and then replaced the CD with *The Baltic Falcon* and scrolled down to the passage I was looking for. Peter talking my father through his interpretation of the Leningrad Symphony. Shostakovich was of course my father's heroic genius who'd kept his suitcase packed every night in readiness for the 2 am. knock announcing the NKVD, and the 7th was his patriotic masterwork. In case I had been really thick and didn't get it, *the play that shall not be named* was the Scottish Play, or Macbeth, which I remembered that Shostakovich had transposed to Russia in his opera *Lady Macbeth of Mtsensk*. Macbeth had resonated throughout this epic.

To hammer the point home, the *'Vanity on the Marsh'* too was Petersburg; the fabulous city that Peter the Great had built upon a mosquito-ridden bog that became Petrograd and then Leningrad before reverting to the original name with the fall of the USSR. The heroine in question was evidently Hans-Peter's fair Lett heroine, Lilya Litvak, the female fighter pilot who, he'd said, had flown her Yakovlev Yak-1 fighter in valiant defence of that city. *'I would have saddled up my Yak and flown wing to wing with Litvak, Johann,'* he'd told my father, even though John had argued that she'd actually flown on another front, in defence of Stalingrad. *Symbolic, Johann!* Or was that 'error' another smoke screen to confuse the enemy?

So far my father's clues had stemmed from our shared musical knowledge. But what of the 'great thaw'? Well, John Thaw was a well-known British film actor, a police action hero who'd starred in *The Sweeney* in his prime, but he'd made a bigger impression in another television series about a solitary, analytical detective whose character in moments of

782

reflection was also given to listening to classical music. I could recall the theme music written for the programme which I believe had spelled out the character's own name in the eponymous code: M-O-R-S-E, *resonating on a single note encoded…..*

By now I had acquired a musical CD of the seventh symphony and it was playing in Emma's walkman as I sat at my laptop. On cue the other clues revealed themselves as Peter had introduced them. A *soft timpanic on Ludwig's great reversal,* Dah-dit-dit-dit: was that 'B' for Beethoven? The exact opposite to Shostakovich's victorious denouement, Dit-dit-dit-dah: *'V-for Victory, like Beethoven 5th's beginning, but more vehement and for Shostakovitch, his so powerful climax!'*

It was all spelled out clearly enough, provided you had a certain background and more particularly, provided you were in possession of *both* CDs. It occurred to me then that Jankaitis may have missed the first CD, and had found the second by chance after I'd left the Linden House: had opened the back of the circular painting, realising I must have taken the earlier one, then sent the second one on to me, copying it first, so that, when prompted by *Cheshire Cat and Caterpillar,* I'd work out the code myself to avoid being framed for a double murder. I assumed that this was a Swiss bank account number, an account that contained much more than 'just' the Romanov billions, now gradually appearing.

Chronologically these number but a third of that of the Beast. I knew that the biblical number of the Beast, that is Satan, was 666, so did that mean 222? Or did it mean a third element of the whole; the number six? *Chronologically…. These number ….*that suggested that the preceding clues numbered six, that is a six-digit number. Very likely a six digit account number of a Kloten bank. The alpha-numeric position of the letter 'B' was 2. The numeric position of 'V' was 22. If you accepted Hans-Peter Neumann's assessment, the number of Dimitri Shostakovich's Great Patriotic War masterpiece, his *heroic masterwork,* was number 7, though many would have considered it his 8th. But his 7th., *The Leningrad Symphony* ends in the powerful hammer blows Dit-dit-dit-dah for victory at Leningrad, re-named from Petersburg and ultimate victory in the Great Patriotic War. So had I found, *chronologically,* 7222? A four digit number. The clue to the *sixth* I already knew was Peter's *'fair heroine of the Vanity…'.* But Litvak's individual digit? What the hell did that mean?

Oh, Clarissa, I've come this far so rapidly on my own, but I could use your GCHQ code-breaking skills right now.

~-~

I looked at the time. I'd have to pick Emma up in an hour, which meant I'd have to leave the house in thirty minutes.

I *Googled* Lily Litvak, finding a wealth of information, but most importantly there was a picture of her Yakovlev fighter on the *Stalingrad* Front. Her Yak 1 fuselage numeral was '44'.

If I was right I now had a six-digit number: 722244. Then again, perhaps I had misread the whole thing and the number was completely wrong. But I didn't think so. Of course I had no idea which bank it applied to and whether another identity or entry code applied.

My interpretation of events firmly connected Jankaitis' sending me the *second* CD to the ransacking of my father's room at the Cedars, most probably by 'Dr. Mitchell' who was searching for the *first* CD. And thence to murder. Without the clues embedded in the first CD the cryptic message in the second made absolutely no sense. And it was specifically aimed at me as the person most likely to be able to decode it, *not* because I was an ace code-breaker, *but because I was my father's daughter.* He knew which prompts to include, which musical and media references would most likely strike a chord with me. It explained the intense look in my father's eye when I visited him at the Cedars. He'd tried unsuccessfully to communicate his secrets to me then and earlier, on the return flight from Lithuania. When I'd been too busy and preoccupied to see beyond the natural frustration of a previously fit man in late middle age, for whom the world had changed in the most drastic way imaginable.

So who was Mitchell? My version of the story cast him as ex-KGB, maybe now a member of the hundred-thousand strong Russian Mafiya. He had to have some reasonably good medical qualifications to have successfully posed as a doctor in the local practice, if for only a few weeks. This suggested KGB thoroughness, attention to detail and training. Possibly this was someone who had been a deep penetration agent for many years, assuming a credible Northern accent; burrowing into and assimilating everything about our culture, ready for a signal to act. Awaiting Kremlin orders that never came in the period of the Cold War. A *Spetsnaz* agent? A very competent and dangerous individual. Just like me perhaps, if I'd not proved faulty.

You might also consider the truss rod CD.

Just what the hell did that sentence mean? Again the good old Internet provided the answer. It seemed it was part of the structure of a guitar! It was a stiffening rod set into the wooden neck to brace against the increased load imparted through wire-string tensioning - when such were fitted. I opened the guitar case. The strings on my father's guitar were some sort of man-made fibre. Nylon, probably. Not wire. So did that imply no truss rod was necessary?

But how could it also be a CD?

However, further investigation would have to wait. It was time to collect Emma.

~-~

As I drove I was planning my next move. Over twenty-four hours had passed since the Cheshire Cat and Caterpillar had left their threatening message on my phone. Their threat to have me arrested for murder had backfired as I was no longer under suspicion from the police of involvement in the deaths of my neighbours and I had a pretty good idea where the crime syndicate who held Tatiana and Lilia had their hideout, rural brothel or whatever it was where they gathered. Whether Mitchell or the two agents who'd posed as Serious Crime squad or MI5 or whomever they'd pretended to be in Ipswich belonged to that gang, I had no idea. Whoever they were they were good, but they weren't *Establishment*.

My mobile rang as I was pulling up outside of the café where Emma was waiting. It was the Suffolk Police with a message that protection in the form of a 'special unit' officer would be sent to stay with us in our new safe house for the time being, arriving this evening. I had mixed feelings about this but I had blundered into the centre of a very extensive police operation and it looked as though my movements were going to be restricted for the present.

Emma was peevish and even more put out when I told her that we'd be having a house guest. The officer duly arrived, a plain clothes police woman with appropriate ID, a police radio and a valise, very reassuring and personable. Armed, she advised me, but I was not to worry and I'd not need to be going out, would I? Alright for supplies, food, toiletries and so forth? We could arrange for deliveries if necessary, *just until this operation was over* remained unspoken, and she'd take care of my car keys. No I didn't have a spare, I lied. Naturally she didn't believe me and asked for my handbag and made a perfunctory examination of the kitchen drawers and other possible places of rapid concealment before settling-down in the lounge to spend the evening, while Emma revised in her room and kept the music down on my orders.

Sergeant Wiltshire had also brought me some mail from Mill Farm. She'd binned the circulars but there was a rates demand and an invoice from Spam. I'd have to pay to have the joinery and plasterwork re-done when all this was over, I thought, remembering the damage. Another letter she'd brought was marked 'Urgent: For Occupier' but turned out to be double glazing advertising and that too went into my bin.

I was racking my brain for a way of getting out and making a reconnaissance of the turn-off on the Beccles Road. It might be one of the sites now under police surveillance for all I knew. If I confessed I could still only tell them that I'd pursued Willis so far in that direction but I'd already denied doing that in some fond hope of finding the twins myself. What, rescuing them at the point of my ancient Tokarev automatic pistol? Rather than waiting for what I presumed would be a simultaneous police swoop on all suspect locations - 'across fifty-five police authorities'? How James Bond my half-baked plan sounded when I spelled it out in my own mind. It wasn't even a plan. And as Slater had reminded me, I had Emma to think about.

Meanwhile I meant to investigate my father's heirloom guitar. The initials 'CD' for Compact Disc had quite another meaning as I'd now recalled from his narrative. It meant it was another *concealment device*, 'spook' terminology as I now understood. I retired to my room leaving Sergeant Wiltshire watching a reality TV show.

Removed from its case, the guitar looked like a perfectly ordinary, anonymous acoustic instrument. A little worn with nylon strings. I turned it over and examined the back for some clue. The shaped piece of wood that helped brace the neck and attached it to the sound case of the instrument drew my attention. It was finely scrolled or decorated with a 'shadow' line that looked almost as though it might contain a circular insert. A 'button'. I pressed it. Nothing. I pressed harder and there was a soft 'click' as the entire back of the instrument released.

I sat on my bed in a slight state of shock, partly from the familiar smell of lubricating oil.

I was looking at what I'd unwrapped from the 'bubble wrap', immobilised against the gently curving instrument back. I realised now that the guitar had been a little heavier than it should have been, but only a little, for it had been cleverly made from lightweight materials, carefully braced and stiffened. The little *Skorpion* too had been lightened in every way possible. The Czech machine pistol's folding stock was aluminium tubing. The two ten-round ammunition clips had their cases drilled for lightness and had been independently concealed in the guitar case itself. The calibre was 7.62, same as the Tokarev, but the rounds were newer. This M61 and the automatic pistol had made me a one-woman arsenal. Not only that, I'd bloody well carried it as an 'alibi' when investigating the caravan parks with the Tokarev shoved into my belt!

But the guitar had yet to reveal its final secret. Inside the hollow neck a metal tube projected – the 'truss rod'. It was a snug fit but I stuck my little finger in and withdrew it without much difficulty. The silencer measured the same length as the *Skorpion* itself. It screwed onto the end of the barrel with a few turns. As I fitted it, the piece of thin cardboard which had been rolled inside the silencer bore, protruded slightly. I withdrew it; another letter from my father. And a small photograph - of 'Mitch'.

My dear Natasha, I hope I am addressing you. If so it is for the last time.

If you've found this then I'm either already dead or otherwise incapacitated because you would not be burdened with this mission otherwise.

Powerful and malign forces have conspired to usurp the Trust which I have been selected to administer, my being the sole heir to its senior position, under which it has been an honour to perform certain acts of disbursement for the benefit of all those families who had suffered under totalitarianism in whatever form. This duty I have dispatched here in Lithuania for nearly a decade.

Now the Mafiya has infiltrated the organisation and there is no going back. In fact I am a virtual prisoner. I have by a single act denied them not only all remaining trust funds of the 'Anastasia Bequest', amounting to some four billion dollars still, but have seized assets of Russian organised crime to the value of a further nineteen billion, all of which is in a numbered Swiss account and untraceable due to my destruction of the means by which I transferred the amount. To cut short a long story, by my own audit I had discovered their on-going money laundering operations.

The bank where these monies are cached is the old established Banque Schneider-Turcat &Cie, Kloten and the password and entry code to view the account is Truffle 962707. Payments and withdrawals as a special client can be made electronically using this code and typing in the six digit account number. This number you may already successfully have worked out, if I know my daughter! Swiss banks are rigorously protected against investigation except where severe tax fraud or the proceeds of international violent crime may be involved. This bank is not suspect nor has it been investigated on behalf of the World Jewish Congress for violations proceeding from the Holocaust and was one of the reasons for choosing it, Natasha, along with their managed account portfolio which delivers 18% PA on a proportion of the original investment.

Finally, if it all goes pear-shaped, the whole deck of cards will fall, ushered by a simple phone call. That number is arrived at by adding twice again the prefix of my hero's symphony of the GPW and cancelling the suffix of that great and friendly Mongolian beast of burden. Remember Samson, Natasha. When the number rings you will be transferred to an extension. Press 'hatch'. The Ignalina area code is 386.

Meanwhile watch out for a smooth bastard, Spetsnaz Colonel Vladimir Kutushin who is socially mobile, probably well-embedded in the middle strata of UK society. Especially watch out for an evil psychotic who might have based himself on Roskov if he is not actually his reincarnation. Even his first name is the same; Nikolai. He is below average height and cannot escape his Georgian accent. One or other of these may be my own Nemesis. Roskov was a hit man for the Chechen Mafiya, creatively obsessive. He is on some symbolic crusade and most certainly mad. You will know him by his serial killer eyes.

Natashka, Alexa told me about the Stasi funding of the Red Path and its eventual dismemberment by the BND after they'd raided their underground training base in West Berlin. They'd kept meticulous records, just like the SS on which the Stasi itself was based, which was fundamental in locating their operatives, most of them. All had bird names. You were *Drossel* by the way. I gather you were intercepted immediately on your return to the UK.

They'd employed a whole range of methods in those Ku'Damm basements: for example, techniques designed for the benefit of those with mental disorder in a perverse mirror-image operation, to break down the personality and create 'compartmented-multiples', programmed schizophrenics. Alexa told me all this. So I know that you were their unwitting dupe; that you suffered sensory deprivation and trans-cranial electromagnetic stimuli when drugged. That specific parts of your brain were targeted by pulses to boost Alpha waves. That you suffered short-term memory loss while other 'memories' would have been implanted; long-term memories and trigger responses to hidden stimuli as well as screen memories to prevent you from recalling what had happened, both during your training and after you'd carried out an operation. That you underwent weapons training and were their star pupil; an unconscious assassin awaiting her implanted key word or phrase to act as instructed under hypnosis.

This work was based on a war time SS-programme headed by Sturmbannführer Klemenz Auer, in a 'black' project housed in a special block at Buchenwald, to which he'd been posted following his previous work evaluating the results of depressurisation, extreme temperature and combustion experiments for the Luftwaffe. The data formed part of a Project Paperclip acquisition at the end of 1945 and it has been since used by the CIA. Their 1950s and '60s MKULTRA project was intended to create their own 'Manchurian Candidates', just like you were supposed to be, my dear.

If I believed the Home Office and the UK civil powers could cope quickly and competently with such labyrinthine conspiracy I would not imperil you. Don't forget there is an Establishment angle with some equally ruthless people who wish to secure the Valkyrie List and destroy it, even though it would have less impact now: you too if they thought you had a copy. The mafiya can still use this for blackmail, even now. I believe that Delcroix has been murdered though he had been arranging to go abroad, with some financial help. His daughter, Amelia, was in hiding last I heard, or gone abroad too. As for Kutushin and Nikolai…Roskov….whatever he calls himself, please, if only for your own safety, and the opportunity arises, kill them both on sight.

You were 'weaponised'. You were to be triggered when a high value target was identified. Red Path's evil plan was to create a small army of sleepwalking killers. They were one cell among many, indirectly connected. They were anti-Western, anti-business, anti-captialist. As such they are ultimately at odds with the Russian Mafiya. The Red Path failed, was obliterated, but it gave you the 'skill sets'. You can do this, I know you can, or I'd not have involved you.

Kutushin's picture is included here, courtesy of the BND, unknown to them.

So it's goodbye my dear. I know we will meet again in some future cluster. I wonder who you'll be next time? Give Emma a kiss from her grandfather.

Johann

~-~

This madness has now become horribly real, incredible though it seems. I read the words again so that I know I am not imagining them and examine the bland face in the photograph for sign that he might be a KGB killer. *I* am not the paranoid schizophrenic despite my early fears. I have been horrendously manipulated and abused but I can think for myself. I am my own woman. Emancipated. Modern. Practical. I can be selective and I refuse to accept any orientalist myth and Dark Age bullshit. But a warning is a warning.

Looking at the core of the message, I understood that if I truncated the number arrived at from the chronology of the Morse Code messages in the symphony of the GPW, *Great Patriotic War*, removed the number of Lilia's 'friendly Yak' - her *Yakovlev* 1 - numbered '44', and added the double seven prefix, I'd conveniently arrive at a Lithuanian telephone number. And so what? I already had that area code for Ignalina and the landline number of the *Linden House* and this wasn't it.

There was a knock at the door. Hastily I slipped the Skorpion under the duvet and dropped the part-dismantled guitar behind the bed.

'Come in!' My voice was a little shaky.

Sergeant Susan Wiltshire opened the door.

'I'll use my sleeping bag on your settee, if that's alright. I've got a book to read so I probably won't sleep much and I don't think anyone can attempt a break-in without rousing me. So I think it will be alright for you to get some rest if you want to. Emma came down for a glass of milk and a biscuit but her light's off so I expect she's asleep.'

'Right. Yes, thanks. I was just going to look in on Emma, but if she's asleep now I'll leave her.'

Wiltshire smiled.

'Ok, well I'll see you in the morning then. Goodnight.'

Damn. I hadn't heard Emma go downstairs. I must have been so wrapped-up in my interpretation of my father's final message that I'd missed her footfall. Damn again, it would have freaked her out if she'd she entered and found me holding a silenced machine pistol. Not to mention there'd been a policewoman downstairs who could have discovered me equally *en flagrante*. The problem was, what was I going to do about finding the twins before the police raids, which might not even involve the Beccles address? Would the reports of other raids tip-off the local criminals and enable them to get away, maybe take the twins with them? I couldn't risk that happening. I was armed. I had an advantage that they'd not be expecting a night time visit. I had to try.

~ _ ~

I carefully let in the clutch and the Vectra started quietly. It was a quarter to midnight and I'd slipped away from the back of the house, locking the kitchen door, left via the garden gate and jogged quietly through the lane to the first gully that led into Station Road where my car was parked. I'd switched on the ignition using my spare key and heaving on the wheel, pushed the far from lightweight car into the middle of the road, slowly gaining momentum on the very slight incline. I jumped in, starting the engine remote from the alert ears of Susan Wiltshire, breathing hard with the exertion. *At least, in my defence, I'm leaving Emma in safe hands this time, DI Geoff Slater.*

As I drove through the dark I pondered my options - was it only yesterday morning I had followed Willis from the trailer park? Now I was in a different car and loaded for bear.

~ _ ~

Anonymous houses were set back from the road opposite the concealed parking spot, their lights visible behind dark hedges and trees. I could hear music faintly playing, a heavy drum-beat. Some aspiring rock musician I assumed. It seemed quite an affluent area. My weapons were distributed under my forest-green Barbour jacket, spare clips and a flashlight weighing down the deep pockets. I headed back for the turn-off hoping it was dark enough to make me invisible; until I was within striking distance of the big house in my imagination, where I hoped my search would end.

Luck was with me in that no vehicle drove past me as I made my way on foot. Anyone walking these lanes would arouse suspicion I was sure. Only cars, not pedestrians came this way at night.

The hairpin turned into the darkened lane which climbed gently to Dower Hill Farm Retreat, as identified by the discreet plaque screwed to a permanently open gate. If I was right about the destination it would seem that farmers were taking 'diversifying' to new lengths. The lane was as dark as my own drive at Mill Farm with tall hedges and trees on either side, hiding any moon that might have assisted progress. My eyes had now become fully accustomed to the night - which was just as well because a car could be heard approaching. I had time enough to slip behind the cover of a tree and crouch down before its headlights raked the hedges. It was coming from Dower Hill. I kept my face turned away from the light as it swept past. I hoped I was well concealed. Time to pull on my black balaclava with the hastily-cut eye and mouth slits – in fact just in time because I had to throw myself flat as two more cars passed me, one from either direction.

I was flagging a little. The rise was gradual but my pace had been brisk and after fifteen minutes lights began appearing like fireflies in the foliage as the lane opened out. Through an open steel gate lay what appeared to be a medium-sized, well-kept park some one-hundred yards across and twice as wide. Several large trees fronted a broad, discreetly lit mansion house; the 'Retreat'. Aka *one people-trafficking hell-hole for Chinese and East European sex slaves*, so I presumed.

Hanging back in the gloom I caught my breath and reviewed the scene. Night lights were dotted about the forecourt and ground-level sodium floods blazed from the boles of two large beeches, fanning light in a wide arc. A car was parked in front of the entrance and a couple of heavy figures peopled the illuminated foyer. A frontal approach was impossible as the observable grassed area was swathed in light. The drive itself was split either side and to the left there appeared to be stables and a cobbled yard, possibly a car park. The drive to the right disappeared into the enveloping darkness. It looked as welcoming as any country hotel except there was no sign identifying it as such: not here, not at the turn-off from the low road. Just that cynical misnomer of a gate plaque suggesting a sanatorium.

How then might this *Paladin* extract two, possibly sick, young women incarcerated in the depths of a fortified and floodlit stone-built mansion?

Keeping to the perimeter trees I circled towards the stable area where a fine cedar cast its broad shadow on the grass. I was hoping they didn't have infra-red cameras or motion sensors. They didn't. They had dobermanns.

The first dog came out of the darkness and took me by surprise. I knew that if it got me by the arm I'd never be able to withdraw the *Skorpion* whose suppressor was my only chance of remaining undetected when defending myself. I crouched and turned away from the charging dog, head down and chin tucked in with my arms half-buried in the bushes, frantically screwing the silencer onto the muzzle. I ensured it was on 'single-shot', cursing my stupidity in not having the foresight to prepare the weapon earlier: above all cursing myself for not having anticipated guard dogs as a first defence.

My behaviour must have surprised the animal which had probably expected me to run, but it only took a few seconds for it to modify its mode of attack. It hit me bodily across the shoulders flattening me and found a grip on my coat collar, yanking me sideways and pulling me helplessly onto my back which blew the air out of my lungs and I lost my grip on the *Skorpion*. Growling deep in its throat, it tried to drag me away from the bushes. It might be lighter than a rottweiler but it had a lot of power in its neck and a formidable bite with the same fearsome aggression and determination. And it was shaking me like a rat. My physique was no match for it. I had a vague impression of another dobermann approaching fast. My throat was exposed and vulnerable and I didn't for a split-second think these animals were trained merely to hold until their handlers arrived. I was half on my side trying to ignore the first dog dragging at my collar, gritting my teeth scrabbling to find the gun. I found it and waited one second until the second animal was almost on me, steadying my aim.

The *Skorpion* kicked and emitted a slight 'pfut'. The round hit square in the chest at a range of two feet, which was pretty lucky in the circumstances. The dog yelped and disappeared from my view. The first dog seemed confused letting go of my collar briefly which allowed me to roll over fast and bring the weapon to bear just as it went for my gun arm. I managed to shoot it in the face and then in the heart, I think, because it laid down and didn't move at all after that. I checked the other dog. It was twitching slightly but I wasn't going to waste a further round on it. Ammunition was strictly limited.

All of this had taken place in seconds, just beyond the capture of the sodium lights. But something might have been seen on CCTV if they had their monitors manned. I moved off rapidly, hugging the perimeter. I'd gone only a couple of yards when I heard a menacing snarl and out of the corner of my eye saw another dark shape approaching fast. I turned to see a big charging rottweiler, growling savagely, its mouth full of daggers, foam flying and hell-bent on my destruction. I stood and faced it.

The *Skorpion* kicked twice as the range closed to almost point blank. I stepped aside and the powerful beast continued straight past, sliding into the bushes with a crash. I had a sudden picture in my mind of Old Kaiser's demise in my father's collected stories of *The Baltic Falcon*. The impression was vivid and perplexing and I put it down to the anxiety of the moment. Christ, I wondered, how many more of these damn things were there? I'd need another clip at this rate.

It briefly occurred to me that I was making a bloodthirsty career of killing guard dogs to add to my CV. But it was probably only a matter of minutes before this canine massacre was discovered and my 'window' for finding the twins would be narrowed.

Headlights swept the frontage and had me ducking into shadow as another car drove up, thankfully not heading for the car park, but rather it made its way around the gravel sweep to park in front of the main doors. My long view confirmed that several figures exited the car and assisted or half-carried someone inside. A busy place considering the hour.

I proceeded to the stables, keeping low behind the several cars parked on the cobbles; a few were typical 'fleet' cars, Mondeos and Vectras, but others were Mercs, Beamers and a Porsche Carrera. Further along in the shadows was the imposing mass of a Bentley.

The rear of the house boasted three storeys, the ground floor being windowless. Twenty-eight windows were located on the upper two floors, all barred. Most were dimly lit. An argument could be made for bars on the basis of security from intruders, but it was clearly a prison, and worse. A fire escape ladder ran up the centre of the rear wall, but just how it could be accessed from the permanently barred windows was not clear.

Turning my attention to the stables I tried a ledge-braced door and found it unlocked. I entered and to my surprise I found I was in a short corridor that opened via another unlocked door into a room with a stone-slabbed floor. I failed to gain an impression of the darkened interior so I shone my small pocket torch around the walls, shielding the beam with my free hand. Iron shackles were hung about at various heights and on one wall a rotatable cartwheel was slung with bondage paraphernalia. In the centre of the space there was a broad table with wrist, neck and ankle restraints at the corners. Various other bits of mobile restraint apparatus, light screens and still and video camera tripods were evident casting grotesque shadows as I briefly flicked the torch on and off.

Posters of girls undergoing sado-sexual torture, swastikas, pseudo-medieval religious symbols or black masses abounded. Among these was an A3 colour blow up of the face of a beautiful Asian and next to it, the unrecognisable horror of what remained: blinded, blackened, melted and featureless, the shocking result of what acid will do when it burns to the bone. A glimpse of that revolting atrocity on arrival would doubtless convince new house girls to comply instantly with every demand.

The muscular shape of a powerful motorcycle crouched in one corner and a large filing cabinet stood in another. I tried a few drawers and one of these rewarded me with a collection of passports, including blank British ones, immigration forms and passport-size photographs; young girls mostly of Asian or Slav appearance. An heavy inner door was locked, somewhat to my relief considering that my imagination had by this time reached overload and I carefully moved back outside.

I scurried towards the main building taking advantage of deep shadow. It seemed logical to climb the fire escape to take a look into some of the windows. Like the legendary SAS I clambered past the first floor windows. High on the ladder an odour I'd been trying to identify was stronger. Unmistakably, from beyond the trees on the night breeze, drifted the stink of a pig farm.

Leaning over and peering to either side, I made out identically arranged bedrooms. One was occupied by a Chinese girl lying motionless. The other appeared to be empty. Climbing to the higher level revealed both upper rooms to be occupied by sex workers and their clients. I found myself staring into the terrified eyes of another Chinese girl lying flat on her back. I'd ducked sharply out of sight but she'd glimpsed my black balaclava'd head and opened her mouth to scream while I hastily shinned back to terra firma. The screams continued faintly as I fled into the shielding dark.

I did not doubt that screaming was a commonplace manifestation in this awful place but suddenly I heard someone whistling: the way one would have summoned a dog, had there been dogs to summon. These escalating events demanded another improvised decision. How could I possibly gain access to this house, armed though I was? Storming in via the front door would be suicidal if the gang, whose number was unknown to me, was armed. And I had no doubt they would be. I had to find a back way in and investigate the rooms.

I continued my hurried exploration of the rear of the property. Aluminium beer barrels were stacked each side of a steel door with no handle which was illuminated by a single low-wattage bulb. Cautiously I pushed at it. It was locked or barred internally. Headlights suddenly blazed to my left and I sank into the shadow of the barrels. The lights moved off behind a screen of trees, beyond which I gained the impression of open farmland. Ignoring this mystifying development I continued exploring the environs and immediately encountered a generator house whose door yielded to my touch. *More slack security and a huge break.* My torch beam revealed a big diesel 'jenny'. I located the master switch and isolated it. If I could knock off the power to the house, the generator would not now automatically kick-in.

I looked up to locate the grid-connection of the mains supply in. Luckily the cable ran close by where I stood, carried by a telegraph pole obligingly fitted with iron foot steps. I hauled myself up close to the cable. I aimed at the porcelain insulator. The 'pfut' of the machine pistol was accompanied by a bright flash and a crackle as the cable parted and retracted under tension, dropping into the bushes. Simultaneously the house and surrounds were plunged into darkness accompanied by the sounds of general unrest within. In a few minutes someone would be coming to find out why the generator had failed to start.

~.~

From my hiding place behind the barrels I heard the rattle and creak of the steel door opening. A figure was moving towards the generator shed, shining a powerful torch before him, swearing to himself in English. Willis!

He opened the shed door and stepped inside. His torch beam had found the switch in the 'off' position. I let him switch it back on. I heard a click, the whirr of a battery-driven priming pump and then the generator started up. He was about to step back but froze. A *Skorpion* muzzle against the back of the neck will have that effect.

'Where are the twins?' My voice was raised just high enough for him to hear over the diesel engine.

'What the f…..?'

'Don't waste your precious time, Willis. Take me to where they're being held and you might continue to breathe. Make any wrong move or call out and you won't.'

'Who the fuck are you?'

I didn't answer; just stepped away from the shed with the gun trained on his back. 'Knock off the switch again and keep your light low.'

He did as he was told. The rattle of the generator subsided.

'Now, which floor are they on?'

'You ain't got a prayer in there,' he said. 'You'll never get 'em out.'

At least this confirmed they were here. Unless he was cleverer than I thought and playing for time. Someone shouted in the darkness, from the house doorway. I jammed the gun into Willis's spine.

'Tell him it's alright. That you can fix it,' I hissed.

'S'orright, Valmir,' Willis called back. 'Just needs re-priming. Go back inside.'

'Right, now move. Take me the quickest way in and up to their rooms, and no detours. We meet anybody on the way and you try anything you get it first. I'm going to be three feet behind you all the way. Keep your light shining ahead.'

We entered the darkened corridor. What smelled like a kitchen lay to one side and then the threshold of an open area with a carpeted staircase visible in the light of his swaying beam. Valmir or somebody called out and shone a torch our way. I shot him from pure adrenaline, which was the only thing left to do by then. He fell with a clatter, his torch bouncing across the floor. It had taken only a moment and I knew I'd crossed a line forever; but then hadn't I been programmed for this all my adult life; an assassin?

'Fuck me!' Willis swore quietly, obviously shaken and shining his torch on the body which was still moving. There seemed a lot of blood already so no doubt I'd hit something important.

Tough.

By my reckoning I had two rounds left in the *Skorpion*. I would be vulnerable when re-loading.

'Keep going. Fast as you like.'

Willis didn't need telling. We made it to the upper floor where he stopped, shining his torch on a door four rooms in.

'That one,' he said. His eyes looked big by the reflected light of his torch.

'Go in.'

He opened the door and I followed him inside.

'Bloody hell's going on?' A Home Counties' voice roused to ire. 'What do you mean just coming in here. What's happened to the bloody lights? Get that torch out of my eyes, damn you.' Blah, blah blah….

Willis's torch illuminated a large, middle-aged naked man; supine, hands cupped over his groin, with two half-dressed, skinny girls either side of him. I barely recognised the Belarus twins. In the torchlight they seemed thinner and paler than when last I'd seen them. Tatiana's face still had some of her old character but Lilia looked spaced-out and listless.

'Tania! Lilia!' I urged them. Grab any clothes you need and get out now. Come with me. Move!'

Tatiana recognised my voice immediately and was voluble in her thanks and almost equally hysterical with both joy and fear. She helped a wobbly Lilia into her jeans and they were jamming their feet into slip-on shoes when the lights came on. Lilia seemed to be coming round a little and was looking wide-eyed at my lash-up combat gear. I could see Willis poised to make a run for the door and moved back to cover him with a warning motion of the gun barrel. There was sudden shouting from downstairs.

'Which is your car?' I asked from behind my balaclava. Home Counties looked quite terrified, manfully shielding his manhood. I suddenly realised that he was wearing bra and stockings and had a belt around his waist. One of his legs was artificial.

'Answer the question or lose whatever you're holding,' I snapped. 'Get the keys, Tania.'

Still no reply from the client.

'Car!' I snarled at him. He seemed unable to speak.

Tania found his keys and held them up. They carried a shiny fob adornment with a familiar 'B'.

'Surprise, surprise,' I said sarcastically. 'Tania, can you handle this?'

I drew out the old automatic.

'Tokarev! Yes, Natasha. My father had such pistol. From *Armiya*.' She reached for the weapon.

'Then let's go.'

Tania stepped up to the bed and for a heart-stopping moment pressed the pistol hard to the 'client's' temple. His face paled and he seemed to shrink, turning his head away and closing his eyes. She snatched up his wallet and phone and moved to the door, looking hard at Willis whose expression betrayed his own sense of fear.

'Out, Willis. Move it. Car park, now!

On the now lit upper floor, doors were opening and heads peering out. Downstairs there were raised voices and the sound of heavy footfalls hammering along the corridor. We ran for the stairs, Willis leading reluctantly. Tania was helping Lilia to stay upright, her gun firmly trained on Willis's back. Bringing up the rear, I fed a new ten-round clip into the *Skorpion* and just flicked it to 'automatic fire' when my mobile phone rang. I grabbed it instinctively to switch it off but decided to answer it on the hoof.

It was Slater's worried voice. Damn, didn't the bloody man ever sleep?

'Sorry to bother you, Natasha, but your landline isn't working? I can't raise Sergeant Wiltshire on the police radio or on her mobile. Could you just check and see if her radio's switched on?'

My blood ran cold.

'It's not a good time right now! But could you get a squad car around there. As fast as possible?' My breathing was obviously laboured.

There was a clear pause before Slater spoke again.

'What the hell are you up to now, Natasha? Where are you speaking from?'

'Just get a car around there *fast*,' I hissed. 'Armed response! For your information I'm at the Dower Hill Farm Retreat outside Beccles, off the A146. It's a major brothel run by a foreign crime syndicate. Full of trafficked and under-age sex-slaves, if you didn't know.'

'Jesus, Natasha.' He called out to someone in the office, *'She's only compromised Pentameter bloody Two! Get out of there immediately!'* he yelled. 'And further….'

I cut him off at the ground floor. Two swarthy Europeans, Albanians or maybe Turks, stared up in amazement as we reached the foot of the stairs. The wounded gang member sat propped against the wall, grey-faced and groaning; very much alive. My bullet had entered above his left collarbone. It seemed I hadn't crossed the line yet! My *Skorpion* covered the two heavies.

'On the floor!' I yelled. 'Down!' The 'heavies' stared dumbly. One with particularly grotesque features, holding a squat sub-machine gun mistakenly raised it. I re-crossed the line with a short burst. The other 'heavy' fled towards front of house, yelling blue murder.

'Outside. Make for the Bentley, at the back,' I shouted, keeping my eyes on the corridor.

Willis obediently led off. Encouragement by example works wonders.

We fanned out on the cobbles heading for the rear of the unlit car park. I turned briefly to see a gunman taking aim from the doorway. I fired another burst. Sparks splashed all over the steel and he ducked back inside just as a whirling downdraught and a strobe light revealed a Bell Jet Ranger whining low overhead to descend on the other side of the trees. A glimmer of torches indicated a landing pad.

'You're driving,' I said to Willis. 'And I will not hesitate to kill you if you drop the keys, hit anything, or even stall the car. Got it?'

The twins piled into the back and I strapped into the front passenger seat with my weapon stuck in Willis's ribs.

'Don't bother strapping in and leave the lights off until we hit the lane,' I said. 'Take it round the back and fucking *floor* it!'

The Bentley scorched out of the car park round the darkened end of the mansion and into the glare of floodlighting to be met with a stream of fire from the front. There was a bang and Willis flinched as all the off-side windows shattered. Lilia screamed, hit by glass and shrapnel from the door as we powered into the lane.

~-~

Shane Willis drove as fast as the rushing headlights would allow, aware that he'd been endangered by the firing from the house as much as from the pressure of the *Skorpion* in his ribs, but I did not doubt for a moment that he would jump me if he could think of any way of taking control of the situation. I tore off my balaclava and shook the hair out of my eyes. I could see he cast a furtive glance, as if he needed confirmation of his captor.

How is Lilia?' I called, not taking my eyes off Willis.

'I do not know how bad she is hurt, perhaps not too much,' said Tania. 'But she is sick, Natasha. And some bastard beat her yesterday. Her face is bruised and her ribs.'

'OK. Willis, ease up. Just drive carefully now. I don't think we're being followed.'

We arrived at the end of the lane.

'Which way?' he asked.

'Turn left. Four hundred yards. There's a lay by. Stop there and switch off the lights.'

We pulled up behind my Vectra. The road was deserted. Behind their double-glazing, the local residents had remained oblivious to the sound of return gunfire from Dower Hill, the gang's un-silenced reports being masked by the sweep of the lane as much by the dense hedges and trees.

We helped Lilia into the back seat of the Vectra. She was bleeding from cuts to her cheek and neck. I kept Willis covered while Tania opened the boot. I invited Willis to get in. I expected some hesitation but he climbed in like a lamb. My marksmanship with the little *Skorpion* seemed to have made an impression.

A transient association. Steiger's attempted Russo-Baltic rescue of Krysia and Kat; one ending in a mercy killing, the other unresolved from reading part two of the saga. The last thing I needed were unhelpful synaptic short-cuts. There was enough present danger to contend and now my overwhelming worry about Emma.

There were plastic cable ties in the Vauxhall toolkit and with these I fastened Willis's thumbs together behind his back and tied his ankles with the nylon tool bag. For good measure I stuffed a far from clean duster between his teeth. He grunted something that sounded like pure hate as I closed the boot lid. *The use of car boots for transporting inconvenient bodies had included Amelia's and Auer's. Now Willis.*

A light strobed in the night sky as nav lights rose above the hillside to the sound of rotors fading to the north. The Jet Ranger.

'What shall we do with him, Natasha?'

An approaching hum attracted my attention. Rising from an easterly direction it quickly became a droning clatter; another helicopter. Police! It turned to circle in the direction of Dower Hill, stabbing its powerful searchlight downwards, behind the trees. Within seconds blue flashing lights appeared behind us and several police vehicles turned off the road into Dower Hill lane, driving at speed, their sirens wailing as they gained the top of the rise.

I got behind the wheel and moved off to find a way back to the A146 that didn't involve passing the turning to Dower Hill Farm and any road block that might have been set up.

'Natasha?' Tatiana asked again.

'He'll give evidence against me of course. For shooting two of the gang. One fatally I believe.'

'What will they do to you for that?'

'Well it'll mean a jail term. Possessing a firearm, taking the law into my own hands; not to mention murder, which they'll probably make stick. There are no extenuating circumstances in British Law. I'd be looking at about fifteen years I suppose, maybe ten if I'm lucky, due to the provocation.'

'But Natasha. They would have killed you if you hadn't fired. Were

800

you supposed to let them shoot you first?'

'They'll say I went armed and looking for trouble.'

Neither the police nor the courts appreciate ordinary citizens acting as judge and executioner, cleaning up the rubbish in society. They'd prefer we all kept quiet in our passive role as victims. Let the police do the job for us. Except that 80% of them are in admin and the others are busy handing out cautions to muggers.

'Natasha, they were all violent rapists. Every bloody one of them rape Lilia and me and rape all the girls when they come first. Thy show us terrifying picture of what will happen to us if we make trouble and beat us anyway, just to show what we can expect if we try to escape or don't do what 'clients' ask. We are illegals and have no status here. We do not exist. We are like ghosts. Ghosts who have sex with twenty men every day, all week, every week. Would be real ghosts before long. It is killing us. Willis did the same. But he had to handcuff me. Lilia fights too, bites him. Bastard.'

'Detective Inspector Slater knows where I was tonight. I told him so that the police would raid the house. Some at least got away in that helicopter. Undoubtedly the gang leaders.'

From what little I'd heard on the phone my action had possibly pre-empted a major operation – *'Pentameter'* or something - a planned raid on many similar sex-slave houses run by organised criminals; timed to prevent tip–offs between the various factions that sold girls on to each other and the suppliers of the 'raw material', mostly from abroad.

'But Natasha. You are Ninja! Brave, like Russian Knight. You must not be arrested because of us. We can escape, get back to Belarus somehow. Disappear. You can dispose of guns. Only evidence would then come from Bastard Willis. Nobody else see your face at house.'

'Yes. Just Bastard Willis,' I agreed grimly.

'Bloody Stalin said *'No man. No problem!'* Natasha,' Tania said softly.

~-~

Lilia needed medical attention. Probably both girls did, for a number of different conditions, without even mentioning leukaemia. I had to deliver them as emergency cases to a hospital regardless.

I knew that what we were doing was completely wrong. It was one thing to kill in self defence and completely unjustified to execute a helpless man in cold blood, whatever he'd done.

But with non English-speaking illegals, humiliated and in terror of the pimps and bullies who'd controlled them, who'd be repatriated as quickly as possible through Yarl's Wood, the possibility of all testifying to what had happened to them and who was responsible couldn't be relied upon. Those girls now in custody, far from home, would be deeply ashamed of the acts they'd been forced to perform as prostitutes. Bearing witness would be an impossible burden for many. In their cultures, family honour mattered above all else and women, already regarded as far less important than men, might refuse to testify in court, fearful that their stories would be broadcast, to the undying shame of their families overseas.

Unless a few of the girls were prepared to speak out, circumstantial evidence alone, the illegal status of their captors and the hoped-for recovery of large sums of money, weapons and drugs would have to be used to prosecute the case. Open and shut? A good defending barrister arguing for cultural relativism might even get the criminals compensation for police brutality.

'Natasha, we cannot let you suffer for us.' Tatiana was speaking low and forcefully. 'I know Lilia needs to go to hospital, but we need to do something first. You are mother, Natasha. You can stop being 'Ninja' now. Go home and take care of Emma.'

We were driving along a deserted, unlit stretch of road with darkened fields on both sides with some woodland. I pulled the car over. *I tried to read what was in those eyes and saw only the stare of a soul looking back at the abyss. Like Nietzsche in the mouth of Klammersdorf. I wondered if this is how Steiger had felt when Kessler led the Commissar Colonel to his execution in the snow, promising to release him.*

On the back seat Lilia appeared semi-conscious. Tatiana was exhausted and weak despite the fire that raged within her. I couldn't run the risk that she'd stumble and fall, that somehow Willis would outwit her, break free, wrestle the automatic from her in the killing field. He was a powerful, desperate man. He'd know he had nothing left to lose by trying and no doubt had been listening intently to what was being said; that was if he could hear anything from inside the boot.

Like grave robbers we opened the boot, like lifting the lid of a tomb and saw Willis staring up at us in the full understanding of his situation, utter terror in the round whites of his eyes. I untied his ankles and motioned him out. He shook his head and scrabbled crabwise, trying to speak through the filthy rag, shaking his head fiercely.

'You can die in there if you want to, or you can come quietly,'

Tatiana snarled. 'Either way you will pay for what you did. For what you are. It is justice.'

I did not recognise this new Tania, who had been the gentlest, most caring creature. I remembered the Russian saying: *To know the mind of another is to enter a dark place*. But who was I to judge her? If I'd gone through what she had I'd want to cut his throat with a potato peeler. I had no doubt as to his involvement in torching the house in Upper Thurston, murdering two children and severely injuring their mother. Here I was facing the old dilemma, seeking revenge over justice on which the stable foundation of our judicial fairness had been erected over time. I was also beside myself with worry about Emma and what I'd find at Elmswell, so you could say the balance of my mind was not what it might have been. If that's any excuse. And yet…..

Tatiana saw my expression.

'Don't judge me, Natasha. I come from a place where murder and rape was done for political ends. Like Zimbabwe, like Sierra Leone, Dafur now. Like in Congo. That savagery continued through two wars. Legacy remains in reputation of KGB and living victims of the gulag. If it seems only to sleep it will rise again. It still works in shadows. I believe Clarissa was murdered because of what she discovered in her Internet searches and from her old GCHQ contacts.'

My eyes widened.

'About Mafiya money, yes, Natasha. No coincidence. Her computer was stolen when we were kidnapped. She ask too many questions in the wrong places and made too many connections. She had 'covert intrusion software' copied on disk from her old job, for international banking network - for tracking large scale movements of money. Also some 'mavericks' she called them, secret contacts. Serious hackers she could rely on. She had told me this. Why are you surprised'

I might have said because everything seemed *too* connected, *too* co-incidental and I'd ceased to believe in co-incidences. I could believe only that things are *never* what they seem, but now action was necessary, not mystery-solving. Willis was shaking his head violently and I was still in a dilemma.

Tatiana continued to cover him with the Tokarev.

'Chrissie got in Willis's way, Natasha,' she said. 'We were disposable witnesses, just fodder. Would have been killed too but they decided we should be worked as prostitute slaves; because we were 'identical' and so more valuable. Some 'clients' found that arousing. Willis had financial trouble. So he sold us to the crime syndicate, gave up just driving illegal work gangs about. Began to work for syndicate himself. It is Mafiya-controlled, I think, but employs only low grade illegals. They only get a small cut of profits. Willis was useful because most of gang spoke only broken English. Naturally there were many perks, including *us* when there were no other clients to satisfy.'

Willis finally spat out his gag.

'You can let me go. I won't say anything. I'll tell you anything you want to know. It was that Nikolai. He's a bloody animal. He killed those two old bitches. It wasn't me. I just lost my temper. I have these rages.... I wanted to find out your address.......'

Tatiana looked at him with contempt.

'This bastard says my sister and me we are too old for top grade hookers. *Da,* you filthy dog! Thirteen year-olds for you, yes! You bastard!'

Willis remained silent.

'Then he boasted that because we were identical twins we might be worth something. He was paid £5000 for us, he told me. He is proud for that. The boss, Arslan, says we will have to work hard to pay back £5000 with interest and also for our 'keep'. We would never pay it off, just some kind of sick joke they taunt young girls with to keep them ......compliant...I think is the word.'

'It is the word, Tania,' I said.

'Natasha, if I wash forever I will not be rid of this pig while he remains alive.'

Hadn't Katarzyna Baroness von Strelitz said as much to Rolf Steiger? When she was chopping wood in a parallel life at Liepus Namas? *Round and round......*

'But this is so...... cold-blooded.' I feel myself shrinking from the act.

'I will take this cup from you, Natasha. You go home then and be mother.'

~-~

Later I dropped the twins off at the nearest A & E. Tania had a few hundred in notes belonging to 'Home Counties' so she was alright for the moment. I entered the number of her newly acquired mobile phone. There were three missed calls and a message: from the owner's wife, evidently. I told Tania I'd contact her as soon as, then tore off to Elmswell, trying to stay in control, in an agony of worry.

My worst fears were confirmed as I entered the village. There were blue lights everywhere. Station Road was blocked by a patrol car with luminous yellow tabards and fluorescent police jackets all over the place and knots of people standing about as if waiting for a celebrity appearance. I was stopped and when I identified myself was bundled into a police car and driven through the plastic tape barrier to my front door. The house was a blaze of light and a stretcher was being carefully loaded into a waiting ambulance. I tore the passenger door open and screamed for my daughter, elbowing two officers out of the way to arrive at the tailgate. The stretcher contained a zipped-up body bag. I felt as if I'd been punched in the stomach and had my liver ripped out. Two officers grabbed my arms. Someone was coming out of the front door.

'Emma! Where is she? WHERE IS SHE?' I screamed.

Slater was talking to me, muffled and afar off, as if from the end of a long tunnel, calming me. The street was swaying and he looked like death himself.

'Alright, Natasha. Alright. It's not your Emma.'

'What happened. Where's my daughter?'

'You can't go inside. This is a crime scene. Forensics has arrived and they'll need to spend some time yet collecting evidence. You can come with me. Where's your car? We'll need that too.'

I surrendered my keys and was put in the back of a police van for a gut-wrenchingly anxious trip to the now familiar Ipswich police station.

~-~

I was sitting opposite DI Slater again, both of us drinking tea although I could barely manage a sip of mine.

I'd already been interrogated by a grim-faced DCI Osborne along with a tired-looking Slater, but the DI was not yet about to let me go and he was determined to go over my statement again. Reaction to the night's events had kicked-in and now my anguish at Emma's disappearance and the circumstances surrounding it had left me in a state of near-paralysis. I was wearing a one-piece cotton overall. The police had found no sign of weapons in my car although there were small glass shards and a trace of blood on the rear seat which wasn't mine and which I'd been invited to explain. My clothing had also traced positive for gun powder residue. I was only half listening. I only knew that, according to Slater, they had no clue what had become of Emma, although I was assured that a wide search was now underway.

'Natasha, you are not under arrest at this moment, but you are very close to it. You answered your mobile from a location that you yourself identified as Dower Hill Farm…Retreat. Corroborated; a fortified brothel, as you confirmed in your reply to my own call. You sounded stressed and breathless to me. As you know, later last night the brothel was raided by armed police. The squad recovered one dead male of Eastern European origin and discovered one severely injured male. Both had suffered gun shot wounds. Scores of cartridges, bullet splashes and holes were in evidence and will be examined in more detail by light of day.'

'We arrested seven clients, one of whom is a pillar of the local community who claims he was robbed and his car was stolen. He now claims he was there in error and that he thought it was a sanatorium offering Thai massage….. all a horrible mistake. His Bentley was discovered with evidence of its having come under fire, abandoned a few hundred yards away from the entrance to the connecting lane. We are now dusting it for prints and the car is being transported to our compound for other evidence to be collected. Before these results are in, I repeat, it will help your case if you can shed light on any of this?'

'No comment.'

'We *are* trying to find, Emma, Natasha. You're not helping yourself by hindering our investigations into this affair. Especially if Emma's disappearance is connected, which at this moment I am prepared to consider.'

I remained silent. I could think of nothing but Emma and what she might be going through.

'I ask you again. Did you locate the two Belarus girls you were searching for, Natasha?'

'No comment.'

'I'll take that as a 'yes' then.'

'Detective Slater. Have you looked into that helicopter departure I described to you earlier.'

'Yes.'

'Well?'

'*I'm* asking the questions here, Natasha. If you want to know what we discovered you'll have to give me something.'

'I'll help you as much as I can. But I'm not going to incriminate myself or others. As far as I'm concerned the scum in that place got what was coming to them. I won't lose any sleep over their fates. The fact is that the gang members who may have escaped by air were probably the big fishes you should be looking for. Russians, Albanians, Tongs, Triads.

806

Who knows? But where would they have gone?'

A horrible connection was building in my mind.

Slater pulled a note book out of his inside pocket and opened it.

'A Norwich-based Jet Ranger Heli-charter firm had been booked to collect a party from a private field located at the map reference provided by GPS conforming to the field adjacent to Dower Hill Farm Retreat.'

'Headed where?'

'Headed back to Norwich Airport where a private charter had been arranged. At very short notice. The duty air traffic controller's statement reports. "A Cayman-registered Cessna Citation 560 of *Falcon Nine Air Charter Ltd.* Departed on 09 at 0145 hrs. Flight Plan filed for EKEB: Esbjerg, Denmark. Eight persons on board plus two crew." The statement continues that the passengers embarked from the western apron without entering the terminal or passing through any formal checking procedure, being regarded as VIPs, and that some had disembarked from the Jet Ranger and others had arrived by road. The car park is at the western side.'

'VIPs? But still, they couldn't have avoided formal processing though Customs, could they?'

'Passport details were faxed through to the Charter desk. They operate a 24 hour service.'

'But….. that's a nonsense. Anyone could have boarded that flight. And why Esbjerg?'

Slater shrugged. 'Apparently it's about maximum range for a Citation when fully laden. Possibly it would refuel there and proceed. Further.'

'Further….?'

'Further east is best guess'

In the pit of my stomach a rat intensified its burrowing.

'Anything else?' My voice was a hoarse whisper.

'Tell me what happened at Dower Hill, Natasha. None of the gang members have papers. Two of them are now actually claiming *asylum*, saying that they were victims, forced to work for the 'syndicate' because of threats made to their families back in Albania, Rumania or wherever. But for most of them it is *omerta*. The mafiya code of silence, with agonisingly fatal consequences for breaking it.'

'Geoff, for God's sake, what else.'

DI Slater took a deep breath.

'The agent for *Falcon Nine*. He reports that the Jet Ranger party had a young woman with them. She was in a wheelchair, reportedly in a coma. He was concerned to make sure she was comfortably seated and the wheel chair was folded and stowed correctly. He said something else.'

My hands were fists. I could feel my fingernails digging into my palms.

'His descriptions of the passengers is rather sketchy. It was very dark of course…but he mentioned the 'little guy' who was taking very special care of the invalid.'

'Yes?'

'Natasha,' Slater was withering. 'My Sergeant, Susan Wiltshire, is in the morgue with two bullets in her heart. A mother herself with two little boys. Callously murdered in the line of duty, assigned to protecting you and your daughter. Your land-line had been cut. She never even had the chance to draw her weapon. Your co-operation is not only expected, it is demanded. By *me*!'

Two in the heart. A close 'grouping', I thought, pushing any feelings of sympathy aside for the moment. Professional. But she was dead and my Emma was still alive. At least I had to hold onto that hope.

'I'm very sorry about your sergeant but I really can't help you with what happened at Station Road, *your* bloody 'safe house' as I understood it.'

My head was reeling but I had one icy thought, something that hadn't registered with me at the time.

'Sergeant Wiltshire kindly collected post from Mill Farm for me on her way there. I didn't ask her to. I only met her that once. She'd just done me a service, as a kind gesture. She'd discarded the circulars, but one letter had been marked 'Urgent'. When I opened it, it was only a 'double glazing circular'. I think it may have been a ploy in case anyone collected the mail. That she may have been followed, to Elmswell and Station Road.' I didn't mention that my own quick visit to Mill Farm might also have been observed.

Slater took this in.

'What else?' I asked again.

'The agent. He mentioned the eyes. He said they looked like Fred West's.'

Rapist's eyes. Serial killer eyes.

~-~

I was allowed to return to Elmswell with my own car after forensics had been all over it. Slater of course knew perfectly well I'd been heavily involved with the mayhem at Dower Hill, the gunpowder residue and the telephone conversation indicated that. But the first interviews with some of the gang members suggested that from their perspective an SAS team had raided the brothel. They identified the leader as a man wearing a black balaclava helmet. It had all happened in seconds and it seemed they could not accept that a woman could have been responsible, despite my having shouted orders at them to 'get down'. A 'culture' thing no doubt, plus the heat of the moment.

With no sign of weapons the Suffolk Police decided not to hold me, knowing they could pick me up again later. They had their hands full following the raid and Emma's kidnapping. Slater had taken over the latter part of the interview himself to try to break me down. He looked fatigued himself to the point of dropping.

One thing he did let drop was a possible ID for the Caterpillar. CCTV images from Ipswich had been layered over data transmitted by the FBI on request. Using their state-of-the-art face recognition software, indications were 90% certain he was a retired, fairly senior CIA intelligence officer, Russian speaking; currently thought to be acting as a security advisor for a Russian oligarch.

I'd rung Tania on *Home Counties'* mobile to check she and Lilia were safe. I searched around the house that had been picked over by Forensics, my stomach in a knot, finding it difficult to think properly, knowing Emma was in the hands of utterly ruthless criminals. The guitar and bubble wrap had disappeared from behind my bed. No doubt the lubricating oil and other residues would be analysed. I half-noted that my new laptop was also missing. I wondered if the police had taken that. I waited in a state of anxiety until dawn. I wasn't hungry but I forced myself to eat a bowl of cereal. I grabbed an apple and headed for Mill Farm, this time conscious that I might be followed myself, but felt safer with some traffic about. It was eight-thirty when I arrived.

Willis was where we'd left him in the mess of my kitchen, tied firmly to a chair that was itself tethered to a heavy radiator so he couldn't move it. He still had a plastic bottle duct-taped to his chest and a drinking straw that passed through a hole in a piece of tape over his mouth. We'd fixed this last night before I'd driven the girls to hospital - so he couldn't shout but wouldn't dehydrate. He looked as if he'd had a bad six hours or so.

I hoped Kelvin's hanged ghost had been keeping him company.

Tania and Lilia were making themselves something to eat from what little was still edible in the pantry and fridge. Lilia looked a little better but the red patches on her face had darkened and she wore a bandage round her head and plasters on her arm. The hospital A & E department had wanted to keep Lilia in for observation but she insisted on leaving after she'd been given some first aid and pain killers. The girls had called for a taxi and returned to Grimwich as planned. It was where we'd hastily dumped Willis and hidden the weapons earlier that morning.

I walked in and ripped the tape from Willis's mouth.

'Where was that flight headed last night and who was on it?' I demanded.

Willis played dumb.

'Jesus, Tania,' I said. 'I am at the end of my tether. Get the *Skorpion* so I can kill the fucker.'

Tania left the room without a word and returned a few minutes later with the M61 and the Tokarev for good measure.

'Natasha, you don't have to do this. It will be better for you if I kill him. Then we will disappear. Become 'ghosts' again.'

Willis was squirming, bravado evaporating.

'Ok, ok! I can't tell you much, but three of 'em took a girl on board. She was drugged. That's all I know. They weren't Turkish. They don't tell me nothin'. They talked Russian or something, mostly.'

'Who were they. The three?'

'I don't know who two were, but one was that twat, Nikolai. He's some sort of Russian anyway. He's mental.'

'Did anyone mention Lithuania?'

'Where's that?'

'Jesus!'

Chapter 55. *Véles & Véjas: Spirits of the Dead.*

A Mythic Wind, and a House of Cards

Tap, tap.

Somewhere an irregular sound was intruding into my consciousness. Like something dripping. I smelled blood and half-opened my eyes to the light. Pain! There was movement. My world, shifting again.

Blood was dripping from my nose onto a metal table and the steel floor beneath me. My head was laid uncomfortably to one side. I felt shoulder and cranial pain. My face was numb and I was breathing loudly through my mouth. I shifted my position and discovered that I was sitting in a chair and my arms seemed to be tied. How peculiar. I peered through my lids again and with a shock found myself looking into those feral eyes of my waking dreams. The eyes of Fred West. Of Charlie Manson. *Werewolf* eyes that I thought of as those of the fabled 'Nikolai', the notorious 'Roskov' who had danced his bloody gavotte through the history of the family Strelitz, and into my schizoid nightmares.

The computer screen was two feet from my face. It looked like my own laptop that I knew had vanished from Station Road. The camera delivering the image to my senses tilted upwards slightly and I saw above his red *Baubas* head, the dark expanse of oil on canvas, the Menulis moon in all her glory and the sword arm of Vytautas, the Lithuanian patron saint: the mounted knight with the double-crossed shield of Orthodoxy slaying forever the black, double-headed Imperial eagle. The painting that Jankaitis had told me was the symbol of Lithuanian statehood and independence that hung atop the staircase of the Linden House.

The camera panned across and there sat the Caterpillar and the Cheshire Cat in the same grey suits they'd worn when they had interviewed me in an Ipswich police cell. The Cat held a laptop on his knees with the screen raised.

'Welcome to our theatre of all possibilities, Natasha,' he said, tinnily, smiling slightly for the first time. 'You can talk. You're on *Skype,* speaker phone. *Conference.*'

'You've led us a merry dance, but I'm sure by now you have interpreted your father's tedious parables that gave us so much trouble.' I recognised this voice - Jankaitis.

Then another, from another place and time told me to pay attention. This new voice came from behind. From above. From somewhere it seemed from my own consciousness. It was Mitchell's. No, it was Vladimir Kutushin's is what it was, without the Northumbrian burr. Without the treacherous hypnotic power of Lindisfarne. My head was throbbing. Gradually I began to recall what had happened at Mill Farm. How long ago had that been…..?

The time at the bottom of the computer screen said 20:57. I assumed it was the same day.

'Watch the screen very carefully, Natasha,' Kutushin said.

My face was hurting now, badly, and my left collarbone felt as though it was broken. But all that was forgotten as the cameraman moved back. Jankaitis, descending the old Linden staircase a step or two, bringing the entire tableau into frame.

Nothing changes for all of our civilised trappings. What can a prehistoric mother have felt to see its child in the massive jaws of a cave hyena? The same primal fear, the same despair and helplessness.

And so the sum of my worst terrors was shockingly revealed, beyond what I could ever have imagined. The evil smile on Roskov's face. The 'Knight of Swords' the tarot card of the archetypal warrior; that great medieval painting who's avenging knight on his white charger that was no help to me in my despair, the ancient oil paint deaf to my silent pleas for mercy. Emma knelt facing me, partly-clothed, stage centre and 'Roskov' stood behind. Her eyes looked dark and empty as if she had already seen the abyss and was resigned. Her bare arms which bore the old marks of her self-harming ran afresh with blood.

The crooning madman. The *Baubas. Raudongevklis* had my child at his mercy.

Red Throat's thin, papery voice seemed to whisper again to me, clear across the Baltic Sea; fish-like, across the Kattegat, over the North Sea, making my flesh creep. The *Iron Wolf*, a lycanthropic fire-eyed demon made flesh. The mythic *Wassermann*…the Water Goblin, who……oh my God!

Der Wassermann. The creature behind Emma's kneeling form held a wicked *kinzhal* at her throat, the blade red with blood.

I screamed with horror and begged with all my power to please not hurt her. That I'd do anything, but please don't hurt my child.

~.~

Kutushin was speaking.

'In the next half hour, Natasha, expect to see Emma's pretty head held high by the hair. Her body thrown down those stairs – symbolically, you know what I mean - at her disobedient mother's feet. I can guarantee it will be an interesting death, and it will satisfy the Gothic fantasy that our friend there dreams about. For him it is a sort of vengeful catharsis. He is quite the historian, though of course criminally insane. Your tiresome father's rambling notes would have explained all that Germanic mythic shit and symbolism, better than I ever could.'

He paused.

'But his tale has certainly inflamed Nikolai Dzherkov there.'

So *that* was his real name.

'We know what you are capable of, so if you attempt any subterfuge or stall for time you will see her tortured and decapitated. Close-up and in Technicolor. The only way this 'Incan rite' can be prevented, Natasha, is if you do exactly as you are told.'

He placed my mobile phone on the chart table next to the laptop. I looked up at the steel framed porthole of the seemingly utilitarian craft in which I was tethered and saw his reflection there behind me and the harbour lights beyond. Two guiding beacons reflecting like familiar lanterns on the calm evening sea.....his salt and pepper hair, still worn too long, his features unfathomable, shadowed from the light of an overhead bulkhead lamp.

'The number is already dialled.' He said. 'All you need do is text the Swiss account number, entry code and whatever password is necessary to access the account. You will also speak the number and password to avoid any confusion. Our friends here will follow those instructions to gain access and *if* they are successful and *if* the balance is what it should be then we will make arrangements for your daughter to be returned safely to you. Otherwise..... my goblin will do what it is goblins do best: fulfilling their frenzied sexual urges.' He raises his voice. 'Won't you, you mad gimp?'

On the screen Nikolai's eye's brimmed redly. His mouth widened in a cracked smile.

Kak zhal, tsaritsa moyevo serdtsa! he began to croon, uttering a string of words in a husky lisp of Russian and possibly English, not that I could follow any of it except that Lenin and Stalin seemed to have been invoked.

Kutushin translated: 'Such a pity for you, my queen, my heart. To be forced to watch the petals torn from your fair English rose. But she is a whore and has betrayed her class. Her punishment it is my sacred duty to fulfil, ordained by Lenin, sanctioned and enshrined by order of the Great Stalin'.

'He believes he is a sort of *apparatchik* 'blood monk', Natasha.' Kutushin spoke quietly. 'That with enough blood sacrifice such as Lenin had ushered in, like Ivan the Terrible before him, the 'God-Tsar' Stalin will return and make Russia great again. He sees Putin as a bloodless ghost behind the scenes. He has a half-formed idea that a Stalin-clone is needed to revivify the Soviet Union in some vampire mother symbiosis that will bring him to life, his inevitable seed re-born. And we let him believe it. And that all of 'this' is about gathering wealth to achieve that aim. He asks nothing but that he be allowed to serve Comrade Stalin's memory. He is quite deranged, but a useful and unquestioning tool, Natasha, so be warned.'

Somehow I found my voice.

'Look, please, just let her go. You have me in your power. You can do what you like with me, but I'm begging you, please just put her on a plane and send her back unharmed. Or at least leave her somewhere safe and tell the police where she is. What have you got to lose.' I was flushing hot and cold, my words coming thickly through the blood in my mouth and the congealing blood in my nose. 'I will give you the access code and the account number. Everything. But release her first. Don't you still have me as your prisoner?'

For a moment Kutushin seemed to be considering it.

'You might just be very brave, Natasha, but I think perhaps you might take us for fools.'

'No, no. Please I will do whatever.....just let her....'

'We've wasted too much time already. *Dlyna demonstratsii, Nikolai! Vyrezat!'* The voice was chillingly even.

On the screen I saw the knife drawn against Emma's throat, the blade withdrawn. Then its tip tight against the blue-whiteness, pushed in. Emma screamed and tried to tear away but was held tight in the arms of the grinning *Baubas*.

I screamed inside and felt close to fainting, my eyes burning with a mother's tears, watching the blood run from Emma's neck. She swayed drunkenly on her knees, shocked now and sobbing, a faint spray of blood expelled with the involuntary effort. She'd seemed heavily drugged but knew enough of what was going on. The *Baubas* lapped dog-like at the blood running from her neck. His tongue seemed unnaturally pointed and long....the hand that held the blade bore an extra finger.

The Afro hooker's comment, the Book of Revelations.....

814

They'd not even tied her to a chair, so secure were they in faraway Lithuania.

'Emma!' I yelled. 'Please be brave. I am following their orders so they won't harm you, darling. Hear me? Be brave, sweetheart.'

There was some sort of recognition. I heard her voice faintly.

'Mum….?'

And then the camera turned again to the Cat and Caterpillar waiting at their computer.

Kutushin untied my hands. 'Over to you, Natasha,' he said, tonelessly. 'Name of the bank.'

I took a deep breath and with a shaking hand clumsily typed in the name *Banque Schneider –Turcat & Cie*, the access code. Then the account number itself.

'What is the password?' This from the Caterpillar sitting at the computer.

'*Truffle*,' I said. The camera was mounting the stairs where Emma still knelt.

'*Truffle*?' The Cat queried.

I confirmed.

'Type it!'

I saw that *Der Wassermann* had dropped Emma to move across to view the computer screen. My head was clearing. I knew perfectly well that Emma would be disposed of immediately they had access to the account and had confirmed its value. I also guessed that my lifeless body would just as swiftly be weighted and dropped overboard in the middle of the North Sea. Or some bleak variation on that theme. The reason we were still just a short distance outside Lowestoft harbour or Great Yarmouth, was to maintain a mobile phone signal to text Lithuania. Of that I was certain.

In these last moments my mind was sharper than it had ever been and my physical pain was forgotten.

'Oh,' I said, nervously. 'I…I think I may have entered a wrong digit in the account number. Let me type it in again.'

'Hold up,' said Kutushin. 'My 'client' here says she wants to amend the account number.'

I'd glimpsed a movement beyond the porthole reflection, between the two lanterns and prayed it was what I hoped for. Everything was now in ultra slow-motion, but my brain was running at the speed of light.

~-~

Just a few hours before we'd had a council of war at Mill Farm. Me, Tania and Lilia, with Willis sitting in the kitchen tied to the chair. I'd had to take him to the toilet. The *Skorpion* jammed into his backbone had inhibited his sphincter to an extent. But now it seemed to have had the opposite effect. I'd been tensed, ready for any sudden moves. He knew that and moved slowly and carefully, his back full of tension too. I observed the detail of his tattooed forearm, where the indentation of the recent plaster clearly showed, a thick snake coiled out of a naked girl with the inscription *Seed of the Serpent*. Lilia tied him firmly again while Tania and I covered him with our weapons.

Tania said that it was precisely a war situation. The best outcome for my own safety was if Willis 'ceased to exist'.

'He is bad man and the world will not miss him. You have rest of your life to live, Natasha. Emma needs you, she does not need to visit you in prison for years and years.'

Emma was missing, kidnapped. I believed her to be in Eastern Europe. I had discovered the secret that my father had arranged for me to discover. Something which the 'KGB *Mafiya*' syndicate had also stumbled across but which they couldn't decipher from the complicated system of clues he'd left - which he hoped I'd be able to fathom. Because some of those were personal, associated with our common love of great classical music and various esoteric references. Others were clinchers which were hidden in clever concealment devices. An acoustic guitar for example.

The 'syndicate' had known about the second 'icon', but not until after they'd lost the first! It seems they had shown the same faith in me that my father had shown, that I'd crack the conundrum…….. the ultimate vindication of his trust at the end.

Somebody, I suspect the bogus Dr. Mitchell, had broken into my father's room at the Cedars, and not having found what he was looking for, had murdered him in cold blood, completing what they'd already started in Lithuania. Meanwhile Mill Farm had been ransacked and my printed copies of *The Baltic Falcon* had been taken. The second icon was sent to me in order that I might solve the enigma while various psychological events were engineered, presumably intended to unhinge me. Perhaps this was a prelude to having me 'sectioned' under the Mental Health Act again, which would have rendered me susceptible to more manipulation on the inside, coupled with my fears for Emma on the outside.

Kidnapping Emma might not have been in the primary plan, but it was a powerful lever. In fact I could not conceive of one *more* powerful.

But why hadn't they just picked her up on her way home from school? Why break into the 'safe' house and murder a police woman? I was certain that they'd wanted the latest data on my computer that they'd stolen - anything based on my own interpretation of both *The Siberian Eagle* and the other disk for clues to the bank details. It was no longer a meagre $5,000,000,000 they had been 'cheated' out of. They'd felt the need to show their power. To demonstrate their ruthlessness, having been foiled in their undoubted intention to grab me as well. This I told Tania and Lilia.

But I'd been *elsewhere*, amateurishly raiding one of the many overseas Russian mafiya money-making operations to release these captives from their sexual-slavery who were my grateful allies.

'The question now is, when will the next contact be made and isn't it time to tell the police everything? Even if it means facing the consequences of my actions of the night, Tania? All I want is to get Emma back safe and sound.'

'I do not believe so, Natasha. From tonight we are outlaws, yes, but we face a more terrifying thing that is beyond all laws and is secretly protected within the boundaries of the former Soviet Union. It has its tentacles everywhere. Your police are powerless to offer you proper protection. Perhaps they don't fully realise the danger of this evil. In any case you would yourself be prosecuted for murder. If you are in jail they *will* get you in there. I believe this to be true before God.'

I was about to reply when Lilia cried out, 'Someone comes here, look!'

I turned and looked out of the kitchen window to see Polish Fred's shiny Morris Minor pick-up pull into the yard. This was not unexpected as Fred had been kind enough to look after not only Emma's pony but Chrissie's donkey and goat from Grimstone House. I'd told him that there was plenty of feed in the stable. The old man opened the pick-up door just as another car appeared from behind. Someone climbed out and for a moment I became totally immobile, every emotion seemed to rage through me like a torrent and my knees became like jelly.

There was a shout from Tania and I saw her raise the Tokarev.

'No!' I screamed but then I realised what she was aiming at. I didn't hear shots but I saw old Fred stagger and fall and the other man running. Tania was quickly at the door and fired the automatic which discharged and jammed. I cursed the old ammunition and the fact I only had a couple of shots left in the *Skorpion*. I rushed past Tania who was trying to clear the stoppage.

I ran in the direction I'd seen two hurrying figures depart and flattened myself against the farmhouse wall as two shots were fired. There was a cry and I moved forward with the *Skorpion* raised only to confront a figure with a pickaxe handle who swung at me. I fired my last two rounds point-blank into his chest and he expired, but I'd already received a fearful blow across my left shoulder and heard a crack as my clavicle separated. I dropped the gun and as my knees went a hand grabbed me by the collar and half dragged and half carried me back towards the kitchen. I had a momentary impression of a one-handed fight involving the two girls and my captor before I was dropped onto the kitchen flags.

Later I recalled sitting in a chair in considerable pain with Willis standing over me, literally frothing at the mouth, shouting and another, taller, man standing behind. Suddenly Willis punched me hard, full in the face. The world exploded in violet light and I felt a brief agony as my nose was smashed. I remembered only his fist drawn back again. Vaguely I recalled a syringe stuck in my arm, then nothing else until the tap, tap of blood dripping onto the floor and on the chart table in the cabin of some vessel.

~-~

Now it seemed that all was up. I had no cards to play except one, and that was a despairing and vengeful reaction to what could only be my worst fears realised and my own painful death momentarily postponed.

Timing in the theatre is everything; so too in the theatre of life. So I played my last card. I looked out of the porthole where I'd seen the light. Now there was only darkness. But I contrived a subtle reaction, as if I'd just seen something. A kind of quick double-take and then a sly glance towards Kutushin, as if to gauge his reaction. In truth it didn't matter if I'd seen something out there or not. He was distracted enough to move forward and stare out of the port. My mind had already been made up and I'd stealthily 'topped and tailed' the connection to Lithuania, added the prefix and the 'double four' suffix, as my father had instructed. I only had to hit the 'hatch' key and pray, come what may.

Kutushin called. 'Willis, get up on deck and see if you can see anything.'

From somewhere in a lower section Willis's muscular frame emerged wearing an orange anorak. I ventured a swift look. He looked as seasick

818

as someone who'd been through a Force 8. I supposed the gentle motion of the boat could provoke sickness in anyone unused to such a movement and I was feeling pretty sick myself but I hadn't considered that the sea had had much to do with it.

Willis clambered on deck and called out that a boat had motored past about three hundred yards away and was turning. The computer screen suddenly became alive with movement and whoops of jubilation. It seemed that the Mafiosi on the landing at the Linden House had struck their pot of gold. I heard Jankaitis shouting for Vlad. They'd evidently checked their bank balance and it was not wanting!

Kutushin was torn between investigating the mysterious motor boat and responding to the celebratory uproar in Lithuania. As a good soldier and *Spetsnaz* he decided to check on security. He looked at me and decided there was nothing I could possibly do and I would keep. Apart from which he wouldn't want to risk a shot that might be heard from a nearby craft and though he could kill me without a sound I suspected that he wanted me conscious, to witness the murder of my daughter. I suspected that my father had been right. 'Roskov' might be a psychopathic demon but he, Kutushin, was just as evil. Hence my father's warning that both of them should be shot on sight! I wondered what insight he had had on these two and what part they had played, that he'd recognised in the downfall of the Trust. I knew Kutushin had murdered my father and shot old Fred at Mill Farm. I only knew from Willis that 'Roskov' had murdered both Clarissa and Chrissie. Willis was complicit and they were peas from the same pod; one all too human and the other hardly human at all, it seemed.

Kutushin pulled himself up on deck. The computer I hoped was close enough for me to speak to Emma. Jankaitis was calling for Vlad. I told him that he was on deck and would be down in a moment. I had a request, a message to give to Emma. Jankaitis said he'd relay it; magnanimous in victory. I said, no, I just wanted to tell her that I loved her. Jankaitis was human at least, and I heard the smile in his voice as he agreed. He dragged her to her feet and I saw the cut in her neck and her dark distant eyes looking at a picture of me with my smashed and bloody nose via the webcam.

Jankaitis and the two grey suits from Lewis Carrol made a quorum of top Russian mafiya along with their trained Baubas killer and only my daughter's life stayed my hand. They were standing a little behind her, drinking vodka, the big medieval canvas was visible beyond with 'Roskov' looking up in what appeared to be thoughtful contemplation of the huge work.

'Can you hear me, Emma?'

After a pause Emma's dyed-black head nodded mutely.

'Darling, I can only say this once. See the big doors?'

Her eyes lifted and she nodded again.

'Is there a key in the lock?' Please let there be a key there, I prayed as I've never prayed in my life.

She squinted against the light from the chandelier. Slowly she nodded again. I could hear footfalls on the deck above.

'Listen carefully Emma. With all your strength. With all your courage I want you to sprint down the stairs to those doors turn the key, get out and run for your life away from the house. Do you hear me?'

Again the black head nodded. I saw her lungs fill.

'Emma, on a count of three. One. Two. THREE! Go Emma! *Go!*'

There was a blur on the screen as she moved sideways. A shout from the landing – Jankaitis screaming in Russian and the Baubas bounding after her. I heard another yell and a commotion on the stairs. Someone seems to have jerked the computer because the next thing the screen was fuzzy. I could have sworn that the painting moved, seeming almost to dissolve into something else. A blur of shining white. I blinked. There seemed to be a flicker of light, like a candle flame reflecting its gleam in the dark canvas and then it was gone. *I heard Kutushin descending the ladder behind me.* Heard the thin raspy voice of the *Baubas*, but it did not seem triumphal; not as though he'd caught my daughter in his snaring arms. Rather it had gained some power, but its sound was more the voice of a rabbit when the fox has come. I listened intently for the rattle of a lock and the slam of a door. *Heard Kutushin's step on the bottom rung.* The other voices seemed confused, anxious. I projected myself keenly into that place and sensed no victory there. I waited for my thudding heartbeats to tell me *when*.

Then pressed '*hatch*'.

The screen did not change. Nothing had happened. Kutushin pushed me aside.

He demanded in Russian to know what was going on there. Jankaitis's face briefly appeared with a worried and puzzled expression. He was evidently explaining that something had occurred and Emma's name was mentioned but I could not make it out when the whole image seemed to wobble and vibrate, plaster dust and debris fell and then a bright flame appeared. There came a scream and a rumble, abruptly cut off as the screen went black.

Kutushin stared at the screen in disbelief. Then he turned to me.

'What happened?' he demanded.

I turned on him in cold triumph.

What had happened was that Soviet sappers had mined the Linden House and many other Baltic palaces in 1941; to kill as many German officers of von Leeb's Army Group North as possible during *Barbarossa*. They'd done an excellent job. But their bomb timers had failed and the explosives were only discovered years later in a secret sub-basement, when my father had had the house restored to administer the fund for the benefit of the thousands, families who'd suffered under the tyranny of Kutushin's erstwhile masters. He'd disarmed the explosives, but those bombs were concreted in place and would have been too unstable to remove. Then, unbenown to the Russian mafiya, as my father grew more aware that they were stealthily gaining control, he'd gathered information from a radical jihadist website - anonymously via an internet café. He'd wired up a mobile phone ringer with new detonators inserted into packs of C4 obtained on the black market, and scabbed them onto the old bombs. '*Remember Samson,*' he'd written, '*It's a house of cards!*' My daughter was either alive or dead, by my own action. By my own defiant hand on a mobile phone key.

I was shaking. All I said to Kutushin was, 'You'd forgotten your own bloody history!'

His face was a mask of white anger in the flux of the searchlight beam that flooded the cabin not a moment too soon. Willis had been shouting I now recalled, but his voice had been overpowered by the thoughts in my head and my scorching hatred turned on Kutushin, murderer of my off-beat, brilliant father.

With a snarl he grabbed my left arm sending excruciating pain through my injured shoulder. He dragged me to the companionway ladder and pushed me up onto the deck. One of HM's Customs and Excise launches was hove to, engines burbling, its bow searchlight trained blindingly on our long motor launch, moored without riding lights. The loud hailer commanded our attention with its metallic cry of '*Armed police!*', informing us to remain as we were, that they would be sending a party aboard.

Kutushin snapped orders to Willis. In seconds the deck vibrated as two powerful engines burst into life. I was held in front of the Spetsnaz agent with his own automatic pistol tight against my temple. He was holding me up as I was in so much pain from my collar bone and shoulder injury. My eyes were downcast and I just wanted to sink to the deck and sleep, though my mind was floating upon its own dark sea to a loathsome island of misery of my own creation.

'Natasha.' A voice came over the hailer. 'Stay calm!'

'If you try anything or she tries to jump I will shoot her before she hits the water,' shouted Kutushin. 'Willis, cast off anchor.'

I was aware of a dim red spot tracking up my chest, over the wreckage of my nose and upwards. Kutushin was tall. I am not. He had a good grip on me, but not good enough to withstand a hollow point to the forehead. I didn't hear the rifle's crack. I was thrust forwards or I'd kicked backwards - either way I going into the water. The impact, the shock of the low sea temperature took my breath away and I involuntarily screamed with the pain from my shoulder, swallowing salt water, coming up once - retching, going down for a second time, left arm not working. I struggled to make my muscles respond, feeling ancient and broken while an inner voice repeated 'I'm drowning, Daddy!' Then hands were pulling me into an inflatable before transferring me painfully into the well deck of the launch. I heard the engines roar and then we were racing in pursuit of the blacked-out craft whose pale rooster tail streamed in the darkness. We had been delayed by they're manhandling me aboard along with the crew of the inflatable which they'd left bobbing in our wake to expedite the chase.

My heart rate had dropped in reflex to the icy water and I was slipping in and out of consciousness, having difficulty in believing that the man with his arm in a sling, holding me gently actually with a tired and seasick DI Slater next to him, was none other than Simeon. My ex.

~-~

'So what do you really think of Crete?'

On the warm terrace with the Minoan bull mosaic and acrobatic dancing girls we sat at a table 'neath Athena's tree, and watched the sun slip down the sky to a tide-less sea. Aerobatic swallows chirruped excitedly, chasing invisible insects around the olives and the white walls. Below, the pretty harbour was littered with painted fishing boats. The rugged coastline was turning blue as the light faded from the sky. Twinkling lights flickered on in ones and twos in the hills and around the harbour front. A few evening seabirds sailed around the cliffs, snickering on balmy air, heavy-scented with hibiscus.

'Is it always as lovely as this?' I murmured.

'To me it is, made the more so by you're being here.'

My life suddenly had a five-year plan. I couldn't think further than that in truth. But it had changed out of recognition in the last few months. It had begun to change without my knowing it when Emma had emailed Simeon that we were in crisis, that her mother was losing it 'big time'. He'd turned up in Grimwich that morning looking for the elusive Mill Farm and had run across Polish Fred who'd taken him to the kitchen door and then taken a bullet. It was Simeon's sudden appearance in the kitchen window which had pole-axed me and sent my emotions into orbit. Two others had then appeared in a rush, armed; a gun and an axe handle. My stolen laptop had provided Kutushin and Co. with the information that Emma had intended to meet him that day at our remote smallholding, away from the 'safe house' - to discuss her going to live with him and to try to resolve my obsessive behaviour following my father's death.

I'd had to find somewhere to dump Willis and decide our plan of action that would avoid my being jailed for murder. Mill Farm had seemed a good base and a rendezvous for Tania and Lilia as it had already been trashed by the syndicate and would presumably have been of no further interest. Whether Kutushin had made a lucky guess that I'd be there, in order to abduct me, or whether he'd intended to try to grab Simeon as further leverage, playing on feelings I might still have for him, or to use him to influence me in some way, I would never know.

Kutushin had got lucky; abducted me, the twins, and reclaimed Willis as an instant replacement for the pickaxe handle-wielding thug - who I'd point-blank shot dead, though he *had* succeeded in breaking my collar bone.

Simeon had walked into this ambush and been taken by surprise, suffering two gunshot wounds, thankfully superficial although they bled impressively. He'd played dead until the Shogun had left and dragged himself bloodily to the telephone and dialled. He'd called for an ambulance for himself and for Fred, who was still breathing. He then rang the police and before losing consciousness he'd told them that he'd heard Lowestoft harbour mentioned in some agitation by the taller of the two killers. He also saw three women being roughly loaded into the vehicle, bleeding and in various stages of consciousness. One of them he recognised as me.

Simeon had suffered 9.0 mm flesh wounds: one to his upper back and one round through the fleshy part of his left shoulder and had lost a fair amount of blood. He had been interviewed by Slater immediately he'd been transfused, stitched and was around from the anaesthetic. Pale as death, still he'd rallied, discharged himself and insisted on going with Slater to Lowestoft harbour, said if he couldn't accompany the police he'd make a bloody nuisance of himself driving around the harbour area himself, bleeding, with one arm in a sling if necessary. Slater told him that the whole Morris/Stewart-Hedges axis was a bleeding nuisance anyway and took him along *and to hell with Health and Safety and Home Office protocol.* By evening they'd found a bloodstained Shogun and moved away from the landward side of the harbour and the various boats that were tied up within, to the outer harbour and moorings. By nightfall the search had led them to the low-lying silhouette of the grey ex-naval launch anchored without lights a mile from the harbour entrance.

They'd hailed the launch and the police marksman on board had taken an opportune shot. Little attempt had been made to talk Vladimir Kutushin down. Submission, given the head count and carnage from Grimstone House and Beccles, to Elmswell and Mill Farm had not been uppermost on the agenda. One mercilessly gunned-down policewoman and mother would have been enough for DI Slater, so I believed. There were few enough witnesses and all had felt the same way. Slater, myself and the North Sea.

Willis had roared blindly on into the dark and had managed to collide spectacularly with the vast hull of a Felixtowe-bound container ship whose lights he'd apparently not seen. Or else had *been* driven by some fear that drained all sense and caution from his mind. Really the collision was a mystery. The cold bodies of Tania and Lilia were then lying in the bottom of the launch ready for a sea burial, which would have been my own fate, I was sure, so I liked to think that the last thing he would have seen was the word MAERSK in twenty-foot letters and known it was his NEMESIS.

~-~

Emma strolled onto the patio holding hands with her new smiling-eyed, young Adonis. Emma's Gothic hair colour had washed out, sun-bleached back to blonde. She'd continued with her swimming too, now that her wrist was healed. It had been a bad break, the distal ends of the radius and ulna snapped and jammed under the proximal ends. But now just the imprint of her plaster remained. Those old cuts on her arms had healed perfectly too, as only young skin can.

She moved now with an easy grace and was happier and healthier than ever I could remember. They were planning on going to a disco in town. Not that there were many. Or maybe they'd drink ouzo and dance a languid dance in the evening's cool of Diskos beach. Either way they went with our blessing, Emma promising to wear a helmet on the pillion of his *Vespa*.

I look down into the clear waters of the bay. A pretty blue and white Cessna seaplane has landed in a wash of foam and a launch has gone out to tow it in to the landing stage. I think of my father and his love of flying. He'd told me once that his dream machine would be a *Hispano-Suiza* V-8 *Nieuport-Delage 'flotteur catamaran'*. A fantasy tandem two-seater sea-biplane in 'Bugatti Blue'. The florid description had stuck in my mind as a child. I'd thought that nostalgia was actually overrated, and for sure my father had uttered a sentimentalised view of the past through his collating of Steiger's diary - from before the Revolution at least. But no one could have accused him of romanticising the events that followed, though seen from a Right Wing perspective, as once I'd have described it.

'You know, the bullshit wasn't all one-sided, Simeon. I had so many things in my past that I had tried to conceal.' *Things that that warred within me, buried deep in my subconscious.*

'I did know, Natasha. But in the end I had to get away. Secrets and lies, heart. They eat you up inside. I'm also 'clean' now, by the way.'

But now I think I did know. Perhaps he'd been one of the watchers, a backpacking student consulting his *Rough Guide* or the departure screen, witness to her other self stumbling through the arcades of Tempelhof trying to make sense of her missing time, overwhelmed by the seeming stridency of sounds and vivid colours, experiencing what she now knew were flashback memories from the LSD. Her stalker that she'd never suspected. Something she'd filed in an inaccessible fold in her memory where she'd always felt something had been wrong with the picture of his life and their life together, yet no stranger than the slip-sliding mosaic of her own. Operating above and beyond the call, had he *actually married her* as part of his own deep cover? While working both sides of the street. Like old Prometheus, Merlin himself. She'd tried and failed to analyse how they'd met; what it was that had brought them together and decided that as he could charm a crocodile out of its armour and subconsciously she'd been as vulnerable as a snail without its shell. That after Berlin she'd been his for the taking.

Was that disarming quality, a trick to fascinate and enslave, something they taught you in the service of the Crown or the Kremlin? *Whose spook were you Simeon? Were you a Sergei?* Were you public or grammar school as you variously presented or had you been schooled on the

Volga? Were you really a 'Rupert', an ex-Para with hints of unspoken training at Shrewsbury for the undercover service? Or was it all cleverly mimicked much further east, a *spion* with the same type of DNA, building the long-term sleeper you became until Glasnost and the rest brought the whole edifice down. You were human at least and perhaps in the end considered that the devils of the West were preferable to the angels of the KGB, especially after the fall. Or else they'd closed my case and decided I'd been de-activated long since and the high priority target was a myth. Almost as big as the myth of the Romanov gold which was perhaps the only target that the mafiya were seeking and believed I was heir to, or had knowledge of its whereabouts – and I was already known to both sides. It was my clever father who'd led them a merry dance with his cut-outs and arm's length operation, until they'd infiltrated him too. You'd decided to make a deliberate hash of things and cut and run to Crete with your partner in crime when it all got too much, and your handlers or controllers and their chain of command abandoned you too. New broom at 'Lego Land on Thames' was it? The same thinking on the River that deposed Clarissa from GHQ, Cheltenham after the end of the Cold War? Or did your Russian boss simply make his own pact with Mammon and abandon you and your fellow conspirators to the winds of fate?

So was it me or your daughter Emma's frantic pleas, or the lure of a fortune that I suddenly had access to that brought you back in the nick of time to act the hero? Were you part of it all, my lover, but had fallen out with the *Spetsnaz* sleepers when they threw in with the mafiya? Were you all in it together? Were you all part of a plot that went wrong at Mill Farm when Kutushin shot you? Or did you have a father's love for Emma and something left in your heart for me? Before we make again the 'beast with two backs', I need to know the truth. And be sure there'll be an ironclad pre-nup. Whatever you *were*, if you're for real this time, for home and hearth, perhaps then we will, all of us, be freed from our monsters.

I understand that there was a parallel operation with me at the centre, while 'they' waited patiently or impatiently to discover what it was I was supposed to do since they no longer had their own foolproof *Enigma* device as in days of yore. Was I still primed to explode or would I make their fortune, those little cadres, wheels within wheels that operated out of the Thames blockhouse or Moscow Centre and their deadly associates? Did I really think I could get away with it, with all those resources on my tail, with or without Simeon, a complex turncoat who'd been working other ops. while pretending to hide away, Crete being a cover story though he'd spent his time there well, some of it in rehab.

He tells me some of this and I fill in the rest. His own breakdown under the strain was real; serving twin masters, both in decline, his human fallibility with me, and the realisation that our masters are the best dissimulators of all and that honour among thieves is a slender thing. That honest coppers like Slater find themselves marginalized, silenced and squeezed between the various agencies but can sometimes shine like beacons in the dark. And he had saved my life at some risk to his own or his career, had he not?

~-~

The returning crew of the Citation from Vilnius had been interviewed on landing at Norwich. They'd seen a big old Russian An 2 cabin biplane embark their recent passengers with the invalid girl, and fly north. An urgent police message to Lithuania had sent the anti-terror squad into action.

Back then I could see those tall black doors in my mind through which I prayed she had run, through which young Arkadi had rushed all those years before, praying tearfully for succour, while inside *Roskov's Latgale Wolves* had been crucifying Kristian, torturing, raping, murdering in an orgy of lust and cruelty beyond belief.

Eighty-eight years later, through that same hellish portal, fled my Emma.

~-~

Her high vantage point in the trees had given a clear view of the activity around the lake. They'd dragged someone out; long gothic hair spread on the grass. A black-clad figure was bent over the body, pumping the chest. The back of his armoured vest bore white capitals, the word 'ARAS'. She wondered what it meant.

'It means *Eagle*,' said the voice in her mind. 'The one giving CPR is called Azu. That's Azuola. It means Oak Tree. A good name for a sturdy officer.'

'Who are they?'

'Lithuanian Special Forces. They're a SWAT team, hand-picked. They specialise in hostage situations. Mafiya hunters. Their helicopters are over there.'

She turned to look. Two dark helos sat on the lawn in front of the smoking crater and what was left of the burning mansion. Her mother always said she could sleep through an earthquake. Armoured response vehicles were parked nearby. Far away she could hear the wail of sirens. Blue lights flickered on the horizon. She looked back to the lake. A dozen or more ARAS were combing the trees and shrubs, walking around the further shore. All carried machine pistols. She was surprised at how well she could see in the dark.

There was a triumphal shout close at hand. The patient had vomited water and was moving, retching, gasping for air.

'Time to go, Emma,' said the voice.

Emma turned to look but there was no one there in the tree and she was wet and freezing cold, gazing upwards into a stranger's face that was flushed with exertion, smiling in relief.

'You will be OK now, Emma,' he said.

Emma tried to speak.

'Lie still and get breath. I need to fix your arm a bit. First I give you shot, OK?'

Emma nodded. The pain in her wrist was so sharp she barely felt the needle. Very quickly there came a feeling of euphoria. Wrapped in a thermal blanket she felt herself drifting. Then she was on a stretcher being put into one of the helicopters, her rescuer by her side.

'Thank you, Azu.' She said.

Lieutenant Azuola Kairis stared at her in amazement.

'How do you know my name?' He asked in astonishment.

She didn't answer, just smiled in her sleep.

~-~

For me in an agony of uncertainty, the most wonderful moment had been when I'd heard Emma's voice on the telephone from the local Lithuanian hospital to the Ipswich police station where I sat, utterly exhausted and distraught. 'Mum…it's me. I'm alright now. Don't worry.'

Like Steiger I had closed my fists and looked upwards and cried, but my heart was full not broken. Unlike Steiger, I affirmed that indeed, there *is* a God. There *is*!

~-~

I'm glad to report that tough old Polish Fred recovered from his gunshot wound, although it took some time to heal.

Like the House of Usher, the great house of Strelitz had fallen, sundered from its foundation by two tremendous explosions. Situated on a geological fault, it had split and fallen inwards on itself.

Subterranean pressure, a subducting platelet may have caused the piezo-luminescence: the glowing mists on the little lake and the phantoms and wraiths that had haunted the house. Perhaps down the years such pressures had created those anomalies in the mind. Like the one I'd glimpsed on the laptop. A white image that seemed to shimmer, wraith-like out of the great medieval painted knight, Lord of the Winds. The tarot warrior knight Chrissie had said was good to have on one's side. Was there a momentary impression of Sergeant's original painting there? Princess Sophie's sainted presence invoked by the flickering of Kristian Graf von Strelitz's candle, from the 'ritual of the stair'.

What I wondered had frightened the *Baubas* so that he'd screamed, terror struck *before* the explosions that gave Emma a vital start? Was it the cool stare of Sophie that *unmanned* him? If you could use that expression of something that looked like it could tear branches from a tree. Had Gagool flown, shrieking into his face? Had he seen the vengeful mask of the Graf? Or was the sword arm of the Knight Vytautas raised to strike?

Or is it all a fantasy?

Interpol's report from Lithuania described the total collapse of the Linden House. Like the 'house of cards' my father had predicted. The power of Samson in the temple.

The investigation was continuing to determine if the collapse had been caused by the spontaneous ignition of mines, unstable buried explosives, concreted into the foundations or by an electrical impulse triggering a detonator system wired into those old explosive charges, based, it was believed, on two five-hundred kilogram Russian bombs from the 'Great Patriotic War'. The remains of several bodies were eventually recovered, some unidentifiable, others known members of the Russian Mafiya. Two of these were ex-CIA, defectors playing for the highest stakes. No body matching the description of the 'goblin'; Nikolai Pavlovich Dzherkov, aka, as far as *I* was concerned, the *Baubas, N. S. Roskov, Red Throat, Iron Wolf* or *Der Wassermann* had been recovered from the lake or the surrounding area at the time of writing.

I've found time to weep, and still do sometimes for the memory of the two Belarus beauties who'd suffered terribly and died at the hands of Kutushin and Willis. Protected in the lower hull, their relatively intact bodies were recovered from the among the floating wreckage by the Customs launch along with Willis's smashed frame and that of Kutushin, whose corpse had been carried at full-throttle on that last wild ride to a marine collision off the East Anglian coast.

I liked to think that Willis's hands had tried in vain to turn the wheel, held fast by the grip of two other pairs of hands; a final spirited act, inspired by the *Véjas*, the Baltic wind spirit who blows the ungodly into oblivion.

Whether we believe in wave or particle, some things seem able to exist in two places at once. Perhaps there's no such thing as time. Perhaps everything is just happening 'now', just in different dimensions; people and events sometimes leaking between. Is all created just 'in the moment' within our limited perceptions, including memories of past events?

How might we explain Emma's experience, when she'd found the courage to flee down the Linden staircase, with the Baubas in close pursuit?

She told me how two angels had guided her, one each side, seeming not to touch the ground. She'd made it to the doors and struggled with the key, panicking because it wouldn't turn. Their cool hands had calmed her, speaking softly in their Slav accents, they'd helped her twist it in the lock, even as she felt the breath hot upon her neck and hands clutching at her body. Before the greater heat of the flame.

Had Krystina and Katarzyna, the long dead Baronesses of Liepus Namas and the Kuznetsowa Estate come to her rescue in that house of dreadful memories, invoked by powerful emotion and terror? An answer to my prayers? Had they come to save their little stepsister who long ago they'd *failed* to save? Or were they phantasms; electrically-generated by known subterranean pressures within the strata?

I wonder about the 'particle-wave energy' of the murdered Belarus twins, Tatiana and Lilia, so brave and resourceful and so wronged. Had they telepathically received my desperate prayers for a daughter's release from an impossible escape situation and had their so recently departed spirits taken control of events in Lithuania as simultaneously they steered Willis to his fatal impact? As to Lenin and his treatise on dialectical materialism, Gorbunov's compassionless Antichrist: if he'd had all the answers his Brutal Experiment might actually have succeeded! Yet we and he are more complex than electro-chemical beings of flesh and blood and may yet have to atone for our transgressions.

Operation Pentameter 2 was a success despite the ripples left from my pre-emptive strike in Suffolk. I was just peripheral. Across fifty-five police authorities, eight hundred and twenty-two brothels and other premises were closed and more than one hundred and fifty foreign women and young girls were rescued, no thanks to my interference, though I don't think I hampered it in reality. Over five hundred arrests were made. But it was accepted that it had been the tip of a much bigger iceberg. My new best friend the *Skorpion* had disappeared into the depths of the North Sea along with the Tokarev. No witness survived from my raid on Dower Hill Farm other than one or two criminals who swore that they'd been hit by 'special forces', so it seemed I was in the clear.

No one had expected the gut-wrenching horror of the operation at Dower: the abortions carried out and the 'donations' from the 'superfluous' sex workers in the 'clinic' stables, adjacent the 'film studio' with its Internet link. The convenient pig farm for disposal of the evidence, the powerful courier bike discovered on site. On the satchel draped over the pillion, a label; HUMAN ORGANS WITH CARE, provided eloquent testimony of the awfulness they'd found there, opening up a whole new line of investigation.

Now I had a vast fortune in an untraceable Swiss account to deal with, though some of it was spread around, the Cayman Islands for one, and I could afford some pretty impressive security.

We're in a sort of extended, self-imposed 'witness protection bubble' here and everywhere we'll travel. But it's discreet, recruited from a reliable and highly regarded agency, its operatives both well rewarded and well armed. The least I could do, I thought, was continue my father's work from this idyll, with my family around me. Emma continues her studies here with Internet access.

Every day my mind seems clearer. My old demons fade into the background. Simeon's injuries have almost healed and so have mine, apart from my nose is a different shape. I wasn't sure I liked it at first. Emma told me '*Get over it!*', then smiled and hugged me and I knew that she was back! I thanked God and Azu of the Lithuanian SWAT team, that my Emma, armed with her courage, had come through it all.

I realised too that deep down I still loved Simeon, and have decided to let things play out naturally, for now. His full and devious legend was for him to tell in his own time as he wished.

The question still tantalised me, whether my dad was right about cluster re-incarnation.

It seemed mad that he had he really convinced himself that he was the reincarnation of an alleged ancestor, von Moritz. But the Belarus twins; were they those same souls who had lived as Krysia and Kat? The recovered bodies showed that the twins had been strangled when they lain bound in the forward cabin of the launch. But during the post mortems, copies of which I'd received via Geoff Slater whose maverick approach to duty had effectively recruited me; Lilia, the elder, was found to have had a slight deformation at the back of her skull, the only physical difference between them, concealed beneath her hair, perhaps from a forceps delivery.

But it looked eerily like an old trauma-from the *inside*! I could not forget how Krysia had died on the field of battle, in a macabre reprise of their younger love's summer idyll, pistol barrel between her lips. The back of her skull blown-off in an act of mercy.

By his hand Steiger had released her spirit and in time would release the goblin lodged in his own injured brain, much as I'd rid myself of mine. For the 'three' of us, our *'troika'*, it had been traumatic and painful. I wondered briefly if the *Baubas* was really a manifestation of the Id, something demonic and malformed, released under extreme psychological trauma across the years: a *Mr Hyde* perhaps to Klammersdorf's *Dr. Jeckyll*, but I probably malign that poor, troubled soul upon whose hanged, sun-blacked corpse the crows had pecked and clustered.

Lilia and Tatiana *had* acquired leukacmia, probably from Chernobyl fallout while their cells divided in the womb: as they'd always known.

I wondered what had happened to Kat. And poor Graczy. Had she survived her treatment at the hands of Roskov's Wolves? Her body had not been reported at the scene of the massacre, witness Katya's pursuit of her abductors. Had her torso been thrown into Katya's cattle truck to drive her insane, the signature scarring on its back; AL:VB? Was that an illusion or had she suffered some equally miserable, cold and bloody fate?

But what did that make *me*? Given my part in these theatricals - even to the extent of my being saved from drowning: did my mind contain the spirit of Steiger? I recalled my father's description of Steiger's dream at Yarmouth, his 'ghost in another's reality' where he'd witnessed, in his imagination, those tragic girls strangled at sea. I seemed to have inherited a fighting streak. But then my dad had that too. So did all the Wiking Freikorps pilots in his *Kameradschaft of the Jasta*, fighting a greater evil as they saw it.

The imperialistic age-old struggle for *Lebensraum* or whatever they thought they'd fought for, must never be rehabilitated the way that Leninism-Stalinism has, undergoing its cosmetic makeover in the New Russia, where the poor suffer. It's about land and resources as well as ideas and flourishes still in Africa where Marxism is a chameleon and the poor suffer. In the West it is about control and has moved into the realms of greener-than-thou environmentalism, whose zealots have nothing left to learn from those old Bolshevists, I think, while cynical big business invests in the myth for the dividends it offers at the taxpayers' expense. With media and school level propaganda it may yet deal a greater blow to the hard-won and rigorous advances of Western science, its culture, freedom and happiness, than Communism ever achieved and millions more will suffer as a result.

So, do we each live our lives over until we get it 'right'? Beads threaded on the timeless string of unbreakable memory, as Tania had said, until we'd worked out our karmas? Are we really spiritual beings who, on occasion, drop into human experience?

I recalled a part of my father's diary, from his effects. That he was increasingly aware of the sound of wood being chopped at the Big House, in the old courtyard at the rear, though no one was seen; nor yet a woodpile. That he felt a presence there in his room. But had it not been Katya's room, perhaps? Or Krysia's.

Who was his 'charming Lithuanian tutor', his path to his old identity through language? Was it Katya that whispered in his ear?

What previous lives had been lived? Kessler, Alexa, Harry, James; Count Wieniawa-Klimaszinski, once a Jagiellonian king. And the others? Who or what had they since become? Emma and I had both cheated fate on the Lindisfarne causeway. Later, *she too* had nearly drowned. Maybe the parallels are there in subtext for those who would look. I even wondered which leg von Ritter had been missing…...I'd like to have asked Clarissa what she thought about it all. But first I'd have to find a planchette!

And Steiger whose 'filament' it was bound all these stories together? His 1926 expeditionary role - where I was later to 'discover him' in the second icon: flying over the permafrost of the Ob River delta…. I wondered on his eventual fate. Wondered about the whole concept of reality, consciousness and truth.

I'd asked Emma whose voice it was she'd heard in her mind as her soul floated in the trees: or in the 'Philosophers' Tree' as she'd once referred to it, but had then forgotten that phrase. She said she'd sensed a male presence. Was it perhaps my father who had come to comfort her? She said she didn't think so, but that it was someone well-disposed, who seemed to belong to the House of Linden. The Graf? Or Rolf Steiger himself?

~_~

Geoff Slater had told me of the report made by Lithuanian Special

Forces after they'd made a thorough search of the grounds at Liepus Namas. Next to the big AN-2 passenger biplane, the aircraft which had transported Emma from Vilnius, they'd come upon a small hangar under the trees. Inside was a powerful single-seater biplane, fully-fuelled, with a long range petrol tank slung under its belly. He'd few further details, other than that the report mentioned in passing the lightning flashes, terminating in stylised raptors, painted on the fuselage.

I'd seen only the fluorescent windsock on my visit, and had recalled my father's first love. Of flying. I mused on the deal he must have made with its owner, James Delcroix, before he'd disappeared, perhaps gone into hiding himself. There was still the matter of the Valkyrie list and he must have needed money quickly if powerful forces within the British Establishment were on his trail and the old engine-less *Tigerfalk* would have been a tempting lure for my father. The engine log book among his effects revealed that it had been retro-fitted with a 165 hp. American-built Warner Scarab radial in place of the original 160 hp. Siemens. The KFZ-1 had been listed in the British Civil Aviation Register in 1989 as 'G-KFZI', a new identity for old D-2058: initialled appropriately for a design from the *Kessler Flugzeugbau GmbH*, proprietor a one-eyed surviving ex-*Freikorps Kampfflieger*, living out his later years in his Swiss lakeside *Schloss*. My father had shipped or flown the still UK –registered biplane to the Baltic in the 1990s where for him it must have represented an ultimate high: the perfect stress buster to assuage a mid-life crisis. I could imagine him happily looping and rolling in the pale Lithuanian sky, inverted over the lakes and meadows of his idyllic retreat.

They'd found a map in the cockpit. Apparently there was a track-line drawn straight to Norwich. This was my father's lightning escape route. He'd been coming home. To me. But they'd got to him first, Jankaitis and co. It all made terrible sense finally.

Steiger's Tigerfalk restored in original colours with 'Rundflug' tail striping.

This beautifully restored vintage aeroplane was the last physical link with my father. I couldn't just leave it to rot in Lithuania and knew no-one who could fly it, so I arranged for some aeronautical engineers from Vilnius to drain the fuel, carefully dismantle and pack the biplane in specially built wooden crates for shipping to the UK; for storage, until I could think what to do with it. I even harboured the mad idea of learning to fly so that I could eventually acquire the skill to fly it myself. To see what he had seen in the beauty of flight for its own sake in a highly manoeuvrable, unique machine. It was an appealing thought. I could afford it now at any rate!

~-~

I'd returned briefly with an escort to Mill Farm. One last look and to gather up some things of sentimental value. Not much, but then where I was going it would mean a new life. Not under Witness Protection as such, but with a new identity at least.

The fields around about and the little meadow were in full summer growth; waving red tassels of maiden grass, silky plumes and feathery 'squirrel tail' all dancing on the breeze. For a moment I thought I detected another movement through the tall grasses, as if a fox were moving there. I shuddered, instantly back in Lithuania where red haired spirits roamed their oceans of blowing grassland, invoking an unspeakable creature possibly still at large. The day had become darker of a sudden and I couldn't wait to leave.

But there was one other act I needed to perform before leaving the shores of these Islands I'd called home.

Wearing a headscarf to cover my injuries I visited my father's grave at Yarmouth, laid flowers there and asked forgiveness. Ho's insidious voice came back to me, over the music of the sea in my headphones, where I'd hung weightless, in grey limbo among the solenoids, or in the Lilly tank, asking who it was had given me unconditional love. My father, I had replied, and he'd thrown moon dust in my eyes; told me it was a lie and that the one I'd trusted most had taken my childhood from me. That worst thing, abused a powerless infant. This false memory, deeply implanted, though never articulated, was the cruellest thing they could have done to me. It broke me and then they reconstructed me, building a different creature of me though outwardly unchanged.

My haunted memory that had contrived the 'incubus', Ho, the ideological mesmerist, who'd whispered into my youthful and impressionable mind, *'Hush, Princess'* - was but a product of my altered state, a phantom presence induced at moments of stress or LSD flashbacks that coincided with the appearance of that deranged stalker, illusionist; incarnation of Lithuanian mythology and a tool of the 'evil genius' behind my mental anguish. He too had enjoyed playing the game, to twist my mind, making me malleable: Roskov, personified, was no more or less a creature than he was a powerful blunt instrument and fiendish manifestation of *Organised Crime.*

Through psychological warfare they had pushed me to reveal what I didn't know I knew. Until I'd decoded 'Johann's Quatrains'.

So, my father, I beg forgiveness for ever doubting you. For even one moment thinking you'd betrayed me in that shameful way.

~-~

My nose had healed and some other minor work had changed me just a little. I supposed I deluded myself that I looked five years younger too.....

Hopefully, if we kept moving, no sniper's red laser would track its way to my heart, though I knew their tentacles were everywhere and neither were police forces free from corruption wherever we laid our heads. But, God willing, no more mysterious white owls, no messengers from the moon would come again to steal my memory away as I lay in my lover's arms.

On cue the moon rose in its magnificence over the jewelled Cretan hills.

A beautiful lantern, hanging in the Mediterranean sky.

Chapter 56. *Coda*

It's later.

I am staring upwards at the turning clouds, drifting without volition on a river of memory. Sometimes the river meanders about oxbow lakes, peaceful backwaters where I would linger and I glimpse again the intelligent eye of a raven inspecting me through a hole in the sky. Sometimes I hurtle through rapids, propelled at light speed round boulders black and dense as the corpses of super-compressed stars which draw me in, then catapult me back through space time to pinpoints of astonishment, perhaps through hypno-regression at which Chrissie too was adept.

That exquisite image of the lantern moon remained from those recent shards of my 'selective amnesia' as had been implied when I was eventually placed under Axel Metz. It was the last memory held dear when I awoke in a mainland hospital side ward. A massive headache, my arms bandaged, my head held together with steel screws and my ankles chained to the bed. An armed Greek policeman was visible through the corridor window.

I was lulled by the sedatives, but not enough to stop from going near crazy when they'd interviewed me. My man was dead and I was in the frame for his murder. They'd found me in the shadow of Athena's tree, at the bottom of the terrace steps, with a fractured skull. I had apparently attempted suicide after finding my daughter in her bath, wrists slashed like my own, but worse was to be revealed....

They were always adept at murder, Clarissa had said. They would make it look like suicide while discrediting the deceased. It was a game to them.

So if it was a murder/suicide pact Simeon had changed his mind as his corpse bore evidence of a mighty struggle. I remembered idly watching the seaplane at the jetty. I tried hard to think about events as they'd unfolded. *The pilot is helping the two passengers in business suits with their laptop cases. There's a car. Emma's young Adonis sitting on his motor scooter. His arm is raised, pointing then he's riding off along the beach. There's no-one on the pillion. The car drives out of sight behind a shoulder of rock and the nearby villa.*

That car would be taking the only road, winding upwards. I now know it had also contained my daughter. Alarm bells would have been ringing loudly in my mind. Suddenly I'm hit by a taser…I seem to remember someone swinging a baseball bat and wondered how I had acted in the last few minutes left to me, if I'd been able to react at all paralysed by the taser, frozen by the baleful stare of the *Wassermann*.

~-~

I cannot remember any of our highly paid security people being present that evening, just flickering snapshot images of my headless daughter in her tub of blood and Simeon with a bullet hole in his skull, bloodstained knife in bloody fingers; but these scenes might have been implanted at interview.

I cling to the pain, like an old enemy because it's real, perhaps the only reality I can rely on from the rest of my legend, so vivid are the delusions from which I suffer. Nothing else can touch me now. No thing can be guaranteed but the here and now, from moment to moment, so I believe. So much else had been seeded in my mind over time with malicious intent.

And it was my fingerprints that Cretan Homicide had lifted from the murder weapon.

An ancient Russian keepsake.

A 1930s Tokarev.

For good measure… you bastards!

I take my stolen palette knife which I've sharpened like a razor and hold it to my arm. I draw down sharply, and again. I feel the blood expressing and sigh, for Emma. So close now…

End

Captions to illustrations

1. Contents Page
Standard German helmet escutcheoned with the Vytis Knight of Lithuania
2. *Der Mönch am Meer*
The Monk by the Sea is a recurring theme in *The Baltic Falcon* representing the isolation of a soul in torment and indecision whose mind bears too great a burden for his head. An image inspired by the German Romantic painter, Caspar David Friedrich. - p20
3. The *Standart*
The Grand Imperial Yacht of the Tsar of all the Russias, *Standart*, leaves Kronstadt harbour. Extremely technically advanced,built by Burmeister & Wain of Copenhagen, this most elegant ship of state was the original and finest of her kind and though inspiring others, none came close to equalling her perfection. At Easter in 1909, the Empress Alexandra Feodorova was presented a Carl Fabergé egg in which an exquisite gold and platinum model of *Standart* sailed upon a sea of rock crystal; the egg supported by twin, black, double-headed eagles, referencing the Imperial figureheads at her bow, stands upon the tails of two dolphins. She is gone now, existing only in paintings, photographs and dreams; and as shipbuilders' models - and what fabulous models they are. - p56
4. The von Moritz *Flitzer* at Staaken
Bearing the blue/white diamonds of the *Bayerische Wappenschild*, the von Moritz Flitzer Z-1 is seen at Staaken Aerodrome in about 1927. The rudder bears the Death or Glory pennant of the 1st. Fighter Aviation Group of the Imperial Russian Air Service, that of his erstwhile respected enemy. The wings are covered in war-surplus lozenge-patterned fabric. (Archive Neumann) - p77
5. *The Baltic Falcon*
The Baltic Falcon, a painting by the Lithuanian artist V. Kestautis, shows a Great Icelandic Falcon on a circular oak panel, which was a concealment device containing a CD through which this story eventuated. - p113
6. Der Kalte Mond
Both the full moon and the round white face of a barn owl are common leitmotifs in *The Baltic Falcon*; implanted screen memories that hide awful secrets deep within the labyrinths of the mind. - p136

7. Kessler's *Kobold*

The only known photograph of the first Kessler type to be built in Germany, der Kobold (Goblin): built Staaken, Berlin, in 1922 in compliance with the treaty obligations of the *Versaillesdiktat* limiting aero-engines to 100 hp. output. First registered in 1925, Ernst Kessler used this machine for aerobatic flying exhibitions with the *Luftzirkus Berlin*. (Archive Hans-Peter Neumann) - p145

8. Ramstein

The tragic 1988 airshow accident at US air base Ramstein, West Germany, was the single worst event of its kind ever recorded. - p162

9. Peter Fechter

Peter Fechter was not alone among those hopefuls trying to escape the oppression and fear of Cold War East Germany, but his newspaper photograph as he lay bleeding his life away in the kill-zone in the shadow of the Berlin Wall exemplified the merciless tyranny of Soviet rule. - p179

10. The KFZ-1 *Tigerfalk* was the last of the Kessler biplanes which briefly starred as an aerobatic machine in the '30s, only to fade into obscurity until rediscovered in the 1960s, mysteriously, in East Anglia.   - p183

11. The lone, unnamed female figure in the snowfield is the first recurrent image which Steiger experiences, as does Natasha, in dreams, in the contemporary period. - p204

12. The figure treads the shoreline, searches his soul and his memory like a beachcomber monk, for the truth he fears but must confront. - p211

13. Rolf is driven to his destiny. - p232

14. Austrian-built Albatros as flown by Steiger.

OEF 253-series Albatros D.III as flown by Steiger on the Italian Front and later in Ukraine: an excellent fighter. Progressive power increases by Austro-Daimler, factory removal of the spinner and introduction of the 'bullet nose' which improved propeller efficiency significantly raised the all-round performance of this machine. The small flag in the cockpit probably indicates that the machine guns are armed. (Archive Neumann) - p269

15. Etrich *Taube*

The Taube was the first really successful design in Germany both as a civilian and a military machine. Elegant in design and built by several manufacturers, it was nonetheless made obsolescent by rapid technical advances soon after the outbreak of war. - p456

16. Stalin's image is towed by a 'troika' of Polikarpov PO-2s. This malignant cult of the personality was taken to monstrous extremes later in Red China and North Korea. - p528

17. Soviet Fokker D.VII

Fokker D.VIIs were officially purchased by the USSR in early 1922, but individual machines of all types were liable to be captured and pressed into service. - p597

18. Out-of-body phenomena, the transmigration of souls and telepathy are among the prevailing metaphysical events that Steiger, Morris, Natasha and Emma struggle to comprehend. - p636

19. The Tigerfalk is still in existence in the UK. - p632

20. Arkadi is awarded the Silver Star - p712

21.Albatros L.17 (D.II) fighter refurbished by Kessler Flygmaskinsfabrik A.B. in Sweden. This aeroplane has the later 'bullet nose' featured by the Austro-Hungarian 253-series machines. The swastikas indicate a visit to Finland in 1922, when Kessler attempted to interest the Finns in acquiring fighters of this type. Despite improvements, including a more powerful engine, the D.II was considered obsolete and French-built Gourdou-Lesseure parasol monoplane fighters and British Martinsyde F.4 Buzzards were already on order. - p753

22. Tigerfalk biplane in Lithuania, ready for dismantling and shipping to the UK. - p834